# The Sleepy Hollow Family Almanac

—a novel by—

## Kris D'Agostino

ALGONQUI

Published by
Algonquin Books of Chapel Hill
Post Office Box 2225
Chapel Hill, North Carolina 27515-2225

a division of
Workman Publishing
225 Varick Street
New York, New York 10014

This is a work of fiction. While, as in all fiction, the literary
perceptions and insights are based on experience, all names,
characters, places, and incidents either are products of the
author's imagination or are used fictitiously.

LIBRARY OF CONGRESS CATALOGING-IN-PUBLICATION DATA
D'Agostino, Kris, [date]
  The Sleepy Hollow family almanac: a novel by Kris D'Agostino.—
1st. ed.
    p. cm.
  ISBN 978-1-56512-951-1
  1. Young men—Fiction.  2. Families—Fiction.  3. Life change
events—Fiction.  4. Maturation (Psychology)—Fiction.  5. Sleepy
Hollow (N.Y.)—Fiction.  6. Domestic fiction.  I. Title.
  PS3604.A3335 2012
  813'.6—dc22                                      2011038421

10 9 8 7 6 5 4 3 2 1
First Edition

A.S. helped me through a tough year.
My parents and my brothers helped me
through all the tough years.

*For the ones condemned to drift or else be kept from drifting.*

—Bob Dylan

# The Sleepy Hollow Family Almanac

# ≪ 1 ≫

I work with retards.

This is fact in more ways than one. It is fact because I am a teaching assistant at a preschool for autistic kids. It is fact because family, friends, and most of the people who populate my life are idiots.

"Peepee," Arham says. He is smiling in a very unnatural way.

"No peepee," I tell him. I grab the small chair on which he sits and pull it closer to me. "You just went," I add under my breath. Arham continues to smile. He's a cute kid, Middle Eastern, Pakistani, or something. His hair smells like peanuts, cumin.

I'm not a preschool teacher. The road that led me here was long and circuitous, fraught with disappointment and regret. My job title is, as stated on my paychecks, "Teaching Assistant." My mother basically thrust the whole thing upon me—under threat of losing the free bed and board I have been exploiting since moving back to my parents' house last year. Although I'm not particularly happy with this job, I haven't been able to summon the proper motivation to do anything about it. I have no idea what I'm supposed to be doing with myself. I have no money. I spend what little I make on weed, student loans, LPs, and the laundry list of bills I've racked up. Life is basically standing still. Stalled out. Or something along those lines. It has made me angry. I am angry all the time. And the fact that I can't focus that anger on any one thing, any one person, other than myself, makes me that much more dispirited.

There is a lap desk resting on my thighs. I sit with one of these for hours, every day. I'm not sure why I can't have a table, but I try not to ask too many questions around here. I shift from one cheek to the other to keep my ass from getting numb and check the clock on the wall: 3:20. Ten more minutes and the school day will be over. Ten more minutes and I will be holding Arham's hand, leading him across the grass to bus number 52. The bus that takes him home.

I shuffle a stack of twenty index cards, all laminated, all displaying various colored polygons. It's shape time for Arham, one of the many programs I attempt to teach him on a daily basis. I place two of the cards on the lap desk. One shows a red star, the other a blue circle. I couldn't get the printer to work properly, so the star looks like a melting pinecone.

I take a breath and check the clock again. Still 3:20.

"Point to the star," I say.

Arham's smile widens.

I have been using bits of cookie all afternoon as small rewards when he behaves well. By this point, a dark circle of brownish muck has built up around his lips. I get paper towels to clean him off. When I return to my seat, he has a look of mischief on his face. He says, "Peepee," then falls out of his chair onto the floor. What little patience I arrived with at eight this morning is gone. I lunge after him. The lap desk falls. Index cards scatter. Arham is excited because I have reacted to him. He has successfully gotten me down to his level. Arham has the attention span of a fourteen-month-old. He's on the spectrum. Autistic, special, slow, handicapped, disabled, annoying, possessing intellectual qualities on par with my grandmother's—whatever you want to call it.

He lies on his back, giggling that high-pitched girlish giggle I've been listening to since the school year began. I grab his miniature frame by the shoulders and attempt to hoist him to his feet. The fucking kid weighs maybe twenty-five pounds.

"Peepee," he blurts out. This time it's accompanied by a volley of spit and chewed cookie bits. A large glob lands just below the neckline of his Looney Tunes T-shirt. Another splatters on my forearm.

I look over at Angela and her student, future Stanford-Binet all-star Hendrick Ramirez. Hendrick is Puerto Rican, three years old, the same age as Arham. Hendrick isn't autistic. He is merely crippled by massive behavior and attention problems. As if this is somehow better.

Angela and I are employees of the John W. Manley School in Sleepy Hollow, New York. There are forty or so kids here, shipped in from various parts of the county. We work with them in semi-isolation, one kid per teacher, two kids per room, so as not to overwhelm anyone. Angela and I share a front room with two large floor-to-ceiling windows looking

out on a very green, very long sloping hill. For normal people this would be nice, these large windows. But Arham has
a thing with birds and clouds and trees. He wants to eat
them. To stop him from constantly banging his head on the
glass, I have been forced to hang sheets of colored craft paper over the windows, blocking his view. The paper is thin,
though, and creates an uncanny kaleidoscope effect on the
floors and walls. I don't mind this.

Spring break is two days away. I just need to make it to
the end of the week.

I take a deep breath. Arham continues to dribble mushy
discharge onto my arm. I grab the front of his shirt and wipe
some cookie-spit paste across Daffy Duck's beak.

Little Hendrick Ramirez is now standing on his chair,
demanding I stop manhandling Arham.

"No!" he tells me, pointing a tiny finger in my direction.
His accent stretches the *o* and for a second he reminds me of
those guys I see camped out on the sidewalks in Port Chester
playing dominoes, eating chicken feet. Hendrick is wearing
a shiny plastic fireman's hat, which makes him much less
mysterious.

"No, yourself," I say.

Angela has put her pen down and is looking at me. I mouth
*Sorry,* like it's not my fault. Arham's giggling increases as he
tries to squirm away from me. He keeps talking about his
desire to make peepee.

I yank him harder than I should and force him back into
his seat. His smile is still there, but behind it I can see he's
confused. He struggles to get up and I pin his arms to his
sides. Tiny veins, so small they look drawn on, pop out along

his neck and he scrunches his eyes to little slits, won't look at me.

"Pee. Pee," he says, more of a breath than a word, pushing himself off his chair as far as he can.

"Yeah, yeah," I say.

Hendrick seizes the moment and disappears behind me, grabbing my plastic container of treats. I'm forked. Either I have to let Arham go, at which point he'll fall back onto the floor, or I can let Hendrick help himself to as many Gummi-Bears, M&M's, and Cheetos as he can cram into his mouth before Angela gets to him.

I drop Arham, which apparently he wasn't expecting, because for a moment, as he sails through the air, his smile vanishes and he looks completely baffled. He hits the deck, banging his head on the lap desk.

"Ouch. Ouch," he says, rubbing his temple.

Hendrick sees me coming and tosses the container into the air. Gummi-Bears disperse across the carpet. M&M's scatter. Hendrick takes off his fireman's hat and stands giving me the evil eye. I reach down to start picking up the mess, and as I do, Hendrick winds up and hits my hand as hard as he can with the helmet.

"Broccoli!" he yells, rolling the *r* with a look of profound ecstasy on his face. *Broccoli* is his favorite word.

If I had a gun, I would shoot everyone in the room, including myself.

My supervisor, Ceci, appears in the doorway. I imagine we've been making a racket.

"Is everything all right in here?" she asks. She is wearing her hair up in a ponytail today.

I sit on the floor, holding my throbbing hand, red and blue and green light from the craft paper spilling across my body. Ceci straddles the safety gate we use to keep the retards confined like barnyard animals.

She bends over and starts to help gather the fallen candy and snacks. I see through her cotton skirt that she's wearing a thong.

ARHAM IS GONE. Hendrick is gone. My fingers hurt.

I'm sitting outside at a picnic table. I'm sweating without really moving. My hair is matted all around my head. I refuse to cut it, mainly because it pisses my mother off.

The John W. Manley School employee handbook dictates that no one is allowed to clock out until four on the dot. Our supervisors are very clear about this at weekly staff meetings. In nonviolent protest I have begun staging sit-ins at the picnic table, silently letting the final ten minutes of the day expire.

I count the moments till I can leave. I emphasize each second by picking flakes of red paint off the table. After work, I'm meeting a Realtor to look at apartments. I'm anxious, filled with a strong urge to just take the first place I'm shown, anything, as long as it isn't my parents' house. I've been riding the seesaw of false hope and delusion all day: upward swings of happy thoughts about the prospect of once again living life outside that house, followed almost immediately by the dreadful remembrance that it's all a big farce I'm orchestrating because I don't actually have the money to rent my own place. My apartment hunt is nothing more than a waste of this Realtor's time, my time.

Thinking about all of this conjures images of my aunt Corrine. Before she lost her mind (the fate of every Moretti, it seems), Corrine worked in real estate. She was the one who put my parents in their current home. The house where I grew up. The house where I once again find myself living.

Corrine isn't really my aunt. She's my grandmother's cousin, so I don't know what that makes her to me. She's seventy years old and lives down the street from my family. I drive by her house every day on my way to work. She's fond of wearing oversize navy snow boots while watering the same patch of desolate garden in her front yard. I usually smile and wave if she sees me and try to forget that as a child I was made to kiss this woman's cheek on holidays. Aunt Corrine is not well. Of course, from my perspective at least, most people in my family are not well. At a YMCA line-dancing class last weekend, a widower named Stan asked Corrine to be his dancing partner. She called my mother at three o'clock that morning to inform us she was engaged.

Corrine woke many relatives that night, spreading the good news.

Last winter, during my mother's annual Christmas party, I found Corrine standing out in the backyard, shivering. There were tears in her eyes. I asked her what she was doing.

"Looking for Lloyd," she muttered. "Have you seen him?" Lloyd was her husband.

"He's been dead for nine years," I informed her. She blinked at me, confusion welling up in her gaze. "I haven't seen him. Let's check inside." I ushered her back into the house.

She's not well, and her brother Harold (this is a guy who

had a new mattress delivered over a year ago and still hasn't carried it inside off his porch) has found a solution to her dementia-related problems. He's gone ahead and secured a new place for her to live, and from what I understand, Aunt Corrine has signed a very long lease. As of this morning, she's a permanent resident of the Four Winds Hospital over in Katonah.

I'm not sure who's going to water Corrine's fallow flower-beds now that she's been relieved of that duty. In forty-six years I'll be her age. I wonder if I'll bow out of the race in similar fashion.

BACK INSIDE THE SCHOOL, I head to the staff kitchen to get some water. Angela is there, sitting at the table, looking exhausted.

"Sorry about earlier," I say.

"It's okay."

She is slouched forward with one hand propping her head up.

"I shouldn't have let things get out of control."

"Around here, it happens," Angela says. "Don't worry."

I fill a cup with water from the cooler and sit down across the table from her. I check the time. Although I've stopped wearing the watch my grandmother gave me as a college graduation present, my cell phone tells me it's 3:55.

"Can I ask you a question?"

She sits back and looks at me.

"Sure."

"Is this the job you saw for yourself when you left El Salvador?"

She seems to turn the question over for a minute.

"No," she says.

"Is your life better because you left?"

"I have more money here than I could ever have there."

"Is this what you imagined? The John W. Manley School?"

She shakes her head.

"No."

"My life looks absolutely nothing like what I thought it would."

Why am I telling this woman these things? Sure, we sit in the same room together for hours every day, but we hardly ever speak more than a few words to each other. The only explanation is that I'm losing it.

"Life doesn't follow the plan you lay out," Angela says.

"Yeah, well, at least you don't have to deal with your family here. My family is killing me."

"Are you kidding? My mother calls five times a day and gets mad when I can't talk for an hour. I send money back, for her, for my father, for *his* new wife, for my sister and her kids."

"You know where my money goes?" I tell her. "Student loans. I'm broke all the time. I'm angry all the time."

"Bills. Calling cards. Babysitter. Food. Heat," Angela is ticking off her expenses one finger at a time.

"I live with my parents."

"I have two kids. No husband."

"I think this talk is depressing us."

We both laugh at the absurdity of it all.

"Family is family," Angela says. "Sometimes you need them."

"I don't," I say. "I want out."

Angela doesn't respond. Maybe she's right, but at the moment, life just feels like a mountain of frustration. I finish my water and check my cell phone again. Time to go.

I WALK INTO my supervisor's office, to where the time sheets are pinned with a thumbtack to the wall. Ceci is on the phone. By the tone of her voice I surmise she's talking to her fiancé.

"That sounds like a great idea," she says. She oohs and aahs. God knows what these two nimrods are discussing. She makes a lovey-dovey face. *He can't see you, asshole,* I think. She doesn't even look at me as I pull down the time sheet and sign out. I put the time as 4:05.

"You look hot today," I tell her as I tack the folder back to the wall. Ceci cups her hand over the receiver.

"What's that?"

"I said, 'See you tomorrow,'" I call out as I slip through the door.

"Listen, Cal. I'd like you to present a graph next month. It's been a while."

"Sure thing," I say, but really I'm gone. I'm out of her office before she finishes her sentence, past the main doors and down the very long, very green sloping lawn to the parking lot. I climb into my hatchback and turn on the radio. It feels like a British postpunk evening, so I rummage around the garbage littering the floor of the car until I find something to fit that bill. I listen to *Entertainment!* Angular guitars, tin can drums, chugging, staccato bass lines. It sounds like heaven, and I'm off, shifting into reverse and pulling out of the lot faster than I should. Tires screech and I'm around the corner heading down Route 9 toward Yonkers. When I hit Palmer Avenue, I have a brief moment of guilt. I should really go home and see if my father needs help. I shouldn't be trying to pass myself off as a renter with good credit or savings of any kind. But then again, he always needs help. They're always looking for something from me in that house. It sucks you in. Fuck it.

When the light changes to green, I continue. I'll keep playing out the charade. I'll pretend I'm something I'm not.

# ≪ 2 ≫

She opens the door. Her blouse comes down just far enough in the front so I don't have to try very hard to imagine what her breasts look like. We step into the apartment. Her name is Pam Kittredge and she immediately tells me about other rentals she has access to. I tell her I wish to see them all.

"What do you do for a living?" she asks as I follow her to the kitchen, which is separated by an island counter from the living room.

"I'm a teacher." It's only half a lie, and it doesn't matter anyway, because my financially crippling student loans and barely existent salary prevent me from having anywhere near the sum needed to sign the lease, which would require me to pay the broker's fee, security deposit, and first month's rent up front.

"That's great," she says. "The landlord is definitely looking for someone responsible."

"I'm that person," I say.

"And what do your parents do?"

"Well, my father is sort of out of work at the moment," I tell her.

"He was laid off?"

"More like disability."

"I see," Pam says. She sees nothing.

I sum up my mother's existence with a vague "She makes sure the bills get paid."

The place is cavernous. Exactly what I had in mind. Giant raw space with exposed piping overhead and colossal paneled windows looking out on an industrial park across the street.

"These lofts are getting popular," Pam tells me. "Like a blank canvas. You can do whatever you want in here."

The previous tenant constructed a corner bedroom with drywall, the sides of which don't quite reach the ceiling.

"The building is full of artists and musicians," Pam says. "All sorts of creative people."

"Sounds like my kind of crowd," I say. Yes. Creativity. Artistry. These are the things missing from my life, keeping me from achieving wholeness and contentment. These are the kind of people I want to associate with. The kind of people I know I can ingratiate myself with if only given the chance. They will surely give me the push out of postadolescence I apparently refuse to give myself. They will show me something other than the America-as-high-school I have come to inhabit.

It is an old building. Built before the war, she tells me. Was once a clothing warehouse. I make a big show of inspecting the amenities. I open and shut the fridge many times. I put my hand in the freezer and let it stay there for a while. I don't know why I do this, but I nod when I finish, as if pleased with my findings. I flick all the light switches and note the rows of naked bulbs overhead. I go into the bathroom and shut the door. I turn the lock. I flush the toilet and watch the water spin away. I run the faucet and the showerhead. I gauge the pressure. Pam shows me to the laundry room just down the hall. I inquire about direct sunlight. I ask about rain leakage. Are pets allowed? What utilities are included? I ask every question I think a potential renter might ask. I pretend that if satisfied with her answers I might say, *I'll take it.*

I ask her if there is roof access.

"I'll have to check on that," she says.

We caravan. Her in her Camry, me in the hatchback, to another building on the other side of town, where I see a different rental. Afterward I thank Pam in the parking lot.

"You related to Kathleen Moretti?" she says, giving my hand a hearty pump while simultaneously looking over my information on her clipboard.

"My mother. Why?"

"No reason," Pam says. With what appears to be sleight of hand, the clipboard is tucked into her bag, my hand is dropped, and I'm holding her business card. "I showed a few houses down Dobbs Ferry to a Kathleen Moretti last week."

"Must be someone else," I tell this Pam. "My parents have enough on their plates without throwing a new house into the equation."

"If you say so," she says as we part ways. "Let me know soon. These places turn over pretty quick."

EASTER IS TWO weeks away, but my mother is in the living room, delicately lining the mantel with her treasured collection of elaborately painted ceramic eggs. I see two giant boxes of decorations at her feet. I start to open my mouth to ask if and why Pam Kittredge took her to look at houses, but think better of it. My mother gets extremely agitated when I bring up the subject of my moving out. She thinks I want her to lend me money.

"Little early, isn't it?" I say to all the ornaments.

"You never know who'll be stopping by to judge," she says. "Helene Miller's had her decorations out for weeks."

"Ah, yes."

"I'm starting dinner," my mother says, but I'm halfway up the stairs. I pass Inez, our maid, on the landing. We exchange greetings. She has a duster in hand, no doubt on her way to the TV room to embark on her weekly cleaning of the entertainment center while my father lies supine, himself a piece of furniture in need of dusting.

I find two envelopes on the mattress in my room. The first, a monthly statement from Sallie Mae. I try to pretend it isn't there. The second is a letter from my father, who's fond of leaving notes instead of initiating direct contact. Messages from the next room.

I lie on the floor, listening to old country records. I have always held the slide guitar in high esteem. It sounds to me like wild animals crying atop windswept plateaus. A nameless city where there is no language, only intense glances and stares. A place where nods and gestures convey all human emotion.

This is what the letter says:

*Calvin,*

*I always wondered why old people read the obituaries. Perhaps we are hoping to see other people's ages when they bite it. I'm not afraid to die. I'm actually getting prepared. I'll be fifty-five next year and all of this is tiring. I have a theory that as human beings get older, chemicals are released into the brain to prepare us for the end. Sort of like how the nurse lubes your ass up before the anus-cam. It makes the whole thing a lot easier to swallow. Easier, not enjoyable. We don't remember birth. I don't think we will remember our own death. Dying. What petrifies me about dying is the aloneness of it. I have always thought about dying in some hotel room, a million miles away from home. Utterly alone. I have spent more time in hotel rooms than I have at home. I need you to promise me, just you and I. Promise me that you will be with me, maybe holding my hand, when I go. I don't care when or where, just get there and see me off. Don't let me go alone. I promise I will try to wait for you. Find me. You're the one that understands me.*

*Dad*

I roll onto my back, look up at the ceiling fan.

Our house makes noises. It always has. The walls creak and settle. Wood splinters without warning. There are footsteps at odd hours of the night. Pipes sound symphonies from behind the drywall.

Sallie Mae has informed me my loan payment is due in two weeks. I am someone who does not like to delay pain gratification, so I write out a check immediately. It's startling how much of my salary is sucked up by this debt. Four years in the undergraduate incubator plus the four-month failed social experiment I like to call "grad school" plus off-campus housing plus many, many burritos equals over $45,000 to repay. At my current income, I'm looking at full financial independence at around age sixty-seven. Between music (I try to buy only vinyl records these days) and weed and pharmaceutical drugs and movie tickets and cell phone bills and credit card bills and video rentals and trying to have a normal social life, I struggle to save a few measly dollars a month.

I navigate the computer's Internet browser to my online bank statement and assay my current finances. I shuffle fifty bucks from checking to savings, bringing the total up to a whopping $567.88. I consider moving another fifty but quickly remember the list of albums I want to purchase over the weekend at the record fair at SUNY Purchase and how happy this will make me. How it will help to (briefly) make me forget just exactly where I've wound up living once again. I need to maintain some level of quality of life in the present, in addition to saving for the future. I vow to buy all the records on my list ASAP. Mental health is crucial. Not just for the children. This is something we are told at John W. Manley School staff meetings all the time.

I delete a few out-of-date porn bookmarks from the toolbar and play online Scrabble for ten minutes before quitting in disgust at a string of extremely low-scoring word combinations.

I resume lying on the floor. I listen to records. I listen

to *Jailbreak*. I listen to *Peace Sells . . . But Who's Buying?* I listen to *Shake Some Action*. I grab the Moleskine notebook from its place under my pillow and flip it open. The first ten pages are dedicated to the ever-growing list of movies I've watched. Since college, I've recorded, in high OCD fashion, the date and name of every film that passes before my eyes. I flip past this part. I flip past the section of notes concerning my father, all the bizarre things he's done in the past eight months:

1. *Watering the flowers in front of our house at three in the morning.*
2. *Crying during telephone commercials depicting long-distance romances.*
3. *Twenty-one-hour-a-day sleep cycles.*
4. *Sitting at the kitchen table staring at old flight logs for hours.*
5. *Unfurling massive Jeppesen aeronautical charts across the living room floor and following navigation lines with his fingers in delicate, precise increments.*
6. *Constant proclamations of "I'm dying" and "God help us."*
7. *His encounter with one of the immigrants working for our landscaping company: "If they have to put me on dialysis, I'm going to shoot myself with this gun." "Sí, señor."*

I flip past these passages. Past the section listing, verbatim, every forehead-slap-inducing thing my brother has recently said in my presence, along with estimated dates.

Some highlights:

- *"Don't worry, the woman I marry won't be allowed to work."* —*9.25.04*
- *"What do you think about these cowboy boots?"* —*3.29.05*
- *"How much would I have to pay some faggy artist to do a portrait of me dressed like a samurai?"* —*8.10.05*
- *"Calvin is such a liberal."* —*10.14.04, 11.2.04, 12.23.04, 12.24.04, 12.25.04, 2.13.05, 7.16.05, 11.01.05*
- *"I need to hit the gym double-time from now till Halloween so I look authentic in my Spartan costume."* —*9.08.05*
- *"I know my sneakers are a size too small. It's because I don't want my feet to get any bigger."* —*6.18.04*

I flip beyond all of this. To the back of the notebook. A column of numbers is listed:

*θ*
*~~125.23~~*
*~~245.36~~*
*~~369.76~~*
*~~446.32~~*
*517.88*

I cross out the 517.88 and write the new figure, 567.88. I close the notebook and place it back under my pillow. Somewhere in the depths of my head, down the long corridor of what seems like eternity, I can see a small flicker of light, a pinnacle of happiness. It looks like $2,000. This is the modest sum I've calculated I'll need in order to secure an apartment of my own. To rejoin the outside world. Ten months to a year is my projected deadline. This financial time frame, of course, does not figure in birthday and Christmas donations from family members, which could speed things up.

My mother knows a sage, this truly bizarre woman who goes by the name Brigitte DeMeyer. Since the illness started, she comes over a few times a week for "wellness sessions" with my father. At her request, they've begun to tape pieces of paper, marked with elaborate drawings of the letter *S*, all over the house. *S*'s on the washer-dryer, *S*'s under paintings, on the toilet. *S*'s above every light switch. Fancy red *S* cards dangle on the chandelier in the dining room, float above the dashboard GPS system in the SUV, stare out from ornate mirrors.

"When you see an *S*, it means smile," Brigitte has told us. "It means you can feel *safe. Secure.* These are words to embrace, to live with," she says. "*Shelter,*" she says.

My dad walks around the house forcing his mouth to react to these little scraps of paper. I'll find him in front of the flat-screen in the family room watching reruns of *Law & Order.*

"Real murder trials are just like this," he'll tell me.

"Don't forget to smile," I'll say, pointing to the large purple *S* hanging from the television.

He'll turn his head, look at me for a moment, and do this weird thing where he smiles, then frowns in rapid succession, his mustache twitching above his lips. Then he'll usually fall asleep at the commercial break.

• • •

MY MOTHER CALLS Brigitte her "spiritual adviser," her "healer," in touch with both this world and the next.

"She sees things," my mother tells me. "She sees more than we do. I have a feeling when she's around."

"Her hand in your pocket," I say.

"Everything is connected," my mother says.

My father is skeptical and reluctant, but he doesn't put up much of a fight when my mother brings Brigitte around to help him maintain a positive outlook during this time of spiritual complexity. Dressed like a Gypsy, gems dangling from her ears, shawls and scarves and kerchiefs wrapped about her, this Brigitte will approach me with open palms on her way into the house.

"I'm waiting for you to come talk with me," she will say.

"I don't really know what you want to talk about."

"There is so much to discuss. When you're ready. Whenever that may be. I'm waiting. The aura in this house needs to stay strong for him. All of you must stay strong."

"Stay strong," I say. "Got it."

# ≪ **3** ≫

The gun is a single-action Colt .45. Holds six bullets and can be used to play Russian roulette. He carries it around with him. Keeps it tucked in the folds of his bathrobe or the billowing pockets of his plaid pajama pants. He believes something is going to happen.

He has a mustache. He has always had a mustache. It's a pilot thing. An unspoken code they all follow in order to identify one another across bars in foreign hotels, in strange cities, in fog-shrouded hangars, in waiting rooms, at the supermarket. Every time they blow their noses, they are reminded of who they are. It is the sort of solidarity I look for everywhere but am without.

"I missed you today," he says to me.

"Missed me?"

We are in the TV room, waiting for my mother to scream, "Dinner!" at the top of her lungs.

"I went hiking up around Fahnestock," he says, fingering the mustache. "Your mother let me fire five shots into a sycamore. I thought of you. You would have had fun."

"Is it entirely legal to fire your gun in a state park?"

"I doubt it," he says. "The blowback is exhilarating. It has the smell of hot metal. It makes me happy. And your mother and that witch doctor, Brigitte, believe in happiness. They believe in its healing powers. As do I, but to a much lesser extent."

My father unmutes the television as *Law & Order* returns from a commercial, and the room is filled with the sound of lawyers. I feel the presence of the paper *S*'s hanging around us.

When it first started, he took pictures with a digital camera, to chronicle the loss of his hair, posting them on a bulletin board he'd hung on the door of the upstairs bathroom. Day one showed little, if any, development, but following the pictures and imagining them playing out like a flip book, by day fourteen, one could witness an interesting pattern forming around the crown of his head. Wrapped in his trademark bathrobe, not even bothering to dry off, he brings down clumps of hair from the shower to show us. He gathers the fallen curls in a cereal bowl and examines them. Defying all logic, the mustache survives.

As things progress, he has turned to nature, to apocalyptic survival. He reads things like *Wilderness Survival for the Modern Man* and *Prepared* magazine and *The Great Outdoorsman*. He has turned the garage into a bunker, bursting with stockpiled bags of rice, an arsenal of bolt-action rifles. He has purchased multiple tents and sleeping bags—each designed for various weather conditions—lanterns, a drum of 87-octane gasoline, flashlights, snakebite antivenom, collapsible pots for cooking in the wild, strike-anywhere matches, a water filtration system. He has arranged everything carefully. He keeps inventory on a clipboard and makes daily inspections to assure that in the event of an emergency, a flash flood, a mustard-gas attack, or nuclear annihilation, he will be able to carry on. The cancer started on his spine.

At dinner, an argument erupts between my siblings.

"The woman is a racist," Chip (short for Charles) says. He is holding a piece of sausage in his hand, waving it around.

"Because she made you buy a ticket?" Elissa asks.

"No. Because I'm white and I needed to get home and my monthly had just expired the day before and I didn't have time to get a new one and she saw an opportunity to exert power over the little world of the commuter train where she thinks she's queen."

"Wally Czerkowski was there and he said you were acting like an asshole," I say.

"What's that guy doing on the train?" Chip asks. "He doesn't have a job." My brother stuffs the hunk of sausage into his mouth. He chews in a very precise manner. His teeth are whiter than cocaine, thanks to three hours spent recently in the dentist's chair. They sparkle when he talks.

"People can ride the train and not have jobs," I say. "People do other things."

"I'm on that train every day," Chip continues, ignoring me. "I work. Every day I see this woman. We have looked in each other's eyes at seven in the morning. She knows me. It's not like I'm a scumbag trying to scam a free ride. It's because I'm white. And I commute and I wear a suit. She resents that. I need to ride the train. It's a necessity. I don't enjoy it. I don't enjoy spending a hundred and sixty-three dollars on that train pass. It had just expired. I was gonna buy a new one that night. Most people would let it slide. It's called courtesy, humanity, empathy. Not this woman. She's going to ask me to pay the ten dollars for a ticket?"

"Like you empathize with her position?" Elissa asks. She huffs.

"What position?"

"That's her job," I say.

"It's her job to racially profile me?" Chip throws up his hands, confused.

"Please don't tell anyone outside this family that you think you're being racially profiled," Elissa says.

"Thank God Mrs. Stone and Mrs. Cunningham were there to defend me when she called the cops," Chip says with a look of concern.

"Oh, Mrs. Stone is such a wonderful person!" our mother says suddenly, very loud. "And so beautiful." She looks around the table.

"Those are rich, white suburban housewives. You're talking about first-world problems," Elissa says. She impales some string beans on her fork, eats them. "I feel bad for that poor train conductor, that's who I feel bad for, she's probably a single mother. And she has to put up with you every day."

"Why does she have to be a single mother?" I ask. "Because she's black?"

"Look who's the racist now," Chip says.

"Please," Elissa says.

"Please," our father says.

"She called the cops," Chip says. "She used her little walkie-talkie to call the cops. She was going to have them throw me off the train."

"She called the cops because you refused to pay for a ticket," Elissa says. "If you get on the train, you have a ticket or you buy one. It's not optional."

A platter of sausage, meatballs, and braciole smothered with gravy sits in the center of the table. It is surrounded by bowls of steamed vegetables.

"Why do you cook so much meat if Chip is the only one who eats it?" I ask.

"Your father likes the smell," our mother says.

"No, I don't," our father says. "I like the smell of gunpowder. And mesquite chips. Emergency blankets, that sort of thing."

"I'm going to write a letter to Metro-North, that's what I'm going to do," Chip says.

"Maybe you should," our mother says.

"Reverse discrimination," Chip says. "It happens all the time."

"I would like everyone to stop talking about the incident on the train," our father says. "I tire of hearing about it."

He reaches across the table and jabs at a sausage.

"James," our mother says.

He drops the meat and returns to his broccoli, his spinach. His mustache twitches.

For a moment, no one says anything. I take a sip of water.

"I don't know how, but I'm going to get that woman," Chip says.

"Get her what?" I ask.

"You are such an asshole," Elissa says. "Reverse discrimination? What a joke."

My father digs into the folds of his bathrobe. His hand emerges gripping the gun. Very casually, he places it on the table and looks around the dining room at us all. We look at the gun.

"I tire of the train story," he says slowly.

The words hang there. Once, he rode a camel and saw the pyramids.

"If that's loaded," our mother says, "I'm going to be really pissed."

My mother is mostly a mild-mannered woman. However, on occasion, owing to some highly capricious Italian lineage, she has been known to "fly off the handle," as my father likes to put it. I watch her stare at the gun. I wonder if this is one of those times.

After dinner I smoke a joint in the third-floor bathroom. Blow the smoke out the window. I get my daily dose of Internet porn. My room is sparse. One wall of shelving houses my record collection. Shelves on a second wall are filled with books, half of which I have never read. There are lots of posters.

I fall asleep. I dream that the molecules of my body become unhinged and drift apart, scattered by the wind, and because of this, in my dream, I am unable to go to work.

THE YEARS ROLL BY. They *have* been rolling by. I can trace my life (all twenty-four years of it) and see how I've come to the place I'm at now. It mostly feels arbitrary, as if every choice was made randomly, or without regard for the consequences. Or even realizing there would be consequences. Truthfully, I might not even have the fortitude to change anything if ever given the chance to do it over again.

I attended a small, extremely expensive, Jesuit-run liberal arts university in Connecticut, whose name is not worth mentioning. I majored in film, graduated in four years, and had little to speak of in the way of life experience.

Unequipped to face the real world postcollege, I bought myself two more years by enrolling in an MFA film-studies program at another very expensive liberal arts university, this time in Boston. Unfortunately, I hated the city, hated the assholes in my program, and hated the professors. John Galkin was the head of the department. His big claim to fame was that he once wrote a screenplay for a notoriously panned modernization of *Moby-Dick*, which starred George Hamilton and was set on a yacht in 1970s Florida. Galkin and I got off on the wrong foot when I insulted his taste in classic cinema by announcing to our class that I found *Citizen Kane* boring. Later in the semester we butted heads again when he handed me back a forty-page term paper and told me I had a week to rewrite it or he was going to fail me. "You use too many commas," he said. "This is unacceptable." With one foot already out the door, I sat on the paper for the week and handed it back unchanged, not one comma removed. He gave me an A–, which confirmed my suspicions that he was just handing out grades. I started to spend a lot of time riding the T around the city, listening to hardcore punk on my Walkman.

I took the train home to Sleepy Hollow that year to see

my family for Thanksgiving. Chip was finishing his MBA at UConn in Storrs, Connecticut. Elissa was a junior at Sleepy Hollow High and had just been suspended for throwing paint on the principal's fur coat.

When I returned to Boston, the first snowfall of the year was blanketing New England. As my train approached the city and the skyline came into view, I began to feel an inexplicable anxiety about what I had decided to do with my life. I went to a few more classes, mostly just sitting with my notebook closed, daydreaming. I wrote a letter to my parents telling them I was dropping out of school. I dropped out of school. Most of my loans were not refunded, leaving me with even more tuition debt. I spent the last of my money wandering around Harvard Square harassing street performers and buying records. I ran out of money. I had no job, nor a desire to get one. I sublet my Boston room, packed up my record collection, and returned, dejected, to my childhood home, a failure.

Back in my parents' house, it wasn't long before I started acting like my high school self. I did nothing, just sat around the house moaning. I drove around till all hours, listening to music and smoking weed with my best friend, Wally Czerkowski (who was also jobless and living at home). I cloistered myself in my room and watched movies until my eyeballs hurt. "Get a job," my mother told me on a daily basis. After two weeks, completely fed up with my idleness, she contacted a friend and finagled a job for me at the John W. Manley School for Autistic Children. I began work as a teaching assistant. I was shown the basics of applied behavior analysis, a form of early childhood intervention similar

to training a dog by way of migraine-inducing repetition.
As I started my new job, Chip finished his degree. Added it
to his wall of accolades. He had a job at a prominent Manhattan bank lined up months before he finished school. My
brother can be summed up thus: type A to the extreme,
vain, egotistical, money hungry, tasteless, insecure, vapid,
demanding, yet somehow a lovable, charismatic rascal. If
I'm honest, I'd say I possess a lot of these characteristics as
well, I just don't have his drive to succeed, which makes for
an unfortunate combination.

My father's decline began around the same time—with
intense back pain he could not get rid of. He was working in
the yard one Sunday and had to stop because of the discomfort. From there, it all happened fast. Tentatively diagnosed
with a herniated disk, he underwent a series of MRIs. The
MRIs revealed a lesion on his spine. An oncologist told us
it was multiple myeloma. None of us had ever heard of it.
Within twenty-four hours he was radiated and simultaneously started on chemotherapy protocol. Three weeks later
he was home. His hair began to thin, then fall out. Soon
after that, my mother scheduled the first of many "wellness
sessions" with Brigitte. The S's made their first appearance
in our house. Chip moved back home to be with our father.

That was six months ago. I am still here. In this house.
We are all here.

I am reading an article in the local newspaper about America's weight problem. I learn the average woman is a size 14.

Through the open window in my bedroom I hear loud splattering noises coming from the backyard, the sound of hissing air. It's Thursday evening. I didn't think anyone was home. I was enjoying a moment of solitude. I had made secret plans to screen a videotape Wally had lent me of a Japanese guy challenging a grizzly bear to a hot dog-eating contest. I drop the newspaper and get up off the floor to see what the racket is.

A committee somewhere has declared Sleepy Hollow to be Tree City USA, and I live on what can only be described as Tree Street USA. Towering oaks, gray birches, and elms ring our property. At the edge of the yard, near the wood fence demarcating what we own from what the Hansons own, stand two life-size cardboard cutouts, sparkling in the gathering dusk. One is a picture of Elissa. She is smiling. The other is me. A photo taken two years ago. I am in my college graduation gown. I am not smiling. These giant photographs are remnants from Chip's twenty-seventh birthday party. He insisted on having one made for all of us. Even our grandmother.

The sound of paintballs and compressed carbon dioxide ripples out again and I see a splatter of green explode across the crotch of my cardboard cutout.

When we moved here fourteen years ago the entire house was blue. Every room a different shade. The stairs covered in blue carpet. The garage stood in teal glory. The wood siding an enchanting cerulean. The banisters were robin's egg. All the toilets: periwinkle. Now only the downstairs bathroom and the garage remain blue. My room had been the cats' room. Ms. Schaffer, the old lady who lived here before us, had a dozen cats and she let them pee everywhere. To this day we have not been able to get rid of the smell from all that cat urine.

I walk into my brother's bedroom and find him and our father giggling, leaning out an open window firing paintball guns down into the backyard.

"I have got to get out of this house," I say.

"You and me both," my father says.

"You've got paint in your mustache," I say, pointing.

"Did I get it?" he asks, rubbing his face with his free hand.

"I thought you two were going to the grocery store," I say.

"We don't take orders from your mother anymore," our father says. "Plus, this is therapeutic for me."

"Who told you that?"

"I told myself," he says, cinching the belt on his bathrobe tighter. I turn to my brother.

"Can you please throw those things away?" I ask, indicating the cutouts. "It's eerie."

"We have to keep them. For nostalgia. We'll look back at these times and laugh," Chip says. "Don't worry, I'll clean them," he adds.

"You're too kind," I say.

Chip fires another volley of paintballs. His cell phone is on the bed and suddenly it comes to life, emitting an electronic squeal that sounds like a monkey wielding a machine gun through static distortion. He has one of those phones with a built-in walkie-talkie feature. I don't know what people call this feature because I've never bothered to find out. But I do know that it enables my brother to be in constant contact with the Algonquin Round Table of intellectuals he calls friends. This phone, or at least the walkie-talkie part of it, makes a harsh, fuzzy squelch every time it's activated. It is the bane of my existence. One of the banes anyway.

"What is the point of that goddamn phone? Why do you need to be able to walkie-talkie people?"

"What phone?" he asks. A gold chain around his neck reads "Gangsta."

"Can you not act like a complete shithead?"

"I resent that," he says. "Have you taken a shower recently?" he asks, changing the subject.

"I'm talking about the phone. The annoying phone," I say, but I check my armpits anyway.

My father closes one of his eyes and aims. He fires. I see my cutout head turn green.

"I need to take at least two showers a day," Chip goes on.

"When I get up in the morning. Definitely when I get back from the gym, and usually I take one before bed."

"I'm well aware of your two-hour, prebed beauty process."

"Have you noticed how much our family sweats?" he asks me. Our father nods in agreement. "Have you seen Dad after he's been on the treadmill? Or Mom when she carries in the groceries?"

"Mom sweats carrying in the groceries because you never help her."

He stops for a minute to take off the wife beater he's wearing. "They're not my groceries."

"You eat them," I say.

"Touché." He turns away from me at this point and examines his neck muscles in the mirror, scrunching his face up in a ridiculous way designed, I imagine, to impressively flex certain muscles. I study him. As usual, I am at a complete loss. For the moment, he has forgotten about the cell phone, about showers and sweating. He turns to face me and flexes again, pivoting on one knee, holding his arms in an S shape. I can't help but smile.

"Look at this!" he calls out. "Look at this!" He strains to bring up the bulges of his arms and back, to justify all the time he spends at the gym. "Dad and I are going to loosen up and listen to some dance music," he says. "You should unwind with us."

"I hate that fucking phone," I say. I leave the room.

I'm not even two steps away when the music begins to blast, rattling the light fixtures in the hallway.

• • •

THE TRUTH IS, I don't help with the groceries either.

She's in the kitchen. At the table.

Like me, she's plagued by bills, by thoughts of *How much is left?* and *Can we make this work?*

An accordion file has exploded its contents around her. She looks small, engulfed in all that paper. Her hand on her forehead, her reading glasses at the edge of her nose.

I take a glass out of the cupboard and fill it with orange juice to the point where even one more drop will cause an overflow. I waddle over to the table, careful not to spill. I sit sipping loudly. No hands. I just lean into it. Maybe now is the right time to ask her about Pam Kittredge.

"When taking care of your father finally kills me," my mother says, "you can save money on a coffin. Just wrap me in all this bullshit." She pushes a stack of what looks like hospital bills out of her way.

"It's grim," I say.

"You have no idea." A little laugh gives way to the water-works. I'm used to it by now. He cries during *Law & Order*, she cries crunching the numbers.

"Mom."

"I'm fine."

"You sure?"

"Not even a little bit."

"Have you been house hunting?" I say, surprised at my own bluntness.

She picks up her head to look at me and I feel like a child. Why did I pour so much orange juice?

"Why are you asking me that?" she says.

"I need to move out," I say.

"Oh God, Calvin." She stands. "Don't start." She leaves the bills and goes to the cabinet where all of his prescription bottles are housed in a large wicker bread basket. She begins to organize tomorrow's doses. "Between your brother's overcompensating. Your sister acting like your sister. And your father"—here she pauses—"painting this house with the brush of depression, I cannot deal. There's no money for you. The money is running out for all of us."

"Mom."

"I see the future. It's me, here, alone. With him. And it won't be him that dies. He'll be fine. He'll live. It'll be me that dies. It'll be me the cancer kills."

"Mom, this isn't the conversation I wanted to have," I say. "I'm not his wife."

"You're not," she says.

"The woman showed me some apartments," I say. "She said she'd taken you to look at houses."

She is crying again. Opening bottles and crying. Dropping pills into little plastic cases and crying. Her back to me.

"Six months at forty percent. And every doctor in that goddamn city ordering more tests and different drugs. I've fallen behind."

"What does that mean?"

"On our mortgage payments."

"How far behind?" I ask.

"It's bad."

"Have you missed a payment?"

"Not yet," she says. "But if he doesn't go back to work or if something doesn't change, it's in foreclosure before the end of the year."

"You're joking," I say, but then she is looking at me and I know. She wipes her nose, and as quickly as she started crying, she stops. The anger flickers across her face and is gone. She takes the pill cases and puts them on top of the fridge. Morning, lunch, dinner, bedtime. The cycle of his days.

I dump the rest of my orange juice into the sink and stand looking out the window at the garage. She comes back to the table, to the papers.

"Who else knows?" I ask.

"Chip knows a little," she says. "Don't say anything yet," she adds. "I was getting ready to tell everyone anyway. It's not like anything's set in stone. I'm just trying to keep every base covered."

Part of me wants to run to the hatchback and drive. Pick up Wally, get high, listen to music, and just drive.

I GO TO my bedroom. I open the notebook. I write:

*I had a parakeet when I was in the eighth grade. He was a small blue-feathered thing, a smattering of black spots around his chest.*

*I forget exactly how I acquired the bird. I think it was a birthday present or something. At the time, I was really into reading fantasy novels. The Dragonlance series was my all-time favorite. Epic tales about elves and wizards battling dragons and the forces of evil, nonsense like that. I recently encountered a dusty copy of one of those books while looking for some records in the attic and reread the first few pages. I cringed and tried to convince myself that reading Drag- onlance was not the sole reason I remained a virgin until nineteen.*

*When I got the parakeet I immediately gave it the name Tanis. Tanis was one of the main characters in the Dragonlance saga. He was half-elf, which meant of course his mother had been an elf, his father a human (or maybe it was the other way around). Their passionate union had created Tanis: half-elf, half-man. The tragic nature of Tanis's existence lay in the fact that he was a bastard. He was alone. Accepted by neither mankind nor elfkind. An outsider forever. I identified with him. Not the bastard part, the outsider part. We kept Tanis in a corner of the living room. My grandmother on my mother's side, the only grandparent I have who's still alive, cared for him.*

*"Tanis?" she asked, dumping a handful of sunflower seeds into the parakeet's cage. "What kind of a name is Tanis?"*

*"He was a great warrior," I explained. "But he had trouble finding true love."*

*"That's no name for a little bird," my grandmother said, frowning, rattling Tanis's cage with her finger. "A little cute birdie like this. I'll call him Pretty Boy. Won't I, Pretty Boy?"*

*She nodded her head and whistled a song to Tanis.*

*The bird chirped and bounced around on its perch.*

*"I don't think Tanis likes being called Pretty Boy," I said.*

*"Nonsense," my grandmother said.*

*From then on she called Tanis Pretty Boy. I tried to get her to stop, but it was no use. She spent so much time with the bird, feeding him, washing his cage, changing the newspaper when he crapped all over it. She talked to him like you talk to a baby. "Hellooooo, Pretty Boy," she'd say in this insane high-pitched voice. "How is my little Pretty Boy today?" The bird would peep and explode shit onto the Arts and Leisure section. "That's right! Little Pretty Boy is hungry, isn't he?" And so forth.*

*Rather quickly I lost interest in Tanis Half-Elven. I had other things to worry about. Pornography was rapidly becoming my favorite activity.*

*One day I came home from school and found Tanis at the bottom of his cage. He had died. There was mottling on his head and the majority of his feathers had fallen out. Some rare disease, my parents speculated.*

*My grandmother wept for the bird. I feigned grief and gave her a big hug. I buried Tanis in the backyard, under the big oak tree we have out there. I said a few words because it was my understanding that when a pet died you were supposed to say a few words. My little sister, seven at the time, helped dig the hole.*

*"So long, Tanis," I said. Elissa stood beside me holding the shovel. "Your namesake led a confused life, uncertain of who he was, where he belonged. You did, too. Some called you Tanis. Some called you Pretty Boy. There wasn't enough time for you to let us know which one you liked better."*

*My parents must've thought I was really upset about the bird croaking, because not long after, I found another parakeet living in Tanis's cage. My grandmother whistled and fed the new bird little pieces of lettuce, made faces like she was trying to communicate with it telepathically.*

*"You're a lucky bird," she shrieked. "That's right. A very lucky bird indeed. What should we call our new friend?"*

*"Tanis Two?" I suggested. It didn't matter.*

*"Ugh," my grandmother said. "No. That won't do at all."*

*She whistled a song and the bird cheeped its head off.*

*"We'll call him Lucky Boy," she exclaimed suddenly, as if a lightbulb had screwed itself into her brain.*

*"Why is he so lucky?"*

*"Because Pretty Boy got sick and passed away," my grandmother said solemnly. "But Lucky Boy will live a long, healthy life."*

*I rolled my eyes, went upstairs to the computer.*

*A few weeks went by and Lucky Boy's feathers started to fall out. It wasn't long before I dug a second hole under the oak tree and said a few words for him.*

*Ten years later, when I learned my father had cancer, I cried. It was on a ramp leading down into the Quik park on Seventy-First, near the building where we'd waited for the MRI results. I leaned against a wall and wept. People walking by slowed to look at me. I took my sunglasses off, wiped my eyes. Chip stood a few feet away, pretending to be waiting for the attendant.*

*My father was up on the sidewalk. I could see his outline against the sun. Once, he had traveled to Cambodia and gone in a canoe up the Mekong River. Once, he had built our deck with his bare hands.*

The next day at work I am in a better mood because it is Friday. We are almost officially on vacation. During story time I sit on a child-size stool and read to a group of retards about a little bird born with only one wing. Broken Bird, he is called, and he is shunned by his friends and family. He flees to the city to live a life of depressed solitude. He meets another bird there that has also been cursed with only one wing. He thought he was the only one. She thought she was the only one. They fall in love and have normal birds as offspring. As I read, Tyrone, a four-year-old with Asperger's syndrome, gets sick and throws up on Arham.

# ≪ 5 ≫

Wally and I have gotten hold of some Vicodin.

David Liebman, our friend, our suburban compatriot, our fellow immature, slacking BA holder, has to have knee surgery. Doctors remove cartilage from one of his legs, put it in a culture, grow it, skillfully implant it in his other leg. Afterward he is required to lie around on the couch for weeks, self-medicating and doing various leg stretches. He is issued this bizarre contraption: the Painease 5000, a lattice of flexible bracing mounted on a motorized plastic frame. It straps to his leg, sprockets and cogs meshing together, forcing his knee to slowly bend, slowly release, slowly bend, slowly release, ad nauseam. To complicate matters further, his parents have foolishly planned a vacation for the week immediately following David's voyage under the scalpel. Isaac and Joan, a psychiatrist and divorce lawyer respectively, deem Wally and me responsible enough to care for David in their absence, to aid in his recovery. His father has procured copious amber pill bottles in David's name to keep his pain at bay.

"I've spoken to the Futtermans across the street," Isaac tells us. "They said you're welcome to use their shower. It has a bench, so David won't have to stand."

We are sprawled on the floor, not paying attention, engrossed in a History Channel piece connecting Nazi Germany to the rise of Saddam Hussein. It is a Tuesday.

"The numbers where we'll be are on the fridge," Joan says. "Oh, and you can always call Grandma Emmy in Peekskill. In case there's an emergency."

"David?" Isaac asks. "Are you listening to us?"

"Yeah, Dad," David says, but it's hard to hear over the sound of the TV. Rommel is racing tanks across North Africa. Then they are gone.

The Painease 5000 whirs and groans, leeched to David's leg like a robotic parasite, his knee flexing and unflexing at an excruciatingly slow pace.

"Does it hurt?" I ask him.

"Only if I stop taking the pills," he says, his eyes fluttering with sleep.

"Which ones?"

"Any of them," he says with a gesture like he is waving good-bye to the room. His mouth hangs open and his breathing eases. He drifts off.

I gather up the bottles that are scattered across the rug and read the labels one by one, nodding with satisfaction. I arrange them in a line like little pain-relieving soldiers. I imagine myself as a pharmacist, doling out pills to people in agony, people in need. I imagine myself working in a medevac tent during World War II. I am in charge of medicating recent amputees, keeping them cognizant, keeping them pain-free. Or better yet, I am in charge of selecting who becomes an amputee. Which limbs are too far gone.

"I'd make a good pharmacist," I say aloud to no one.

"I'd make a good tail gunner," Wally says, his hands grasping imaginary guns. He makes cannon noises with his mouth. On television, a man in a well-tailored suit stands in front of a wall-size map of Iraq.

"According to biographers, Saddam never forgot the tensions within the first Baathist government," he says, his accent thick, British. He knows things we don't.

Wally and I last about fifteen minutes. We tire of the television, the drab curtains David's mother has chosen to match the upholstery, the ticking of the grandfather clock. I sneak a bottle into my pocket. We leave.

It doesn't take long for the pills to kick in. The Vicodin is a gateway to a strange world where everything slows, gears down, and we hear things no one else can. We walk through the strip mall, travelers lost in a beautiful dream, giddy and elated, though we don't know why. There is an air of superiority in our movements. I am somehow immune to the problems of the working world. I am above it all. I don't have to deal with my family's issues. Anyone's issues. It is spring break. I have the week off. We go to Carvel, eat ice cream out of waffle cones, and imagine the girls behind the counter want our phone numbers.

I ask Wally to drive. He has blond hair, blue eyes. He is of Polish descent. Since his graduation from a similar small northeastern liberal arts college, he has staunchly refused to seek employment. His parents pay his loans. He mooches drugs off everyone and is, all in all, heading down a much darker path than me. He seems to never think about the future. I tend to think of nothing but.

The hatchback bounces along Route 9. We shoot over the Tappan Zee toward Nyack, heading for Harriman State Park. We seem to be traveling at a gingerly pace, as if Wally wants to capture every detail of highway asphalt passing beneath us.

"There're a lot of hawks in the sky today," I say, pressing a finger to the window, tilting my head back. "It's unsettling."

They circle above the car like dive-bombers, darting and swooping from the limbs of trees, avian acrobats swimming through air. I am convinced they are just biding their time, hatching a plot to attack us. I study the trees, trying to get a jump on the birds.

"I'll get the jump on these birds," I say, reassuring Wally. "You just get us to the woods. I'll worry about the birds."

"I'm not worried about the birds," Wally says.

Then my mood shifts completely. I feel joyous, bubbly. I'm not so much concerned with sinister birds. I reevaluate the trees. I look for myself in their boughs, search for humanity in those myriad leaves. As if I might discover the components of human emotion.

We park near some other cars, half in a ditch, half on the street. Traipsing over fallen trees and boulders, we follow a broken path to the center of a large limestone outcropping overlooking the lake. I collect five rocks and throw them, one by one, into the black water. I look at my face in the ripples.

"This is the best Tuesday of my life," Wally says to no one.

I sit. I lean back. I watch the wind tear across the lake. Far away, on the other side, I think I can see a cave.

By a complete stroke of grand luck, whimsy, we encounter Doug M. and his troop of live-action role players: a bunch of guys who obsess over Dungeons & Dragons and use terms like "gem mint condition." We know they are worse off than we are. Bigger losers than Wally or I can ever hope to be. While we have temporarily retrograded back to our high school selves, they will stay this way forever. It is comforting to be around them sometimes.

"Oh," Wally says. He is beaming, stumbling awkwardly to his feet, clutching a shrub for support. "The LARPers are here. Look at them." He is bursting with emotion.

I swivel on my limestone seat and feel it, too. I am speechless.

A dozen men, boys, young adults, creep from behind bushes, appearing amid the foliage where seconds earlier they had not been. Dressed in chain mail hauberks, horned Viking helmets, fur loincloths, velvety cloaks adorned with crescent moons, monk robes. They carry battle-axes, bludgeons, quarterstaffs, weighty sabers, morning stars, lances, rondels. It is magnificent to behold. They speak like kings to each other. They are kings. They sparkle. They are no longer the losers I so frequently dub them.

As Wally and I look on, the warriors split into two distinct groups and square off, hesitantly waving their weapons in the air. They eye each other with fierce delight. I am not exactly sure what is happening, but it is clear a battle is taking shape before us.

"Quickly, or I'll be forced to annihilate you all!" I hear one of them yell: an oversize collegiate with a Prince Valiant haircut and an enormous sword. He shouts with a fake accent, his voice ringing out above the wind. "Draw your blade. I can see in your eyes you have a warrior's strength!" he thunders.

Doug M., dressed like a knight, lifts the hinged visor on his rusty basinet and shouts back: "But not a warrior's courage!"

"Draw your blade!"

"Your father sent us here to rescue you," one of the wizards shrieks suddenly from a few paces behind everything. He steps forward. His staff has a red orb taped to the top of it. Clearly battery powered, it is blinking like a traffic light. "You are in the embassy of the royal city." His voice is high, effeminate, wizardly.

"I shall not draw my blade against the lord," Doug M. responds.

"Hey, Doug," Wally calls out. "You gonna be at that warehouse party tonight?"

"This is not real," the wizard warns, waving his staff. The orb jiggles, threatens to fall off.

"You'll draw your blade against all the lords of the White City!" Prince Valiant says. His minions jitter at his side, waiting for commands.

"If I must," the wizard says, "I will use my lightning-bolt spell."

"Coward!" someone yells out of nowhere. "Scum!"

"I am a priest of the light!" the wizard protests. His eyes are afraid. They dance from face to face. I have no sympathy for him.

"Draw your blade!" Prince Valiant says.

"No!" Doug M. yells. It doesn't matter.

Prince Valiant rushes forward, his mop of hair bouncing across his forehead.

"They draw against us," he screams. "Destroy them all!"

I gasp and try to step backward as the warriors clash. My body is so alive it can't move.

It all seems very real. Death is surely imminent, though the weapons make no sound as the warriors swat at each other.

"Kill the evil!" someone shouts.

"Ow, Julian! That hurt!"

"Suck it up, Kurt!"

"Kill the evil!"

"Run away!"

"Attack!"

The dialogue disintegrates into a jumbled mess of screams and laughter and indecipherable gibberish. The wizard prances about, calling out, "Lightning bolt. Lightning bolt." The only ones who seem to stay in character are Prince Valiant and Doug M.

I turn to Wally. His eyes are wide, flat stones.

"As far as I can tell," I say, holding a finger up, "Doug M. is some kind of king and he's trying to protect that lady from those elves over there that want to take her captive."

"I don't see any lady," Wally says, squinting in the sunlight.

"She's there," I say. "Her name is Gretchen or Gretel or something. I saw her once at the public pool. She'd fallen on the pavement outside the snack shack and there was a hole in her head."

"Is she attractive?" Wally questions, his voice arcing out over the lake behind us. I can almost see the words.

"I don't know," I say. "She wears a hat to cover the hole."
I never understood this hat. Why cover the one thing that
makes you unique? Webbed feet? A cause for celebration.
Giant ears? Beautiful. A lazy eye that wanders and travels
along its own lines of vision? Something to be proud of. Six
fingers. Auxiliary nipples. Wally and I lack that sort of defin-
ing characteristic. Our faces are blandish, nebbishy, stand-
offish, a thousand "ishes" that keep us in the background,
blurred. Our bodies are forgettable. We go to parties and the
next day no one can remember having seen us there.

The battle ends just as it began. The role-playing knights,
the kings and wizards, mages and peasant farmers, the Vi-
kings, the noblemen, retreat into the woods, following paths
to their parents' cars. They drive off in tandem, a funeral
procession back to whatever painful realities await them. I
hear catcalls, hooting, hollering. Someone wants to know
where the "mead celebration" will be taking place. Wally
and I nod to each other as the sun dips below the trees.

## ≪ 6 ≫

We have time to kill before the party, so Wally and I swing by David's to make sure he's still breathing. We find him right where we left him, splayed out on the couch in what appears at first glance to be a coma, watching a documentary on the cosmos, entitled *Cosmos*.

"I've seen this," I tell him. "Carl Sagan narrates. It's thirteen hours long."

"Everything's been seen before by someone," David says, narrowing his eyes to little slits so he can scrutinize our faces.

"What does that mean?" Wally asks.

"Don't listen to me. I'm very emotional right now."

"Is it the pain?" I ask. "Are you medicating?"

"Do you need anything?" Wally asks.

"It's the pain, isn't it?" I ask. "We've had an exhilarating day."

"I could use some water," David says. "It takes me forever to get to the kitchen on my own."

"Okay, great," Wally says. "Water. Got it. Great. Coming right up."

The Vicodin torpor has worn off at this point. My limbs have come back to me, intact. Wally returns with a glass.

"Should we stay with him?"

I watch as a meteor hurls through space and collides with another meteor.

"He'll be fine," I say.

I pilot the hatchback to 7-Eleven for the purchasing of beers. We arrive at the warehouse just after nightfall. Part of an eerie industrial park. Abandoned and unused, seated behind the railroad tracks on the outskirts of Oscawana. I don't know what adventurous soul first discovered the spot, but over time it has become a regular destination for mischievous denizens of the county. The place of choice for secret rendezvous, displaced college frat parties, meetings of clandestine organizations, unbridled romantic exploration. For many, it is the wellspring of regret. Wally and I often waste idle daylight hours here smoking weed and wandering around, climbing the dilapidated infrastructure and breaking windowpanes. It was here I took Patti Reynolds behind a gravel pile one summer during college. I put my hand down her pants.

Cars are everywhere, parked at odd angles. Headlight beams crisscross, casting yellow light on the people, the dirt. Wally and I awkwardly make our way through the crowd. I bump into more than a few people. I recognize many faces from the woods. Where earlier they had been regal, inspiring even, now they are unremarkable. Only Doug M. retains any sort of glorious air. Wally and I join him. He is perched on the hood of his 1971 Chevy Nova, arms folded across his chest. Even though he no longer wears a basinet and his broadsword is now a pink wine cooler, he still looks kingly. A massive, rotund man with a wild crown of bushy hair. I imagine trumpet fanfare playing when he enters a room. Gretchen or Gretel or whatever her name is stands nearby, half lurking in the shadows, a baseball cap pulled down over her eyes.

"It's Hole in the Head," I whisper to Wally as we drop our six-pack into the cooler and exhume colder cans from the bottom.

"That was some battle today in the woods," Wally says.

"Yes, it was," Doug M. says. He finishes the last of his wine cooler in one sip and tosses the empty bottle over his shoulder with a casual elegance. "Gabby was almost slain," he says.

"Gabby," I say, her true name returning to me.

"What?" she says, stepping out of the shadows. She tilts her head back so her big eyes can peer right at us all. I see the sight of her visibly shakes Wally. Fear comes into his face.

"Nothing," I say quickly, stifling a laugh. I try to sip some beer and look natural. "I was just saying your name, is all."

"What about my name?" she asks.

"Take it easy," Doug M. tells her out of the side of his mouth.

"It's crowded tonight," Wally says.

"Baseball game over in Fishkill." Doug M. nods. "High school kids celebrating the victory."

"I saw you once," I say to Gabby. "At the public pool."

"You one of the ones who laughed?"

"I can't remember."

"Well, the joke's over."

"Clearly," I say.

"There is no joke," Wally adds. He kicks some dirt. "No joke at all."

"I gained enough experience points today to move up a level," Doug M. says, prying the cap off another wine cooler he produces from some hidden pocket in his clothing. "I'm a master swordsman now."

"I knew it," Wally says. "You looked very confident out there."

Gabby glares at me. I am filled with an urge to run away. Her eyes seem to pierce straight into my brain. I scan the nearby crowds, hoping for a familiar face, anyone I can rush off to say hello to, extricating myself from the current milieu.

I spot Elissa. She is standing with a group of angsty-looking teens.

"There's my sister," I say, seeing my escape.

I make my way over to the group of kids, who are huddled together like refugees. They are dressed darkly. Dark hooded sweatshirts, dark pants, boots. They talk with their heads down, eyes trained to the ground. They make no acknowledgment of my presence as I insert myself into their cluster. Only my sister stands out, wearing her standard garb: T-shirt with holes all over it, jeans, sneakers from Goodwill. She looks older than seventeen. She salutes when she sees me.

"You're not drinking?"

"Nah," she says. "Not tonight."

"What's with them?" I ask.

"These are my friends from after-school activity clubs. We're all in the Stratego Club, the Punk History Awareness Club, the Nihilism Club, and the Godard Is Overrated Club. They're upset because apparently two of them showed up to this week's Nihilism Club meeting, breaking a two-year streak of zero attendance."

"I was curious," one of these glum characters says.

"Cheer up, men," I tell them. "Is it that bad?" I finish my beer and hurl the bottle as far as I can into the gloomy expanse of the factory behind us. I wait to hear it shatter.

"Yes, it's that bad," another kid says. He looks thoroughly dejected. I have seen this look before. "It's put the whole club in a paradox. We shouldn't care enough to show up and we certainly shouldn't care enough to care that someone did show up."

"We're frauds," a third says. He is carefully pushing dirt into a pile with his boot tip.

"These guys are usually much more fun," Elissa says. Without really talking about it, we leave the circle of depressed nihilists and walk into a dark patch of shadow under a mass of toppled I beams. I notice, not far away, a bonfire is being lit. Old two-by-fours with rusty nails, tree branches, and broken crates. Planks of wet, graying wood pried off the warehouse windows, other assorted lumber, erected to form something like a funeral pyre, set ablaze by drunkards.

"Dad's a little off," Elissa says. Her face is lit up by flickering yellow and orange light.

"I'm pretty sure he's always been this way," I say, shaking

my head. "He just kept it under wraps. Now he's got an excuse to be as weird as he wants."

"He and Chip went cosmic bowling tonight."

"Since when did they start spending so much time together?"

"Chip says it's all part of the recovery process," Elissa says. Kids in leather baseball jackets are pumping their fists in the air, flailing their bodies around the fire. An improvised tribal ritual.

"They're all completely bonkers," I say. I shake my head.

"I realize this," Elissa tells me.

We both watch flames envelop wood. I see that Wally and Doug M. have crept toward the excitement and are lurking behind the celebration. They stare with delight, with wide grins. I know their thoughts: superiority and self-consciousness, amusement and horror, longing and repulsion.

"Dad wrote me a letter," I say. "He asked me to hold his hand if he dies."

"He's in a bad way."

"They both are."

"What can we do?"

"Save ourselves?" I ask. And seriously, I want to know if that's the answer.

"If I tell you something," Elissa asks, "can you keep it a secret?"

"I can try," I say, thinking perhaps she's already learned our mother might have to sell the house. Saves me having to break the news myself, even though I said I wouldn't.

But Elissa doesn't mention the house or bills or money.

She says, "I'm pregnant."

I stand waiting for the warm sensation of brains oozing out the side of my head. The jocks begin chanting, loudly, invoking some kind of higher power to grant them more home victories.

"What are you thinking?" she asks.

"I'm waiting for my brains to ooze out of my head."

"Be serious."

"I am being serious," I say. "That's heavy news."

"No shit it's heavy. I'm heavy."

"Not yet."

"I don't know what I should do."

"You're fucked."

"I realize this."

"He is going to flip."

"I realize this, Cal."

"Grandma will faint."

"I'm prepared for this. I'm prepared to place pillows behind her when I deliver the news."

"I see Mom crying."

"I have already bought a box of tissues."

"I can help you, if you need support, but only to a certain point. I'm not very good with these kinds of things."

"What kinds of things?"

"Life things. Important life things that have meaning, repercussions. Anything that involves talking to other people in a meaningful way. Any confrontation where feelings are concerned."

# ≪ 7 ≫

I come home to find my father has erected a geodesic shelter in the backyard. "It's not a tent." He was very clear about this distinction at the sporting goods store when I joined him on one of his first survival-related shopping sprees. "It's a geodesic shelter. I'm done with tents."

He is awake, sitting beneath the unzipped mouth of the tent, looking at the stars. His face is cast in shadow, but I can still see the lines where his mouth ends, the hard shape of his jowls. He has grown bony in his illness. His cheeks and nose and chin have sunken. In his forties, these features were swelling. His belly was on the move back then. His love handles. His whole body was expanding. Now, at fifty-four, his spine full of malignant plasma cells, he has become slight.

His medication causes mood swings. Bouts of uncontrolled sobbing come on without warning. Empty, draining depression followed by periods of manic goofiness. He says strange and puzzling things to the mailman. He laughs at inappropriate times during movies. He leaves letters on my bed. He draws unfounded parallels between himself and dead celebrities, such as Kurt Cobain.

My father is a pilot. His illness has grounded him. Having no professional responsibilities, he frets over inconsequential things. He obsesses about late fees at the video store. He gets angry when my mother fails to return from the supermarket with the correct beans for his survival bunker. He is afraid of death. He ponders the coming apocalypse. He waits for the darkening of the skies with a Zoloft in hand.

I approach his encampment.

"This is such a cry for attention," I tell him.

"I'm dying," he says, cupping his head in his hands. His voice rises the few bars preceding a whimper.

"You're not dying."

"Don't yell at me, all right?"

"I'm not yelling," I say. "Sooner or later, though, you're gonna have to shape up."

"Funny, coming from you," he says.

I sit near him. He has an emergency blanket wrapped across his shoulders. His head shines in the moonlight. It is a nice night. The houses around us are dark. People are asleep in their beds. Our neighbors do not worry about things while they sleep. I am convinced of this.

"Your sister's not home yet," my father says.

"I guess not."

He clicks a flashlight on, pointing it directly in my face before placing it in the grass, aimed at the sky, a miniature searchlight.

"The world's ending," he says. He pulls the .45 out of his pajama pocket and holds it over the light, turning it, cradling it in his fragile hands. "It won't be long before they're executing people on public television."

"I think we've got a while before they're executing people on public television."

"I can feel it coming," he says.

"Your brain isn't working properly," I say.

"Five years. Maybe eight, if we're lucky, but I doubt it."

"Promise me you won't think about it too much. It's not good for your depression."

"Okay."

"Okay, what?"

"Okay, I won't think about it too much."

"Everything's gonna be fine," I say. "I swear."

"If I can't go back to work," he says, "if they won't let me fly, nothing's going to be fine."

If my mother has kept him in the dark about the state of their finances, then I don't want to talk about the house. I don't want to talk about the money. And if he knows? If he's already woven possibly losing his house into his web of depression? I still don't want to talk about the money.

"How was bowling?" I ask.

"Bowling was bowling," he says. "It cost sixty dollars, I didn't break a hundred and fell down three times."

"At least you're out doing something."

"God help us," he moans.

"What are you upset about?"

"The transplant," he says.

"It's okay to be nervous about it," I tell him. "I'm nervous. But it will be fine."

"If it doesn't work . . ."

"The doctors know what they're doing."

"They don't have a fucking clue," he says. "And afterward I'll never pass a stress test. The FAA won't give me back my clearance. The money will run out. Your mother's a fool."

"Mom's not as naive as you think, Dad," I say. "She's pretty much spearheading the fight to keep everything from falling apart."

"Everything *will* fall apart."

"Try not to be so negative."

"Wanna hold it?" my father says, offering up the gun.

I take it from him. Feel its weight.

I look up. I see a few stars and the blinking lights of a plane heading toward La Guardia or JFK.

"Falcon Nine Hundred. Three engines," he says absent-mindedly. My father loves to do this, identify aircraft as they streak across the sky. I hear the crack in his voice and then he begins. A low wail, quiet, like a child.

"Give me a break, Dad," I say. He cocks his head to look at me through his hands. I set the gun down in the grass. "You're not going to die. Okay? You have to stop telling yourself you are. Suck it up. Things could be worse. At least we're all together."

"You hate it here," he says.

"Sometimes it isn't so bad."

"It's pretty bad," he says.

"You aren't alone," I say. "You won't be alone."

"Be there when I die, okay?"

"Come on, Dad. Don't talk like that. It's not gonna be anytime soon, but of course I will."

Footsteps near the house. I swing the flashlight around and freeze Elissa where she stands, key in door.

"Get that light out of my face." I lower the beam, and in the darkness she says, "What are you idiots doing out here?"

ONCE AGAIN IT is morning and I decide to skip the whole showering thing. A vacationer is entitled to a certain smell, a conscious rejection of hygiene to differentiate these idle days from those working days.

Wally and I consume what's left of the Vicodin. We pilfer David's weed stash (kept in a plastic jar at the back of his sock drawer). We laze about, pretending to keep him company. He occupies the whole couch, reclining in knee-recovery position: on his back, pillows supporting all appendages, dressed only in underwear, empty beer cans, the scars on his knees like zippers. He has already abandoned his flexing exercises. The Painease 5000 is nowhere to be seen. I flip through channels until I discover *The Texas Chainsaw Massacre 2*.

"The mind is a powerful agent of recovery," David announces amid the haze of smoke.

"I'm not acknowledging your presence until you put some pants on," Wally says.

"This is my house," David says.

"This is your parents' house," I say.

"They're not here," David says.

"Still," Wally says.

"Still," David says. "Do you know how long it takes me to hobble to my room? Show me pants and I'll wear them."

"Later," Wally says.

"What happened to the Painease Five Thousand?" I ask.

"Got rid of it," David says.

"You threw it out?" Wally says, aghast. "It's for your own good, man."

"It's behind the couch," David says. "I'm using my mind from now on as the primary instrument of my recovery."

"You're supposed to be flexing that leg," I say. "We're in charge."

"I'm flexing my mind," David says. "If the mind is strong, the rest will take care of itself."

"I give up on you," I say.

"As soon as I get better I'm going to order some salvia," David says.

"Count me in," Wally says.

I turn my attention to the television. My face has gone slack and it's getting hard to focus on any one thing in the room without everything going blurry. I find squinting helps. Leatherface tears the roof off a car and severs the top of the driver's head. An eruption of blood follows.

"I worship this movie," I say.

"I'm nauseous," Wally says.

I sit up, or rather, very slowly I force myself into something resembling a seated position.

"What's gonna happen to us?" I ask.

"In what context?" David asks.

"In the context of life," I say. "A year from now I'll be twenty-five. My father got *married* when he was twenty-five. He bought a *house*. I have nothing to show for it."

"We don't want those things," Wally says.

"*You* don't," I say.

"You *do*?"

"Perhaps you're jealous of your own father?" David asks.

"I'm not," I say. "That's not the point."

There comes a part where Leatherface is literally carving someone into sausage.

"It feels like there's a fog drifting through my brain right now," David says.

"Doesn't it ever scare you to think what it's gonna be like in, say, ten years?" I ask.

"Never," Wally says.

"I'll most likely be dead in ten years," David says.

"I'm asking seriously," I say. "This little club we have here. Is this it?"

"Do you want more?" Wally asks, pushing at the air in front of his face with his fingers. He doesn't like talking about this kind of stuff.

"I just don't want to be *here*."

"Thanks," David says.

"I don't mind," Wally says.

"But when does *this* end?" I say. "And *how*?"

"It doesn't," Wally says.

"Maybe we need to grow up," I say. "At least a little. Maybe it isn't all about us."

"If you haven't already made the leap into the world where responsible people live," Wally says, "you never will."

"I could grow up whenever I want. I could stop all this at any time," I say. "I have complete control."

"You control nothing," Wally says.

"I could become an adult. Really move into adulthood. If

I decided to, I could help my family with the *real* problems they have. My sister is having a *baby* and I'm pretty sure she wants to keep it. My father is convinced this cancer is going to kill him. My mother claims she can't keep paying the mortgage on our house. Those are tangible, real-world problems. Problems I might be able to be a part of solving. Or at least try."

"I wouldn't," Wally says.

"Just like that, you'd turn away from your family?" David asks.

"If it meant keeping my sanity," Wally says.

"Maybe I'm supposed to be in that house," I say. "Maybe I'm the catalyst for change. For love. I can love them all. Love everyone."

"That's the pills talking," Wally says.

"It's not just that. I'm torn," I say. "It's an existential dilemma of the soul."

"Fuck it," Wally says.

"Be that person," David says. "If that's what you want. Help them. However you can."

"I just might," I say.

ACROSS THE DINNER table, I watch Elissa. Waiting for her to slip. To let some revealing nugget about her preggo status out of the bag. She lets me down by talking for what seems like hours about the awful state of the country's current presidential administration.

"You liberals," Chip says, his usual dismissal to anything my sister or I have to say about politics.

Chip clears the plates by himself—so helpful. Our mother

extracts a tray of freshly baked brownies from the oven. She sets them in the middle of the table, along with a tub of vanilla ice cream and hot fudge.

"Oh, no," our father moans.

"Not tonight, Mom," I say.

"You guessed it," she says. "Family meeting."

"Do we have to?" Elissa asks, looking slightly worried.

"It's mandatory."

As soon as everyone has heaped brownie sundae into bowls, my mother commences.

"I don't really know how to bring this up, so I'm just going to put it out there. Calvin already knows part of it." My heart beats faster, thinking perhaps she knows about Elissa and it's all over with, but instead she talks about the house. "I met with a real estate broker last week," she tells us all.

"Why?" Elissa asks.

Chip is devouring his sundae.

"Because if things keep going the way they're going," our mother says, "the bank is going to foreclose on this house."

"I knew it," our father says. His ice cream is melting in the bowl. He hasn't touched it. "Kathy, I told you. It's all over with. We're gonna wind up on the street."

He thumps his forehead onto the table and keeps it there.

"Don't overreact, Jim," our mother says.

"You said you had it all under control," he says to the floor.

"I did," she says. "I do. But the medical bills are piling up. Plus credit cards, taxes, food. Everything."

"How long have you kept this from me?" he asks.

"If I had told you two months ago, would it have mattered?" she asks. "You wouldn't be sitting here in your bathrobe?"

"Well, what are you saying?" our father asks.

"You don't seem to want to get better," she says.

"I have cancer," he says.

"Treatable cancer," she says. "They all say you have a good chance. That's all we keep hearing."

"How bad is the mortgage?" is all he says.

"If we default, it doesn't mean we're destitute," she says.

"What about the money I've given you?" Chip asks.

"What money?" I ask. This is news to me.

"Your brother's doing well at his job," our mother says. "He's been helping out a little with the bills."

"More than a little," Chip says, finishing his dessert.

"Since when?" I ask.

"For a while," our mother says. "And I really appreciate what Chip is doing, but it might not be enough in the end."

"And everyone laughed when I put all that rice in the garage," our father says.

"We're still laughing," I say.

"It won't be so funny when we're living off it," he says.

"We can't just give up," Elissa says.

"No one's giving up, sweetie," our mother says. "We need to regroup, is all. Figure out a way to stay together."

"Calvin doesn't care," Chip says. "He'd be happy if the house went down."

"That isn't true," I say. "All I ever said was we can't all live here forever. It isn't normal."

"You talk a lot," Chip says, "but I'm the only one throwing in most of my salary to help keep everyone together. In this house, I'm the selfless one."

"What would you like me to do?"

"Your brother doesn't want you to do anything," our mother says.

"I have nothing to give," I say.

"I'm sure you have something squirreled away," Chip says. I shoot him what in my mind is the most withering glance I can muster.

"I might need that money," I say.

"For what?" he asks.

"Stop now," our father says.

"No one is asking you for anything, Calvin," our mother says. "I don't expect anything. I just think everyone needs to be aware of what's going on around here. This affects all of us."

"Yeah, it does," Elissa says. "What's gonna happen to us if we can't keep the house?"

"We'll figure something out," our mother says.

"Oh God," our father moans, finally lifting his head off the table.

"It's not just us," Elissa continues. "What if there were . . ." She trails off.

*Don't break it to them now,* I think. And she must be thinking the same thing because she doesn't say anything else.

In the silence, our father reaches out a shaky hand. His spoon clinks in the bowl. He scoops some melted ice cream into his mouth.

THE SEESAW GOES up and down. Flashes of inspiration and hopefulness are trailed by groundswells of bleak anxiety. In my notebook I try to write out some bizarro version of Moretti life. In some other house. Where everyone is healthy and in good spirits and no one carries firearms or forgets to wear a condom. Life isn't so bad in the notebook because I can mete out whatever fate I deem appropriate for all of us.

My week of vacation rolls on. Days go by like tiny windows of color. Flowering, brilliant, florid peaks of productivity and inspiration. I take up my guitar, dream of writing pensive ballads to magically disintegrate girls' pants. I pick five novels off the shelf and lay them on the floor. Famous, grand works of literature's fine, storied past.

*I will read all of these this month,* I tell myself.

Then come the death-defying spells of lethargy. Couches, sitcom reruns, junk food. I indulge in seventies horror films. I write the films in my notebook, date the entries. I make phone calls to see who has drugs. I visit friends. I accompany my grandmother to the grocery store.

# ≪ 8 ≫

On the way, I get into a debate with her about technology. It begins when I turn on the radio and start flipping stations.

"Don't fool with that," my grandmother says, swatting at my hand. "I have it just the way I want it."

We are heading down Route 9 through the picturesque commercial district of Tarrytown, which takes all of three minutes.

"I'm not fooling with anything," I say.

"You're fooling with my radio player," she says. "It took Grandma a very long time to find those songs."

"Do you have any idea how a radio works?" I ask. "Even the vaguest concept?" She doesn't answer. "You hit the button until it goes to the station you want. See, look, 88.5, that's the one you like. It's right here, it's not going anywhere."

I've had this argument with her before. She believes once you tune in a frequency on the radio, you have to leave it there forever.

"This is my car," she says, getting frustrated. "Turn the

radio off now, you're making Grandma upset. That crazy music of yours."

"Fine," I say. I turn off the radio. The Hudson River rolls by. I catch glimpses of it down side streets. The Palisades yawn on the far side of the water. I lean my head against the window. The doctors have told us Dad has a 68 percent chance of successfully getting the cancer into remission, but before that can happen he must undergo a painful stem cell transplant, which entails not only the procedure but three weeks of isolation. He is not looking forward to it. I don't like the thought of losing him. I wish I had said something to him about the letter he wrote me. I promise myself I'll bring it up, but I know I never will. I try to think about what Elissa's baby might look like, which is hard, considering I have no idea who the father is. Regardless of that piece of the puzzle, perhaps there's a chance it will defy the paternal traits of our family and embrace those of our mother: Fine blond hair. Soft features. Blue eyes.

I lift my head and look at the smudge of grease I've left on the glass. I push the button that raises the back of my seat to get a better view of tedious suburbia, restored Victorian houses.

"Will you stop fooling with everything," my grandmother says. "You're going to break it."

"Oy," I say. "This is painful."

"We're not Jewish," she says. "Just sit still, we're almost there."

She turns her attention back to driving. She narrows her eyes into little slits and scrunches up her nose.

"What are you doing?" I ask.

"Squinting," she says. "I'm having trouble seeing the lines."

"Should you even be driving?" I say, raising my eyebrows and sitting up, more attentive now. "Where are your glasses?"

"I left them at home." She is hunched forward, clutching the steering wheel with all her might.

"I'll drive back," I say. "Jesus."

"Watch it," my grandmother says. "He hears you."

I LIKE SUPERMARKETS. I feel at home in supermarkets. It's strange because most of the time I dread being in public. I am not a fan of crowds. I sit in the back of movie theaters. I am awkward when placing orders at restaurants. I have a tendency to leave social gatherings abruptly, without saying good-bye to anyone. I lurk and slink in the shadows. I enjoy eavesdropping on strangers.

Supermarkets are anonymous. Neatly organized shelves, immediate access to brownie mix, powdered lemonade varieties and fruit juices, assortments of bread, guys behind the meat slicer, prepackaged taco kits, select cheeses, depressed lobsters, teenage checkout girls.

"You should eat more meat," my grandmothers says holding an entire turkey in her hands, turning it over and over like she's trying to roast it with her eyes.

"I eat fish," I say. "I like shrimp."

She frowns. "Where do you get your protein from? You need protein."

"What do you know about protein?" I ask.

"There was a wonderful article in *Reader's Digest*," she

says. She returns the turkey to its ranks among the other turkeys.

"*Reader's Digest* sucks," I tell her. "I'm gonna get some cookies."

"Tsss," my grandmother says, giving me a disapproving look. "There's certainly no protein in cookies," she adds.

"I'm not eatin' 'em for the protein," I say to her, but already I'm gone, around the corner, heading down the dessert aisle. I'm surrounded by colorful arrays of chocolate and sweets, granola bars and artificially preserved cakes, wafers and doughnuts. Everything wrapped in foil and plastic, sealed up to survive nuclear winter. I take my time selecting. Chocolate chip. Double chocolate chip. No chips. Fudge. Circle. Square. Oval.

I take a package of gingersnaps and stand there looking at it. I remember when Elissa was younger we used to sneak gingersnaps out of the jar and sit out back with glasses of milk. Elissa held the shovel. I wrapped Tanis in paper towel and laid him in the dirt. She helped me pack my records when I went off to Boston for grad school. She came with our mother to pick me up when I dropped out. She told me not to worry. She dances in front of her mirror. She twirls her hair around her fingers when she's nervous. She steeps two tea bags at once in her mug. She smiles and she cries and the telephone rings in the middle of the night. Caught with a can of spray paint. Caught stealing clothes. Caught doing something wild. The wild child—my sister. Officer at the door, understanding smile. "She's a wild one." Breaking curfew, lack of motivation at school, dirty clothes, but somehow always pulling it off. Always talking her way out of things, quelling our parents, making it impossible to get angry with her.

And if we lose the house? No one could say it was my fault. It's not like my pitching in $567.88 will have the bank walking away satisfied. Or is it something larger than that? The fear of responsibility? Immaturity rearing some heretofore unseen face? No, that face has been around for a while. She needs a safe place to have this baby, if she's going to have it. He needs a safe place to recover, if he recovers. How much are these gingersnaps anyway? Four dollars and sixty-eight cents. I stand and try to weigh the importance of things. The importance of living my own life versus the importance of doing the right thing, assuming I know what the right thing is. Maybe it's an easy decision, depending on how you look at it.

I'm surrounded by chocolate and cookies and frosting and flour sifters, rolling pins, the sugar and sugar substitutes. I feel everything flowing in strange, circular organization. Everything in life seems to converge here with the desserts. So much of me wants out of that house, away from it all. If I stay? Is it just a string of long nights at his bedside ahead? Holding his hand when he's going through a rough patch. Holding her hand in the delivery room. Holding all of their hands, shepherding them through their problems. Is that the right thing? I'd be no help in that regard anyway. The truth is I have no idea what I'm going to do. Even less of an idea about what's going to happen.

"YOU'RE TALKING CRAZY," Elissa says through a mouthful of strawberry ice cream. We're seated on the back porch, in lawn chairs. The sun is setting. Colors are everywhere.

"But don't you see?" I say. "If I keep living here, if I don't get out, where will it end? What stops it from turning into forever?"

Elissa looks down at the pint of ice cream in her hands and frowns. She puts it on the wrought-iron table, licks the spoon. I keep going.

"Chip thinks he's doing the right thing giving them money, and that's great, but he *likes* living here. He *likes* spending time with Dad."

"You like that, too," Elissa points out.

"You know what I mean."

"Where will you go?" she asks. She takes a stray lock of hair and curls it around and around. Her jeans are dirty.

"I don't know," I say. "I'm not even sure I should go any-where, that's what's getting to me."

"But where *would* you go?"

"Anywhere I can afford."

"Quite a plan," Elissa says.

"I was just starting to get some money saved up," I say. "And now all this."

"Feel like you'd be deserting us?"

"Sort of."

"You're here now, Calvin," my sister says.

"That's the problem," I tell her.

"You talk like it only affects you."

"You're seventeen, Elissa, it's fine for you to be here."

"At least you and Chip got through college. You see Mom and Dad shelling out for tuition now?"

"College?" I say.

"Why not?" she says.

"You're pregnant."

"After," she says.

"So you're keeping it?"

"I like to think I'm taking responsibility."

"The girl who intentionally misspelled her name on the SATs is all grown up?"

"Don't hassle me, okay?"

"You'll be the only freshman with a kid," I say.

"It doesn't matter now anyway," she says.

"So then what *are* you going to do?"

"I'm going to try my best to help them," she says. She says it spontaneously, without even thinking.

"Tell me how."

"I could get a job," she says.

"Back at Hot Topic?"

"I'm not working there. Ever again. Don't even mention it," Elissa says. I open my mouth to suggest something else. "Or Videorama," she says, beating me to it. "People who rent movies are weird."

Just off the deck, the kitchen window is open slightly. Our mother stands at the sink, starting to fix dinner. Directly behind Elissa and me, through glass sliding doors that lead to the family room, our father is asleep, sprawled across the sectional.

"I'm really worried about everything," Elissa says.

"When are you gonna tell them?" I ask.

Elissa stands, walks to look in on him. I join her. Together we watch the folds of his robe rise and fall with shallow breaths.

"I can't seem to bring myself to add more to this mess," she says.

"It is a mess," I say.

"I was thinking I should wait till after the transplant."

"That might not be such a bad idea," I tell her. I put my hand on her shoulder. I feel collarbone through T-shirt, fragile, delicate. As quickly as I do it, I regret the gesture and drop my hand.

"Are we gonna make it?" Elissa asks.

I think about the question for a long time and fight back some tears bubbling to the surface.

"I hope so," I say.

The screen door pops open and our grandmother is standing there. Her apron has an enormous lobster on it whose claws look like they are pinching her nipples.

"There's a letter for you, Cal," she says, waving an envelope.

## ≪ 9 ≫

I stand looking at the letter for a long time. It's postmarked only a few days ago.

I tear the thing open. Inside, printed on heavy, off-white card stock, is a formal invitation to Chris Hillman's wedding, to take place on September 23.

I think about the one time Chris got a boner in gym class. It was in eighth grade, during gymnastics week. Leaping onto the pommel horse. Falling from the pommel horse. Walking across the balance beam. Falling from the balance beam. Hanging limply off the still rings while Mr. Schizarro, the PE teacher, taunted us from the ground until we fell from the still rings.

The boner Chris Hillman got during those glorious floor exercises became something of a myth. It popped up in the middle of a tumbling exercise. Mr. Schizarro was kneeling next to the springboard, banging his hand on the blue mat, screaming at us to run toward him. When we hit the board and sailed into the air, the idea was to flip forward as Schizarro snatched with his greasy claws and helped us land in a bridge position, heads tilted, stomachs pointing toward the ceiling. Chris's turn saw him bolt down the mat like a madman and leap with all his might. Schizarro took hold of him in midflight and guided his body down. And there it was. Hillman, held suspended, quivering slightly, his back arched like a cat's, palms resting on the ground, head steady, belly and pelvis thrust forward. And an erection as clear as day pushing against the confines of his navy gym shorts. Boners were relatively new to us back then. The laughter grew slowly, from a few stifled chuckles to a full and steady roar. Hillman's face turned beet red and he bolted into the locker room.

I was a nerd then, as I am now. I traveled with a group of kids who were seriously into Dungeons & Dragons. We weren't LARPers. There was no dressing up involved, just intense gaming. I was an elf. I had exceptional dexterity and a bow and arrow—stolen from the den of an ogre. An über-geek with inch-thick glasses named Arthur Kornberg was the Dungeon Master. Together with Max Whitman, Leonard Morgenstern, Charles DiDomenico, and Chris Hillman, we formed something of a dork supergroup. Girls snickered at our ill-fitting attire and fondness for sweatpants. Our T-shirts displayed such witticisms as "I've Got Level 14 Charisma" and "Show Me Your Dice." We were never invited to parties, stayed in on the weekends, talked passionately about horror movies. We stood on the cusp of high school, that giant labyrinth where older kids smoked cigarettes, loitered in the parking lot, made out with each other.

We didn't know it, but our little crew of losers wouldn't survive past the eighth grade. Arthur went off to genius school in Manhattan. Leonard, to a Catholic preparatory somewhere in Texas when his parents deemed Sleepy

Hollow too "liberal." Max Whitman was arrested for stealing his neighbor's car and wound up in juvenile hall. No
one saw much of him after that. Charles DiDomenico moved
two towns over, to Croton, and got really involved in drama
club. Only Chris Hillman and I made it to Sleepy Hollow
Memorial High. For me, high school was a chance to start
fresh, a place where I could sculpt a new Calvin and shed my
Poindexter status. I stopped playing D&D. I started hanging out with a different crowd, the "cool" kids. I wandered
the streets on weekend nights. I listened to classic rock. My
T-shirts grew sloganless. My clothing got tighter. I discovered pot. I learned if you smoked enough of it, everything
became suddenly and inexplicably hilarious. Every movie
ticket purchase was an enormous feat, an exercise in nu-
anced and exquisite contract negotiation. Every trip to the
mall, a staggering journey filled with lingerie-display ogling
and teriyaki chicken in the food court.

Chris Hillman and I had a falling-out freshman year
when he accused me of being "too cool" to be his friend.

"You think you're hot shit," he told me outside the deli
near school. He picked an acorn up off the ground and with
unprovoked aggression, pegged me in the head with it. He
rode off on his bicycle. Aside from cordialities in the hallway, we haven't spoken since. So why does he want me at
his wedding all these years later? What does it mean? Have
I been invited in error? Does he have some horrible, sham-
ing retribution in store? Does he have any idea how bad his
timing is? Who decides to get married right in the middle of
the most trying time in Moretti family history?

My grandmother slices eggplant, dips the slices in egg
and flour, tosses them into a frying pan. They sizzle.

My mother washes spinach in the sink. "I heard his fiancé is three years older than him," she says, fisting the spinach into a pot of garlic and oil.

"What's her name?" my grandmother asks. I look at the card.

"Marie Gold."

"It was probably Goldstein when her people came over on the boat," she says. She pulls cooked eggplant slices from the pan with a fork and lays them in a bed of paper towels.

"Your people came over on a boat, too," I remind her.

"That's different," she says.

"How is it different?" I ask.

"My mother scrubbed floors for nickels," she says. Her giant spectacles, rimmed with translucent red plastic, are starting to fog with steam from the eggplant. "On her hands and knees. Don't talk to me about hardship." There is sweat on her forehead.

"You should open a window," I say.

My father appears in the hallway, heading slowly for the garage with his clipboard. He pauses to look in at us. His robe is not cinched tight enough and I can see his distended stomach.

"Inventory?" I ask. He holds the clipboard up as an answer and continues on, out the back door.

"Where is the reception?" my mother asks once he's gone. She's lit the burner under the spinach and is pouring salt into the pot. "I'm sure it's costing a fortune."

"I don't care how much it costs," I say, throwing my hands up. "I'm asking, why do you think I've been invited? We aren't friends."

"He's such a smart boy, that Chris Hillman," my grandmother says. Her pile of eggplant slices has grown to a sizable mound. Oil soaks the paper towels. "He went to Harvard, you know."

"How is it," I say, "you remember where he went to school, but the other day you couldn't remember that I was teaching at a preschool?"

"You don't forget a thing like Harvard," my grandmother says. She takes her glasses off and lets them fall across her enormous bosom, where they dangle from one of those jeweled chains librarians wear.

"He went to Yale," my mother corrects.

"Whatever," I say. "He got a boner in gym class once. What do you say to a person like that?"

"He's in law school," my grandmother says, shaking her head. "Probably going to make a lot of money."

"We should ask him for a loan," my mother says.

"I'm aware of how much this family values financial success," I say.

"As long as he's happy," my grandmother says.

"*You* should be happy," my mother says, stirring the spinach as it cooks down. "I hear people are dying to get invited to this wedding. It's the talk of the town."

"You mean the talk of the country club?" I say.

"Sadly, as part of our savings plan, your father and I have canceled our membership at the club," my mother says.

"Tough sacrifices," I say.

"I'm trying to make them," she says.

"There's no way in hell I'm going to this wedding."

"I think you should go," my mother says. "And I think you should take your father."

"You're joking," I say.

She pulls a piece of spinach from the pot with her bare hands and tastes it.

"That's good," she says. She licks her lips.

"Why wouldn't you want to go?" my grandmother says. "You might meet someone. Lots of single girls at weddings, you know."

"I'm not interested in meeting anyone who owns a pantsuit."

At dinner my father shows us three of his newest paintings. They are passed around the table. The first is dominated by a green landscape. The shadowy figure of a man lies on the ground with a flower growing out of his stomach. Neither Chip nor Elissa has anything to say about it.

"Who is that supposed to be?" I ask.

"That's me," my father says, rubbing his eyes. He has pieces of eggplant in his mustache, but I don't tell him.

The other two paintings are composed of violent slashing lines and random circular splatters in a range of dark greens and purples and blues.

I eat more spinach than I have ever consumed at one sitting in my life. I don't touch any of the eggplant or pasta. I grab the real estate section of the newspaper and hide up in the third-floor bathroom, feeling guilty and looking for cheap apartment rentals. I flush the invitation to Chris Hillman's wedding down the toilet. I watch the late movie, *Stroszek*. Inside my Moleskine notebook, at the bottom of the movie list, I write: *Stroszek—04.09.06*.

Spring break is over. The retards haunt my dreams, calling out to me, drooling on me.

# ≪ **10** ≫

Work. Monday. I spend my lunch half hour talking with Georgie, the thirty-five-year-old hip-hop enthusiast who lives with his mother in the Dunwoodie section of Yonkers. A lot of his free time is spent in pursuit of the perfect neck fade. He has a gold chain collection. He supplements his assistant teacher's salary with a modest amount of marijuana trafficking. He is fond of wearing Yankees jerseys four sizes too big for his body, drives a Camaro.

"How's business?" I ask.

Georgie nods his head. "Pretty good," he says. "Stocked up on this Asian shit. Real nice. Save you some?"

"Yeah, maybe," I say. "Payday's coming."

"Ain't gonna be selling much once summer comes around," he tells me. "Getting outta here."

"We all are," I say.

"For real. I got my record almost done. It's only a matter of time now." He waves his hands in the air, gesturing over the parking lot, the trees, the nail salon across the street, as if he is scooping it all up, at once owning and dismissing everything.

"What's the plan?" I ask.

"Aside from rapping?" he asks. He answers his own question. "Getting another job," he says. "There's a shit ton of money to be made in private tutoring, son."

"So I've heard," I say.

"Think about it," Georgie says. He puts a finger to his temple. "These nut bags? They don't want to leave the house. They hate it. They throw a fit half the time they get dragged down here, spit all over themselves. Whack you with a chair. Whatever. So? Go to them. Their own turf. Makes perfect sense. They feel better. Keep the cattle calm. Motto number one."

"I hear that," I tell him. "You've put a lot of thought into this."

"That's what I'm talking about," Georgie says. He crams half a tuna sandwich into his mouth. "I'm always thinking next level."

Back in the classroom, I find Arham is having a better afternoon than usual. Today he is a sponge. I decide to work on his greetings. I take him by the hand. I lead him through the halls of the John W. Manley School. We say hello to everyone we come across. I make sure Arham maintains eye contact. I make sure that the people we see squat down to his level. That they take care to say clearly, "Hello, Arham." To which he must reply, "Hello, _____." This ideal interaction happens maybe 10 percent of the time. Mostly he stares at the walls, points at things we pass, calling out their names loudly. "Chair!" "Microwave!" "Door!" "Woman!" He speaks with utter confidence but a complete lack of conception. He speaks because his mind has soldered together the visual connections. Beyond that, there is nothing. Dim and elusive for the rest of his life. I envy him in ways I don't want to get into.

On our journey we find Ceci coming out of the teachers' lounge (a small room that smells like cigarettes). Inside the teachers' lounge one can find a refrigerator, jars of instant coffee, Splenda in the drawers, two couches, and a sign that says NO SMOKING.

Ceci lowers herself onto her haunches. I've been avoiding her all day because I haven't even started working on the graph I promised her I'd present. Her hair looks like it has recently been dyed or cut or both. It flows over the shoulders of her blouse. I can see a little bit of her back. The top of her panties.

"Hello, Arham," she says, staring straight into his eyes.

"Peepee," he says.

She touches his arm. "Hello, Ceci," she corrects him. "Hello, Arham," she repeats.

He pauses. Raises his eyebrows.

"Hello. Ceci," he ventures. He smiles, rubs his face with his hand.

"Very good, little man," Ceci says. "You're so special."

She stands, straightening her collar.

"How are things with your dad?" she asks.

"He's going in for his stem cell transplant soon."

"I hope it goes well," she says.

"Thank you," I say.

"Listen, Cal," she says in the tone I have come to know as

the herald of uncomfortable work talk. "Everyone here loves you. You know that, and I would love to promote you. Give you more money."

"I could use it," I say.

"I know. But I'd like to see a little more from you," she says. "More investment in the school. In the kids."

Arham is squirming beside me, slithering around my legs. I've got only a few more seconds before he rams his head into something.

"I feel pretty invested," I tell her.

"But are you excited?" she asks, slapping my arm in what I imagine she thinks is a jocular manner. "Are you having a good time?"

"Yeah," I say. "It's a good fit for me right now."

"What about the future?" she asks. "That's what I really mean. Where do you see yourself in five years?"

"Do we have to have this conversation right now?" I ask. Arham is now pulling on my arm, urging me to let him move. He is antsy. I am antsy.

"Have you thought at all about going back to school?" she asks. "I might even be able to convince them to pay."

"At this very moment," I say, "my idea of financial responsibility is to never incur another ounce of student loan debt in this lifetime."

"You're good at this," she says. She sort of half points at Arham.

"I'll think about it," I say. She turns to go but thinks twice about it.

"Got that graph ready?" she says. I knew it was coming.

"I have a few things that aren't completely where I'd like them to be."

"Well, you're off the hook at the moment," Ceci says, "Tracy really wants to present the progress she's been making with Samantha's fine motor skills. I told her she can go ahead and get it ready for this month."

"I swear I will present a graph before summer," I say.

"I'm gonna hold you to it," she says. She walks off, leaving Arham and me alone in the hallway. Her heels click like daggers.

"You are so hot," I say, under my breath. I look down at Arham. The index finger of his right hand is knuckle deep in his nose.

"Don't pick your nose," I tell him. "It's gross."

"Bathroom," he says, pointing at the door to the ladies' room.

"Good job, buddy," I say. "That's the bathroom."

I DIRECT ARHAM to a free spot on the rug. I check the clock to confirm that indeed there is only one more hour until the bell rings. Music time. We're all here. Everyone from our side of the building. Georgie and his pupil, a little girl named Shaynequa, who at the moment is spinning around and around in circles on the rug while Georgie stares off into space. Robyn and young, gifted Franklin. Elaine drags Tyrone into the room. He is screaming about something, but since he has the language capacity of a stapler, she has no idea what his problem is. Tracy enters, Samantha in tow. Samantha isn't watching where she's going and Tracy isn't watching Samantha, so I'm not surprised when Samantha trips over Tyrone and they both go down in a heap.

Tony, the music teacher, finishes pulling his hair back into a tidy ponytail and strums his guitar a few times, tuning up. Shaynequa stops in her tracks. She stares at Tony and the guitar as if she hasn't seen him and it every Monday for the past seven months. She takes a few steps forward, falls on her face. Georgie doesn't move to help her. Angela ushers little Hendrick Ramirez into the room. He is wearing his plastic fireman's hat, business as usual for him. He is complaining about being made to attend music.

"I don't like this," he says, waving a finger at Tony. "I don't like you. My papi come here and get you."

"Thank you for that," Tony says. Eventually everyone is seated, somewhat in a circle, though it looks more like a dented egg. Tony takes a seat on one of the small chairs and plays some chords. He sings, "I once had a rooster, my rooster had me." His voice floats out over the kids, enchants them, draws their faces up. They sit, mouths open, eyes twirling. For these twenty minutes my mind can wander. Tony has the reins. "I fed my rooster on a greenberry tree," he sings.

Georgie keeps time, playing drums on his knees, closing his eyes as if he is really moved by the farm song.

"My rooster goes cock-a-doodle-doo. A doodle-dee, doodle-dee, doodle-dee, doo." Tony hits the chords and smiles, looking around the room. Angela sings along.

How am I going to get out of this wedding? Why am I even thinking about it? Just forget it. Just don't deal with it. It's not important. Deal instead with things that are within your power to change. Deal with your family. Try to help them. Isn't that what adults do? Isn't that the mark of maturity—the ability to forget what's forgettable and shoulder something harder? Something outside the comfort zone? Struggling outside the comfort zone. Surely I've read about that somewhere. I can do it. I can be more than I currently am. I might get lost in the course of helping them, I might never have money or a place to call my own, and four out of five girls consider guys who live with their parents undatable (I've read that somewhere, too), but I could hold my head high. There is a risk, though. If I join them in their quest to live on in that house? If I give them money? If I keep saving and put those savings toward the mortgage, or whatever needs a money Band-Aid, and the bank forecloses in spite of that? What then? It's the equivalent of throwing my money into a wishing well. I'd be no closer to living on my own and we could still lose the house.

Tony sings on. He sings about a cat. "I once had a cat," the song goes. "My cat had me." And so on. A dog, a cow, a goat all make appearances. Ceci stands in the doorway, checking in. I catch her eye and we smile and nod at one another, but I'm sure we're smiling about very different things.

In the car, waiting at lights on the way home, I look at myself in the rearview mirror.

"Just do *something.*"

I'M STRUCK WITH the idea while sitting on the toilet in the third-floor bathroom. There's maybe a way to have it all. I see a way. Ceci's advice is good advice. She's right. I am in need of a new job, a higher salary—just not at the John W. Manley School.

I sit with the newspaper and go through the want ads, hoping to find a new line of work. Something more suited to my interests, my life goals. Whatever those might be. I'm troubled to find nothing even remotely interesting or, for that matter, attainable. A few publishing jobs, all requiring two to three years' experience in the field. A handful of executives are looking to pay between $20K and $25K for assistants who'll book flights, make hotel reservations, pay bills, and shuttle their children to and from private school. Live-in nanny? Cash manager? Continuous improvement co-ordinator? Information technology project manager? Web developer (pro bono)? Insurance agent? Accounting assistant? Phlebotomist? Bilingual administrative consultant? Research events creator? Quality-control technician? No-pay externships? No-pay internships?

Surely there is a job somewhere in need of my vast, impractical background in liberal arts. Where are the filmmakers? The photographers? The art gallery curators? Where is the golden ticket that will earn me the $57,116.40 ($41,220.85 + $15,895.55 estimated amount of accrued interest to be paid during repayment = $57,116.40) I need to get out of debt? The pay dirt I could use to alleviate my family's looming financial demise? The entry-level job that pays more than it did in 1975? The company in whose employ I would earn valuable self-worth, confidence, life meaning? I take a few deep breaths and open the bathroom window, which looks out onto the driveway, our family cars. The garage.

Finally, in dismayed frustration, I turn to the apartment listings, where I manage to find a few rentals that look within reach, should I decide, in the end, to keep what I save for myself.

I look forward to the next time Wally and I can take some pills and watch horror movies.

# ≪ **11** ≫

I write about sleep:

*I go to sleep. I often sleep when there's not much else to do.*
*My bed is a mattress on the floor. I dream. I've been told only*
*boring people talk about their dreams. I have a dream where*
*I'm not strong enough. I need to fire a gun. I need to kill*
*something. But in the dream, I'm not strong enough. It looks*
*like a monster, this thing I have to kill. A mutant hybrid of*
*monster and celebrity. I'm not sure which celebrity, some fe-*
*male pop star, tabloid queen, reality TV contestant. Someone*
*famous for being rich. A globe-trotting heiress traveling the*
*world in search of endless weekends. My dream assailant is*
*enormous, so much bigger than I am, bearing down on me*
*across moist earth. She lopes, shuffling her feet, slouched. A*
*teenage jet-setting zombie supermodel with dyed blond hair.*
*Veins and pulsing coils all fused and meshed together. A*
*webbed lattice of innards beneath translucent, glowing skin.*
*She closes in. A gun is always in my hand. I have to fire it to*

*kill this thing and save myself. I level the gun and put my finger on the trigger. I'm not strong enough. I squeeze, struggling fruitlessly, gripping with both hands, squeezing and squeezing, but I'm too weak. And I wake up.*

MY FATHER AND Chip are sprawled on the couch in the TV room. They lie opposite one another, their legs entwined, all parallel lines. The two of them share a bizarre notion that family closeness translates to physicality. They are fond of hugging. Group hugs. Family hugs. They enjoy petting and back rubs.

I take a seat on the sectional as far from them as possible.

"I had the dream about human weakness again," I say.

"My life is a dream about weakness," my father says.

"Do you think I'm dreaming about my own weakness?" I ask. "My own physical weakness? Am I sick? Some neurological disease? Is there illness in my future?"

"I'm dying," my father says. "Maybe the dream is about me?"

"You should hit the gym with me," Chip suggests. "That's how I stay so healthy." I don't look at him, but I'm sure he's raised a flexed muscle.

"I'm learning now to live without my dreams," our father says. He runs a hand across his head, feels the stubble there. "How long till my hair comes back? That's a question."

I look at him. He's lost a lot of weight. Lost almost his entire potbelly. The undersides of his arms sag, making him look older than he actually is.

"You need to cheer up," I say.

"They scheduled the transplant," he says. "Ten days away. That's a reality now, too."

"You should be glad to get it over with."

"Everyone will have to wear a mask and gloves when they come to see me in isolation. That'll be fun. I have that to worry about."

"I'll come every day," Chip says, rubbing his feet against our father's legs.

"I'd like that," the old man says.

Elissa appears in the doorway, home from her various after-school activities. She rubs her head, twirling a finger in her hair. For a second I think she has come to break the bad news.

"My little girl," our father says. He smiles slightly, a faint twitch of lip and mustache. "Give us a hug."

Elissa falls onto the couch, into his arms. He envelops her with his blanket. Chip moves to join them. A group pile-on. A hug of epic proportions. They lie there, all wrapped arms.

"I love you guys," our father says, his voice muffled through layers of clothing and flesh and blanket.

"Gross," I say.

"I love you, too," he adds.

MY GRANDMOTHER MAKES chicken salad sandwiches. I eat one at the kitchen table with her and my mother. Somewhere between the two of them arguing about the appropriate number of wedding guests a couple may invite without sacrificing elegance and sophistication, and a lengthy back-and-forth commentary on the economic state of the country ("It has something to do with all these illegals. I'm sure of it," my grandmother says, waving a cautionary finger at the wall), I have a moment of weakness. I can't take it anymore and decide on the spot to rent one of the apartments

Pam showed me before the break. Not the loft in Port Chester—it's too much of a financial impossibility—but the other one, the small studio in the microscopic hamlet of Montrose, a twenty-mile journey north of Sleepy Hollow. It has a price tag of $1,000 a month, totally out of my budget, but I'm not sure I can stand another minute with my family.

It's the seventeenth of the month. I go to my computer and check to see if the John W. Manley School's direct deposit of my bimonthly paycheck installment has gone through. It has. I send off a loan payment and calculate about $145 can be moved into my savings account. I transfer the money and write the new figure in my notebook. I cross out "567.88" and write "712.88" in its place.

Her business card is wedged within the pages. I dial the number.

"Pam Kittredge," she says. Her voice is bright and cheerful.

"Hi, Pam," I say. "This is Calvin Moretti here. You showed me some apartments a few weeks ago."

"A few weeks?" she says in the same indifferent, happy tone. "Okay."

"Ah, well, I was wondering about your finder's fee."

"What exactly were you wondering?"

"Well, see, I really want to take one of the apartments. I have the first month's rent. And I can get the security. I can borrow it, I think, maybe, from my folks."

"You'll need them to cosign as guarantors," Pam points out.

"Okay, yeah, sure," I say. "I don't think they'll have a problem with that." I just can't seem to tell this woman anything but outright lies.

"Good," Pam says. "I'll just need copies of your last four pay stubs, your social, and fifty dollars for our credit check."

"Yeah, well, I was wondering about the finder's fee."

"What exactly were you wondering?"

"I wanted to see if we could possibly work out some kind of payment plan. Maybe I could give part of it to you now and part of it to you later in the year or something?"

"Oh, I'm sorry," Pam says. "It doesn't work like that."

"It doesn't?" I ask.

"What did you say your name was again?" she asks.

"Calvin. Moretti," I say.

"Listen, Calvin," Pam says, not unfriendly. "It seems to me like you might have to work out some finance issues before we can get you set up with a place. Why don't you check back with me when you've got a little more money to work with."

"That may be never," I say. "But thanks."

She hangs up. I hang up. I pace around my bedroom. I look at all the records on the shelves and wonder how much I could get if I sold them all. Who am I kidding? Some of those are first presses. Limited editions. Colored vinyl. Clear vinyl. Clear marble colored vinyl. Rare Japanese imports. Hard-to-find collector's items. Far too sentimentally valuable to ever sell.

BRIGITTE VISITS A final time before the transplant to make sure my father's life energy is composed and ready to absorb everything coming his way. It is a special session, which both my parents attend. She ushers them upstairs into their bedroom and closes the door. I am not privy to what goes on in there.

As my father prepares for the transplant, their mortgage crisis seems to be forgotten. Someone presses pause and we talk about nothing else but the impending procedure.

An hour passes and Brigitte emerges again, a satisfied look on her face, her earrings shimmering. I watch her drift down the stairs. Her eyes are ringed in dark makeup. She moves with a floating grace, on soft slipper feet. Her clothing jingles.

"Is he ready?" I ask.

"He is," she tells me. "Are you?"

"I don't have anything to get ready for."

"Don't you?" she asks.

"Not that I know of," I say.

"Remember," she says, "I'm here if you want to talk. I feel your energy. It's good. I'm waiting."

And then she moves to the front door. I open it for her and she glides past.

# ≪ 12 ≫

We take him to the hospital. All of us. I help my mother pack some things.

"He got this in Saudi Arabia," she says, about the small plastic alarm clock on the night table. We pack some paperbacks, airport fiction espionage stories about submarines and nuclear weapons—his favorite. We pack a toothbrush. His mustache comb. We pack underwear and T-shirts. A pair of khakis.

"You're wasting your time with those pants," he tells us.

He wears his trademark bathrobe in the car. None of us talk much. Even Chip is silent. Down through the Bronx, over the Triborough into Manhattan, and I look mostly at the buildings lining the FDR. We've been here many times over the past year. Exit at Seventy-Second. Head downtown. New York Presbyterian's main entrance is off York Avenue, on Sixty-Eighth. When my grandmother's appendix burst last Christmas, we took her here. When Chip, playing hockey, shattered his wrist so badly the bone was protruding, we took him here. This is where all my father's doctors are.

My mother knows the way but insists on programming the GPS. A bell sounds as we turn the corner.

"Your destination is ahead," a soft female robotic voice says from the dashboard.

At the entrance he's given a wheelchair and I push him into the main lobby.

We're stopped by security. There is a problem regarding the gun.

"I don't understand," my father tells the guard.

"What exactly don't you understand?" the guard says, raising an eyebrow, his giant hands resting on his hips. He wears large sunglasses.

"I might be dying," my father says.

"Patients aren't allowed to carry firearms in the hospital, sir," the guard says. He looks around at all of us.

"Don't look at me," I say. "I told him not to bring it."

Elissa is behind me. Chip is holding the suitcase with my father's things. My mother comes out of the café waving a brown paper bag.

"I got bananas, an orange, and two bottles of water," she proclaims.

"Dad brought his gun," Elissa says.

Our mother lowers the bag.

"Un-fucking-believable," she says.

A large nurse wearing blue scrubs, hair in a bun, waddles up to join us.

"Is everything okay here?" she asks.

"This guy thinks he's coming in with a firearm."

"Don't look at me," I tell the nurse. We all look at my father.

"It's fully registered," he says. "Completely legal."

"Sir," the nurse says, an edge of impatience creeping into her voice. "I can't admit you into the hospital with a weapon."

"In fact," the security guard chimes in, "I'm gonna have to confiscate it."

"Oh, no," my father says.

"Oh, yes," the security guard says. He nods. I see everyone in the reflection of his sunglasses. He steps aside to admit a group of people talking loudly in what sounds like Polish. "What I should do," he adds, "is call the NYPD. Have them come down here, do a voucher check on the thing. But. Since I recognize you all and your wife always says hello to me, I'm doing you a favor." Everyone waits.

"Fine," my father says. He reaches into the folds of his bathrobe and extracts the revolver. He caresses it softly, the way one would a puppy, and then places it gently in the outstretched hand of the security guard.

"Wise move," the guard says.

"Very good," the nurse says.

"Can we go in now?" Chip says. The nurse nods, flashes her practiced smile.

"If you'd all follow me, we can get you where you need to go," she says. We follow her to the large information desk. She takes her place behind a computer and punches buttons.

"Your name?" she asks.

"James Moretti," my mother says. The nurse types.

"Okay, excellent," she says. "You need to head to radiology. Take the G bank of elevators to the seventh floor, follow the signs."

Elissa says, "We know the way."

HE LUCKS OUT and gets a single overlooking the East River. I
see a garbage barge floating down toward Buttermilk Channel, drifting under the arch of the Fifty-Ninth Street Bridge.
I see the aerial tramway there, moving like a slug. Dusk is
settling in. Lights are appearing.

"I have to take a leak," Chip says, dropping the suitcase
on the bed.

My mother begins to set up the room, unpacking the
things she felt compelled to bring. She lines the windowsill with over a dozen framed pictures. She pauses next to
me for a minute, takes in the scenery outside the window.
Roosevelt Island in all its creepy solitude.

"Beautiful night," she says. The toilet flushes and Chip
comes out of the bathroom, zipping up his fly. His hair looks
freshly gelled.

"This city is a dump," he says. "I bet you can see trash
floating by." He joins us at the window. He points down into
the dark water below. "Yup, look at that. There. See that
shit? What is that?"

"It's the East River," I say.

"Total dump of a town," Chip says. He shakes his head.

"Can someone help me into bed?" our father asks. His
wheelchair is parked near the nightstand. He sits slouched
in it.

Elissa goes to him. She puts her arms around him. Supporting under his shoulders, she hoists him gingerly onto
the edge of the bed, where he sits, wincing in pain.

"Oh God," he moans. "My fucking back is killing me."

I move the suitcase onto the floor so he can lie down.

"Look," he says, pointing at the darkening sky. "Jets flying approaches into La Guardia." We all look. A plane is coming in low just above the buildings beyond the bridge. Landing lights flash. The dull rumbling of its engines.

"Boeing," the old man says. "Seven Sixty-Seven. Two engines, under the wing. Big boy."

A nurse comes in carrying a neatly folded hospital gown and slippers.

"Put these on, please, Mr. Moretti," she says softly.

He is pressing all the buttons on the remote control for the television, which is mounted to a metal frame on the wall.

"The TV isn't working," he says.

"You have to pay for it," the nurse says.

"We went through this last time, honey," my mother reminds him.

"Oh, yeah," he says, letting the remote fall from his hand, so that it dangles off the wall, tethered by its plastic chord.

"I'll have it turned on," the nurse says. "The doctor will be in to talk to you."

Nurses must work on their smiles at home.

Once she leaves, Chip and Elissa help him change. They take off his sneakers. They take off his bathrobe. I unfold the gown while he lies in his underwear, his legs white and thin. He is made of wet paper. I hand the gown to Elissa. She covers him, wrapping the ends behind his back. She ties the strings together and eases him down, his face scrunching in and out of painful expressions.

Our mother finishes erecting the shrine of pictures and busies herself arranging "get well soon" cards. She stacks the paperbacks.

"I brought you a pad and pen," she says, holding up a Moleskine notebook, just like mine. "You can write about what happens here. I think it would be good for you. Cathartic."

"I don't want to," my father says, waving a hand at her.

"Suit yourself." She puts the notebook down on the table next to the cards. She returns to the suitcase and takes out my father's leather carryall. He's had the same bag since I was a kid. He takes it with him whenever he flies. Navy blue with maroon trim. She dumps its contents into the drawer on the night table. She hangs his clothes in the closet.

"I'm cold," he says.

Elissa takes the sheet out from under his body and drapes it over him. She takes a chair and moves it to the bedside and sits with her feet propped up, her hand on his leg. Chip pushes a few pictures aside and seats himself on the windowsill, his head against the glass. We watch our mother move around the room, putting knickknacks in every available space.

"Kathy," my father says. "You didn't need to bring all this shit."

"I want you to feel at home," she says.

"It's a hospital, Mom," I say.

"Still," she says. She pauses for a moment in midstride, considering the stuffed teddy bear in her hand. She looks at it for a second before placing it on a shelf in the closet.

"Where's the bag *I* packed?" he asks.

"Oh, for God's sake," she says. "You don't need a first-aid kit in a hospital. It's embarrassing."

"It's not a first aid kit," he says. "It's my binoculars and a blanket and some other stuff I want to have with me. Where is it?"

"It's right here," she says, taking a small orange sack from one of the suitcases and placing it on the bedside table next to a framed picture of the Empire State Building.

"Thank you," he says. He caresses the bag. He tilts the picture frame over onto its face. My mother immediately stands it back up and slides it out of his reach.

My father tries the TV again. This time it flickers to life. He turns to the Food Network.

It is an hour before Dr. Nadoo arrives to brief us. He is a slight, spectacled Indian man with delicate features. His face is soft, experienced, and he has an air of wisdom about him. The kind of person you feel comfortable entrusting important health decisions to.

"Hello. You're all here. Very nice to see you," he says when he comes in. "Nice to see you again, Kathleen," he tells my mother. Elissa takes her feet off the bed and stands. Chip gets up. Everyone shakes hands. I don't think any of us are sure where to be or what to do.

"Hey, Doctor," my father says.

"How are you feeling?" Dr. Nadoo asks.

"My back is killing me," he says. "That's nothing new."

Dr. Nadoo nods. He glances at his clipboard. He lifts the top page and checks something off with his pen.

"Okay," the doctor says. "Very good." He comes around to stand at my father's bedside. "Can you sit up, please?" he asks. He takes the stethoscope from around his neck and checks the old man's heartbeat. My father takes deep breaths, in and out. Nadoo nods some more and wrinkles his brow. He presses on various spots of my father's torso, asking, "Does this hurt?" He takes a blood pressure reading.

"Okay," Nadoo says at last. "Everything looks fine. The nurse is going to come in and take blood. I want to check a few things. If everything is good on that end, we can start the chemo in maybe an hour. Are you ready?"

My father does not look ready at all.

"I guess," he says. He looks down at the sheet covering his legs.

"I'll see you soon, then."

The doctor heads for the hallway.

"Do I get dinner?" my father asks.

Nadoo stops in the doorway and looks back.

"I'm afraid not," he says, and he leaves.

In between jerk-off sessions last night on the Internet, I read up on the procedure my father is about to undergo. Autologous stem cell transplant. Which basically means that a week ago, doctors harvested stem cells from my father's spine and froze them. Now his immune system must be brought down to zero and the stem cells reintroduced into his body. The chemo he will be dosed with tonight and tomorrow will severely cripple his white blood cell count, enabling a smooth acceptance of the stem cells. Then he'll spend three weeks in isolation, building his body's defenses back up.

The John W. Manley School has been very understanding about my father's illness. It's Thursday night and I've taken tomorrow off so I can be here with him in the wake of the intense blast of chemotherapy he is about to experience.

The same nurse from earlier returns and fills three vials with blood from my father's left arm. He makes faces the whole time like a little boy afraid of needles. I have to admit I don't enjoy looking either.

When she's finished, we wait some more. He turns up the volume on the TV and we watch Mario Batali make linguine with clam sauce.

Dr. Nadoo comes back around eight thirty, this time with two interns in tow, a collection of nurses, and Dr. Schore, who is head of the stem cell team in charge of administering the transplant. A few minutes of introductions, and once again my mother, Chip, Elissa, and I hover about, trying not to get in anyone's way.

When it all began, on one of his first overnight stays at the hospital, a shunt was installed in my father's chest. His portal vein was tapped permanently just below the collarbone. Through this passage, his stem cells were harvested to be cultured and grown. He claims that after a week or so, the skin healed over the place where the shunt had been sutured, and he now feels like he is partially robotic. When he undergoes the second half of the transplant process, the reintroduction of stem cells into his body, it will be conducted through this same entryway.

We watch as the bags of chemo drugs are hooked into a tube protruding from the square of tape surrounding the port. Dr. Schore suggests the addition of antinausea medicine along with the chemo.

"Most of the time it does nothing," he says.

It isn't long before I can't be in the room anymore and I excuse myself.

"I have to eat, Mom," I say. "I don't feel well."

Chip and Elissa join me and the three of us walk in silence out of radiology and down the G elevators to the cafeteria on the basement level. The cafeteria itself is closed, but there is a bank of vending machines filled with everything from tuna salad sandwiches to cheesecake. I don't eat anything.

*When I was thirteen, I played a year of Little League baseball.*
*Mostly as an unspoken favor to my father. They stuck me*
*in right field, the only position where I might possibly avoid*
*all contact with the ball. I batted seventh in the order. Once,*
*during a game toward the end of the season, a fastball hit me*
*square in the nose, knocking the plastic helmet off my head*
*and splaying me out in the dirt. When I came to, I could taste*
*blood in my mouth. My father was squatting over me, along*
*with Coach Ruggiero and half the team. He put his hand un-*
*der my head, told me not to move. I didn't want to get up. I*
*would've stayed there forever. I have never felt as safe as I did*
*lying there with a broken nose.*

I WANDER THE HALLS. I walk past rooms somewhere deep in cardiology. I examine charts. I stop and look into rooms. I poke my head inside quickly to catch a face. I try to make eye contact if I can, to better gauge the condition of the patients within. I guess what it is they suffer from. What sickness has put them here. I invent imaginary scenarios. Bedside family vigils. Estranged lovers appear in the middle of the night for one last sweaty entanglement. Wills are written. Cats are endowed with large sums of money. The patients are old, young, middle-aged, twentysomethings, thirtysomethings. They have barely begun their lives. They have accomplished everything. They leave legacies behind. They leave nothing behind.

I walk past rooms, three beds deep, all filled with the somber, expressionless faces of people who barely even notice I've breached their privacy. A cute orderly eyes me suspiciously from behind a food cart.

"Can I help you?" she asks. Her voice is soft.

She tilts her head to the side, waiting for me to step out of the way so she can deliver dinner.

"I think I'm lost," I say.

"It happens," she says. She squeezes past, not bothering to deal with me any further. I continue my journey. I wind through what appears to be an MRI unit and then a pediatric wing. I pause outside an OT room to watch a little girl in a hospital gown bounce up and down on a giant orange ball.

"There's nothing wrong with her," I say, but there's no one listening.

I head back the way I came, follow signs to the G elevators, those bastions of familiarity. I take a wrong turn somehow and find myself in more unknown territory. These corridors are foreign to me. Plastic map placards are of no use. A room ahead glowing bright and blue. Bright, soft blue light spilling out onto the linoleum. They're showing movies inside, I think. I take my time getting there and stand for a moment, looking in. There's a technician, a short Asian guy, seated before a large monitor displaying static.

"Check it out," he says, turning to me with an odd expression, as if he has been waiting for me.

"I know you?" I ask him.

"Nah, man," he says. He motions me closer.

I step into the room. It's small, with one wall made entirely of glass, through which I see a billowing hunk of machinery, a white cushioned bed, fitted inside a man-size tube.

"MRI?" I ask.

"Nope," the technician says. He has glassy, lost eyes. He presses a button underneath the monitor, and undulating blue and white pulses replace the static. Moving things. Like amoebas or jellyfish. Cells.

"Beautiful, man," he says. "Breathtaking."

I stand next to him. We don't say anything for a while. We just watch the forms on the monitor change and grow and curl on top of each other. The amorphous blobs fold inside themselves, are reborn into newer things. Different things. It all fits.

"What is it?" I ask.

"Everything," he says, and he says it like he can't believe I didn't know.

"WHERE'VE YOU BEEN?" my brother asks when I finally wind my way back to our father's bedside.

I can hear him vomiting inside the bathroom. I take a seat in one of the plastic chairs near the closet and wait. He emerges moments later, wiping his mouth. My mother is at his side, hands bolstering his upper body, hobbling with him in a bizarre dance, the IV stand rolling behind them.

Chip stops pacing back and forth in front of the windows to watch this shambling procession back to the bed. "You okay?" he asks.

"No," my father says. I can see tears in his eyes.

"They weren't kidding about that antinausea medicine," my mother says.

Elissa is asleep in a chair. She looks peaceful. Her hair is a tangle of knots. I have a strong urge to wake her up and make her comb it.

"Chemo's all done for tonight," my mother says, once she has tucked the old man back under the blue sheet and adjusted the contours of the bed to his liking.

"Thank God," he says. He coughs dully a few times, rubs his face with his hands. "I should have brushed my teeth while I was in there."

"It's okay," my mother says.

"You guys don't have to stay," he says. "I'm exhausted. I'm just gonna go to sleep. If I can."

I stand up and come around to the side of the bed and look at him. One of his arms is above the sheet, folded across his chest. His veins are at attention like a maze of worms beneath the sagging skin of his forearm. I reach down and trace the bulges with my finger. I don't know why I do this.

"Chip," he says, "will you bring me the blanket I packed?"

My brother goes to the table where the orange bag sits and unzips it. He takes out a plastic package containing a safety blanket. Together, my brother and I unfold it and drape it over the frail body before us.

"Thank you, boys," he says.

We don't say anything else. My mother rouses Elissa. We move around the room, gathering the garbage that has accumulated over the few hours we've been here. The four of us huddle in the doorway and look back for a moment. He is already asleep.

## ≪ **13** ≫

They come for him the next day. He panics. He is an anxious mess. The doctors huddle, murmuring. The whole thing is almost called off.

"This isn't going to work," my father says. His face sags, his eyes fill with tears.

"You're acting like a baby," my mother says. "Don't start. You have to be strong, Jim."

"Come on, Dad," I say. "It'll be fine."

His hands shake. He worries them together.

Dr. Nadoo is here, Dr. Schore, their teams of nurses and interns and assorted hangers-on. Elissa and Chip and our mother. All of us. A convention. Everyone standing clumsily around the bed. There must be a dozen clipboards.

"Okay, Jim," Dr. Schore says, his face stern and frozen, like he'd rather be elsewhere. I can see lint in his beard. "You have nothing to worry about. We do this all the time. It's nothing new."

"But how do we know we haven't missed the window of

opportunity?" my father asks. "The cells are probably all dead by now." He moans. He buries his face into the leathery pocket his hands make when he clinches them together.

"You really have nothing to be anxious about," Dr. Schore says in his genteel, measured way. It is the lexicon of all doctors to speak in soothing, noncommittal phrases at times like this. "The worst is over. You already went through the chemo. This is nothing compared to the chemo."

"I don't want to do it," he says quickly. "If they're dead, you'll be putting dead things into my body. My body doesn't want dead things."

Dr. Schore lifts his glasses, rubs his eyes in frustration. "We're wasting time here," he says. He turns to one of the nurses. "Doris, can you get some morphine in him. We've got to get moving on this." Doris, a rounded, middle-aged woman with curly blond hair, nods and clicks the self-medication button two times with a sausage finger.

A few heads turn and glance at the clock. It's 1:13. The sun, high above the Fifty-Ninth Street Bridge, is bursting in the windows.

"These guys know what they're doing," Chip adds.

"Dad," Elissa says, "everything's gonna be okay."

Elissa squeezes between Dr. Schore and one of the clip-boarded interns to take our father's hand in her own. It is only then that he begins to calm. He weeps unabashedly but quietly. He seems oblivious to the fact that the room is crowded with lab-coated men and women eager to attach tubes to him.

Soon, his red-rimmed eyes grow slack and his head cants

to the left and he stops crying and doesn't say much of anything. Elissa continues to hold his hand until she is asked to
move out of the way.

The bag seems to materialize out of nowhere, passed
along from intern to nurse to Dr. Nadoo to intern until it
reaches Dr. Schore. A light pink color, like weak lemonade,
with a sticker that reads MORETTI, JAMES A. Schore turns the
bag around in his hands.

"What are you looking for?" I ask him. He cocks his head
at me, birdlike. He doesn't answer. He hands the stem cell
liquid to Doris, who hangs it next to the saline bag on the IV
stand. She selects the correct tube from the drawers by the
sink. She pulls down the top of my father's gown to expose
the chest port. She disconnects the saline tube and swaps
the two, starting the drip again.

"There we go," she says, rubbing her gloved hands together, latex upon latex making an unnatural sound. "Easy
as pie."

"Now what?" Chip asks.

"We wait," our mother says.

"Exactly," Dr. Nadoo says. He nods in satisfaction and
points a finger at the door. He and his team file out into
the hallway, followed closely by Dr. Schore and the rest of
them. Doris tells us she will be back to check on him in a
little while.

"Oh God," he moans, but it is low, almost inaudible. He
is exhausted. He must be exhausted. He gives himself over
to sleep. He makes sharp yelps from inside whatever visions
his brain is conjuring. Night terrors. He stirs now and then.

I watch the clear pink liquid drain from the bag and move through the snaking tube into his chest, his body.

He sleeps.

My mother takes a seat next to him and seems to fall into a trance, her gaze moving slowly from his face to the IV and back again to his face. She says nothing. Machines in the room beep and it is one of those times when I'm happy we are together. Sometimes, being present is enough, and if nothing else, we are here. All of us.

## ≪ **14** ≫

A week after the transplant. A week into his twenty-one days of isolation. All visitors must don surgical masks and paper skullcaps. They must remove their shoes and put on cloth slippers. Touch as little as possible. His immune system is on the mend, slowly climbing back to normal levels. Word from the doctors on high is the stem cells are holding and his white blood cell count is returning.

I hike into the woods with Elissa and Doug M. After work, Doug M. picks Elissa and me up in his Nova and we drive across the Tappan Zee. Gabby comes, too.

"Hello," I say, surprised to see her when I get in the car.

"Whatever," she says, her blue eyes hidden beneath the bill of her baseball cap.

We traverse a dense stretch of forest. White paint ticks on the sides of rocks and trees mark the Appalachian Trail, a path that stretches some two thousand miles from Maine to Georgia.

Doug M. leads us. A portly, noble guide. We pass a stream and a patch of stone formations like crooked teeth. We wind up a steep hill and negotiate short, curling switchbacks. We come to a large plateau of enormous flat rocks, running at least three hundred yards to a cliff overlooking the entire park. The lake is visible below and the cliff wall dropping off to the forest floor. The tops of trees are visible, swaying in the wind.

"I can't believe we made it all the way up here," Elissa says.

"It wasn't that hard," Doug M. says.

"I could stay forever," Elissa says. She walks forward, toward the edge. I follow her, rolling my eyes as I go. "Let's camp," she yells back as the wind picks up. Her hair flies into her face.

"We don't have sleeping bags," I tell her.

"So what?" she says. The wind gusts again. Gabby's hat flies off her head and she turns to follow it frantically. For the first time, I really see her hair: long and blond, straight and peppered with brown. She turns after the runaway hat so quickly I don't get a chance to see the hole in her head.

"Follow that hat," Doug M. says.

Gabby recovers the hat and the four of us make our way toward the edge of the plateau. We can go no farther. Beyond us, the rolling forest and hills stretch off to the horizon, where the sun and orange sky meet the treetops. I toe the cliff line. Let my foot dangle over the side. Doug M. walks with his hands on his stomach, leaning back slightly. He looks more like a king than ever. He turns his head this way and that, squinting in the wan sunlight. He undoes his pants and urinates off the side of the rock ledge.

"There might be people down there," Gabby tells him.

"Fuck 'em," he says. "Let 'em come get me. I'm a warrior."

Elissa gathers small rocks from the ground around

her. She draws back her thin arm and, one by one, flings them out into the air. I watch them arc, falling through the branches. Everything is glowing yellow and dull as the sun begins its dip. Behind us, our shadows are long. Mine seems to belong to a much more handsome version of myself. *My shadow is attractive*, I think.

We stand looking out over all of creation, or at least all of Harriman State Park, New York. Gabby holds a hand to her head. She's returned her hat to its familiar spot. She pulls her hair into a ponytail and threads it through the back of the hat. She and Elissa are laughing, pointing toward the lake. I can't hear what they're saying. It doesn't seem to matter. I walk over to join them.

"Can you believe we're only twenty miles from home?" Elissa says.

"Unbelievable," I say.

"Don't be a jerk," Gabby says, pushing me slightly. "It's beautiful. Admit it."

"I admit it," I say. And then none of us speak for a long time. We just stand there, listening to the wind, which has picked up so strongly I have to turn my head to take a breath. Elissa edges closer to me, puts her hand through my arm. I am a whole head taller than her.

"You should enjoy this," she tells me.

"I am enjoying it," I say.

"It's time I told them," she says. "Told him."

"The longer you wait, the harder it will be," I say.

"Part of me thinks he'll be happy about it," she says. "That it will be good for him."

"He acts like a grown-up baby," I say.

"And you wouldn't?" my sister says. "He can't fly, which is

like the only thing he actually loves to do. He can't pay the bills. He can barely walk."

"If he didn't sit around feeling sorry for himself," I say, "he might actually get better."

"You'll come with me?"

"Yeah," I say.

I try to imagine her in six months: swollen belly contrasted against her thin frame and angled features. I'm waiting for her to say something to make me feel better about my situation. I'm waiting for her to tell me everything will be okay. And then she does.

"It won't last," she says. "Whatever it is you're afraid you'll get yourself into. It won't last. Nothing does."

"But how much time will I lose in the process?"

"One day you might look back and be happy you have the memories."

"I don't know what I'm afraid of," I say.

"It's more than just the house," she says.

"When did you get so smart?" I say, giving her a little nudge with my shoulder.

"I was born this way."

My sister is a person who can enjoy the present. Something I have never been able to do. I am always too focused on the future, even when I have no idea what the future has in store. She is right, though. It is beautiful here and I don't want to ruin the moment by talking too much. So I shut up. I look at my sister. I'll help, I decide. Finding a new job is the solution. Keep saving money. Give the money to them. To the house. To whatever they want to put it toward. I will do the selfless thing. For once. I will do the thing my instincts tell me not to do. The right thing.

Gabby is beside us now.

"We're on top of the world here," she says.

"I wish I had a throne to sit on," Doug M. is yelling behind us, his arms raised in triumph.

"We better head back to the car before it gets too dark," I say, but I am the last one to start walking.

EVERYONE EXPRESSES HIS or her concern. At work, Georgie informs me that my father is in his prayers. Georgie tells me this during music time with Tony. He leans over. In a hushed voice, says, "He's in my prayers, dog." Georgie hits his chest a few times, indicating roughly the placement of his heart.

"You're in mine," I say. This confuses Georgie and he turns his attention back to Tony, back to the guitar and singing.

In the front room, with its colored paper over the windows, Arham and I sit staring at each other in silence. Angela and Hendrick are hard at work across the rug.

"You ready to do some learning?" I ask the little man.

"Yeah," Arham says. He is smiling from ear to ear. I take the lap desk off the floor and place it across my thighs.

"Numbers or colors?" I ask.

"Colors," he says. "Peepee?"

"Colors it is," I say. "No peepee."

Arham nods, as if everything makes sense to him. I hold up the first card. A red triangle.

"Triangle," he says. His eyes go slightly cross for a brief second.

"Red," I say. I put the card down on the lap desk and then pick it up again. Arham looks at it, licking his lips.

"Red," he says.

"Good job, buddy," I say. "Good job." I hand him a large piece of Oreo cookie, which he inhales with one chomp of his tiny jaws. We continue through the exercise. Out of twenty examples, Arham gets fifteen correct. Not bad. When we finish, he is slumping slightly in his seat. His head lolling with exhaustion. Our day is almost over and he is tired.

"We can stop," I say to him.

"Peepee?" he asks. I think he is telling the truth. Usually when there is no task at hand for him to get out of doing, a request for peepee can be taken seriously.

"Okay," I say. "Let's go." I put the lap desk and cards on the ground and close the rewards container. I start to stand up, but the little man has other things in mind.

"Hug," he says. He springs out of his seat, throwing his arms around my neck, smooshing his face against mine. I can smell a nauseating mixture of Cheetos and cookies. I lose my balance and we both fall to the ground, laughing. He is cracking up.

"Oh, oh, oh, oh, oh, oh," he is saying. Over and over again. He rolls away from me, giggling. The sun shining through the craft-papered windows is blue and green and red and it casts colored light on his face and hair. He takes my hand and leads me to the bathroom. Fortunately for me, Arham is capable of peeing without assistance. His parents make sure to dress him solely in sweatpants and sweatshirts, easy elastic waistbands. No confusing buttons or strings or zippers. Today he is wearing New York Jets contraband and, of course, his favorite pair of hand-me-down shoes, pink ballet slippers that once belonged to his older sister.

# ≪ **15** ≫

Everything appears to be in its proper place. Two sets of glass doors separating isolation room from hallway. Two sets of glass doors segregating germs and microbes and other unwanted particles from the sterile bubble he now dwells inside.

On my way from the elevator, a nurse with a soft smile and vacant eyes hands me a plastic bag containing all the necessary attire to wear while visiting. I feel silly in the latex gloves, mask, and cloth booties. I look at my reflection in the doors and am embarrassed that I still dress like a teenager: dirty jeans, T-shirt. I spend a couple of seconds trying to get the surgical cap to look right, but my head is too small, my hair too greasy.

I go in.

I look at him. He's drifting in and out of sleep. The Food Network blasts at top volume from the TV bolted to the ceiling. I take the remote and lower the sound to a respectable background level. He doesn't seem to notice me at first. His face is gaunt. His eyes are sunken farther back in his head.

His head is smooth peach fuzz. His skin has turned that jaundiced color I thought was reserved only for the dead. The room smells clean, antiseptic. It makes me slightly nauseated.

"Calvin," my father says. He pats a free space on the mattress next to him.

"I'll just sit here," I tell him, lowering myself into a chair near the windows. His new view isn't as spectacular as the first room he was in. York Avenue and the east side of Sloan-Kettering have replaced the looming span of the Queensboro Bridge. "How're you feeling?" I ask him. He makes a face like he doesn't know how he feels and for a while we don't say anything to one another. Every so often he moans.

"Oh God," he says.

"Oh God what?" I ask.

"I'm dying," he says.

"Jesus Christ, Dad," I say. "You're not dying. You're gonna be fine, just stop talking like that. It's in your mind. The doctors are saying it worked."

"Eh," he says.

We both turn our attention to the television and watch the tail end of an *Iron Chef* episode. I can hear him start to snore. He is asleep. I stand and walk to the window, look at traffic below. When I lean my head against the glass, I can see all the way up York Avenue into Spanish Harlem.

On the nightstand next to his bed, there are a bunch of "get well" cards my mother has arranged into a shrine, along with some books on spiritual well-being she has purchased for him. He refuses to even glance at them, but it doesn't matter, my mother feels satisfied simply because the books are in his presence, as if by some miracle the information contained on their pages will permeate my father's brain while he is sleeping. Underneath, I can see the notebook she gave him when we first came to the hospital. There are drips of dried paint across the front of it and a pen closed within, marking the place where he last wrote. I remember him saying he would never use the notebook. I open it. There are at least twenty pages of entries, including an extensive list of songs he would like played at his funeral. He's also made some watercolor sketches and penned numerous lines of poetry and a short essay about his favorite corkscrew.

As I read these things, I feel like I'm trespassing.

When I was twelve years old I found some nudie mags in the closet of my parents' bedroom. I don't know why I had gone in there in the first place, but once inside, I became exhilarated. I kept one ear always on the door, listening for footsteps on the stairs. The magazines were in a cardboard box under some blankets. When I found them, I felt like I was invading my father's privacy. Even though I don't put the notebook down, I have that same feeling now.

The sound of someone else in the room startles me out of my thoughts. It's Elissa. She is holding one of the green surgical caps in her hands. She slides nervously through the door. Her feet, encased in the sterile booties, make a soft whooshing sound as she walks. I put the notebook back where I found it and return to my chair.

"How's he doing?" she asks.

"The same," I say, not really knowing what that means. "I think you're supposed to put that on."

"It looks so stupid," she says, smiling, putting the cap over her hair and tucking her ponytail up into the back of it.

"You look great, sweetie," our father says. He is awake again. His face brightens in Elissa's presence and he pats the empty space beside him, just as he had when I came in the room. Elissa goes directly to him. She hugs his dwindling body and takes his hand in hers.

"Rub my back," he pleads. "It's fucking killing me." He rolls slightly onto his side and looks over his shoulder at her like a needy child.

"Okay, Dad," she says. "Just for a little while, though." She kneads her hands over his shoulders and squeezes in the places he tells her. He groans in ecstatic pain.

"You couldn't pay me to do that," I say.

"You don't care about me," my father says.

"Oh, I care about you," I say. "Just not enough to touch you."

When Elissa finishes rubbing his back, she turns to me and says, "I was wondering if I could talk to Dad alone for a little while." My cue to exit.

"Yeah, sure," I say, standing up. "I'm hungry anyway."

I am nervous for her. For all of us. I hope he takes it well.

"Do you guys need anything from the cafeteria?" I ask.

"I'm fine," Elissa says. Her face has taken on the soft, girlish qualities she seems able to summon at will for just such delicate situations as this. I'm sure it won't be the last time she delivers bad news to our father.

"WHAT DID HE DO?" I ask as I drive her to school.

"He cried for a while," Elissa says. "But I'm not sure he was crying about the baby."

"He wasn't angry?" I ask.

"No," she says.

"What exactly did you say to him, though? What were the words you used?"

"I told him he was going to be a grandfather," she says. She holds her backpack in her lap. Her face looks like it's gotten a little puffier. Aside from that, she is unchanged. She pulls a package of Twinkies out of her bag and shovels them into her mouth.

"Jeez, Elissa," I say.

"It's unreal how much I've been eating," she says. "Ever since the morning sickness stopped, my appetite is enormous."

"Pregnancy will do that," I tell her.

## ≪ 16 ≫

I make a list of everything in the attic:

*Boxes and boxes and boxes. An old rocking horse. A high
chair with a little white steering wheel. Toy soldiers covered
in dust. Stacks of framed pictures. Grandma and Grandpa on
the shores of Cape Cod. Chip, Elissa, and me in front of the
Louvre. Our parents' wedding. Birthdays. Graduations. Proms.
Hundreds of thirty-five-millimeter slides, just everywhere.
Major moments. Frozen time. Milk crates full of my father's
record collection (which I ransacked for any decent albums
long ago). A dresser full of winter attire. Wool sweaters, hats,
scarves, gloves, snow pants, ski boots, skis. Old stereo components in various stages of disrepair. Luggage, so much luggage. Heaps of decorations: Thanksgiving, Christmas, Easter,
Halloween, Valentine's Day. My mother decorates the house
almost weekly—there is always something to celebrate. An old
television set with a thirteen-channel dial. Magazines piled in a
loose mound, saved for some unknown purpose. File cabinets
stuffed with papers. Notebooks. Textbooks. Cookbooks. Letters. Folding chairs. Blankets. Cobwebs.*

I find solace in the attic. There are so many boxes up here. I kneel before a bookshelf on the far wall, near the only window. I feel dust in the back of my throat. I open the window. It's barely big enough to stick my head out, but the breeze feels good against the stale air. I take the lid off a cardboard box labeled *Calvin School Stuff.* Inside are report cards, standardized test scores, photos, book reports, drawings from art class. Anything my mother could get her hands on and preserve. Ours is a house where nothing is ever thrown away. Everything is sacred, irreplaceable, of possible future use. I lay out a series of class pictures spanning from second to fifth grade. Chris Hillman and I went to Siwanoy Elementary together. In all the photos he is seated two or three kids away from me, his blond hair tightly cropped, combed nicely to one side. His smile seems to exude and embrace his nerdiness. I remember his valedictory speech, outlining the merits of social responsibility, the importance of community. He'll be a lawyer soon. And a husband. I heard his fiancée's parents are helping them buy a house in Nanuet, across the Tappan Zee.

There were others who'd come up the educational ranks with me. Christian Rafelson joined the navy right out of high school. Tara Walsh—married at twenty-two, kid at twenty-three—went to cosmetology school and works at a salon in White Plains. Peter Wells, captain of the varsity hockey team, selling real estate in San Diego. Monica Pearce, tall, blond, extremely attractive, the wellspring of many a nighttime jerk-off session, still tall, blond, and extremely attractive, married to a douche bag, working at a PR firm in Manhattan, living in a two-bedroom off the park, purchased for her by her parents as a wedding gift. There's a good chance I'm the sole alumnus from Sleepy Hollow Memorial High School's graduating class of 2000 who's living back home with nothing to show for his life.

Thinking about all of this tips the seesaw on its never-ending back-and-forth journey between staying and going. I'm still convinced I need to take the altruistic route. Give what little I save to my mother, to my father, even to Chip. Keep the house. Keep a place for Elissa to bring the baby home to.

Of course, I waver in my conviction. The seesaw has two sides. I'm jealous of anyone who doesn't have money problems. Or health problems. Or both. I'm jealous even of my classmates who seem to have set up miserable lives for themselves. At least they have lives. I'm convinced of this. Any life is better than aimlessness. I should just move out. They'll be fine without me. And the seesaw floats up, up, up, toward hopefulness, toward the feeling that tells me everything will be okay. I can find a better job. I can help them keep the house. Between Chip helping and Elissa and me and 40 percent of my father's salary, the mortgage will get paid. And he'll get better. He'll be fine. They'll all be fine. The *baby* will be the catalyst for love in this house. It won't have to fall on my shoulders.

I go to the well-used file cabinet—the place where my mother archives all the financial papers that cross her desk.

From a folder labeled *Winter '06* I pull a sheaf of mortgage bills, half of which are second and third notices. It looks like she's rolled the school taxes and property taxes into the house—$9,455 is the average amount of each bill. I find a letter, written by her, asking the bank to wave the late fees, explaining about my father's illness and the loss of the majority of his salary. It isn't just mortgage bills either. There is life insurance. Gas and electric from Con Ed. Credit card bills. Landscaping. Snow removal. Spraying of the trees for insects. Emergency hospital visits. Planned hospital visits. MRIs. CAT scans. Chemo. There's even a bill for the wig she bought him, which of course he had nearly peed his pants laughing over and refused to wear.

She's got things pretty well organized. I can follow the papers on the house back three years (a length of time suggested by the IRS) and see how my parents fell back on their home equity line of credit to pay for things like college tuition, vacations, various credit card debts, and, most recently, those portions of his medical bills not covered by insurance. The whole mess is daunting. It sprawls beyond even my grasp of what the word *debt* means. At this point, the house, which they purchased in 1992 for $299K, has appreciated to $1.2 million, but they owe nearly that much, so even if they sold tomorrow, they'd walk away with barely anything. And just as quickly, the seesaw reaches the top of its fulcrum and the weight of it all sends my whole thought process in the opposite direction. No amount of money I save will make a difference. In all likelihood it's past any sort of fixable state. Still, it isn't about that. It's about being more present. It's about making myself available. Or at least trying to make myself available. Whatever I give is really just a symbol.

I take a last look at all the papers. There is one bill, from the Yonkers Water Company, for $312.67. It's a third notice and some kind of warning is attached. Two quarterly statements my mother hasn't gotten around to paying. It may have been missed in the deluge of invoices she encounters.

I put the other bills back in their folders. I close the drawers of the file cabinet. I fold the water company invoice and put it in my back pocket.

I go back to my bedroom. I can't sleep, so I put things in the notebook. I concentrate to make straight freehand lines. I use a fine-point Sharpie to draw tiny floor plans of our house. I make sure to include window and door positions, staircases, cabinets, the kitchen and dining room tables, televisions. I indicate the location of each and every paper *S* with small red stars. I tally fifty-three in total. Fifty-three indicators of safety. Spheres of well-being. I wonder if at this point he even notices these small reminders to stay positive, wear a smile.

I take the letter he wrote me from my sock drawer. The one where he said he felt closer to the end of his life than to the beginning. I cut out the words, trim them as close and tidy as I can with a scissors, and paste them into the notebook.

I start a new section. A section dedicated to the breakdown of expenses for our household. I title it "Family Finances." I try to determine everything we are paying for that isn't absolutely necessary. To identify where, if possible, we can cut back on spending. Try to embark on some sort of family-wide savings plan. It is a sense of guilt and dread and confusion driving me to do this. It isn't long before I'm overcome with fatigue and crawl into bed.

Later, in the middle of the night, I wander back to the kitchen, hungry. As I fix a turkey sandwich, I get sidetracked looking at all the pill bottles in the cabinet. I study their names. Strange, alien-sounding things: Revlimid, Decadron, Biaxin, Colace, Senokot. I research their side effects on the Internet. I squirrel away small stashes of the more interesting ones for myself, doling them out when I feel adventurous, lonely, angry, happy. Doling them out pretty much whenever I feel like it.

THEY RUN TESTS that seem to have no purpose at all. Write down numbers. Consult charts. Check graphs against other graphs. Watch as he blows into various tubes. Nod their heads. Scratch their chins. Tell us his immune system has recovered sufficiently. Tell us the stem cells have taken just fine, and as far as they can tell, the myeloma is moving into hiding. Tell us that if the cancer continues its retreat, with a little luck he can return to work by the end of the summer.

He comes home. They do not give him back his gun.

He still looks sick, his face and body sunken and withered, his hair just beginning to show the faintest traces of reemergence. Still, he's on the other side of the fence, they say, over all the big humps. Everything is steady, for the moment.

I send off a loan payment. I take a second blank check and make it out to the Yonkers Water Company in the amount of $312.67. I sign it. I figure if I use the hundred dollars I would normally spend on the purchasing of weed and various other methods of escapism, plus a little from what would be my monthly savings allotment, I can cover this one bill. I can do that much. I write everything in the book. Same routine.

I shuttle what I think I can spare into my savings account. Cross out the old, pencil in the new: ~~712.88~~. 888.13.

In the living room, I find my mother hanging decorations for the Fourth of July. Red, white, and blue things. Freedom-related trinkets.

"Jesus Christ, it isn't even June," I say to her.

"I've got a spare moment *now*," she says. "I'm hanging the decorations *now*."

"You're the boss," I say. She is staring at me. I take the check and the bill from my pocket and hold it out for her.

"What's that?" she asks.

"I found a bill," I say. "One I think maybe you missed."

"I'm bound to miss a few," she says.

"I want to pay it for you."

"It's not necessary, Calvin," she says.

I step forward with the check still in my hand.

"Just let me," I say. "I'll feel good about it."

She seems to be thinking it over. She takes the papers from me.

"Why are you snooping around in the bills?" she asks.

"I don't know," I say. "I thought if I had a better idea about how much we spend a month, I could think of some way to chip in."

She accepts this explanation. She looks over what I have given her.

"This is too much, Calvin," she says. "Really."

She keeps folding and unfolding the bill. I'm not really sure she knows what to say.

"Just take it, okay?" I tell her.

"How did I forget to pay the water?" she says.

"It happens."

She looks at me now.

"Thank you," she says.

I go to my bedroom.

When I lay my head down for sleep, I'm filled with a deep sense of contentment. One that stays with me all the following day.

WALLY THINKS HE should get a job.

"My father keeps telling me it's a good idea," he says.

"You did graduate from college," I tell him. "Most often it's the next step."

"I know that. I'm aware of that. I just don't see anything I want to do."

"You majored in history," I say. "There's always teaching."

"You need a master's to teach," he says.

"It helps," I say.

"We just need to get out of this beat town," Wally says.

"And go where?"

"Wherever we want."

"I can't," I say. "I've embarked on a mission."

"To save the house," he says. "Save the family."

"To grow up," I say.

"Never happen."

"Maybe not for you."

"Why do you refuse to accept this?" he says.

"You'll see," I say.

"You'll fail."

"But I'll try."

"The difference is debatable."

"I can't leave," I say. "I need to be around."

"Just for a little while," Wally says.

"I don't have money for a little while."

"We'll live off the land."

"You mean mooch?" I ask.

"Yes, mooch," Wally says. "Let's take a trip."

"I can't," I say.

We drive through the streets of Tarrytown, passing a joint back and forth. We listen to music. The sky is clear. I turn off North Broadway, drive past the library and down the long slope of Palmer Avenue. I pull into the parking lot of Kingsland Point. A few streetlamps cast orange pools of light. A group of teenagers talk loudly and laugh nearby, clustered around a picnic table. There is no one else in sight. I park and let the car idle. We roll down the windows. I turn off the radio and we finish the joint, throw the roach onto the ground.

"Sometimes I think my brother's right," I tell Wally. "He doesn't analyze things the way I do. He just does. He got it in his head that he wants to help my parents keep their house and he's doing it."

"Your brother's never been right about anything in his life," Wally says.

"He's right about this."

"I should get a job in a record store," he says.

"Art is the only truth there is," I point out. I like to pretend I know what a statement like this means. Art as truth. It's only half a joke.

The kids at the picnic table start smashing bottles. The sound echoes out over the river.

"Everything you need to know about human existence can be learned from movies," Wally says.

"Books and film. Music. These are the things we obsess over so we don't have to deal with real life," I say.

"These are the things," Wally says.

"He'll be home from the hospital soon," I say.

The water glints in the moonlight.

A cop car drifts up to the picnic table, materializing from the shadows at the other end of the parking lot. The kids bolt, fleeing into the darkness.

The spotlight follows them for a moment, but the cops don't bother to give chase. The light turns in our direction.

"Park closes at dusk," a voice booms. "Time to go."

I nod my head and wave. I put the hatchback in reverse and we are gone.

*"UN. FUCKING. BELIEVABLE."* My mother is screaming so loud she is drowning out *Jeopardy!* So loud my father stirs from his sleep at the other end of the couch and waves a hand at her.

"She told you?" I ask.

"No. She told *him*," my mother says. "She tells him everything. She always did. *He* told me. And apparently you already knew."

"Are you mad?"

"Family meeting," she says.

"No. No. Mom, not tonight."

"*Now*," my mother says.

"Do we have to?" my father asks, rolling over onto stomach, hiding his face in protest.

She doesn't answer. She just walks out.

We gather in the kitchen. Chip, in sweatpants, checks out his reflection in the windowpanes. Our father fiddles with the ends of his bathrobe. Elissa is looking sheepish at the head of the table. I sit with my notebook, hoping to show them all some of the expenses I've deemed unnecessary, possible cutbacks in Moretti family spending. Our mother is holding a plate of store-bought chocolate chip cookies. No homemade enticements this time.

"Go ahead and tell them," she says, practically throwing the plate onto the table.

"They already know," Elissa says.

"Know what?" Chip asks.

"I'm pregnant."

"That's a good one," Chip says.

"She's serious," I tell him.

"Are you fucking kidding me?" He chokes a little on the cookie he's cramming into his mouth.

"*She*," our mother says, "is not kidding."

"It's true," Elissa says.

"Are you getting the hook?" Chip asks.

"Come on now, Chip," our father says.

"It's a legitimate question," our mother says. "What *are* you going to do?"

"I'm going to keep it," Elissa says. She stands up. "I fucked up. I'm taking responsibility."

"You sound like a right-wing Christian," I tell her.

"No, I don't," she says.

"Now might not be the best time to be all *grown up*," Chip says.

"It's the right thing," our father says.

"Am I the only one here with a clear head?" our mother says, throwing up her hands. "This is insanity."

"I think Mom's a little freaked out at the idea of being a grandma," I say.

"Yes. It's freaking me out," she says. "It's not just that. It's the house. Everything." And she is crying, or rather, the red in her eyes is clearly visible. That place just before tears.

"We'll figure something out, Mom," Elissa says.

"I've lived here for fourteen years," she says.

"Mom, I know you don't want to sell this house," Chip says. "I don't want to lose it either."

"It might be out of our hands," I say.

"It's easy for you to say that," she says. "You act like this isn't your home anymore anyway."

"That isn't true," I say. "I'm gonna help. I've decided to help."

Our mother cries. Not a big show, just wet eyes.

"It'll be okay," Elissa says. She takes our mother's hand in hers.

"How will it be okay?" Chip asks.

"Dad's stress test is coming up. His numbers look good. Don't they?" I say. "There's a chance he'll be flying again."

"When? A year from now?" Chip says.

"I remember not too long ago you telling me I needed to be a little more supportive," I point out.

"He never leaves the house," Chip goes on. "He wears a bathrobe all day."

"It's comfortable," our father says.

"He *wants* to stay sick," my brother says.

"I'm sure," I say, "if they asked him to fly again, he'd get dressed."

"Perhaps," the old man says.

"We're so fucked," Chip says. "All the money I've sacrificed. Down the drain."

"Don't talk like that," our mother says.

"How should I talk?" Chip asks. "I'm the only one really doing anything tangible to help around here."

"Just because you're in a position to financially pitch in," I say, "doesn't mean you're the only one helping."

"Oh, yeah?" he asks. "What are you doing?"

"For starters, I'm trying to find a better job. Something that pays more."

"Honey, you don't have to," my mother says.

"It makes sense, though," I say. "If I was making more, I could support myself better. I could find a place of my own without any help from you or Dad. Every penny you have could go to the house."

"It's always about you," Chip says. "Isn't it?"

"No, it isn't," I say. "Look." I pull my notebook out of my pocket. I flip it open to the "Family Finances" section. "I've been looking over all the bills. And we spend a lot of money on stuff we don't need."

"Like what?" my mother asks.

"I don't know, lots of stuff," I say. "Canceling the country club got me thinking. But there's other things we could do without. Cut the maid loose, for starters. Maybe get rid of one of the cars."

"I barely have time to get your father to all his appointments," my mother is saying. "You want me to clean the whole house by myself on top of that?"

"We could all clean," I say.

"Maybe everyone just needs to fess up and admit the house is a done deal," Chip says. "The sooner we start figuring out where we're all going next, the better off we'll be."

"Where will we go?" Elissa asks.

"Somewhere smaller," Chip says. "Somewhere we can *afford* to live. Right now, that isn't here."

"Come on, Mom, stop crying," I say. "Please."

"I'm fine," she says.

The whole thing has taken a heavy toll on her and I can see something I've been missing this whole time. She doesn't want to move. She, more than any of us, is attached to this house, to all its weird noises and creaks. The cat-pee smell. The teal garage. All of it.

"Let's stop now," our father says. "I don't want to talk about this anymore. You're upsetting your mother."

But by then, there is really nothing left to say anyway.

IT'S LATER AND I find my brother in his bedroom watching the Mets.

"Now you like baseball?" I say.

"I got money on the game," he says.

"You've taken up gambling?" I ask.

"Looks that way," he says. He waves his hand like he wants me to go away.

"Take a ride with me," I say. He looks at me and says nothing. "For Elissa," I add.

In the car, my brother and I indulge in the only common musical bond we have, N.W.A. We listen to "8 Ball." We listen to "Straight Outta Compton." Maybe we share other more important things, but contemplating what they might be seems too daunting a task at the moment.

Stars in the sky tonight. The moon lights up the houses dotting the hills on either side of the river and there are hardly any cars on the Tappan Zee Bridge.

Most of the shops in the mall have already closed. We walk past handfuls of dimly lit storefronts with clerks hunched over cash registers, trying to balance out the day's sales. We ride the escalator to the top floor. Barnes & Noble is a burning testament to man's desire to do his shopping in large, pulsing chain stores.

It takes a while for Chip and me to find the parenting and family section. Neither of us will stoop to ask any of the numerous employees we walk past for assistance. Eventually we find ourselves in front of a wall lined with books on pregnancy, baby names, postnatal and postpartum care, fertility, motherhood. I scan the titles, trying to guess which one would be best. They all seem pretty apropos. *I'm Pregnant! A Week-by-Week Guide from Conception to Birth. Great Expectations: Your All-in-One Resource for Pregnancy and Childbirth. Oh, Baby, the Places You'll Go!*

"How 'bout this one?" Chip says. He grabs one at random and hands it to me. *The Mocha Manual to a Fabulous Pregnancy.*

"This is for black women, I think," I say, giving it back to him.

"Well, I don't know," he says, reexamining the cover before returning it to the shelf. I catch the eye of a middle-aged woman whose name tag reads "Doris."

"Excuse me, Doris," I say. She smiles what I imagine is a smile right out of the employee handbook and comes to stand between my brother and me.

"How can I help you gentlemen?" Doris asks.

"Do you sell any pregnancy books for teenagers?" I ask.

"I don't think so," Doris says. Her smile wavers only slightly.

"Our sister's pregnant," Chip says.

"I think most of these are probably written for women of all ages," Doris says.

"All right then," I say. I grab the one that Barnes & Noble has the most copies of: *What to Expect When You're Expecting.* "This will do," I say.

"Excellent choice," Doris says.

"Let's roll," Chip says.

Back home, we present the book to Elissa.

"I hate to burst your bubble," she says, "but Mom and I already got a bunch of these. But thank you, seriously, it makes me really happy that you did this for me."

My brother and I don't say anything. It's about other things, maybe. Doing something together, for someone else, someone other than ourselves. Something I'm trying to do more of.

## ≪ **17** ≫

My mother gets a dog. A Yorkshire terrier.

"It will be good for your father," she says. "Bring some happiness to this house. I think. I hope."

The dog arrives and is almost immediately the most annoying thing I've had to deal with in a long time. My sister names her Emma.

Her ears stick straight up like antennas and her eyes follow anything that moves. Her favorite activity seems to be trying to lick people's noses. She is adorable and her adorableness is intolerable. She is full of boundless energy, a bundle of hyperactive rambunctiousness that has no limit. I fight a constant urge to kick her across the room.

My grandmother sings to the dog. Makes faces at it. Talks to it like you talk to a baby.

In the living room I lie on the floor, on my back, staring at the light fixtures. Emma prances around my head like a prizefighter, bobbing and weaving, licking my cheeks, my chin, trying to fit my nose into her tiny mouth. Occasionally

I swat at her and she bounces out of reach, then scampers forward, nipping away.

"She's definitely irritating enough to be part of this family," I say.

"You're so grumpy," Elissa says.

Our father pads in from the TV room, holding his bathrobe tight around his waist, dragging a blanket behind him. He is like a child roused from a nap.

"Can you shut up?" he asks. "I'm sleeping."

"Dad, you can't just lie around the house," I say. "You should be out doing stuff. The doctors say it's good for the remission."

"Doctors don't know anything," he says. He grimaces. He runs his free hand through the tiny amount of hair that has returned to his head. "I'm dying." He squats down on his haunches and tickles the floor with his fingers, making a sucking noise between his teeth. "Here, Emma. Here, sweet girl," he says.

The dog drops back a moment and stares at him, head cocked, deep in thought. Her tail wags. She darts forward, attacking his hand. He smiles. He sits down, crosses his legs, and scoops the dog up into his arms, cradling her like a baby. He scratches Emma's belly, and her hind leg twitches with pleasure.

"We can barely take care of ourselves," I say. "And now we've got another living thing to look after." I stand up and start off toward the kitchen.

"Cal," Elissa calls after me, "don't be so angry."

"I'm not cleaning up any poop. I'm saying that right now so everyone is clear."

In the kitchen, I find my mother and grandmother, fixing dinner. The smell of peppers and onions is everywhere, as is, of course, the smell of garlic.

"The idea is to spend less money," I say, plunking myself down in a chair at the dinner table.

"The dog makes everyone feel good," my mother says. She wipes her hands on her apron.

"It doesn't make me feel good," I say.

"You're in the minority there," she says.

"Little Emma needs us to take care of her," my grandmother says.

The all-too-common feeling of claustrophobia creeps in. How can I help if they refuse to use common sense?

It's like I've known only this house and these people all my life. Maybe I won't ever know anything else. Maybe I'm not supposed to. The scariest thing: that somehow I'm meant to be here, at this kitchen table, forever, for all time, watching these two women make chicken cacciatore. I picture a future where my parents manage to hold on to the house and I help them do it. I could, in essence, be indenturing myself to a lifetime of postadolescence with no hope of anything more.

I stand up quickly, grab my keys off the countertop, and am out the back door without answering anyone's queries as to where I'm going or when I'll be back. I am unconcerned that dinner is almost ready.

The car smells like socks and recently smoked joints. I grab the nearest tape, Infest's 1987 demo. I pop it in. I crank the volume. I back out of the driveway too quickly and don't see Chip come running around the corner until I'm almost on top of him. I slam on the brakes and he makes a grand gesture, pretends I've hit him. He howls in fake agony. Bursts out laughing. I roll the window down, lower the music.

"Very funny," I say.

"I know, I know," he says, catching his breath.

"Where are you coming from?" I ask. I wave a hand up and down, indicating his outfit: mesh shorts, wife beater, running shoes, headband.

"Work," he says. "I found a way to get an extra mile of cardio a day. I run to and from the train." He pats his briefcase affectionately. "My suit," he says.

I roll the window back up without saying anything else and pull away, turning the stereo up even louder than before. My brother fades in the rearview mirror, watching me go, until he is nothing more than a blurry figure on the sidewalk. I turn a corner and he is gone.

WE TAKE ADVANTAGE of a particularly nice day. We bring the children outside. To the playground: A bed of wood chips and safety-padded climbing apparatuses, rubberized benches surrounded by wooden fencing. A romper room for those not capable of romping without causing severe bodily harm to themselves and others.

I take Arham by the hand and lead him into the bright morning sunlight. He laughs manically and runs in circles for a while, waving his hands at the sky, at the clouds. He opens and closes his tiny fists in an attempt to grab it all, pull it down. He falls. He picks himself up again. I pretend to be a monster. I chase him, making gurgling noises and lurching about like a zombie. I catch him and hoist him into the air as he shrieks with laughter.

"Gotcha," I say. He bubbles with joy and I spin him round and round and then send him on his way. He runs to the slide, wobbling with dizziness. He pauses, steadying himself, before he looks back and laughs some more.

Little Hendrick Ramirez is tugging at my sleeve.

"Be the monster for me," he says.

"Take off the fireman's hat," I say, "and I'll be the monster." He thinks about this.

"I no take off my hat," he says.

"No dice," I tell him. He pivots and runs off. He and Arham take turns scampering up the netting of the climber and hurling themselves down the slide headfirst.

Angela comes over to stand near me.

"You're great with him," she says.

"Think so?" I say.

"Of course," she says.

I look out at the playground.

"I love that little guy," I say.

After yard time, I sit in my small chair with my lap desk. Arham sits in his small chair. We run through some lessons. I show him letters on index cards. He calls them out.

"*A*," he says.

"Good job," I tell him. I hand him a small piece of Doritos from the box.

I present another card.

"*K*," he says.

"Excellent, my man," I say.

Another card.

He tilts his head.

"*P*," he says.

"*Q*," I say. I let the information sink in.

I put the card facedown on the lap desk. I show it to him again.

He tilts his head.

"*Q*," he says.

"Good job," I say. I rub his head. I feed him more chips.

I mark two checks and an *X* for the first three results on my clipboard.

Before I know it, we've gone through five lessons. Letters, colors, actions, pattern recognition, and shapes. The morning session ends and Arham gets on his bus and is gone. I eat my lunch in silence at one of the picnic tables.

Friday afternoons are reserved for staff meetings. This week's gathering is dedicated to an instructive lecture provided by the New York State Department of Health and Mental Hygiene. "Infection Control in the Day-Care Setting." We are promised a mandatory certificate of completion at the end. A piece of paper required by law for caregivers working with children under the age of five. The County of Westchester sends a tall, sallow-faced Polish immigrant named Dr. Francis Valcheck. "Call me Dr. Frank," he tells us all. He peers at us from behind golden wire-rimmed glasses and speaks with a strong accent. We are seated in uncomfortable folding chairs, staring at a projector screen. I give myself ten minutes before my mind completely wanders off into the land of daydreams.

Dr. Frank's presentation begins.

"I am here on my own time," he tells us. "I take this class very seriously. I will not tolerate chitchat. I will not tolerate jokes or giggling or any of that silly stuff. I'm not being paid to be here. You are. This class and the certificate we give you are required of you by law and you must stay until the very end or else I will not give you credit for attendance."

There is a murmur in the back of the room.

"What's that?" Dr. Frank says. He holds a hand to his ear and leans forward, pantomiming as though he is listening for the disrupter. "Are you saying you know more about this stuff than I do?"

Georgie snickers. Dr. Frank points his finger at Georgie. "You think this is funny?"

"No, sir," Georgie says, suddenly straight faced, if not a little embarrassed to be singled out.

"Please, tell me," Dr. Frank continues. "Maybe you are a registered nurse? Hmm? Maybe you are the smartest? Ya? Maybe you want to come up here and lead the class. Do the show? I'll sit down. Take a nap."

"I ain't no nurse," Georgie says.

Dr. Frank stands up tall. He turns his attention back to the entire room.

"Very distracting to have people talking. Giggling," he says. "No more. Please, people. Let's pay attention. There is nothing funny about what I'm going to teach you today."

The good doctor goes on to show us a PowerPoint presentation on how to properly identify certain infectious diseases. The accompanying slides are very disturbing. I'm particularly weirded out by the photos of adult tetanus, which show a naked man whose muscles have locked—back arched, teeth clenched, rigid from head to toe, like a curved metal rod.

"Total prolonged contraction of skeletal muscle fibers, ya?" Dr. Frank says. He doesn't wait for a response. He presses on. He shows us measles, mumps, diphtheria, pertussis, rubella. He shows us the correct ratio of bleach to water required to make a suitable solution for cleaning tabletops and diaper-changing areas and toys. We watch a video detailing the correct way to wash hands. "Count to thirty in your head," a young woman narrates. "Remember to wash hands after any of the following: After arrival at the center. Before eating or handling food. After toileting or assisting children with toileting, and after diaper changing. After contact with any body secretions (nasal or oral secretions, stool, blood, urine, vomit, or skin lesions). After handling an ill child. Use a vigorous friction."

No one makes a peep the entire time. After the slide show, Dr. Frank embarks on a rather lengthy tangent about his childhood in wartime Poland. Several relatives of his weren't able to smuggle themselves to the United States, wound up in concentration camps. "I was very lucky," he tells us all. He raises a finger in warning and waves it around the room. "Very lucky," he says.

An hour later, we are all filing out of the room, certificates in hand, heading to our cars and the weekend. It is the end of one of those days where work doesn't seem so meaningless. A day when infectious diseases can be tamed and controlled. A day when Arham's vacant smile is full of hidden genius and untapped potential. A day when there is hope in even the most lunatic of possibilities.

THE PHONE IS ringing for a while before I remember I'm the only one in the house. I'd successfully persuaded my father to accompany my mother to the movies. I send them to a romantic comedy about a sports reporter who falls in love with the pro tennis player she's assigned to interview. I know they'll both hate it, but it's the first public appearance, aside from hospital/pharmacy/video store trips, that the old man's made in a long time. I even get him to wear a sweat suit and no bathrobe, which takes my promising to DVR the episodes of *Law & Order* he'll be missing. Chip is out in the city with his friends. Elissa, too, has been carted away by a group of obnoxiously chatty girls to "hang out."

It's eleven o'clock, somewhere in that area. I'd fallen asleep with a copy of *Fangoria* draped over my chest. The ceiling fan is whirring and whirring with the sound of the telephone.

"Hello," I say after rolling off my bed and sliding on my stomach across the hardwood floor.

"Cal." It's Elissa.

"What's wrong?"

"I don't want to be here anymore."

"Where?" I ask.

"Over at Grace Reynolds's. A party. He's here."

"Who's he?"

"*Him.*"

Apparently I'm not assessing the situation as quickly as my sister thinks I should be. Then it clicks.

"Oh, okay," I say. I rub my face, trying to motivate myself into a state of readiness. A mind-set of relaxed helpfulness. "Don't panic. I'm on my way. Just stay where you are."

"I'm in the bathroom, on my cell phone," she says. "I don't have a ride and my friends want to stay."

"It's cool," I say. "I'm on my way. I'm leaving right now. Listen to the sound of my keys."

I hang up and walk to the hatchback. Crickets seem to be the only thing I can hear, sawing away to one another. The air is clear and dark.

I drive at a fairly good clip, across town to Kelbourne Avenue, over to Munroe and then finally onto Hunter Avenue. I can see the line of cars parked outside the place. Empty cups and random packs of howling, lurching teens pollute the vicinity. Parents out of town: the crucial ingredient to all successful high school parties.

I park. Walk around back and push through clusters of googly-eyed preps and jocks and a strange contingent of tight-panted, jean-jacket-wearing punks before I'm able to locate the back door and then the kitchen and finally the stairs, which take me up to a dimly lit hallway. Dance music is pumping downstairs. Up here, the floorboards are vibrating with dull bass throbs. I feel the masses of young bodies below, swaying, spinning, gyrating.

I find the bathroom, but Elissa isn't there. I open a bedroom door to a view of two kids making out. His hands on her tits.

"Sorry," I say.

"Pervert," she says before I can close the door.

*Lucky bastard*, I tell myself. I turn to head back down the steps and see Elissa by the window at the end of the hall, in shadows.

"You got here quick," she says.

"You said it was urgent."

"It is."

"Are you all right?"

"Not at all. I'm having trouble breathing. They keep staring at me."

"We'll go."

"Him and his friends. I feel like they want to hurt me."

"No one's gonna hurt you."

"I feel all weird. My heart is pounding. It's gonna kill the baby." She puts her hand on her belly. Leaves it there.

"The baby is fine."

"Everything's all fucked up," she says. She slumps forward a little, in her shoulders. I move to hug her but pull back before I do.

"It'll be fine. We'll just leave."

"What'd I do? I'm just one more problem in a series of unsolvable problems."

"Listen. I understand. I completely agree. It's a shitty situation. But what you're saying, it doesn't have anything to do with the baby. The baby will be fine."

"You don't know that," she says.

"We'll all be okay. You'll see."

"I'm so confused."

"You don't have to figure anything out right now," I say. "You're the one who's always telling me not to think so much. Now is a time for that. Now is a time for no thinking. To listen to your own words."

"I feel all weird."

"It'll pass."

"It's probably the weed."

"You're high?" I say. I can hardly believe what I'm hearing.

"I know," she says. "Don't yell at me, okay? It was, like, one joint. Like, half a joint. I just. . . I don't know. I fucked up."

"You definitely fucked up," I say. I grab her by the shoulder and start shuttling her toward the stairs. "You're smarter than this."

"I hate him," she says.

"You should."

"Thanks for coming."

"It's okay."

"I don't know what I'm doing here."

"All right. Let's go." I take her by the elbow and together we go back downstairs and through the living room. The music is in full force here. A kid in a ridiculous red striped tracksuit is pumping his fists in the air behind turntables in the corner. He drops out the low end for a few seconds on the mixer, then cranks it back up. The crowd cheers wildly and flails about.

I stop along the wall and survey the room. Elissa is looking meek, glassy eyes focused on the floor. I can see now she is pale, sweaty.

"Where is he?" I ask.

"Please, Cal," she says over the noise. "Let's just go." I stare at her. She points to a group of kids hovering near the keg in its ice-filled plastic bucket. They are crowded into a narrow passage near the front door. I drag her toward them. I spot him without her help. I don't even know his name, but I know which one he is. He's the one who can't look at us. The one whose head is aimed at the ground more intensely than Elissa's.

"Hey," I say, pushing him against the wall.

"What's your problem, dude?" he says. His hair is dirty blond. There are freckles around his nose. Hollow eyes.

"My problem is you're a fucking asshole," I say.

A couple of his friends seem to have gathered around and are eyeballing me with hungry stares. They would like nothing more than a fight. It would make their evening memorable. Separate it from all the other nights.

"Cal," Elissa is saying, tugging at my sleeve. "Let's go."

"Dick," I say as I turn and follow my sister out the front door. I'm flush with adrenaline. I spend the entire ride home fantasizing about better last words I could have said to him. Thinking, *I should have punched him.*

IT TAKES ME a while to calm down. I pace around in the kitchen. My father is asleep on the couch in the TV room, home from the movies. I kept my promise. *Law & Order* is replaying itself at top volume, drowning out his snores.

I eat a turkey sandwich. I drink orange juice straight from the container. As I'm closing the refrigerator door, I see Elissa standing near the back stairs. She is dressed in a white T-shirt, running shorts. Her hair pulled up in a ponytail, her stomach swelling underneath it all.

"I'm sorry about that stuff I said," she says. "I don't know what I was talking about."

"No worries," I tell her. "It's understandable. We've all got a lot going on. You especially."

"I want this baby."

"I know," I say. "It's okay to have doubts. It's a big thing."

"It's good for me," she says. "I'm happy about it."

"Okay," I say.

She laughs a little and turns to head upstairs.

"Good night," she says.

"Good night," I say.

*She isn't ready for a child. I'm always amazed at how much more mature Elissa seems than either Chip or I. But a kid? She needs to live her life more. She needs to have the chance to fuck things up in the normal way. Like the rest of us. Having a kid at seventeen is too much of a fuckup too soon. She'll miss out on the chance to build up other more instructive life regrets. She may have made the wrong choice in keeping the baby.*

*It could be that the ability to make any difference—with Elissa, with him, the house—is beyond anything I have to offer. It could be it's only my presence anyone requires. The simple action of being here. To see things through, no matter the outcome. Is that the right thing to do? I keep asking myself the same questions and I keep coming up with the same vague answers. Stick it out and see what happens. The choice entails scary possibilities. And none of them seem to include my ending up happy. I don't want anything bad to happen to my family. I don't want to lose my father. I don't want Elissa to struggle in her life, just as much as I don't want to dash my chances of being happy.*

# ≪ **18** ≫

He gets a new gun.

This time, a smaller, more compact version. A snub-nosed .38.

My father's love of weaponry has always intrigued me. When I was a child, he went on frequent hunting trips with his friends. They'd venture up to the Catskills wielding .22 rifles. They fancied themselves outdoorsmen. He was in shape then. He swam three times a week. He ran every morning. As he grew older and all three kids needed his attention, he had less time to spend on his hobbies. He gave up the outdoor adventures. He gave up exercising. He grew a belly. The cancer brought back his survival instincts, his obsession with a rapidly approaching apocalypse. The assumption that if he dies, so would the world.

I steal my father's gun. Or rather, I borrow it for an afternoon. I don't know why I do this. I'm in the TV room. I see it resting on the coffee table in front of the couch where he is fast asleep: The flat-screen, the sectional couch, him in his bathrobe, snoring. Baby pictures of Elissa, Chip, and me on the walls. A newly framed black-and-white shot of Emma. Against this grand tableau of white suburbia, the gun. Metal and cylinders and bullets. I sit down at his feet quietly, trying not to wake him. He snorts loudly as the weight of my body comes to rest on the couch. His breathing quickens and then relaxes, returning to a steady rhythm. He snores on. I reach a hand out and place it over the gun. I feel the coldness of it. I'm not holding it, but I feel its heaviness. I pick it up. So many connotations. So many meanings for such a small thing. I look at my father's face. The only time he seems at peace is when he is asleep. I look at his mustache. I stand and tuck the gun into the waistline of my jeans. I feel stupid doing this, so I take it out and put it in my back pocket, where it bulges like an inflated wallet.

I PICK WALLY UP. We drive out to the woods. We are sober— no pills, no weed, nothing. It feels good to have my wits about me. My head is clear. I roll the windows down and let the air rush in, filling the car with sound, tossing my hair in every direction.

"It's getting hot these days," Wally says.

"We'll head to Island Pond," I say. "Go swimming."

"Definitely," Wally says. He reaches into his backpack, pulls out a BB gun, an old pump-action, the kind that fires a single pellet at a time. "We can shoot some cans," he says, stroking the gun, pleased with himself.

"Cool," I say.

I pat the .38 in my pocket. I am filled with a sense of manliness because of the gun. It throbs against my hip, separated from my body by only a thin layer of really dirty denim.

We drive seventeen miles west of Tarrytown, over the bridge. We pass the mall in Nyack, the ice rinks in Monticello. We count signs for Harriman State Park. We pass the dairy farm boasting the world's greatest mozzarella cheese. We pass the hot dog stand just off the Thruway. We park at the edge of the woods and enter, full of hope.

Shafts of light cascade down through gaps in the foliage.

"This is truly God's kingdom," Wally says as he rushes through a patch of tall, swaying grass. He runs his hands across the tops of the blades. "It's amazing we don't enjoy this place sober more often."

"I can feel the insects around us," I say.

"See what I mean?" he says. "If we had real lives, we'd have to give this up."

"Would we?" I ask.

"It wouldn't be the same," Wally says. "When you have responsibilities, you're always thinking, *What should I be doing right now?*"

"I think that all the time as it is," I say.

"Then stop," Wally instructs. "Let it go."

"It's not that easy," I say.

"Your sister fucked up," Wally says. "You're father is fucking up by not snapping out of his funk or whatever. You didn't do anything wrong. You don't have to punish yourself. You don't have to stay there."

I'm looking at the back of Wally's head as we hike, really trying to study his posture, the slant of his body. I'm trying to figure out what he's really saying to me. *Do I know this person at all? What common bond brought us together as friends? Does it still exist?*

We listen to the breeze. We reach the pond. We swim. We leave our clothing on the rocks. I am careful not to let Wally see the .38. Not yet.

We wear only our underwear. The water is warm. Occasional pockets of frigidness erupt from unknown depths. There are things living beneath us. Dark things I don't like to think about.

Wally wants to swim out to the tiny island in the middle of the pond. It takes us ten minutes and I make most of the journey on my back.

"I'm doing the reverse doggy paddle," I say through a mouthful of scummy water.

The island is maybe twenty yards in circumference, ringed by rock outcroppings and a few scrawny trees. Wally climbs out of the water and stands triumphantly on top of the island's highest point. He startles a flock of white and gray herons resting in the brush. They flap violently into the air, squawking and confused. I scamper up to dry land, clawing at rocks, and hoist myself onto a flat stretch of limestone.

"We'll call this Bird Island," I say.

I stand. Water runs off my body onto the rock. The sun dries it up as I watch. The pond stretches out before us. The spot where we left our clothing seems a mile away.

"Man, we swam far," Wally says, holding a hand to his forehead, warding off the glare.

"We're fools for never having done this before," I say.

"Fools," Wally says.

After a time, we swim back. We laze about on the mainland rocks, drying our frail bodies in the sun. There is no one else around. I feel as though we are completely isolated from the world. It is a good feeling and for a second I am enjoying myself. I am enjoying the moment as it unfolds, trying not to think about anything else.

"Let's shoot the BB gun," Wally says. He puts his jeans back on and ties his T-shirt around his head like a turban.

I fashion my shirt in a similar way and check to make sure the pistol is still secure in my pocket, and together we wander off along a faint trail. It leads up around the pond to an area of the forest we have never been to before. A broad canopy of trees looms overhead, and here it is cool and inviting, lush sounds all around.

Wally loads a pellet into the BB gun and pumps air into the chamber.

"Hello!" he calls out. Nothing stirs, only the ever-present sound of leaves. He raises his gun and fires at a nearby tree. With a dull sound, the pellet embeds itself in the soft bark.

"Check it out," I say. I take the pistol out of my pocket and hold it awkwardly, not gripping it by the handle, but rather letting it lie flat in my palm.

"Who's is that?" Wally asks.

"My dad's," I tell him.

"Someone would hear," Wally says, looking around.

Branches crunch beneath our feet.

"There's no one out here," I say. I'm not convinced of this, but I say it anyway. I want to fire the gun. "*He* does it all the time," I say. We stand for a while, my arm outstretched, the gun sitting in my hand, neither of us moving, our breathing getting quick and choppy. Slowly I bounce the gun and then take it in my hands, curling my fingers around the handle. I put my back against a tree and raise the barrel. I pounce forward, swinging my body, bringing the gun to bear on the empty forest before me.

"Lemme hold it," Wally says. I hand the pistol over to him. "What kind of gun is this?"

"Snub-nosed thirty-eight," I say. "He took it to the movies last week."

"Will he be pissed?"

"Probably," I say. "It'll be good for him. Keep him on his toes. If anything, me taking the gun will only further convince him that no amount of readiness is going to help."

A rustling in the near distance catches our attention. About a football field away, as if magically conjured on cue, a deer is toeing through the brush. A small thing, bowing its head to the ground.

"A doe," I say, quiet, hoping not to scare it off.

The deer takes a few hesitant steps forward. I'm not sure it has seen us yet.

"Check it out," Wally says. He smiles. He pops out the cylinder of the revolver and empties the six bullets into his hand. He takes one and reloads the gun with a single round. He spins the cylinder and slams it home.

"I'm gonna find out what this deer knows," Wally says.

He raises the gun, so nonchalantly it's like he's merely pointing his finger. The dead click of the hammer.

"Let me try," I say.

Wally surrenders the gun to me. I spin the cylinder. Take aim at the deer. I pull the trigger. The forest erupts in sound, the report echoing out like thunder cracks. The deer looks at us and then falls into the dirt, its legs kicking about.

"Jesus fucking Christ," I say.

We run to the animal. It is in the midst of intense death throes. There is a lot of blood. The deer is violently twitching, its legs flailing this way and that way, leaves stirring up in the ruckus. It snorts loudly, again and again.

"There's nothing we can do," I say.

"Fuck you, Cal," Wally says. His voice is altered now, panicked. "You killed a living thing here. What are the fucking odds of this happening?" He looks at me with pleading eyes. He looks at me like a child who knows he has done wrong.

"One in six," I tell him.

"No, really," he says. "I mean, it has to be like one in a thousand or more."

"No matter how dumb you are," I say, "the math doesn't change."

"Oh, fuck," Wally says.

"It's not dead yet," I say. We watch the deer. Its gyrations lessen, and one of its eyes points straight up at the trees, blinking rapidly. The deer snorts loudly one last time and for a while nothing happens.

And here, if I really think about it, is evidence of something I've been looking for ever since my return to the family homestead. Of course, it was a thing administered by chance, the killing of the deer, but wasn't *I* in control of that chance? Sure, the deer had to be there at precisely the right moment. The bullet had to be in the chamber. The wind or tides or tilt of the earth, or whatever, had to align just so and guide everything home. Yet, wasn't it my hand wielding the gun? Squeezing off the round? In part it was chaos at work—the chamber could have been empty. All right. But it wasn't. And now that it's over with, I can't seem to imagine any other outcome. I'm not able to summon any possibility other than pull trigger, fire bullet, kill deer. It's all laid out in a divine plan from start to finish. So simple. Luck and chaos and uncertainty are part of it, but ultimately I set the thing in motion. And why not carry that over to everything else in my life? Why not link everything I want together into my own plan and then see it through to completion? We expect the same, if not more, out of the retards. We ask them to attempt to learn in the face of almost overwhelming natural instincts to *be idiots*. If they can be better, I can be better. The seesaw swings up and I see a clear path to good things. The family keeps the house. I contribute what little I have to contribute, and when the time is right, I leave, I get my own place. I get everything I want. Everyone is happy and alive and without sadness. The way is so clear.

"This is an important moment," I say.

"We're murderers," Wally says.

"We're men," I say, and I put the gun back in my pocket. It is hot. So hot, in fact, I feel its burn against me, alive.

Clearly I have moved on to some other level of life, a place where Wally has not followed. I see now a gap between us. His inability to move forward. His insistence on staying put without any thought about the future. I'm closer to figuring my life out. I'm trying. Baby steps, I think, are the way. Baby step #1: Don't spend so much time with my friends. Baby step #2: Less weed. Baby step #3: Love everyone. Baby step #4: Save money. Baby step #5: Give money to family. Baby step #6: Move out. Baby step #7: Start life.

"We have to get out of here," Wally says, moving away from the deer. "Someone definitely heard that. This is what happens when I don't get high."

We return to the car without incident. Wally tries to forget what we have done, but I hold it close to me. The deer died because I was in control. We aren't as helpless as we seem. When I get home, in an effort to test my theory of control, I find a reasonably priced home appraiser in Tarrytown and schedule an appointment for the following week. If we are going to lose the house or be forced to sell it, we might as well be armed with as much information and as much foresight as we can gather.

## ≪ **19** ≫

As May draws to a close, I can see the end of the academic year at the John W. Manley School. Special children need special care, so there's no real summer break to look forward to. School officially ends the last week of June. The kids go back out into the world. They sit in their parents' backyards for a brief two-week intermission, floating blissfully in inflatable pools, smearing ice cream all over their faces. Then they return to us, and the process continues through eight weeks of "camp" until September rolls around and the academic calendar starts up again. The only difference between real school and camp is that we aren't required to collect data on the children over the summer. I do not have to chart Arham's progress.

While public school teachers across the country get two whole months devoid of vacant-eyed stares and temper tantrums, we get two lousy weeks. After which it's back to my little chair. Back to watching Arham march across the room to his seat in front of me, his little head barely clearing the cubby shelves. Back to Shaynequa and Hendrick and

Franklin and the little girl whose name I never learned who keeps smearing her own poop on the walls in the OT room.

Still, though, summer is summer and we get half-day Fridays as something of an appeasement. I am looking forward to idle time again. I will sit in the air-conditioning of my parents' house, watching bad movies. I will take my baby steps. I will deal with the frustrations of my family. I will throw myself to their aid. I will figure out how to be helpful. And when it all becomes too much, and only as a last resort, I will attempt to escape boredom by taking drugs. But usually I'm not bored. I have a pretty active imagination, so I'll just take drugs in an effort to become one with nature. Only I hate the idea of becoming one with nature. That dirt. Those squirming bugs. I will stay inside as much as possible. I will battle the heat. I will reverse my hatred of insects and dirt and embrace nature. I will make frequent trips to the state parks of the region. I won't turn my back on anyone. I will get close to everyone. I will be all things to all people. Friend, brother, son, lover. It looks to be a wonderful summer.

"You should get a job painting houses in your spare time," my father says at dinner.

"Why the hell would he want to do that?" my mother asks.

"I did it when I was in high school," my father says.

"He isn't in high school," my mother says.

"He can make some extra money," my father says.

After the incident with Wally in the woods, I returned the gun to my father's bedroom. My father never inquired as to its sudden disappearance that one afternoon. Whether he knew I took it and simply chose not to mention it, or he had no idea, is a mystery to me. I never asked him about it.

I CATCH CHIP in the bathroom in the middle of his bedtime ritual—an insane series of cleansing and beautification treatments of his own design that he has been administering to himself since high school. He is convinced his good looks depend on carrying out this process on a daily basis. He has detailed this regimen to me many times. First he showers, scrubbing his body with different cleansers. He washes his face with an alcohol scrub and then exits the tub, leaving the water running at the hottest temperature. He sits on the toilet for twenty minutes with a towel wrapped around his head. When he has sufficiently "steamed" himself, he washes his face in the sink with three kinds of acne medicine and applies dabs of a tan-colored cream to particularly troublesome spots. He brushes his teeth, flosses, gargles with mouthwash, and shaves his chest, arms, and legs and trims his pubic hair with an electric razor. He opens the door to let the room cool down. He uses Q-tips to clean his ears and nostrils and puts on aftershave.

"You know how much water this wastes?" I remind him as I walk by.

"It's the price one pays to look this good," he says.

I go to my room and lie on the floor listening to Appalachian folk music from the 1920s until I can't keep my eyes open anymore, at which point I crawl into bed and drift off.

The next day, when I get home from work, there is a letter waiting for me on the kitchen table. Another invitation to the Hillman wedding. It's as if by some sadistic courier, some cruel joke, Chris knew I had flushed the first one down the toilet. The worst part about this new invitation is a handwritten note on the back:

*Calvin,*

*Hadn't gotten an RSVP from you yet about the wedding. Really hope you can make it. Feel free to bring a significant other. Just let us know who'll be coming by July 1.*

*Thanks.*

It is signed "Chris Hillman."

I go to the garage with my notebook. I count everything there. All the flashlights and matches, the tents and sleeping bags, the cans of beans, rice bags, and lanterns, the batteries and snakebite antivenom, the first aid kits, all the rifles, pots, and pans, the water bottles. All of it. I make a list. I imagine it is not dissimilar to the list my father keeps. The inventory he has made for himself.

*I have long believed my father to be truly at ease only behind the yolk of an airplane. In his healthier days, away on trips to Europe or Asia or wherever, he'd phone my mother frequently to complain about how much he hated foreign countries, how much he hated being away from all of us. His desire to come home. As a child, I would be passed the phone. "Say hello to your father. He misses you."*

*When he returned from these trips, it didn't take long for him to start complaining about the intolerable boredom and dread of suburban life. "I'm dying to be away again" was an infamous mantra of his. He'd pace around the house, from room to room, observing all of us in our daily routines. He'd point out exactly what it was we were doing wrong. He was the constant critic during my childhood. But in the air, at the helm of the jet, I know he worries about nothing. I know he*

*experiences catharsis of a kind he can never find on the
ground. And now he is not up in the air or down on the
ground. He is nowhere. Relegated to the world of the sick and
the suffering and the weak. Where does that leave him? He is
like the deer. Subject to fate and chance. He needs to see the
other end of that paradigm. I need to show him how to think
like a person wielding a gun.*

I am doomed to never understand my family.

I take the second invitation to the paper shredder in my
father's office. I destroy it, knowing full well that no matter
what I do, I am doomed. Doomed to attend the ceremony,
the reception, all of it.

"MAY I BE EXCUSED?" he asks at the dinner table.

"No, you may not," is my mother's stock reply. "The family is eating together and you are going to sit here and act
normal and be part of dinner."

"You can't just sleep all day," Chip tells him.

"I'm sleeping right now," he says, lifting his shoulders
slightly, cradling his head in his hands.

"Very funny," my mother says.

"I'm fucked," he says. He moans. He starts to cry. His
crying bouts are still frequent. These tearful episodes can
be triggered by anything. A bill arriving in the mail, a phone
call from a doctor's office confirming an appointment, an
episode of *Law & Order* he's already seen. We ignore him.

"The appraiser's coming tomorrow," I tell the table. "Don't
make any sudden messes tonight."

"The house is in good shape," our mother says. "You boys
did good."

For the past two days, in anticipation of the appraiser's judgment, Chip and I have cleaned and organized nearly every section of the house in our spare time. We threw out thirteen heavy-duty garbage bags filled with unused clutter from the basement and junk from our bedrooms and all the common areas. We scrubbed and polished the bathrooms. We picked up around the yard. We did everything we could think of to make the place look its best.

When dinner is over, I rinse plates in the sink and load the dishwasher.

"Need any help?" Chip asks. He's still at the dinner table, reading the *New York Post*.

"I got it," I say.

He stands, folds the paper, and walks over to join me at the sink.

"Can you think of anything else we may have overlooked for tomorrow?" he asks.

"It'll be fine," I say. I rinse the salad bowl and place it on the bottom rack. I close the machine and start the cycle.

"I think so, too," my brother says.

"Can I ask a favor?" I say.

"Of course," Chip says.

"I was thinking maybe you could write a check to pay for this, save Mom and Dad the money. I could give you half, just not right now."

"Sure," Chip says. "No problem."

He pats me on the shoulder in what I'm sure he thinks is a brotherly way.

THE APPRAISER APPRAISES. I'm there to greet the man when he rings the bell. I shake his puffy hand. A smell of cigars hangs about him. Chip covers the $250 fee, as he said he would. My father stays in the TV room the whole time. I tell him to try to keep the volume down. My mother introduces herself to the appraiser, then hangs back, following us from room to room, floor to floor, without saying much.

The house scores points for the modern kitchen, renovated four years ago at our mother's insistence. The deck is, of course, a positive addition. The third-floor bathroom (my sanctuary) brings the total count up to four, a very good number as far as bathrooms are concerned, the appraiser informs us. No central air is a bad thing. No wallpaper on any of the walls is a good thing. No carpeting is another positive. Mold spores in the basement is bad. The appraiser notices the cat pee smell hovering around my bedroom, another deduction. His estimate comes in at a little over $1 million. Just as we suspected. The house has appreciated greatly in the time we have lived here.

The appraiser leaves. I can see my mother is shaken, most likely filled with painful thoughts about the possibility of actually having to leave her home. She goes to the TV room and sits quietly beside my father. I feel good that it is done. For me, the thought of losing the house is sad, but I think it's better to be prepared than to just blindly hold out, waiting helplessly for whatever is coming. It's like wielding the gun: There is some amount of control in every situation. You are never totally powerless. If we have to sell the house, we might as well be in a position to get as much as we possibly can for it. Chip walks around, inspecting the places of interest the appraiser pointed out. He is convinced the house is worth more. Everything revolves around money and the lack of it. All of our problems seem to come from this one open wound. I am convinced more than ever that I need to be making more money. I take up the search for a new job with increased determination and resolve.

I go to and from work. I train the retards. I show Arham his numbers and colors. I take him around the school and encourage him to make eye contact with people when he says hello. I teach him the alphabet. I reward him with Oreos when he successfully recites it back to me. I lie on the floor and listen to records in my bedroom and stare at the light fixtures until I see colored spots on the walls.

# ≪ 20 ≫

It isn't in the mailbox. I see it lying in front of the door as I come home from work. It is addressed to Elissa.

She is sitting in the kitchen, making tea, when I bring it to her. She takes the envelope from me and sits looking at her name, scrawled across the front in large, sloppy letters.

"Asshole," she says.

She tears it open. A sheaf of twenty-dollar bills falls out, along with a handwritten note. She twirls hair between her fingers, spreads the cash out on the table. She reads the note quickly, turns it over, and looks at the back. She reads it again.

"What does it say?" I ask her.

"What do you think it says?"

"What are you gonna do?"

"I'm going to *do* what I was always going to do," she says.

"I'm going over there," I say.

"What for?" She laughs. "To beat him up?"

I think about this for a while.

"I don't know what I'll do," I say finally. "I'll get Wally and David. We'll egg his house or something."

"I'm the one in high school," she reminds me. "It's okay. I'll go. You can drive me."

She directs me up Route 9, through Ossining, into Croton. We do not listen to music. We turn onto a long uphill street running at a severe angle away from the river. Up and up, I can feel the hatchback struggling to make the ascent. Elissa tells me to take a left. We zigzag through narrow roads lined with small houses sitting practically on top of one another. We pass Croton High and a field where a baseball game is under way. We make our way down a dead-end street.

"It's here," she says, pointing. I pull over in front of a white house with a screened porch. The hatchback idles loudly as we sit looking.

"I don't even know this shithead's name," I say.

"Bjorn Copeland," Elissa says.

"He's European?"

"He's not European."

"All right, well, what's the plan?"

"I don't know," Elissa says. She opens her door and gets out. I follow. I walk behind her, noticing the way her stomach has grown. Her gait has become lopsided. The energetic teenage swagger she usually moves with isn't as noticeable. Her strides seem older now.

We mount the steps to the house and march through a screen door onto the porch. A strange smell hangs in the air, like faint remnants of a fire. Elissa rings the bell. We wait. She rings again. No one comes. No sound from inside the house, no movement.

"I don't think anyone's home," I say. Elissa takes the envelope from her back pocket and lays it on the ground. She tears the note up, throws the pieces into the air.

"This was stupid," she says. She turns and together we head back to the car. The sun is setting above us, making its way down past the tree tops. Color is spread across the sky. The wind rustles up through the branches. It feels good on my face.

"Whoa," Elissa says. She stops in the middle of the walkway. Her hand darts to her stomach. She feels around, rubbing her belly, a strange look of concentration on her face.

"Is it time?" I ask. I shuffle my feet awkwardly. I'm not sure if I should run back to start the car or take out my cell phone and call 911.

"No, you moron," she says. "It moved."

AT FIRST I say no. When I see the way she is looking at me, I relent and go with her. Our mother comes, too.

The three of us sit waiting in obstetrics. There are pamphlets. I leaf through one detailing early childhood development and the warning signs of mental retardation.

When I shake Dr. Fine's hand, there is sweat between our palms.

"Is it okay I'm here?" I ask him, not even coming close to looking in his eyes.

"Of course it's okay. My understanding is the father's out of the picture?"

"Very," my mother says.

"I remember when we were looking at ultrasounds of *Elissa*," Dr. Fine says. He laughs at this.

The baby is hard to make out at first, so much gray on the screen. Swirling lines and circles and pulsing parts. Dr. Fine draws the wand slowly over Elissa's belly and the picture becomes clearer.

"See that?" he says, pointing. A large blob is quivering in gray static. "That is the baby's head. And there is the heart."

"It looks confused," I say.

"No, it doesn't," Elissa says.

"In this family it has no choice," our mother says. Everyone looks. The baby floats, tiny. Its heart bumps. We watch it. Elissa's stomach is like taut balloon elastic, a swollen thing covered in blue gel.

"The halfway mark is not far away," Dr. Fine says. "I'm a little concerned about your blood pressure. Bit on the high side. I want us to keep an eye on it. And remember, stick to foods on the list. I'm going to have my secretary put some paperwork together. A few rules you should already be following."

"I'm pretty much fucked for life," Elissa says. Dr. Fine coughs into his hands, makes an uncomfortable chuckle.

"Do you want to know the sex?" he asks. We look at Elissa.

"Let's be surprised," she says.

IN THE PARKING garage, in the car, our mother cries. She turns the engine over and her head drops.

"I'm sorry, Mom," Elissa says. She leans over from the passenger's seat and puts her hand on our mother's arm. "I know how bad my timing is."

"It's not you," she says. "It's your father. I really don't think he's going to be around much longer," she says. She has trouble getting the words out. "He's not doing well at all."

"We know, Mom," I tell her. "But if he doesn't want to get better, there isn't much we can do."

"It's not like we can force him to think positively," Elissa adds. "He's convinced he's dying."

"We need to be tough with him," our mother says. She stops crying abruptly. She wipes her eyes dry. "You don't know what it's like for me," she says. "Every day he moans and cries. He talks about death constantly. He refuses to see a therapist. He doesn't eat. He sleeps all day long. I've taken him to so many doctors I've lost count and they all say the same thing. If he wants to fly again, he needs to convince the FAA he's mentally fit to be in the air, and right now there is no fucking way he's going to do that. Not wearing a bathrobe with a gun in his pocket. Not with a garage full of sleeping bags. It's a total no-win situation." She pulls onto Seventy-First Street and starts the drive home.

"The man needs help," she continues. "He needs to be on medication, but he can't get on medication because the FAA doesn't allow psychiatric drugs to be taken by their pilots. He doesn't take the medication, he won't be able to fly. He does take it, they won't let him."

"It's a shitty situation," I say.

"I need you guys to back me up," our mother says. "If we see him just lying around, moping, we need to make him get up and do things. He needs to start acting normal."

"Cal should take him to that wedding," Elissa says.

"No way," I say. "I'm not going."

"All your friends are gonna be there," our mother says.

"I hate those people."

"Would you think about it, Cal?" my mother says. She turns her head to look right at me. "It would get him out of the house."

"*You* take him to the wedding," I say.

"I wasn't invited," my mother says.

"He'll have to wear a suit," I say.

"We'll get him into a suit," our mother says. "I'll force him if I have to."

"He loves spending time with you," Elissa says.

"He thinks you're the only one who gets him," our mother says.

"I know this," I say.

"He loves you," Elissa says.

"I know this," I say. "I'm completely aware of this."

"You should take him," our mother says. "The two of you should go."

I look out the window. I watch buildings go by.

"I don't want to go," I say.

"Just think about it."

"Maybe," I say.

"Good," my mother says. "I already RSVP'd for you both."

## ≪ **21** ≫

June begins. Elissa starts to put on weight. She continues to eat massive amounts of food. She looks pregnant. It's no joke anymore. There is a realness to it now. There is a shape. Her cheeks puff out. A new calendar is pinned to the door of the upstairs bathroom. It hangs above my father's hair-loss pictograph. Marked with big red *X*'s, counting off the days till she's due. November 13.

Everyone seems to be in a better mood when Elissa is around. My father smiles more in her presence. He asks to feel if the baby is moving. He puts his hand on her stomach and waits. He jerks away when he feels the slightest kick.

"Whoa," he says.

Brigitte's paper *S*'s still decorate most of the house.

One night, Chip steams Elissa's favorite vegetables and even goes so far as to bring home veggie burgers and soy hot dogs from the grocery store.

Following my advice, Inez is let go. Chip and I assume most of the cleaning responsibilities. We clean. We traipse from room to room with feather dusters and Pledge. We dust everything spotless. Emma barks at the vacuum, cowers when I swing the hose in her direction. I take over laundry duty so my mother can dedicate herself fully to keeping my father from sinking deeper into his self-created void. She handles all the finances. For months now, my mother has been looking after Elissa. She has been making sure Elissa gets enough sleep at night. She has been taking Elissa to school in the mornings. Has been consoling her when other kids give her a hard time. Just as earlier in the year, it was my mother who talked to the principal, the teachers, explained the situation to them, assured them Elissa would finish her assignments, take her exams, and be ready for graduation. It was my mother who accompanied Elissa to breast-feeding and childbirth classes from day one. I imagine it like this: A bunch of expectant couples positioned on mats in a cherry-colored room practicing their breathing. Elissa the only one there with her mother as a partner.

"I HAVE TO PEE, like, every five seconds," she says to everyone at dinner. She inhales her food. Afterward she relaxes on the couch with our father. They watch reruns of *Law & Order.* Chip and I join them. We stretch out on the sectional, the four of us. Elissa devours two candy bars.

"Are those things on the list?" I ask.

"They're on *my* list," she says.

"Dr. Fine would disapprove," I say.

"It's no big deal," she says. Her head is propped up on pillows. Her stomach is a mound. She plays with a hole in her jeans.

"Boy or a girl?" Chip asks during a commercial break.

"I told them I didn't want to know," she says.

"That's retarded," Chip says. "What if people start buying clothes for a girl and it turns out to be a boy? How are people gonna know what to get for it?"

"I'm going to build a mobile," our father says. "With little airplanes." He rubs the top of his head, feels the hair there, the beginnings of curls, new and short.

"When exactly are you going to do that?" Chip asks. "You watch TV or sleep all day."

"Not all day," he says. He moans. "Your mother is already on my case. Don't you start, too."

"You've been behaving like a pussy ever since the operation," I tell him. "You aren't sick anymore. You need to start acting like it. You need to get off the couch and do something with yourself."

"Thanks for the advice," he says. He reaches a hand across the empty section of couch between us and tries to touch my arm.

"Don't," I say, pulling away from him.

"You're weird," he says.

"No, I'm not," I say. "*You're* weird."

"Can I lay my head on your shoulder?" he asks.

"No," I tell him.

My mother comes into the room with her cooking apron on, in her hand a wooden spoon, which she points at my father. Some tomato sauce flies onto the carpet.

"James," she says, "I have some good news for you. Cal is taking you to Chris Hillman's wedding. You're his date."

"I love weddings," he says. And that seems to settle it. We are going.

My mother returns to the kitchen.

*Law & Order* comes back on and we all sit watching for a while without speaking.

"I've seen this one," our father says. "I've seen them all."

He reaches his hand out again and touches my arm. This time I don't pull away.

THE WANT AD comes to me through the hazy, dull afterglow of a long day at the John W. Manley School, a fug of weed smoke around my head. The ad stares at me from its newsprint frame, gray and black and inky. I sit on the toilet in the third-floor bathroom. I am careful to ash the joint into the sink. I must stretch forward, leaning off the bowl in an effortful manner, to do this. The real estate section is scattered on the floor before my feet. I've also circled a few houses in what I think might be the family price range. I intend to bring these listings to my mother's attention.

I hold smoke in my lungs. I read and reread the job description. A production assistant is needed at a well-known film company in Manhattan. A company responsible for several of my most favorite dramedies of the past few years. A company whose aesthetic vision has been clearly proven time and time again in the cinematic arena. When the lights go down in the theater, I've come to know and find comfort in said company's opening credits logo. A clockwork horse galloping across a green field while dramatic violins swell and flutter magnificently. Seeing this, I breathe a sigh of relief, knowing there is a good chance the film I'm about to see won't suck. Or at least it won't suck much.

Here was a place where scholarly examination of film

would be encouraged, fostered. No longer would I have to dream of seeking out like-minded cinephiles. I would be surrounded by them on a daily basis. I would be paid to debate the merits of the *Die Hard* franchise. I would find comrades to help bolster my love of schlock horror. Here would be others who understand the importance of bad filmmaking, its critical and paradoxical relationship to all art in general. Lunch breaks would be spent sharing Netflix queue suggestions. Work functions would involve dutifully attending prescreenings, followed by Q&As with the director in secret locations where only those on a list would be allowed admittance. Hobnobbing with producers and industry assholes. Sundance. Telluride. Cannes(!).

I cough on a particularly jarring pocket of smoke. My eyes water. I use my circling red pen to ensnare the ad with several unnecessarily bold rotations.

Later, by the blue glow of the computer screen, I e-mail my résumé, along with what I think to be an extremely passionate cover letter enthusiastically conveying my love of film coupled with my desire to work for said company to the exclusion of all others. I click Send. I lay my head on my pillow, nervous and excited, hoping for an interview. Hoping for good things. Hoping maybe I've found a place where I belong, a place where it all makes sense, a place full of people whose brains operate in the same way as mine.

ELISSA GRADUATES FROM high school over the weekend. The whole family attends the ceremony. I sit in the gathering summer heat, under a bright sun, and watch her walk. A few hundred people are gathered, seated in rows of folding chairs. Digital cameras flash. A few murmurs go up as she passes. Our grandmother weeps. The valedictorian, a redhead with a face full of freckles, stands proudly, gives a speech about following your inner voice, the true essence of being. This is the way to happiness, she tells the gathered multitudes. This is the way to happiness. My father laughs. Covers his mouth with his hand and laughs.

I'M SHOCKED, LITERALLY, when I learn about the interview. I turn the key in the ignition of the hatchback and wait while the engine gets on its feet. The radio has been giving me problems lately. It will only turn on if I pinch together two wires dangling from the underside of the center console. Wally showed this trick to me. I'm still confused as to what exactly happens when these two wires are made to touch. Regardless, I'm sitting in the car, checking my voice mail. A young woman's voice is on the message, pleasant and airy, with something of a southern tinge. She identifies herself as Charlotte and would like to know if I'm available to "come on down" to the offices of the well-known film company at the end of the week to meet with Mrs. so-and-so about the production assistant position. As I listen to this young woman and her delightful news, I bring the wires into joyous union to jump-start the tape deck and am met with a jolt of electricity.

"Fuck," I say. I immediately jam my fingers into my mouth. What comfort this maneuver might result in is beyond me. The phone flies from my hands and is momentarily lost in the pile of tapes and paper on the floor of the passenger seat. The tape deck fires up, blasting *Red Headed*

*Stranger.* I fumble the phone out of the chaos and quickly press 7 to save the message. When I have properly composed myself, I call the offices of the well-known film company. I speak with Charlotte and inform her that Friday works perfectly for my schedule. She pencils me in for eleven thirty. The added bonus is that Friday is the last day of work, with a two-week break following before the start of the summer session. I'll have to take the day off to get to the interview, which means I'll have to miss the last staff meeting of the year. This does not bother me.

It's all coming together.

ON WEDNESDAY, I sit with Arham and the hours go by. The lap desk is cluttered with stacks of laminated index cards. I show him a picture of a man skiing.

"Skiing!" he says.

"Good job, little man," I tell him, rubbing his head. I show him a picture of a woman swimming.

"Swimming!" he says.

"Excellent," I say. I give him a piece of cookie, which he swallows without even chewing. I show him a picture of a man running.

"Driving!" he says.

"Running," I say, correcting him. I put the picture down and pick it back up again, reintroduce it. Arham looks. He scrunches up his eyes.

"Running," he says.

"Nice job," I say. I pat his head. He giggles.

"Pee, pee," he says.

At 3:40, through the colored paper, I see the yellow buses

beginning to arrive. I take Arham by the hand and lead him to number 52. I make sure he has his backpack, his lunch box. I make sure he finds a seat toward the front because he gets carsick sometimes. I wave good-bye to him.

"See you tomorrow," I say.

"Bye-bye," he says, waving his hand.

I take a personal day form from the office and fill it out for Friday. I go to Ceci to deliver the request and clock out. She is sitting at her desk with an unhappy face.

"Just the man I was looking for," she says.

"Something up?" I say. I feign ignorance.

"No more excuses. This Friday. Graph presentation. It's our last staff meeting of the year before camp starts."

"I can't," I say. "This Friday I've got—"

"It's not a choice," Ceci says, cutting me off.

"That's what we tell the kids," I say.

"I know."

I take a breath.

"Okay," I say. "I'll do it. Fuck."

I crumple the personal-day request behind my back.

THE NEXT DAY, I leave work early to accompany my sister to another ob-gyn appointment. More pamphlets. I flip through one chronicling the horrors of sexually transmitted diseases. I flip through one chronicling fetal development from conception to birth. I look at diagrams. I learn that around the sixth week, the baby will have an umbilical cord. A head, eyes, a liver. Until the tenth week, it will be called an embryo. Afterward, a fetus. This is when the vital organs begin to work. This is when the baby's heart pumps. By the nineteenth week, the fetus can sometimes be seen sucking its thumb on the ultrasound.

Elissa holds my father's hand while we wait. It is embarrassing that he is with us, dressed in his bathrobe, but our mother insisted. "It'll be good for him" has become the mantra of our house.

There are two couples in the waiting room with us. Young couples, seated in chairs, flipping through their own pamphlets, glance over at us from time to time. I wonder what they are thinking.

I take my cell phone into the bathroom for some privacy and call Charlotte at the well-known film company.

"I was supposed to come in for an interview tomorrow," I tell her, "but something's come up. I need to reschedule. Any way we can do it first thing Monday?"

Charlotte puts me on hold so she may consult her calendar. Muzak plays in my ear and I take advantage of the break to urinate. I try to pee as quickly as possible. She clicks back on the line as I'm flushing the toilet and I try to get back out into the hallway before she can decipher the sound.

"You're in luck," Charlotte says. "We have a couple of other interviewees scheduled for Monday. How's one thirty?"

"Sure," I say. "Perfect. Thank you very much."

"See you then," she says.

I return to the waiting room. I try to put a beautiful, freckled face to Charlotte's voice and am quite pleased with the mental image I concoct.

When the nurse comes out and calls "Moretti," we all stand together and are herded through the door and down the hallway into the examination room. Shortly, Dr. Fine joins us.

"James," he says when he sees my father, "it's good to see you." The doctor seems to completely ignore my father's attire, his disheveled look. "You'll have to bring me up to date with the myeloma. Kathy told me a little. I'm sure it was rough going."

"It could come back at any time," my father says.

"Positive thoughts," Elissa reminds him. My father looks at her, then back at the doctor.

"I'm feeling okay," he says.

On the screen the baby floats, suspended in darkness, a glowing, giant head with feet and arms. One day it will run through a playground and I will put it on a swing. I will push it as high as it wants to go. I will be an uncle. One day soon I will be an uncle.

Dr. Fine is satisfied with what he sees.

"Everything looks good," he says. "Your blood pressure's still a little high, but we'll see. If it stays where it is, we'll be fine." He wipes the jelly off Elissa's stomach with a cloth. She sits up, pulling her sweatshirt back down.

"I've been having some heartburn," Elissa says.

"Been sneaking anything you shouldn't be eating?" the doctor asks.

"Not really," Elissa says.

Dr. Fine chuckles. "Take some Tums," he says. "And stay away from junk food. Stick to the list. You should know better."

"Okay," Elissa says.

"As far as I'm concerned, this baby is arriving on schedule and perfectly healthy," Dr. Fine says.

OUTSIDE, THE CITY is all muted colors and sunset. We drive up First Avenue. We turn left onto Ninety-Sixth. We head crosstown past prewar walk-ups and luxury condos. I count doormen. I count old ladies walking poodles. I count buses.

"If it's a girl, I want to name her Harper Lee," Elissa says.

"Harper Lee Moretti?" my father asks.

*"To Kill a Mockingbird,"* Elissa says.

"And if it's a boy?" I ask.

"Easy," she says. "James Jr."

My father accelerates through a yellow light and coasts out onto Riverside Drive.

# ≪ 22 ≫

I park the hatchback. I throw it into neutral and contemplate leaving the emergency brake off. Maybe it'll roll away. I look around. Garbage covers most of the seats. Tapes scattered about. Classic rock, gangsta rap, seventies synth prog, grind-core, power violence, doo-wop, bluegrass, folk, stoner rock, psychedelic pop, twee pop, sludge, drone, doom, black metal, thrash metal, horror-movie soundtracks, Bach's Toccata and Fugue in D Minor, Rachmaninoff's Prelude in G Sharp Minor. Sometimes I buy so much music I don't even have time to listen to it. Entire albums sit neglected for months.

It is a dark, gloomy day and I just want it to be over with, I want nothing more than my two weeks of vacation time. My brief respite before the dull tedium of camp ensues. My graph presentation and five-minute lecture to the staff is the one thing standing between freedom and me.

I dig out the folder containing my work from the pile of crap occupying the passenger seat. I scan it one last time, making sure there are no typos. I have decided on a chart showcasing Arham's repertoire of behavior expression throughout the year. It's a doozy, even I have to admit. I glance at the index cards I've prepared to guide my "lecture." My opening paragraph:

> Throughout the year, I have observed Arham Sarkhar on a daily basis, in a classroom setting designed for ABA therapy. I have noted the amount of time Arham has received ABA therapy and the change in his behaviors over the ten-month school year. The behaviors I observed were play skills, communication skills, self-help skills, motor skills, social skills, computer skills, eating behaviors, receptive language, expressive language, and imitation. I then calculated the amount of time Arham received ABA therapy, the independent variable, and the change in the behaviors over that time, the dependent variable.

Basically, what this means is that over the year, I've collected data from every exercise I've run with Arham. Every flash card I've shown him, every letter I've had him write, every person I've made him say hello to while maintaining eye contact. I've marked down every correct response he's delivered and every time he's made a mistake. I've compiled this data into one big, massive graph to show, in essence, how much improvement he's made since September. It is a document of just how close to "normal" Arham has crept since I started working with him.

Data collection is the most important thing that happens in an ABA environment, I have been told this many times at the John W. Manley School. For Ceci, graph interpretation is the equivalent of a fat, long line of cocaine. She lives and dies by graphs. Those little dots and lines light up her eyes and jack her heart rate to aerobic levels. Ceci is in it for the long haul, addicted to the children she teaches. Never losing the drive to get them ready for the cold, hard world that they will someday attempt to join and that will, in the end, reject them.

It starts to rain as I head up the sloping brick walkway into the building.

In the conference room there are at least thirty people. Every teacher. Every assistant. Ceci. Georgie. Angela. They are all here. In the corner there is the usual table of doughnuts and coffee and orange juice we are given at every staff meeting. Outside the windows, I can see it is now pouring, a torrential rain running in thick, fast rivulets down the street.

I position my first transparency on the overhead projector, bringing it into focus for everyone to see. I begin. I tell the room about Arham Sarkhar, my student. I tell them he will soon be four years old. For Christmas I brought him a pair of kids' Nikes because I was sick of seeing his mother send him to school in his sister's old ballet slippers. I tell them Arham loves hugs. I tell them he is missing three front teeth that have yet to come in. I tell them he never fails to smile when I let him know he is doing a good job. I tell them he tries to get out of doing work by pretending he has to urinate. I tell them that over the year, Arham and I have been through a lot together, including an incident where he hit me in the side of the head with a rock during yard time. I tell them that while I don't know all the children at the John W. Manley School as well as I know Arham, I know they are all special and amazing. I mean all of this. I enjoy Arham's company more than I think I let myself believe and I am proud of the progress he's made. A pang of sadness creeps through me because in the back of my mind, I know he's fucked for life. I know most likely his parents won't stick to the tedious regime and structure his education requires. Eventually they will give up sending him to special schools, they will tire of running exercises with him. They will have more important things to deal with. Their other "normal" children will require the bulk of their attention. Arham will be neglected. He will retrograde to the way he was when he came to the John W. Manley School. He will sit in front of the television all day and smile and not ever know that he was once doing so well.

I explain the graph I have made and talk about what the numbers mean. I cite specific areas where Arham has made the most progress. His one-to-one correspondence, for example, is amazing. I have sat and listened to him count to 157 without missing a single number.

When I finish, everyone claps and the rest of the staff meeting unfolds swiftly.

Ceci corners me at the breakfast table, my mouth full of chocolate-glazed.

"That was great, Cal," she says. "Really. Just so good."

"Thanks," I say, swallowing half a doughnut as quickly as I can. For a second it gets stuck in my throat and I need to swallow again to get it down. Ceci hands me a glossy folder, an information packet for Pace University's master's program in applied behavior analysis.

"I went ahead and gathered up some info for you," she says.

I take the folder from her. The cover depicts a group of smiling students seated in a circle across an idyllic campus green.

"I'd love to promote you," Ceci is saying. "Get you on track to be a head teacher. But school policy is you have to be enrolled in a program somewhere. Start working toward your certification."

It's nice to hear her compliment me. Maybe working at John W. Manley could be rewarding in the long run. It feels, at the moment, like a good place to be.

"Okay," I say. "I'll think about it."

"You said that last time I brought this up," she says. "I'm just trying to help. You mentioned you could use more money."

"I could," I say.

She pats my shoulder and walks out of the room. I watch the way her ass moves inside the cream-colored skirt she's wearing. I think about how tonight when I get home, I'll lock myself in the third-floor bathroom and picture that skirt while I jerk off.

I eat two more doughnuts and wait for the buses to arrive.

I TRY TO let Arham have fun today. I don't run any exercises with him. We spend most of the morning playing Connect Four. He has no idea how the game works, but he gets a big kick out of dropping the checkers. He bursts out in uncontrolled fits of laughter every time he lets one fall. I let him give me lots of hugs. We walk through the halls, telling everyone we see to have a nice break.

"Have a nice break," Arham says. "Have a nice break,"

he tells the garbage can outside the bathroom. "Have a nice break," he says to Rosa, the receptionist. "Have a nice break," he tells Julio, the maintenance man. Have a nice break. He is a broken record, but he is happy. I make no attempts to teach him anything.

After lunch, the rain tapers off and the sun comes out from behind the clouds.

We round up everyone in our section. The retards: Arham, Hendrick, Shaynequa, Franklin, Tyrone, and Samantha. The teachers: Georgie, Angela, Robyn, Elaine, Tracy, and me. We traipse to the yard like cattle. Every five feet someone falls or bumps his head. There is screaming and giggling and a few farts, but eventually we make it out there. I close the gate and stand at the monkey bars, leaning against one of the metal poles. Arham spins around and around in circles. I get nauseated just looking at him. Shaynequa runs to him.

"Hug," she says. Arham stops his spinning and the two of them embrace. Shaynequa loses her footing and they both fall into the wood chips, laughing like maniacs. I look at all the kids. I look at Georgie. He is perched on a swing, staring off. The other teachers—Angela, Robyn, Tracy, and Elaine—are hovering around the sandbox, chatting. I feel someone tugging at the bottom of my T-shirt. It wouldn't be Hendrick if he wasn't wearing his plastic fireman's helmet.

"Some people make a really big poop, like my papi," he tells me.

"That's bathroom talk," I say.

"What?" Franklin asks, coming over to us.

"My daddy makes a big poop," Hendrick repeats.

Franklin considers this information.

"My dad's hairy like a buffalo," he says.

Shaynequa and Arham are back on their feet, standing nearby, listening.

"Basketball," Shaynequa says.

"My daddy hits tennis balls," Samantha says.

"Broccoli," Hendrick says.

"My dad likes channel surfing," I tell the kids.

"What's that?" Franklin asks, his hand slithering down his pants.

"It means he likes to watch TV," I say. "Take your hand out of your pants."

"Channel surfing," Franklin repeats. He smells his fingers. "Channel. Surfing. Channel surfing." He says it like a hymn, as if the words themselves give him strength. He marches around, stomping his feet. "Channel surfing," he says, again and again.

It isn't long before the others join him.

"Channel surfing," Shaynequa says. She jumps up and down.

"Channel. Surfing," Arham says.

The six of them huddle close to one another, bouncing around, yelling, "Channel surfing," as loud as they can. Tyrone groans and hollers.

The other teachers approach, trying to figure out what's going on.

A PERIOD OF great uncertainty. A period of illness and pregnancy, of intense family "togethering." I pull out of the parking lot. The squat stucco building dwindles away in the rearview mirror. I will not be back for sixteen days. I'm happy about this. At the same time I'm a little nostalgic. I feel the nagging sensation that, much as I claim to hate that school, much as I tire of Arham saying "peepee," I'll miss him. I'll miss hearing about Georgie's grand plans for the future and Ceci's wedding arrangements. Hendrick's fireman's hat. I will miss them in a quixotic way, a way in which I can romanticize the job into something wholly different from what it really is.

THE NIGHT BEFORE, I stand in front of the mirror trying to cobble together something in the realm of appropriate attire for the job interview. The idea is to lay out my whole outfit before going to bed. Have it all prepared so that in the morning I can sleep in awhile, dress, eat some breakfast, and make my way to the train.

I have one suit. A leftover from my college graduation. I try on the pants. They fit the same as they ever did. I have a white button-down shirt, which came as a hand-me-down from my father, which I had hemmed to fit my thin frame. I comb my hair. I do this for the sake of making a good impression. I will do this again in the morning. I tuck the shirt in and observe. Not bad. I dig through the bottom of my closet and find one of the two ties I own, a green and blue striped thing. I go back to the mirror and hold the tie up against my chest to gauge its fashion effectiveness. I see Chip in the mirror, standing in the doorway, shaking his head.

"Look at you," he says.

"I'm trying," I say. He looks me up and down. He takes the tie out of my hands.

"Follow me," he says. He leads me to his bedroom. *Scarface* posters adorn the walls. A black light is attached to the ceiling and I see he has recently hung a disco ball.

"Stand there," he says, directing me to the full-length mirror near his bed. He opens the door to his closet to reveal the vast array of business attire neatly hanging within. He engages the electric rack and selects a simple black tie. Not too thin, not too wide.

"Very classic," he says, handing it to me.

I take a very long time tying it around my neck. I stand back, smoothing out the shirt beneath.

"Not bad," I say.

"You can't wear those," he says, pointing to my white tube socks.

"I don't have anything else."

He shakes his head and goes to his bureau. He extracts a pair of clean dress socks.

"And shoes?" he asks. I don't say anything and he returns to the closet for black leather dress shoes. I sit on his bed, put the socks on and slip into the shoes. They're surprisingly comfortable.

"Jil Sander," my brother points out. "They cost eight hundred bucks, so don't step in dog shit, okay?"

"I'll try not to," I tell him.

"You can thank me later," he says.

I stand in front of the mirror again.

"I feel like an asshole," I say.

"You look good," my brother tells me.

"I look like *you*." I start to leave but stop in the doorway. "Thanks," I say.

"No problem."

"I mean it," I add.

"I know," he says.

# ≪ **23** ≫

A young girl seated below giant, glowing corporate signage greets me. She speaks into a microphone attached to her ear, announcing my presence. I am greeted moments later by sleekly dressed Charlotte, who is just as attractive as I pictured her. She is tall in high heels. A black skirt and white blouse, dark hair pulled straight back in a ponytail.

Charlotte directs me down several corridors. Past offices and supply closets and copy machines. Past the etiquette of office mannerisms. A way of walking down carpeted hallways, the watercooler, the communal kitchen, where you find the coffee machine. A style of speaking, both stylishly uninformative and nonconfrontational. An air of hushed, false calm and claustrophobia in the three-walled cubicle arrays and laser-printer whirs. In all of my daydreaming about the possibility of working at the well-known film company, in all of my idealized envisioning, I have overlooked the simple fact that it would be, at the end of the day, an office job. Furthermore, an entry-level office job. One that just happens to be at a film company. But still, it is a job I could live with. A job at least in some way connected to a field I care about. Or pretend to care about. It seems a step in the right direction. More money than the John W. Manley School has to offer. More longevity.

My journey with Charlotte ends in a small conference room, where she asks me to sit and make myself comfortable.

"You'll be speaking with Rebecca Quinn," Charlotte says. "Head of production."

"Mrs. Quinn," I say, more to myself than anyone else. "Okay."

"Would you like any coffee?" Charlotte asks. "Water?"

"I'm fine," I say. "Thank you."

And then I'm looking at the back of her head, and her ponytail flips up and down and she is gone. The smell of her perfume is still here and I try my best to bask in all its sexual glory as I wait for the mysterious Mrs. Quinn.

She arrives. A short lady. Midforties. Loose, biblically flowing gray dress. Her neck ensnared in a strand of enormous brown wooden beads. She swirls past me into one of the large seats at the head of the table. She is carrying a stapler and a sheaf of printer paper, which she plunks down in front of her. Her face seems weary and deep. Impossible to read. I'm not sure whether to sit or stand, so I do a sort of half-stand thing, which I know looks extremely awkward, but I'm powerless to stop myself from doing it nonetheless.

"Mr. . . ?"

"Moretti," I say, sitting down finally. "Calvin Moretti."

"A pleasure, Mr. Moretti," Quinn continues. There is what

feels like a long pause before she speaks again. I find myself unable to hold her gaze for very long. My eyes dart between her face and the view of Midtown Manhattan yawning out the windows behind her. "Are you familiar with stapling?" she asks.

"Uh, yes," I say. "I've stapled many times."

She leans forward, pushes the stapler toward me, arching her eyebrow at the stack of paper.

"If you'd be so kind."

I look behind me at the door. I find no help there.

Quinn slumps back in her chair and rocks slightly. The beads of her necklace clink and clank together when she moves. Her hair is littered with impressive gray streaks.

I am slow to gather the papers together. I make a big show of lining up the edges as perfectly as I can. I bang them a few times on the table to get them in order. I pick up the stapler and close its mouth around the upper left corner. Everything goes according to plan. No surprises. The stapler does not explode in my hand. I lay the now-unified stack of papers back on the table.

Mrs. Quinn reaches out a veined hand to take up my work. She seems to be scrutinizing the angle of the staple in relation to the corner of the paper.

She holds it up.

"Allow me to show you what I'm looking for," she says.

"By all means," I say.

A staple remover is revealed from some hidden pocket in her outfit. She undoes my work. She takes the stapler into her hands and clicks off a new round. This time, instead of the angled approach I took, she makes sure her staple is parallel to the top edge of the pages. She slides the new packet across the table.

"I see," I say.

"This is the precision I expect," she says. "Don Caulfield in A and R might have his own way. Maybe he's a little loose. A little easygoing. That's fine. Not in my shop. Perfection. That's what makes money."

"Of course," I say. I'm looking for some way to broach the subject of movies. In my mind, this interview involved my talking about my favorite films. I thought I'd be answering questions like, who was the better editor, Walter Murch or Hal Ashby? Which was the superior film, *Godfather I* or *II*? I was completely unprepared for the stapler business. Surely the real interview would start any minute.

Mrs. Quinn is shaking her head like she understands something very crucial to the moment.

"You have your master's?" she asks.

"Not yet," I say. "I'm hoping to go back to school for film studies in the near future." It was a kind of truth. I did think about it from time to time.

"Your undergraduate degree?"

"Film," I say. "I've been watching movies since I was little. It's something I'm really passionate about."

"Indeed," Quinn says. More awkward silence. My breathing is audible. "You know this job pays very little," she says.

"More than I make now." That was a mistake.

"I'm looking for someone to go the extra mile. Come in early. Stay late if need be. Lots of phone calls. Task juggling. Arrangements. I might even throw a little of my personal billing into the mix."

"It all sounds very exciting," I say. "I'm looking for a job where I have room to grow. And I'm really eager to be around film again."

Mrs. Quinn is nodding at me and I'm not sure why.

She has more questions. They all seem to fall into a strange non-film-related sphere. I'm not quite sure how to respond to any of them. I feel like she is looking through me. When it's over, she thanks me for my time and says she'll be in touch. Charlotte has reappeared almost out of nowhere and is ushering me back into the hallway.

"You live in the city?" I ask, trying to make small talk as we go.

"Brooklyn," she says. Her smell.

"Oh, sure," I say. "Brooklyn."

She stops just short of the reception desk.

"So, I'll hear from you guys soon?" I venture.

"In a couple of weeks, I'd think," Charlotte says. "Mrs. Quinn always likes to take her time with new hires. Better to be sure than regret it later."

"Right," I say. "Makes sense."

"We have your résumé on file," Charlotte says. "Thanks for coming in."

"Thank you," I say.

All the walls in the elevator are mirrors, and if I twist and turn just the right way, I can see the back of my head. I can see the side of my head. I can see myself from every angle.

On the street, I loosen my tie and walk the ten blocks to Grand Central. I breathe easier back here on the street. The interview seems a complete disaster from start to finish. I'm not sure what kind of impression I made, but it certainly can't have been a good one. For all I know, I failed the staple test with flying colors. I disappointed Mrs. Quinn before she's even hired me.

The Hudson Line rockets north, through Morris Heights. University Heights. Marble Hill. Spuyten Duyvil. Riverdale. Ludlow. Yonkers. Glenwood. Greystone. Hastings-on-Hudson. Dobbs Ferry. Ardsley-on-Hudson. Irvington. I watch the trees slide by against the reflection of my face in the window. I hand the conductor my ticket when he comes through. I get off at Tarrytown. My mother is waiting in the SUV to take me home.

"You need to sell this car," I tell her.

"How'd it go?" she asks.

"I have no idea," I say.

I ENTER THE mind-set of total ambitionless slackerdom. I've earned it. I don't have to think about anything on vacation — that's why it's vacation.

I take Emma for lengthy walks. She is growing on me. I've been watching her closely in the few weeks since she joined the family. She has a total disregard for her own personal safety, coupled with an inexhaustible supply of curiosity that drives her into the most daring situations with complete abandon. She hates the mailman. She hates other dogs. She loves my father. She seems skeptical of Chip. All in all she seems to be making the right choices. I see her prance across the kitchen with a cockroach in her mouth. She has no fear.

Things at home remain focused on the big events. The mortgage. The baby. His recovery. Chip and I continue to do as many chores as we can, to elevate some of the burden from our mother. Chip, also, has begun to focus his attentions on helping out with all the paperwork bogging her down. These days, I often see Chip seated at the kitchen table with our mother, flipping through credit card bills and mortgage papers, conversing about which funds can be funneled into the mortgage. My brother investigates my father's stock options. He makes phone calls to our parents' mutual fund and learns that putting him and me through college has drained most of their savings. Seeing him take such an active role makes me even more resolute to secure a job with the well-known film company. To start pulling my own weight.

Elissa continues to *gain* her own weight. Continues to mark off the days on the giant calendar. July, and she is on the downward slope now, a spiral trajectory toward the impending big bang.

"The baby can hear my voice," she tells me, a Twinkie in her hand.

"What have you told it?" I ask.

"How can I explain that to you?" she says.

"You shouldn't be eating that."

"Give me a break," she says. "It's one fucking Twinkie."

Wally and I purchase fireworks on eBay. Single-shot aerial tubes, bottle rockets, skyrockets, missiles, ground spinners, pinwheels and helicopters, flares, fountains, M-80s, sparklers, black snakes, strobes, tiny tanks that shoot sparks. We make plans to set them off in glorious fashion. We invite David Liebman. I ask Doug M. to bring Gabby. We tell Elissa to come, even Chip. We drive to an empty park near the Hudson. We check for cops. We light the pyrotechnics ceremoniously. We "ooh" as they ascend, "aah" as they burst in color and vanish. We wield fire and are thrilled by it. I catch Gabby's eye. I smile at my brother.

I point a Roman candle toward the water. Wally lights it. The wick sizzles. It goes off. Globes of bright, hot flame erupt into the night. They crest outward and sputter away before they ever hit the ground.

## ≪ **24** ≫

Our yearly trip to Grandmother's house in Cape Cod. A ritual observed by the Moretti family since before I was born. A week spent crammed in a tiny cottage built by my maternal grandfather in the sixties. We swim in the ocean, stroll through the mall, eat fried things from the seafloor, play minigolf, walk down Main Street, buy oversize sweatshirts embroidered with "Cape Cod."

I wait for a call from the well-known film company. I wait for news about the job.

My mother is very keen on reminding everyone about the fragile state of things. "Enjoy your time here," she warns. "We may not have the money to come next year." Under her watchful eye, we are implored to enjoy *everything*. We must enjoy our ice cream cones—they may be our last. We must enjoy the beautiful weather, the sand, the boats—we may never see them again. Most importantly, we must enjoy each other—who knows where we'll all be this time next year?

We go to the beach at the end of Sea Street. It's just a small inlet of the larger bay beyond, but once dusk settles and cool air blows in off the islands and the last sunbathers go home, it is the perfect place to relax. My grandmother stays back at the house boiling lobsters for dinner.

We pass through the small plaza, where an elaborate fountain filled with pocket change bears a copper plaque dedicating the beach to JFK. The Kennedy compound is a few miles away, a popular destination for tourists, although eight-foot hedges obscure most of it.

Chip and I sit in the sand. Windbreakers zipped up against the gathering breeze. Our father is on a bench behind us. Elissa and our mother have conspired to slowly break his habit of wearing only pajamas and bathrobes. So, against his will, they've forced him into jeans and a plaid button-down. He cradles his head in his hands. Every so often he looks around. The seawall runs behind him, separating the beach from the parking lot. The sound of waves lapping up onto the shore. Dozens of small sailboats moored out in the bay.

"You like living at home?" I ask Chip.

"I like that the family's all together," he says. He leans forward, pushing his bare feet into the sand. "Italian families stay together. In Italy that's what they do. They live together for as long as they can."

"Well, listen, I think helping them out is pretty noble of you," I say.

"I know you don't like being stuck there," he says in return, "but just being there helps. He needs it."

My brother puts his arms around me, drawing me into a bear hug.

"Get off me," I say, struggling against his grip. He's stronger than me and I have to wait until he lets go.

"You love it," Chip says.

"I do not," I say.

The ferry whistle blows across the water, at the docks, as the seven o'clock Hy-Line departs for Martha's Vineyard.

"Don't you like hugs?" Chip asks.

"I do," I say, "just not from you or Dad."

Down the beach, Elissa and our mother are walking toward us through the shallows. Elissa's sweatpants are rolled up to her knees and she dips her hands into the water to pull up a dead crab. She pantomimes it pinching her throat.

"Think she's gonna be able to handle a kid?" Chip asks.

"She's gonna have a hard time."

"But see, we'll all be there to help her," Chip says. "That's what I'm talking about. Like we were there for Dad."

"You really believe that?" I say.

"Dad?" Chip calls out, over his shoulder. "You okay?"

Our father looks up. "I'm great," he says.

My brother and I sit without talking as the sun inches toward the horizon behind us. We watch Elissa and our mother approach.

"Heads up," Elissa says. She throws the crab into Chip's lap. He bolts to his feet.

"Gross," he says. The women laugh. They go to the bench and sit with Dad. After a while, Chip and I get up to join them. The five of us watch the sky and the boats and the seagulls and all of it.

"Your mother tells me you went for a job interview?" my father says, turning slightly to address me with his eyes.

"Right before we left," I say.

"How did it go?"

"Dunno."

"Is it something you want?"

"I think so," I say. I throw up my hands. "Yeah. It's something I want. It would mean more money. More money I could throw at this house thing."

"I'm sure you did great," my mother says, reaching over to touch my face with her hand. There is a smell of burnt hot dogs on the wind.

"Cal, I need your help," my father says.

"Please, Dad," I say.

"No, really, this time I'm serious," he says. He looks at me again. "I need you to help me write a letter," he says. "So I can get back up in the air."

There are so many boats out on the water. They heel from side to side.

"Sure," I tell him. "I'll help you write a letter."

THE LOBSTERS ARE OVERCOOKED. They have the consistency of rubber cement. Still, they taste pretty good, and by citronella candlelight we dine around the picnic table in the front yard. Chip eats with his hands, tears the lobster apart, licks melted butter off his fingers.

"Delicious," he says.

After dinner, Grandma takes Elissa and Chip to get ice cream. My father and I sit down in the kitchen to write the letter. My mother, faithful archivist of every scrap of Moretti documentation, has collected all the paperwork accumulated throughout the course of his illness. A thick manila folder bursting with doctors' reports, evaluations, and test results, hospital bills, and notarized letters. She drops it on the table with a thud.

"Holy fuck, Mom," I say. "How do you keep track of all this?"

"Welcome to my world," she says. "I'm treating myself to a bath."

"Okay," I say. I spread the papers out onto the table. He sits across from me. He has changed back into his bathrobe. He looks like a teenager awaiting punishment for staying out too late. "First things first," I say. "What exactly do we need to achieve with this letter?"

He seems to ponder the question.

"We need to convince the FAA I'm healthy enough to fly," he says. "I have all the necessary forms, all the doctors' notes, the charts and test results, graphs, scans, X-rays. We just need a cover letter to tie everything together."

"All right," I say. "We can do that."

He shows me an e-mail from his oncologist. In it, a plan is laid out in regard to petitioning the FAA to reinstate his pilot's license. Basically, the doctor points out the trouble spots that need to be addressed. The biggest hurdle appears to be proving that my father is no longer a coronary risk. That he won't keel over from a heart attack because of all the medication he is on and the shock that the stem cell transplant has put his body through. In the eyes of the FAA, a coronary risk is a massive problem for their pilots, one they are very reluctant (with good reason) to overlook.

"I'm fucked," he says.

"No, you aren't," I say, but really I don't know what I'm talking about. "We'll just take another shot at it. Persistence, okay? Don't try to rush anything."

"It's been a year and a half."

"You'll fly again. I promise."

Together we sort through everything, piece by piece, chart by chart. We select what we think is important to include in his application. Anything new the FAA might be interested in knowing. Anything that might sway them to give him a medical clearance.

We leaf through endless blood-work charts. Glucose levels, creatinine levels, protein totals. Lipid panels. HDL versus LDL. Iron count. There is a lengthy typed profile of his case history. The whole disease chronicled from first diagnosis through the stem cell transplant. Included in that is a letter explaining that he has developed hypercoagulability as a result of the myeloma. This means his blood clots too easily—creating even further risk of a heart attack.

Once we have what we consider to be a nice cross section of test results and recommendations and diagrams showing that the cancer has successfully moved into remission, we draft the letter. It is simple, plainspoken. In it, I instruct my father to write about his love of aviation, his passion for flying. I tell him to write about how much he misses the plane, misses running ground checks. Misses engine maintenance. I tell him to write about the time his father took him to an air show in White Plains as a child and how he knew right away that he was meant to fly. I know it is easy for him to write about these things. I have long felt my father is only truly content and worry-free when he is flying. He finds catharsis behind the yoke of a plane, and only there.

When we finish, it is late. The ice cream has all been eaten. Everyone is asleep.

We are alone. The house is quiet around us.

"I still have to pass the nuclear stress test," he says.

"Don't think about it," I tell him.

"It's all I think about," he says.

• • •

AFTER HE HAS gone off to join my mother and the rest of them in slumber land, I sit on the couch with the Pace University information packet spread out across the coffee table. I leaf through its contents. I try to imagine myself sitting in the grass with fellow students, discussing behavior modification for three-year-olds. This is not the future I saw for myself, and I remain confident the well-known film company will be in touch any day with good news. Still, it's always best to have a backup plan—I'm sure I read that somewhere. So plan B is back to grad school. Plan B is the John W. Manley School for the foreseeable future. It isn't a choice I really want to commit to, but it might be the best thing for me and for my family.

There is an application included in the folder. I fill it out. I answer all of the questions. I write the personal statement in my notebook with the intention of later transferring it to the computer. I write about my family. I write about working at the John W. Manley School with Arham and how he has earned a special place in my heart. How my relationship with this tiny person has helped usher a once-lacking sense of selflessness into my life.

The sun is brightening the lower portions of the sky by the time I finish. I put the application papers into a large envelope, the same kind my father and I used for his FAA plea.

Then I go to sleep.

WE COMMITTEE IN the driveway outside the house. Everything is a committee with these people. This time, negotiations revolve around what to take with us to the beach. I suggest a moderate amount of amenities. Chip and my mother are pushing to bring everything we own of a seaside-related nature. They load the SUV with enough gear to shelter, feed, and entertain a small country.

"Thanks for the help, Cal," Chip says as he stacks folding sun chairs.

"I've got everything I need," I say, showing them my towel and magazine.

"What about sunscreen?" my grandmother warns. She has waddled out from the house to deliver us something wrapped in mounds of tinfoil. "You've got to use sunscreen. Grandma spent too much time in the sun as a little girl, and do you know how many cancers the doctors have taken off me?"

"How many, Grandma?" Chip asks.

"Thirty-two," she says. "And counting."

"Jesus," my father says. "Let's go."

"Let's bring the kayak," Chip says.

"We don't need the kayak," I say.

"Yes, we do," Chip insists.

"What a wonderful idea," our mother says. "Elissa can have a nice ride in the kayak. It will be good for the baby."

"How exactly does that work?" I ask.

"It will be soothing," our mother says.

"Please, let's not bring the kayak," I say.

"Put the kayak on top and let's be done with it," our father says. He throws his hands at us in disgust and gets in the car.

"Why's he sitting in the back?" Elissa asks.

"I don't know," our mother says.

"I don't even think they allow kayaks in the water here," I try to point out.

"This is Cape Cod," Chip says. "They allow kayaks everywhere."

"Let's not go nuts here, people," I say. "It's bad enough we have to bring five beach chairs and a giant blanket and three umbrellas and footballs and Frisbees and a cooler and magazines and eight kinds of sunblock and visors and paddleball and God knows what else. Can't we just go to the beach and *relax* like a normal family? Without all the bullshit?"

My father rolls the window down to address us all.

"Your mother wants the kayak. You know the kayak's coming. Why fight it?"

"My head is about to explode," I say.

"Chill, man," Chip says. "It'll be fun."

"Elissa, won't you like a nice ride in the kayak?" our mother asks. Elissa shrugs.

"I made sandwiches," our grandmother says suddenly, thrusting the lumpy tinfoil package into my face.

"We get lunch at the beach, Grandma," I say. This confuses her.

"I went through all the trouble."

"Take the sandwiches," our mother says.

"*Let's go,*" our father says.

At the beach, I swim. Chip, Elissa, and I wade through chest-deep water to a sandbar. The salt feels good drying on my shoulders. The sun is warming. Elissa floats on her back, her stomach bubbling out. The people on the beach are far away.

"You think there are sharks around here?" Chip asks.

"Are you afraid?" I ask.

"Yeah," he says.

"This is the bay," I tell him.

"What about bay sharks?" he asks.

I DECLINE TO join my family on their "fun" walk along the beach.

"Bring me back a grilled cheese from the snack shack," I instruct.

After they depart, I sit watching the umbrella poles. All three of them. I fix my gaze on the one closest to me. I squint. I line it up with a buoy out on the water. I pinpoint its exact position against the horizon. The wind has picked up and is shaking the poles rather violently. They sway and jitter and I am convinced they will uproot themselves in unison at any moment and tumble off toward the parking lot, wreaking havoc, ruining sand castles, and rousing sunbathers from blissful naps. I will have to chase after the umbrellas, a spectacle for all to see. All the girls on the beach. All the mothers. All the grandparents. The handicapped. The overweight. They will watch as I flail around, hopelessly trying to reclaim the runaway shading. I am sweating profusely thinking about this. My fingers are slipping on the magazine. It is suddenly hard to hold. Where are they with the goddamn food already?

To take my mind off this horrifying scenario, I count the number of girls near my chair whom I would have sex with. I stop at eighteen, realizing my standards have fallen to fantastic new lows. My eyes wander back to the umbrella poles. Have they moved a few millimeters upward or am I losing my mind? They seem to be swaying an awful lot in the breeze.

A slender teenager in a flower-patterned two-piece is doing impressive handsprings and cartwheels not ten yards in front of me. Her three sisters, likewise attired, cheer her on. "Again," they say. "Double with a twist this time."

What is it about gymnastics? Body contortions. Lithe, smooth appendages, curling and swinging to meet at the dark, secret vertices of the female anatomy. The sweet, fecund smells that build in those places. The soft, warm embrace. Leotards. Sports bras. Short shorts. Tight material of the stretching kind. Bikinis. These things draw my eye.

The sweat builds. The magazine is nothing more than a pretense now and I don't even bother to send token glances in its direction. I wonder how long, under the guidelines of public etiquette involving felony-aged teens, I am allowed to stare at the girls before I am required to look away. I turn my head to the left and watch an extremely hairy, bald gentleman wince as his wife smears suntan lotion over his already burnt shoulders. Back to the floor exercises. I am openly gawking now as one of the sisters has joined up and both girls are hurling their sleek, tapered bodies through the air. It is as if they are performing solely for my enjoyment. They smile and laugh. Then I remember the umbrellas. Surely they are about to pop forth from their securing and ruin the moment.

My family returns, sand billowing around them as they trudge wearily back to our encampment. I hear them above all the noise of the beach crowd.

"Here's your grilled cheese, dick," Chip says with a smile as he throws a soggy paper bag into my lap. The gymnasts continue their display. Elissa catches me staring.

"Those girls are twelve," she says.

"If that," my father adds.

"Honestly, Calvin," my mother says. "They *are* a little young looking."

"I wasn't staring."

I watch them flip and flop and plop. Arranging themselves once again on the sun chairs and blankets. At least I don't have to worry about the umbrellas anymore. It's someone else's problem now. Let the wind blow them clear to Truro for all I care. We are a family at the beach. Like other families in so many ways, yet unique in our own quirks and strangeness.

ELISSA, CHIP, AND I wander the Cape Cod Mall on Iyannough Road. We try on sunglasses at the sunglasses kiosk. We eat soft-serve ice cream. We scan the titles at the megaplex and decide it would be hilarious to watch *The Devil Wears Prada*. We regret the decision almost immediately. Afterward we drive home in silence, back to the cottage where everyone over the age of thirty is already asleep. I can hear my father snoring from the living room.

Elissa and I are sharing the back room, with its two full-size beds. Chip has opted for the pullout couch in the living room. In the morning, we play minigolf at Pirate's Cove, a pirate-themed tourist trap. When Chip hits his ball off one of the holes into a small lake containing life-size animatronic buccaneers battling on the bows of a fake clipper ship, he accuses us all of conspiring to cheat against him.

The well-known film company never calls and I start to worry. I make Chip drive me to the Internet café on Main Street, in "downtown" Hyannis. I send an e-mail to Charlotte, inquiring as to whether the position has been filled.

• • •

WE SIT OUTSIDE at our favorite clam shack along the Hyannis docks. We open shellfish into our mouths. Our mother makes a toast. She raises her glass of house white. A faint mist drifts in off the bay. Fishermen guide their boats back for the night. Foghorns blare out. A family is posing for snapshots in front of a fake shark. The last traces of sunlight are flickering away. I can't help but notice Elissa drawing stares from other families seated near us. Her appetite is insatiable. Doctor's orders say no shellfish for the pregnant teen, but my sister has no trouble polishing off three hot dogs and a full plate of fries.

"Is that good for the baby?" I ask her.

"It's food," she says, ignoring me.

"Last summer at this time," our mother begins, "we didn't even know your father was sick. And now, with a little luck and a lot of doctors' visits, only a year later, he's still with us. Hopefully we'll all be here again next year."

"With one addition," Elissa says.

Chip and I have beers, our grandmother is drinking seltzer, Elissa and the old man have indulged in virgin piña coladas. We raise our drinks.

"To Jimmy's health," our grandmother says.

"Cheers," Elissa says.

"We love you, Jim," our mother says.

"We love you, Dad," I say.

We clink glasses. We listen to the water lapping against the boats in their slips.

We have no idea.

# ≪ **25** ≫

My father and I mail off the letter to the FAA.

"It's out of our hands," I tell him.

The family returns to Westchester. The John W. Manley School beckons.

There are new faces at summer camp. New students. A whole batch of retards straight off the short bus, in second-hand clothing.

There are new teachers as well. Fresh, bright-eyed women, just exiting grad programs, eager to sink their teeth into the real world of applied behavior analysis. I remain one of the few teaching assistants not currently working toward or already in possession of a master's degree. Yet soon, all that might change.

Of course, all the old faces are back, too. Georgie is here. Ceci is here. Angela is here. We are all here. On the first day, I meet with Ceci in her office. She wants to discuss my future.

"How would you feel about working with Arham for the summer?" she asks. "He's come so far with you. I think it would be such a special thing for you both to keep going together. Tell me what you think."

"Sounds great to me," I say. And I am happy about this.

"If he keeps making the progress he's making with you, I'd like you to think about sticking with him through the coming school year, too. It's not unheard of."

"I have no problems with that," I say.

"Calvin," she says. Switching gears into the tone of *serious* work talk. "I asked around. Like I said I would. If you want, that thing we talked about, going back to get your master's, it's definitely an option."

"Look, I appreciate you looking out for me," I say. "There is a *lot* going on with my family. I don't think it's a good time to really shake things up."

"From what you've told me," she says, "it might be the *best* time."

I start to say, *I'll think about it,* but I stop myself.

Instead I say, "I can't give you an answer right now."

"The Manley School will pay for almost all of it," she says.

"You have to let me think about it," I say.

"It's a great opportunity," she says. "Don't let it slip away." She does the nurturing smile. I think about the application, filled out, sitting in my room, just waiting to be turned in. And that would be it, a done deal, back to school, off down a road of commitment to *something*. Maybe it doesn't matter what I commit to. Perhaps it's the decision itself that matters.

"I won't," I say.

"I'm just saying, we don't offer this to everyone," she says. "We think you're doing a great job. I know someone on the board at Pace. Just get the application back to me and I'll put it in the right hands."

"Ceci, I really appreciate the kind words, but you have to realize I'm not sure if this is for me." I gesture behind me.

"Consider it," she says. "That's all I'm saying."

In the classroom, Arham is wearing the sneakers I bought him. He is bursting with giggles. He runs to me and hugs my knees.

"Hug," he says. "Hug."

"How are you, my little man?" I say to him.

"Okay, okay, okay," he tells me.

THE DAY COMES when he must take the stress test. My parents make the trip into Manhattan alone. The general consensus is it would be overwhelming for him if we all went.

The test consists of electrocardiograph scans and a lengthy treadmill run, coupled with an isotope injection to measure how well his heart muscles function under stress. It's the last big hurdle standing between him and the successful reinstatement of his medical clearance. If he passes the test, the FAA will reopen his case and, with a little luck, aided by the supporting material we sent in the letter, reissue his license. He can return to his job at Transcontinental Air, go off disability, start collecting his full salary instead of 40 percent. Mortgage gets paid. House stays.

I wish him luck. Hug him awkwardly in the driveway.

"There's eggplant in the fridge," my mother says from the car. "Don't forget to walk Emma. We'll be back around six, I think."

"Have fun," I say.

"Yeah, right," I hear my father say. And then they are gone. Shortly after, there is an eruption of horn honking from the street in front of the house. I go to the living room window and see a group of young men all dressed in polo shirts in a black BMW. Chip comes thundering down the stairs carrying his golf bag.

"Where you headed?" I ask as I meet him at the door.

"I'm not even going to answer that," he says. And then he, too, is gone. He piles into the waiting car. There are hoots and hollers as the BMW peels away.

"Three down," I say to myself. And as if the heavens themselves have heard my prayers, the phone rings and I hear Elissa shriek from her bedroom. There is giggling and it isn't long before a car is outside honking for her.

"Jackie's taking me to the mall," Elissa says, waddling down the stairs. "We're gonna look for maternity clothes."

"Want help?"

"It's kind of a girls-only thing," Elissa says.

"Fair enough."

Her T-shirts are beginning to stretch around the budding mound of her stomach. With each month that goes by, she seems to look older and wiser. The pregnancy is very becoming and I've never seen her so happy.

I am utterly alone in the house for the better part of the day. I check my e-mail and see that Charlotte has written me back. My heart drops when I open the message and discover a semiformulated brush-off stating that, indeed, the position has been filled. She thanks me for coming in and says the well-known film company interviewed *many* over-qualified people for the job. It was a tough decision. Nothing stays the same, sure, but nothing much changes either. I feel like complete horseshit. I walk around in circles in my room and have a moment of panic. No extra money for my family. No extra money for me to move out. Nothing changes. I'm stuck here. In this house, with all of them. And worst of all, all I have to give in the way of financial support is a lousy $1,214.45, as of my last count. I am able to make no strides into adulthood. No progress toward being my own man. I do belong at the John W. Manley School. I go to my bedroom and pull the application out of my desk drawer. I call my undergraduate university and request transcripts to be sent. From my notebook, I transcribe my personal statement into Microsoft Word. I print it out. I seal everything up in the envelope and throw it on my bed. The only thing left to do is to hand it over to Ceci. Seal my fate. I'm not there yet, but something tells me I will be soon.

I walk to the bathroom.

"Goddamn stapler," I say to my face in the mirror.

Thoroughly dejected, I spend the rest of the day in a depressed funk. I sulk about. I masturbate eight times in five hours, tying my old record. I watch videos online, compiling a "greatest hits" of my favorite categories. As usual, I try to find women with glasses and knee-high socks. I look for blonds at first, switch to brunettes after a while. I try to take my time with each session, not wanting to rush. I've read this is good practice. A hasty jerk-off can lead to decreased stamina when confronted with the real thing. The fifth time around, I think about Gabby. I fantasize taking off her hat and touching my hand to the hole in her head.

I listen to records. I listen to *Sweetheart of the Rodeo*. I listen to *Pet Sounds*. I listen to *Beggars Banquet*. I listen to *Sabbath Bloody Sabbath*. I lie on the floor in my room in my boxer briefs and turn the stereo way up. I listen to *Larks' Tongues in Aspic*. I listen to *Close to the Edge*. I doze off for a half hour and when I wake I decide to alphabetize my records. I take them off the shelves and separate them, by artist, into twenty-six piles. This takes a while. There are a lot of records. I sort through them all. I stop occasionally to think about what was going on in my life when I acquired certain records. For the most part, I can't remember anything noteworthy about any of them. I look at my room and wonder how much of my life and money I've wasted collecting records, getting lost in music, shying away from forging real relationships with people. I look at the posters on my wall and determine they must all come down. I tear each from its place and crumple it into the garbage. When I finish, I am happy. I'm having a productive day. Getting things done.

I put on one of my father's bathrobes. I wander from room to room. I turn lights on. I turn them off. I stand in front of the piano in the living room and strike keys at random. I turn the television on. I turn it off. I take off the bathrobe. For dinner, I make a grilled cheese sandwich and heat up a can of tomato soup. When I finish eating, I jerk off once more, breaking the record. A very productive day, indeed. I call Wally to see if he wants to go to the movies. We opt for a horror film, some low-budget schlock. When I get home, my parents are sitting at the kitchen table. My father is eating a bowl of cereal. My mother is flipping through channels on the small television on the counter. I hover near the fridge.

"How'd everything go?" I ask.

"He passed," my mother says. "Dr. Nadoo thinks he has a chance at getting his license back."

"Well, that's good news," I say.

"It's wonderful news," my mother says.

My father slurps a heaping mound of cornflakes into his mouth.

"He doesn't look so thrilled," I point out.

"I feel terrible," he says. He wipes a line of milk from his chin.

"Your father's having some anxiety problems," my mother says.

"Still?" I ask. "Everything seems great." As I say this, his head drops and he lowers his face into his hands.

"James," my mother says, "stop crying. You've been crying all day. You need to stop this."

"Everything is fucked," he says.

"Jesus, Dad," I say. "Mom's right. You need to calm down. What's the matter?"

He raises his head, looks at us both. His eyes are weary. His jowls are starting to regain some of the puffiness they possessed before he got sick.

"Something's wrong with me," he says.

I leave them both to their separate worries. I go upstairs. Elissa is in her room, lying on her bed, her hands resting on her belly. She is listening to music.

"Are you having alone time?" I ask from her doorway.

"Just taking a moment," she says. She doesn't move or open her eyes.

I step into her room. I sit on the green and white throw

rug that occupies the space in front of her bookshelf. I lie
on my back.

"Dad passed his stress test," Elissa says.

"I know," I say. "He's downstairs crying about it right
now."

The weeks tumble by. I do not get in their way.

NOTHING IS A better barometer of failure than the success of
other people. Chris Hillman's wedding approaches. I think
about how much money will be dumped into the festivities
as I open a fresh bill from Sallie Mae. I go through the usual
motions. I mail off a payment. I add some money to my savings. I total the new sum in my notebook. I cross out the
old amount and write the new one. I'm up to $1,367.36. This
makes me both happy and depressed at once. There is no job
at the well-known film company to inflate my savings, and
$1,367.36 is just a drop in a very large bucket when taken in
the context of how much is owed on the house. My financial contribution seems paltry, almost meaningless, and I
haven't even given it to them yet.

Elissa is a whale. That much is certain. She spends most
of her time reading now, sitting in the living room with my
father. Her maternal instincts, roused by her pregnancy,
have turned her into the defacto Dad caretaker. Elissa allows him two hours of television watching a day. The rest of
the time she makes sure he spends in more productive, useful pursuits. She takes him on walks. They go to the grocery
store. The library. They sit in the park.

"Today's limit has been reached," she'll say as she turns
off the television. "Let's figure out what we want to do, shall
we?"

"I want to work on the mobile," he might say. In which case, Elissa will shuffle him to the basement, to his workbench, where he has begun constructing the present he promised to make for the baby. He and Elissa take frequent trips to the hobby store so he can purchase scale models of the aircraft he needs. "It's going to have all my favorite planes," he says. He buys tiny F-16s. He buys a Bell X-1, like Chuck Yeager flew to break the sound barrier. He buys a D-21 Tagboard, of Russian design, for spying during the Cold War. He buys a Boeing X-43. The old Fokker EI, a German dogfighter from World War II. A British Spitfire. He sits for hours and glues the models together. He fastens them with fishing line to a wooden cross he has sanded and polished. Over a few weeks' time, the mobile begins to take shape, and I can tell he is proud of what he is doing, proud to be making something for the baby. He brings the work in progress to the dinner table, keeping us informed as to its development. Filling us in on which aircraft he plans to add next.

"I'm working toward ten planes," he says.

For Arham's birthday, his parents send a small cake to school with him. He drops it on the bus, so the left side is dented, but the words "Happy Birthday Arham" can still be made out across the top. I bring him into the main room, where Ceci has gathered some children and their teachers. Tony plays his guitar and we all sing to the little man. He sits beaming. He blows out the candles with a hail of spit and gusto. I give him a big hug, which he seems reluctant to relinquish.

"Happy birthday, Arham," I say to him.

He looks me right in the eyes.

"Happy birthday, Arham," he says.

## ≪ **26** ≫

My father and I drive in silence. Twenty minutes on 117 and we are there. The reception hall is enormous, tucked up among the tall trees in Chappaqua. A place called Silver Springs.

I'm shocked to find I actually enjoy wearing the tuxedo I've rented. It fits me better than I could have hoped, and when I check everything out in the mirror before departure, I find myself satisfied. Maybe I am finally growing into my lanky frame. Maybe I'm getting some looks, after all these years.

The parking lot teems with Sleepy Hollow High alumni. Faces from the past. Each filling me with pangs of dread. These are people I hated seven years ago and certainly haven't grown any fonder of since. I linger in the car, unable to bring myself to even open the door and get out. I see Christian Rafelson, hair buzzed perfectly smooth, waving his hands in the air, apparently in the midst of some grand enchanting yarn that has Tara Walsh, Danielle Fusaro, and Monica Pearce enraptured. They all burst out laughing at something he says. A few of the "guys" loiter near the entrance, smoking. I watch John Wellington adjust his sizable gut around the waist of his pants so he can demonstrate for Paul Workman and Joe Fleischner the proper upward motion of a golf swing. Of course, the few people I wish were in attendance haven't been invited.

My father bangs on the window.

"Let's go," he says.

It is odd to see him dressed in a tuxedo. I'm surprised at how handsome he looks. His face betrays a decent amount of exhaustion and he still has the sallow hue of sickness, but it isn't as bad as it once was. The mustache is trimmed nicely.

"I'm coming," I say. I hesitate for another second before getting out. "I can't believe I'm here."

"There will be cake," my father says.

"You can't eat cake," I tell him.

He marches off. I follow, reluctantly stopping to say hello to everyone who notices me. I have eight versions of the same conversation before I even get inside. They all go something like this:

PERSON I WENT TO HIGH SCHOOL WITH: Oh my God, Calvin Moretti! How are you?

ME: Fine. Pretty good.

PERSON I WENT TO HIGH SCHOOL WITH: What are you doing these days?

ME: Teaching at a preschool.

PERSON I WENT TO HIGH SCHOOL WITH: Wow, that is so cute!

ME: I suppose. And you?

PERSON I WENT TO HIGH SCHOOL WITH: I work for *blah blah blah* doing *blah blah blah* and I just got a raise and I've been there for three years now, so they definitely owed me, and hey, by the way, I'm sorry to hear about your dad, and how's he doing?

ME: He's right over there.

PERSON I WENT TO HIGH SCHOOL WITH: Oh, man. He doesn't look so good.

ME: That's what he says.

PERSON I WENT TO HIGH SCHOOL WITH: Wild.

ME: Wild.

PERSON I WENT TO HIGH SCHOOL WITH: Well. It really is nice to see you.

ME: It is nice to see you, too.

I STAND TOWARD the back, as much in the shadows as possible, but it's hard because the banquet hall is cavernous and filled with sunshine pouring through every window. I watch as the band sound-checks. There is a loud spike of feedback from the microphone as the singer plugs into the PA. I squint to get a better look at the drummer as he takes a seat behind his kit. He looks like Arthur Kornberg, the Dungeon Master. It can't be. Then again, it must be—the resemblance is too uncanny. I walk toward the stage. The singer is saying, "Test," into the microphone over and over. I stand silently while the guitarist changes a string.

"What kind of stuff are you guys playing today?" I ask, just lobbing the question into the air for any of them to field.

"All sorts of crap," the bass player, a stocky, balding

investment-banker type with a Santa Claus tie says. "The bride gave us an extensive list of *great* suggestions," he adds.

"I'd like to suggest a heavy D&D theme," I say.

Arthur looks up from his stool and stops twirling his sticks.

"I'd like to suggest *Dark Side of the Moon*. In its entirety," I say.

"That would be rad," he says. He still wears the same enormous clear-rimmed glasses he wore when we were in the sixth grade. "Calvin?" he asks.

"Arthur Kornberg," I say. "The Dungeon Master." I step up onto the stage and Arthur comes out from behind his floor tom and bass drum and we do one of those awkward hugs only two guys who aren't good at human contact are capable of pulling off.

"Still gaming?" I ask.

"About to make the move to straight-up LARPing," Arthur says.

"You always were the nerdiest," I tell him.

"You should come out," Arthur says.

"It's not for me."

"What is for you?"

"That's what I'm trying to figure out."

"It's a tough nut."

"How weird is it to see all these people?"

"So weird," Arthur says. "Like an episode of the *Twilight Zone* that's going to last five hours."

"How long you been doing this?" I ask, motioning to the rest of the band.

"It's only our second wedding," he says. "Hard-core wasn't paying enough."

"It never does," I say. "You were in a band?"

"Female Blood," he says.

"You were in Female Blood?" I ask. "I saw you guys. Like, three years ago in Cambridge, at the Middle East. Your singer threw up on himself. I can't believe I didn't recognize you."

"My longhair phase," Arthur says. "We broke up." He pushes his glasses up with the tip of a finger and scrunches his nose like there's a booger lodged there that's making him uncomfortable.

"Shit, man," I say. "If I had known it was you, I'd have said hello."

"Eh," Arthur says. "No sweat."

"Well," I say, looking around for my father. I spot him standing at one of the hors d'oeuvre tables, staring into a bowl of punch. "I gotta go corral my dad. He's not well."

"I heard," Arthur says. "Good luck with all that."

"Looking forward to the set," I say with a salute.

"Don't look too hard," Arthur says.

I SEE CHRIS from across the room. He and Marie have taken the first dance. The guests are all seated at their tables watching. He lifts her arm into the air, holding it daintily by the fingertips. He twirls her. The band plays "Wonderful Tonight" and does a halfway decent job of it.

"His moves are all wrong," I tell my father, who is sitting next to me. The plate of food he was served a half hour ago is still untouched. Our tablemates are two of Chris's male cousins whose names I have already forgotten. They are both extremely excited about a new sailing vessel their family has acquired on Martha's Vineyard.

"A thirty-foot schooner," Cousin #1 tells us.

"You know what makes it a schooner, don't you?" Cousin #2 adds.

"Fore and aft sails," my father says out of nowhere. He rubs his mustache. "I'd love to get my hands on that boat."

"You know a lot about seamanship?" Cousin #1 asks.

"I'd sail into the sunset," my father says.

"Maybe Buffy will let you come out for a jaunt this summer," Cousin #2 says.

"Who the fuck is Buffy?" my father asks.

"Our mother," Cousin #2 says.

"Do you sail?" Cousin #1 asks.

"I fly," my father says.

"He's been sick," I say.

"Pity," Cousin #2 says. "Seeing the water race by off the side of the hull is the most liberating feeling in the world."

"I'd like to be *under* water," my father says.

"A scuba man," Cousin #1 says.

The band moves on to the next number, "Lady in Red." The tables have begun to clear out as most of the guests find their way to the dance floor. They sway, slowly, affectionately. There is a collective glow to everyone. They are really enjoying themselves. I see their eyes, their smiles. Outside, the sun is setting, but its colors are still in the sky. Orange and red and purple are everywhere.

Cousin #1 and Cousin #2 excuse themselves.

"We're off to find some tail," one of them says.

"Godspeed," I tell them.

• • •

THE CAKE ARRIVES. A massive thing, towering as tall as a man or more likely a midget, but still, *towering* is a word that suits it. A plastic bride and groom grace its summit. The cake is cut. Chris and Marie gobble up the first slices. They pose for photos with the cake. They embrace. He dips her, low, toward the parquet. He kisses her neck. Flashes pop. A few cheers go up from a rowdy group of drunken male spectators who I can only assume are Chris's frat brothers from Yale.

Cake is being delivered to all who wish to consume cake. Hillman's best man, a large, hulking figure with Ken doll hair, rises from his seat and clanks a spoon to his Champagne glass for attention.

"Greetings, everyone," he begins. "For those of you who don't know me, my name is Chad Pennington. I was Chris's roommate freshman year. And captain of the Yale rugby team." He pauses here for a moment to let this information sink in.

"Yale rugby rules," someone yells out.

Pennington surveys the room before continuing, making eye contact with people, something he perhaps learned in a public-speaking class. His body wavers slightly. Massive shoulders seem to test the very limit of elasticity his suit will allow. His head lolls a little and it is clear he has parted ways with sobriety much earlier in the day. He raises his glass. He tilts it too much and spills Champagne onto his lapel.

"Man down," someone yells out.

Pennington lowers his glass, realizing, I think, that he still has a speech to deliver before the actual toast.

"Welcome," he continues. "This really is a special day. When

I met Chris, I don't think he'd ever kissed a girl. He was a real nerd." He pauses here. "Not much has changed." Ah, the punch line. A few chuckles arise from the audience, all seated in their assigned places, shoveling cake into their mouths.

I HEAD TO the bathroom and go through the painful procedure of pulling my dick out of the tuxedo fly. I pee for what seems like hours, relishing the wonderful feeling of release. On my way out I almost collide head-on with the groom.

"Oh, what's up?" I say. Chris seems to be pleased we have bumped into one another. He extends a hand and I shake it as firmly as I can.

"Hey, Calvin," he says. "I'm glad you could make it."

"Yeah, me, too," I say. "Having a good time."

"How's your father holding up?"

"He's eating cake, I think," I say. "Congratulations," I add.

"Thank you," Chris says. His blond hair is neatly combed to one side. His tux fits him very well and he has lost most of the dorkish qualities that plagued him as a teenager. He looks like a man.

"So was it scary?" I ask.

"A little."

"You feel any different?"

"I feel good," he says.

"It must be nice to know what you want," I say.

"I suppose," he says.

"I'm glad things are going well for you," I tell him.

"So what's new with you?" he asks.

"I work at a preschool for retarded kids. Live with my parents."

"It'll turn itself around," Chris says. "It always does. Hey, I'm about to explode." He opens the door and starts into to the bathroom. He pauses. "Hey," he says, "I didn't think you'd actually come. It was my mother's idea to invite you. I thought you'd have no interest. Kind of thought we disliked each other. For what it's worth, I'm sorry I hit you in the head with that acorn."

"It's your wedding day," I say. "All is forgiven."

I GO TO the bar and get a third glass of wine and one for my father.

"Here," I say, handing him the drink. "You can have this, but if Mom finds out, I'll never forgive you."

"Understood," he says. He takes the glass from me and sips it slowly.

I see he has helped himself to a second slice of cake. I take the plate from him and put it on an adjacent table.

"You can't have any more cake, though," I say. "Mom would kill me if she knew you even had one piece."

My father and I sit for a moment without talking. We drink our wine.

"You think I'm crazy?" he asks.

"I think you're depressed."

He nods his head. He looks around the room. We both do. The dance floor undulates with bodies. Some drift off to the bar. Others linger out on the large balcony, cigarettes dangling from their lips. Others have gathered in make-shift huddles, instinctively drawn into their old high school cliques. I have lost track of Chris Hillman. The band does a swinging version of "Can You Feel the Love Tonight." My father smooths his shirt out with his hands, adjusts the angle of his bow tie.

"I hate tuxedos," he says. "When your mother and I got married, in *1973*, I wore a white suit. With bell-bottoms. Everything's gotten so jumbled up."

"They were never so ordinary to begin with," I tell him.

"How are you holding up?" he asks.

"Terribly," I say. "I have no idea what I'm doing."

"Who does?" my father says.

"I have no girlfriend."

"Consider yourself lucky."

"My friends are letting me down."

"They always do."

"I contribute nothing toward keeping the house from going under," I say.

"You're there," my father says. "That counts for something."

"But I can't help with money," I say. "Not like Chip is helping with money."

"There are other ways," he says.

"What I really want," I say, "is to know how it feels to be passionate about something. To pick a path and go with it and not think so much about what's next."

"It never stops," he says.

"I wish it would."

"I don't know what to tell you."

"You don't have to tell me anything," I say.

"It's a tough nut," my father says, echoing the exact words Arthur Kornberg said to me earlier in the evening.

"I basically refuse to take any responsibility onto my plate."

"Everyone has responsibility," my father says. "Whether they want it or not."

"Some people have more than others," I say. "Look at you. You got a family. A house. Car insurance. Life insurance. A mortgage."

"About to go into default," he points out.

"Why did you decide to shoulder all that?"

"I didn't think there was any other way to do it," he says.

"There's always another way," I say.

He laughs.

"I was too scared of *not* getting married," he says. "I was terrified of being alone."

"Are all men just little boys forever?" I ask.

"I know you took the gun," he says. He wipes his eyes with the back of his hand.

"I wanted to shoot it."

"I know the feeling."

"Can I tell you, though, Dad? Here's the thing with shooting the gun. I realized something I've been overlooking all this time. We may be more in control than we think. Of everything. Of what happens to us."

"We're not in control of anything," he says.

"Because you don't see it working out in your head," I tell him. "You don't see it happening the way you want it to happen."

"I don't want to be sick anymore," he says.

"Then don't act like it's going to come back," I say. "Give yourself that much."

"And after that?" he asks.

"After that, what happens, happens. You can't stop it or change it. But at least you didn't play a part in it."

"You're as confused as your mother," he says.

"It's like with the house," I go on. "We're in control. We can leave anytime. We don't have to wait for the bank."

"I don't want to go," he says. "Your mother doesn't want to go."

"I know, Dad," I say. "I don't want to lose the house either. I'm just saying."

"What are we gonna do?"

"We'll figure something out."

"I know this has been a tough year," he says. "For everyone. And I'm sorry for that."

"It's not your fault," I tell him. "It's mine. It's no one's."

THE BAND SEGUES into "What a Wonderful World" as Chris and his mother take the dance floor. They pivot and turn in slow motion. Tears well up in the eyes of onlookers. A touching moment between mother and son.

Cousin #1 and Cousin #2 return from their pussy hunt. They each double-fist pieces of cake.

"No dice?" I ask as they take their seats.

"Bunch of hags out there," Cousin #1 says.

"This is getting boring," Cousin #2 says. "Someone needs to liven things up around here."

My father leans forward, motioning for us all to do the same. He looks over his shoulder. He opens his coat and flashes the butt of the revolver, the snub-nosed, jutting from the waistline of his pants.

"I could take care of that," he says.

The cousins seem excited. Their eyes widen.

"Oh, Jesus fucking Christ, Dad," I say.

"Relax," he says, waving his hand at me and closing his jacket back up. "I'm just joking around."

"You're a wild one," Cousin #2 says.

"I like that," Cousin #1 says. They finish their cake. They rise again and are gone. Off in search of more alcohol. It is only a few minutes before a man in a security uniform approaches our table.

"Excuse me, gentlemen," he says. His arms are thick and bulging inside the sleeves of his shirt.

"Yes, Officer?" my father says.

"I'm not a police officer," the security guard says.

"You have a very striking presence," my father says.

Chris Hillman has finished the dance with his mother. The singer announces that the next number will be the band's last. They begin to play a rousing rendition of "Everlasting Love."

"I've been informed by some of the guests that you have a firearm on your person," the security guard says. He has his hands on the back of my father's chair, and he leans in close as he says this, as if it is a secret he wants to share with us.

"That's correct," my father says. He tries to say it casually, but it just comes out weird. "It's fully registered," he adds. The security guard raises an eyebrow.

"I'm gonna have to ask you to leave, sir," he says. "Both of you."

"What did I do?" I ask. My father opens his coat again and takes the pistol out. Somewhere nearby a woman gasps.

"It's not a big deal," he says.

He puts the gun down on the table, a little too hard maybe, or maybe his finger is on the trigger and all the excitement makes him twitch, or maybe it's something more inexplicable. Divine intervention. For whatever reason—I'll never know—the gun decides to go off.

Everyone is staring at me. Every neck in the place seems craned in my direction. The security guard's mouth is slack, as if it has become unhinged.

"Ouch. Ouch," I say. I look down at the small, ragged hole in the shoulder of my tuxedo jacket.

I stand up. The room is very strange looking. I'm not on any drugs. No pills or weed or lines of blow or sacred shamanistic herbs. I'm sober, but everything is different. Nothing is where it should be. The tables are drifting apart. I see Arthur standing at the edge of the stage with his drumsticks in hand. Once, we were friends. Once, he was the Dungeon Master. And the deer kicked its legs all over the place. Twitched and flapped. Its eyes spun round in their sockets like ball bearings. We scooped dirt with shovels, Elissa and I. Threw it down into the hole and listened to it spatter across the shoe box with Tanis inside, wrapped in his paper-towel death shroud. Is there any control? Am I completely misleading myself? Is all life just random and arbitrary? Who gets cancer? Who loses their house? Who dies? Who lives? Who is happy? Who walks in agony and malcontented despair? An inch one way, maybe it isn't my shoulder. An inch the other way, it's a tree and the deer runs off. A few dollars more. A condom.

It feels like minutes later. Or is it hours? I'm in the back of

an ambulance. A large black man is seated beside me, holding my hand. I realize he's just taking my pulse. He drops
my hand and looks into my eyes.

"You're gonna be fine," he says. His voice is deep and
soothing like my grandmother singing to me when I was a
child and couldn't fall asleep. I'm having no trouble sleeping
now. Through the ambulance windows I watch the head-
lights of cars blur and splice into one another.

"Did we leave my father?" I ask.

"I don't know," the black man says.

I feel close to him. This large, soothing, dark-skinned,
compassionate emergency technician. I feel safe and numb
and at ease. My arm and my shoulder have gone away from
the rest of me.

We both fired the gun with unintended results. My father
and I. Things happen. You have to puzzle out what to do
afterward.

# ≪ **27** ≫

Light creeps up the wall. For the most part, the room is empty. Bed and IV. I watch their shadows retreat downward across the floor, elongating and falling out of proportion as the sun rises above the East River. There is another bed, but it is unoccupied. I don't recognize this part of the hospital. I can see out into the hallway. Nurses scuttle back and forth. No one checks on me.

I'm going to have to jerk off with my left hand for a while. A challenge I am looking forward to overcoming.

I count saline drips. I pinpoint how many there are in a minute. I close my eyes and listen to the cardiac monitor. I fall asleep.

When I wake up, my eyes are caked shut. I open them slowly. I do everything slowly. My mother is sitting at my bedside.

"Before you ask, my shoulder is fucking killing me. And I feel like shit," I tell her.

"I don't trust any doctor in Westchester."

"Yes," I say. "I'm very aware of your stance on the medical profession outside New York City."

"I don't want some quack taking care of my son," she says. "You're going to be fine."

"That's a relief," I say.

"They had to remove the bullet," she says. "Small surgery."

"What day is it?"

"It's Tuesday," she says. "You slept most of yesterday."

"Did I say anything funny?" I ask.

"People always say funny things when they're on morphine," my mother says. "Your father recited plotlines from *Law & Order*."

"Where is he?" I ask.

"He's at home," she says. "He's embarrassed to see you. He feels so guilty."

"I'm not mad at him," I say. "He needs help, Mom."

"We all do," my mother says.

"What happened?" I ask.

"In the end, nothing," my mother says. "Cops came. They took the gun, brought him to the station. The Hillmans wouldn't press charges, so they let him go. Naturally, his pistol permit has been revoked."

"It's so humiliating being part of this family."

"You were passed out," she says. "I was the one who had to go fetch him."

The pain in my shoulder fluctuates from mild to excruciating.

"How long do I have to stay here?"

"I don't know," my mother says.

"Work?"

"I called them. Spoke to a wonderful woman. They completely understand."

"They're always so understanding."

"They said to rest up and everything will be waiting for you when you go back."

"I'm hungry," I say.

"I'll get you something," my mother says.

"Can you bring me some paper, too?" I ask.

"Sure, dear," she says, and she is gone.

THE PAIN MEDICATION they have me on causes strange thought patterns that I want to capture for transcription into my notebook at a later time.

*Junior year of college I spent a week in North Carolina visiting my classmate Doug Gordon. We were close then, but I've lost touch with him since.*

*Life is constantly turning on itself and eating up the spot where it was only moments before. Life as Ouroboros. Life as inescapable tedium. Life as family. Maybe that's the whole point.*

*I remember the drive down from Durham to the town where Doug lived. It was a long stretch of old road where most of the houses had front yards littered with mattresses, rusting car chassis. I wanted to live in those houses. The people were free inside there, I could just tell. They lived like free people.*

*We wasted a lot of time in Chapel Hill. At the university there.*

*We'd walk through the quad, admiring the Douglas fir.*

*We'd pick out the best-looking girls as they rushed from one*
*class to the next, holding their books like babies, and then*
*we'd complain about how unapproachable they seemed.*
*We'd sit against the mossy stone walls lining the campus and*
*discuss the fact that our ilk seemed nowhere to be found. We*
*were supremely alone, dejected young men and we felt it was*
*better that way. I feel this still. I feel it now, in the hospital,*
*recovering from a gunshot wound to my shoulder, adminis-*
*tered by my own father. I feel I belong here. It was, in all like-*
*lihood, inevitable that I follow him.*

IT ENDS UP being another day before they send me home. I
leave the hospital just after 9 a.m., my right shoulder encased in mounds of gauze and tape, a sling keeping the
whole mess in place.

My father drives in with Chip to pick me up. They have
Emma with them. She goes into a frenzy when I get in the
car, pounces into my lap, licking my face.

"They gave me drugs," I say.

Percocet and Tylenol with codeine. All I had to do to get
them was complain about the pain in my arm and wince
whenever I was in a doctor's presence. It is the first time I
have legitimately scored prescription drugs. I shake one of
the bottles with my good hand.

"Share," Chip says from the backseat. "My legs are killing
me from the gym."

"Get your own," I tell him.

"Your mother thought it would be a good idea for me to
come," my father says.

"I seem to recall you saying something about not taking orders from Mom," I tell him.

"Maybe I wanted to come," he says.

"It's a nice day," I say.

"You hate me?" my father asks.

"I don't hate you," I say. "I don't hate you at all," I tell him again. "I'm just tired."

"We're all tired, I think," he says.

"Business as usual for this family," Chip says.

"Shut up," my father says.

Emma throws her front paws up on the window and stares at the taxis whizzing by on the FDR.

# ≪ **28** ≫

She steals my sock. I chase her through the kitchen, into the dining room, out to the living room. She scampers under the piano and won't come out. I see her under there, the sock dangling from her mouth. She looks at me.

"Give me the sock, you shithead," I tell her. I get down on my knees, pain shoots up through my shoulder, and I pause to adjust the sling. I reach with my left arm, my good arm, and try to grab her. She backs up against the wall, out of reach. When I crawl under the piano, she bolts to the side, rounds the corner back into the kitchen.

"The dog has my sock," I call out. I remember I am home alone, having opted out of a family trip to the mall. "Fuck," I say.

I back out from under the piano. I stand up too quickly and bang my shoulder. The pain is excruciating. I roll on my back, squeezing my eyes shut as hard as I can. When I open them, I see tiny points of light everywhere I look.

It takes me forever to stand up. Despite my pledge to do fewer drugs, the pain drives me to the bathroom, where I take a Percocet. Surely I'm allowed such indiscretions following a gunshot wound?

I look at the scrap of paper hanging from the mirror, a giant letter *S* inscribed on it. I throw it in the garbage. I flush the toilet for no reason.

"That asshole should have come by," I say.

I DRIVE TO his house. I remember the way. I speed up the curling streets of Croton, climbing higher and higher, away from the twinkling Hudson. Turning the wheel is awkward with one hand, and it's painful. I'm not supposed to be driving. I'm supposed to be taking it easy.

I park. I watch the porch for a while. I watch the windows. I look for signs of movement inside, a signal of some kind, telling me what to do next. My arm is throbbing from shoulder to elbow. I drum my fingers on the steering wheel. I leave the keys in the ignition. I get out and walk across the front lawn and march up the steps. I stand on the porch, ringing the bell. I don't know what I plan to do. It feels like a long time goes by before the lock turns and the big red door swings open and Bjorn is standing there in gym shorts and a tank top. Wild, sweaty hair is matted all around his forehead. He is breathing heavy.

"You?" he says.

"Me," I say.

"What?"

"Why are you all sweaty?"

He looks behind him.

"I was on the treadmill," he says.

"Elissa Moretti," I say.

"What about her?"

"You should have come by. To see how she's doing. See how they're doing."

He looks at me for a moment. His mouth is turned up a little at the ends, like he's smiling, but he isn't smiling.

"What?" he says.

"You should have come by," I tell him. I hit him in the face as hard as I can with my good arm, my good hand. I've never punched anyone in my life. It feels okay. The dull sound of knuckle hitting cheekbone. An intense pain rockets up my forearm. He falls to one knee and I'm on top of him. His arms are around my waist, and we hit the deck, flop around on top of one another. My arm comes loose from the sling. It's all gone numb. Something jerks me and I'm being dragged to my feet from behind.

"Just hold on a minute," a man's voice is saying.

And at the same time, Bjorn is yelling, "This guy is fucking crazy." He spits blood. He holds a hand to his bleeding lips.

"Get your hands off me," I say. I wave my good arm and squirm until the man releases his grip. I stumble a few feet. I nearly fall.

I turn and swing my arms, warding them both off. I feel the wound opening under the bandages. The warm sensation of fresh blood, the slipperiness of it.

"Son," the man says, "you're in a world of trouble."

"He fucking punched me," Bjorn says in disbelief.

I stand there, catching my breath, clutching my shoulder, pressing hard against the gauze beneath my sweater.

"Go get the phone," Bjorn's father says. "Call the police."

"I'm bleeding," Bjorn says.

"Just do it," his father says.

"You do it," Bjorn says. He spits more blood. "I'm gonna kick his ass." He advances toward me. His father grabs him by the shirt and drags him through the front door, into the house.

"Call the police," he says. "Now."

My bearings are coming back to me. I turn and run as fast as I can to the hatchback. I fumble for a second with the handle, then I'm inside and I'm shutting the door and I'm starting the engine and I'm wrenching into first gear and peeling off. I look in the rearview mirror, half expecting Old Man Copeland to bolt into the street after me. He doesn't. Just houses and trees, getting smaller and smaller, and then I'm through a stop sign and around a corner and I'm gone.

THE FOUR WINDS HOSPITAL is set back behind black wrought-iron gates. From the road, I see brick through the trees. Soothing glimpses of the vast, secluded complex. I see swatches of roof. Shingling, old and noble. It has the feel of a college campus. Ivy growing over brick.

I drive up past the main entrance. The grounds are littered with patients and nurses out taking midafternoon strolls. An elderly man, hunched over a walker, is escorted by a young lady in pink scrubs toward a bench near a small pond. Others, many others, are being led to various resting places. Tranquil spots selected to promote relaxation and recovery. Momentary escape from inside thoughts. I look to see if Aunt Corrine is among those permitted access to fresh air. She is nowhere in sight.

I put on my turn signal even though there aren't any other cars in sight. I coast into the visitors' parking lot. I sit for a moment, listening to the radio. I turn off the radio. My face hurts, and from the looks of it I'll have a black eye soon, though I don't remember Bjorn getting any shots in. My arm hurts. My sling is in tatters. I jury-rig it into working condition. Both my hands ache.

"What are you doing here?" I ask the rearview mirror.

I take the keys out of the ignition and walk across the lawn.

The lobby smells like a library. Stale paper and ancient wood. There is sweet, gentle Muzak coming from speakers in the ceiling. Low tones, calming and jarring at the same time. A girl in a swivel chair behind the reception window spins toward me as I approach, as if she senses my movements before I make them. I look at her. We share an unspoken bond and I feel a stirring in my stomach that gives me hope. This girl can see my weakness. She will accept me and show me to a place, a room, a support group, a doctor's office. She will tell me why I am here. She will help find the missing pieces. And if she can't do these things personally, she knows who can. She knows what to do. I am safe in her hands.

"Hi there," the girl says. Her name tag reads "Veronica."

"Hello, Veronica," I say.

"Can I help you?" she asks.

"My aunt is a patient," I say. "I was hoping I could say hello to her."

"Of course," this girl, Veronica, says. Her eyes seem to dance in her head. She wears a necklace. A small silver butcher's knife dangling between her breasts, inside the collar of her blouse. She is looking at me with concern.

"I'm fine," I say.

"You look like you got the shit kicked out of you."

"I'm fine," I say. I touch my face. I touch my lip. "I'm fine," I say again.

"You don't look fine," Veronica says.

"Maybe a bathroom?"

"It's right there," she says, pointing down the hall behind me.

I run cold water and splash my face a few times. I stick out my tongue and look for something, although I'm not sure what exactly I'm looking for. My eyes are tired. I do look like I've had the shit kicked out of me. I head back out to the lobby.

"You look the same," Veronica tells me.

"I feel the same."

"What's your aunt's name?"

I look at her necklace. I look into her dancing eyes.

"Corrine Jones."

Veronica punches some keys on her computer. She clicks her mouse.

"Building Four. Across the lawn, near the gym."

"Thank you, Veronica," I say.

"You're welcome."

I turn and leave. Back out to the lawn, the Muzak ringing dully in my ears.

Because of a genetic malfunction in her ovaries, Aunt Corrine was forced to adopt. A baby girl she named Grace. Grace had black hair. Dark circles under her eyes at the age of nine. She was a few years older than me. Grace would babysit me sometimes. We'd play a game where Grace would put a toy car in her underwear and I would take it out. She'd put the car in my underwear and take it out.

"You get hair down there," Grace told me.

"You don't have any," I said.

"It'll happen."

Grace went on to become a heroin addict. She dropped out of high school, had a kid before she turned twenty-one. I have no idea where she is now.

A male nurse at reception in Building Four holds a clipboard. Glasses dangle from a chain around his neck. He shows me to Corrine's room.

"Four twenty-six is just at the end of the hall here and to your left," he says, pointing with his pen. "Past the water fountain. You can't miss it. Dinner is in half an hour, just so you know. Try not to stay too long."

"I won't," I say.

I make as little noise as possible as I walk. I don't want to disturb the delicate illusion of sanity hanging in the air. I let my heels fall slowly, purposefully. I bring my toes down gently. I try to breathe only when necessary.

I stand outside her door for a long time. I knock, and when nothing happens, I turn the knob and go inside. Corrine is standing at the window, peering out at trees and landscaping. Green shrubbery. She looks at me, her movements slow and drawn out. She wears a pale green sundress, slippers. Her face is a map of lines and furrows. A bookshelf on the far wall is filled with knickknacks. Empty picture frames, porcelain animals.

"Calvin," she says.

"Hi, Aunt Corrine," I say.

"I'm waiting for a new washer-dryer," she tells me.

I look at the door behind me.

"How's Grace?" I ask.

"Can't remember the last time I saw her."

"She doesn't visit?"

"Not once. I'm not even sure she knows I'm here. We don't talk. She went to Rochester to be with the kid's father."

"Jesus."

"God is here. I think."

"You don't really believe that."

"If you could feel the things I feel."

"All I feel is pain in my shoulder."

"What happened there?"

"My father shot me. He's going through some things. Trying to work them out."

"Jimmy always was a little odd," Corrine says. She walks to the bookshelf and arranges a set of miniature bells in a straight line. "Even when he was younger," she adds.

"I didn't know him then," I say.

"You know him now."

"So people don't change?"

"In my experience, they don't."

"Is happiness achievable?"

"I'm happy."

"But you're here."

"Is it any better out there?"

"I think the general consensus is that it's better out there."

"They let me do whatever I want. I take swim classes.

Sunday night movies in the community room. Refreshments. There's even a nature trail. It's quiet all the time."

"It's never quiet in my house."

"That's real life."

"I could use a break from it."

"There is no break."

"You're taking a break."

Corrine sits on the bed. She bites her fingers. Outside, light is disappearing from the sky.

"Is Lloyd seeing anyone new?" Corrine asks.

"Lloyd's dead."

"He is, isn't he?"

"For a while now. I'm sorry to have to keep reminding you."

"I like thinking about him," she says.

"I don't know why I came."

"I'm glad for the company. I don't see much of anyone. What's the news out there?"

"Trying to figure out how to hold on to our house," I say.

"Times are tough," she says.

"Family's getting bigger," I add.

"Overeating?"

"Elissa's pregnant."

"She's a bit young, isn't she?"

"Yeah, she is."

"Like Grace."

"Not really. Aunt Corrine?"

"Yeah?"

"I used to dread having to kiss you hello when I was little. I'm sorry for that."

"You did? Well, no worries. We can forget. We can just worry about right now."

I leave her then. I kiss her forehead slowly, and although the wrinkles of her brow are rough and leathery under my lips and she smells faintly of urine, I smile when I pull my face away. I hug her until she lets go. In truth, I hardly know this woman at all, but down some path of family lineage we share something. It is strange for me to show up like this, to be in her room, but it feels like a step in the right direction.

I stop back at the main building on my way out and see Veronica, still seated behind her computer screen. She smiles when she sees me.

"Hi there," she says.

"Hello again. So what's involved in getting a room here?"

"How long you planning to stay?"

"As long as it takes."

"You want two twins or queen size?"

"As long as I can smoke in the room."

"There's no smoking on the premises," Veronica says.

"Does the Muzak ever stop?"

"It's on a loop."

"You're not taking me seriously," I say.

"I'm not," she says.

In the car I put my head against the steering wheel. I dig through the tapes on the floor. I listen to deep soul music from Mississippi towns like Vicksburg, Indianola, Coahoma. Places I've never been to but have a clear picture of in my head. Hot and sweaty, thick with history. Spanish moss growing on the trees. Hedgerows. People own their houses free and clear.

My arm pulses with pain.

# ≪ **29** ≫

When I get home, I half expect to see flashing lights outside the house. Officers waiting to take me in. There's nothing like that.

I find my family in the living room. My mother is sitting in one of the wing chairs flanking the fireplace, Emma curled in her lap. Elissa is lying on the floor, her head propped by a pillow, her hands resting atop her belly. My father is on the sofa with his reading glasses on, but he's not reading anything.

"Oh my God, Cal," my mother says, "what happened to your face?"

"I don't want to talk about it right now," I say.

My mother puts the dog down and comes over for a motherly inspection of my wounds. I brush her off.

"Stop, Mom," I say. "I'm fine."

Instead she retrieves an ice pack from the fridge and hands it to me.

"Join us for family time," our father says.

"Brigitte thinks it's a good idea for us all to spend at least a half hour together each day," our mother says.

"You look really bad," Elissa says.

"Can we please just let it go?" I say.

I lie down on the couch. I put the ice pack on my face. I use the tops of my father's legs as a pillow. I am careful not to move my arm too much. He strokes my hair and I don't tell him to stop. It doesn't bother me. The day has been a dream, waking and dozing, waking and dozing. Chip comes thundering down the stairs from his bedroom.

"I'm here," he announces.

"We're glad to see you," our father says.

"Your face is all fucked up," he tells me.

"So is yours," I say.

"He won't tell us what happened," our mother says.

"He obviously got beat up," Chip says.

"Just let me rest for a second," I say.

My brother paces around. He grabs a Duraflame from the wicker basket next to the mantel.

"Should I make a fire?" he asks.

"It's not cold out," our mother says.

"A fire would be nice," Elissa says.

"A fire would be nice," I say.

"You look like shit," Chip says.

"You already pointed that out," I say.

"It needed to be said again," he says.

I close my eyes. I feel them wanting to stay shut. A nameless weight spreads out into my limbs. I close my eyes. I am confident that when I open them again, everyone will still be here, in this room, and we will be okay. We will be happy with who we are.

• • •

OF COURSE HE COMES. The next day. Friday. Old Man Copeland. I see him through the glass of the front door, his large
frame blocking out most of the sunlight. Before the doorbell
even rings, I am heading up to my room, most likely to hide
under my covers.

I pause at the top of the stairs, out of sight. I duck my
head to get a look at what is going on down there. I wait for
whatever is coming.

My mother lets him in and he stands in the foyer, his
arms dangling at his sides. His face is flecked with sweat.
Elissa and my father are in the family room. The TV is on
at top volume.

"Can I help you?" my mother begins.

"You most certainly can," Copeland says. "Does a Calvin
Moretti live here?"

"He most certainly does."

"Are you his mother?"

"I most certainly am," she says in that voice of hers, that
appeasing, calm voice of hers. The one she uses on police
officers when she gets pulled over for speeding. The one she
uses to talk her way out of sticky situations.

"He's in a lot of trouble," Copeland says.

"What'd he do?"

"What he did was physically assault my seventeen-year-
old son on the porch of our house yesterday."

"Calvin," my mother calls out. I take a few breaths and
descend the stairs to join them. I can feel my face blushing
as I go. My palms sweat.

"This man . . ." My mother motions in his direction.

"John Copeland," he says.

"This man, John Copeland," she continues. She stops for a moment. Her hand moves to her chin and she thinks about something for a second. "I'm sorry, did you say your name is Copeland?" she asks.

"John Copeland. My son is Bjorn. He's out there in the car. The boy's too darn afraid to come up here himself."

We all pause for a moment to glance back out the door, across the yard to the street, where Bjorn is indeed sitting in the passenger seat of a silver Escort.

My mother is mulling something over in her head. When she speaks again, her voice has modulated from calm and even to pressure-cooker temper-tantrum mode.

"You've got a lot of nerve showing up here, you know that, asshole?" she says, and even I am afraid of her tone.

"I'm an asshole?" Copeland says, aghast. "I've got a lot of nerve? I've got a lot of nerve?" He says it the second time for effect, maybe, or maybe because he can't believe what he's hearing. "I'm gonna call the cops. He'll go to jail."

"Before anyone goes to jail," my mother says as she moves to put herself between me and Old Man Copeland. She is close to him, almost right in his face. "Before you make any calls, I'd have a talk with your son about what he's been up to."

"What is that supposed to mean?" Copeland says.

"It means," my mother says, screaming now, "little Bjorn's had a good time recently and we're stuck with the bills." She pauses here for effect. "You come to *my* house and threaten to call the cops on *my* son. I have a husband, sitting on the couch in there"—she points to the TV room—"recovering from cancer. Maybe I'll make a phone call or two myself.

Maybe you'd like to be a grandfather? Buy the kid some clothes. Take it to the doctor. Pay for schoolbooks. Take it to the zoo. How does that sound?"

I am smiling behind her, trying not to let Copeland see. He stands there with his arms dangling and I don't think he has the slightest notion what to say. He is flabbergasted. He shifts his weight from one leg to the other and opens his mouth, but succeeds only in emitting a strange gust of air, like a whistle.

"I think it's time for you to leave now," my mother says. She is holding the front door open, signaling for him to exit. I can see her knuckles are white where she is gripping the knob.

"Sorry," Copeland manages.

"Bye now," my mother says. And just like that, Copeland is out the door and heading across the walk with his head hung and his mind most likely awhirl with questions. I see Bjorn sit up straight as his father plops down behind the steering wheel.

"Asshole," my mother calls out.

The engine starts and they drive off. I'm shaking with adrenaline.

I DON'T SMOKE a joint in the third-floor bathroom. I don't look at Internet porn. I don't think about houses or coming or going. I don't think about the future. I don't hand over my grad school application to Ceci. It just sits in the envelope, waiting. I can't bring myself to do it. Not with all that's happening.

I go out to the deck and sit on the steps leading down to

the backyard. My shoulder still throbs from the previous day's run-in with the Copeland family.

I sit, alternating my gaze between the birches and oaks and elms. My arm is in its sling.

My mother comes outside. As she opens the back door, Emma bolts out, darting across the grass in frantic circles. My head spins just watching her. Emma stops for a moment to take a leak, continues running. My mother sits down next to me, cradling herself against the slight chill in the air.

"I broke my arm once when I was in the eighth grade," she says. "Volleyball."

"I didn't know you played volleyball."

"I wasn't very good. Only did it to make my father happy. All I remember is how much the cast itched."

"These bandages aren't too comfortable," I say, lifting my arm as much as the pain will allow. I adjust my shoulder inside the gauze. I wait till she looks at me. "What are we gonna do, Mom?" I ask.

"I don't know," she says. "Wait for a letter from the FAA, I suppose. Take it from there."

"If he doesn't get clearance," I say, "it's going to be bad."

"He's made it through worse news," she says.

"I feel so bad for him," I say. "He loves it so much."

"If they don't let him fly, we'll deal with it."

"You've said it yourself. We could always let the bank fore-close. It'll take them a year or more to get us out of here. We have time."

"His medical could come through," she says. "It's not out of the question."

"He's in no fit state to fly," I say.

"Maybe so," she says.

Emma runs in circles on the lawn.

"I've been saving up money for a little while," I say.

"I'm glad to hear it," she says. "I know how hard it is for you to be stuck here."

"I want to give it to you and Dad," I say. "For the house. For whatever you need."

She touches my shoulder.

"I appreciate it," she says, "but I've been thinking. It isn't right for me to expect you and Chip to bail us out."

"Moving out isn't at the top of my list anymore," I say. "Elissa needs a place to bring that baby home to."

"She'll have a place," my mother says. "Whether it's here or somewhere new."

"She needs it," I say.

"Listen, Cal," my mother says. "I'm not going to lie. It's been nice having you around. All of you."

"We drive each other crazy."

"We laugh a lot, too," she points out. "He likes having you guys around. Sometimes I think it may be the only thing that keeps him going."

"We can't all live here together forever," I say. "Chip and Elissa, too. At some point it's gonna be just the two of you. He has to figure out what he's living for. Or else there's no point."

"I used to think if I could just keep us all together, everything would work itself out," she says. "I'm learning that isn't the answer. It's just . . . you don't know what it's like to be alone with him. Really alone. He whines and cries. Tells me he's dying from the moment he wakes up till the moment he goes to bed. It is endless."

"I'm sorry, Mom. I know it's a lot on your plate."

"No. I'm the one who should be sorry. It was wrong of me to make you feel like you needed to be here. All of you. He's my husband."

"He's my father," I say. "I want to be here. Plus, I feel guilty. About this." I raise my bandages. "This is the last thing he needs right now."

"It's all right," she says. "In a way, it might not be such a bad thing. I think it was a wake-up call for him. He's been in his own little world for so long."

"I'm sorry," I say. "Really I am."

"It's not your fault," she says. "I want you to know that you don't have to stay. Start your life."

"I want to help," I say. "I really do. With the house. With all of it."

"Do me a favor, then," she says.

"Anything," I say.

Emma catches sight of a squirrel crawling up one of the tree trunks. She launches into a barking frenzy.

AND SO OVER the weekend I accompany my mother and Chip and Pam Kittredge on a morning-long outing to view houses. The parade seems endless. Most of the houses in what Chip has deemed our price range are depressing. One after another. We are shown a dozen listings. We look at single-family houses, multifamily houses, condos, adequately sized apartments. We look at Tudors, brick, stucco, plastic siding.

We inspect basements and garages. Survey lawns and yards. Decks and porches. We see enclosed sitting rooms. We talk about attic space and storage. One bathroom. One and a half bathrooms. Two bedrooms. Three bedrooms. This one has a large living room, which really makes up for the fact that the kitchen is so tiny . . . The neighborhood here is just marvelous . . . Very up and coming . . . Lots of young couples fleeing the city . . . They say the elementary school down the block is one of the best in the county, you know, for when . . . That fireplace works . . . Here, let me open the flue . . . And of course they'll be fixing that . . . I'll have to check . . .

Chip is all questions. He wants to know about heating and utility expenses. Property tax and closing costs. He wants to know about square footage and fees. Hidden costs.

"How much lower than asking can we come in?" he ponders.

Pam rides in the SUV with us, directing us from house to house, describing the neighborhoods as if we haven't been driving up and down Route 9 along the Hudson River valley all our lives. Hastings-on-Hudson, Ardsley, Irvington, Dobbs Ferry, Tarrytown. We tour all of western Westchester County. My mother's face betrays nothing about what she's thinking. There is an eagerness in me that is hard to contain. I want to find a place. Just one that feels right, that feels like it could work. So I can know that they're safe. That even if they lose the house, they have something to fall back on, a plan of some kind.

Most of the houses need work. A few are in good condition. Only one really strikes me as a possible place I can see my parents downsizing to and being happy. A small, quaint three-bedroom, two bath Victorian on the border of Yonkers and Hastings. Attached garage and a small back porch, where I picture my father sitting on spring days, daydreaming about airplanes or whatever it is he daydreams about. Best of all, there is enough room for everyone. Elissa and the baby. If Chip insists on living at home for the rest of his life, there's a room for him. For me, there is couch space when I come to visit.

When it's all done and Pam has driven off in her little car, the three of us sit down to lunch at a pizza place in Tarrytown.

"That was fun," I say.

"I don't like that woman," Chip says, dumping way too much red pepper onto his slice.

"She's fine," I say.

"They're all out to get you," he says.

"Realtors?" my mother asks.

"Women," Chip says.

"The Victorian in Hastings was by far the best," I say.

"I liked that one, too," my mother says. She hasn't touched her pizza.

"We'll see," Chip says. "We have to crunch the numbers."

"Nothing is certain," my mother says. "We don't *have* to move. Not yet."

"Be realistic, Mom," Chip says.

"I am being realistic," she says. "Your father doesn't want to sell. I don't want to sell. We haven't missed a payment. Yet. We haven't defaulted. If he gets his job back, it could change things. Don't be so eager for us to move."

"I'm the one who *made* the last mortgage payment, so you

don't have to remind me," Chip says. "And by the way, at this point, we're paying interest only. Not a good sign."

"If we stay and the bank forecloses," our mother says, "it will take a year or more for them to get us out."

"*Or*," Chip says, "we sell *before* they foreclose, take what little we can scrape together after paying off, and start fresh somewhere else. Somewhere we can afford."

"By then, he could be working again," our mother points out. "If not, Medicare takes over. Disability. A lot could happen."

"Yeah," Chip says. "A lot of other stuff could happen, too. Stuff we haven't even thought of."

"He hasn't worked in nearly a year, Mom," I say. "If he doesn't get that medical, you know what's going to happen."

She starts to cry.

"Okay," I say. "I'm sorry. Let's stop now. We'll play it by ear. When he hears from the FAA, we'll look everything over. See where we're at. We need to keep all the doors open, right?"

"I suppose," Chip says.

Our mother excuses herself to use the bathroom. As soon as she is out of earshot, Chip starts in.

"She's losing her mind," he says. "You see that, right?"

"She's got a lot going on," I say.

"They're clinging to this house," he says. "They're petrified of change. We need to step in and do something."

"Like what?" I ask.

"Persuade them to sell," he says. "Talk them into down-sizing."

"Chip," I say, "they love that house. It means a lot to them."

"They can't afford it," he says.

"I agree with you," I say. "But it isn't right to just give up."

By this point, our mother returns and we fall silent.

She sits staring at her pizza, as if waiting for answers to appear in the pooling oil.

# ≪ **30** ≫

I watch a movie. *The Prowler.* 1981. Directed by Joseph Zito. A plot summary might read something like this: masked killer who likes to wear World War II army fatigues brutally slaughters a group of college kids too busy getting it on at the annual spring dance to really notice. I go to my bedroom to retrieve my notebook from its spot under my pillow but am surprised to find it isn't there. I remember leaving it up in the third-floor bathroom.

From the hallway, I hear Elissa crying. I am very familiar with the sound. I hate when my sister cries. Even worse when it's my fault.

I thought I was the only one in the house who actually made use of those facilities on the third floor. Apparently I was wrong. She read the whole thing. Every thought I've penned about her or Chip or our parents. Every jerk-off fantasy. All the movies. The stuff about her not being ready for a baby. The stuff about the house and our family finances. All the strange things running through my head, spewed out in black or blue ink on the pages of that tiny book.

She's sitting on her bed, wrapped in her green blanket. Her hair is in her face. Tear streaks down her cheeks. She looks at me like a child. She has her finger in the middle of the notebook. She closes it and wipes her nose.

"What the fuck?" is all she says.

I am standing awkwardly in the threshold. First I try leaning against the doorframe. This feels very weird. I try to thrust my good arm into the depths of my pant pocket. This is too casual. I don't really know what to do.

"You weren't supposed to read that," I say.

"Even if I wasn't," she says.

"It doesn't mean anything. That's not really how I feel."

"I don't care what you write about *me*," she says.

"You don't?" I ask.

"All this stuff about Dad," she says. "You know how fragile he is right now. How do you think he'd feel if he read some of the stuff in here? If he knew you went through *his* journal?"

"You just read mine," I say, incredulous.

"It's not the same. He's sick. It's a violation."

"This is ridiculous."

"You throw us all under the bus," she says.

"I don't."

"You tell me one thing to my face. Everything's gonna be fine. Don't eat Twinkies. Don't smoke weed. The baby. Think of the baby. But you don't think I'm ready."

"It's not like that."

"If you thought I was making a mistake, why not tell me to my face?"

"Because I'm not good at talking to people," I say. "You know me."

"This," she says, holding up the notebook, "is fucked up."

"It's me working out the bullshit in my head. The things I've *said* to you, they're what really count. Not what I write in there."

"This hasn't been easy for me. Everyone's so worried about Dad."

"You're not alone."

"How am I supposed to believe that now?"

"Elissa. It doesn't mean anything. I'm usually stoned when I write in there."

"Blame it on the weed," she says. And then she turns her head toward the windows and I know what this means. She's done talking.

"Come on," I say.

"Fuck you," she says.

I stand for a while longer, then realize I can't think of another thing to say.

I go downstairs and pace around the living room. My father is in the basement working on the baby's mobile. Without really thinking about it, I head down there and continue my pacing behind him at the workbench. He is in his pajamas.

"Almost done here," he says. He has a paintbrush in his hand and is streaking blue paint onto the tail of an F/A-18 Hornet. The finishing touches. I see for the first time that not only has he assembled the ten model airplanes, but he's painted the detailing as well. And he's done a surprisingly good job.

"You did all these by hand?" I ask him.

He steps aside and shows me his work.

"Your old man has still got it," he says.

"Looks good."

He cleans the brush on a paper towel.

"I used to pace when I got upset, too," he says.

"Elissa and I had a fight,"

"Wanna talk about it?" he asks.

"Not really," I say. "I just need to move around."

He nods his head and turns to search through the paint box for another brush.

"Make it up to her," he says over his shoulder. "She's in a tough spot."

"I know," I say. "I will."

But I never do. Elissa and I don't talk about the notebook again. When I go back up to my room, I find she's thrown it on my bed. I put it back under my pillow.

She stays in her room the rest of the night with the door closed. She's still in there the next morning when I leave for work.

At the dinner table we don't exchange more than a few meaningless cordialities. "I feel fine" and "Yes, the baby is still squirming nonstop" are all I can manage to get out of her.

I GO BACK to work. I've been two weeks convalescing. Aside from having to answer a constant assault of annoying questions and a few embarrassing retellings of the ordeal, things fall quickly into the old routine.

"Shot by your own father," Georgie says on one of the first days I'm back. "That's some deep shit."

"The deepest," I tell him.

It takes another two weeks for my face to look normal again.

I go to a handful of physical therapy sessions at the YMCA. I drive myself. Twice a week. I lift meager weights with my right arm. I roll my sleeves up over my shoulder and touch the pink lump where a small, quarter-size scar has formed.

My therapist is a tall black guy named Dwayne. His biceps ripple beneath his shirt.

"Higher," he tells me. I lift the dumbbell higher. "Good," he says. "Excellent."

I pull elastic bands in varying degrees of resistance. I stretch. Dwayne stands beside me. Together we see each exercise through to completion. Afterward I sit in the steam room. I let sweat roll down my body. I am on the mend.

Days. Weeks. Halloween. The John W. Manley School requires its staff to wear costumes. There is a party for the kids. I pretend I am a doctor. I wear scrubs and a stethoscope, a surgical mask.

"Isn't that theme a little played out around here?" Chip says.

I regain most of my mobility. I begin to think of myself as the guy shot by his own father. The stuff of mythically humorous proportions. Suburban folklore.

The cops never come for me. We don't hear from the Copelands again. I have my mother to thank for that.

Elissa stays pregnant and mad.

I TAKE MY grandmother to pick up her new eyeglasses.

"Bifocals," she tells me as we drive. "That means two different lenses."

I park the car and help her onto the sidewalk. She stares at a bus stop billboard of Osama bin Laden. Above his turban, the words ENEMY OF FREEDOM are inscribed. A recruitment poster for the US Army. My grandmother stands before it, hovering and tottering on her squat legs. She squints.

"It's a picture of God," she says, waving a hand at the billboard.

"I don't know about that, Grandma," I say.

"I think you're wrong," she says, moving on toward the optometrist's office.

On the way out, with her new bifocals firmly seated across her nose, she inspects the poster again. She looks at me.

"Who is that man?" she asks.

At home, my mother is waiting in the kitchen for me. The look on her face is one I have seen before. It hasn't changed since high school. It is the look that lets me know I fucked up.

"You realize your sister is going to give birth any day?"

"I realize this," I say.

"So your idea of helping out, of making sure she's healthy and ready for this huge thing to happen, is to upset her?"

"What did she say?" I ask.

"She didn't *say* anything," my mother says. "She's been sulking around. You don't think I notice?"

"How should I know?" I say.

"Whatever you did," my mother says, "undo it."

"She won't talk to me."

"It's not good for her to be upset. Not in the state she's in. It's not good for the baby."

"Okay. I get it."

"If this is how you plan to help, don't bother."

"I fucked up," I say.

"This is not what I need right now," she says.

She gets up from the table. She sets a pot of water to boil on the stove and digs a box of spaghetti out of a cabinet.

Elissa is in the doorway, out of nowhere, leaning against the wall. She has a strange look on her face.

"Have you been listening?" I say.

"Mom," she says. "I don't feel so good." Her face is sweaty.

"Oh my God," my mother says, dropping the spaghetti onto the floor. "Is it time?"

"I don't know," Elissa says.

And my mother is running to her and holding her.

"Call an ambulance," she says to me.

I pick up the phone and dial. I tell the dispatcher who I am. I give our address. I'm assured help is on the way.

My mother and I walk Elissa to the living room and lay her down on the couch. I get her a glass of water. She is pale. She is damp all over and seems very close to losing consciousness.

"Where's your father?" my mother asks, panicky.

I run into the TV room. He is on the couch.

"It's Elissa," I say.

"What's wrong?" he asks. He sits up as quickly as he can and then hoists himself to his feet. I can see the strain on his face.

"I have no idea," I say.

We sit with her until the ambulance arrives. We follow in the SUV.

"I'll drive," I say.

She is taken to St. John's Riverside Hospital, in Yonkers. She is put into intensive care. They call Dr. Fine at his home, and within the hour, he is with us. "Hypertension" is the word being thrown around. They tell us she has to stay in the hospital for the duration of the pregnancy. Her blood pressure. Two weeks, they say, and she'll be home with the baby. Dr. Fine wants to monitor her closely.

"She needs rest," he tells us. "She has to be calm. Relaxed. This could be serious, but I think we've got a handle on it now."

We sit with her for the remainder of visiting hours. My father strokes her hair. She is awake but exhausted and falls in and out of sleep while we are there. When the time comes, my mother refuses to leave. Absolutely refuses, almost throws a fit.

"We have to leave her, Kathy," Dad says. "You can't stay all night."

"I can," she says. "I will."

"We'll take good care of her," Dr. Fine assures her.

"Kathy," my father says. He takes her hand. "We have to go. I'll come back first thing tomorrow."

"You promise?" Elissa asks from her bed.

"What else do I have to do?" he says to her.

In the car, heading back home up Route 9, my mother drives and complains.

"I hate the idea of her being in some Westchester hospital," she says.

"We know your disdain for all doctors outside the borough of Manhattan," my father says.

"They're quacks," she says.

"Well, Dr. Fine is a New York doctor," I remind her. "He drove up from the city to see her."

"That's the only reason I left her there," my mother says.

IT MAKES PERFECT sense to me. The blood pressure scare with my sister is the wake-up call my father needed more than anything. More than shooting me in the shoulder. I can see the ordeal gives him strength. I notice the change in little ways at first.

Almost immediately, he stops wearing the bathrobe. He digs out his L.L. Bean relaxed-fit jeans. His flannel shirts. His argyle socks and boat shoes. He combs his hair and spends every moment of every day with her. There are some, like Chip, who say it's about time. My mother doesn't really offer an opinion one way or another. I think maybe she's scared of jinxing the whole thing. He drives himself down to the hospital in the mornings. He reads to Elissa. He keeps her up to date with worthy news from the home front. She is scared. She confides in him. The future is a mystery for both of them, and it's only logical that with her now in the hospital, the bond between them strengthens. Our mother puts in as much visiting time as she can between bill paying and housekeeping. I try to help her out by continuing to clean the house and by fixing my own dinners. Chip makes appearances at the hospital most nights after he gets home from work. Elissa's room fills with stuffed animals and balloons and "get well" cards. There is an outpouring of support from almost everyone we know.

The Saturday after Elissa goes to the hospital, my mother comes to me while I'm watching *Jeopardy!* in the TV room.

"I think he's ready," she says.

"For what?" I ask.

She walks to the TV and takes the piece of paper with the letter *S* down.

Okay. I help her. We walk through the house taking down all the *S*'s. We take them down off every light switch and mirror and picture frame. We take them down wherever we find them. We go to the SUV and take the *S* off the rearview mirror. We take them all down.

"It kills me to say it," my mother says, "but her going to the hospital is exactly what he needed."

"He's shaping up," I say. "Let's hope it sticks."

# ≪ 31 ≫

The wood panels on the door have warped and splintered over the years. The whole thing groans and creaks as Chip turns the handle and lifts. Teal paint chips fall to the blacktop. No one says anything. We just stand and take in the vast accumulation of survival equipment our father has amassed over the past eight months. It is almost an hour before we get the bulk of it out into the driveway.

My brother is dressed in matching green sweatpants and sweatshirt, headband, wristbands. His hair is neatly gelled to pointy perfection. His tips have been recently frosted.

"You look great," I tell him.

"Always," he says. He and I lift the drum of gasoline onto a dolly and wheel it to the SUV. We fold the seats down and hoist it into the back. Our mother sits in a lawn chair beside the garage, digging through a manila folder full of receipts.

"Jesus Christ, Jim," she says. "This is why we're broke."

"Technically this stuff is all useful," our father says. He is carefully laying his rifle collection on a painter's tarp. He picks one up. "You sling back the bolt like this," he says, showing us how to check and clear the chamber of any rounds. Chip and I nod. We take the rifles one at a time. Expensive lever-actions from the turn of the century, ornate-handled shotguns, nonfunctioning World War II carbines, bolt-action Winchesters, Spencers, Lee-Enfields, Lloyds. The scope-fitted Krag-Jørgensen. An old Swiss K31. As we clean them, he tells us the history behind each gun.

"That one I got from my father, just before he died. Actually, a good number of these were his. Some from Italy. A few even saw action."

"You don't have to get rid of them," Chip says, wiping sweat from his forehead.

"I want to," our father says. He strokes his mustache in thought. He smiles, then frowns.

"Your father needs to think positively about the future," our mother says, receipts in hand. "Brigitte says dwelling in the past isn't healthy. Your father needs to move on with his life. To a new place."

My brother and I polish the guns, putting them back on the tarp as we go, moving down the line, rifle after rifle, until they are all clean.

We tackle the bowels of the garage.

"Give me a hand with these," Chip calls out. I venture in and together we carry out thirty-pound army-supply rice sacks. We stack them on top of each other in the car, next to the gasoline. Chip adjusts his headband in the side-view mirror. Our father oversees the work, directing us here and there. We load two hundred cans of beans.

With the food rations done, we sort the merchandise from the sporting goods store. Most of it is still in boxes, unopened, dusty. We wipe down packages of geodesic shelters and lanterns, flashlights, first aid kits, sleeping rolls, bug repellent, compasses, water jugs, collapsible pots and frying pans, thermoses, natural hemp soaps, a propane oven, metal utensils, tongs, waterproof strike-anywhere matches, can openers, mixing bowls, measuring cups, aluminum foil, trash bags and clothing pins, Tupperware containers.

"So what's the plan?" I say.

Our mother stands, tucking the folder of receipts under her arm. She surveys the scene.

"Beans and rice to the soup kitchen in Mount Vernon," she says, pointing. "Gasoline to the Exxon station. Camping shit back to the store."

"You have the receipts for all this?" I ask.

"What do you think?" she says.

"They'll take it back," Chip says. "They have to, we never used it."

"We don't need this stuff anymore," our father says.

"We never did," our mother says.

"I hope you're right," our father says.

"What about the guns?" Chip asks.

"eBay," our father says. "

"Let's go," our mother says, slamming the car doors shut.

THE SEESAW GOES up and it goes down. It always has.

A letter comes in the mail with this return address:

US Department of Transportation
Federal Aviation Administration
PO Box 26080
Oklahoma City, OK 73125

I give the envelope to my mother and she brings it into the kitchen and gives it to my father.

It's from the FAA's Aeromedical Certification Division. His case has been reevaluated based on recent medical results they've received. The papers we sent. The letter we wrote. His medical clearance has been denied.

"Dad. I'm sorry." It's one of those times when I have no idea what to say. No way to be of comfort. And when he cries, I cry, too, and it's so appropriate there's almost a beauty to it.

The four of us around the kitchen table.

The letter lies like a stone.

"I didn't see this coming," Chip says.

"I'll never fly again," my father says. His hands are in the pockets of his jeans. His face is all furrowed lines.

"You don't know that," I say, but it's such a lie I don't even convince myself.

My mother doesn't speak. I can see tears gathering in her eyes.

"You were wrong," my father tells me. "I knew. You lied to me."

"I didn't," I say. "I didn't lie to you, Dad."

"I just want to hit fast-forward," he says.

"Fast-forward through what?" Chip asks.

"All of it," he says. "I'm done."

"What are we gonna do?" my mother says, finally speaking.

"We looked at houses," I say. "We know what's out there. We know we have options."

"Our options are getting fewer and fewer," Chip says.

"We're together," I say. "We'll be okay."

They all just look at me.

# ≪ **32** ≫

The cold weather is here to stay.

He will never fly again. It is a time of great loss. Of expectations dashed. And all of it on the eve of Elissa's delivery. The baby whose arrival now carries possibly the last vestiges of hope for us all.

My father is visited by Thurston Krants, CFO of Transcontinental Air, as well as the head of the flight department, a man they call "Tig." Arthur Tiglowski. The men sit in the dining room of our house and offer my father the terms of early retirement they have drawn up. He is out. Someone has already been hired in his absence. They saw it coming, maybe, long before any of us. Continuing 40 percent till he turns sixty-five. Medicare and Social Security for the rest of it. Health coverage for my mother stops the day he dies.

He doesn't make a fuss. He signs their papers. He shakes their hands and accepts their condolences. If he is upset, he doesn't show it. After they're gone, he mails his old medical certificate back to the FAA in the self-addressed stamped envelope they provided for just this purpose.

I wait for the baby steps *he* has taken — the cleaning out of the garage, the retiring of the bathrobe, the selling of the guns — I wait for them to abruptly reverse. It doesn't happen. My father retreats to the sanctuary he has established in Elissa's hospital room. He watches over her with conviction. My mother buries herself in the bills, scouring over them for anything she may have missed, any way to connect the dots, now that all the numbers have been laid before her.

It takes a lot of self-motivation, but I steel my nerves and stop by Ceci's office Friday morning. I drop the envelope onto her desk.

"I'll do it," I say.

"You sure?" she says.

"I don't know if I have a choice at this point," I say.

"I'm sure you can start classes spring semester."

"Great," I say.

I still haven't spent more than a few moments visiting my sister. She's still angry about the notebook and I don't want to make her angrier. Dr. Fine said relaxation and calm. I want to give her that. I plan to apologize at the appropriate time.

HAVING RESIGNED MYSELF to a lifetime with children, I feel I've earned a little indiscretion. It's all become too much for me. I am the one who reverses the baby steps. Never before have I wanted so badly to obliterate my mind.

I seek solace in the friends I'm positive I've outgrown. I tell myself it's just for one night, then back to the quest for adulthood. I need to turn my brain off. For a little while.

David Liebman is mobile again. I hardly saw him all summer, but here he is again, limping around, dragging his feet, and talking about how great it is to be moving again, to be able to go wherever he pleases.

"I'm a hostage set free from months of captivity," he says. He is wearing blue spandex knee supports.

"We're proud of you," I tell him.

"You walk like a gimp," Wally says.

"Mobility factor isn't a hundred percent," David says.

"Have you taken up volleyball?" Wally asks.

David nods. He produces a small metal tin from his pocket and holds it aloft. "You should be nice to me," he says. "I bring gifts."

"Praise," I say.

David opens the tin. Inside is a black, flaky mound of dried, crushed leaves. It looks like coal, shattered into a thousand tiny pieces.

Salvia. Over the years, it has become a rare treat for us. Wally and I are both too unmotivated to track it down, but David knows a place online. Salvia is a completely legal herb that can be bought over the counter in some states. When vaporized with a high-temperature flame and smoked out of a bong, it induces anywhere from five to thirty minutes' worth of monstrously intense visual hallucinations. Like taking LSD without the eight-hour commitment. I hate psychedelic drugs for that very reason: I don't like surrendering so much control. I enjoy prescription meds to numb the senses and relax major motor muscles. I blow the occasional line. Once, I freebased Special K in college and spent the better part of a night yelling at furniture.

Aficionados claim the Mazatec Indians in Oaxaca chewed salvia leaves to facilitate shamanic divination visions. I like to pretend I am part of this grand tradition. Lost in our woodland suburbia, divining my own future, interpreting omens thrust upon me by circumstances out of my control. Omens consisting of illness and genetics.

Wally's parents, Polish immigrants with an insatiable thirst for family history, have gone away to attend a genealogy conference in Tampa, where Victor, Wally's father, is to deliver a lecture about the origins of his ancestry and the exhausting Czerkowski migration over the Carpathian Mountains of Romania, across the Kraków-Częstochowa Uplands, coming, finally, to plant roots in the foothills of the Sudety. As a clan, the Czerkowskis had led an arduous existence before braving the Atlantic to prosper as fur coat salesmen. I have listened to both Victor and Wally go on and on about what life for their grandfathers and great-grandfathers was like. What struggles they overcame, how they survived.

"Kogo to obchodzi," I'd say. The only Polish I know. It translates roughly to, "I don't care."

We rendezvous with Doug M. and the enigmatic Gabby, who I secretly hoped would be in attendance. We try our luck at the Public House, one of Tarrytown's two bars. A large group of rowdy fraternity brothers begin to pantomime various athletic stances. We grow paranoid and self-conscious. We leave.

We arrive at Wally's around midnight. The house is empty and silent.

The five of us settle into a large room in the basement.

"I'm making this the entertainment center of the house," Wally tells us.

"The vibe here is interesting," Doug M. says, surveying the room with a grand sweep of his hands.

"This is a dungeon," David says.

A large TV on a wooden base, decrepit couches scattered about. A warped Ping-Pong table. A stereo system. Washer-dryer in the far corner. All of Wally's records are on the floor, arranged in small stacks, occupying most of the open wall space. David hobbles to the record player. He selects and plays a series of old 45s. "Denise" by Randy and the Rainbows, "Then He Kissed Me" by the Crystals, "Walk Away Renee" by the Left Banke, "Gee" by the Crows. "Get a Job" by the Silhouettes. Others.

Wally is in the middle of the room, legs crossed in the lotus position. Pretending to meditate.

"I'm ready," he says. He seems to think his mind is capable of achieving a higher level of functioning. I am in no position to tell him otherwise.

"Bong's in my bag," David says, pointing to the knapsack he's been carrying with him all night.

"Nice," Doug M. says. He presides over the room like a king. His throne, the couch.

"Trumpets should announce your arrival," I tell him.

"They're playing as we speak," he says.

Gabby is admiring the glasswork on David's fifteen-inch bong, its red and blue designs swirling like webbing. I have to admit I hate bongs, always have. They fall too firmly into the realm of weed culture for my liking. I don't really consider myself a stoner. In fact, I dislike the subculture of people whose identity revolves around their obsession with weed. They hang posters of Bob Marley and make sure to announce whenever the clock strikes 4:20. They wear hemp necklaces. They tout articles about the health benefits of marijuana and advocate its legalization. I don't care about any of that. I just like to get stoned.

"We need ice," Wally says, springing to his feet. He darts off into another room and returns with his hands full of ice cubes, which he deposits in the chamber of the bong.

"Excellent," David says. He seats himself between Wally and Gabby on the rug. Doug M. and I join. A cultish-looking circle. David draws the tin of salvia from his pocket and stuffs a heaping pinch into the bowl. He holds the butane flame to the stem. The flaky black leaves ignite, turn to glowing orange embers. The cylinder fills with smoke, and David yanks the stem, sucks the smoke up, and holds it for what seems like forever before expelling it into our faces. He coughs violently.

"Harsh," he manages to say.

The bong makes its way around to everyone. We keep the burning smoke in our lungs for as long as we can. When we finish, Doug M. sets the bong down on the carpet and turns the TV on. PBS is showing a special about the usefulness of speed bumps.

"Speed bumps," Wally says. He erupts in a fit of laughter so vicious his eyes water and his face reddens. I join him, unable to keep myself from laughing, although I'm not exactly sure what we're laughing at.

"What is with those things?" I say through the tears streaming down my cheeks. I stumble to my feet and walk a few paces before falling to my knees in front of an end table. My eyes perceive a patterned layer of shimmering Day-Glo blobs on top of its lacquered surface. I see an ant, moving slowly, heading toward a ceramic lamp. The ant just inches its way along, beautiful and awe inspiring—the simplicity of unfettered travel. This ant is *going* somewhere. This ant has an objective, a purpose, like everything else in the world. The ant seems completely unfazed by the vastness around it, oblivious. I laugh even harder at this, roar with laughter, and suddenly, almost at the same moment, I realize how horrifying it is. I stand. My body tingles everywhere. All my appendages feel like they've fallen asleep. I see a pattern of golden spades across my skin. They pulse with a sunspottish intensity that keeps moving and changing. I am in a dream. My own dream about death and Wally's basement. I can hear the dryer in the corner going and going. I am in a dream. I have died. This is what being dead is like. Death means you have no control over your body, it means your mind pulls you in the direction it wants to go and you have no choice but to follow it. My body wants to go to the right. Unseen forces in the room are pulling me to the right, toward the wall. I try to fight. It is impossible.

"I can't turn left," I say. "Something's wrong. I can't turn left."

"You're turning now," Wally says.

"You're doing it," Gabby says.

"Something's not right," I say.

I spin in a circle in the middle of the room, convinced I'm not moving at all.

"Everything's fine," Doug M. says. He is lying facedown on the floor.

"My eyes have a mind of their own," I say.

David comes over and puts his arms around me. "It's cool, man," he tells me. "Calm down."

I stumble in his embrace and together we slide to the floor. I try to remember what just happened, but my short-term memory has gone out the window. My face keeps pulling itself to the right and my eyes keep pulling themselves to the right. I rub my hands over my face, but I can't feel a thing. I start to cry. I slap the ground. I am a child again, throwing a tantrum.

"Cal," Gabby says, "you're fine. There's nothing wrong with you."

She starts laughing while she is saying this and it scares me even more.

"Don't do that," I say through my tears.

"I'm not laughing at you," she says. "I'm just . . ." She trails off, lost in a thought she doesn't feel it's necessary to explain. I want to see the hole in her head, but I'm afraid of what might happen if I take her hat off. I touch her shoulder. I squeeze her cheek.

"Quit it," she says. She pushes me away.

"I want it to stop," I say. "I want to go to the hospital."

"We can't go to the hospital," Wally says. He shakes his head. He stands up and goes to the wall. He sways in front of the dryer. He lowers his head to the metal, rests his face against it.

"This is where it all happens," he says.

"I need medical attention," I say, throwing my hands

up in the air. "I can't turn around and I'm dead. My heart stopped beating."

David is slouched in the La-Z-Boy. He seems so far away, completely unreachable. His legs in their shiny spandex knee supports are propped on the footrest. His eyes are falling from his head. He lifts a hand and waves it like a conductor's baton. He looks up at the ceiling.

"The roof is coming off," he says.

"Everything's changing," Wally says.

Everyone seems to be traversing new landscapes of the mind, venturing to places larger than this basement room.

I stumble to a standing position and do my best to exit. I head upstairs to the living room. There are no lights here and I bump into many things on my way to the couch. I fall to pieces, swallowed up by the cushions. I wipe tears from my face and curl into a ball. My eyes adjust to the moonlight. I can hear someone nearby. Gabby comes out of the shadows. She kneels down in front of my face, her eyes so green, so deep. Her baseball cap is pushed up off her forehead. The scar is visible, small and pinkish, round like a quarter, but her hair is falling across it in such a way that it seems completely natural. She was born to wear the scar. It is part of her DNA, her soul. The scar makes all the sense in the world right now, and through the tears, through the short-term memory loss and the needling sensation still plaguing my extremities, I focus on that one thing.

"I'm dying," I tell her.

"You're not dying," she says. She touches my face, pushes my hair back with her hand.

"Just rest," she says. "Forget it. Try to sleep."

"I'm going to sleep," I say. "I'm going to sleep forever."
And I close my eyes.

When I wake, Gabby is in my arms. I'm not sure how this happened, but she's there nonetheless. I am holding her. Her head is resting on my chest. We are fully clothed and the room is cast in shadows and pools of moonlight spilling in from the windows. Everything is blue. The grandfather clock ticks loudly. Carefully, so as not to wake her, I slide out of our embrace and stand. My head is swirling, the events of the night foggy and sticky and moving into the past. My crying episode seems a memory. The color spots are gone and I feel slightly normal again. I touch my chest, run my fingers down my arms, feel my legs, my calves. I check that my dick has not fallen off. As far as I can tell, I did not die. I am whole. I am happy about this discovery. There is still hope. I walk into the kitchen, go down the wooden steps, and follow the glow of the TV back to the room where everything started. David is asleep in the La-Z-Boy, reclined in the same position I had last seen him in. Doug M. is sprawled out on the floor, facedown, snoring loudly. An infomercial boasts a clothing steamer that can be owned for three easy payments of $29.95. Wally is nowhere to be found. I imagine at some point he made it to his bedroom.

I return to the living room. I sit on the couch, not really knowing what to do. Gabby's hat is on the floor. Her hair spills across her face. She stirs in her sleep and reaches out. Touches me. She gropes around and pulls me down into her arms. It happens very quickly, and before I know it, we are kissing. Wet, middle-of-the-night kisses caught in shadow worlds between waking and sleeping. Somewhere in pleasant limbo. She guides my hand to her breasts. Her T-shirt is off, and I have my mouth on her nipple, firm under my tongue. I brush my cheeks against her chest and yank her pants off with a fluid motion even I am startled by. It's been a long time since I tasted a girl, but I haven't forgotten how much I enjoy it. For a while, there seems to be no sound except our breathing. I run my hands over her ass. I explore every curve I encounter in the dark. When I finally put myself inside her, it seems like hours have gone by. She breathes so heavily into my ear that it feels like she's trying to tell me something.

"What?" I ask her, my voice flushed and throaty.

"Fuck me harder," she says. I consent. I fuck her harder and then I come.

"Did I just come inside you?"

"I'm on birth control."

"Thank God."

We dress slowly and fall asleep again in each other's arms. There is only the faintest trace of pain from the scar on my shoulder.

As I drift off, I wonder if the whole thing was a product of the salvia, of drugs. A mirage that will be gone by morning. Something done by ghosts. I wonder if either of us will remember it at all.

TWO DAYS LATER, I call Doug M. on my lunch break and ask him how I can get ahold of Gabby.

"I heard what you two did," he says.

"Just give me her number."

"Your girlfriend is a sensitive subject."

"She's not my girlfriend," I say. "It was just a onetime thing."

"You had a bad trip, my friend," he says.

"What's the number?"

"Get it yourself," he says. "She's at work as we speak."

"Oh, really," I say.

"Café Tarrytown," Doug M. says.

I hang up.

I make the ten-minute drive down Route 9 from the John W. Manley School. I park in front of the café.

"Be cool," I tell myself before getting out.

There are a few people scattered around at the tables, drinking lattes, eating sandwiches. Gabby is coming out from behind the counter with a soda in her hands when she sees me. Her baseball cap is pulled down over her eyes.

"Hey," she says. She stops, just stands there with the soda.

"How are things?" I ask

"Okay, I guess."

She brings the drink to an old man sitting alone near the windows. She goes back behind the counter. I follow her.

"I never come to this place," I tell her. I can't really think of anything in the way of conversation.

"I know," she says.

"I guess you would," I say.

"Want some food?"

"Yes, as a matter of fact." I look at the menu, written on a large chalkboard behind the cash register. "Veggie burger," I tell her, "with fries."

She writes my order down and goes into the kitchen to put it through. I sit at an empty table, and when she comes back she sits across from me.

"Wally's in here all the time," she says, wiping her hands on her apron.

"Yeah. I haven't been hanging out much with those guys lately. Been trying to help out the family. Things are all wacky at my house," I say. "Plus, that salvia nightmare threw me off my game. I may never go back."

"Big words," Gabby says.

"Big man," I say.

"It's all talk."

"I'm in a rut," I say. As I'm talking, it dawns on me that the seed of what I'm saying has been growing in the back of my mind for a while now.

"You need to get back on track. Isn't that what they say?"

"That is what they say. I think I need to make a big change. Something radical."

"Change is scary," Gabby says.

"It is," I say.

"Leave the country," she says.

"I might have to."

She puts her hand on the table. Not far from mine. I want to hold it but haven't the guts.

"You're confused, I think."

"Very."

"You need to think about all this."

"I do."

"How's your sister?" she asks.

"Ready to blow."

"And your father?"

"He lost his job."

"You must be so sick of the same questions," Gabby says.

"Depends who's asking them."

"Is that a compliment?"

"Yes," I say.

"Did he really shoot you?"

"He did."

"It hurt?"

"Very much."

The bell on the door jingles and jangles as a herd of high school kids spill in. Gabby has to go off and take orders. I watch her. She delivers a tuna melt. She delivers drinks. She grabs my veggie burger and drops the plate at my table.

"Give me a call," she says. "If you want." She's written her number on the check. I stare at her ass as she goes. I shovel fries into my mouth. When I finish eating, I stuff her number into my pocket. I leave a big tip. I leave contemplating the notion of something big happening in my life, something profound enough to shake me out of the rut I've fallen into.

I get back to work just in time for the start of the afternoon session.

# ≪ **33** ≫

I am lying on the floor listening to black metal. I listen to *Tentacles of Whorror*. I listen to *Codex Necro*. I listen to *Filosofem*. My mother has already come in three times and asked me to turn it down. I ignore her.

"This is the music of insanity," she says from the doorway.

"Then it should replace the cuckoo clock as our family anthem," I tell her.

"For you," she says, handing me the cordless phone.

"Hello?"

My mother is lingering in the doorway, listening. I shoo her away with my hand. She doesn't move.

"Hello, Calvin? Pam Kittredge here."

"Oh, hey, Pam."

"How's everything been? How's the family?"

"My father lost his job. My sister's in the hospital with pregnancy complications. I'm getting over a bullet wound. Everything's really good."

There is silence on the other end of the phone.

"I'm just kidding," I say, realizing how insane all of that must sound.

"Oh. Well. I thought I'd check in with you," Pam says. "We haven't spoken in a while and a couple of fantastic places up around Montrose have come in. I could take you around."

"Thanks, Pam," I say. "I'm gonna hold off for the moment. Until everything gets settled around here."

"Sure thing," she says. "Just thought I'd check in. Tell your mother to give me a call Monday—we can get started on the paperwork."

"What paperwork?"

"A few things I need for the listing."

"I'll tell her," I say. I hang up.

My mother is still in the doorway.

"What listing, Mom?"

My mother touches her face.

"You're father and I are putting the house on the market," she says. "Your brother thinks it's a good idea. Just to see if we get any interest. We don't *have* to sell. But it's not looking good."

She is clearly uncomfortable talking about this and I don't want to get her upset. I cannot imagine what she is thinking. I'm sure it was not an easy decision for her. She has lived here, as we all have, for more than fourteen years.

"It's okay, Mom," I say.

She shakes her head, says nothing more. She walks away. When she is gone, I turn the music back up.

IT IS EARLY evening and I am in the kitchen when it happens. Sitting at the table skinning fruit as precisely as I can.

I carefully work a paring knife around the circumference of an apple. I see how long an unbroken curl of skin I can produce.

"I could do this professionally," I tell my mother, who is furiously cleaning the countertops with a Dustbuster, the noise of the motor all but drowning out my voice. She stops vacuuming.

"What did you say?" she asks.

"I said I could be a professional fruit peeler. Look at this." I hold up a lengthy twirl of apple skin. The phone rings. My mother answers it.

"Oh my God," she says after a moment. She hangs up. "Okay. That was your father at the hospital. It's time."

She's frozen in the middle of the kitchen, Dustbuster in her hand.

"Where's Chip?" she asks.

"At work," I say.

"Okay. It's just us. Let's go."

"I'll drive," I say. I grab the keys off the table and head to the SUV. I realize my mother has not left the house. I go back inside. She is still standing in the middle of the kitchen.

"We gotta go," I say. My mother looks at me. She puts the Dustbuster in the fridge. "Ma, you just put the Dustbuster in the fridge."

"I know. I'll get it later."

She moves quickly past me.

"Can I drive fast?" I ask as I back out into the street. "I feel like I should drive fast."

"Just go," my mother says.

"I'll drive fast, but efficient."

I try to drive as fast as possible without flipping the car. From the backseat, my mother calls Chip and tells him what's happening. He says he'll leave work immediately and meet us there.

"ELISSA JANE MORETTI," our mother tells the nurse. We wait while her chart is called up. We are directed to the maternity ward, where they have moved her. Room 1256.

My father is already with her. He is dressed in khaki pants and a polo shirt, his hair combed to one side. He looks more collected than I have seen him in a while. I hug him.

I take her hand. My palm is damp and slippery.

"I'm sorry about all that shit," I tell her.

"It doesn't matter," she says, breathing in and out quickly, trying to control the pain. "Forget it."

A nurse with blond hair and many earrings comes in. "How far apart are the contractions?"

"I don't know," Elissa says. "Like, ten minutes?"

My sister looks pale. She yelps.

"All right," the nurse says. "My name is Nancy. I'm going to ask you a few more questions so I know where we're at. Okay?"

"Okay," Elissa says.

"Looks like"—Nancy consults a chart—"your water broke an hour ago?"

"Yes," Elissa says.

"Okay, good," Nancy says. "When did you last eat?"

"I don't know," Elissa says. "One o'clock maybe. Lunch. I had a sandwich."

"Just sit tight. We paged Dr. Fine. He's on his way."

"Thank you," our mother says. She is standing near the bed. I'm not sure any of us know what to do. Elissa cries out in pain and takes a deep breath, closes her eyes. Our mother moves closer to her, strokes her forehead.

"I'm going to ask everyone to leave the room so we can get Elissa prepped," Nancy says.

"I'm staying," our mother says.

"Fine," Nancy says.

My father and I head to the lounge down the hall. There are three sofas, a half-dozen cushioned chairs. A line of vending machines. A television bolted to the ceiling. DVD player on a shelf. There are videos to watch while you wait. Last year's most popular romantic comedies, last year's box office hits. Christmas wreaths and garlands are hanging tastefully from things. There are blinking lights coiled around the clock on the far wall. Nurses and orderlies and doctors flutter about. Carts are wheeled here and there. We are not the only family having a baby tonight. A handful of other people are here, all with the same look: false bravery in the face of the unknown.

Twenty minutes go by and Chip shows up. He is dressed in his work attire: suit pants, white button-down shirt, black tie.

"What'd I miss?" he asks when he comes into the room. He has a small teddy bear with him.

"Not much," our father says. "Doctor's on his way."

Nancy comes to the lounge and tells us we can visit a little longer, but once the doctor arrives we'll have to leave again.

Chip and I follow our father down the hall to Elissa's room. Our father walks to her bedside.

"How's my little girl?" he asks. He kisses her forehead.

"Kinda painful here, Dad," she says.

Chip puts the stuffed animal in her arms.

My mother hails a nurse walking by in the hallway.

"Where's Dr. Fine?" she asks. "He needs to be here now."

"I'll check for you, ma'am," the nurse says.

I slump into one of the chairs near the windows. Our view is of the Hudson River. I see the lights of houses on the far side.

Another twenty minutes go by before Dr. Fine arrives with Nancy, the nurse, behind him.

"Sorry for the delay," he says. "You hanging in there?"

"I think so," Elissa says. She winces in pain. "That was a big one," she says.

Dr. Fine takes my sister's blood pressure.

"It's high," he says. He rubs his big hands together.

"My feet hurt," Elissa says.

"Let me take a look," Dr. Fine says. He pulls back the sheet. He feels her feet. "They're swollen," he says. "Okay, I want to get moving. We're going to really keep a close watch on things. We may have to move quickly and take the baby sooner than expected."

"Is everything okay?" I ask.

"Yes," Dr. Fine says. "Everything's okay." He tells Nancy to start an IV. "A precaution against Elissa becoming dehydrated." He checks her blood pressure again. Another nurse arrives and an ultrasound transducer is strapped to Elissa's abdomen to monitor the baby's heartbeat.

"It's time for everyone to leave," Dr. Fine says.

"I want Mom," Elissa says.

"Sure, baby," our mother says.

We are slow to leave—my father, Chip, and I. The men. We shuffle back to the lounge. I lie on one of the couches. Chip paces back and forth in front of the vending machines.

"I don't remember being this anxious when you were born," my father tells me, taking a seat in the row of chairs across from me. It is three dismal hours before Nancy comes into the lounge and talks to us. "How is she?" my father asks.

"Dr. Fine is doing everything he can. There've been some unforeseen developments."

"Unforeseen?" I ask.

"The doctor is going to perform a C-section to get the baby out," she says.

"What are you telling us?" Chip asks, standing up.

"I don't have all of the information right now," Nancy says. "More specialists are being called in to assist. I assure you I will be back to keep you updated."

"I want to see her," my father says. He starts to head out of the lounge.

"Mr. Moretti," Nancy says, "you can't go into the delivery room right now. We're going to send Mrs. Moretti out here to wait as well. The doctors need space to work. I assure you that everyone is working as hard as they can to make sure Elissa and the baby are safe."

My father doesn't say anything. Smile. Frown. And Nancy is gone again. We try to relax. Soon my mother is escorted into the lounge to join us. We ask her questions, trying to figure out what is happening, but she has little information to give us. Elissa's blood pressure is too high. The doctors are doing what they can. I lie back on the couch. My shoulder aches, remembering its own recent trauma. After a long time I manage to doze off.

I OPEN MY eyes slowly. To flaming light exploding from the fluorescent bulbs in the ceiling, and then it all comes into sharp focus. My father is on his feet. He is talking urgently to the nurse in front of him. Urgency in the air. Chip looks at me.

"What's happening?" I ask, but my voice gets lost somewhere.

When they come down the hall, I know. I don't know how, but I know. Something lacking from their faces. A certain way the nurse won't look right at us when she talks, but rather looks past us at something on the wall, some faraway speck of light only she can see. We huddle together and listen. She speaks from a place of great altitude, a place where I long to be. And still, I know. The way Dr. Fine puts his hands in his pockets. The way his eyes seem to hold maps of red inside their curving. It is complicated, he says, or rather, a complication. Preeclampsia, someone else says. They didn't see it coming. There was no way to see it coming. Her blood pressure got too high and there was nothing they could do. The baby lived. Emergency cesarean saved the baby. A little boy.

And when you see your sister and she is in front of you one minute and behind a curtain the next and gone the next, you are suddenly reminded how nothing is ever the same for very long, and all those things you dwelled on yesterday are today just empty, trivial irrelevancies. All your worries are taken from you and replaced with what feels like a heart attack, a power outage of all the things you're made of. You try to get through the swinging doors and into the room where you last saw her. They are wrong. It's someone else. You'll show them. You'll find her and she'll be sitting there in the bed and you'll point and say, *See, that's her. She's fine.* But you know. And no one saw it coming. Hypertension and special surgery and words you don't know the meaning of and then you can never say another thing to her. The hospital becomes a different world. This is the way it goes. You are looking at the linoleum tiles. Green and white and green and white. You think of all the days to follow. How will you fill them up?

Imagine the scene in any number of ways. However it's supposed to play out. Picture these things if it helps. Make a list so you won't ever forget: Mother collapsing into Father's arms. He tries his best to hold her up with what strength he can gather, he himself not terribly far removed from the hospital. Some other family's congratulatory balloons are suspended in the air and they seem like laughter. Taunting, joking laughter. All sound is going away now. Brother is crying. He is in the corner crying so that maybe no one will see. There is a failure of bravery now. We are not so strong.

I ASK HIM, "Are we going to make it?"

I ask him again and again.

I keep asking, and he tells me, "I think so."

In the hospital, we stand for a while. The two of us. In front of the glass wall that separates outside contagions from the newborns, rolled in white cloth, their faces scrunched and pink, eyes clamped shut, dealing with the shock of being squeezed from their safe, dark void. Slowly grasping the fact that they'll never be so comfortable again.

We stand awkwardly.

"It doesn't seem real," he says.

"No," I say. "It doesn't."

"Which one?" he asks. "I can't read from here."

I scan the names.

"He's that one there." I point to the second crib from the left.

I look at my father. His mustache is tidy and handsome. His face has most of its roundness back, most of its color. His hands seem like the hands of a man who is getting older, but they no longer look like the hands of sickness. More and more he is starting to get his looks back, his old self. The man I've known all my life. Only now his eyes are filled with sadness. A new pain he hadn't known existed up to this point.

And here we are. He looks over at me and does the half smile, half frown I have come to know so well in twenty-four years. His mustache twitches, and after a while he turns back to look at the babies. His hand finds its way to my shoulder, where it stays for a long time.

And then, surprisingly, there is silence. Silence for a long time. Silence in the car coming home from the hospital. Quiet, dark houses drifting by. A silence in the driveway, where I hear our footfalls on gravel. And in the house, in the living room, on the stairs, to the bedrooms. Stillness echoing and deep. It is like coming home after a long trip, a readjustment to something familiar but at the same time foreign and distant and cold. I walk from room to room, touching things. We are home, but *home* is a loaded, relative word and it doesn't really feel like home at the moment. It feels like someone else's home. And the silence only leads to more silence. My mother sits in her bedroom with the television on mute. My father sits in the family room with the television on mute. Chip stays longer at the gym. My grandmother cleans around us, trying to maintain some level of normalcy in the house. No one has much of anything to say. It takes too much effort to think of anything to talk about except the one thing. But when it comes to her, what is there to say?

Take-out food and casseroles from friends and from people on the block and movie rentals and condolences at the supermarket and time off from work and all of us silently blaming ourselves, thinking we could have done more or said more or stepped in on her behalf somehow. I listen to records without hearing the words. I dwell on this fact: the last real conversation I had with her was an argument.

## ≪ 34 ≫

For two weeks, most of what happens has an unnatural fluidity. I don't go to work. They are very understanding. Arham is placed in the hands of a substitute. The baby, a little boy, James Jr., like she wanted, comes home after spending his first three days in a neonatal incubator. He is healthy, they say. My father hangs the mobile from the ceiling. It dangles above the crib, which we have set up in her room.

I float through the proceedings. I touch things. A chair, the wall, sheets on my bed, doorknobs, towels in the bathroom, the scar on my shoulder. I stand in front of the mirror and comb my hair. I do this for my mother. Not for tradition or appearance, not for any reason other than for her. I wear a tie and I stand in our living room and I talk to people. At the church I feel arms around me and I talk to people. They put their arms around me. There is a disconnect, though, as if nothing has any significance. Wally and David come by after the service. Doug M. turns up. Aunts and uncles. Cousins. Neighbors. The Hillmans. Everyone comes by. They put their arms around me. People bring food and flowers and cards and it all piles up in the dining room. A note in the mail from the John W. Manley School signed by Ceci and Georgie and most of the children. I can barely look anyone in the eye. I say little. I go to my room and stay there for long periods of time. I close the door. I listen to records through headphones. I pick certain songs, put them on repeat.

Our house makes noises. It always has. The walls creak and settle. I listen to the pipes.

"YOU ARE SAFE," Brigitte says. "Close your eyes now and say, 'I am safe.'"

I close my eyes. "I am safe."

"You are safe," Brigitte says again.

"I am safe."

"You are safe in this place. This room. You are safe in your body," Brigitte says.

"I am safe."

"Picture this thing I am telling you. You are standing at a lake. Can you see it?"

"Yes."

"What does it look like?"

"It's big," I say. "I can barely see the other side. There are trees, rocks, and—I don't know—blue skies overhead. Something like that."

"What are you wearing?" Brigitte asks.

"I don't know," I say. "A bathing suit."

"Who else is there?"

"I'm alone."

"Good. Excellent. Now, as I count to three, I want you to

dive into that lake. Are you ready? One. Two. Three. Dive into that lake. Swim to the bottom. Imagine you can hold your breath forever. It is not a problem. Swim down. Dive."

"I'm swimming," I say. "I'm diving."

I hear her clap her hands together.

"What do you see at the bottom?"

"Darkness," I say. My eyes are still closed. "It's very dark. There are some tree trunks, fallen tree trunks. Mud. Murk."

"Okay. Okay," Brigitte says. "Now I want you to take off your bathing suit. Imagine that you are naked there."

I shift in the chair. I wring my hands together.

"You are naked and it is only you who is there in this lake bottom," Brigitte goes on. "Look at yourself, your nakedness."

"Okay," I say. I swallow hard. Feel a knot rise up in my stomach.

"Breathe in, please," Brigitte says. "Fill your stomach with breath. Imagine there is a lion in your stomach and fill that lion with air until it is too big to fit inside you."

I do this. I breathe through my nose, thinking about a lion. I breathe and breathe until I am all air.

"Good," Brigitte says. "Hold it. Hold it. And now . . . open the lion's mouth in your stomach and breathe out through the lion's mouth, breathe out through your stomach."

I exhale. I feel myself relax slightly.

"Open your eyes," Brigitte says.

I open my eyes, rub my hands against them, get used to the light in her living room. We are alone in this place. Brigitte's house. I came because I didn't know what else to do.

"Tell me, how do you feel?" she asks.

"I feel angry. I feel confused."

"What do those feelings look like?"

"Like my sister. Like James Jr."

"What color is your anger?"

"Purple?"

"Good. This is good."

"It feels horrible."

"I want you to use this. Use these feelings. Stay in the moment. Imagine the worst, the saddest moment you've had these last weeks. And go there and stand there and be in that feeling."

"I'm there. I'm there all the time."

"And what are you doing there?"

"I'm holding Baby James."

"Where is your sister?"

"Gone."

I'm crying, but it's a soft crying that I keep just barely in check. It's inside.

"What have you been doing with yourself to deal with this?"

"I've been going to the woods more."

"What's in the woods?"

"I don't know."

"You are looking for something. We'll explore this."

"Okay."

"What do you see when you are there?"

"It depends on what drugs I've taken."

She looks at me as if she doesn't understand.

"It depends on the mood I'm in," I say. I wipe my eyes.

"Okay," Brigitte says. "Okay. That's enough for today."

"I want to be honest with you," I say.

"I would appreciate that."

"I don't know how much of this I buy into. This aura stuff. Spirits or whatever."

"It doesn't matter. We're not talking about *spirits* now. We're talking about *you*."

"Just wanted to say that."

"I want you to do something for me."

"Okay."

"Try to visualize things. See everything first in your mind. When images come to you, when they come to your mind, be they good or sad or happy or scary, don't push them away. Make them into what you want. Hold on to them. And when you are ready, I promise, you'll see all is well. All will be well. You are safe."

Brigitte stands and so I stand. The walls here are lined with tribal masks and bells and paintings of forests and wind chimes and it smells of Nag Champa and I can hear my heartbeat and she tells me that love is all around me and that the people I care about are all around me. No one has gone away. And then I leave. And I don't feel silly. I don't feel like talking with her was a waste of time. I feel strangely at ease for a moment. If only for a moment.

IT'S THE TIME of day when all the light is gone, but it still isn't dark yet. The time of transition, when sadness is most aware of its own power. I go to Elissa's room. I do that thing where I stand and look at the posters on her wall because it's my understanding that this is a thing you do when someone dies. I sit on her bed, with all her stuff. The blanket folded near her pillows. The green one she used to wrap herself in when she was cold. Her CDs and books, stacked neatly on the shelf, and a bandanna draped over the lamp on her night table, throwing red shadows onto the walls and floor. The crib. I stay for a while. No one walks by, and I'm glad for this. I'm not sure what I would say to anyone who saw me in here.

Grief is disappointment. Grief is failure. Grief is dealing *with.* It's moving on or not moving on. It's my father's mustache. That way he smiles, then immediately frowns. It's the dirt we threw in the hole over Tanis, the parakeet. It's little James. James Jr. It's his eyes when he opens them, his face when he's asleep. It's all of us pulling together to take care of him. It's Chip heating up formula at the kitchen stove to feed him. It's my father rocking him in the middle of the night to stop him from screaming. It's my mother holding him and humming softly, his tiny hand curling around her finger, Emma lounging at her feet. It's all of this and it's none of it.

I'm getting by. I'm visualizing. Doing what Brigitte suggested. Or at least trying. I'm seeing things the way I want them to be. I'm not rushing anything. Or at least I'm trying not to rush anything. I am here. I am in the now. I am not trying to figure it all out at once. I am taking it step by step. I am getting by.

I SIT AT the kitchen table eating a peanut butter and jelly sandwich. I'm eating it with little heart. Hardly any enjoyment. My mother wanders in and gathers things from the counter—her pocketbook, her scarf, her keys. I see that she looks so tired. It's present in her body, her posture. All the weariness and dread and grief and anxiety boiled down to some giant kernel of blame and stuffed in her pocket. My mother is sad. She walks out the back door without putting her coat on. I sit for a while, chewing. When I don't hear the car start, I go after her.

It is cold. The coldness you feel accompanying confusion. A tight sensation in the spine. Things turning off inside you.

I find her standing in the driveway, crying. She has one hand against the side of the house, bracing herself. Her other hand is gripping her pocketbook.

"Come inside, Mom."

"We're out of toilet paper."

"Well, the car's back that way," I say.

"What?" she asks.

"Chip'll go," I say. "I'll go. It doesn't matter."

"I should never have let her."

"How were you going to stop her?"

"I could have stopped it."

"Elissa always went against the grain," I say. "She wanted that baby. You can't do that to yourself."

"We should have known better. All this time, we thought it was your father we were losing."

She looks at me, but I can't meet her gaze. I stare at the shrubs she's planted where the driveway ends. Where the pavement curls away to grass.

"I couldn't take care of her," she says. "How can I take care of him now?"

"He needs to take care of himself," I say. "He's coming around. Look, he stopped wearing the bathrobe. That's a big deal and you helped him get there. You stayed on top of him."

My mother wipes her eyes with the back of her hand. She stops crying. She sniffles. I take a step toward her, as if maybe I want to hug her. But I don't.

"We should have looked out for her more," she says. Her voice is small, throaty. "You did everything right."

At this, she starts to cry again. As quickly as she stopped, it turns back on.

"The house is gone," she tells me, and it's hard for her to get the words out.

She composes herself a bit. Her nose is running. I feel like crawling into a hole.

"When?"

"We accepted a bid yesterday."

"I mean, how long do we have?"

"Who knows? Depending on what the bank does? Sixty days."

"Have you told Chip?"

"He's taking me to sign papers at the end of the week. It's over."

I open my mouth, but I can't think of anything to say.

## ≪ **35** ≫

She is slow to decorate the house. Slow to bring down the boxes from the attic. She moves about with a long-instilled sense of purpose. Automatic routine. She drapes tinsel and garland. She arranges nutcrackers. She ties mistletoe to the dining room chandelier, where until only recently a piece of paper inscribed with a giant letter *S* had hung. I help her wrap the front bushes in lights. A wreath goes up on the front door. My father drives into town and returns with a modest tree from the guy selling them out of a parking lot. I help him put it in the stand. Chip comes home from work and all four of us hang decorations. I stand on a stepladder and place a star at the very top. When we're done, we sit in the living room and admire our work. No one says anything.

It will be James Jr.'s first Christmas. I feel like buying him as many presents as I can afford. I feel like showering him with gifts.

ON THE SECOND Monday of December I'm in the teachers' lounge getting my lunch when Ceci comes in. She's wearing a white button-down and jeans. I can see just enough of her tits.

"How you holding up?" she says. She grabs a mug out of the cabinet and fills it with lukewarm coffee. She stirs in a packet of sugar.

"Okay, I guess." I move past her. As I open the fridge, my hand brushes against her leg. "Sorry," I say. I take out the cheese sandwich I brought with me.

"I bet you're looking forward to the break," she says. "Be good to be around your family."

"I guess. Yeah," I say. "It's gonna be weird, though."

"I know," Ceci says. She sips her coffee. "I'm sorry. I don't really know what to say."

"It's okay," I say. "There's nothing to say." She leans against the side of the fridge, slouching into it, her back arched slightly, pushing her breasts forward against her shirt. She looks suddenly and openly vulnerable. She wants to be held. She wants me to hold her. She is making an inviting face. She leans against the side of the fridge. She looks like she wants to be kissed. I'm suddenly very close to her. I lean in quickly and put my lips on hers. She steps back, away from me. She lets go of her coffee mug and it clatters to the ground. It doesn't break, but coffee goes everywhere.

"Fuck," I say. "I'm sorry. I'm sorry."

She doesn't say anything. For a while she stands holding her hand to her mouth. She looks at the mug, the pool of coffee spreading on the tile. She leaves the lounge abruptly, the door slamming behind her. I grab paper towels and clean up the mess.

I don't see her for the rest of the day. At three thirty, I take

Arham down the hill to bus number 52. I make sure he gets his favorite seat near the front. I rub his head.

"Hug," he says. I hug him. I wave good-bye from the curb and watch as the bus drives off. For a few minutes I sit outside in the cold at the red picnic table. I look at my breath in the air. I visualize everything in my head. Walk myself through it. And then I go to Ceci's office. I knock softly. Through the window in the door, I can see her sitting at her desk. She's on the phone, but she hangs up quickly and waves me in.

"Can we talk?" I say, as I open the door.

"Sure," she says. We barely make eye contact.

I step in. I sit in one of the chairs near her desk. It's green and soft and I slump into it. I look outside mostly. A few of the school buses have yet to depart. I see Angela helping Hendrick across the lawn. Georgie is saying good-bye to Shaynequa.

"I don't know what came over me," I say.

"You've got a lot going on," Ceci says. "I realize that."

"If you wanna fire me, I would completely understand. I think you should."

"I'm not going to fire you, Calvin."

"You should. I want you to."

"No, you don't."

"Yes, I do. I can't work here anymore."

"Look, I understand," Ceci says. "You've been through a lot. I'd be behaving strangely, too, if I were in your position."

"It's more than that," I say. "I'm not going to come back after the break." I look at the floor. I look at Ceci. She frowns.

She leans back in her chair. She swivels forward, moving closer to me. She straightens her ponytail.

"Because of what happened in the lounge?"

"It's something I've been thinking about doing for a while," I say. "I need to figure out some family stuff and I need time to do that."

"So take some time," she says. "Use the holidays to think about it. I'd hate to lose you. Don't do anything rash, not until you've thought it through."

"I have thought it through."

"So you're just going to give up?" she asks. "Everything we worked out? The whole thing?"

"I don't know that my heart was ever in it to begin with," I say. "I'm sorry."

"What about Arham?"

"You can't do that to me," I say. "I've got enough people to worry about without taking him on, too."

"He's come so far with you."

"I know. And he'll go further with someone else. Someone who actually wants to do this."

"You don't want to be a teacher?"

"No," I say. "Listen, I love working here. This has been an amazing experience for me and I've learned so much. And I'll miss that little guy and I won't forget him or any of these kids anytime soon, but when I close my eyes, this isn't what I see myself doing."

"What do you see yourself doing?"

"I have no idea," I say. "Right now I need to be home. I have to help out if I can. There's a baby to look after."

"I wish you'd change your mind," Ceci says. She puts her hands on the table and plays with her engagement ring, spinning it around and around.

"I'm sorry to spring this on you," I say. "It's a shitty thing to do, I know."

What about going back to school?"

"It's not for me."

"What can I say?" Ceci says. "I'm disappointed."

"I'm sorry I disappointed you."

Ceci throws up her hands. "All right. Finish out the month. Type up a letter."

There isn't anything left for us to talk about, and silence settles in. I am slow to get up from the soft green chair. I am slow to leave her office.

I GO OUT to the hatchback.

I want to start the engine and drive. Just keep driving. Cross the Tappan Zee and head north until there's no more road. As long as I keep going, everything will be fine. Perpetual motion is the answer. It keeps everything outside the car at bay. If I can somehow stay inside that cocoon forever, there will be no problems. As long as I never get where I'm going, it will all be okay. It will be manageable.

Instead, I drive to a spot I know, on Van Wart Avenue. I park. The bridge is in the short distance. Sloping hills dotted with quiet houses on the western bank of the Hudson. Cars coming and going, a certain order of motion, of other people's lives, not my own. Where they are going, who they love, what their lives look like, I have no idea.

It would be something, if I could do it, if I could just turn my back and leave.

The hatchback idles shakily, the engine humming.

I'm done at the John W. Manley School. That much I'm certain of. No grad school. No Pace University. I'm walking away.

The murky, uncertain future is a scary thing to contemplate and I can't really see the path before me. I miss her.

I release the emergency brake and put the hatchback in gear.

I remember we're low on formula, so I swing by the store for some cans of Similac.

CHRISTMAS COMES AND goes. It is hard on everyone and there is a pall of subdued quiet to everything. My mother cooks a modest dinner. It's just us. No relatives. No party. We exchange small gifts. Chip, in a valiant effort at keeping the status quo, gives me an NRA belt buckle. A pewter eagle clutching two rifles in its talons, with the inscription "Use it or lose it." He finds this very amusing. I give him an oversize Knicks jersey with the name "Moretti" on the back, which he has been dropping hints about wanting.

I shower James Jr. with presents, just like I planned. Reusable diapers, a new blanket, little footed pajamas. At the mall, my father and I decide to go dutch on an unnecessarily large stuffed giraffe.

It isn't the best holiday we've ever spent as a family, but I feel in a weird way it's not the worst either. There is a certain closeness I feel to everyone. I'm on the seesaw, as always. It oscillates now between intense feelings of guilt about my secret plan to desert them and skin-crawling moments of despair when I want to bolt from the house and never come back. I haven't fully committed to any real course of action, nor have I told anyone that I'm thinking of going away for a while.

I have $1,791.45 in my savings account. My last paycheck from the John W. Manley School should be on its way shortly. In my notebook, I do a quick breakdown of my "finances." All divvied up, there are three months of Sallie Mae payments, plus a little left over for me to live off, if I eat nothing but cheese sandwiches and sleep on couches. I don't plan on smoking weed for a while, so there's a cutback. If I decide to go, I'll probably just take a few changes of clothes, my Walkman, some tapes, my notebook. Up and down. I am adrift in limbo. I have been there for some time.

THE REST OF the house is quiet. My mother is at the grocery store.

I am in the kitchen, warming a bottle. I listen to the walls. I wait for a pipe to clang.

Upstairs, the baby is crying. I hear my father's hushed voice. I tilt my head, trying to make out what he's saying. I turn off the stove. I climb the stairs to the second floor.

My father is in Elissa's room. He is at the window, rocking James Jr. gently in his arms. After a while, the baby is quiet.

"Lunchtime," I say, stepping into the room.

My father is smiling at the baby, making faces.

James Jr. begins to squirm again.

"Want me to take him?"

My father hands the baby over to me. I cradle his head in my hand and rest his tiny body in the crook of my arm, the bottle in my free hand. I've gotten quite good at this maneuver of holding bottle and baby at the same time. It is a delicate ballet that causes me a little discomfort—the shoulder will be stiff forever, I think. Still, though, it is accomplished. I sway back and forth.

"There you go," I say, guiding the rubber nipple into James Jr.'s mouth.

The baby moans softly and begins to drink. After a moment, he coughs and spits up a little onto my arm.

"Gross," I say, but it doesn't bother me. I hold the baby to my chest. His head smells like talcum powder. I turn back to the window. The garage seems far away, across the yard. The trees are bare and shaking in the wind. I decide then, at that exact instant, that I will stay. The radical move I will make, the thing I will do to shake myself out of the rut I've fallen into, will not be to run away. I will do the opposite. It will be the harder thing, sure. It will be the choice that means more work and more responsibility, and yet, it also seems to fit well with the proclamations I made to Dave and Wally that day in Dave's living room—eons ago, it feels—when I told them I could grow up whenever I wanted. When I told them "adulthood" was a challenge you either took on or shied away from. I will be that person. I will help out instead of hinder. I will be there for people, even if it means sacrificing some things. Even if it means putting off my own happiness for a little while. I am needed. There are people whom I care about—love—who need me.

We need each other, for we are moving. We are leaving

this house. My parents have decided on the Victorian, the one on the Yonkers-Hastings border. Things will be changing yet again. I will change with them, as best I can. And at the same time, I know I won't be here forever either. Elissa was right. She always was. Nothing stays the same. Nothing lasts. There is no true permanence in this life. Things begin. Things end. I will move out when the time is right. When it makes sense, I will have a life outside my family. It is inevitable. Until then, I will be here. We will all be here.

James Jr. stirs in my arms and stops drinking from the bottle. His eyes open. He looks right at me.

I CALL GABBY'S cell phone. It goes to voice mail. I'm happy about this. I leave a message. I put the ball in her court, as they say.

"Sorry I've been a little out of the loop," I say. "There's a lot going on. Don't know if you've heard. Maybe you have. Okay. So, we're moving. That's happening. There's a lot of stuff to pack up. Stuff to throw away. I'd like to see you, after we get moved. If you feel like it. Or whatever. Yeah, so call me back, I guess. Okay. Bye." I hang up.

"Fucking idiot," I tell myself.

THE HOUSE IS full of boxes. Boxes and boxes. In the living room. In the foyer. Everything in its proper box. My mother has labeled all of them. *Kitchen Stuff. Books. FRAGILE— Fine China. Baby's Stuff. Chip's Clothing. Cal's Records.*

Chip is out in the driveway yelling at the movers, a pair of burly men in back braces who seem completely detached from the emotions of the day.

"Careful with those wing chairs," he is telling them.

There is a Dumpster behind the moving truck, full to the brim with the things we are not taking with us. Things we are shedding.

I walk through the house. Meals we've eaten in the kitchen. Movies we've watched in the TV room. The feel of the stairs underfoot. The second step from the top makes a sound like the creak of a door. No one ever got around to fixing the leaky kitchen faucet. I go to my bedroom. Chip's bedroom. The baby's room. All empty now. Echoes everywhere.

There's no third-floor bathroom in the new house. I'll have to make some adjustments. We all will. The piano in the living room has been sold, hauled away already. No space for it where we're going. The pool table in the basement makes the cut. Chip is very happy about this. He has grand plans to create a "man cave" in the basement. Chip has taken over the financing for the new mortgage. He's worked out a roughly sixty-forty split between him and our parents. For the time being, my father's disability and Chip's salary will join forces to pay the bills. It's a good thing he's around. Having no job at the moment, I'm back to freeloading.

In time, you come to know a place. After a year. After decades. You know it so well you forget you know it so well. You stop seeing it for what it is. And then one day you are walking through it for the last time.

I don't want to think about it, but I do. I allow myself a little bit of nostalgia, which normally I hate. I look in the closets. I flick on lights and look at the fixtures. There is dust in some of the corners. There are cracks in walls that will have to be plastered over.

My mother is in her bedroom putting the last of her clothing into boxes. My father is sitting on their bed, which has been stripped to the bare mattress. He is holding James Jr.

"Please try to keep Chip from insulting the movers too much," my mother says.

"The baby is completely unfazed by all of this," my father says.

"Do you guys need any help in here?"

"We're almost done," my mother says. She is holding a pink dress. One I haven't seen her wear in years. "Do I want this?" she asks.

"I don't know," I tell her.

From outside, there is the sound of a horn blaring.

I go to the window. Chip is hanging out of the driver's side of the moving truck, leaning on the steering wheel. I throw up the sash and stick my head out. The air is cold.

"What's the problem?" I yell.

He lays off the horn.

"Let's go already," he calls out. "These boxes aren't moving themselves."

*There's a feeling of wanting to be closer to things. Of wanting to keep them a certain way. Call it an ache, felt only when the passage of time is clearly visible. Or when, at the edge of change, you are reluctant to let a particular moment go. The idea is to hold on to time. To live inside it. But this can never really be. The moment is always gone. Even before you've thought to cling to it.*

# ACKNOWLEDGMENTS

These people read and encouraged and listened and spoke and were colossally responsible for aiding this book into existence.

Without whom I would be lost:

Tim O'Connell, Ethan Bassoff, Matt Lombardi, Chuck Adams (and the entire Algonquin team), Josh Anzano, Dave Liebowitz, Steve Moore, Steve Lowenthal, M.P. "Snakeman 5000" Berdan, Ron "Morelli 1" Morelli, Justin Jarboe, Stephen Walsh, Morgan Workman, Melissa Mamatos, Minju Pak, Marina Robinson, Matt Cowal, David Gates, Jon Dee, Darcey Steinke, and everyone at Beginnings Nursery—especially Jane, Claudine, LeeAnn, Lilla, and Ellen.

I love you all. Peace.

# The Sleepy Hollow Family Almanac

A Note from the Author

Questions for Discussion

# A NOTE FROM THE AUTHOR

When people want to know if my novel is autobiographical, I always feel like saying, "What work of fiction isn't?" It's all based on something, even when it's not.

The wackiest and thereby most vexing period of my life (so far) was my midtwenties. I found that handful of years, roughly from twenty-three to twenty-six, and the extended period of postcollege floundering that went with it, to be stranger and far more coming-of-age than high school and my teen years (encapsulated for me by a white suburban upper-middle-class bubble) ever were. I knew I wanted to try and express the emotions, the anxiety, the excitement, the antsy-ness, the wonder—and the lurking, unspecified dread—that informed that period.

My father really does have multiple myeloma. My family really did lose their house. I really did work at a preschool for autistic kids. My grandmother really did mistake a picture of Osama bin Laden for God. My brother really did think he was reverse discriminated against by a Metro-North train conductor. But almost everything else in the book is exaggeration, or complete invention. I do not have a sister. I rarely smoke weed. I don't know any live-action role players. My father did not carry a gun around in his bathrobe, although it might have been interesting if he had.

I graduated from college in May 2000. And much like Calvin Moretti, when it was over, I had no idea what to do with myself. I knew one thing: I didn't want a job. Furthermore, I had no idea how to get one. Nor did I know what people actually *did* at "real" jobs. So I decided to go back to school. Get a master's. Two more years of partying, I thought. I started a film MFA at Boston University. I was twenty-one. Long story short, I dropped out after a year and wound up living back home after being on my own for five years. My youngest brother, Tom, was still in high school. Almost immediately, I retrograded back to my high school self—both in how I viewed life and how I dealt with my parents and the people around me. I was jobless, broke, and largely without motivation. The next eight months became, without a doubt, the strangest and most surreal and intensely formative period of my entire life. I was completely adrift in the world without any direction in which to steer myself. No one was forcing me to grow up. It didn't seem like I had to. I'm a huge fan of coming-of-age stories. But I felt like I hadn't read any books (or watched any films) that took on this idea of my generation's grossly delayed plunge into adulthood. When I did come across some piece of art that attempted to tackle the subject, there was often a romance component as the fulcrum. Or the thing would be bogged down by pointless pop-culture reference. Or, worst of all, it would fall back on grossly inaccurate and contrived dialogue to attempt to convey how young people talk to each other. A sort of "look how cool and hip and funny they are" mentality. I wanted to consciously avoid those trappings. I didn't want love to be a motivator for Calvin. I didn't want friends, or "good times," or anything like that. What I wanted to do was put on the page a snippet of someone's life at a crossroads.

I was also really interested in the generational divide I saw between my parents and me. My father was a home-owner, had a career, and had his first child (me) all before he turned thirty. I'm about to turn thirty-three and have done none of those things. This strikes me as noteworthy, or at least of some interest. Before starting to write *Sleepy Hollow*, I looked back at novels and films I liked that I thought fit the bill. Art about people who were too old to be experiencing the feelings they were experiencing. At twenty-three, I should have been moving past any coming-of-age experiences. But there I was, trying to puzzle out in which direction I wanted my life to go. And *where* I wanted it to go.

Why does anyone write anything? There are more answers to that question than there are books in the world, and none of them really get at the amorphous motivations that drive people to make art. Or at least I don't think they do. The truth is, I wrote *The Sleepy Hollow Family Almanac* because I couldn't write anything else. When I sat down in front of my computer and started typing, these were the characters I could conjure, this was the story that I knew how to tell, because these were the things that were happening around me. These were the people who populated my life, for better or for worse.

QUESTIONS FOR DISCUSSION

1. Calvin Moretti is a twenty-four-year-old who has returned home because he can't seem to find his way in the world. At the beginning of the novel, he states, "Life is basically standing still. Stalled out" (page 2). What does Calvin's plight say about him, and about his generation? Are his feelings age-specific, or is there a universal quality to them? How might Calvin's father, James, have been different at twenty-four?

2. James states that Calvin is the only person who understands him. How do father and son express similar feelings, despite their very different circumstances?

3. Calvin's mother, Kathleen, seems to be the center pin holding the family together, yet she, too, shows a somewhat "flaky" side by bringing Brigitte, a spiritualist, into the home to counsel the family—and James in particular—about the crisis they are facing. Do you feel that Kathleen has a firm grip on reality? What do you think would happen to her if Chip and Calvin and Elissa all decided to move out of their Sleepy Hollow home?

4. At one point Calvin's father, James, says, "I'm learning now to live without my dreams" (page 92). Do you think this declaration speaks solely to the loss of his job as a commercial pilot? What kind of statement might the author be trying to make about the status of the American middle class in contemporary society?

5. Many people prioritize their lives by keeping lists, but Calvin seems to be obsessed with list making. How do you think Cal's obsession is connected to how out of control his life has become?

6. The novel opens with Calvin stating, "I work with retards." What does he mean by that? How does that statement make you feel about Calvin's character initially? Do your feelings about him change as the book progresses?

7. Arham, Calvin's charge at the preschool for autistic kids, is a minor character who nonetheless plays an influential role in Cal's maturation. How do you feel about Calvin's relationship with Arham? Do you think that one day Calvin might achieve enough maturity to be a father himself?

8. Is Calvin's father, James, a "mature" person in the sense of being a responsible figurehead for his family? If your answer is yes, how do you rationalize the ever-present gun and his careless use of it? If no, what role do you think his status as a breadwinner played in holding the family together, both financially and emotionally? What other factors might have made up for his seeming immaturity?

9. Calvin and his friends dabble in recreational drug use to help them escape the mundane lives they feel stuck inside. Do you think this drug use is a result of their current stations in life, or do you view it as part of the problem? Do you think it is something that will continue in Calvin's life, or will he eventually move beyond it?

10. As Elissa's pregnancy draws to an end, James discovers a new resolve and a determination to care for himself and the baby. How do you feel about this new child's future in the Moretti household? In general, how do new responsibilities change the way we view ourselves and our families?

11. There are many novels that delve into the lives of contemporary dysfunctional families. Can you compare this novel to others you've read? Would you say that the members of the Moretti family—and the relationships among them—seem realistic? Why or why not?

12. In chapter 11 (pages 91–92), Calvin describes a recurring dream in which he has to kill an approaching monster, but he lacks the strength to pull the trigger, no matter how hard he tries. How does this dream tie into Calvin's real-world fears and anxieties? How does it relate to what happens with his father's gun later in the book (i.e., the shooting of the deer and the accidental shooting at the wedding)?

13. Romance, or the desire for romance, is largely absent from Calvin's thoughts and desires. He doesn't seem to want or need a girlfriend. Do you think this is peculiar to Calvin,

or is it a reflection of the isolation felt by many in his generation? What do you think the author is saying about the way Calvin navigates the world? What do you think the author is saying about the future of romance?

14. In many regards, this novel is about, if not the end of the American Dream, the diminishing of the bright, rich future many of us were raised to expect. How do you feel about the future of the Moretti family? What do you think will happen to these characters?

15. Calvin claims to be bad at "life things. Important life things that have meaning, repercussions. Anything that involves talking to people in a meaningful way. Any confrontation where feelings are concerned" (page 56). Do you think he is right about this? By the end of the novel, has he changed? What do you see as Calvin's future?

Kris D'Agostino lives in Brooklyn, New York. This is his first novel.

Join us at **AlgonquinBooksBlog.com** for the latest news on all of our stellar titles, including weekly giveaways, behind-the-scenes snapshots, book and author updates, original videos, media praise, detailed tour information, and other exclusive material.

You'll also find information about the **Algonquin Book Club**, a selection of the perfect books—from award winners to international bestsellers—to stimulate engaging and lively discussion. Helpful book group materials are available, including

**Book excerpts**
**Downloadable discussion guides**
**Author interviews**
**Original author essays**
**Live author chats and live-streaming interviews**
**Book club tips and ideas**
**Wine and recipe pairings**

**twitter** Follow us on **twitter.com/AlgonquinBooks**
**facebook** Become a fan on **facebook.com/AlgonquinBooks**

# The Sleepy Hollow Family Almanac

# CONSPIRACIES, COVER-UPS, AND CRIMES

# CONSPIRACIES, COVER-UPS, AND CRIMES

Political Manipulation and
Mind Control in America

BY
JONATHAN VANKIN

Paragon House Publishers
NEW YORK

First edition, 1991

Published in the United States by
Paragon House
90 Fifth Avenue
New York, NY 10011

Copyright © 1992 by Paragon House

Library of Congress Cataloging-in-Publication Data
Vankin, Jonathan, 1962–
Conspiracies, cover-ups, and crimes : the secret files of
political manipulation and mind control in America / by Jonathan
Vankin. — 1st ed.
p.     cm.
Includes bibliographical references and index.
ISBN 1-55778-384-5
1. United States—Politics and government—1945–   2. Conspiracies—
United States—History—20th century.   3. Manipulative behavior—
United States—History—20th century.   I. Title.
E743.V36   1991
364.1'0973—dc20                               91-8064
                                                CIP

Manufactured in the United States of America

To my parents,
LARRY AND JEAN VANKIN,
with love, for everything.

# CONTENTS

# *Acknowledgments*

When you go to the library and look up "conspiracy theories," you don't find much. The research for this book, therefore, was more a process of accumulation than systematic investigation. I relied almost as much on people chatting with me and handing me stuff as on my own digging. The list of those people is very long, and I don't remember everyone, but thanks to you all.

There are a few people I must single out by name, two in particular. Ken Swezey was so essential to developing my ideas and direction for this book that he deserves more than just a humble thank you. He did even more than help. It must sound like a terrible cliché to say that without Ken this book never would have been possible. But it's true. Without Ken this book would never have been written. I was originally writing the book for Ken's small imprint, Blast Books. Not only was he willing to encourage me to write my first book, he had enough faith in the project to bring it to the attention of Paragon House.

That brings me to Evelyn Fazio, my editor at Paragon. About Evelyn, too, I can truthfully say that this book wouldn't have been written without her. She was enthusiastic about the project from the start. Her confidence in me was something I never thought I'd experience as a first-time book writer. She was always there with reassuring words, and I needed many.

Also at the top of my list is Don Kennison, of both Blast Books and Paragon House. He offered research help, ideas, and all-important moral support.

Of all the people who helped with my research, my colleague John Whalen, media columnist at *Metro*, deserves top billing. Much gratitude also to Eric London, who read my rough draft and gave me exactly the type of criticism I needed.

Finally, thanks to Dan Reichert for being my friend for an extremely long time; to Hal March for the same thing (and for innu-

merable hours of conversation in the world's coolest record store); and to Brent Filson, my mentor.

Saving the best for last, my most special thanks to Coleen Curran, who read every chapter as soon as it came out of the word processor, and did the impossible through this entire ordeal: She lived with me. Most remarkable of all, she still does.

Jonathan Vankin
Santa Clara, California
December 1990

# Introduction

## THE THRESHOLD OF BELIEF

*Ignorance ... brought about anguish and terror. And the anguish grew solid like a fog and no one was able to see.*

The Gospel of Truth, 17:10
NAG HAMMADI BIBLE

Is there something rotten in America? Ever since the political assassinations of the 1960s, Vietnam, Watergate, and, more recently, the Iran-Contra affair and the Persian Gulf War, there has been a growing feeling among many Americans that something is terribly wrong. But what is it?

*Conspiracies, Cover-ups, and Crimes* is a journey through the blood-red and midnight-blue netherworld where governments mingle with gangsters, and democracies enter secret partnerships with Nazis; where presidents deal drugs, respectable businessmen run billion-dollar rackets, and shadowy secret societies pull the strings of public officials. It is about the dark area usually covered by the term, "conspiracy theory."

*Conspiracies, Cover-Ups, and Crimes* is the first comprehensive and objective exploration of "conspiracy theory," the last real political heresy. Who really killed J.F.K.? Were we told the truth about the "mass suicide" at Jonestown? Did the CIA have a hand in bombing Pan American flight 103? Did the Nazis ever really surrender? Is the government manufacturing human robots to carry out assassinations? Is there a secret, evil force manipulating our everyday lives?

Crazy questions, perhaps. But in writing this book, I've interviewed a variety of Americans who have devoted their lives to answering those questions nonetheless. Are they crazy people? The answers may surprise you. After profiling a number of "conspiracy theorists," I'll explain the conspiracies themselves, presenting the evidence gathered by conspiracy researchers, and letting the reader decide where fact becomes fiction and fiction all too factual. While the book tries to present no final answers, I came away from this project asking questions about America and my own place in it that I'd never dared ask before.

B etween 1963 and 1981, there were six attempts on the lives of presidents or presidential candidates. When that happens in other countries, we shake our heads at the primitive ways of "banana republics." Here, every recent assassination attempt has been attributed to madmen (or madwomen) acting alone. Get rid of the crazy people, and the system still works. Perhaps we should change a law or two, make it tougher for them to get guns, but otherwise the country is stable.

To maintain this belief, we must also place faith in the institutions that comprise the amorphous entity called "the system"—government, business, media, academia. Those institutions provide us with our way of life and all the information we need to live it, but lately an unshakable faith in their benevolence and stability has been hard to justify.

There is something about America that makes conspiracy theories inevitable. Something that makes them necessary. The word conspiracy derives from Latin roots which translate roughly as "breathing together." Sounds healthy, but the idea is heresy. In America, the word used to describe conspiracy theories is "paranoid." Conspiracies are delusions. Believe in them and you are mentally ill.

But is there value to these ideas after all? Would we be shutting ourselves off to a fuller understanding of America by understanding conspiracy theory as a symptom of mental illness?

Stalinist as it sounds, treating unorthodox ideas as psychiatric ailments, this diagnosis of conspiracy theories is distinctly Ameri-

can. We like to believe that our American system is unique, that unlike most countries around the world we have a system that works. Things may go wrong, sometimes terrible things, but they are caused by minor malfunctions, not by flaws in the system itself.

That is why, when we face awesome crises like the savings and loan robbery, the defense-contracting scam, or even constitutional collapses like Iran-Contra or Watergate, we never ask the obvious question: How in our democracy could these things happen? Instead, we change a few laws, prosecute a few villains, then declare that the system is repairing itself. Nevertheless, participation in politics has never been lower, because, I believe, people have a gut-level feeling of helplessness.

I've heard it said that the most dangerous thing about conspiracy theories is that they create a feeling of helplessness. If everything that goes wrong is caused by a conspiracy, then there is nothing anyone can do about it. The people in this book are evidence to the contrary. They are activists, constantly working on, thinking about, and searching for the real causes of helplessness gripping America.

In the past century, we have experienced an overwhelming social transformation. We are moving toward what one scholar, Bertram Grass, calls "friendly fascism." We may already be there. When the difference between lies and truth no longer means anything, we become easy to manipulate—fair game for "mass media, world spanning corporations, armies and intelligence agencies," he wrote. "Meanwhile, the majority of people have little part in the decisions that affect their families, workplaces, schools, neighborhoods, towns, cities, country, and the world."

In the first part of this book I've profiled a variety of Americans who reject the illusion of "friendliness," what appears to be a new insidious form of control. In the second part, I explore the ideas of these Americans. My intention is not to endorse—and certainly not to discredit—any one conspiracy theory or the broad conspiracy that seems to emerge throughout Part Two.

This book is an attempt to delve into a way of seeing the world that is far different from the one we're all used to. In this strange

and not very comforting view, fantasy and fact shift positions with disconcerting, but delightful, regularity. I've attempted here a kind of mental new journalism of total immersion into the subject. I've steeped my mind in conspiracy theories, figuring the only way to truly understand them is to see the world from their point of view. Despite the pervasive paranoia that can result from these explorations, I'm fairly confident that I've emerged with my sanity intact.

So consider this a voyage, like Darwin on the *Beagle*, through environments rarely explored, stopping to take samples along the way and coming back to port with a new understanding of our environment, our history, and ourselves.

In a scolding editorial about a congressional committee's finding in 1979 that President John F. Kennedy was assassinated by a conspiracy, the *New York Times* declared that the problem was not the committee's finding but its choice of vocabulary. "The problem," said the paper of record, "is the word. The word is freighted with dark connotations of malevolence."

The *Times*'s attitude toward *conspiracy*, though typical, is disheartening. As scary as some of this stuff is, I also find it exhilarating. As important as I believe it is to explore dangerous ideas, I also find it fascinating. The word "conspiracy" may be a "problem" for some, but only because it represents the unknown, mystery, and risk. Those are the things that grip the human mind and bring it to life. These ideas can only be a problem for those who wish to keep our minds under control.

# Part One

# THE
# RESEARCHERS

# 1

## "I Am a Breeding Experiment"

*"Did you shoot the President?"*
*"I didn't shoot anybody. No, Sir."*

> Exchange between a newsman
> and Lee Harvey Oswald moments
> before Oswald was shot dead.

Sometime around Easter 1959, a young marine named Kerry Wendell Thornley struck up a friendship with his company's resident misfit. The misfit was sometimes called "comrade" by the other marines at El Toro Annex just outside Santa Ana, California, because he was unreserved in his admiration for Karl Marx and communism. His real name was Lee Harvey Oswald.

Oswald openly subscribed to communist newspapers. On a Marine base, that was more than enough to make him an outcast. His introverted personality and penchant for cracking jokes in an exaggerated Russian accent secured his position as what Thornley called "the outfit eightball . . . what in the Army they called a yard bird and in the Marine Corps a shit bird." He had no true friends, but among his acquaintances on the base Thornley was one of the steadiest.

Oswald was "a jarhead private with a swab in hand, slopping soapy water over the wooden plank porch of the operation hut," Kerry wrote in 1965. "With this picture there is a vague feeling of sympathy that might find expression in the question: Why are they picking on that poor guy?"

And who was Kerry Thornley? Kerry Thornley is still trying to figure that out more than thirty years later. In 1959, he was an aspiring writer from Los Angeles, a barracks' intellectual serving his tour in the military after a year at the University of Southern California.

In retrospect it was a propitious pairing—Thornley and Oswald. The next four years of Oswald's life, which were also its last four years, marked him as one of the most bizarre figures in American history. And Thornley, in a different and far more obscure way, would leave his own palm print on the cultural brainscape. The assassination of President Kennedy would change them both profoundly, more even than it altered the American consciousness forever. It ended the existence of Lee Harvey Oswald, accused of the crime and murdered on national television two days later.

For Kerry Thornley, on the other hand, the assassination at first seemed a stroke of morbid good fortune. At first. He was no admirer of Kennedy and admits to celebrating at the news of Kennedy's death. More important, the sudden if posthumous fame of his eccentric marine buddy appeared to be a remarkable coincidence that would give Thornley's literary career a big break.

Thornley had already written a novel, a story of a marine's disillusionment with his country. The protagonist of Thornley's novel, *The Idle Warriors,* was a fictionalized version of Lee Harvey Oswald.

The novel never found a publisher, but this does not revoke Kerry Thornley's odd distinction of being the only author to write a book about Oswald *before* the Kennedy assassination. Thornley kept an open mind, but he had no reason to doubt that Oswald, whom he remembered as a malcontent, killed Kennedy all by himself.

Thornley's association with the president's alleged assassin has long ceased to seem a coincidence to him, or particularly good fortune (though it did get him a commission to write a nonfiction book called *Oswald,* which was published in 1965). He has come to believe that he was, against his will and without his knowledge, part of the conspiracy that killed Kennedy. And not only that. The plot, or rather the master plot of which the assassination was but one

result, was hatched before he was born. He has been a coerced conspirator since his prenatal days.

Thornley and Oswald, too. This plot still continues. In 1981, Thornley wrote another book—as yet unpublished—about what he believes was his part in the conspiracy. At the time he wrote it, Thornley thought that the conspirators first began to manipulate him when he became friendly with Oswald. He now believes that this association was a part, not the start, of the operation.

"Since then, I've realized that I'm the product of a German breeding experiment. My mother and father were spies for Japan during the war. I learned enough about intelligence community cant and so forth that I can decipher what was going on in my early environment," Thornley said to me, once I had tracked him down by phone.

"What I think they were trying to do was create a monarchy in this country. I think they came over here originally with that purpose."

A breeding experiment?

"Oswald was, too," Thornley says. "We both were."


This would be a good time to take a step back. Let's leave the "breeding experiment" thing for a while, because even more than most conspiracy theorists, Kerry Thornley is an easy guy to poke fun at. His ideas can't be done justice in pithy snippets like "he thinks he's a breeding experiment." When I last tried to make contact with Thornley, after being out of touch for about a year, he said that he didn't want to talk on the phone because the only phone he can use is in his landlady's living room and "last time we talked she and her son sniggered at the far-out things I was saying through the whole conversation."

Writer Bob Black once remarked to Thornley, "You used to satirize conspiracy theories; now you believe in them." Black reports that Thornley "solemnly agreed." Nonetheless, I still wonder if it's all a put-on. Is Thornley's intricate conspiratorial autobiography an elaborate mind game he plays with himself and anyone who'll join in? Or is he really an intelligence agent, with a macabre

cover story for his role in the J.F.K. conspiracy? Or could the story be true? Is Kerry Thornley a helpless pawn in a game beyond anyone's comprehension, who somehow figured out what has been happening to him? If it could happen to him, what about the rest of us?

I raise these questions not because Thornley's theories are remarkably strange. For the most part, they're no stranger than a lot of the other stuff I've come across in researching this book. But unlike some of the other characters herein, whose stone-faced sincerity is unimpeachable, Thornley has a history as something of a philosophical jester. This history makes his encounter with Oswald and its aftermath all the more a conundrum.

In the 1950s, during a philosophical argument in a bowling alley, Thornley and his friend Greg Hill invented a bogus religion they called "The Discordian Society." To be a Discordian, one must worship Eris, the Greek goddess of chaos and discord. Most religions are unworkable because they impose order on the senseless course of human events. Discordianism, Thornley and Hill therefore resolved, would worship disorder.

This seems a commonsense proposition, if a rather Swiftian one. Thornley and Hill wrote a little Bible (Hill wrote most of it) called *Principia Discordia*. The book became a kind of underground classic. It gained in stature when Robert Anton Wilson and Robert Shea quoted liberally from it in their best-selling science fiction novel *The Illuminatus Trilogy* (a satire of conspiracy theories, in which the Illuminati are, fittingly, sinister conspirators and the Discordian Society must rescue the world). Wilson and Shea dedicated the first book of the *Trilogy* to Thornley and Hill.

The *Principia Discordia* gained enough notoriety to propel it through five editions, and it's still in print today. In what must surely be one of the most twisted examples of synchronicity in this whole tale, for reasons which will soon become evident, Hill is reported to have first run off the *Principia* on a Xerox machine in the office of New Orleans District Attorney Jim Garrison a few months before the Kennedy assassination in 1963.

To readers of what is sometimes described as the "marginal" press—the busy subculture of fanzines and similar self-published tracts—Thornley is known for his impassioned and occasionally

incoherent (though always funny) rants that appear in every issue of *Factsheet Five* magazine and on his own irregularly published broadsides, *Kultcha* and *Decadent Worker*. In these highly unusual writings, Thornley reveals himself as an anarchist thinker with a heavily conspiratorial perspective unique even among anarchists. But anarchism is just the culmination of a long intellectual quest.

Despite the subversive wit of Discordian "guerrilla ontology" (as Discordian dabblers like to call that particular line of thought), Thornley classified himself as an "I-Like-Ike" conservative during the late 1950s. He slithered out of that phase, through traditional liberalism and into Marxism during his marine stint. While he was immersed in his "Marxist" period, Thornley heard a news report about a young ex-marine who defected to the Soviet Union.

The defector, as is etched in the brain of every Kennedy conspiracy aficionado, was Thornley's former buddy Lee Oswald.

Oswald's defection was ostensibly the result of his growing disaffection with the American way after serving at a Marine base in Japan. It echoed the alienation Thornley was feeling at the time. He served at the same Japanese base after Oswald had been there and left: Atsugi, home of the supersecret U-2 spy plane (an odd assignment for a sympathizer like Oswald). Observing how Americans interacted with their hosts in a foreign land, Thornley seethed. Oswald's defection to the USSR gave Thornley the inspiration for *The Idle Warriors,* and he promised whoever would listen that the book would be "a poor man's *Ugly American* which would 'blow the lid off' the situation resulting from peacetime stationing of troops in the Far East."

*The Idle Warriors* would turn out to be the center of Thornley's life for the next few years. But its ideological theme changed even before he began writing it. On the ship back to the States once his tour in Japan was up, Kerry picked up *Atlas Shrugged,* the philosophical novel by Ayn Rand. Pitting diametrically opposed Randian "Objectivism" and degenerate "collectivism" against each other and a backdrop of melodrama, *Atlas Shrugged* changed Kerry's outlook once again.

Thornley was now a confirmed "*laissez-faire* capitalist." In theory. Not in practice. Honorably discharged from the marines, he

adopted a Bohemian life-style—prided himself in it, actually. He supported himself as a waiter, a doorman, and later a hobo. When I first reached him, he was washing dishes in a Mexican restaurant. His reliance on menial jobs or no job at all, despite his noteworthy intellect, has stirred suspicion of Kerry Thornley, as we shall soon see.

Thornley's service at Atsugi was just one of the many times Kerry Wendell Thornley stepped in the footprints of Lee Harvey Oswald. Back in the states, after some time in his native California, Kerry moved to New Orleans. His stay in New Orleans was to be the crucial episode of his life. Some of what happened to him at that time did not take on significance until a decade later. There was one incident that would begin to haunt him sooner.

According to Thornley, in the fall of 1963, when he had just returned from a few months out of town, he was in a restaurant called the Bourbon House in the French Quarter. He was at a corner table talking to a man. He can't remember who.

As Thornley told it in 1976, a woman named Barbara Reid, "whose reputation as a voodoo worker had reached my ears but with whom I was not then well acquainted," came over to him.

"Have you ever been in radio work?" she asked.

Thornley said that he hadn't.

"Well, you should be in radio," said the voodoo lady. "You have a lovely voice."

Kerry, unmoved by flirtation, said thanks. He went back to his conversation. With whom was he talking? After the Kennedy assassination, Barbara Reid said that Thornley was conversing with Lee Harvey Oswald. She told this to New Orleans District Attorney Jim Garrison. Five years later, on February 8, 1968, Garrison called Thornley to testify before a grand jury. Garrison's investigation into the J.F.K. assassination was by then national news, and the subject of national controversy. Garrison quizzed Thornley about his alleged acquaintance with Oswald in New Orleans. Thornley maintained, as he always had and still does, that he had not seen Oswald since 1959.

Thornley and Oswald's rather casual friendship came to a

screeching halt when Thornley made a sarcastic remark, in response to one of Oswald's incessant gripes about life in the marines, in America, or something. "Come the revolution," Thornley chided, "you will change all that."

Oswald, looking "like a betrayed Caesar," as Kerry told the Warren Commission, shrieked at him "Not you too, Thornley!" and stalked away. Thornley never spoke to him again.

That was Thornley's recollection, noted as early as two days after the assassination, when the FBI interviewed him at Arnaud's Restaurant in New Orleans, where he was a waiter. He repeated the same account to the Warren Commission in his testimony of May 18, 1964. He still tells the same story.

Garrison wasn't buying it. As Thornley repeatedly denied meeting Oswald in New Orleans, Garrison just as doggedly prodded him. He had arrived at a conclusion about Thornley in advance, and the twenty-nine-year-old free-lance writer wasn't confirming it. Garrison still holds to that conclusion with the same conviction that Thornley still refutes it.

Garrison's conclusion was, and is, that Thornley was the man calling himself "Oswald" who, accompanied by a big, scary-looking Cuban tried to buy ten pickup trucks from a Ford dealership in New Orleans in early 1961. The real Lee Oswald was still in the Soviet Union. In all likelihood, the trucks were going to be used in the Bay of Pigs raid, or some such covert anti-Cuban operation, because the fake Oswald and his tough-guy cohort said they were from a group called "Friends of a Democratic Cuba."

This was one of many "second Oswald" incidents prior to the assassination, and Garrison thought Thornley was playing Oswald in this one and possibly others. The D.A. even calls Thornley an Oswald "look-alike."

Judging by photos of Thornley from back then, that's a real stretch. The resemblance is passing at best—imaginary, if you ask me. In any case, Garrison or at least people around him were so keen to prove Thornley could have impersonated Oswald that a reputed Garrison associate, Harold Weisberg—a writer who by 1968 had already written four conspiracy books about the assassination—asked a California artist to "touch up" photos of Thornley to make him look more like Oswald. Weisberg's letter

making this suspicious request was typed by one of Garrison's secretaries. When the letter was leaked to the press, Garrison's office denied having anything to do with it.

"Was Thornley an agent of the intelligence community?" Garrison asks in his most recent book. "Had he impersonated Oswald or coached others to do so?"

That was what Thornley was up against when he encountered Jim Garrison. At first, Thornley thought he would be helping Garrison. When he refused to admit meeting Oswald in New Orleans, Garrison indicted him for perjury. It was not exactly a secret indictment. Garrison spared nothing in smearing Thornley well before any trial. He sent forth a press release on February 21, 1968, stating flatly that "Kerry Thornley and Lee Oswald were both part of the covert federal operation operating in New Orleans." He noted that Thornley was one of "a number of young men who have been identified as CIA employees."

"I can tell you this flatly: I'm not a CIA agent," said Thornley when he was arrested at his home (then in Tampa) the next day. "Why does he think I am? One of the reasons is that I went to Arlington, Virginia, after leaving New Orleans. Another is that I have the education to hold white collar jobs, but don't."

Garrison was also intrigued by *The Idle Warriors*. "As luck would have it," Garrison snidely observed, "the man he wrote about ended up being charged with assassinating the president."

If only Garrison had known that the insane Bible of Discordianism had been first published on a Xerox machine in his very own office. What would his reaction have been then? Thornley mentions that, for a while, Garrison theorized that the Discordian Society itself was a CIA operation. In 1976, Thornley said that he thought that was "very funny and completely absurd" of Garrison. In 1989, he might not have been so sure.

Garrison eventually dropped the perjury charges. Thornley never stood trial. The ordeal was a jarring one. Extremely disturbing to Thornley were the numerous apparent coincidences, seen as highly sinister by Garrison, between his travels and Oswald's. Or those of an Oswald impersonator.

Though Thornley denied meeting Oswald in New Orleans, it was undeniable that they were there at the same time in late 1963. This baffled Kerry. Oswald had made headlines that summer, when Thornley was out of the city. Oswald was passing out leaflets for the "Fair Play for Cuba Committee," a real organization of which he was the only New Orleans member. It is now widely believed, and was by Garrison, that Oswald's New Orleans chapter was a front—some sort of government operation with Oswald as its agent.

Whatever Oswald's real motives, he had been in a street corner brawl with an anti-Communist Cuban. In retrospect, it's likely that this incident was staged. Again, whatever its real reason, it put Oswald in the news and made him briefly a local celebrity, appearing on local newscasts as a spokesman for Marxism.

Yet when Thornley returned to New Orleans in September, no one thought to mention to him, "That marine buddy of yours who you're writing a book about is in town," though most of his friends knew the gist of his work in progress. This was all the more strange because Thornley, from news reports of Oswald's return from the Soviet Union, knew he'd gone to Dallas and was considering a trip there to see him. Thornley hoped to elicit some details that would flesh out the ending of *The Idle Warriors*.

Another convergence: While Thornley was out of New Orleans, after visiting his parents in Whittier, California, he traveled to Mexico City. He returned from Mexico, he told the Warren Commission, on September 3 or 4, 1963. About three weeks later, in Mexico City, Lee Harvey Oswald, or someone claiming to be him, appeared at the Cuban consulate and threw a very conspicuous tantrum. He wanted to travel to Cuba, and he wanted a visa right away. When he couldn't get it, he had a fit.

In a book called *High Treason*, Robert J. Groden, who was a photographic consultant to the House Select Committee on Assassinations, published what he says are photos, presumably taken by the CIA, of the man identified as Oswald in Mexico City. They are not photos of Oswald (and they sure aren't Kerry Thornley), so this incident may also be part of a frame-up.

Garrison points out that when Thornley moved to New Orleans, he moved directly to a neighborhood occupied by a cadre of intel-

ligence agents. Some of the most startling coincidences came from
Thornley himself, in his 1976 recollections.

Oswald's "Fair Play for Cuba" address was 544 Camp Street, the
same building as the offices of Guy Bannister, ostensibly a private
investigator. Actually Bannister was a right-wing crazy who appears to have been working for some intelligence agency on anti-
Cuban subterfuge. His secretary reported that Oswald often visited
the office, and on the very day that JFK was murdered one of
Bannister's employees told the FBI that Bannister and David
Ferrie—another far-right CIA operative, who also worked for the
Mafia—were somehow involved in the assassination. Even the
House Select Committee on Assassinations, reluctant as it was to
find any conspiracy, found these two characters worth investigat-
ing. Oswald's almost certain link to Ferrie went back to when
Oswald was a teenager when they were both in a unit of the New
Orleans Civil Air Patrol.

Without going through all of the evidence amassed by a phalanx
of researchers over the years (Garrison not least among them),
suffice to say that it indicates that Bannister and Ferrie were
coordinating some kind of intelligence operation out of 544 Camp
Street, an operation that was probably intended to target Castro,
but may well have turned against Kennedy. And the consensus is
that Lee Oswald, possibly without knowing all of what he was
involved with, was part of that operation. Was Kerry Thornley?

Garrison is convinced of it. Thornley protested, but by the
mid-1970s he didn't know what to believe. He recalled meeting
Bannister at the Bourbon House as early as 1961. Bannister, Thornley recalled, was introduced as "a man with a great interest in
literature." So Thornley, remarkably, began to tell him all about his
book in which Oswald was the main character. Thornley also
remembered going to a party where he met David Ferrie. Was he
being manipulated?

When he appeared before the Warren Commission, Thornley
was quite satisfied that Oswald was Kennedy's lone killer. He was
still convinced a year later when his book *Oswald* came out. A
tabloid in Los Angeles ran some excerpts from the book. A graduate student at UCLA named David Lifton saw the excerpts.
Lifton's avocation was collecting evidence to criticize the Warren

Report. He tracked down Kerry, who was then a doorman at an L.A. high rise called Glen Towers.

This apartment building posed another puzzle that had significance to Thornley only in retrospect. According to Thornley, "the most colorful resident" of Glen Towers was John Roselli. One of the country's most powerful mobsters, Roselli it would later be revealed, was part of the CIA's assassination plot against Castro. His intimacy with the CIA's dirtiest dealings made Roselli a posthumous object of suspicion in the Kennedy assassination. Shortly before he was to testify before the House Select Committee on Assassinations, which assembled in the mid-1970s, Roselli was found chopped into pieces, floating in a metal drum off the Florida coast.

Thornley said that Roselli told him the CIA "killed their own president."

Thornley didn't know quite what to make of his casual conversations with Roselli, but with David Lifton's help, his thought was going through troubling transformations at that time. Lifton and Thornley had a series of meetings and struck up a friendship. Lifton confronted Thornley with enough evidence that Thornley felt he could "no longer hide from myself the probability that either Lee Oswald was innocent or he had not acted alone."

The evidence Lifton laid out would soon become standard stuff in writings by the many critics of the Warren Report. When Lifton showed it to Thornley, it was revolutionary. By the time Thornley met with Jim Garrison, he believed that there was a conspiracy in the assassination. He did not believe that he had played any part in that conspiracy, even unwittingly. It was Lifton, then, who thought Thornley had been "set up previous to the assassination as an alternate patsy."

It was largely at Lifton's urging that Thornley cooperated with Jim Garrison. Before Thornley got involved with Garrison, Lifton held high hopes for the New Orleans D.A.'s investigation. But a couple of meetings with Garrison, followed by the indictment of Kerry Thornley, left Lifton bitterly disillusioned. Thornley as well. But where Lifton went on to pursue his own rigorously factual assassination investigation, which culminated in his 1980 best-seller *Best Evidence*, Thornley was personally involved in the drama, and rather than investigate, he meditated.

In the course of Thornley's reflections, something that he had not told the Warren Commission, and certainly not Jim Garrison, began to take on drastic importance. Besides his chat with the alleged Oswald at the Bourbon House in September, 1963, Thornley had other mysterious conversations in New Orleans.

In 1961, a friend of Thornley's introduced him to a pipe-smoking, bald man named (Thornley was told) Gary Kirstein. Like Thornley, Kirstein was a writer (again, this is what Thornley was told). At the time, the only thing memorable about Kirstein, who was kind of a Neanderthal racist, was that he was planning to write a book with the curious title *Hitler Was a Good Guy.*

Thornley recalled the content of his more notable conversations with Kirstein. The rekindled memory was astonishing: They had debated how to assassinate President Kennedy. Hypothetically, of course. They were talking as two writers discussing how it would be done in a novel. Kerry had blotted out this macabre recollection for a decade.

"I was so bored," Thornley now recalls. "He basically predicted everything to me that was going to happen in the next twenty years, including the Manson family, the war in Vietnam, and so on and so forth. All of which at the time I did not believe a word of. If I'd known that I was making history I would have been so excited. I was actually just bored to tears.

"I thought he was a nut," Thornley says, remembering his initial impressions of Kirstein. "I just didn't think he had it together. I thought he was just some asshole who was probably a little bit sadistic and didn't have anything else to do, so he was just playing with my mind. That's what I thought. To me, his whole worldview was so foreign to my nonconspiratorial worldview at that time that he just seemed to me like a psychologically degenerate individual."

This gossamer "Gary Kirstein" is the catalyst of Thornley's conspiratorial scenario. Thornley still isn't sure who Kirstein really was. He believes he might have been E. Howard Hunt, the CIA master spook who became a public figure as a shadow dweller of the Watergate scandal. Playing around with this possibility, Thornley authored an article in 1973 called, "Did the Plumbers Plug J.F.K.,

Too?" After the piece was published in an Atlanta underground newspaper, Thornley received a couple of strange anonymous phone calls.

One of the callers asked, "Kerry, do you know who this is?" Thornley said he didn't.

"Good," said the caller, and hung up. The voice on the other end of the line brought back eerie memories. It sounded similar to the voice of that man Thornley had talked to in New Orleans a decade before. He decided he could keep his recollections to himself no longer.

Two years later, after searching his memories for every bit of information they would yield, Thornley went to the Atlanta police, who were then looking into new allegations about the murder of Martin Luther King, Jr. He remembered Kirstein had also talked about killing King. The idea, Thornley remembered, repelled him and he didn't want to discuss it even hypothetically. In 1975, he was beginning to see connections between the assassinations of Kennedy and King.

Twelve days after making his statement to the police, Thornley was attacked by two men in ski masks who pistol-whipped him in the face and, weirdly, stole all of his identification.

Thornley had nothing solid to prove that the robbers attacked him with the intention of stealing his I.D. But he had his suspicions. He wondered if his I.D. might be used—by whom?—to create a "second Thornley," not unlike the "second Oswald," who Jim Garrison still suspects may have been, at least once, played by Kerry Thornley.

The mysterious phone call. The stolen I.D. The refreshed memories of Gary Kirstein. The series of coincidences linking Thornley to Lee Harvey Oswald. Things coalesced in Thornley's brain.

"He was always repeating himself," Thornley recalls of his "Conversations with the Devil of Sauerkraut and Philosopher-Kings" (the title of Chapter One of Thornley's book about his Kirstein experience). "There were things he wanted me to remember. What the CIA calls programming somebody."

In 1981, Thornley thought Kirstein was the first intelligence agent who tried to program him. His readings and meditations have caused him to dig deeper in the decade since he wrote his un-

published book about Gary Kirstein. He now believes he knows who his first controller was.

"There were five or six things that my mother always said over and over all the time," Thornley reminisces. (*Mother?* Mother!) "One of them is that, when they put a child out for adoption, they usually pick parents that physically resemble the natural parents. Whenever she could, she brought that up. And another was, 'Kerry's not very observant.' And I gradually realized that what she was saying over and over was not evidence of senility. There were certain things she wanted me to remember."

By studying his own genealogy, Thornley says he has found that instead of Irish, as his name sounds, his family is actually of German and Swiss descent. He also believes they were part of the Vril Society. The Vrils were a proto-Nazi occult group that had connections to Aleister Crowley's Golden Dawn. They tried to make contact with a race of alien gods who lived in the center of the Earth, believing that the gods were fathers of the "master race." Kerry Thornley takes it from there. Like all good Nazis, he says, the Vrils are working "to create a super race." That is the purpose of their "breeding experiments."

"The Vril Society isn't technically genocidal," he says. "As far as I've been able to tell, the philosophy behind it is to breed people the same way that other animals are bred, to create ones that are more intelligent, healthier etc., etc., etc. Within every race, they're breeding. It's not quite such a simpleminded type of thing as was going on under Hitler."

The experiment that produced both him and Oswald, Thornley concludes, was a Vril-Nazi attempt at eugenics. Thornley, however says that he is "what they call a mutant, because I didn't turn out to be a racist. . . . I wasn't turning out to be the good Nazi they hoped I would be."

Because he is the output of what must be a very important process to Nazi cultists carrying out these experiments, Thornley has been under surveillance since birth, he says. A "bugging device" was planted on his body when he came into the world. He came to that realization after being teased by strangers for an embarrassing sexual experience that could only have been recorded by some device hidden on his person.

People have been checking up on him, monitoring and terrorizing him all along. The enigmatic "Gary Kirstein" may have been foremost among his controllers.

"Whatever it is, I've lived this long because the Nazis happen to like my genes," he says. "Twenty years ago, the guy I talked to in New Orleans predicted a lot of the stuff I've been going through, particularly once I realized that I was somehow involved in the Kennedy assassination. Basically, he told me I'd be persecuted to the end of my life. I probably will be. I'm getting used to it, I guess."

So there is the tale of Kerry Thornley, first known as a footnote to one of the century's pivotal episodes, who now believes he is one of the "Boys from Brazil." His own introspection has been supplemented by ceaseless reading, and among his readings are expositions by Mae Brussell. Brussell's article, "Nazi Connections to the JFK Assassination," rings familiar after Thornley's account of his meetings with "Gary Kirstein." Frankly, Thornley's theory would explain a lot of the anomalies that have cropped up in Thornley's life, although it's hardly the most concise and probable explanation.

I still wonder, and have never really answered for myself, whether Thornley means his theory literally. Thornley is always the intellectual explorer, but his one dogma appears to be this, as stated in a recent scribbling (he is still a voluminous writer, *compelled* to write): "Every human being is—either because of evolution or an innate way of nature—born into this world with an enlightened consciousness that is curious, loving, ecstatic, freedom loving and erotic, and early social conditioning obliterates and fractures it."

In the dark reality of Thornleyism, I wonder if the conspiracy against Kerry Thornley is a metaphor for the larger conspiracy against human nature. Social conditioning taken to ghastly extremes. Perhaps a metaphor come true.

Robert Anton Wilson, whose *Illuminatus Trilogy* gave Thornley a dose of underground acclaim, once explicated Thornley's satirical Discordian religion. One achieves "Discordian enlightenment," Wilson states, when one realizes that Discordian doctrines are not

literally true, *"but neither is anything else."* Reality is determined by its interpreter.

Thornley's memories and speculations are his evidence for his own current version of reality. His "breeding experiment" hypothesis fits his evidence as well as any other. Is it literally true? If not, what is?

"A lot of order is projected, according to Greg Hill," Thornley says, referring back to his old cohort in Discordianism from the days of bowling-alley philosophy debates.

"I think there's some truth to that. And Greg is probably, I think, an arch-conspirator, you know."

# 2

# VOTESCAM

*O good voter, unspeakable imbecile, poor
dupe . . .*

OCTAVE MIRBEAU,
*Voter's Strike!*

On election night, when the three major television networks
announce the next president, the winner they announce is not
chosen by the voters of the United States. He is the selection of the
three networks themselves, through a company they own jointly
with Associated Press and United Press International.

That company is called News Election Service (NES). Its address
is 212 Cortland Street, New York City. Its phone number is (212)
693-6001. News Election Service provides "unofficial" vote tallies
to its five owners in all presidential, congressional, and guber-
natorial elections. NES is the only source Americans have to find
out how they, as a people, voted. County and city election supervisors don't come out with the official totals until weeks later.
Those results are rarely reported in the national media.

The U.S. government does not tabulate a single vote. The government has granted NES a legal monopoly, exempt from antitrust
laws, to count the votes privately.

Those are the facts.

Even an average citizen should be a bit unsettled by the prospect
of a single consortium providing all the data used by competing
news organizations to discern winners and losers in national elections. To Kenneth F. Collier and his equally obsessed older brother
James, the possibilities are apocalyptic.

19

Ken and Jim Collier's discovery of NES in 1988 was the apex of a pyramid they had been assembling for nearly twenty years. Other stones in the awesome structure: Richard Nixon, John F. Kennedy, George Bush, the CIA, Supreme Court Justice Antonin Scalia, Washington *Post* publisher Katherine Graham, "60 Minutes" reporter Mike Wallace, and just about everyone who has anything to do with administering, tabulating, reporting on, and running in American elections.

In their self-proclaimed crusade to prove "Votescam" (as they've pithily christened the conspiracy) the Colliers have filed a string of lawsuits, *pro se,* against the Republican National Committee and other big-time defendants. The RNC offered a reward for evidence of vote fraud. The Colliers say they have evidence, but the RNC won't pay up, depriving the brothers of both the reward money and, they claim, a Pulitzer Prize with all its attendant benefits. So they sued for $250 million.

They've traveled from coast to coast, depending on the kindness of strangers—people who believe their own local election officials are cheaters. The Colliers come in and offer to prove it. They've haunted warehouses, slept in VW buses, set up their office in the middle of a sidewalk, and for a while lived in the Library of Congress. One person who lodged Ken Collier for a period of weeks told me he finally had to kick Collier out of the house. The person called Collier a "con man," but it seems to me that if the Colliers are trying to engineer a get-rich-quick scheme, they've picked a funny way to go about it.

Almost all of the Colliers' writing on Votescam has been published by two newspapers. The Liberty Lobby tabloid *Spotlight,* voice of the ultraright "Populist Party," ran a continuing series of Votescam articles from 1984 until 1988 (the Colliers insist that Votescam is a "nonpartisan" issue, and indeed there seems to be no detectable ideology in their writing, even in *Spotlight*). A small community newspaper in Hialeah, Florida, called the *Home News* is also a regular outlet. Collier articles with headlines like "Herald Fabricates Story," "The Case against Judge Scalia," and "The Real Roots of Watergate" break up the folksiness of the forty-four-year-old *Home News*, which mostly fills its columns with city council debates, high school sports, and garden club meetings.

In 1989, the brothers compiled the entirety of their research into 326 pages of manuscript—including a plethora of reprinted memos, clippings, court transcripts, and magazine articles. Their unpublished book is called, appropriately enough, *Votescam*. The ordinary person's one chance to take part in democracy, the vote, has been stolen, says the book. Every significant election in the country, the Colliers believe, is fixed. And not by rogue opportunists or even Boss Tweed–style strong-arm "machines," but by a sophisticated web of computer experts, media executives, and political operatives, all under the coordination of the Central Intelligence Agency.

"There isn't one single person in public office who earned their way there," said Ken Collier, when I interviewed him. "That's why the environment sucks. That's why there's the drug scene. That's why there's so many criminals and crooked politicians. Everything that's happened is because the vote is totally rotten. Rotted through to the core."

Like many conspiracy researchers, the Colliers can trace their life's mission back to one single event. Unlike many researchers, that event was not the J.F.K. assassination. Later, they would find a place for the pivotal assassination in their scenario. But the Colliers' revelation came on a date that lives in infamy for them alone: September 8, 1970, in Dade County, Florida.

The events of that day appeared innocent enough. The Democratic party in Dade County held its primary election for the U.S. House seat held by veteran congressman Claude Pepper. Pepper, who remained in Congress up to his death in 1989, was entrenched. He had no Republican opponent. The Democratic primary between Pepper and a hopelessly obscure opponent was *de facto* the final election, and a mere formality even in that regard.

The shock, to the Collier brothers, came soon after the polls closed at 7:00 P.M. Two of Miami's three television news stations projected Pepper the winner almost immediately. Nothing spectacular about that. They could have picked Pepper to win days before the election. What was remarkable were the exact predictions of Pepper's victory margin, and of the total voter turnout. At 7:24, one station projected a turnout less than 550 votes away from the eventual count of 96,499. In that same time span, less than half

an hour, the stations called several other races on the ballot to within a percentage point of the final totals.

Unbelievable accuracy. But perhaps explainable as a marvel of technology, the genius of statisticians, or at least a mind-boggling stroke of luck. Until a University of Miami professor overseeing the projections announced one other fact: The projections were based on numbers from a single, computerized voting machine. Not one precinct, but one lone machine.

There was a third television station in Miami, but it was reported to suffer a computer malfunction on election night and waited until late in the evening to broadcast election results phoned in from county headquarters. By that time, televisions were off. Dade County received its results not from the courthouse, but from a single machine somewhere. Not even the professor who collected the spewing data knew where that machine was.

Most voters in Dade County watched the election returns with indifference. There were no big political surprises, least of all in the Claude Pepper race. The dazzling speed and precision of the local stations' projections went largely ignored. Except, of course, by the Colliers, who were mortified. They had more than an average voter's interest in the race. Claude Pepper's hopelessly obscure opponent was Ken Collier.

The brothers Collier, sons of a Royal Oak, Michigan businessman, were both journalists. Jim had worked for the Miami *News* (though like so many impoverished reporters, he has already defected to public relations). Ken wrote features for the New York *Daily News*. In 1970, they caught the ear of an editor at Dell Publishing with a book proposal about running a grass-roots political campaign. The main chunk of research, they proposed, would consist of actually running such a campaign. And so Ken decided to take on the venerable Claude Pepper with Jim as his campaign manager and with no fund-raising. The whole campaign cost $120 and consisted mainly of gumshoe canvassing, talking to nearly every voter in the eighteenth congressional district.

"It was a random thing that I happened to decide to run in the year 1970," Ken told a radio interviewer in 1988. "But they had never used prognostications like this prior to that time in Florida. And when they did, it seems like we stumbled into the pilot project

of the methodology that has since 1970 absolutely, completely, taken over the United States voting system."

According to the Colliers, the process used on a limited scale that evening in Miami has been expanded into an Olympian system that allows the three major television networks to "monolithically control" any election worth controlling—that is, most of them.

"What do they do? They wait 'til the polls close. They announce who's going to win in virtually every race, they announce what percentage these people are going to get. They are virtually *never* wrong. And the key to remember is once you have been named, you can rest assured you will be the winner. And later on, if only these networks can have some sort of mechanism whereby they could make the actual vote turn out the way they projected it nationwide, they would have the same setup they had down in Dade County, where they would announce who won early on, then meddle with the election results later to make sure they turned out that way."

Into the picture steps News Election Service, the only mechanism in existence for counting national votes on election night, the only one in contact with every voting jurisdiction in the nation. The Colliers are the only researchers I've come across who make an issue out of NES, but the company is a conspiracy theorists' dream—or nightmare.

As mentioned above, NES operates exactly the way the most imaginative conspiracy theorists believe all media operate. The ABC, NBC, and CBS networks, together with the AP and UPI, own the company jointly. Associated Press is a nonprofit co-op of a large number of daily newspapers, and UPI serves many of the rest. Local television and radio stations take most of their election returns from network tabulations. NES is a very real "cabal." Every media outlet in the United States acts in concert, at least on election nights.

NES has a full-time staff of fourteen. On election nights, that number swells to approximately ninety thousand employees, most of them posted at local precincts phoning in vote totals as they're announced. Others answer the phones and enter these totals into

the NES computer. The government has no such computer. Only the privately held NES counts the votes. I called NES's executive director, Robert Flaherty, and asked him whether his company was run for profit. He wouldn't answer. His only response was "I don't think that's part of your story."

The Colliers find the existence of a "master computer" that records every vote in the United States more than coincidentally reminiscent of that single, mysterious voting machine in Dade County whose printouts were the basis for preternaturally precise vote-total predictions. The Colliers hold an even more ominous suspicion that the NES computer can "talk back" by phone lines to vote tabulation computers in cities and counties across the country.

"I don't know for sure that they're all connected to one. The immutable fact is that if they can do it, they will do it," Collier explains. "Computers are all linked. If you have a telephone number, you can get into most computers."

NES was conceived in 1964, in part as a cost-saving measure by the three major television networks (it was originally called Network Election Service), but largely to solidify the public's confidence in network vote tallies and projections by insuring uniformity. In the California Republican primary that year, television networks projected Barry Goldwater the winner on election night, while newspapers reported Nelson Rockefeller victorious in their morning editions. The networks themselves could vary widely in their return reports.

"Many television executives believe the public has been both confused and skeptical over seeing different sets of running totals on the networks' screens," the *New York Times* reported.

The networks (the two print syndicates were soon added to the setup) wanted the figures transmitted over their airwaves to be irrefutable. With all the networks—and later the print media— deriving their information from a central computer bank, with no alternative source, how could they be anything but?

"The master tally boards . . . would probably come to be accepted as the final authority on the outcome of races," the *Times* declared.

The "news media pool" was first tried in the 1964 general election. Most of the 130,000 vote counters were volunteers from civic

groups. Twenty thousand newspaper reporters acted as coordinators. NES central was located at New York's Edson Hotel. Vote-tallying substations were set up in such select sites as an insurance company headquarters and a Masonic temple. When polls closed, the newly formed system shaved almost ninety minutes off the time needed to count votes in the 1960 election.

News Election Service had its goal *circa* 1964 to report final results within a half hour of final poll closing time. Now, of course, they go much faster than that. In the 1988 election, CBS was first out of the gate, making its projection at 9:17 Eastern time, with polls still open in eleven states. ABC followed just three minutes later.

All of these light-speed results are, naturally, "unofficial." The Collier brothers would say, "fraudulent." County clerks take a month or more to verify their counts and issue an official tally. Plenty of time, the Colliers say, for any necessary fudging and finagling. And there may be none needed. Discrepancies are a matter of course throughout the nation's thousands of voting precincts. The major networks rarely bother to report on such mundane matters. So who's going to know? The idea, according to Ken and Jim Collier, is to get the predetermined winner announced as speedily and authoritatively as possible. NES provides the centralized apparatus to do just that.

One rationale behind maintaining a vote-counting monopoly is to insure "accuracy," but in 1968, when Richard Nixon defeated Hubert Humphrey by a margin that could be measured in angstroms, the role of NES became a good deal more shadowy.

At one point in the tally, the NES computer began spewing out totals that were at the time described as "erroneous." They included comedian/candidate Dick Gregory receiving one million votes when, the New York *Times* said, "His total was actually 18,000." The mistakes were described as something that "can happen to anyone."

NES turned off its "erroneous" computer and switched on a backup system, which ran much slower. After much waiting, the new machine put Nixon ahead by roughly forty thousand votes, with just six percent of the votes left to be counted. Suddenly, independent news reporters found over fifty-three thousand Hum-

phrey votes cast by a Democratic splinter party in Alabama. When the votes were added to Humphrey's total, they put him in the lead. Undaunted, the Associated Press conducted its own state-by-state survey of "the best available sources of election data" (presumably, NES also makes use of the "best available sources") and found Nixon winning again. And that's how it turned out.

What exactly was going on inside the "master computer" at NES? The company's director blamed software, even though the machine had run a twelve-hour test flawlessly just the day before using the same programming. Could the software have been altered? Substituted? Or was the fiasco caused by a routine "bug," which just happened to appear at the most inconvenient possible time? At this point, it's more a question of what we *can* know than what we *do* know.

My own feeling is that with all the snafus and screwups, the real winner of the 1968 presidential election will never be certain. I do know this: Liberal warhorse Humphrey died without fulfilling his dream of becoming president, while Nixon is still hanging around, his loyal crony George Bush in the White House.

"Nixon has more power now than when he was president," proffers Ken Collier. "He's the elder statesman."

The Colliers look at "The Great Dade Election Rig" of 1970 as a trial run for a new, streamlined method of election rigging. Could the presidential election two years before have been the nearly botched rig job that convinced the conspirators of election banditry to concoct a slicker modus operandi?

Computers tabulate fifty-four percent of the votes cast in the United States. Sure, paper ballot elections were stolen all the time, and lever voting machines are invitations to chicanery. But there's something sinister about computers. Though most professionals in the field, as one would expect, insist that computers are far less vulnerable to manipulation than old ways of voting, the invisibility of their functions and the esoteric language they speak makes that assertion impossible to accept.

Even executives of computer-election companies will admit that their systems are "vulnerable," although they're reticent to make

public statements to that effect. One executive told me, right after asserting that there's never been a proven case of computer election fraud, "there's probably been some we don't know about."

Even if "we" do find out, there's still little chance that the fraud will be prosecuted. A former chief assistant attorney general in California points out that without a conspirator willing to inform on his comrades or an upset so stunning as to immediately arouse suspicion, there's little hope of ferreting out a vote fraud operation.

There are very few elections that qualify as major upsets anymore. Preelection polling tempers the climate of opinion effectively enough to take care of that. As for turncoat conspirators, if the conspiracy works there are no turncoats. A good conspiracy is an unprovable conspiracy. It remains a conspiracy "theory." To even talk about it is "paranoid."

"If you did it right, no one would ever know," said the same state prosecutor, Steve White. "You just change a few votes in a few precincts in a few states and no one would ever know."

Maybe it's already happened, say the Collier brothers. In their unpublished book, they note that a turnaround of just 535,000 votes distributed correctly in eleven states would have handed Massachusetts Governor Michael Dukakis the 1988 presidential election, defeating George Bush in the electoral college.

Bush may have received an earlier Votescam benefit, the Colliers hypothesize, a rare election that *was* a significant upset. According to the Colliers, the favor came courtesy of New Hampshire Governor John Sununu, who had staked his political future on Bush before the then–vice president was a clear people's choice (if he ever was).

Bush had lost the Iowa Republican Caucus, the first round of the 1988 presidential primaries, to Senate Majority Leader Bob Dole. As Bush entered the New Hampshire primary, pollsters placed him behind Dole in that state, too. These were "days when things were darker," Bush said in his acceptance of the Republican presidential nomination six months later. His campaign was fizzling.

Despite his apparent deficit in public opinion, Bush won a decisive nine-point victory in the New Hampshire primary, reanimated his campaign, and more or less coasted to the nomination and presidency. The press attributed this remarkable turnaround to the

contrary nature of New Hampshire voters and Dole's allegedly "mean" public image.

Ken and Jim Collier tell a different story.

Sununu was later rewarded with an appointment as Bush's chief of staff, often considered the second most powerful job in the country. He is a *computer engineer* who had been a member of the Center for Strategic and International Studies, a Washington think tank the Colliers believe to be linked to the CIA. The Colliers also posit the CIA as the umbrella over NES, for reasons we'll get to before the chapter is through.

"All John Sununu had to do," they write, "was get access to the on-air script of (the networks') election unit to *script-in* George Bush as the 'projected' winner based on exit polls; step two: commandeer the mainframe master computer (NES) . . . so that the final official totals in county and state computers can be manipulated over a sixty-day period to reflect the early projections of a Bush victory.

"It is the prescription for the covert stealing of America."

Even though Ken Collier insists that vote-fraud researchers who preoccupy themselves with computer voting are "obsolete," the New Hampshire primary-rig scenario turns on the "Shouptronic" voting machines used in Manchester, New Hampshire, from which early returns were taken. The Shouptronic's most advantageous feature is the speed with which it tabulates votes. Multiple machines can send results to a central computer instantly over telephone lines or even by satellite.

Shouptronic is essentially an automatic teller machine for voters. All votes are recorded by button pressing. The Shouptronic leaves no physical record of votes. Like all computer vote counters, its programming is top secret.

As solid a source as Robert J. Naegle, author of the federal government's national standards for computerized vote counting, is alarmed by the secrecy masking computer election software.

"They act like it was something handed down on stone tablets," he says. "It should be in the public domain."

The Shouptronic is named for its company's owner, Ransom

Shoup II. In 1979, Mr. Shoup was convicted of conspiracy and obstruction of justice relating to a Philadelphia election under investigation by the FBI. That election was tabulated by old-fashioned lever machines, which also leave no "paper trail" of marked ballots. Shoup was hit with a ten thousand dollar fine and sentenced to three years in prison, suspended.

Another computer voting company, Votomatic, maker of Computer Election Services (now known as Business Records Corporation Election Services), emerged unscathed from a Justice Department antitrust investigation in 1981. The president of the company quipped, "We had to get Ronald Reagan elected to get this thing killed." The remark was supposed to be a joke. Forty percent of American voters vote on CES systems.

CES machines have been described as relying on "a heap of spaghetti code that is so messy and so complex that it might easily contain hidden mechanisms for being quietly reprogrammed 'on the fly.'" A computer consultant hired by the plaintiffs in a suit against CES described the way a CES computer runs its program as "a shell game."

Votomatic has one especially troubling drawback. On election night 1982 in Miami, Ken and Jim Collier captured the problem on videotape. This "Votescam Video" has been the Colliers' Exhibit A ever since. They've showed it to reporters at major television networks, and evangelical talk show host Pat Robertson paid them 2,500 dollars for broadcast rights to the tape. Robertson aired a portion of the tape.

The problem with Votomatic, captured on the Colliers' tape, is something called "hanging chad." The perforated squares on Votomatic computer ballot cards are, for some reason, called "chad." When a voter fails to punch it out completely, it hangs on the card.

To solve this problem and allow the computer to read the cards, election workers routinely remove hanging chad. The registrar of voters in Santa Clara County, California, says that "five percent or less" of all Votomatic cards have hanging chad, and election workers don't pull it off unless it is hanging by one or two corners.

The vision of local ladies from the League of Women Voters deciding how voters have voted, putting holes in perforated ballots

with tweezers was an astounding proposition to the Colliers. When they talked their way into the Miami counting room on November 2, 1982, toting video camera with tape rolling, that's exactly what they found. *Prima facie* evidence of tampering, they believed, and Jim started shouting "Vote fraud! Vote fraud!" for the benefit of the camera. The Colliers were forced out of the room.

The Votescam Video is the basis for James and Kenneth Collier's lawsuit against the Republican National Committee. The video led them to Washington, where, through sheer force of will, they convinced an ABC legal reporter to screen it. But ABC never picked up the story.

The Colliers were not surprised. They added ABC to their list of defendants in one of their *pro se* lawsuits, along with the League of Women Voters and the RNC. Then they invoked the federal RICO (Racketeer Influenced and Corrupt Organizations) statute to charge the troika with a racketeering vote-fraud conspiracy.

Backed by the *Home News*, Ken and Jim sued Antonin Scalia, whom President Reagan appointed to the Supreme Court in 1986. Ken Collier testified at Scalia's senate confirmation hearing, where, under oath, he accused Scalia of sandbagging his lawsuits against the RNC. Scalia, say the Colliers, wrote a "killer memo" recommending that aspects of the suit be dismissed. He placed the memo in court records without following legal procedure, the Colliers contend, thus using his authority as a federal judge to shield Votescam from public scrutiny.

"He acted without jurisdiction to cause to come into existence a 'counterfeit concurrence' which contained self-serving prejudicial language exonerating friends and colleagues who had been party-defendants in the three cases, causing lower court judges to take judicial note of the tainted document and summarily dismiss those cases," Ken testified in the prepared portion of his statement.

The brothers' antipathy toward Scalia dates back to April 23, 1971, when they sent a telegram to then-president Nixon detailing the Great Dade Vote Rig. Scalia was in charge of the White House telecommunications office at that time, and the Colliers are convinced that he grabbed the telegram, took it to Nixon personally, and instead of suggesting an investigation of vote fraud persuaded the president to cover it up.

The telegram led to Watergate, the break-in compelled by Nixon's fear that the Democrats were going to use some Votescam connivance of their own and he would be cheated out of reelection in 1972.

"He never invoked that as a reason for Watergate," says Ken Collier. "But, instead, he had his brother buy into the company that was putting out all the software back when that's the way they were doing it." The California company was CES.

For a while, Watergate was the cornerstone of Votescam, but the Colliers seem to replace cornerstones rather frequently without letting the edifice of their Votescam scenario crumble. After linking Watergate to Votescam, they took the big leap back to the muddy pool from which all contemporary American conspiracy theory crawls: the Kennedy assassination.

The creation of NES was part of a CIA operation to control the media. The agency needed to hush up its involvement in the killing of J.F.K., so it created its own "media desk," which maintains hegemony to this day. The Colliers last year shot a new video in Dealy Plaza revealing a sewer grating in the grassy knoll—the area from which assassination researchers have long believed the shot striking Kennedy in the head was fired.

Beneath the sewer grating is a "sniper's nest" says Ken Collier, concealed by grass and brush. The drain leading out of the grassy knoll is a perfect escape route.

And Votescam spirals on through time.


The Colliers have now spent two full decades tracing Votescam. They've been flat broke most of the time, and Jim lay for a while near death with a stomach tumor. The tumor was diagnosed not as cancer, but as an outgrowth of stress. Killed—almost—by Votescam.

When I contacted the Colliers, they were somewhere in New York, trying to find a publisher for their finished book. They've packaged the manuscript replete with cover graphic. An American eagle, its beak is curled in a sinister sneer. They wanted me to help them. They wanted me to call the editor of the *New Yorker* on their behalf to recommend that he publish an excerpt from *Votescam*. I

told them that, somehow, I didn't think my opinions would carry much clout with the *New Yorker*'s management, if I could even get through on the phone (it was tough enough just tracking down the elusive Ken and Jim Collier).

"It's not even a quest," said Ken of their twenty-year endeavor. "It's a simple report. The book will blow your mind because if you didn't have some reason not to publish it, you'd publish it because it's so vital. It goes right to the core, heart of the democracy. The vote. The winners, the senators, the congressmen, the ones that go ninety-eight to ninety-nine percent incumbency every single time—it's all because it is truly a clique, a club.

"Ultimately it might come out. I don't see how though. Everyone with anything to hide is at the top with billions to gain. Even if we had the book out, you would never see an interview on network television. You couldn't publicize it. Why? Because the networks are the ones that do it. The networks are the ones that count all the votes for senate, for the president, for congress. You don't necessarily even believe it until you see it yourself. Why twenty years? I don't know."

I had the feeling, talking to Ken, that the Colliers were nearing the desperation point. I couldn't worry about them. They'd been there, and past it, before. The Colliers still hope that Votescam will be their road back. At the same time, strangely, they know they have no hope. Once Votescam hit them like a gnostic vision, there was no returning to the world of consensus.

In the course of one conversation, Ken Collier recoiled from the label "conspiracy theorist," then turned around and announced, "The newspapers are all corrupt, and at this point I'll say that and I don't care what anyone thinks." The Colliers' pessimism is as confirmed as their perseverance.

That may be the final paradox of Votescam.

# 3

# GET LAROUCHE!

*The stealthiness of the enemy and his
ubiquity!
I saw that we must copy it.
In our own way of course.*

ADOLF HITLER

Lyndon Hermyle LaRouche, Jr., could have stepped fully formed
from the pages of Marvel Comics. His devotees see him as the lone
hero who can save the world from forces of evil raging out of
control. To adversaries, he is a sinister genius bent on global domination. In the real world these days, he's a federal prisoner.

LaRouche has spent immeasurable energy constructing an aura
of personal importance. Every studied nuance says "executive":
meticulously tailored suits, salon-clipped thinning hair, a fixed
smirk of contempt for all those intellectually inferior (which is
everybody), and a tight circle of disciples, who, far more than a
"cult," are an efficient machine converting his innumerable
schemes to reality. How it all came crumbling around him is a
story whose plot is helical to say the least, leading from the school
yards of Lynn, Massachusetts, to the secret chambers of British
aristocracy, through the fertile ferment of Lyndon LaRouche's
mind.

LaRouche began life as the son of New Hampshire Quakers. The
family moved to Lynn, an industrial, ethnic burg, when Lyndon,
Jr., was ten. When World War II hit, he was a conscientious
objector, as the family religion demanded. Then he suddenly

33

changed his mind and enlisted in the Army anyway. His tours of duty were spent in medical units around India and Burma.

There's some speculation that LaRouche may actually have been an Office of Strategic Services (OSS) intelligence agent—an intriguing hypothesis, considering that he was also a Marxist. He claimed to be, anyway. Somewhere along the line, he became a hardened anti-Stalinist and swayed toward Trotskyism. Never satisfied with the Marxist groups he encountered, put off by their hypocrisy and vacillation, he started his own group. In the late 1960s, LaRouche's no-prisoners style of leftism attracted a few radical academics, but most were repulsed in 1973 when LaRouche began his "Operation Mop Up" baseball-bat attacks against members of the more traditional left. His henchmen raided more than seventy gatherings of groups like the American Communist Party and the Socialist Workers Party (a little irony there—LaRouche had been a full-fledged SWP member from 1948 to 1963).

By then, leftists were convinced that LaRouche belonged nowhere in their ranks, that he was at least a provocateur, at worst a dedicated fascist. He did nothing to alter that impression. His writings and speeches in the mid-1970s mark a mutation in LaRouche's public thinking, usually characterized as a swing from the radical left to the extreme right.

His alliance in 1977 with CIA-connected mercenary and "security specialist" Mitch WerBell, who ran a paramilitary training camp for LaRouchians, as well as later contacts with KKK big shot Roy Frankhouser and others of that ilk, confirmed LaRouche's "swing to the right." But the physiognomy of LaRouchism displays characteristics evolved far beyond most known species of right-wing extremism. LaRouche transcends classification and scoffs at "left-right" distinctions. "I don't believe," he sneers, "the seating arrangements of the French National Assembly of 1793 have permanently frozen politics for the end of time."

While most kids his age were preoccupied with the exploits of Babe Ruth or Gary Cooper, young LaRouche, shunned by his schoolmates, was a pennant-waving fan of German philosopher Immanuel Kant. While this failed to win him a date to the junior

prom, it did provide LaRouche with the philosophical basis for his swelling *weltanschaung*.

"The problem with most of the conspiracy buffs is Americans don't know much about history, and they don't understand historical processes. Therefore they come up with simplistic kinds of conspiracies and they don't understand what the word conspiracy really means," says LaRouche. "Since I had a philosophical background as a young man, I recognized what the problem was. It was philosophical. I always look at these things from a political, philosophical standpoint, rather than how most people look at them. So that takes me to the evidence a little more directly than most people."

LaRouche's "philosophical background" is like a pair of X-ray specs. It lets him see through the shroud of politics, history, and current affairs to the naked truth, which is an eternal struggle between two philosophies—rationalism (good) and empircism (evil). Their adherents are united in two opposed conspiracies.

LaRouche starts with Kant's "moral imperative," that the only moral "maxim" is one that could be formulated as universal law. Stated simply, if an action is not right for everybody, it isn't right for anybody. Or, to look at it another way, if something is morally right for anyone, then it must be right for everyone. Murder, to take an example, is morally wrong, because "Thou shalt murder" could never be a universal law.

LaRouche, who has an acute techno fetish, updated Kant for the postindustrial world, composing the prime directive of LaRouchism: "the promotion of scientific and technological progress not only in our own country, but the right of developing nations to the same principles that we're committed to."

LaRouche sees technocracy as the proper goal of global politics. The title of LaRouche's book, *There Are No Limits to Growth*, says it all. We don't need less industry; we need more. We shouldn't be phasing out nuclear power; we should be accelerating it. We shouldn't be trying to curtail the world's population; we need *more* people to make technology work. All limits to growth are artificial and unnatural. There is no danger to the environment. Technology *is* ecology.

Technology is also morality. As societies become technological,

LaRouche believes, they place more cultural value on rational thinking. As they place more value on rationality, they become more moral. Kant says that all moral laws can be discovered through the rational process. LaRouche extrapolates from Kant: Technology is rationality in action, *ergo* technological development equals moral action.

"Wherever populations have become more rational in this fashion they have become more moral," LaRouche wrote. "The converse is more emphatically true. Technological pessimism . . . promotes cultural pessimism [which] unleashes all of the devils of which a population is capable of becoming."

One of the terms in the LaRouchian lexicon, a language that sounds something like conventional political discourse, but not quite, is "Malthusian." What LaRouche calls "neo-Malthusianism" is close to what's usually called "Social Darwinism." LaRouche loathes Thomas Malthus, the British economist who coined the phrase "survival of the fittest," later appropriated by Charles Darwin, who turned what was supposed to be an economic principle into a hypothetical natural law. In LaRouche's technotopia, there's an abundance of industrial-produced everything, so there's no competition for resources—no "survival of the fittest."

This thinking leads LaRouche to include in his dogma support for "beam weapons," the Strategic Defense Initiative—"my proposal" he calls it—as well as nuclear power, especially the as-yet-untamable fusion variety. He really pushed the limits with his latest cause. When he was running for president in 1988, his fourth campaign, he bought a half hour of network prime time to explain his plan for colonizing Mars. He called it the "Mars driver project," and declared it the only conceivable means to unite the country, accelerate technological innovation, restore the economy, and save the planet.

The nay sayers to these brilliant ideas, the "pessimists," are the empiricists: David Hume, John Locke, John Stuart Mill, Thomas Hobbes, Bertrand Russell. They and their philosophical ilk, in LaRouche's interpretation, base their moral reasoning not on rationality but on experience (empirical facts, hence the term, "empiricism").

Experience is a muddy thing. If we base our moral judgments on our experience, then we'll confuse things that *feel* good with things that *are* good, morally. Empiricist morality, as LaRouche reads it, is governed by "irrational hedonism."

So repelled by empiricism was schoolboy LaRouche, and so convinced by Kant, that when his adolescent schoolmates taunted him—they called him "big head"—he lashed back by calling them "unwitting followers of David Hume."

Thus was born the LaRouchian conspiracy theory. History's bad guys have been the "irrational hedonists" of empiricism, whose "pessimism" has spawned all of the evils mankind has endured in its nasty, brutish, and, so far, short existence. If their conspiracy succeeds, the human race will plunge into an anarchic abyss. The LaRouchian term is "New Dark Ages." The tool they'll use to cast us into darkness, he believes, just may be a nuclear holocaust.

One shouldn't get the idea that this awesome and complex conspiracy is perpetrated by a bunch of dead philosophers. Hume and the empiricists are no more than shills for evil ideology. The conspiracy predates these British philosophers, but it is uniquely British. Lately, its deadliest exponent, in LaRouche's view, is Henry Kissinger.

"Henry's career has always been, since he got out of the war as a tool of Chatham House, that section of British Intelligence . . . Kissinger is essentially an agent of Chatham House. He's essentially a British agent or an agent of British influence who has been funded to a large degree and sponsored by Nelson Rockefeller and to some degree, less so I think, by David (Rockefeller)."

Chatham House is headquarters of and another name for the Royal Institute of International Affairs, a British counterpart to the Council on Foreign Relations. LaRouche says that Kissinger's government training at Harvard came under the auspices of Chatham House.

The British have been keepers of this "irrationalist" flame for centuries. LaRouche traces the conspiracy's British lineage back to fourteenth-century Scottish King Robert Bruce. Bruce was the

originator of Scottish Freemasonry. He was under the heavy influence of the Knights Templars, whom he seems to have been harboring from the persecution they faced in Europe at that time.

The Templar connection links Bruce with the ancient tradition of gnosticism—or, to put it in LaRouche's terms, irrationalism. Oddly, LaRouche considers the Templars "humanists," that is to say, on the right side. Bruce's Templar faction were "renegades," and Bruce himself is "the direct ancestor, by unbroken lineage, of all the men of evil in England."

When LaRouche says that Bruce is forefather to the present-day irrationalist conspiracy—the conspiracy responsible for the world's opium traffic and its resulting subjugation of entire nations, including the United States—he means it. "The leading controllers of the opium war against the United States are not only connected by interlocking directorates and other business ties, but by ties of "blood" that constitute this web under *one* family."

Rationality, he believes, will save the world from the British conspirators. In LaRouche's opinion, the world's leading rationalist now sits in Lyndon LaRouche's jail cell in Rochester, Minnesota. A political prisoner of the forces of darkness.

From the rationalist vs. empiricist premise, LaRouche's reasoning behind such conclusions as his widely publicized "Queen of England pushes drugs" zinger is relatively clear—as clear as anything can be in the fog that hangs over a battleground of dueling conspiracies.

LaRouche combats the conspiracy with an intricate counter-conspiracy of his own devising. Now, he believes, he is suffering for it. He began serving a fifteen-year sentence for federal tax and credit fraud convictions on January 27, 1989. He was sixty-six years old when he reported to prison.

"Who's the conspiracy theorist," asks LaRouche's Boston lawyer, Odin Anderson. "LaRouche or the U.S. government?"

Though the numbers of LaRouche's followers are usually estimated at around one thousand (domestically—there are overseas LaRouchians as well), his network has consisted of at least sixteen political organizations and twelve publications—even a software

company. His "Fusion Energy Foundation" and its now-defunct magazine, *Fusion*, gained a readership of respected scientists and dealt seriously with nuclear fusion technology. The newsweekly, *Executive Intelligence Review*, sometimes beats the mainstream press to major stories and reports on regions of the world most ethnocentric American media ignore.

His private intelligence organization has the respect of even LaRouche's harshest detractors, sometimes rivaling the official intelligence community. "That doesn't mean we're running the biggest spy net in the world. It means we are able to think better than they are," LaRouche boasts.

Boston was the site of his first trial, where the government sought to expose LaRouche's underworld financial-political machine, devouring the life's savings of little old ladies to underwrite the vaulting political ambition of its central figure, LaRouche.

LaRouche's lawyers countered by outlining a government conspiracy to destroy LaRouche, a "Get LaRouche Task Force" created at high levels of the administration. While most media had made a practice of dismissing LaRouche's theories, to their bemusement LaRouche's "paranoia" began to look more and more like reality as the Boston trial progressed. Eventually, it became such a morass that the judge declared a mistrial.

"The government got caught with its hand in the cookie jar, failing to disclose exculpatory evidence," says Anderson.

Just as LaRouche had suspected, there was a full trough of internal government memos—including one between Iran-Contra conspirators Richard Secord and Oliver North—showing an apparently concerted effort to keep LaRouche under surveillance. LaRouche surmised that he'd been framed.

The LaRouche defense team tried to show that the credit-fraud and tax crimes LaRouche faced were the result of government skulduggery. The government, they said, had placed infiltrators deep in LaRouche's organization. Numerous documents came out to support that claim. LaRouche claimed that more than informants, these infiltrators actually committed the various illegalities and improprieties that he was being tried for.

Among the motives proposed by LaRouche's lawyers for this government operation was that LaRouche and Oliver North were

apparently competing for the same pool of cash. While North and his surrogates were smooth talking wealthy senior citizens and right-wing tycoons for funds to ship to the Nicaraguan contras, LaRouche's supporters were doggedly combing that same constituency to fund their leader's presidential campaign.

The government's true motives were much darker and deeper, says Lyndon LaRouche. Though LaRouche, who affects the image of a high-tech CEO, must now don undignified jailhouse skivvies, his confidence remains regal. He experiences not the slightest doubt as to the origins of his current predicament. The mastermind of the frame-up, he's certain, is that Chatham House chiseler, Henry Kissinger.

On August 19, 1982, Kissinger wrote a brief note to William Webster, then director of the FBI. In its entirety, the two-paragraph letter with the salutation "Dear Bill" reads: "I appreciated your letter forwarding the flyer which has been circulated by Lyndon LaRouche, Jr. Because these people have been getting increasingly obnoxious, I have taken the liberty of asking my lawyer, Bill Rogers, to get in touch with you to ask your advice, especially with respect to security.

"It was good to see you at the Grove, and I look forward to the chance to visit again when I am next in Washington."

The "flyer" could have been any one of a number of LaRouchian anti-Henry tracts. Undoubtedly this particular flyer was "Kissinger: The Politics of Faggotry." In it, LaRouche drew connections between the Roman Empire, Studio 54 (famed hangout for coke-snorting squalid socialites), Red-baiting homosexual mob lawyer Roy Cohn, and Kissinger. The purpose, apparently, was to demonstrate how Kissinger's policies are shaped by the overriding fact that he is a "faggot." Or at least by the fact that he has "the personality of a faggot," as LaRouche later testified when he realized that he'd have a hard time certifying his claims about Kissinger's sexual orientation.

Kissinger signed his letter to Webster with "warm regards," but to LaRouche this was hot stuff. Kissinger's letter, he believes, started the FBI on its "get LaRouche" campaign of spying and persecution that eventually led to his incarceration.

The creepy thing is, he's right.

At least it looks that way. Just a few months later, Webster asked one of his underlings to figure out how the FBI could start a probe of LaRouche, "under the guidelines or otherwise."

One of his many problems, LaRouche says, is that he opposed the administration's Nicaraguan contra war. "We opposed it because it stank, not for any other reason. I said, 'What do you want to do, start a war with the Jesuit order? You idiots!' "

Not that LaRouche had any sympathy for the Sandinistas or Catholic Liberation Theology under which "the Soviets came in very happily and merrily." He felt that politically there were better ways to handle the problem than the contra operation. As he put it, in a flash of common sense, "You don't just go in there and start shooting up Jesuits."

How LaRouche's reasoning runs from the Jesuits to Oliver North to Henry Kissinger is not simple. North was a "throwaway" for CIA director William Casey, who was "covering for somebody." That "somebody" may have been Reagan. Not Ronnie (as the chummy LaRouche likes to call him). Nancy. She was supposedly "under the very strong influence of the circles of Armand Hammer. . . . She's an idiot," LaRouche offers, genteel as always. "This is one of the problems I ran into. The president is pussy whipped."

Hammer, the pro-Soviet industrialist, provides the necessary link to the New Dark Ages ideology of which Soviet foreign policy is an embodiment. Kissinger, as an agent of Chatham House, comes from the same "irrationalist" skein.

Unlike the John Birchers, who view Kissinger as a traitor and commie mole but no more than that, LaRouche sees Kissinger as his nemesis in a most personal sense. Kissinger was "coordinating most of the dirty operations run against me internationally," since the spring of 1975, when LaRouche, who dabbles in the foreign policy game himself, began stepping on Kissinger's diplomatic toes.

To hear LaRouche tell it: "The indicated prompting of this is that I made a trip to Bagdhad and from Bagdhad back to Germany in April of 1975. What I launched at that point were two projects. One, to attempt to set up a new approach to Israeli-Palestinian relations, to secure a negotiated peace based on something like that which has been called the Middle East Marshall Plan. Shimon Peres

and others in Israel were interested in that. Some Arabs were interested, particularly some of the so-called moderate PLO people. We thought we had something going and Kissinger didn't like that.

"At the same time I had proposed that as part of doing business in the Middle East, this was the time to make a general monetary reform, to go back to a gold-reserve basis rather than a floating exchange rate system, which was in effect at that time. So Kissinger from that period was on my tail. So at that point I began to take notice of Kissinger. I took notice of him as a person who was personally committed to being my adversary."

LaRouche also claims to have angered Kissinger by investigating the real reasons behind Israel's 1982 invasion of Lebanon. LaRouche assumes it was Reagan's secretary of state Alexander Haig who gave the Israelis the go-ahead, and because Haig is a Kissinger protégé, "we assumed this had to be a Kissinger scenario that was used."

So LaRouche and his crew of civilian spies set out on what he calls "a journalistic sort of investigation." As usual, they came back with bedazzling results.

"What we caught them at was a land scam operation. We got Henry Kissinger Associates and Henry personally deeply involved in this. What they were doing was using thuggery to induce Palestinians to give up their land at bargain prices on the West Bank. Then [Ariel] Sharon over at the [Israeli] defense ministry was certifying this land as Israeli defense territory. . . . It was the most profitable real-estate swindle in the world. I said, 'Look, we've got to turn this stuff over to our friends at the National Security Council. It's a matter of national security.' But Henry found out about this and became furious."

One supposes that even Henry Kissinger at his wiliest would have a tough time driving up property values on the West Bank— the view's not bad, but the neighborhood's a little shabby. Oddly enough, LaRouche's "discovery," that Kissinger induced the invasion of Lebanon to make a quick killing off rigged real estate, is one of his more mundane postulates.

On the wilder side, there's his assertion that the Grateful Dead, rather than simply an aging, boring rock band, is actually "a British

Intelligence operation." The British, it seems, have been using sex and drugs and rock 'n' roll to pave the way for a postnuclear population.

"That was an Allen Dulles–period operation which was run, together with the Occult Bureau types in British Intelligence, such as Aldous Huxley," he calmly explains. "This is part of this satanism business. Call it the counterculture. Call it the Dionysius model of the counterculture. Rock is essentially a revival of the ancient Dionysic, Bacchic ritual. It does have a relationship to the alpha rhythms of the brain. If combined with a little alcohol and more, shall we say, mood-shaping substances, with youth, with funny sex, this does produce a personality change of a countercultural type."

"This satanism business" has become LaRouche's latest pet peeve. He alleges that the canon of New York's Episcopal archdiocese "was a regular visitor of a notorious Manhattan homosexual and satanic cult-practicing club called the Mineshaft. Here (the canon) had his own room where little boys were shamelessly abused."

In the preceding brief passage are three of LaRouche's more noxious themes: Anglophobia (the Episcopal church, the U.S. version of the Church of England), satanism, and homosexuality, with special attention paid to pederasty. It was shouted accusations that "your husband sleeps with little boys" that once prompted Nancy Kissinger to throw a right to the jaw of a vociferous LaRouche follower in Newark Airport back in 1982. That incident prompted Kissinger to worry about LaRouche's people becoming "increasingly obnoxious."

A fixation on sexuality, or, perhaps more correct to say, a revulsion at sexuality, was once one of LaRouche's main themes. For public consumption at least, he has toned it down as of late, but his charge that Kissinger is a "faggot" is hardly atypical. He's branded entire movements, the Puerto Rican nationalists, for example, as "sexually impotent." Reportedly, masturbation is in violation of LaRouchian tenets and can get a follower kicked out of the group. He has also insisted on sanctioning all relationships into which his followers enter, and "unauthorized" liaisons have been dealt with cruelly.

Sex, drugs, Dionysian revelry—anything that can be broadly defined as "countercultural"—is to LaRouche not a natural rebellion of youth, not an expression of real alienation, but a deliberately planned attack on modernity (i.e., morality) by forces who want to create a malleable populace, ready to follow orders once the structure of rational-technological society has been obliterated.

"Another word for it: New Age," he says. "The longer term: Age of Aquarius. People were experimenting with various utopian models, constructing small groups experimentally which were considered New Age types. How to create experimental types that might survive the aftermath of a general nuclear war."

"Conspiracy essentially means either a common purpose, a common philosophical and practical purpose, or a set of common and conflicting purposes which cause people to work together for common ends as well as conflicting ones," explains Lyndon LaRouche. "And conspiracy is a general term which can mean a great number of things. One can't say, 'There is a conspiracy.' One has to say, 'What do you mean by a conspiracy? What kind?' "

As LaRouche battles empiricists, British imperialists, and spaced-out touchy-feely types united by the common purpose of creating a primitive, hedonistic neo-Roman Empire, he has done well in forming his own allegiances with people in high places.

For that reason, and others, he is often the subject of speculation by other conspiracy researchers, who are given to mistrusting one another, who wonder if LaRouche himself is an agent of something . . . larger.

"He was in army intelligence," says conspiracy researcher John Judge whom we'll meet in chapter seven. "I've thought that for many years from the earliest stuff he did. I also felt he was put up by the Rockefellers, because you know some of the Rockefellers are Navy intelligence."

LaRouche has met with heads of state in Mexico and India (he somehow worked his way in to hold talks with Indira Gandhi) and has sold himself in Latin America as a respectable advocate of debt relief—something Latin American leaders are only too happy to hear. While he was on the outs with Jimmy Carter, a president who

was the consensus selection of the Trilateral Commission (he is said to have once mulled over the possibility of assassinating Carter), LaRouche was received kindly by the Reagan administration. At least in the beginning.

There was a taint of double-cross to the Reagan administration's prosecution of LaRouche. LaRouche and his supporters met often with important officials in the Reagan administration and the CIA. He was even admitted to the CIA's sanctified Langley, Virginia, headquarters on at least one occasion.

Confronted with the administration's frequent contacts with LaRouche, the president's press secretary Larry Speakes allowed only that the administration would meet with "any American citizen" who could provide "helpful" information. The ability of LaRouche's private intelligence operation to come up with a helpful hint here and there is hard to deny.

LaRouche also helped to get Reagan elected. He popularized George Bush's Trilateral Commission membership and "blue blood" pedigree, which devastated then–front-running Bush in the 1980 New Hampshire primary. The LaRouchians embrace attack politics like a holy crusade. Their eagerness to smear Bush let Reagan reap its benefits without soiling his hands.

LaRouche claims to have been "very much involved with the National Security Council" in 1982, developing his "beam weapon" proposal. Whether his influence was as profound as he wants the world to believe, who knows? What does seem certain is that the Reaganites saw something they liked in LaRouche. He met with several high-level NSC aides, and even had one over for dinner at his mansion in Leesburg, Virginia. Even in the days before Reagan, LaRouche used his friend Mitch WerBell to cultivate a network of contacts in the CIA.

LaRouche's own followers were a formidable intelligence gathering force. They spent endless hours on the phone, displaying the kind of perseverance that the hungriest cub reporter only dreams about. Throwing in healthy doses of deception (sometimes posing as journalists from more respectable news organizations), their untiring labor paid off in interviews with a wide range of policy makers. But they had the mentality of spies, not conventional journalists who never try to break the parameters of credibility.

With information gleaned from their telephone conversations, they are often able to come up with intelligence data even professionals find quite useful.

Supreme Court justice David Souter, when he was attorney general of New Hampshire, used information passed to him by LaRouche's private spies to help cripple the Clamshell Alliance, an antinuclear group fighting to stop construction of the Seabrook nuclear power plant. New Hampshire's state police recommended the LaRouche agents to Souter as "very well-informed gentlemen." Philadelphia mayor Frank Rizzo found the LaRouchies useful as he prepared for "terrorists" to attack bicentennial celebrations back in 1976.

There is no doubt that LaRouche's effort to construct a counterconspiracy is the reason he now serves what amounts to a life sentence in federal prison.

He was convicted after his second trial, in Alexandria, Virginia. The judge in that trial would not allow LaRouche's lawyers to use government sabotage as his defense. That issue is what made the Boston mistrial an epic.

I'm in no position to pass judgment on LaRouche's guilt or innocence on the charges of credit fraud and tax evasion. His jurors, I would say, are. When his four-month Boston trial on those charges ended with the judge calling the whole thing off, the jury decided they had to settle things in their own minds, and they took a straw poll. Unanimously, they agreed that there was "too much question of government misconduct," and that government plants "may have been involved in some of this fraud to discredit [LaRouche]."

Their verdict was completely unofficial, of course. But they found Lyndon LaRouche not guilty.

# 4

# UFOs in the Garden
# of Eden

*As flies to wanton boys are we to the gods;*
*They kill us for their sport.*

WILLIAM SHAKESPEARE
*King Lear*, Act Four, Scene One

William Bramley's law office is an uncharismatic cubicle in a cozy complex tucked away on the outskirts of San Jose, California. A desk, a couple of chairs, blank white walls, and a window are all the amenities his modest practice requires, along with the portable computer and copy machine he keeps at home where he would much rather work.

Bramley keeps his office as understated as his ambitions. Driven not by the desire to pull down six figures as a partner in some heavy-hitting urban firm, the thirty-six-year-old Bramley, who has lived in and around San Jose since he was a teenager, dreams instead of salting away just enough to buy a plot of land along the Oregon coast and move to quieter climes.

Even his demeanor seems too temperate for the contentious civil courtrooms where he makes his living. With a calm voice and light blue eyes that don't always rise to meet yours, Bramley is ill fitted to the mold of a big-city attorney. As unlikely as he is a model for "L.A. Law," William Bramley is even less suited for the role he assumed early in 1990: prelate to an American underground of UFO believers.

"I guess I've become kind of the historian of the movement,"

drawls a bemused Bramley. His unfamiliar cult status leaves him unimpressed, and a little uneasy. In fact, "William Bramley" isn't even his real name. Rather, it's a *nom de plume* the lawyer assumed for the book that has conferred upon him his newfound renown, a fat volume he published himself and embossed with the grandiose title *The Gods of Eden*.

He doesn't want his secret identity revealed because he worries that judges, on whose whim his success in the legal profession depends, would take him less than seriously if they knew he had spent seven years devising an all-encompassing conspiracy theory in which the masterminds of the plot are . . .

Well, let's put it this way: One of the reasons the book has become so popular among hard-nosed UFOlogists is that *Gods of Eden* is not another slavish paean to the great saucer faith. There is only one chapter in Bramley's book—the first—that addresses the question of whether UFOs are real. The book contains but a single example of those familiar could-be-anything photos purporting to depict a flying saucer.

Most of the illustrations chosen by Bramley are plates lifted from an old edition of Milton's *Paradise Lost*.

Bramley's 535-page tome, which includes a fifteen-page bibliography, is not another cumbersome catalogue of close encounters, an awestruck account of alien abduction or a New Agey prophecy of messianic star children come to save us from ourselves. Instead, this camera-shy attorney has formulated a unified field theory of human history, tying virtually every turn of events since the garden of his book's title to an unseen oligarchy of UFO overlords Bramley identifies only as "The Custodians."

Here is his thesis: "Human beings appear to be a slave race breeding on an isolated planet in a small galaxy. As such, the human race was once a source of labor for an extraterrestrial civilization and still remains a possession today. To keep control over its possession and to maintain Earth as something of a prison, that other civilization has bred a never-ending conflict between human beings, has promoted spiritual decay, and has erected on Earth conditions of unremitting physical hardship."

Pretty potent stuff, for a torts lawyer. Bramley is acutely aware that, as he says in his book, he is "wide open to ridicule for

expressing such a hypothesis." Hence, he keeps his real name under wraps. He takes pains to maintain a decidedly nonwacky tone in his prose, has never seen a UFO, and protests that he was never a UFO true believer nor particularly fascinated by conspiracy theories. When he started working on the book, he insists, UFOs were not even on his outline.

The question, then, is how a levelheaded member of the bar like Bramley can devise such a bleak, belief-defying theory. But first, it is necessary to digress. We need to discuss the whole question of UFOs. Most conspiracy theories have their basis, at least, in something undeniably real: assassinations, big banks, intelligence agencies, or whatever. With UFO theories, the footing is not so firm. Are they real? Are they a massive hoax? A delusion? If real, what are they? Spaceships from another world? Projections of the collective unconscious? Sinister and supersecret government experiments?

Whatever they are, or aren't, UFOs always lead into the idea of conspiracy. While there are many serious students of, say, CIA malfeasance, who are not conspiracy theorists, anyone who approaches the UFO "problem" finds a conspiracy of some sort. But that is only one reason why this book, which is about exploring territory where the possible melts into the unthinkable, contains a chapter about a topic that many serious observers and scientists find utterly unbelievable.

Another, more important reason is the simple lesson UFO theories can teach us: What we know about the reality we have to deal with every day is nothing compared to what we don't know. And to what we can never know.

More than most conspiracy theories, UFOs are an intellectually treacherous subject. Credibility is precious currency, and it is quickly spent when UFOs are the topic of discussion. There are many things about the world we just don't understand completely yet; that should be an innocuous and self-evident statement. But even suggest that the UFO phenomenon may be one of those things, and suddenly you'll find yourself the target of suspicious glances and skeptical innuendo. Are you one of those believers,

they wonder? One of those nuts? This despite the fact that a majority of the American people believe that extraterrestrial spacecraft actually visit li'l ol' planet Earth. Like truth, credibility is not a democracy.

With my own somewhat tenuous credibility at stake for including a chapter on UFO conspiracies in a book whose subject already tiptoes on the fringe, I want to answer here the same question I get—and anyone else gets—when trying to talk about the topic with the slightest hint of seriousness. "Do you believe in UFOs?"

If I could, I'd strike the word "believe" from the English language. Since what we understand about the empirical world is based on probability and supposition, not certainty, "belief" is a faulty state of mind, except when dealing with the obvious.

To the question "Do you believe in UFOs?" the answer, therefore, has to be yes. Obviously, there are flying objects that go unidentified. That, of course, is not what the question really means. When people ask, "Do you believe in UFOs?" what they're really asking is "Do you believe that space creatures patrol the planet in flying saucers?"

That's an empirical question. So my answer has to be no, I don't believe in UFOs, but I don't completely disbelieve in them either. I find it highly unlikely that spacemen from another planet have traveled to Earth. There are too many factors against it, not least of which are the laws of physics. On the other hand, even though the vast majority of UFO encounters appear explainable, a few are not. Can I say for sure that these few are not actual brushes with visitors from another world? No, I can't. I'm pretty confident that they are not, but I can't be *certain*. To be certain is to be dishonest.

What I do know is that there are thousands, millions of people convinced that UFOs are space aliens. Why? Any supposition we make about the physical world comes from our experience. We are convinced gravity exists because things fall. We stick to the ground. *Ergo*, gravity is real.

We all experience gravity. Not as many of us have experienced UFO contact (I never have, in case you were wondering). People who are convinced that UFOs are real have been convinced by experience. Discounting out-and-out hoaxes (of which there are

undoubtedly plenty), the question becomes: *what* have these people experienced?

Attempts at objective investigations of UFO sightings, abductions, crashes, and so on have gone nowhere over the years. The physical evidence is usually ambiguous, pseudoscientific, or subsumed by the politics of this touchy topic. Yet we're still left with these "contactees" and their experience.

John Keel, mentor to many a UFO theoretician, posed the apt question in his book *UFOs: Operation Trojan Horse:* "How do you investigate something that doesn't exist?"

"The answer," Keel continued, "is that you investigate and study the people who have experienced these things. You don't investigate them by checking their reliability. You study the medical and psychological effects of their experiences."

Essentially, that was William Bramley's approach. Not to investigate contemporary cases, but historical ones. Tracing the written record back to Mesopotamia and Sumeria, Bramley noted what people throughout history actually said about celestial phenomena, how they actually reacted to lights in the sky and "gods" flying down from heaven.

Bramley did not begin by looking for UFOs. He started with a single question, one that could be answered any number of ways, and finished with his Grand Theory. He got from the first point to the rather distant second much the same way many conspiracy researchers come to their unorthodox conclusions.

Clichés to the contrary, most conspiracy theories are born not of "paranoia" but from a kind of hopeful curiosity. Conspiracy theorists usually get started by trying to understand the inequities and horrors that have fogged the human spectacle for all of recorded time. Why are things this way, they wonder, and must they be this way?

"I got interested in the problem of war," says the matter-of-fact Bramley. As an undergraduate in the early 1970s, he majored in sociology at the University of California, Santa Barbara. He says he was "always what you'd call liberal," but never highly active politi-

cally, especially by the standards of that era. A decade after he graduated, whiling away his time wondering where his life was headed (he hadn't got his law degree by then), he succumbed to perpetual student syndrome and embarked on a book project that would be an extension of his collegiate focus.

"My idea was to kind of go through history and see where you have people profiting and benefiting from war who were not directly involved in it. Just do a sociological study of that problem and maybe offer a solution to resolving it—some way to take the profit out of it."

Applying the intellect of a future lawyer, Bramley figured that all wars must have some motive. There had to be something in it for someone. He quickly shot down his own preliminary hypothesis, however. He came across numerous wars in history that appeared to be motivated by no tangible objectives.

"I started getting into these bizarre things where there didn't seem to be anything more than ideology," Bramley says. "You look for the profit and you look for the political advantage, and it's just not there. That's when you start to get into religion. So you ask, 'Where did these religions start?'

"I started looking into how these religions all seem to have a common nexus: secret societies," Bramley explains. "That's when things started getting a little off the track."

Secret societies: that inescapable theme. Bramley's "Gods of Eden" theory is a twist on the legend that secret societies have been the guiding force behind human history. There is, as Bramley notes, a religious component to secret societies and, therefore, to secret-society conspiracy theories. But even "secular" conspiracy theorists, who focus on such tangible (by comparison) entities as the U.S. intelligence community, attribute the qualities of a secret society to the CIA and like bodies.

Bramley turned up numerous historical personages linked to or belonging to secret societies. Freemasonry has been a preoccupation of more than a few American presidents: George Washington, Harry Truman, Theodore Roosevelt, Ronald Reagan, and others. Other politicians, too. Jesse Jackson, of all people, is a Masonic inductee.

While it's an axiom of conspiratoriology that secret societies of

one form or another are at the core of the story-behind-the-story, there's no agreement on who's behind the secret societies. Bramley's conjecture is that secret societies originated as a prehistoric cult of snake worshippers dedicated to freeing humanity from the snare of the brutal "Custodians." Defeated in this effort, the "Brotherhood of the Snake" was then infiltrated by Custodial agents, and turned against mankind. It survives today, in its diverse incarnations, as the secret societies that allegedly manipulate human events.

Bramley's theories of snake-worshipping cults and their relationship to secret societies are factual enough. The snake is one of the oldest religious symbols known to man. Hidden in the Bible is the surprising detail that Moses founded a snake-worshipping cult, and that a sect of Jews made sacrifices to the snake for several hundred years. As pagan symbols always are, the snake was redefined as a symbol of evil by modern religions. To continue their religion, snake cultists formed secret societies to dodge persecution. One of the few places the snake symbol survives with its original meaning, that of a healer, is on the emblem of the American Medical Association.

But we're getting ahead of ourselves again. Even when he hit on the secret society thesis, Bramley still had not uncovered the UFO connection that, unbeknownst to him, he was being drawn inexorably toward.

He hadn't been quite ready for his secret society revelation, so it was with a bit of trepidation that he pushed on through library stacks in search of details to flesh out this esoteric topic. All the secret societies—Masons, Rosicrucians, Persian and Asian sects, ancient mystery cults, pagans, snake worshippers—as different as they appeared on the surface, the more his intellectual adventure steamed ahead, the more Bramley found that the societies shared common beliefs and motifs.

The "All-Seeing Eye" was one frequently recurring symbol. It now peers from the back of every U.S. dollar bill, as well as, oddly enough, from the emblem of the Marxist government of Ethiopia. Bramley found that, as all conspiracy mongers are aware, the eye is a sacred symbol in Freemasonry. But it goes back even further. It represented God's eye in early Christianity and the "Eye of Horus"

in ancient Egyptian religion. The eye even appeared on early versions of the Confederate flag before the U.S. Civil War. Where was the link?

"Eventually you run into these things—people they call the gods," Bramley says. He traced mythology back to Sumerian tablets, then found that the same stories dated into prehistory. The characters in various stories had different names, but were disconcertingly similar.

"There were very human gods who used to fly around in the air," Bramley says. "Then, somewhere along the line, I read something about the ancient astronauts theory. Here were people who were speculating those gods were members of an extraterrestrial society."

When an amateur researcher finds himself whisked away by the chariots of the Gods, that aged icon, credibility, begins to become a problem. "This is where I just ended my research," Bramley says. "I didn't want to get into it."


Bramley was not the first to conflate ancient mythology with modern UFOlogy. As Keel notes, "Many leading UFOlogists suspect that innumerable historical incidents branded as religious phenomena may actually be misunderstood UFO activity."

The Bible is the source of several such incidents. Ezekiel's "wheel," which according to the scriptural account dispatched four odd-looking creatures upon its descent from the sky, is most often cited, but there are quite a few others.

The "pillar of fire" that guided the Israelites out of Egypt is another bizarre celestial phenomena recounted in the Bible. Elijah, another major prophet, was watched over by guardian angels in the form of flying fireballs and was finally carried away in a "chariot of fire." Could the brimstone barrage that flattened Sodom and Gomorrah have been a nuclear device from an alien spacecraft? And just what was that "burning bush" that held such detailed conversations with Moses, anyway?

No less an authority than Carl Sagan, who is one of the most dogmatic and—for some unknown reason—respected UFO debunkers, once called for an historical investigation of ancient myths

to see if they yielded clues to early contact with extraterrestrial visitors.

These close encounters of the allegorical kind are not exclusive to the Bible. Almost every culture features religious myths involving strange creatures, gods, and chariots from the sky. There are innumerable explanations for the frequency of such stories. Fertile human imagination is certainly one. Take them at face value, however, and they are what they are: UFO reports.

While what we think of today as the UFO phenomenon began in 1947, the historical record of unusual heavenly happenings runs uninterrupted. Joseph Smith, founder of the Mormon church, received his life's mission in a visit from a heavenly messenger. The Book of Mormon is supposedly a translation of writings Smith found on a set of mysterious tablets he unearthed at a location given to him by this visitor. Also in the nineteenth century, coincidentally (or maybe not), there were a series of unexplained "airships" sighted over parts of the United States.

Charles Fort, the brilliant turn-of-the-century writer who invented the category of "unexplained phenomena," catalogued a handful of nineteenth-century "lights in the sky" incidents, which read exactly like more recent UFO sightings, even though Fort was writing over thirty years before the term "UFO" was concocted.

Fort's wonderful books dealt with the unexplained phenomena of nature—events that science refused to explain, because they did not fit. Fort didn't try to explain them, or debunk them. All belief systems exclude something, he thought. Strange phenomena were proof to Fort that there is a deeper reality that science has excluded.

Fort was an inspiration to Keel, who founded the New York "Fortean Society." Bramley, on the other hand, didn't discover Fort until he was into the third draft of *Gods of Eden*, and when I met him he hadn't even heard of John Keel. His journey to the heart of the conspiracy was a solo flight.


Bramley stopped his spare-time quest when he found no escape from the "ancient astronauts" theory. He came across so many of these historical UFO tales that he figured going on would only get him into trouble. After a hiatus from his project, Bramley began to

squirm with curiosity. "I finally confronted it and said, 'That's strange, but that's what it seems to be.'"

Having traced the origins of secret societies back to age-old tales of aerobatic humanoid gods, Bramley decided to work forward again. He wanted to see if he could track the secret society network, the "Brotherhood of the Snake," from ancient times to the present, correlating its beliefs and activities with historical UFO stories. "And I was just stunned," Bramley says. "Because I could."

To do Bramley's book-length argument justice in a short summary is not possible. A selected example will have to suffice, even though the one I'm going to choose is one Bramley is sensitive about. His theories on the Black Death of the Middle Ages have been a popular topic of discussion on radio programs that have featured him as a guest. Bramley doesn't like to see them taken out of context.

"Anybody who has read the book, by the time they get to the chapter on the Black Death, they've understood all that stuff beforehand and they could see how I could arrive at that conclusion. But if you just launch into that with somebody who's not exposed to the earlier stuff, it becomes totally unreal to them," Bramley warns.

With that caveat—and with the hope that anyone reading *this* book already expects unreal conclusions—here is Bramley's theory on the Black Death, the plague that wiped out a sizable slice of the European population in the thirteenth and fourteenth centuries.

The generally accepted explanation is that the plague was spread by rats in the unimaginably unhygienic conditions of the times. Bramley's research contradicts the "rodent theory." A "minority of cases seem to be related to the presence of vermin," he found. Far more common, his research revealed, were reports of odoriferous "mists" preceding outbreaks of the disease. Also coinciding with certain outbreaks, Bramley discovered, were—lo and behold— reports of strange lights in the sky.

The foreboding aerial anomalies were described in contemporary writings as "meteors" or "comets." Bramley points out that back then anything moving across the sky not identifiable as a bird or the sun was called a "comet."

These "comets" left deadly trails that killed trees and vegetation as well as people. Bramley connects these accounts with Mesopotamian writings that mention flying "gods" who scorched the landscape, and quotes numerous historical passages describing "mists" and "fogs" that were blamed for outbreaks of disease going back to ancient Greece, where Hippocrates himself advocated communal bonfires as a method of clearing the air of the noxious clouds.

Other historical sources uncovered by the scholarly barrister from San Jose indicate that the mists were exuded by mysterious "demons" who strolled into villages clad in black, wielding instruments usually referred to as "scythes." The scythes, Bramley speculates, may actually have been some sort of spraying device that spewed toxins.

The "Grim Reaper" caricature derives from those descriptions. Seasoned UFO aficionados will recognize the archetype of the "Men in Black," those macabre agents whose alleged appearance often coincides with saucer sightings.

From those accounts, Bramley surmised that the plague was the result of something other than poor medieval municipal sanitation services. It was a deliberate act of biological warfare perpetrated by the Custodians. The ranchers, for some reason known only to themselves, were reducing the herd.

That's the best example I could find of how Bramley links historical events to the postulated airborne superrace. The plague episode is exemplary of his thesis that, as Charles Fort put it, "we are property." Bramley spent nearly a decade of his life devising this thesis and accruing evidence to support it. Then came decision time.

"I had to decide whether I wanted to publish all of this," Bramley laughs. "I mean, it could be embarrassing to be associated with ideas like that!"

For others, it could be more than embarrassing. I interviewed a pilot who claimed to have been employed by "a number of government agencies" in Southeast Asia. In his contact with various friends in the military and intelligence communities, he became aware that the U.S. government has already made contact with an

extraterrestrial race, and that there were over one hundred people at a saucer landing on a U.S. Air Force base outside of London, England, in 1980.

He wondered, "If this stuff is going on, why don't I know more about it?" He "called in a few favors" from his shadowy buddies, and pieced together a story of massive government cover-ups and "programming of the population for the last forty years." After he dared to give a few public lectures on the topic, he was called in by his employer—he was then a cargo pilot—and asked, "Do you really believe this stuff?" He said that he did. He was fired.

I haven't given this particular fellow's name because he has a new job with a different company, and I have no desire to cost him that one, too. Suffice to say that he bears one of the best-known names in aviation. In any case, he is but one advocate of the widespread "government cover-up" UFO conspiracy theory.

It is true that the U.S. government took a strong interest in the UFO phenomenon. The now famous Air Force "Project Blue Book" compiled a thick compendium of UFO incidents. An eyebrow-cocking footnote to Project Blue Book: Despite its astonishing thoroughness, nowhere does it mention the "Roswell incident," the first and most exhaustively researched "saucer crash." Not surprisingly, there has never been definitive verification that a spacecraft, or any craft, crashed as alleged near Roswell, New Mexico, on July 2, 1947. But something weird did happen there, and the military at the time took more than a passing interest. The case still gets occasional publicity. Yet the Blue Book files are silent about it.

Government agencies have aroused ominous suspicions, perhaps rightly so, by going out of their way to discredit UFO reports. In 1954, the CIA set up the "Robertson Panel," named for its chairman, Dr. H. P. Robertson. The committee was at least a spiritual ancestor to the Warren Commission, as by all accounts it had reached its conclusions in advance.

Somewhat more candid than its Kennedy assassination counterpart, the Robertson Panel openly advocated a policy of "debunking" the UFO phenomenon with the stated aim of reducing public "susceptibility to hostile propaganda." The panel's frankness may or may not have something to do with the fact that, unlike the

Warren Commission, which thrust its report with authority into the public forum, the Robertson Panel's full findings were secret for twenty-five years.

One of the most thoughtful and credible (there's that word again) UFO researchers, French astronomer Jacques Vallee, believes that the government may have good reason to obscure the truth behind UFOs. Like John Keel, Vallee sees little evidence to convince him that UFOs are probes from another planet. His scenario is even more frightening than the dark theories of malevolent extraterrestrial superbeings propounded by the reclusive William Bramley.

"UFOs are real," Vallee wrote in his 1979 manifesto, *Messengers of Deception*. "They are an application of psychotronic technology; that is, they are physical devices used to affect human consciousness."

Vallee takes Keel's advice and delves into the psychology of UFO contactees, and the cults they form and that form around them. The contactees are victims, he proffers, used by some controlling power to effect deep social changes in human society.

It is true that there are totalitarian overtones, and sometimes more than overtones, to the beliefs of many contactees. What's even more sinister, some of the early contactees, particularly the founders of a movement called "I AM" in the 1930s, were open fascists and anti-Semites who draped proto-Hitlerian "Jewish conspiracy" ideology in an extraterrestrial cloak. "I AM" was a forerunner to the more recently fashionable "New Age."

William Bramley doesn't fit in there anywhere. I've been cautioned to "be careful" when dealing with these suspiciously nazified UFO ideas, but to me what is remarkable about William Bramley is that he is the opposite of a zealot, ideologue, or zombie-faced cultist. His politics are, if anything, mainstream progressive. When last I spoke to him, he doubted that he would bother to write a follow-up to *Gods of Eden*, so casual is his commitment to the UFO cause. His desire for personal secrecy is a discretion to shield his "real life," not the clandestine tactic of a cryptototalitarian.

Bramley is interesting precisely because he is so boring. His is a normal intellect that came into contact with abnormal aspects of reality few people have the energy or courage to confront. When we do confront them, the world becomes, to borrow the title of a John

Keel book, a "Disneyland of the Gods." Given how little human beings comprehend of what's really going on out there, anything, to the adventurous mind, can seem possible. The danger is not in trying to know more, no matter how wild the attempt, but in the conviction that knowledge is all but complete, with only details left to fill in. What we know is insignificant, and there is a human hunger for answers. A healthy hunger.

If a logical, meticulous trial lawyer like the pseudononymous William Bramley can reach such an outrageous conclusion after seven years of research, it proves not that he's crazy or a fascist, but that the limits of our understanding are exceeded only by the boundaries of curiosity.

# 5

# THE INVISIBLE GOVERNMENT

*Can you look in the mirror, or into the faces
of your children or grandchildren, and say
that you were too busy to become involved? Are you not willing to give your
time and money when our Founding Fathers pledged their lives, their fortunes and
their sacred honor to oppose the New
World Order?*

GARY ALLEN
*Say "No" to the
New World Order*

**M**uch has changed for the John Birch Society since 1960, when it
was the nation's most fearsome regiment of right-wing militants.
They worked to impeach Earl Warren. They called Eisenhower a
dirty Red. They staged a campaign to repeal the income tax. No
more. By the late 1980s, the Birch Society was something closer to a
preservation society of parochialism in an America long since mutated into a cultural black widow's web.

"There's hope that we can turn this thing around," says Jack
McManus, the Birch Society's spokesman since 1973 (and a member since 1964). "We can accomplish the goals of saving our country and saving the constitutional republic our founding fathers gave
us. And one of the reasons for hope is the fact that it is a conspiracy."

"**I**'ve been looking for a way to build and sell a house in a biblical way, without having to charge interest," mused the man behind the counter at the John Birch Society bookstore. He was a chunky fellow in a flannel shirt and a smile that said "Southern hospitality," even though he was in northern California. He held six paper dollars in his hand, fanning them like playing cards. They were the receipts from his one sale of the day, and he had nowhere to put them. No cash register, no counter, no change, except for a box of coins. It's a bright and clean little shop, uncontaminated by customers. "When you look at it, really, in this country, with all the interest we have to pay, we're all slaves," he said.

The gray-haired lady who'd stopped by to chat, looking like she'd come straight from telling Tom Sawyer to whitewash the picket fence, grabbed the six paper dollars in his hand and ruffled them disdainfully.

"*This* is credit," she warned. "See here where it says, 'Federal Reserve Note.' If they want to do away with credit, they'll have to do away with *that*."

The "American Opinion" bookstores, though not actually operated by the society, are the only outlets devoted exclusively to Birch-sanctioned literature. So ready are they to spread the word, that a good chunk of their stock lists an asking price of "free." The four hundred American Opinion stores across America will still take your six bucks for a crisp new copy of *The Blue Book of the John Birch Society*, now in its twenty-third printing. They sell flags, too, and that brings in a little more of that paper money.

The folks who work in the shops—it just seems right to call them "shops" and "folks"—often work there for free. They're usually downright friendly. Their compensation is conversation, even in little bits. A tad here about Citibank forcing South Dakota to repeal its usury laws so it can set up a national credit card business. A morsel there about getting the truth out to the young generation, because they're the ones who need it most.

If not a conspiracy, the evils Birchers see perpetrated against our national heritage would be unstoppable forces of history. The

America of John Birch and Robert Welch would be left pathetically in the dusty past.

Robert Henry Winborne Welch, Jr., Massachusetts candy and jelly magnate, was the founder and self-proclaimed "dictatorial boss" of the John Birch Society. John Morrison Birch, military intelligence officer, never knew of the society's existence. He was killed in 1945, at age twenty-seven, by Chinese Communists while on a spying mission in North China.

Welch, who died in January of 1985 at the age of eighty-five, was born in North Carolina. He claimed a lineage of farmers and Baptist preachers going back to 1720. He moved to Boston in 1919, after an eight-year education at the University of North Carolina, the U.S. Naval Academy, and Harvard Law School. He never received his law degree. He went into business and became one of the country's largest candy makers. Throughout his career, politics, not sucrose, was his passion.

Welch had long been fascinated by Birch, authoring a biography of the fundamentalist Baptist missionary turned anti-Communist spy, four years before founding the society. Welch never knew Birch, but for his original society "Council" Welch selected Lt. Gen. Charles B. Stone, III, Birch's military unit commander. Welch decided that Birch was not merely a spy killed on an espionage mission in hostile territory. He was the first American soldier to die in World War III, the struggle against world communism. If there was ever any doubt that Birch would have agreed, his parents gave the society their public support.

The John Birch Society began when Welch invited eleven well-to-do, conservative industrialists to a meeting in Indianapolis, on December 8, 1958. There, he harangued them for two days with the "incontrovertible and deadly" truth that had been cooking in his fudge maker's brain for years. On the first day, he outlined the aims of "the Communist conspiracy." On the second day, he detailed his plans for a new organization dedicated to battling the alleged conspiracy in the United States political arena. Curiously, Welch acknowledged that this plan involved using the same techniques used by the Communist conspirators themselves: letter-writing campaigns, propaganda publications, and front organizations.

These speeches were published as the *Blue Book*, often called

Welch's *Mein Kampf,* which quickly became required reading for all Birch initiates. But it was an unpublished book, which, when the media discovered it, made Welch one of the country's most visible and controversial figures. That book was called *The Politician,* and it, too, is sometimes called Welch's *Mein Kampf.* (Likening Welch to Hitler was not uncommon in those days, and though he, like all Birchers, considered such rhetoric yet another element of the Communist smear campaign against him, his own statements about the Birch Society being a "monolithic organization" under "complete authoritative control," with Robert Welch as the authority, invited the comparison.)

*The Politician* was the book in which Welch made his instantly notorious allegations that President Dwight D. Eisenhower was a Communist agent, saying he had been "planted in (the presidency) by the Communists." He also called General George Catlett Marshall (he of the famous Plan), "a conscious, deliberate, dedicated agent of the Soviet conspiracy." He doled out likewise vituperation to numerous other political figures.

Even Barry Goldwater, a friend and admirer of Welch, advised Welch to "burn" the privately circulated manuscript, but Welch didn't listen and his unfinished book, which he claimed had nothing to do with the John Birch Society, turned this frumpy, bald little businessman into a national celebrity.

Celebrity was nothing Welch craved. He conceived of the John Birch Society as, if not a secret society, then at least one shy of media scrutiny. It took two years before any national media even noticed the society's existence. Welch himself has been described as a painfully shy man with absolutely no gift for public speaking, an odd trait in light of the hundreds of speeches he gave in his career as Bircher in chief.

His talks were nothing more than readings from his pamphlets and books. He'd drone on for up to three hours, convinced that his message was so important that listeners would endure any hardship to hear it. He once lectured to a group of businessmen in Florida in an enclosed lecture hall, forbidding, for some reason, any windows to be opened. He was dreadfully doctrinaire, refusing to answer questions from the audience when he found the questions too pointed.

Welch was a cantankerous sort, given to complaining about his bad accommodations when traveling and his incompetent underlings back at the office, but he could be oblivious to the oppressive conditions of sweltering gymnasiums and lecture halls where he delivered his gospel, eyes rarely glancing up from the text.

Unlikely as it seems, celebrity is what Welch got, and the Birch Society, embodied in his presence, became an object of national fascination. One newspaper asserted that the Birchers "provoked the most heated public controversy since the heyday of the late Senator Joseph R. McCarthy."

One of the most furious melees involved the Army's major general Edwin A. Walker. A highly decorated veteran, Walker was fired from his command of the 24th Infantry in Augsburg, Germany, in 1961, when an overseas newspaper reported that he was indoctrinating his troops with Birchian ideas. He later resigned from the Army.

Welch's *The Life of John Birch* was required reading for soldiers in Walker's "special warfare" program designed to teach them proper ideals of Americanism. Walker had also been lecturing his troops on who the real Americans were. He called former president Harry Truman "definitely pink," along with Eleanor Roosevelt, Edward R. Murrow, and Eric Sevareid.

This was the same General Walker who, two years later, would duck a bullet flying through the window of his Dallas home, allegedly fired by one Lee Harvey Oswald. If Walker staged his own attempted murder, and he may have—he was the original source for *the* claim that Oswald fired the shot—then the Birch Society itself is implicated in a significant and sinister conspiracy of its own.

For Robert Welch, celebrity brought criticism, even from friends. Barry Goldwater publicly disavowed Welch's more extreme positions, particularly the slur on Eisenhower contained in *The Politician*. Welch's allegations about Eisenhower's loyalty also led the conservative National Association of Manufacturers to censure the Birch Society, even though a Birch council member was also on the NAM board.

The Birch Society still protests that Welch's remarks on Eisenhower's alleged crimson tint were taken out of context, suggested only as a possible explanation for Eisenhower's upsettingly

moderate (to Birchers) policies. Birchers insist that Welch gener-
ously granted Eisenhower the benefit of the doubt. He allowed that
likable ol' Ike could have been a mere dupe or an outright fool,
rather than a dedicated Communist agent.

Off the record, some of Welch's acquaintances questioned his
practice of labeling everyone and everything not in sympathy with
the society as part of the conspiracy. "We should use a rifle instead
of a shotgun, perhaps," suggested one.

The John Birch Society still takes its shots, but no longer struts
into the saloon guns drawn. "If you measured our strength in
numbers, we're not doing well anywhere," says McManus. "But
anyone who says anything and means it sounds like a crowd."

The society's headquarters moved in July 1989 to Appleton,
Wisconsin, hometown of Birchian tragic hero senator Joseph
McCarthy. "A delightful irony," quips McManus. The home base
had been previously divided between San Diego, California (lair to
many a right-winger), and Belmont, Massachusetts. Membership is
loaded into places like Idaho, which has twenty percent more
Birchers per capita than the union's other states and sixty John
Birch Society chapters, at last report. There are eight chapters in
Oklahoma City, with fifteen to twenty members apiece. Total
Birch membership is reported to be down to about fifty thousand
(from a high of twice that many in the 1960s) in three thousand
chapters.

But the Birch Society is not letting itself die out like a clan of
Shakers. At ten summer camps spread through the country, the
society enrolls about one thousand children and teenagers. They're
given a regime of softball, swimming, and conspiracy.

"We've got truth on our side, and there are more good people in
this country than bad," says Jack McManus. "History is made by
the dedicated few."

McManus's words would be anathema to political scientists who
see history as a process of competing views struggling to reach an
accommodation. History as a creation of the "dedicated few" is the
mentality of crusaders and conspiracy theorists. In the idealized
vision of political science, the "process" is paramount, in which

two political parties, one "liberal" and one "conservative," share a total commitment to fair and open debate. Within that agreed-upon framework, they smooth their differences into a consensus. The product of this process, like noodles oozing from a pasta maker, is national policy.

John Bunzel, author of the 1967 book *Anti-Politics in America,* explained the right-wing conspiratorial mind-set as opposed to that seamless system; therefore, it is not only antidemocratic, but "antipolitical" as well.

"Early in our history fear of a 'democracy of the people' was the motivating force behind those who lashed out against what they felt was the 'conspiracy of the immigrants,' " Bunzel wrote. Conspiracy mongers were motivated, he says, by a loathing of immigrants and the horror that their "foreign" culture would subvert the American way of life, whatever that may be.

Fear of foreign influence was the motivation for early "nativist" political parties, of which the so-called "Know-Nothings" were the first. Was the root of revulsion at foreigners a fear of "democracy of the people"? The question is rather more complicated than Bunzel makes it out to be.

The Know-Nothing Party was founded in the early part of the nineteenth century by writer Ned Buntline, whose only other achievement was fictionalizing the exploits of a cowboy named William Cody to create the American Hero "Buffalo Bill." Named the American Republican Party, they, like the Birchers more than a century later, modeled themselves along the agoraphobic lines of a secret society. When asked about the party's activities, a member was supposed to say, "I know nothing."

The Know-Nothings had one policy: to ban immigrants, especially Catholics, from holding any kind of public office or becoming U.S. citizens. The Vatican, they believed, was organizing a conspiracy to subvert the United States from within and thus "extend its sphere of influence." A typical pamphlet, "Startling Facts for Native Americans Called Know-Nothings," explicated how the scourge of "Popery," led by its "Popish" priests, would accomplish its goals.

"There is abundant proof," the pamphlet asserted, "that a foreign conspiracy has been organized in Catholic Europe to embar-

rass and overthrow the institutions of this country. . . . The valley of the Mississippi has been mapped as well as surveyed by the Jesuits of the Vatican, and Popish cardinals are rejoicing in the prospect of the entire subjection of this land of freedom and intelligence to Papal supremacy."

The "Papists" realized that America was becoming the "center of civilization," the Know-Nothings surmised, and set their "Popish" designs on it to "compensate" for their "losses in the old world," by conquering the new one.

Know-Nothing anti-Catholic fixation never died, though the party faded away. Manic Christian comic books drawn by Jack Chick show the pope as a high-tech anti-Christ, with a supercomputer keeping tabs on good Christians, who are hunted down and tortured into recantation.

The Know-Nothing Party in its day extended its influence beyond comic books—or whatever their nineteenth-century equivalent would have been. No fewer than seventy-five Know-Nothings served in Congress, many more in state legislatures. Millard Filmore, a former president, tried to reclaim the White House in 1856 as an "American Party" candidate. He scored twenty-one percent of the vote.

Did all this success come to the nativists because of a widespread fear of "democracy of the people"? If there had ever been such a "people's democracy," as Bunzel thought there was, there would be no nativism. The anticonspiratorial struggle was not so much a struggle to exclude certain people from the political process, as it was a battle over control of political institutions, the permanent institutions of power already in place in the then-fledgling U.S.A. They were unabashed servants of those institutions. They may have been antidemocratic, at least with regards to "democracy of the people," but they were not antipolitical. They were expressly political and, like the McCarthyites, used the political tools of the American system.

"Advocating the largest freedom in matters of religion, we view no sect with prejudice or favor. We are organized for political purposes and cannot recognize the existence of sects," the Know-Nothings wrote. The Know-Nothing claim to be bigotry free finds an echo in 1990, when Louisiana politician David Duke, a former

Ku Klux Klan grand wizard, claims no animosity toward blacks or Jews. He merely seeks to protect white citizens—the citizens already in control of the nation's political and economic system.

Historical treatment of Know-Nothings as a prototypical "hate group," and the media's handling of Duke as a persistent, if noxious, outsider given to lying about his own racism miss a critical point. Conspiracy theories are not an aberration in American history. Conspiracy theories *are* American history.

Some form of "right-wing" conspiracy theory—which usually means a conspiracy theory in which the conspirators are some breed of social outsiders—has always been the fabric weaving together the sheer cloth of American political unity. To the Know-Nothings, the outsiders were Catholics. To the Birchers, they were Communists. To Christian fundamentalists, they are "secular humanists." To ultraright survivalists, they are Jews. In the common parlance of acceptable political debate, they are "special interests," which usually means minorities and ethnic groups. The conspiracy theory is constant.

The difference between mainstream Reaganite conservatives and John Birchers is that besides the "fringe groups" none dare call it conspiracy theory. The Birchers do dare, and by calling it conspiracy they make their targets not only outsiders, but insiders.

"We believe that the conspiracy we're fighting is a conspiracy above Communism," says McManus. "Communism is its chief arm, but at the heart of it is a powerful clique of individuals that mean to rule the world. They've created a lot of 'isms.' Communism, socialism, syndicalism, taking power with labor unions. Other isms."

The Birch version of the Illuminati story is actually one of the yarn's most sober spinnings. Adam Weishaupt founded the Illuminati on May 1, 1776, "which is why Communists and socialists celebrate May Day." Concerned more with contemporary politics than history, the Birch Society doesn't bother filling in the fluorescent colors that other tellers of the Illuminati tale swab on liberally.

Gary Allen touched on the Illuminati in his definitive rendition of the Birch theory, *None Dare Call It Conspiracy*. He discusses

antecedents to the supposedly Illuminist Council on Foreign Relations, particularly the "secret society" of the Round Table established, Allen says, in the will of British colonialist diamond king Cecil Rhodes.

"It should be noted that the originator of this type of secret society was Adam Weishaupt, the monster who founded the Order of Illuminati . . . for the purpose of conspiracy to control the world. The role of Weishaupt's Illuminists in such horrors as the Reign of Terror is unquestioned, and the techniques of the Illuminati have long been recognized as models for Communist methodology."

The Illuminati, however, weren't always players in Birchian conspiracy theory. At the outset, Robert Welch was content simply to talk about "the Communist conspiracy" without delving into any more detail than that. Allen apparently picked up the tale from Welch, who gleaned his ideas about the "monster" Weishaupt and his cabal from the writings of Nesta Webster, Victorian England's conspiratologist in residence, and the eighteenth-century journalist John Robinson.

For Welch and Gary Allen, "Illuminati" was too esoteric a term. They preferred "Insiders." In looking for a properly descriptive buzzword, Welch rejected "Luminist," but almost settled on the puzzling "Supercom" (apparently short for Super Communist). He dropped "Supercom" when he realized that its similarity to "Superman" gave it "a comic-page flavor which was not helpful."

The Insiders are the spiritual descendants of the Illuminati, inheritors of the conspiratorial crest. They have names like Rothschild, Ford, Morgan, and Rockefeller. "An *Insider* is consciously a member of an international Master Conspiracy of long standing," Welch wrote.

The most important of the Insiders' regular meeting places in the conspiracy's modern era is the Henry Pratt House, on West 68th Street in Manhattan, home to the Council on Foreign Relations (CFR). Since its founding in the aftermath of World War I, the CFR has been the preeminent intermediary between the world of high finance, big oil, corporate elitism, and the U.S. government. Its members slide smoothly into cabinet-level jobs in Republican and Democratic administrations. The policies promulgated in

its quarterly journal, *Foreign Affairs*, become U.S. government policy.

Through the CFR and its offshoot, David Rockefeller's Trilateral Commission, the Insiders program a destructive course for America.

The goal of the Council on Foreign Relations is to establish a "One World Government," or a "New World Order," according to Birch theory. Sounds pleasant, but the reality, Birchers say, will be a commie/illuminoid nightmare with the Insiders in charge. The grand design of the Insiders is nothing short of total world power.

World government will redistribute the world's wealth among all nations, resulting in "a reduced standard of living for Americans." Worse yet, there will "no longer be any freedom of movement, freedom of worship, private property rights, free speech, or the right to publish." Finally, the New World Order will "be enforced by agents of the world government in the same way that agents of the Kremlin enforce their rule throughout Soviet Russia today."

Intimidating prospects, made more so by the council's own proclamations. Mixed in among articles on Peruvian political upheavals, international monetary policy, and East-West relations, *Foreign Affairs* occasionally carries a piece like "The Hard Road to World Order," which appeared in the April 1974 issue and was authored by Richard N. Gardner of Columbia University, sending tremors quaking through the Birch Society's ranks.

"In short, the 'house of world order' will have to be built from the bottom up rather than from the top down," says Professor Gardner. "An end run around national sovereignty, eroding it piece by piece, will accomplish much more than the old-fashioned frontal assault."

Gardner goes on to describe as "hopeful" the fact that "technological, economic, and political interests" are dragging individual governments toward some form of world government or world order. No matter that Gardner calls for a "world structure that secures peace, advances human rights, and provides the conditions for economic progress."

Nor that another CFR member protests that the council is an

idyllic "marketplace of ideas related to American foreign policy . . . an exciting, creative, and intellectually stimulating institution," whose opposition comes from those egg-sucking unfortunates "not invited to be members." The Birchers are having none of it.

"The reality of socialism is that it is not a movement to divide the wealth, as its superrich promoters would have us believe, but a movement to consolidate and control wealth," wrote Gary Allen. "If you control the apex, the power pinnacle of a world government, you have the ultimate monopoly."

In *None Dare Call It Conspiracy*, Allen details how multinational cartels literally built the Soviet Empire. "The Federal Reserve–CFR Insiders began pushing to open up Communist Russia to U.S. traders soon after the revolution."

He details how the Rockefellers' Standard Oil and Chase Manhattan Bank bought into the young Soviet Union as early as 1922, purchasing huge swaths of oil fields and setting up an American-Russian Chamber of Commerce. With these early investments, Allen asserts, the Insiders literally purchased control of the Communist world. Their master plan was to use socialism, with its centralized economic control, to take over the rest of the world and set up their "One World Government," a "New World Order."

What ended up happening looks like exactly the opposite. The capitalist world took over the communist countries. But the end result is still the "New World Order." The Birchers see the whole series of shocking events as a scam.

Former CFR member George Bush and his military machinations in the Middle East are especially alarming to the Birchers, designed as they are to create a "New World Order."

"Remember, war is big government's best friend," said McManus on a radio interview during the Saudi Arabian troop buildup in late 1990. Most troubling to McManus was the role of the United Nations in guiding the operation—"the U.N., founded by a pack of Communists." If Gary Allen were alive, he would share McManus's revulsion.

Allen, who died in 1986, was a former Stanford University football player, high school teacher, and self-proclaimed practicing leftist until he ran into John Stormer. The aptly named Stormer (whom we'll meet more formally in the next chapter) was a hard-line

conservative polemicist whose book, *None Dare Call It Treason*, was the Goldwater Republican's bible. Allen was an instant convert; apparently, his reverence for Stormer's work was so great that Allen named his own most famous book—the above-mentioned *None Dare Call It Conspiracy*—after Stormer's.

Stormer's book contained the usual and numerous indictments of the CFR, but lacked the Illuminati angle. Allen added that later, inspired by Robert Welch. Stormer, in turn, derived much of his CFR information from Dan Smoot, a former FBI agent whose "Dan Smoot Report" newsletter continually updated the machinations of pinkos in power. Smoot's book *The Invisible Government* was one of the first to lay down the anti-CFR law. In his reasonably dry (for this sort of thing) account of the CFR network, Smoot never goes into the "Round Table" legacy to which the CFR, according to Allen, owes its existence. When Smoot wrote his book, the Birch theory hadn't developed its intricate nuances. Nonetheless, he does go into considerable detail about the "interlock" between the CFR and a formidable list of liberal organizations, including usual suspects such as the American Civil Liberties Union (ACLU), the National Association for the Advancement of Colored People (NAACP), Americans for Democratic Action, and SANE Nuclear Policy, Inc. The latter organization was connected with Bertrand Russell, whom Smoot calls a "British pro-Communist socialist." He also cites, approvingly, a newspaper editorial calling Americans for Democratic Action "an organization strikingly like the British Fabian Socialists."

Birch-inspired or approved writings never go too far in singling out the "British" as masterminds of the conspiracy, but occasionally references to the conspiracy's "Anglophile" bent do crop up. Names like Cecil Rhodes and Lord Alfred Milner ("front man for the Rothschilds") figure prominently. The Anglophobic strains running through the Birch conspiracy theory erupt to the surface in the thinking of other theorists, particularly Lyndon LaRouche. As the Birch theory developed, it settled comfortably into that tradition.

The Birchers do not shy away from naming prominent Jews as conspirators, but, on an official level anyway, they recoil from any expressions of anti-Semitism. One former John Birch Society em-

ployee has criticized the Birch leadership for tolerating anti-Semites in the society's ranks so long as bigoted members don't spread their views around publicly or embarrass the organization. The society sees the charges of anti-Semitism and bigotry as part of an organized smear campaign, which peaked along with the society's notoriety in the early 1960s.

"Our Jewish members were very upset when they heard we were anti-Semites, and our black members said, 'This is ridiculous,'" says Jack McManus. "The smear campaign did its work. It was very effective, and we realize that."

During Welch's reign, several anti-Semites who later went on to become prominent in the always-active field of Jew hatred either left the John Birch Society in disillusionment with the society's refusal to attack the Jews, or in direct conflict with Robert Welch over the same issue. Willis Carto, who went on to found the Liberty Lobby and the Institute for Historical Review, was a member in the early days and wrote a couple of articles for Welch's *American Opinion* magazine. Others included William Pierce, who quit the society to link up with George Lincoln Rockwell's American Nazi Party, and Ben Klassen, author of *The White Man's Bible*, who upon quitting called the society "a smokescreen for the Jews." Paramilitary rightist (he founded the Minutemen) Robert DePugh was kicked out of the society in 1964, when the Birchers realized that he was plotting guerrilla warfare. And Tom Metzger, skinhead leader and former Ku Klux Klan grand dragon who somehow became the designated hater on national television talk shows such as "Oprah," "Donahue," "The Morton Downey, Jr., Show" and "Geraldo" (Metzger was on stage during the legendary Geraldo Rivera nose-breaking extravaganza), was also a Bircher for a while.

Though the society has fingered the Anti-Defamation League (ADL) of B'nai B'rith as an arm of the conspiracy because of the way the ADL monitors right-wing groups, it did start a "Jewish Society of Americanists" to make Jewish right-wingers feel more at home.

Welch and his heirs in the John Birch Society leadership have been scrupulous in avoiding any perceptible hints of anti-Semitism. Whether that's just a P.R. ploy I can't say, but I don't believe so.

Warns Jack McManus, "No one has anything to fear from us but the Establishment."

The irony of the ultraconservative Birch Society's rabid hatred for the Establishment is that the Establishment is by its nature conservative. By the time of the "Reagan revolution," conservatives had mastered the subterranean craft of public relations. The folks-and-shops American provincialism that binds the rank and file of the John Birch Society became official P.R. of the administration. Savvy conservatives learned to use conspiracy theory in subtle ways, resurrecting the nativism of the nineteenth century, adapting it shrewdly to the configurations of a mass, technological society. As they came to political power, their Birch-style "Insider" theory became more than a searching explanation for the puzzling American predicament. It is a tool of power, the quasi-official conspiracy theory of the United States.

# 6

# NONE DARE CALL IT TREASON

*The United States has had more light than
any other country on this planet. God has
placed his hand upon America.*

JIMMY SWAGGART

In a crisp blue blazer, sporting a smartly trimmed white handlebar mustache, the old man looked like a colonel from the First World War. John Stormer saw him approach. It was 4:30 in the afternoon. Stormer had finished a lecture a few minutes earlier. He'd been lecturing without much interruption since 10:30 that morning. He'd start up again after dinner.

He was taking a well-deserved break, alone in the corner of a large function room at the Sheraton-Lincoln Hotel in Worcester, Massachusetts. Worcester was but one stop on a perpetual tour with his traveling seminar "Understanding the Times." Each two-day conference may feature up to fourteen hour-long speeches by Stormer. He lectures on the encroaching presence of international communism, the Communist influence in the U.S. government, media, and education system, and what Americans can do to combat the menace.

Mr. Mustache, the colonel, was eager to consume that message, and to laud the man who served it to him. "That was a great speech," says the colonel in a crackling voice, congratulatory hand extended. "And you know, Jack McManus always says if you want to know what's really goin' on in politics, you've got to see who's writin' the checks. And who's writin' the checks is the Federal Reserve!"

A tall, good-humored, round-faced fellow, Stormer laughs nervously. He seems slightly embarrassed. "Well, yes. That's part of it," he proffers. Stormer shakes the old man's hand and sends him on his way.

I was sitting near Stormer, watching him converse with a parade of hand shakers and back slappers. All very routine, but that particular exchange surprised me for its mundanity. I'd expected a more ardent affirmation of this admirer's antifed outburst.

That the Federal Reserve occupies the nucleus of a conspiracy to siphon America's wealth from the working man to the wealthy few is an article of faith among denizens of the conservative milieu to whom Stormer is a demigod. His rivet-hard right-wing rhetoric is crystallized in lectures titled with ominous queries: "Why Are Our Leaders Betraying Us?" "How Do They Plan to Get Us?" and "What Can We Do to Return America to Its Heritage as a Nation under God?"

Yet in those speeches, Stormer breezes by such conspiratorial superstars as the Council on Foreign Relations (CFR) and the Rockefeller family as if they were incidental players in the game of world power. He was almost embarrassed to mention them at all.

The quick and otherwise forgettable exchange between John Stormer and the colonel, I thought, was a succinct demonstration of a division in conservatism. There are hard-core conspiratorialists, the Birch Society most famously. They are "fringe groups." But their conspiracy theory in a sort of acid-washed form has become mainstream political currency. The softer version of the Birch/nativist theory has become a staple of Republican administration propaganda. The proponents of the more palatable version of the theory get themselves taken more seriously than the Birchers. They get the message out. Televangelists such as Pat Robertson, who ran for president in 1988, and the now-discredited Jimmy Swaggart had a ready audience of millions. Most of their viewers were, I would guess, honestly religious people. Their sincere Christian beliefs were easily exploited by the likes of Robertson and Swaggart, and more lately Larry Lea, who calls for an "army" of believers to combat, physically if necessary, homosexuals and other heathen. The preachers raised, if not an army, then at least a vast coterie of voters to prop up the conservative agenda.

Stormer is another proponent. So are Jesse Helms, Pat Buchanan, Phyllis Schlafly, and Howard Philips, to name a few. And let's not forget the best known conservative of all, Ronald Reagan.

The Birchers and their ilk are "fanatics," scorned by all who've been admitted within the boundaries of acceptable political discourse. The "conservatives," on the other hand, are not only accepted within those bounds in America, they've accrued an impressive measure of political power. Helms, of course, is a veteran of the U.S. Senate. Philips and Buchanan have held administration positions in the federal government and continue to hold sway with their opinions for hire in newspapers and on television. Stormer's profile is lower these days, but the author of *None Dare Call It Treason* and his "Understanding the Times" road show are sought after by conservative klatches around the nation.

The conservative conspiracy theory enjoyed its peak of power in the early 1980s. Now it is, at least partially, in remission. Witness the 1988 presidential campaign in which George Bush got considerable mileage from his repeated indictments of the American Civil Liberties Union (ACLU). Pat Buchanan, who is not only one of the most conservative but, due to his televised ubiquity, one of the most influential political commentators in the country, called the ACLU an "anti-Christian organization" on national television.

The nerve Bush struck was the fear of conspiracy, the fear that "outsiders" or "special interests" will take over American institutions. The ACLU was part of the conspiracy to undermine what Bush called "mainstream" American values. It was the skillful use of conspiracy theory as propaganda that allowed Ronald Reagan, a man backed from the start by the defense-corporate Establishment, to run for president as an antigovernment candidate, lambasting "Washington" as the enemy with the same vitriol he spewed at the Soviets.

The difference between "right-wing fanatics" and "conservatives" is more packaging than product. Birchers see an active, organized network of Insiders working purposefully to overthrow the American government from within. The conservatives see our society becoming imbued with beliefs, attitudes, and opinions that can only lead to America's downfall. The "fringe" right-wing con-

spiracy theory holds that communism is being forcibly injected into the American mainstream. The acceptable-propaganda theory warns that subversion is quietly percolating through the American membrane.

Conservatives such as Stormer express discomfort with their brethren in the Birch Society. Ted Temple, a leading conservative activist in the heart of supposedly "liberal" Massachusetts, is hasty to add, when declaring his opposition to "One World Government," "I'm not a conspiracy theorist, a John Bircher." Temple prefers a more positive definition of his political faith: "I'd say conservative as defined now is one believing in less government, equal opportunity, a strong defense, and traditional family values."

Americans have been conditioned to reject "conspiracy theories," unless they're disguised as something else, but a French observer saw the essence of American conservatism immediately. Guy Sorman distilled it thusly: "The growth of big government was neither accidental nor necessary, but functionally organized as a project of a society strongly influenced by European socialism. . . . The groundwork for this outburst of leftist ideology was carefully prepared by the media and the universities. . . ."

What the Birchers believe is what conservative propagandists want the country to believe. Communism could never take hold in a country on its own merits. Communism, they both believe, is a prima facie evil needing billions of dollars worth of overt and covert coercion to establish itself as a national form of government—as if the same couldn't be said for any ideology.

Mainstream conservatives pay less attention to the machinations of the Rockefellers, the CFR, and that clique. They save their suspicions for more amorphous entities. The conspiracy to subvert America is "much broader" than the influence of a few think tanks for the rich and shadowy. Stormer focuses instead on a "conspiracy of shared values," as he calls it.

"If you teach people something, then you don't have to control them," he tells a rapt Thursday afternoon audience in New England. "We have millions of Americans who think they're good, loyal Americans who, in their fundamental beliefs, are Marxists."

How did they get that way? What is the mysterious "conspiracy of shared values" that can turn a red-blooded son of Uncle Sam into a pawn of Mother Russia? As foggy as the "shared values" notion sounds, there are tangible villains in the conservative conspiracy theory.

More dastardly than the ACLU is the American educational system, embodied by the National Education Association (NEA). No less an influential conservative than Ronald Reagan has accused the NEA of plotting to install a "federal school system with everything from curriculum to textbooks dictated by Washington." It was his fear of NEA domination that led Reagan during his presidency to all but cripple the U.S. Department of Education. The only purpose of the agency was "federal regulation of our schools under the domination of the National Education Association," he believed.

The mission of the NEA is to "completely destroy" the "dying laissez-faire," and to subject "all of us" to "a large degree of social control." The words are not Reagan's, or John Stormer's, though Stormer quotes them eagerly in *None Dare Call It Treason*. They belong to Dr. Willard Givens, who was executive secretary of the NEA from 1935 until 1952.

Even the California State Legislature, much to Stormer's delight, once excoriated the NEA for publishing social science textbooks by "Communist front organizations" and authors.

That was more than fifty years ago. But conservative antipathy toward the NEA hasn't subsided with the passage of the century. And understandably not. The "propaganda front of the radical left," participated in a 1982 "Peace Day" demonstration that received public endorsement from Gus Hall, America's most venerable Communist. If the NEA wasn't in step with Hall's radical agenda, asks conservative writer Sally D. Reed, why was the NEA's president marching in the Peace Day parade? "My own suspicion," speculates Reed, "is that the NEA is so friendly toward Soviet totalitarianism because it sees that any opposition to the Soviet Union would stand in the way of its goal of a collectivized world government." In other words, the NEA's design is to indoctrinate American youngsters with "one worldism," what Reed calls "global education."

"Its intended purposes sound harmless enough," writes Reed, "sensitizing students to the interdependency of the world's people, emphasizing human rights for everyone, and enhancing the student's appreciation for cultural diversity and philosophical pluralism." In fact, she continues, "globalism is aimed at inculcating young minds with political attitudes that are conducive to the creation of a socialist world order—you know, a United Nations, where every nation has one vote and we all share the wealth no matter what our contribution is."

How different is that from Jack McManus's statement in his pamphlet *The Insiders?* "The real goal . . . is to make the United States into a carbon copy of a Communist state, and then merge all nations into a one-world system ruled by a powerful few."

This exact viewpoint finds its way into the *Congressional Record*, courtesy of Jesse Helms. He delivered an anti-*glasnost* rant on the floor of the Senate in 1987, in which he warned that "the influence of establishment insiders over our foreign policy has become a fact of life in our time. . . . The viewpoint of the establishment today is called globalism. Not so long ago this viewpoint was called the 'one world' view by its critics. The phrase is no longer fashionable among sophisticates; yet the phrase 'one world' is still apt because nothing has changed in the minds and actions of those promoting policies consistent with its fundamental tenets."

The most durable and beloved spokesman for the conspiracy theory was Ronald Reagan. He began preaching its tenets when he was hired as a corporate shill by defense-contracting General Electric in the early 1960s, and subsequently turned into one of Barry Goldwater's most visible supporters, which in turn opened Reagan's own portal into electoral politics.

Backed by GE's corporate dollars, Reagan traversed the country giving slightly modified versions of one basic speech, a speech that drew on the thinking of Robert Welch and Phyllis Schlafly, who were in concordance on the thesis that Eisenhower had sold out America. Come 1964, when *None Dare Call It Treason* began to rack up paperback sales that would have put it high on the best-seller list had paperbacks been so included, Reagan drew on John

Stormer as well. While still on GE's payroll, he gave his speech to an assembly of the Christian Anti-Communist Crusade, a right-wing group whose infamy rivaled that of the John Birch Society.

Reagan continued to sound the conspiratorial themes, couched in his comforting storybook imagery, while president. The more receptive his audience, the freer he felt to let loose, so when he spoke to a convention of evangelicals in 1983, he unleashed what became his most notable piece of conspiratorial rhetoric. He suggested that the nuclear freeze movement, very much in favor at the time, was nothing but a means for the Communists to achieve their "objectives," their "global desires." As if for good measure, he declared the Communists to be "the focus of evil in the modern world" and cautioned against ignoring "the aggressive impulses of an evil empire."

When the conspiracy propaganda diminished in usefulness to Reagan, the conservative believers from whom he drew his material began to turn on him. The propaganda was never aimed at them. They were its inspiration and when Reagan left that form of propaganda behind, they were disenfranchised. Reagan himself, through negligence or ignorance they believed, was becoming part of the very conspiracy he was elected to destroy. Portly Howard Philips, a man with the face of a German shepherd and the voice of an FM disc jockey, is a former Nixon aide who founded the Conservative Caucus (one of the right-wing lobbying groups that leapt to power in the early 1980s). He believes that it was really the Rockefellers' boy George Bush running the show all along.

"Bush got a lot of praise for being loyal to Reagan," he says. "In fact, Reagan was loyal to Bush. . . . I would say Bush probably had more input over policy from 1981 to 1988 than Reagan did, certainly with personnel."

Bush, then, probably had something to do with picking George Schultz as secretary of state. "Schultz was the worst secretary of state from the conservative anti-Communist perspective that we ever had," Philips proclaims. "He was simply an errand boy for the commercial establishment."

Philips also made news, when Reagan and Gorbachev were indulging in one of their summit meetings, by calling Reagan "a

useful idiot for Soviet propaganda." The old anti-Communist warrior, as far as conservatives were concerned, had turned into a dupe for the Reds.

"If you really want to know what's going on in politics, follow the money," says Howard Philips. "And that is the great untold story. I'm sure there are large elements of treason. . . . I'm sure we've had our share of spies and traitors, but worse than the traitors are people who for reasons of greed rather than betrayal advance policies that are detrimental to the cause of liberty in our country."

Such market-driven traitors, according to Philips, include David Rockefeller, Armand Hammer, and grain tycoon Dwayne Andreas—the same Establishment "One Worlders" condemned in far sharper terms by the Birchers.

Besides the education establishment and the commercial establishment, the third big player in both the hard-core and soft-core versions of conservative conspiracy theory is the media establishment. The leading conservative media assassin is Reed Irvine, whose group Accuracy in Media, founded in 1969, organizes boycotts of sponsors for programming it considers too left wing. While the AIM program sounds like a throwback to the "Red Channels" era of 1950s TV, Irvine maintains that "our media are still being manipulated by time-worn Marxist tricks."

Recent issues of AIM's twice-monthly bulletin "AIM Report" contain headlines such as "Has Walter Cronkite Been Bought?" and "CBS Is Bankrupt—Morally."

As a supposed investigator of "left-wing propaganda," Irvine is a loudmouthed example of how conservative conspiracy theory is itself propaganda, kind of an official government conspiracy theory. Irvine himself belongs to the American Council for World Freedom, an offshoot of the World Anti-Communist League. That group is tied to an international web of right-wing terrorism and propaganda, and sometimes looks like a worldwide fascist conspiracy tied in with elements of the CIA, Central American death squads, and other unsavory elements.

Irvine often targets programming that advocates conspiracy the-

ories, if they are conspiracy theories that challenge the status quo. AIM went after the 1988 NBC television movie "Shootdown," which had as its theme the possibility that KAL-007 (the commercial 747 that in 1983 strayed into Soviet airspace and was shot down) was actually on a spy mission for the CIA. That exact thesis was argued in the book *Shootdown* by British writer R. W. Johnson. Because NBC didn't insure that the movie had "a balanced script giving sufficient weight to the nonconspiratorial side," AIM directed one of its letter-writing campaigns at the show's prime sponsor, the Johnson and Johnson corporation. Johnson and Johnson responded with what amounted to an apology.

AIM spends most of its energy battling the major television networks, which, Irvine says, are "ill-equipped to screen out Communist or other propaganda inimical to our country's interests."

With piquant frequency, conservatives such as Irvine are linked to organizations that seem to be the support system for the very "Establishment" they accuse of Commie treason. The CIA for instance. Who these days is more closely identified with the CIA than "conservative" ACLU-basher George Bush? It has also been said that the Rockefellers' Exxon, in some countries at least, is indistinguishable from the CIA. While it's true that conservatives often paint the CIA as a left-leaning organization, more objective observers see palpable links between the agency and right-wing causes.

When the whole picture comes into view, right and left start to look meaningless. Conspiracy theory can be used as propaganda by the powerful, or it can be the result of independent inquiry into the roots of power. The conservative conspiracy theory is the most public and popular, but it doesn't call itself conspiracy theory. There is a legal definition of conspiracy in this country, however, and that, too, has come under attack from conservatives (and by civil libertarians). It has been used to put mobsters behind bars, as well as Wall Street wheeler-dealers. One can understand why certain elements of the right and the "Establishment" wouldn't enjoy having the concept of conspiracy entrenched in law.

The legal definition of conspiracy first came into discredit in 1967, when New Orleans District Attorney Jim Garrison put it to

work against an accused plotter in the assassination of President Kennedy. All Garrison really did was put into official legal documents the work of a number of researchers before him and since, for whom the Kennedy assassination was the event inspiring all contemporary conspiracy theories. Of those amateur investigators, none was more unrelenting than one housewife in the seaside resort town of Carmel, California.

# 7

# THERE IS NO WORD FOR
# RATIONAL FEAR

*The better the state is established the*
*fainter is humanity. To make the individ-*
*ual **uncomfortable**, that is my task.*

FRIEDRICH NIETZSCHE,
*Twilight of the Idols*

Mae Brussell, sixty-six years old, died on October 3, 1988 of
cancer. At her gravesite, David Emory, one of many who look on
Brussell as a hero of the twentieth century, delivered a vengeful
eulogy laden with vows to track down her murderers. Can cancer
be induced? U.S. intelligence agents have likely considered using
cancer and other "natural causes" as untraceable forms of killing.
But was Mae Brussell a victim of oncological assassination? Two
years after her death, Emory remained convinced that her cancer
was "no accident."

In the spring of 1988, after seventeen years of broadcasting a
weekly program of news, theories, and conspiratorial commentary
called "World Watchers International," Brussell suddenly dropped
off the air. She had received a death threat, she explained. That in
itself was nothing remarkable. In her career of conspiracy research,
she named so many politicians, business leaders, distinguished citizens, and American institutions as complicitous in the ongoing
coup d'état that death threats were almost as routine as ridicule.

In 1988, for the first time, she was really scared. A man who is

said to have identified himself as "a fascist and proud of it" threatened to visit her at home to "blow your head off." Something about him gave the threat sickening authenticity. Brussell immediately quit broadcasting.

Around the same time, surreal incidents began to haunt Brussell: break-ins at her home with nothing stolen, but furniture moved around; a jigsaw puzzle piece taped to the wall and a handwritten note, "We were here." She felt the onset of the sickness that would later kill her, already convinced that she was being monitored from a house on her street in Carmel, California. The day she died, a house on her street burned down. Was it the same house?

If in fact some mysterious power paid Brussell close attention, she worked hard to earn it. Her legend—and since her death it has become as much folklore as fact—begins on November 23, 1963. Brussell was at that time "just a housewife interested in tennis courts and dance lessons and orthodontia for my children." She had little reason for any other worries. Her great-grandfather started the I. Magnin department store chain, and her father was Hollywood Rabbi-to-the-stars Edgar Magnin.

The assassination of President Kennedy put all normal functions on hold for housewives and husbands throughout the nation, but it was the sight of Lee Harvey Oswald that would alter Brussell's life.

The television was on, with the arrested Oswald parading before the Brussell family. Brussell's daughter Bonnie, though she was a small child, could see that Oswald had been beaten. The little girl wrapped up a teddy bear to send to the abused, accused assassin. Two days later, Brussell watched horrified as Oswald was murdered on national television. The horror did not fade, and she needed to salve it. As soon as the Warren Commission published its evidence, she wrote a check for eighty-six dollars and ordered all twenty-six volumes.

The evidence, it turned out, was so voluminous as to be almost useless, because the commission, for reasons of its own, published it without an index. Rather than write off her investment to experience and return to the universe of tennis courts and braces, Mae compiled her own index. She not only indexed the twenty-six volumes, she cross-referenced them. Still not satisfied, she began annotating the volumes as well. The process produced twenty-

seven thousand typed pages of notes and took nine years. By then, Mae Brussell's worldview was altered beyond all previous recognition.

In ferreting out every morsel from the Warren Report, supplementing her research with untold amounts of reading from the *New York Times* to *Soldier of Fortune*, Brussell discovered not merely a conspiracy of a few renegade CIA agents, Mafiosi, and Castro haters behind Kennedy's death, but a vast, invisible institutional structure layered into the very fabric of the U.S. political system.

Comprising the government within a government were not just spies, gangsters, and Cubans, but Nazis. Mae found that many of the commission witnesses—whose testimony established Oswald as a "lone nut"—had never even spoken to Oswald, or knew him only slightly. The bulk of them were White Russian émigrés living in Dallas. Extreme in their anti-Communism, they were often affiliated with groups set up by the SS in World War II—Eastern European ethnic armies used by the Nazis to carry out their dirtiest work.

Brussell also discovered an episode from history rarely reported in the media, and not often taught in universities. Those same collaborationist groups were absorbed after the war by United States intelligence agencies. They hooked up with the spy net of German General Reinhard Gehlen, Hitler's Eastern Front espionage chief. Gehlen made a secret deal with the U.S. government after the war, thus avoiding capture and possible prosecution. Far from facing trial, Gehlen and his entire espionage agency traded bosses—from Hitler to Uncle Sam.

"This is a story of how key Nazis . . . anticipated military disaster and laid plans to transplant nazism, intact but disguised, in havens in the West," wrote Mae Brussell in 1983. She didn't author too many articles, but this one, "The Nazi Connection to the John F. Kennedy Assassination" (in *The Rebel*, a short-lived political magazine published by *Hustler* impresario Larry Flynt), was definitive, albeit convoluted.

"It is a story that climaxes in Dallas on November 22, 1963, when John Kennedy was struck down," Brussell's article continued. "And it is a story with an aftermath—America's slide to the brink of fascism."

Many of Brussell's findings have been corroborated by recent books: *Blowback*, about the Gehlen organization, and *The Belarus Secret*, chronicling U.S. importation of Eastern European fascists, as well as a handful of others. The Cold War was manipulated, to some extent manufactured, by front-line Nazis and their henchmen.

When Brussell was forced off the air, beginning to feel sick, and dying, Nazis and JFK were old news. Her latest project, the one that her devotees feel induced her fatal traumas, was a study of Satanic cults—within the U.S. military. The hidden fascist oligarchy had progressed far beyond the need for patsies like Oswald. They were now able, Brussell asserted, to hypnotically program assassins.

Satanic cults are the state of the art in brainwashing. With drugs, sex, and violence, they strip any semblance of moral thought. They are perfect for use in creating killers. The United States military, Brussell found, was using them. Perhaps that discovery was too much for the conspirators to endure.

Despite corroboration of her premise—the Nazi link to the U.S. government—Brussell remains alone, long after her death, in connecting the Nazi network to the Kennedy assassination and its calamitous consequences. Her theories are supported only by former colleagues such as Dave Emory. For ten years, he has been broadcasting his own "Radio Free America" series, ferreting out all things fascist.

"Along with George Seldes," Emory proclaims, "Mae was the most brilliant political intellect of the twentieth century. Period. And I'll state that for the record. One of the problems Mae encountered was she used an unconventional format broadcast-wise. A lot of the criticism Mae endured was really criticism of *how* she said what she said. Her style, rather than what she had to say."

Emory enjoys describing his own conspiracy research as "pedantic." Brussell's was, if anything, dithyrambic. Her programs were not for the uninitiated, and even the initiated could have a hard time following along at home. She baked clippings, speculations, little-known facts, and occasionally unsupported assertions into an

informational pudding so rich and thick it was difficult to stomach. She could be confusing and esoteric about her facts. Reading her writing is even more befuddling than listening to her tapes. But her message can't be missed, and her restless intellect was always at the fore. Listening to Mae Brussell, you knew that you were hearing the workings of an engaged mind. Synchronizing your own with hers was a task of a higher level.

Mae Brussell was a deeply busy person—not the superficial over-scheduling that passes for a busy life in our society, but, rather, her mind required constant input and she never had trouble finding it. She subscribed to, and friends swear she read, twelve daily news-papers and more than 150 magazines. She clipped them, never tiring, running off photocopies for cross-referencing. She treated the vast amounts of information flowing daily through the media the same way she treated the Warren Report. By the time of her death, she had amassed thirty-nine file cabinets of clippings in her home.

"She led a remarkable life," says Emory. "In addition to doing all of her work—and she was remarkably productive—she was an avid photographer, a collector of art. She led the most complete exis-tence of anyone I've ever known and she was a tremendously strong human being. And that helps create a cult of personality.

"I think a lot of people literally worshipped Mae for her strength. I admired her for her strength, but she was worshipped by a lot of people."


Emory's eyes, when he takes off his secret-service style mirrored shades, are close-set eyes that dart nervously from corner to corner, then fix and pierce. These are not the eyes of a man on a mission, the eyes of a man on the lookout. Emory has none of the look of a spy, with his ungainly lemon yellow baseball cap pulled down to cover his ears, a toothpick protruding from between his lips ("surrogate cigarette," says the former smoker), and the paunch of a working man over forty. "Style is not my strong suit," Emory announces in his signature sardonic baritone. "Information is." "What the show is about is not Dave Emory," he repeats. "It's about the informa-tion."

Information is Emory's favorite word. He always pronounces it *inforMAY-shun.* "*InforMAY-shun.*" The breath must roll up from the diaphragm to deliver it correctly, with the proper reverence.

"We're going to take a short musical break," Emory will tell his listeners, before spinning some avant jazz or folk-protest record. "Then we'll be back with more *inforMAY-shun.*"

Across the San Francisco Bay Area, his listeners absorb the *inforMAY-shun*: This is the truth we've never been told, and it may be too late to learn. The U.S. is spiraling into fascism, and fast. The government is corrupt, compromised. The military, the intelligence community, and the law enforcement system are overrun by Nazis and quislings. Get in the way of the juggernaut, and you die. More than a scandal, the "outlaw national security establishment" has become a health hazard.

Knotted with contradictions, Emory can be ogling some California beauty in jogging shorts one minute, and the next announcing his intention to "head for the hills in New Mexico or Vermont" to escape the imminent drop of fascism's iron fist. Supporting himself as a short-order chef, supplemented by a small inheritance from his mother, he'll state that he plans to spend the next decade in pursuit of some real money, then reconsider, noting the futility of self-betterment "with this country going fascist."

The country is going fascist. Emory offers that observation as casually as one might comment, "Prices are going up." From his two decades of digging, the trend toward fascism—no, not a trend; the country is being deliberately driven that way—has assumed *a priori* standing.

"During the 1970s, as I began reading about the various materials that I feature on my program, I came to the conclusion that *if* people were reading not enough of them were reading," says Emory, between sips of wine in the Sizzler restaurant where he works part-time. Despite a degree from Amherst College in 1971, Emory has worked nothing but blue-collar jobs since graduating. He double majored in psychology and English, and his literary bent permeates his radio program; he reads extended passages on the air from political books and relevant newspaper articles.

"Where I learned about the stuff was from reading, and it became apparent to me that most people simply were not reading or the

public's perceptions could not remain as they are. My feeling is that the printed medium is the final arbiter of truth, and that's why what I do could be thought of a sort of a hybrid operation. It is radio, yet printed material is featured. I don't hold myself up as the ultimate exemplar of truth. The ultimate verification is to come from the printed medium."

Unlikely as the wooded, college campus radio station setting seems, through this secluded sluice flows the information. Emory commences each broadcast with a caveat that "the information presented" will be unlike the type most news consumers are accustomed to receiving. As their tap into this subterranean spring, listeners are eager to extract all the wisdom they can from Emory. Pity the caller who questions him critically—the word arrogant has been applied to Dave Emory more than once. But for those honest knowledge seekers who phone in during his time slot, he'll willingly oblige.

His listeners' numbers are unknown. KFJC, which airs Emory's weekly "One Step Beyond" talkathon, is a ragged, noncommercial station with no access to ratings or listener surveys. But they are out there, the audience, enough to jam the phone lines every Sunday night.

"Yeah, hi, Dave. Just heard you talking about the guns . . ."

Even Emory's offhand remarks snare the imagination of his audience. He'd made a crack about gun control; a Bay Area man had been murdered at a party by a skinhead with a knife. If the victim had been carrying a gun, Emory suggested, he might still be alive. "Are you suggesting bringing guns to parties?" the caller inquires.

"Well, I'm not saying bring them to parties, but ask yourself this: If somebody comes to stab you, would you rather have a gun on you or not? It's a question you have to decide for yourself."

"I completely agree," the caller chimes. "I think that clearly the powers that be are trying to take our weapons away."

"I'll give you a couple of anecdotes, one from my experience and one from the late Mae Brussell's," intones Emory. "After Mae was receiving her death threats and after she was driven off the air, and before she was overtaken by cancer, she went out and had signed up for shooting lessons and she was going to buy a gun, and she was going to carry it with her at all times."

"No kidding," says the caller with evident surprise. Mae Brussell, the compassionate housewife, self-described airwave existentialist, dithyrambic mistress of monologue, often called the queen of conspiracy theories—she contrived to carry a gun? Mae planned to pack a piece?

"No kidding at all," Emory assures. "And last year, at the same time Mae was being threatened, I was receiving a number of interesting activities. A couple of times there were indications that people had entered my apartment. There was some blood smeared on my front door. A lot of weird phone calls, people would call and hang up and the usual sort of low level harassment. At that time I borrowed a gun from a friend of mine in law enforcement, and a box of shells and a speed loader so that I could put six extra rounds in.

"This goes back to my observation at the top of the broadcast. People are not really aware of the forces around them that threaten their existence at any given time, and as an activist, in a sense someone who is out front, I'm running into them perhaps a little earlier or to a somewhat greater extent at this stage of the game than you are. But ultimately what goes around comes around. You could be pursuing your software company, but then if the federal government or people in it want to take it away you may not have recourse. I'm not saying you're going to have to shoot 'em. But ultimately you're going to have to make a stand.

"In a normal civilized society, there shouldn't be a need for something like that, but this isn't a normal, civilized society. When you're facing organized political terrorism, well, you make up your own mind. I think you're going to want access to a gun when the time comes."

"Both the left and rightists are trying to take my guns away from me," complains another telephone voice, distant and shrill as radio phone-ins always sound. "What hope do we have as individuals?"

"Well, I would say keep your powder dry," advises Emory.

By now, Emory's employment history has become a point of political pride. He feels he knows how the working class thinks and feels, because he *is* a blue-collar guy, despite his Amherst College education. His working-class outlook is one he has had to grow into. For a time, he thought of himself as nothing more than "a

failed scholar," living in the low-rent district of Allston-Brighton, Massachusetts, a working neighborhood of Boston heavily inhabited by college students.

Consistent with his affinity for hard-hat polity, Emory's mistrust of traditional left-wing political activists, particularly 1960s' pranksters like Abbie Hoffman and their 1990s' counterparts on the fringes of the environmental and gay rights movements, can lapse into outright hatred. The American left, he'll assert waving a fearsome fist, is purely elitist, with no regard for the working people. Worse than that, the tactics and attitude of the traditional left are so certain to drive the working class rightward, leftists couldn't serve the right wing better if they were covert agents.

Emory believes that some of them are. He's aired suspicions about Abbie Hoffman and Gloria Steinem. The Reverend William Sloane Coffin, longtime activist and now president of the antinuke group SANE/Freeze, was in the CIA, and Emory suspects that revered left-wing journalist I. F. Stone might have been. Earth First!, the once-obscure environmental direct-action group that got headlines in 1990 when two of its leaders were injured by a car bomb, is loaded, Emory fears, with agents provocateurs.

The correct form of political activism as far as Emory is concerned is "communication" and making people aware of *inforMAY-shun*—which not coincidentally is the means of activism he has chosen. The term "conspiracy theorist" is anathema to Emory; it's "stigmatized," or "a term of derision," like "calling a woman a 'sweet chick.' "

"It makes people who are interested in this material look like a bunch of "Get Smart" fanatics sitting around watching reruns playing with their propeller beanies," Emory sniffs. He is a "political researcher," even a "scholar," who takes a certain satisfaction in being labeled "pedantic."

When Watergate hit, Emory began his studies, consuming whatever he could find regarding the hidden inner workings of the government. The first connections were obvious. The Watergate burglars were anti-Castro Cubans and CIA agents whose history in intelligence dated back to the Bay of Pigs. Why were these specialists soiling themselves with a third-rate burglary? As the scandal

unfurled and Emory read on, more connections emerged. E. Howard Hunt, the CIA executive who apparently engineered the break-in, was also a coordinator of the Bay of Pigs. More revelations came as the 1970s—which ironically have been dismissed as the decade when "nothing happened"—rolled on.

Numerous journalists and finally the House Select Committee on Assassinations tied the Bay of Pigs, anti-Castro/CIA cadre to the assassination of President Kennedy. The House committee concluded that there was "probably" a conspiracy behind the Kennedy assassination and, though it declined to name any conspirators, investigated several CIA, Cuban, and organized crime figures as possible suspects.

All of these revelations took months or years to come out. Even then, they saw little attention from the above-ground media. But in August, 1972, a scant two months after the Watergate break-in, Mae Brussell published an article in a magazine called *The Realist*. Normally a journal of political satire edited by yippie humorist Paul Krassner, *The Realist* on three occasions took time out for Brussell's surreal revelations. Her first article was called "Why Was Martha Mitchell Kidnapped?" In it, Brussell spelled out the entire scenario behind Watergate.

Emory moved to California in the late 1970s, and in 1980 he met Mae Brussell. As a scholar, he felt "failed" no longer.

"**I**'m an existentialist," Mae Brussell, a former Stanford philosophy major, once said. "I believe that each of us in the last analysis is on our own. The newspapers I read—you can read them, too. These men can't kill all of you. You've got to get smart because if you don't, you'll all be at the end of that gun yourselves."

For every Dave Emory Brussell inspired, every independent researcher, she had a gaggle of slavish devotees. These were disciples, some straight from the bug-eyed and stringy-haired school that also seems to spawn Lyndon LaRouche's lower-level foot-soldiers. To encourage a healthier legacy, on her deathbed she authorized that a research center be created in her name, donating her overstuffed files and plenary political library.

Emory donated money to starting up the center, but the curatorship went to John Judge, with whom Emory has been embroiled in a simmering feud since 1984.

Judge also managed to get himself some lecture bookings and onto radio talk shows. According to Tom Davis, a longtime friend of Brussell's whose mail-order book service is one of the best sources for political books, Judge and Emory had been "competing for radio kudos" since at least 1984, when they were interviewed jointly on Los Angeles station KPFA and ended up in a vocal shoving match, won by the indomitable larynx of Dave Emory.

Emory swears that his differences with Judge are no mere "personality conflict." He makes a series of charges against Judge, which, frankly, sound like flights of fancy and in any case are unconfirmable and therefore unprintable (Judge is, after all, unlike the subjects of most conspiracy theories, a private individual). Emory has not been shy about publicizing his opinion that the center was infiltrated by the intelligence community, and has said so on the air. Not as wild an allegation as it sounds, given the government's addiction to monitoring and harassing activists of all stripes. True or not, Emory's charges are a measure of how shattered Mae Brussell's death left him. Not only does he stick by his contention that Brussell was murdered by a cancer potion, he once told me, "I think I know who slipped her the mickey."

The Mae Brussell Research Center was set up in Santa Cruz, California. Judge, a Washington, D.C., native (in the conspiracy milieu, he's a suspect on that basis alone), moved cross-country in 1988 to set it up and begin fund-raising.

He collected thousands, somewhere in the mid–five figures, then a series of personal conflicts and health problems drove him back to the East Coast. The center collapsed, to be resurrected by Davis and some associates as the Mae Brussell Library in Seaside, California.

There was a string of problems with the center, one of them Judge's refusal to open it to the public. According to Davis, the new library will be open. But, says Davis, "one of the problems was Dave Emory."

Davis says he personally implored Emory, to whom the Mae Brussell Research Center will always be "so-called," not to attack

the center on his show. In the fall of 1989, Emory burst. Restraining himself for a year, he could no longer hold it in and went on the air accusing Judge of financial improprieties and other sordid acts. In private, Emory is even more vitriolic.

Whatever the objective reality of the Mae Brussell Research Center controversy, the version that navigates the canals of Dave Emory's brain is another of his many traumas.

John Judge does not appear to be a very traumatizing person. Bushy of beard, scraggly of pony tail and hefty of weight, he resembles nothing more than a leftover hippie. Standing on stage at a Berkeley nightclub, there to celebrate a tribute to the late Abbie Hoffman, Judge launches into his theory of Hoffman's murder. The coroner said suicide. Judge says the autopsy is inconsistent with that conclusion and, besides, why would happy-go-lucky Abbie off himself?

"He was depressed!" comes an angry woman's voice through the smoky haze. Judge stammers, but continues. The coroner who did Abbie's autopsy was the same one who covered up the murder—disguised as a car accident—of television journalist Jessica Savitch.

"She was a coke head!" the same voice shrieks. Judge, normally somewhat jaded, becomes impassioned. He gestures emphatically at the audience, which is rustling uneasily, unsure whether to cheer the heckler on and boo this conspiracy nut off the stage—or do exactly the reverse.

"No, I don't have the name of the person who killed Abbie Hoffman," Judge declares. "But if you don't think that kind of thing happens here, you don't know where you're living!"

The audience makes up its mind. It applauds Judge heartily as he stomps off. "I don't know if she was a plant or just an idiot," he says afterward. "But that's what they're going to say about everyone whom they kill in this decade. He was a coke head."

A precocious, somewhat maladjusted child of civilian Defense Department employees, Judge's career as a conspiracy researcher began at the age of ten, when his folks would drop him off in the Pentagon library.

"I didn't have a lot of friends and made friends out of books," he recalls. "I was growing up with neighbors from the CIA, NASA, Defense, understanding that there was a covert or sub-rosa reality to the government. And liking to do research . . . I had a twelfth-grade reading level by sixth grade. They wanted to boost me up in grades, but my mother wouldn't do it. She didn't want me to lose my social milieu."

Emory has one word for Judge's research: "garbage." Yet there are few factual points where they disagree except perhaps that Judge speaks at Abbie Hoffman memorial benefits, while Emory considers Hoffman a CIA provocateur. The difference as far as I can determine is a matter of personalities and of style. Emory makes it a point of honor to read his printed sources on the air. Judge is adverse even to using footnotes, feeling they're all part of the corrupt academic game.

Emory grants scant room for hope, with his melodramatic threats to pitch civilization and head for the hills, his ideology teetering on the brink of survivalism. Judge believes that the ultimate purpose of the fascist conspiracy is to "camouflage" the surplus of material goods created by industrialization. Without the swinging fist of capitalist-fascism, the world's wealth would be equitably distributed and we'd be living in something akin to paradise.

"To concentrate the wealth and maintain power, it's necessary to create a commoditized consumer society that wastes the material," Judge explains. "Also, to highlight war and war production, which is the ultimate capitalist product because it destroys other products, can only be used once and it brings in tremendous profit."

Emory veritably sneers at the appellation, "conspiracy theory." Judge embraces it. He runs a mail-order service for his articles and related literature. The name of the service is "Conspiracy!"

"Big deal," he shrugs. "Conspiracy. You don't think human history operates that way. How do you think the class carries out its will? All Adam Smith's magic hand, or do they have some schleppers to do their dirty work? And if they do, don't they have names, don't they have addresses and histories? Eventually you unearth a net of people who do certain things, who have interests aligned to money.

"I operate on that level. I don't operate on the level of looking around and saying all of history is a secret plot in a boardroom. But history is a concentration of power and wealth in certain hands, an aggregation of wealth from quite a while ago. And that concentration is going to do certain things to protect itself."

Emory and Judge have one common denominator—Mae Brussell. With her, they share a nightmarish vision of how far the "concentration of wealth" will go, and has gone—what "certain things" it will do.

From the Kennedy assassination to the Jonestown massacre to the bombing of Pan Am 103. Assassinations by induced cancer, hypnoprogrammed gunmen roaming suburban schoolyards, biological warfare weapons (AIDS, for one). Not even the crust of the earth is safe from manipulation. Invoking his signature slogan, "food for thought and grounds for further research" (his catchall for pure speculation), Emory noted that the 7.1 San Francisco earthquake of 1989, a 5.4 earthquake in the same area just two months earlier, and the rapacious Armenian earthquake of December 1988 had one thing in common. During each quake, the U.S. space shuttle was in orbit.

Earthquakes coinciding with shuttle flights could be chalked up to happenstance, Emory is well aware. Yet there remains the nagging problem that, according to Emory, some military weapons experts have predicted that seismic manipulation would render nuclear warheads obsolete in the twenty-first century. And Judge alleges that spy master general Reinhard Gehlen advocated weather warfare as a cleaner means of genocide, replacing the inefficient and unpopular extermination camps.

In the early 1970s, Mae Brussell predicted that the intention of the subterranean ruling class was to install Ronald Reagan in the White House. She said she was "laughed out of auditoriums" for publicizing this prediction. Reagan, then governor of California, was thought of much the way Dan Quayle is today, as a brainless boob beloved of right-wing extremists, but with no real national possibilities.

"The candidate is selected twenty years in advance," she said in early 1988, "and there is no stopping him." She pointed out that the predetermined ascendant to Reagan's seat would be George Bush.

Under Reagan and his successor, the country has been transformed from a creditor nation to a debtor, and the world's largest debtor at that. The national deficit is larger than ever and making matters worse, the Defense contracting, HUD, and Savings and Loan scandals amount to a large-scale, unprecedented looting of the national treasury. In Ian Fleming's *Goldfinger*, James Bond stops a criminal conspiracy from looting Fort Knox. That was fiction. Under Reagan and Bush, it really happened and there was no James Bond. In his place were David Emory, John Judge, and, for a while, Mae Brussell, howling at the moon.

"During the Great Depression, there were all sorts of Keyensian options that were open to us," says Emory. "They are not open to us anymore. Given the fact that America operates under the law of supply and demand, given an economic crunch, the comfort and perceived well-being of the American middle class is going to depend on their continued access to a sufficient number of goodies to preserve that illusion.

"I think what's going to happen is the number of goodies will be kept accessible by reducing the number of people competing for those goodies. I expect in this country to see large-scale eliminations of population." The extermination option has already been exercised he says, and the American people are blissfully unaware. The general public never questioned the "utterly preposterous" cover story of the Jonestown massacre, for example, despite the fact that many friends and relatives of the dead believed that Jonestown was some kind of government experiment. An aide to gunneddown congressman Leo Ryan found evidence that the CIA was involved. No coverage. No outrage.

"Granted that was down in Guyana, so people aren't going to investigate it, but are people going to investigate it if it's up in the Sierras?" says Emory. "Or how many people will go to Montana?

"It would in my opinion be very possible to round people up, put them in concentration camps, and *gas* them without having the public aware of it."

"If other people come up with stuff, it's called history," com-

plains John Judge. "If we come up with it, it's called conspiracy theory. Then the model they tend to discount or lump you with is that you're personally paranoid. There isn't even a *word* in the English language for realistic or rational fear."

If Emory's hopes for Mae Brussell's place in history come true, such a word will exist someday. I don't know what it would be, and I'm not optimistic that she will ever be recognized as, in Emory's words, "the Albert Einstein of political science." Then again, there was a time when you could say something similar about Albert Einstein.

"Intellectual culture," notes Dave Emory, the ominous voice in the night, "is by its very nature reactionary, and what Mae had to say went against the grain." The same is true for Emory's own research, and John Judge's. Mae Brussell may never find the mass acceptance that Emory says she deserves. If she does, she will do for the rest of us what she's already done for him. She not merely, as he puts it, "redefined the proper channels of inquiry in political science," she redefined reality.

Reality may never be the same.

# 8

# SHADOW PLAY IN NEW ORLEANS

*It's exactly like a chess problem. The Warren Commission moved the same pieces back and forth and got nowhere. I made a new move and solved the problem.*

JIM GARRISON

There were more than forty reporters by the pool at New Orleans' Fontainebleu Motel. They were waiting for the district attorney, a six-foot-six, pipe-puffing, pistol-packing politician, worthy to shoulder the tradition of high-living Louisiana politics. Often sighted lounging at the city's Playboy Club, he was also the scourge of Bourbon Street. A fighter pilot in World War II, he was discharged for psychological reasons during a tour of duty in Korea. When he ran for district attorney, he defeated a criminal court judge who had been the legal community's 3:1 favorite—by a 2:1 margin.

As renowned as the D.A. had become, his notoriety did not traverse the boundaries of New Orleans, where populism is as potent as voodoo. He knew that was about to change when he saw the swarm of reporters. Under his breath he whispered, "My God." It was February 20, 1967.

Garrison called the press conference to elaborate on his statements of two days earlier, statements he had made in aggravation after the *New Orleans States-Item* revealed the secret of Garrison's most sensational and daring stunt yet. He'd raided strip joints,

unseated judges, and faced down the mayor. But in late 1966 and early 1967, his office had been forebodingly silent.

Checking public records, where Garrison's expenditures were recorded, a couple of *States-Item* reporters found some unusual travel vouchers totaling eight thousand dollars. Where were Garrison's men going? Piecing together facts and rumors, they came out with a startling story. Three years after the Warren Commission concluded that Lee Harvey Oswald acted alone, the New Orleans district attorney was conducting his own investigation into the assassination of President John F. Kennedy.

The paper followed up its story with an editorial demanding an explanation from Garrison, implying unsubtly that he was gearing up not a solid case, but a grab at national media coverage.

Garrison shrugged off the revelations about his investigation as inevitable. The editorial's personal tone, on the other hand, infuriated him. He blasted back. Yes, he was conducting an investigation into a New Orleans–based conspiracy behind the president's murder and more than that, he proclaimed. "There will be arrests."

Arrests. The assassination of President Kennedy was less than four years into history. His successor was still in the White House, a constant reminder that a U.S. president had been murdered, and no one had ever been tried for the crime. There were no answers. The Warren Commission had satisfied some, at least in government circles, but it left much of the public with a queasy feeling. In 1966, an attorney named Mark Lane came out with a book that took a long ride on the best-seller list. Titled *Rush to Judgement*, it found enough holes, inconsistencies, and errors in the Warren Commission findings to set off a nationwide debate.

Tagged as a "Warren Report critic," Lane obviously believed there was a conspiracy in the assassination. Yet he never specified what the conspiracy might consist of. While he helped sharpen that vague uneasiness about the Warren Commission report, he created as much confusion as he quelled. And then came the district attorney of New Orleans: "There will be arrests."

Either the mystery would finally be solved, or this man was the most brazen opportunist in political history. Whichever, it made an irresistible story. When Garrison called a press conference at a private motel (where he'd be safe in barring the "irresponsible"

*States-Item*), the national media was there. His switchboard was deluged with calls from as far away as Moscow. Six years before, Garrison was a nobody city attorney with no political backing and an irrational urge to run for D.A. Over the next two years, he would become one of the country's most controversial public figures.

Twenty years after Garrison held his poolside press conference, Daniel P. Sheehan filed an affidavit with a federal court in Florida. Chief attorney for a nonprofit law firm called the Christic Institute, Sheehan was at least as obscure as Garrison, and the case he proposed to try—in civil court, not criminal—was an assassination case, but a little-known one. The allegations made by Sheehan, the result of a private investigation, were nonetheless as nerveracking as anything envisioned by Garrison.

The assassination cabal fingered by Garrison is the same underground empire unearthed in the Sheehan affidavit. It had not disbanded with Kennedy's assassination. According to Sheehan's narrative, the conspiracy was still in business. He found it hard at work in Central America, where, in the 1980s, the contra war was still hot.

From Garrison to Sheehan, New Orleans to Nicaragua, the more things remain the same, the more they've changed. If I understand what Garrison and Sheehan say—each in his own inimicable idiom—there has been one small group of men in charge of not only the American government but the American psyche. The shots to Kennedy's brain were the first wounds to our collective mind. The crossfire continued through the morally murky and bloody events of the three decades since. These days, sometimes it seems, our own brains have been blown away.

Jim Garrison sprang from nowhere to national infamy on that February day in 1967, but his entrance into New Orleans politics was equally confounding. As suited as he seems to that city, he was born seventy years ago in Denison, Iowa. His name was Earling Carothers Garrison. He didn't do much growing up in the corn country. When he was three, his parents split and his mother hustled the future conspiracy theorist to Chicago. After a while, his

father snatched him and took him back to Iowa. A legal battle ended with the boy in his mother's custody, back in the Windy City.

He served his tour in World War II, then went to Tulane University, where he earned his law degree. At Tulane, he insisted that people call him, simply, "Jim." He later changed his name legally to "Jim Garrison."

Garrison went to work as an assistant prosecutor in the New Orleans D.A.'s office, but his real sights were set on his boss's job. In 1961, after a couple of failed attempts at lesser offices, Garrison performed a political miracle. With no significant political support and just as little name recognition, Garrison drew on his considerable abilities as a political thespian. Vigorous, confident, and youthful, Garrison offered himself as a clear choice against the entrenched incumbent, Richard Dowling. He chided Dowling as "The Great Emancipator," for what Garrison said was Dowling's disposition to let felons go free.

Dowling did his own cause no good. A democratic patrician whiling away his latter years in what appeared to be secure public office, he wallowed in a stereotype of his own making. When Garrison blasted him for retaining his private practice with a prominent firm while in office, Dowling replied that he could not maintain a life-style befitting his stature on his paltry fifteen thousand dollar public salary. If the voters didn't like this comfy arrangement, Dowling declared, they could go right ahead and elect themselves a "new boy."

Jim Garrison was that new boy.

Grand flourishes continued once Garrison took office. He began "cleaning up" Bourbon Street, arresting homosexuals, prostitutes, and B-girls, putting the sleazier joints out of business, pressuring the more classy to further refine their ambience.

When the city's criminal court judges, a panel of eight, tried to bring Garrison under their control by cutting off his vice-busting cash flow, Garrison refused to be chastened. He challenged the judges' integrity, suggesting that there may have been "racketeer influence" in their decision. He also ridiculed the judges' work ethic, or lack thereof, needling them for taking over two hundred holidays in a year. The judges sued him for defamation. Garrison

held his ground right through to the Supreme Court, where he won a landmark decision upholding the right to criticize public officials.

He announced his candidacy for state attorney general, but let the filing deadline pass without doing anything. He insinuated that he might run for mayor against Victor Schiro, whom he'd crossed during the D.A.'s race. Schiro responded by investigating Garrison for corruption. Garrison parried with an investigation of the mayor.

When the state legislature failed to pass one of Garrison's pet bills, he wondered aloud if the legislators had been bribed. The legislature censured Garrison, and he responded with characteristic *cojones* calling the censure "an honor."

In 1965, he won a second term, crushing his opponent, who just happened to be one of the allegedly goldbricking judges Garrison had previously humiliated. Returned to office, he turned his public-relations bazooka on the New Orleans police, who he felt were not adequately supportive of his crackdown on Bourbon Street vice. The cops returned serve, arresting Linda Brigette, a stripper who danced in a club owned by a Garrison ally. Garrison prosecuted her but she never served any time, and soon he was lobbying the new governor (who was elected with Garrison's help) for her unconditional pardon.

Such was the turbulent tenure of Jim Garrison, district attorney, man about town. Until November 1966. Then the grandstanding ceased, the pyrotechnics fizzled. The towering figure clad in white dinner jacket barhopping the French Quarter was gone. Garrison vanished from public view, even changing his unlisted phone number.

He broke his silence three months later. "There will be arrests."

The secret investigation in 1966, the one that led Garrison to announce in May 1967 that he and his staff "solved the assassination weeks ago . . . we know the key individuals, cities involved, and how it was done," was not the first time Garrison had peeked into the assassination mystery. On November 23, 1963, one short day after J.F.K. died, Garrison decided to check out whether Lee Harvey Oswald had any associates in New Orleans. Oswald, as we

detailed earlier, spent the summer of 1963 in New Orleans, his hometown.

A couple of stories whetted Garrison's suspicions. He had heard that an acquaintance of his, a normally levelheaded if extremely right-wing private investigator named Guy Bannister, had spontaneously pistol-whipped a drinking buddy the day of the assassination. The buddy was Jack Martin, another P.I. Martin, the story went, triggered the assault by taunting Bannister. There had been certain people frequenting Bannister's office that summer, Martin chided. He told Bannister he would remember who they were. Bannister responded by trying to pound the memory out of Martin's head with a gun butt.

Bannister's office was at 544 Camp Street in New Orleans, the address made famous by Oswald, who stamped it on his Fair Play for Cuba handouts. Putting the two facts together, Garrison—along with a lot of other people—figured that Bannister was running Oswald as a front. Bannister, it would turn out, had CIA connections. The theory expanded: Oswald was being set up as a fake Marxist, giving him a prefabricated motive for the assassination.

Those musings would all come much later. In 1963, Garrison was intrigued by Jack Martin's tales, and Martin was well known to spin them. A New Orleans *States-Item* reporter once termed Martin "as full of that well-known waste material as a yule hen." The same reporter also noted, however, that Martin did have "the friendship and confidence of reputable, well-placed individuals . . . he must be taken with a grain of salt leavened by a grain of confidence."

Martin told of another Bannister operative, a flying ace named David Ferrie, who, on the evening of November 22, drove all night through the rain to Houston, Texas. According to Martin, Ferrie was to fly the J.F.K. assassins over the Mexican border. Presumably his flight would be the second leg of the shooters' getaway. When Ferrie got back to New Orleans a couple of days later, Garrison had him arrested and turned over to the FBI. Ferrie was quickly released.

In 1967, after Ferrie died suddenly, Garrison beatified him as "one of history's most important individuals." Perhaps. Perhaps not. One thing is certain; Ferrie was one of New Orleans' most bizarre individuals. His reputation as an aerobatic adventurer was

local legend. Much of his derring-do was performed under contract to the CIA. Ferrie was both a fanatical anti-Communist and a well-known night crawler on the New Orleans homosexual party circuit. When some of Ferrie's exploits with teenage males became public in 1962, he lost his job at Eastern Airlines.

In all likelihood, Ferrie knew Oswald since the accused assassin was a teenager. Oswald served in a Civil Air Patrol unit commanded by Ferrie, who was said to have the boys under his command mesmerized.

The most strikingly strange trait Ferrie flaunted was his face. Somehow, he had lost all his hair, all over his body. He once said it was burned off in a plane crash. He once said he lost it due to a rare tropical disease. Ferrie's macabre attempt to compensate for this deficiency consisted of dressing for Halloween every day. He wore a badly fitting scarlet toupee and scribbled on Groucho Marxian eyebrows with greasepaint. To match his Dadaesque visage, he adopted the fashion sensibilities of a circus clown.

A true nut case, Ferrie took up cancer research as one of his hobbies. His apartment was filled with caged mice, on which he carried out a regimen of unusual experiments, the nature of which is not quite clear.

The FBI cleared Ferrie. Garrison saw no reason to dispute the findings of the largest law enforcement agency in the land. He forgot all about it.

At least, he says he forgot all about it. When the news of his 1966 investigation broke, Ferrie surfaced again. Panicking, he went to the local media and announced that he was Garrison's suspect and that he was completely innocent. Two days after Garrison's press conference at the Fontainebleau Motel, David Ferrie was found naked under a sheet in bed at home, dead.

Ferrie's curiously timed demise was the one event that turned the Garrison investigation from a sideshow to serious business. The coroner ruled that death came from a cerebral aneurism, noting that Ferrie had actually suffered one before, with no apparent ill effects—a medical rarity.

Garrison announced that Ferrie's death was suicide—Ferrie figured the game was up, and snuffed himself. Proponents of the "strange deaths" hypothesis find it more likely that Ferrie was

murdered by an insidious method that could disguise the death as natural.

Within hours after Ferrie's body was found, his close friend Aladio del Valle, a Cuban exile, was discovered shot through the heart in Miami.

Most of the press expected that Garrison, whom they took for a grandstander anyway, would now claim victory as verified by the "suicide" of his star witness and suspect, and get back to the business of busting burlesque houses and aggravating local politicians.

Jim Garrison double-crossed his detractors again. Less than two weeks after "one of history's most important individuals" was discovered cold and unclothed, Garrison made good on his promise that "there will be arrests."

Clay Shaw was a pillar of the New Orleans business community. Garrison pilloried him. The case against Shaw began on May 1, 1967, with his arrest on charges of conspiracy in the murder of President John F. Kennedy, and ended exactly two years later, with his acquittal.

"I continued to believe that Shaw had participated in the conspiracy to kill the president," writes Garrison in his autobiography, "his role having been essentially to set up Lee Oswald as the patsy." But he had an impossible time establishing Shaw's motivations. Garrison attempted to tie him in with Ferrie, Oswald, the New Orleans homosexual underground, and, of course, the CIA. Publicly, the businessman was known as a moderate liberal who felt favorably toward Kennedy. To make the case tougher, Shaw appears to have committed perjury by denying on the stand that he had known David Ferrie.

Garrison's failure to pin even a small part of the postulated J.F.K. conspiracy on Shaw was widely read as a repudiation of conspiracy theories. It was not. Much of the evidence Garrison gathered goes far toward supporting a conspiracy.

Nonetheless, damage was done. It wasn't simply that Garrison lost his case. It was the way he lost it. His best witness, Perry Russo, claimed he'd been in a meeting at which Shaw, Oswald, and Ferrie discussed assassinating the president. Russo was caught in

contradictory statements, and Garrison tried to sculpt his testimony with hypnotism and drugs. Another witness who testified he'd seen Shaw and Oswald together admitted he was on heroin at the time. Garrison also relied heavily on a notation in Shaw's address book, a post office box number for someone called "Lee Odom" in Dallas, Texas. Garrison said he found the same P.O. number, sans identification, in Oswald's little black book and, furthermore, he contended, the number was actually a coded version of Jack Ruby's phone number.

Pretty flimsy stuff on which to base the criminal case of the century. All the while, Garrison marched on with shoulders back, chest out, chin up, without a qualm that his conduct was bringing down not only his whole prosecution, but justifiably or not, an entire movement.

The taint of Jim Garrison sticks to assassination conspiracy theories. Things did not have to turn out that way.

Whether Garrison had the goods on Shaw for sure can never be known. Shaw died in 1974. Witnesses saw ambulance attendants carrying a covered body on a stretcher *into* Shaw's house before he was found, and no autopsy was ever performed. Ferrie died; Bannister died of a heart attack; and another of his associates was thrown out—or fell out—of a Panama hotel room in 1964. That was Maurice Gatlin, Sr., who was also connected with the CIA and its anti-Communist activities in Latin America. Even with the lead players six feet under, and Garrison stereotyped in the media as a man eloping with his own ambition, there are still suggestive remnants from the Jim Garrison investigation.

In 1979, Richard Helms, zipper-lipped former CIA director, finally admitted that Clay Shaw had in fact been what he called a "part-time contact" of the agency. Shaw's CIA connections had been confirmed four years earlier when whistle-blower Victor Marchetti, Helms' one-time deputy, described how Helms fretted throughout Garrison's probe, worried that Shaw's cover would be blown. That doesn't necessarily mean Shaw had anything to do with the Kennedy assassination. It does mean that he wasn't telling his whole story, and neither was the CIA.

One of Garrison's earliest and harshest detractors, Warren Report skeptic Edward Jay Epstein, accuses Garrison of numerous "self-fulfilling prophecies." Garrison's major theme, once he became a national media personage replete with an appearance on Johnny Carson's "Tonight Show" and a lengthy interview in *Playboy* magazine, was CIA "news suppression." In Epstein's view, Garrison was using this charge as a convenient out whenever he was devoid of evidence to support an allegation. That is, Garrison would make unsubstantiated allegations, claiming that supporting evidence was in the hands of the CIA. When the CIA didn't cough it up, that proved that the CIA was covering it up. The cover-up, or "second conspiracy," allowed Garrison to cite nonexistent evidence to support virtually any charge.

That's how Epstein saw it. He was right to take Garrison to task for this clever twist of sophistry. Even so, there was more to the story than Garrisonian demagoguery.

Garrison asserted perhaps somewhat recklessly that Oswald worked for U.S. intelligence agencies. True, he did base this conclusion on, as Epstein wrote, "[his] own private interpretation of 'missing' or classified documents he had never seen."

Tom Bethell was the man who brought those secret documents to Garrison's attention. Bethell, a British schoolteacher and jazz buff, was in New Orleans to study the city's musical heritage. He got sidetracked by a strange fascination with Garrison's theory (Bethell is now an editor of the conservative political magazine *The American Spectator*). At Garrison's behest, Bethell went to Washington and dug through the National Archives. He turned up over 350 Warren Commission documents that were still classified. Of those, he noted twenty-nine that, based upon their headings, appeared to be of particular interest.

The CIA, according to Bethell's list, had a secret document containing information on Oswald's knowledge of the U-2 spy plane program, begging the question, why would a ne'er-do-well private have any knowledge of the U-2 plane? Also in the classified files was a document recording "statements of George De-Mohrenschildt re: assassination." DeMohrenschildt was the White Russian émigré who became Oswald's friend and mentor after Oswald returned from his odd "defection" to the Soviet Union. He

was also CIA connected. Why would the CIA keep secret his comments regarding the assassination?

One of the nonclassified documents Bethell found contained a notarized statement by a state department official who said he had received information on Oswald from the CIA a month prior to the assassination. While the mere fact that the Oswald file was classified does not "prove" any of Garrison's claims, why the CIA would be interested in this supposedly alienated loser with a failing marriage and few friends seems a fair question.

Nor is it unreasonable to infer that the CIA would take such an interest because the agency is interested in keeping track of its agents—or the agents of other intelligence agencies. There's often speculation that Oswald worked for some branch of military intelligence, possibly Naval Intelligence, since he was a marine. Guy Bannister, reportedly Oswald's controller, was a Naval Intelligence vet in addition to his work for the CIA and his employment by the FBI.

More than a decade after Garrison first made news, the House Select Committee on Assassinations interviewed a former CIA employee who said he was "convinced" that Oswald "had been recruited by the agency to infiltrate the Soviet Union." The committee questioned Richard Helms, who acknowledged that the CIA had a file on Oswald, but that it was a "dummy file," just a folder, nothing in it. He was not asked if the folder had ever contained anything, or why the CIA would keep even an empty file on a disaffected loner like Oswald.

Again, Garrison's public motor mouthing obscured and discredited an aspect of the case that deserved serious investigation. He chose to make his case in the papers, rather than the courtroom.

Garrison had more curious evidence. In the three weeks before the assassination, Ferrie (the alleged would-be getaway pilot for the J.F.K. killers) deposited seven thousand dollars in the bank, Garrison discovered. Jack Ruby, Oswald's killer, had a similar financial windfall around the same time. Garrison was also right in his allegation that the wealthy Shaw and Ferrie knew each other. In Robert Groden's book *High Treason*, there are photos of the pair at what the author says is a gay party.

David Ferrie, in addition to being a CIA operative, worked for

New Orleans mob boss Carlos Marcello. On the morning of the assassination, before he jumped in his car and took off for Houston, Ferrie was in a courtroom watching Marcello fight off another of Attorney General Robert Kennedy's deportation attempts. Marcello had previously made what at least one of his associates considered a serious threat against President Kennedy's life, as had Marcello's mob associate Santos Trafficante—one of the CIA's contacts in its Castro hit plots. The FBI learned of Marcello's threat and dismissed it. In 1979, when the Select Committee on Assassinations heard about this incident, it characterized the FBI's reaction as "deficient."

Garrison for some reason never displayed any interest in Ferrie's mob ties, only in his homosexual and intelligence contacts. For that and other reasons, Garrison himself has been suspected of taking more than a prosecutorial interest in organized crime.

John Roselli was one of the CIA's main connections to the mob. He was strangled and dismembered shortly before he was to testify to the Assassinations Committee. When the committee came out in 1979 with its report, it noted that Garrison and Roselli met within the month after Ferrie's fortuitously timed death. The "secret meeting" took place in a Las Vegas hotel.

Garrison dismisses the committee's notation as "absolutely false," the work of the "disinformation machinery of the government's main clandestine operation." Being targeted by this formidable opponent, remarks Garrison in his autobiography, is "no small honor."

Not surprisingly, Garrison labels all attempts to link him with organized crime as "canards." Both *Look* and *Life* magazines ran articles during his investigation, insinuating that Garrison owes favors to Carlos Marcello, who, according to the allegations, gave Garrison some meaty perks.

Not only does Garrison deny any ties to organized crime, he has come forth with Hooveresque denials that organized crime exists in New Orleans. In his autobiography, Garrison says he never found "any evidence that [Marcello] was the Mafia kingpin the Justice Department says he is."

On the other hand, as Garrison himself points out, it was not much of a friendly overture to the underworld when he stamped

out numbers running and flattened the brothel business in New
Orleans. Author William Turner has reported that Garrison once
refused a sizable Mafia bribe.

Through the mob allegations, through his many confrontations
with powerful politicians, through his battles with the national
media, Jim Garrison never fell too far out of favor with the New
Orleans voters. He won three terms as D.A., finally losing a race in
1973. His constituents didn't let him stay down for long. He was
elected to the appellate bench in 1977, and after serving a ten-year
term, was elected to another one. Today, he is a judge on the
Louisiana Court of Appeals.

None of that has quelled the skepticism of Garrison's doubters,
who ask if Garrison's blasé approach to David Ferrie in 1963 had
less to do with his faith in the FBI's omniscience than with Ferrie's
underworld connections.

An even darker suspicion sprung from the Left. As Garrison's
case frayed, the notion appeared that despite Garrison's vitupera-
tive tirades against the Warren Commission, his investigation and
theirs may have more than a little in common. Could Jim Garrison,
the new skeptics asked, be part of a second-level cover-up designed
to discredit legitimate inquiries into an assassination conspiracy?
Intended or not, Garrison produced that unfortunate effect.

To diehards, Garrison is still a hero, a man against the system
who fought courageously in pursuit of truth against a Big Brother
federal government determined to uphold its own destructive fiction. To his credit, Garrison was the only law enforcement official
to attempt a prosecution of any kind in the most important American murder case of the century. To his shame, he blew it.

For most people, even for serious researchers into the Kennedy
assassination of whom there remain plenty, Garrison is an historical
curiosity. In many ways, he is as complex and confused a character
as Lee Harvey Oswald, a blight of contradictions, not completely
cognizant of his own mission. Maybe, just maybe, he had cracked
one of history's most cryptic cases. At this point, it doesn't matter.
There is another lawyer crusading on the conspiracy trail who has
tracked the plot from New Orleans to Nicaragua.

# 9

# SUING THE SECRET TEAM

*Nothing could hurt us! We'd become a corporation an' unner business law corporations are defined as immortal beings! HA HA! We're IMMORTAL! WE NEVER DIE!*

> Speech by a drunken American Eagle from *Brought to Light* by Alan Moore and Bill Sienkiewicz

Daniel Sheehan, who studied at Harvard Divinity School, has his spiritual side, but since 1986 he has been chasing spooks. The forty-five page affidavit he filed in a Florida federal court is now the eye in a pyramid of a conspiracy theory called the "Secret Team." But the "Secret Team" is more than a theory. It is a corporeal group of men with names and addresses. Names that can be listed on a civil lawsuit under "defendants." Addresses where they can be served subpoenas.

Sheehan is chief counsel for the Christic Institute, a Washington, D.C.–based shoestring-budget, public-interest law firm and self-described "interfaith public policy center" that takes up cases, and causes, with some socially conscious tilt. Before the founding of the Christics, Sheehan always leaned in that direction. He was fired from his first job, a plum that most law school grads would kill for, at a big-time Wall Street litigation firm. They said he was doing too much *pro bono*. He was defending rioting prison inmates and Black Panthers. Not Wall Street style. He spent a year working for

headline-hounding trial lawyer F. Lee Bailey, but that experience fell short of his ideals as well. Sheehan was lost in the law in 1973.

Almost two decades later, Sheehan looks like he never drifted away from that era. I saw him in late 1989 at one of his many fund-raising lecture stops. He had the bushy hair and sideburns of a legal aide to the Watergate Committee. A tan sportcoat and a sunny yellow wide tie topped off the anachronism. Politically, he lives in the early 1970s.

The 1970s are a decade much ridiculed—the "nothing happened" decade. Actually, it was an era of American soul-searching and gut spilling, of intense self-examination, something that vanished in the cash-fixated 1980s. This was not the narcissistic personal self-examination memorialized as the "Me Decade"; that came later. The last years of Vietnam and the Nixon-Ford days brought on a national, political self-scrutiny that this country could use today. The aversion to meaningful introspection in the 1980s and 1990s is Sheehan's frustration.

Watergate opened a crack into the nocturnal world of clandestine politics and allowed a splinter of light to shine through. The crack threatened to widen into a chasm with the Church Committee's probe of the CIA, the Rockefeller Commission, and House Select Committee on Assassinations.

The secret government was being seductively stripped, and Sheehan was aroused. He was on the five-lawyer team that defended the *New York Times* in the Pentagon Papers case. After dropping out of divinity school, he worked for the American Civil Liberties Union and defended Native Americans from Wounded Knee, the radical-Catholic Berrigan brothers, and Dick Gregory.

In 1976, Sheehan took over a civil lawsuit brought by the parents of a young woman who had been killed in a car accident—Karen Silkwood. She died en route to give evidence to the Atomic Energy Commission about dangerous practices at the nuclear power plant where she was employed. Silkwood, apparently, was contaminated by radiation. The government never heard her evidence. Her friends and family believed she was not an accident victim, but that she had been murdered. Sheehan agreed. His opponent in the case was Kerr-McGee, a gigantic energy company.

Sheehan shoved the corporate monolith and dislodged it, winning a civil suit and vindicating Silkwood. Although the lawsuit did not prove that Silkwood was murdered, it was another foray for Sheehan into the demonic inner workings of the corporate-government establishment. His latest adventure, the "Secret Team" suit, bores right to the black heart of that monster.

Sheehan now alleges that he has identified the shadow government, the group of ruthless men who really run the country, and who have been in that position at least since the assassination of President Kennedy. Watergate allowed a peek behind the veil of secrecy. The Christic Institute lawsuit paints a portrait—nude. But outside of Danny Sheehan and his devotees, the nation is averting its eyes.

Sheehan's clients are two American journalists. In 1984, Tony Avrigan and Martha Honey were in Honduras covering a press conference. The speaker was Eden Pastora, a contra, but not a typical one. Fed up with CIA manipulation of the contra cause, he wanted to break away and start his own movement. At the press conference called to announce his intentions, a bomb went off. One American reporter was killed. Avrigan was badly injured.

The husband-and-wife reporters began to investigate the bombing, an investigation joined by the Christic Institute when it took them on as plaintiffs. They discovered that the attempt on Pastora's life was not, as it had originally been portrayed, Sandinista sponsored. The culprits were Pastora's rival contras, or, more precisely, the invisible institution behind the contras. That nameless entity was a chimera of CIA agents and Columbian cocaine kingpins, soulless mercenaries and fanatical ideologues, multinational businessmen and guttersnipe thugs. Sheehan labeled this chthonic enterprise "The Secret Team."

The Avrigan-Honey/Sheehan-Christic lawsuit names twenty-nine men as participants in the Secret Team. The term itself was the title of a book by Col. L. Fletcher Prouty, former liaison officer connecting the CIA and the Pentagon. In a position to know, Prouty wrote that the government is actually operated by just such

a "team." The twenty-nine individuals listed in the lawsuit are not Sheehan's true targets. The reeking maw of a system that disgorged them is what he really aims to shut down.

Included on the list of defendants are names well known to trackers of the Iran-Contra trail: Richard Secord, the retired general who was the Iran-Contra congressional committee's leadoff witness; John Hull, CIA operative whose Costa Rican ranch was allegedly a drug and gun runners' airport; and Albert Hakim, the elusive arms dealer who helped pull the Iranian arms deals together. Also on the list were such masterminds as Ted "The Blonde Ghost" Shackley, former CIA covert operations chief often credited with setting up the agency's Laotian opium smuggling connections, and General John Singlaub, leader of the fascistically tinged World Anti-Communist League.

The allegations in Sheehan's affidavit come from a private investigation with close to seventy sources, many deep inside the CIA and the defense establishment, Sheehan says. One of the few sources he names is Edwin Wilson, the supposedly "renegade" CIA man now in jail for selling arms to Libya. Sheehan has assembled assertions, information, and innuendo, and he has written a story. Like Jim Garrison, Sheehan is struggling to reify his theory in the firm ground of law. He has a tool unavailable to Garrison. The federal Racketeer-Influenced and Corrupt Organizations Act (RICO) allows Sheehan to accuse the Secret Team of "a pattern of racketeering" that includes every transgression against man and nature from drug smuggling to murder to coup d'état. They trade not only in narcotics, missiles, and money, but in nations and lives, hearts and minds.

"By any definition," says Sheehan's affidavit, "these defendants, alleged merchants of heroin and terrorism, are organized criminals on a scale larger than life."

A florid, torrid rhetorician, Sheehan's sweeping proclamations have been both the greatest risk to his credibility and his most powerful means of winning support—support the Christic Institute urgently needs. The case cost something like forty thousand dollars per week to maintain, even with Sheehan and Sara Nelson— his wife and the institute's director—taking salaries under twenty thousand dollars per year.

On February 3, 1989, a U.S. District Court judge tossed the lawsuit out of court and ordered the institute to pay one million dollars in attorney's fees to the defendants. Whether or not that total included the sixty thousand dollars Richard Secord reportedly spent on propaganda to discredit the institute is not clear. But the case continued. At this writing, it is still awaiting its day in court, before a panel of three appellate judges in Atlanta. Like the horizon, that day never seems to get any closer, no matter how far forward Dan Sheehan moves.

Sheehan insists that fear among the Secret Teamsters is peaking as his chance of getting the Christic case heard increases. He has been successful in provoking outrage from the defendants. John Singlaub's animosity toward the Christics is not something he hides. He once said that, if he could, he'd "ask for an air strike to blow the bastards away." Ted Schackley has called the institute "malevolent" in an article he wrote for *Defense and Diplomacy*. John Hull rants that the Christics are nothing but a Commie front.

Their power is threatened by public exposure, Sheehan says. His affidavit makes only a brief mention of the J.F.K. assassination, but in his public appearances Sheehan is unequivocal. Once the Secret Team is exposed, so, too, will the conspiracy behind the deaths of John Kennedy, Robert Kennedy, and Martin Luther King, Jr.—as well as the drug epidemic and the vast stupefying of America produced by disillusionment combined with deliberate policies that strengthen the forces of violence while ignoring basic human needs.

Jim Garrison and Daniel Sheehan were never after a single group of criminals. The Secret Team theory is not merely a gangster novel; it is a biblical epic. The conspirators are not simply greedy or power mad; they are the agents of an almost alchemical social, political, and psychological transformation. They created a world of twilight, torture, and mendacity. Their world is now our world.

Whether the conspiracy theories derive from faith, fact, or a mixture thereof, the world we live in is unavoidably real, and it seems to get less livable all the time. If only we could understand it, we might be able to find our way through. But in a society where the obfuscation of elitist "experts" passes for understanding, the

relative clarity of even the most convoluted conspiracy theories—
and the Secret Team theory is not exactly crystalline in its
simplicity—will always be thrown out of court.

Part Two of this book looks at the flip side of popular reality.
What follows is as exhaustive a compendium of American conspiracy theories as I could compile. Rather than list every theory, and
attribute it to a particular theorist—an impossible task, with the
endless overlap among them—I've let the conspiracy theorists
guide me to the "evidence" itself. Most of the material in the
following chapters comes from mainstream or slightly off-center
sources.

Journalists like to think of themselves as a skeptical lot. This is a
flawed self-image. The thickest pack of American journalists are all
too credulous when dealing with government officials, technical
experts, and other official sources. They save their vaunted "skepticism" for ideas that feel unfamiliar to them. Conspiracy theories are
treated with the most rigorous skepticism.

Conspiracy theories should be approached skeptically. But
there's no fairness. Skepticism should apply equally to official and
unofficial information. To explain American conspiracy theories,
over the next eight chapters, I've had to rectify this imbalance. I've
opened myself to conspiracy theories, and applied total skepticism
to official stories.

Dan Sheehan has been trying in court to prove how this nation
has been corrupted by a conspiracy. He is using the system as it was
designed, to change what the system has become. Before the system
can be changed from within, I believe, there has to be a change in
the way we think about our country. The second part of this book is
the result of an experiment in making that change: within myself,
because, for each of us, that's where it all must begin.

*Part Two*

# THE
# CONSPIRACY

# 10

# Coup D'État in the U.S.A.

*There is no doubt now there was a conspiracy, yet most of us are not very angry about it. The conspiracy to kill the president of the United States was also a conspiracy against the democratic system—and thus a conspiracy against **you**. I think you should get very angry about that.*

> Gaeton Fonzi
> Investigator, House Select Committee on Assassinations

Assassination is a special kind of killing. Not murder for money, not murder for revenge. Assassins kill for political control. One bullet and a whole nation—government policies, economy, zeitgeist, and all—can be altered.

History is speckled with assassinations—from Julius Caesar to the shooting of Austrian archduke Francis Ferdinand, which set off the First World War. In other countries, assassination is part of the political process.

Not in America. In America, our assassins are like our serial killers—roving lunatics who crisscross the country stalking their prey. They cause politicians a few nervous hours, but they're no threat to the American way of life. They have no motives. Therefore their actions, traumatic as an earthquake or a tornado, are just as meaningless. The consequences of their senseless violence is mere historical chance. Or so we'd like to think.

123

Assassination conspiracies, of all conspiracy theory genres, drill into America's rawest nerve. They shatter the foundation of our national ego, the firm American faith in our moral superiority. We like to think of ourselves as the world's original, and most stable, democracy. It is a comforting notion: Because we're always in the right, nothing can ever go wrong. Other countries change their political system through murder; ours is immune to its influence. Political murder is impractical, not to mention uncouth.

But American chauvinism is only one reason assassination conspiracy theories cut so deep. Another is more paradoxical. The very plausibility of assassination conspiracies is what makes them so hard to swallow. The more real our fears, the greater our psychological defenses. Assassination theories are terrifying because they could be true.

As difficult as it would be to maintain a massive conspiracy to rule the world, a limited conspiracy against one person is easy to assemble. Yet eliminating one person can be a most powerful means of controlling a whole society of people. If President John F. Kennedy was killed by a conspiracy, this doesn't necessarily mean that there is a permanent, global conspiracy. But killing Kennedy was a good step toward ruling America, which rules a large part of the world.

The United States Congress, in the form of the House Select Committee on Assassinations, took the official position that J.F.K. was "probably" assassinated by a conspiracy. The committee reluctantly acknowledged the most limited kind of conspiracy—a conspiracy of two people, Lee Harvey Oswald and an unknown accomplice. But the committee investigated any number of Mafia and intelligence community characters on its road to that conclusion. The congressmen clearly suspected something bigger, although they lacked the will to specify what.

Even a larger conspiracy involving criminals and intelligence agents does not mean that there is an all-consuming, illuminati conspiracy. It doesn't mean there isn't one either. Researchers such as Mae Brussell and Dave Emory place the Mafia-CIA brotherhood into a sprawling network of Nazis and fascists who gained their grip on the U.S. government after World War II, when the U.S. collab-

orated with thousands of Nazis to set up the then-burgeoning Cold War national security establishment.

That's the problem with admitting even the tiniest conspiracy. Once you step into the forest, there's no telling where the trails will lead. Perhaps our government can be controlled by a shrewd group of killers. There have been more than a few political assassinations in recent decades, including one of an American president. Perhaps the coup d'état has already been carried out.

The official mythology of American politics prefers a combination of two different theories of history. For lack of better labels, let's call them the "process" theory and the "accident" theory.

The "accident" theory gave us the "lone nut" political assassin. If all assassinations are merely the work of crazies acting on their own, then there is no such thing as a coup d'état. When lone nuts appear, it's the fault of psychology, not politics. Such random occurrences may cause a few policies to shift, but they don't affect the American system.

One noteworthy policy change: Six weeks before his death, President Kennedy announced a new policy of "Vietnamization." The growing conflict in Indochina, he declared, would be turned over to the Vietnamese. Americans—who were already sinking into the morass—would be pulled out before it was too late. Kennedy even confided to advisers that after his reelection he would embark on a full-scale withdrawal from Vietnam, to be finished by 1965.

Two days after J.F.K.'s assassination, on November 24, 1963, new president Lyndon Johnson—in one of his first official acts as commander in chief—issued National Security Action Memo Number 273. The directive completely discarded Kennedy's peace plans. Everyone knows the rest of that story.

The "lone nut" doctrine is dogma, and assassination conspiracy theories heresy, because madmen have no political motives. "Lone nuts" strip assassinations of their meaning: Violence *can* change the American system.

Typical of academics is the psychoanalysis of assassination conspiracy theories offered by G. William Domhoff: "We all have a tremendous tendency to want to get caught up in believing that

there's some secret evil cause for all of the obvious ills of the world." Conspiracy theories "encourage a belief that if we get rid of a few bad people, everything would be well in the world," he muses.

This school of thought sees conspiracy theories as some sort of psychological defense mechanism, but, armchair analysis aside, the personality quirks of conspiracy theorists hardly serve as refutation of the odd facts they uncover. How they string those facts together is more a matter of the way they see the world—a different viewpoint, not a mental defect.

If the J.F.K. assassination was the work of lone nut Lee Harvey Oswald, acting out of some personal sense of disgruntlement and alienation, then the whole Vietnam War was an accident. But what if the assassination was carried out by a conspiracy? Could escalating the war, for reasons of ideology and corporate profiteering, have been one of the conspirators' motivations? Then wouldn't the Vietnam War be an event planned by individuals outside the American system of electoral politics, of check and balance? The American system, it would appear, could have been altered by that cross fire in Dallas. And, more importantly, by the people who planned it.

The history of American assassination conspiracy theories starts on November 22, 1963. The killing of John F. Kennedy was not the first time an American president was assassinated. Nor was it the first time that the possibility of conspiracy was mentioned in connection with a presidential assassination. Eight people besides John Wilkes Booth were convicted of conspiring to assassinate Abraham Lincoln. Four were hanged.

The Kennedy assassination was different. More modern.

There is a whole generation of students in college now who were born after the 1960s were over, born in a world in which the Beatles had already broken up. A world in which Richard Nixon had already been president and, rather than carrying out his promise to end the Vietnam War, was dropping bombs on Cambodia instead. The love-in at Woodstock had already happened; peace marches and civil disobedience had been replaced by orgies of hatred and burning cities.

Something new and malignant had surfaced in America. It first appeared when Kennedy's head was blown open as he rode in an uncovered limousine through a grimy section of Dallas, on a route, incidentally, that he had never planned to take.

Political scientist Bradley Klein gave a concise description of the American metamorphosis when I interviewed him for a story I wrote on the assassination's twenty-fifth anniversary in 1988. "It was a different world," he said, of the days before Dallas. "It was a world in which people still had savings and you got by with a family of four on one income. There was a sense of America's place in the world. Now things have become vicious and ugly and nasty."

Doesn't it feel like there's a direct path from Dallas to the brutal state of society today?

The path leads from the assassination through Vietnam, the assassination of Martin Luther King, Jr., which led to several years of rioting, and the slaying of Robert Kennedy—without which Richard Nixon would almost certainly never have been president. The calamities continue, through Watergate, another national trauma. The same year, conservative Democratic presidential contender George Wallace was shot and paralyzed. Together with the Watergate dirty tricks campaign, the Wallace shooting insured that Nixon would be president for a second term.

Watergate was followed by all sorts of sordid revelations about the CIA—including its plethora of attempts in cahoots with the Mafia to knock off Fidel Castro. There was conflict in the Middle East, which led to a false "gas shortage." Oil companies were able to jack up prices several hundred percent. They enriched themselves, consolidated power, and unleashed oppressive inflation.

In a later chapter, we'll see links between oil companies and the CIA. As early as the 1950s, the National Security Council had authored a secret directive designating multinational oil companies "instruments" of U.S. foreign policy. Big oil companies were put beyond the reach of U.S. law.

The overthrow of American-backed Shah Reza Pahlavi of Iran by a radical Islamic uprising came next. The Iranian revolutionaries seized an embassy full of American hostages and destroyed the administration of President Jimmy Carter. Carter's "Desert One" attempted rescue mission only made matters worse. The rescue

copters crashed in the Iranian desert. One of the players in the Desert One scenario was General Richard Secord, who would become a public figure a few years later, as one of the Iran-Contra conspirators.

Mixed into this parade of perdition were assorted terrorist killings, hijackings, and kidnappings in the U.S. and abroad, which reinforced American feelings of national irrelevance, individual impotence, and governmental iniquity.

It is a logical fallacy to assume that outcome and motive are necessarily the same. Nonetheless, after the Kennedy killing, the United States petrified into a permanent war economy. The Vietnam War segued quickly into the renewed Cold War. Even when our Eastern Bloc "enemies" loosened up, President Bush warned that there would be no "peace dividend" from reduced military spending. Of every America federal tax dollar, more than twenty-five cents goes to the defense budget. Huge defense contracting companies siphon trillions from the economy. The money goes to no productive use, crippling the capacity for individual enterprise and, with it, the American spirit. Draw your own conclusions.

The harvest of these sad seeds was the cynical and shallow Reagan 1980s. Political involvement dropped to record lows, while power grew ever more centralized in a shrinking number of gigantic corporations. Freed from public oversight, the corporations acted almost as nations unto themselves. The weak ones died while the strong merged. The corporate takeover of America concentrated economic power in the hands of a few, but showed its most anti-democratic effects in the media business. Not only money, but information—the air, water, and food of democracy—came under the control of elite interests.

Americans turned inward. Our spirit crushed and hope for a better world so remote it became unfashionable, we substituted consumerism for meaningful political liberty. "Greed is good," became the credo, but more sensible citizens wondered if they weren't living in a nation turned inside out.

Logically, it is rather a reductio ad absurdum to blame the whole bleak panorama of the past thirty years on the assassination of President Kennedy. Nor could it all be the preplanned result of a conspiracy. Is anyone really that forward-looking to plan such a

string of events? Still, it is only natural to ask how it all happened. If there was a conspiracy behind the Kennedy assassination, it must have had a motive. If that motive was more than a vendetta, if it was control of the country, would the conspirators stop with one murder to maintain that control?

Is America in the pocket of its own killer cabal, one much cleaner and quieter than the gangs who rule the "banana republics" we hold in contempt? Are we a nation in the grip of kinder, gentler death squads?

The Kennedy assassination happened almost three decades ago, which is not a very long time when you think about the breadth of history. But I can't think of any other single event that has been the subject of such voluminous writing, research, and contemplation in the first thirty years after it occurred. There are probably hundreds of books about the Kennedy assassination. New ones are published every year. Combine these books with shorter articles, television programs, and radio talk shows, and I would guess that there are thousands of pieces of work from scholarly to speculative to fictional devoted to the J.F.K. assassination.

Most are dedicated to the proposition that there was a conspiracy involved. To summarize all the evidence and arguments, obviously, is beyond the reach of this short space. Suffice to say that suspicion has been stirring since the moment Kennedy's head snapped backward from the impact of a bullet that hit him from in front.

On the famous Zapruder film, an eight-millimeter home movie of the assassination taken by a Dallas businessman, you quite clearly see Kennedy's head lurch violently backward at the precise instant that a geyser of blood and brains erupts from the right side of his head.

The Warren Commission insisted that Kennedy had been struck only from behind. The anomaly fascinated UCLA graduate engineering student David Lifton. Laws of physics require that an object struck from in front be propelled backward. Lifton couldn't accept that these laws of physics were suspended at the moment a bullet struck Kennedy's head.

That single observation altered Lifton's life. He devoted the next

fifteen years to scraping through the assassination's medical evidence. By the time he was finished, and his work culminated in the best-seller *Best Evidence*, the backward head snap was the least of the peculiarities Lifton had uncovered. His conclusion that Kennedy's body was shanghaied once it arrived from Dallas at Bethesda Naval Hospital, then medically altered to eliminate evidence of shots from in front, is still one of the most debated hypotheses of the J.F.K. conspiracy. But no one has yet been able to refute fully Lifton's findings.

Who was on the Warren Commission, the government body that scripted the tale of Lee Harvey Oswald, "lone nut"? Lyndon Johnson appointed the Warren Commission to quell national trepidation. "Out of the nation's need for facts, the Warren Commission was born," Johnson earnestly stated. The commission was headed by United States chief justice Earl Warren. It also included former CIA director Allen Dulles. Dulles had been removed from his CIA fiefdom in 1961—by Kennedy.

Gerald Ford was also on the commission. Ford later became an unelected president of the United States when Richard Nixon resigned and handed him the job. Nixon had appointed Ford vice president to fill the slot vacated by the disgraced Spiro Agnew.

Ford pardoned Nixon unconditionally for any crimes he had committed in connection with Watergate, even though Nixon had never been charged with any crimes. The pardon insured that he never would be. Nixon, who had been narrowly defeated by Kennedy in the 1960 presidential election, was in Dallas the day before Kennedy arrived, as corporate lawyer for Pepsi at a bottlers' convention. While in town, he garnered much ink after a few death threats, but, in true macho Republican style, he refused to add any new bodyguards to his entourage.

One researcher I've interviewed, Trowbridge Ford, believes Nixon's bravado was a setup, goading the self-consciously virile Kennedy into eschewing simple security measures while riding through Dallas. The ploy also diverted the attention of the secret service.

"I think he knew the president was going to be assassinated," says Trowbridge Ford. He also believes that Nixon's worried references to "the Bay of Pigs thing," sprinkled throughout the Water-

gate tapes and White House correspondence, are euphemistic references to Dallas. "You can't say 'Dallas' because if you say 'Dallas,' people are going to say 'My God! Dallas!' So you say, 'The Bay of Pigs thing—that's a consequence of the Bay of Pigs thing.'"

Did Gerald Ford become president as a political payback for keeping "the Bay of Pigs thing" under wraps?

Trowbridge Ford (no relation to the president—that is, none that I know of) is far from the only researcher to draw a line from the Bay of Pigs fiasco in 1961, to the Kennedy assassination in 1963, to Watergate nine years later. In November 1973, while Nixon was still president, University of California at Berkeley professor Peter Dale Scott published an article "From Dallas to Watergate: The Longest Cover-Up," in muckraking *Ramparts* magazine. "I believe that a full exposure of the Watergate conspiracy will help us to understand what happened in Dallas, and also to understand the covert forces which later mired America in a criminal war in Southeast Asia," Scott wrote. "[W]hat links the scandal of Watergate to the assassination in Dallas is the increasingly ominous symbiosis between U.S. intelligence networks and the forces of organized crime."

It is, Scott wrote, "no coincidence" that most of Watergate's shadow players dwell in the same "conspiratorial world" that led to the Bay of Pigs, the Castro assassination plots involving CIA-mob teamwork, the gun- and drug-running syndicates formed in pre-revolutionary Cuba (later transplanted to Miami), and the Kennedy assassination cover-up.

Richard Nixon, topping that roster, instigated the Bay of Pigs plan in the Eisenhower administration. Through his friend Bebe Rebozo, who laundered illegal contributions to Nixon from (among others) Howard Hughes, Nixon is linked to international narcotics and gambling operations. Rebozo's business associate "Big Al" Polizzi, named in 1964 congressional hearings as "one of the most influential figures of the underworld in the United States," is one link. Miami's Keyes Realty Company, which bought land for mob bosses, Cuban government officials, and Nixon, is another. Nixon's curious cooperation with the mob-infested Teamsters Union and his pardon of Teamster boss Jimmy Hoffa are other crime connections.

While Nixon was in Dallas working for Pepsi, he may have met with right-wing oilman Clint Murchison. The Texan oil magnate was part of an elite Texas circle of power that included H. L. Hunt—who once tried to finance a death squad to assassinate leftist activists and who paid for publication of the book *Krushchev Killed Kennedy*. Lyndon Johnson and John Connally can also be counted among the Texas power brokers of the time.

Murchison was a close political and personal friend of J. Edgar Hoover. The legendary lawman made regular visits to Murchison's estate. Murchison was also tied to the Teamsters, into whose pension fund he was allowed to dip, and to underworld financial kingpin Meyer Lansky. Murchison's direct tie to the Kennedy assassination cover-up is his company, Great Southwest. The company's lawyers took on a curious client following the assassination: Marina Oswald, Soviet wife of Lee Harvey Oswald. They even housed her in a hotel owned by Great Southwest. The House Select Committee on Assassinations found it probable that Marina's Murchison-connected lawyer told her exactly what to say in her testimony to the Warren Commission.

One of Marina's most important pieces of testimony was her allegation that Oswald was the unknown gunman in an attempted shooting of General Edwin A. Walker in Dallas a few months before the assassination. The Warren Commission used her revelation as key evidence to establish Oswald's deranged motives.

Remember Walker, the general relieved of his command for indoctrinating his troops with John Birch Society literature? He was another widget in the Dallas machinery of right-wing extremism.

What the commission could not explain was how Oswald's guilt in the Walker near miss, supposedly Marina's secret, was reported in a German neo-Nazi rag, *Deutsche National-Zeitung und Soldaten-Zeitung*, just one week after the assassination. The paper had phoned Walker the day after Kennedy was killed. From him, or from other sources, the German "journalists" heard not only that Oswald fired the shot, but that he was arrested for it—get this— along with Jack Ruby!

Unable to fathom that twisted tale, the Warren Commission wrote it off as "fabrication."

Odd as it may seem for a German ultraright propaganda sheet to phone an American retired general right after the assassination of the U.S. president, for that paper there was nothing unusual about it. Its editor, Gerhard Frey, was a friend of Walker's through circles of the American and international right. They even shared the status of "journalist." Walker was military editor of the *American Mercury*, a Birchesque paper, in 1963.

H. L. Hunt, a big Nixon bankroller, tried persuading Nixon to pick Gerald Ford as his running mate in 1968. Earl Cabell, the mayor of Dallas when Kennedy was killed, was another element in this Texas oligarchy. Cabell's brother Charles was deputy director of the CIA—until he was fired, by President Kennedy.

CIA adventurers E. Howard Hunt (no relation to H. L.), Frank Sturgis, and others—the "Cubans" of Watergate break-in fame—had proven connections to both the Bay of Pigs and Watergate. Oddly enough, one of the Cubans was a vice president of Keyes Realty. Not by coincidence, these creatures also lurk around the Kennedy assassination.

Sturgis, a member of the CIA-Mafia kill-Castro clique, fed disinformation to a Miami journalist right after the assassination. His false tip led to news stories that Fidel Castro had ordered the Kennedy hit. Hunt recruited Cubans for the Bay of Pigs invasion. He was a CIA agent in Mexico City, according to findings of reporter Tad Szulc, when Lee Harvey Oswald or someone calling himself that name made a scene at the Cuban embassy there (described in Chapter 1). Hunt may also have been in Dallas on November 22, 1963. One of three distinguished-looking "tramps" photographed "under arrest" after the assassination looks uncannily like Hunt. But Hunt strongly denies being in Dallas or Mexico.

The tramps were never booked. Their names remain unknown. Despite being arrested, photographs show they were not handcuffed nor did the arresting officers restrain them in any way.

As for assassination theorist Trowbridge Ford, he was forced into "early retirement" from Holy Cross. The school saw him, he says, as "that Kennedy nut, the asshole of the faculty." He believes that his retirement came at the behest of Holy Cross trustee Edward Bennet Williams. A well-placed (to say the least) Washington law-

yer, Williams, now deceased, represented clients as diverse as the *Washington Post* when it broke the Watergate story, and CIA chief Richard Helms, one of Watergate's cover-up artists.

Ford developed most of his theories combing through "the public record." For observers closer to the crime, forced retirement is a fate they would have welcomed.

Since the mid 1960s, researchers have been enthralled by the "suspicious deaths" theory. More than one hundred witnesses to, alleged participants in, or investigators of the assassination supposedly died "suspiciously." Some are more "suspicious" than others, but here's a sampling:

The majority of eyewitnesses that day heard shots from in front of the president (the "grassy knoll"). Some saw possible assassins— none matching Oswald's description. Lee Bowers, Jr., was in a railroad control tower overlooking Dealy Plaza, where Kennedy was shot. He saw two men standing behind the fence on the grassy knoll before and immediately after the shooting. He saw a car driving around back there, its driver speaking on what looked like a two-way radio. Bowers died in a one-car accident three years later.

James Worrell told the Warren Commission he heard "the fourth shot" (Oswald was supposed to have fired just three) and saw a man in a dark coat run from the Texas School Book Depository. Worrell was killed by a car while riding a motorcycle in 1966. Richard Carr corroborated Worrell's testimony. He didn't die, but survived a stabbing and an attempted car bombing (three sticks of dynamite didn't explode).

The list goes on and on. Not all of the people on the list were eyewitnesses. Some were suspected of involvement in a higher level of the conspiracy—George DeMohrenschildt, for example. He was a White Russian émigré with intelligence connections who took Lee Harvey Oswald as his protégé. It was an odd relationship, considering that Oswald was supposed to be a Marxist who had returned from defection to the Soviet Union. DeMohrenschildt died of a gunshot wound, presumably self-inflicted, the same day a congressional investigator located him, and the same day he was to be

interviewed by longtime Warren Commission skeptic Edward Jay Epstein.

Congressman Hale Boggs was a member of the Warren Commission. He had his doubts about elements of the commission's conclusions, the "single-bullet theory" especially. He also had information on the FBI's surveillance of Warren Report critics, which prompted him to accuse the bureau of "Gestapo tactics." Flying over Alaska, he was on a plane that simply vanished.

Mobsters Sam Giancana and John Roselli were murdered shortly after getting slapped with congressional subpoenas. Both were key to the CIA-Mafia liaison. Clay Shaw, the only person ever tried for conspiracy in the J.F.K. killing (by Jim Garrison, who failed to get a conviction partly because his star witness, David Ferrie, was dead), was found dead in his home. No cause of death could be determined; Shaw's body was embalmed too quickly.

The witness most conspicuously dead is Lee Harvey Oswald himself, shot by low-level mobster Jack Ruby. A prodigious hustler, Ruby had his own busload of bizarre connections in crime and government. During a break in his trial, Ruby sighed, "The world will never know the true facts of what occurred."

He did offer to tell his story to the Warren Commission if the government would transfer him to Washington, D.C., out of harm's way. The commission refused. Instead, Gerald Ford traveled to Ruby's Dallas jail, and heard nothing but babble.

Ruby died of cancer in 1967. The cancer, he contended, had been administered to him by injection.

For months leading up to his assassination, oil companies and other big corporate interests had been lobbying Kennedy to step up, not cut back, the Vietnam effort. In May, Socony Mobil lobbyist William Henderson presented a paper at a conference sponsored in part by the Asia Society. The president of the Asia Society was John D. Rockefeller, III. The Rockefeller family is the leading oil family in America, and owned much of the stock in Socony Mobil. Henderson's paper called for a "final commitment" to Vietnam. Socony Mobil made over half of its profits from operations in the Far East.

None of this should be a revelation. The oil companies and big banks (Rockefeller-run Chase Manhattan for one) were unabashed in their desire to protect investments in the region. Adopting publicly expressed wishes of the country's most powerful corporations as United States foreign policy was nothing new. Kennedy posed a threat to that system. He was easily disposed of.

Any number of astute analysts have scrutinized the fearsome power of the corporate state. Professor Bertram Gross's book *Friendly Fascism* is an outstanding example of power-structure scholarship. Like most in his field, and in academia generally, Gross rejects the idea of a "a single central conspiracy."

If the Kennedy assassination was a conspiracy, however, it suggests that the various factions of the power structure are capable of coalescing into a "central conspiracy" if the need arises. Once that possibility is granted, the difference between a faceless corporate machine and a conspiracy to run the country becomes merely semantic.

According to Jim Garrison, the oil-banking-military cabal creates dreadfully real structures to enforce its will. He noted that Clay Shaw was a director of Permindex (short for Permanent Industrial Exhibits), an enigmatic Swedish company set up, it claimed, for the promotion of international industrial exchange. Garrison saw a darker purpose.

*Nomenclature of an Assassination Cabal*, a manuscript that circulates among conspiracy researchers, takes Garrison's scenario to its extremes, combining Garrison's findings with underpublicized Warren Commission evidence and all kinds of corporate documentation from Switzerland, codifying the Permindex conspiracy legend.

Permindex, the book argues, is actually a private assassination bureau. It works in cooperation with a top secret department of the FBI called Division Five. Among the numerous and illustrious financiers of Permindex are Clint Murchison and H. L. Hunt.

Regardless of Garrison's credence (even his critics acknowledge that he turned up salient facts), or the scholarly standards of underground xeroxes such as *Nomenclature*, there are too many facts that don't add up. Too much weirdness engulfs the Kennedy assassination—and evident attempts to cover up who really did it.

To coldly dismiss the conspiracy angle is pure dogmatism. There is as much evidence for conspiracy as for the "lone nut" theory.

There are motives galore. CIA cold warriors and anti-Castro Cubans had a grudge against Kennedy for back stabbing them on the Nixon-sponsored Bay of Pigs invasion. The CIA had an extra beef: Kennedy had become appalled at its outrageous conduct. He vowed to smash the CIA's power and started by firing Allen Dulles.

The Mafia had its own vendetta against Kennedy for letting his brother carry out the vigorous, almost fanatical prosecutions that J. Edgar Hoover had shunned. In fact, Hoover had prominent friends with underworld ties, though he publicly denied that the Mafia was real. Chicago boss Giancana had reason to feel sharply betrayed. His vote-rigging probably meant Kennedy's margin of victory in the razor-close 1960 election.

Oilmen such as Murchison and H. L. Hunt had a grievance of their own with Kennedy. They were ultraright ideologues who despised the president, but they had an even more compelling motive. The oil depletion allowance let them multiply their wealth to unthinkable dimensions. Kennedy had promised to strip that allowance.

J. Edgar Hoover bore a disdain for the Kennedys that is well known. Their unwillingness to control their sexual escapades provided Hoover with copious stuffing for his file cabinets. According to one book, rather tenuous in its credibility, Hoover hired a hit squad. "Mr. Hoover had decided that the courts of the United States did not properly administer justice the way he thought they should," an alleged member of the squad claims. "Mr. Hoover had a way to deal with that. He found ways to make the guilty parties disappear."

At the same time, Hoover maintained an alliance with Interpol, the international police organization commandeered by Nazis in 1938 and according to some investigators, still infiltrated by the remnants of the Third Reich.

The Nazi network extends to the upper rim of the American defense establishment. In chapter 17, we'll discuss "Operation Paperclip," the government's program to recruit top Nazi scientists and engineers. The Germans supercharged the U.S. defense indus-

try and many assumed high-level positions with defense contracting corporations.

We've discussed what the military-industrial complex gained from Kennedy's death. The Vietnam War, Lyndon Johnson's and Richard Nixon's gift to history, was a bounty the defense industry never would have enjoyed had Kennedy lived.

Johnson and Nixon received a modest little perk of their own from the assassination: the presidency of the United States. Johnson plunged into the presidency as soon as Kennedy was certified dead. Nixon had to wait. Things didn't come as easily for him.

Nixon was big oil's candidate, the CIA's liaison with congress, a friend of the FBI, and a fellow traveler with organized crime. For those forces to keep their grip on America, one assassination could never be enough.

In the words of L.B.J.'s former press secretary Bill Moyers, commenting on the CIA's affair with the Mafia, "Once we decide that anything goes, anything can come home to haunt us."

# 11

# KINDER, GENTLER DEATH SQUADS

*These men should be equipped with weapons and should march slightly behind the innocent and gullible participants.*

Instructions for assassins in a CIA guerrilla warfare manual

Robert F. Kennedy died on June 6, 1968, from a bullet fired into his head. The bullet came from two inches behind his right ear. Sirhan Bishara Sirhan, convicted of firing that shot, stood in front of Kennedy when he pulled the trigger. No witness saw him come closer than a few feet.

The young senator was celebrating his victory in the California Democratic presidential primary at the Ambassador Hotel in Los Angeles when he was gunned down. With California secure, Kennedy would have won the Democratic nomination for president.

His prospective Republican opponent, Richard Nixon, had already been cheated out of the presidency once by a Kennedy boy. He would not be deprived again. Nixon tiptoed to a whisper-width victory over Hubert Humphrey that November. It's hard to imagine that he would have beaten Bobby Kennedy.

Humphrey was the weakest candidate the Democrats could run, with his wishy-washy platform on the war. How many opponents of the Vietnam War, who would have voted without reservation for Kennedy, simply stayed away from the polls?

For the second time in five years, the American electoral system was altered by violence.

Sirhan was written off as another solitary wacko. How he could have fired at Kennedy from a spot where he never stood went unexplained. The coroner who located the fatal wound, Thomas Noguchi, was fired from his job. After a hearing, misconduct charges against him were found baseless, and Noguchi got his job back.

Someone in the pantry of the Ambassador Hotel *was* standing to Kennedy's immediate right rear when Sirhan attacked. That person had a gun, and admitted drawing it. His name is Thane Eugene Cesar. In June 1968, he was a twenty-six-year-old plumber employed by the Lockheed corporation. He was moonlighting as a security guard, and it was in that capacity that he carried a gun to within inches of the likely next president of the United States.

Though he admits drawing the gun, Cesar has always denied firing it. Almost always. In *The Second Gun*, a documentary by journalist Ted Charac, a friend of Cesar's says the security guard told him he did fire, and was concerned that his action would have "repercussions." Cesar's clip-on tie was found lying next to the senator's bleeding body.

There has been speculation, most recently from investigative reporter Dan Moldea, that Cesar shot Kennedy accidentally. That's possible, of course. Nonetheless, Cesar was no fan of Kennedy. He was one of thousands of rightists who loathed Kennedy. He had ties to right-wing groups. The exact nature of his work for Lockheed, the nation's largest defense contractor, is also cloudy. The same friend who heard Cesar say he fired has also said that Cesar worked in an "off-limits" area of Lockheed, open only to "special people."

Cesar, according to crime reporter David Scheim, had connections to the mob. If that's true, it dovetails with the fact that Sirhan's chief attorney once represented gangster Johnny Roselli—the same bigwig who worked with the CIA to kill Castro—who told Kerry Thornley that the CIA "killed their own president," and who was hacked to pieces and stuffed in a floating drum just before he was scheduled to testify before the House Select Committee on Assassinations.

There were other creepy characters in the pantry, which was stuffed with more than seventy-five people. There was a Pakistani named Ali Ahmand, who was seen standing right behind Kennedy. Former CIA contractor Robert Morrow thinks Ahmand may have fired the head shot from a gun disguised as a Nikon camera. Morrow remembers seeing such weapons while working for the CIA.

Most infamous on the roster of accomplices is the ethereal "woman in the polka-dot dress." A number of people saw this woman, and more than one heard her say, "We shot him," as Kennedy lay on the floor. The polka-dot lady fled the pantry immediately. On her way, she passed Sandra Serrano, then twenty years old and chairperson of Youth for Kennedy in Pasadena. Serrano recognized the woman. She had seen her just moments earlier walking toward the pantry with a slim young man. Serrano identified the man as Sirhan.

As the polka-dot lady rushed by Serrano, she uttered her infamous, "We shot him." Serrano, who said the woman appeared "pleased," asked who had been shot.

"Senator Kennedy," the polka-dot lady replied, then disappeared.

Serrano was the only witness who clung to the polka-dot lady story. For her determination, she was rewarded with weeks of intensive, often abusive questioning by the Los Angeles Police Department, culminating in a lie detector test that had more in common with a tribunal of the Spanish Inquisition. The "tester," Enrique "Hank" Hernandez, badgered her relentlessly. At one point he pleaded with her not to "shame [R.F.K.'s] death by keeping this thing up," and accused her of having no sympathy for Kennedy's family.

Hernandez warned Serrano to recant her "lie," lest it become "a deep wound that will grow with you like a disease, like cancer." Practically in tears, Serrano stuck by her memory. But when Hernandez, like some kind of shaman, implored Serrano to "let this thing that is going to grow with you and is going to make you an old woman before your time come out of you," she finally cracked.

"It's too messed up," Serrano cried. "Even I can't remember what happened anymore."

Shortly thereafter, Hernandez triumphantly announced that Serrano had admitted her polka-dot lady story to be "pure fabrication."

Treating Serrano like a medieval heretic was only one in a series of strange procedures the LAPD took in the R.F.K. investigation. Declaring from the outset that they wouldn't allow "another Dallas," investigators ignored or dismissed several damning dollops of evidence, the impossible angle of the fatal shot not least among those. They also ignored extra bullets found in the pantry. There were more bullets in there than Sirhan's gun contained.

The LAPD may well have been linked to the CIA, which infiltrated numerous police departments in the 1960s, and is thought to have trained LAPD officers in clandestine methods. Manuel Pena, head of the department's "Special Unit Senator," which conducted the assassination investigation, worked for an "international development" unit of the LAPD. Congressional investigators later exposed that unit as a cover for CIA activities in Southeast Asia and Latin America.

Hank Hernandez, Sandra Serrano's inquisitor, worked for the same unit. He bragged to Serrano that he had administered tests in "South America, Vietnam, and Europe." He claimed to have lie tested "the dictator in Caracas, Venezuela," Marcos Perez Jiminez.

Why those far reaches of the globe fall under the jurisdiction of the Los Angeles Police Department is, shall we say, uncertain. If Hernandez was telling the truth about his far-flung assignments, he must have been working for someone else.

And what about Sirhan Sirhan? Didn't he confess to the killing? He leapt to his feet in the courtroom and shouted, "I killed Robert Kennedy with twenty years malice aforethought!" (Quite a claim, considering he was only twenty-four.) Isn't that self-incriminating enough?

Actually, Sirhan never remembered shooting Kennedy. He confessed, he said, because "all the evidence has proved" that he was the assassin. He failed as well to recall keeping the bizarre notebooks found in his apartment, even though he agrees he must have written them. They contain scribblings like "R.F.K. must die,"

"R.F.K. must be assassinated," and "My determination to eliminate R.F.K. is becoming more the more of an unshakable obsession." He also wrote the unexplained phrase "please pay to the order of" again and again.

The writings were ranting and incoherent. Sirhan, some researchers believe, was under hypnosis at the time of the assassination. That would account for his lapses of memory. It would also make him the perfect patsy, one who actually fired a gun in front of a roomful of witnesses. Much easier to make a frame-up stick when you've got twenty-five or fifty people who saw your fall guy do the crime.

To work such a plot, the conspirators must have control of their agent in both body and mind.

The idea of a mind-controlled assassin, a human robot who'll kill on command, goes back much further than Richard Condon's 1959 novel, *The Manchurian Candidate* (and the classic film of the same title). As early as the thirteenth century, a Persian secret society known as the Hashishim—Assassins—perfected techniques to turn ordinary young men into killers. It is fitting that history appropriated the sect's name for both assassination and hashish. They used drugs to gain control of the minds of their unsuspecting hit men. The bedazzled dupes were the original "lone assassins."

The Assassins unleashed a skein of violence aimed mainly at political leaders, which gave them control over large portions of the Middle East, and brought the sect incredible wealth. In the thirteenth century, nobody was baffled by the wave of lone assassins. Everyone knew who was behind them and why.

In the twentieth century, an equally strange cult, the intelligence community of the United States government, has also experimented with remolding the human mind. The umbrella for these efforts was a program called MKULTRA (pronounced M. K. ULTRA), approved in 1953 by CIA director Allen Dulles at the urging of Richard Helms, who would later become director of the Central Intelligence Agency himself.

MKULTRA was an ultrasensitive program of experiments in search of a drug that could alter human behavior. The program was

not publicized at the time. It didn't come to light until more than twenty years later, when congressional investigators revealed it, and a set of exhaustive Freedom of Information Act requests led to several books on the macabre operation.

MKULTRA gained its notoriety for introducing LSD into America, giving birth to the 1960s counterculture. Its darker purpose was to create the perfect agent, the Manchurian candidate: an agent who would take any order without question, who would be absolutely trustworthy, an agent with no free will.

MKULTRA was just one part of the government's ongoing mind-control effort. Both the CIA and the Army were involved. The Army was more public about it, selling its program as a national security measure, to keep ahead of the Communists, who were known to have developed brainwashing techniques.

The sales pitch for mind control was based on half truths. Various Communist countries had come up with mind-control methods, but they relied on the tried-and-true formula of indoctrination and propaganda, not on psychopharmacology. Either way, the U.S. was ahead. Going back to the days of "Wild Bill" Donovan and the Office of Strategic Services (OSS) (precursor to the CIA), the government was exploring methods of mind control. Always, one of the program's aims was to create human robots—unsuspecting citizens who would act without their knowledge, against their will, as couriers, spies. Assassins?

There are only suggestions that they succeeded in these sinister endeavors. Donald Bain's 1976 book, *The Control of Candy Jones*, details how a former USO pin-up girl was hypnotically transformed into a CIA courier. Her "controller" may have been—according to journalist Walter Bowart—a doctor named William Jennings Bryan, a psychiatrist who had been technical consultant to the film version of *The Manchurian Candidate*. Bryan died in 1977 at the age of fifty, "allegedly," writes Bowart, of a heart attack.

Among assassins, there are three good candidates for Manchurian status. One is Sirhan. The repetitive writing in his notebooks bears the mark of what his defense psychiatrist Dr. Bernard Diamond called "automatic writing." When Diamond interviewed Sirhan under hypnosis, the alleged Kennedy killer would often

write his rambling answers. At one point, Diamond asked him why he was "writing crazy."

Sirhan's scribbled answer: "MIND CONTROL MIND CONTROL MIND CONTROL."

A former U.S. intelligence officer who gave Sirhan a psychological stress evaluation (more sophisticated than an old-fashioned polygraph test) seven years after the R.F.K. assassination is quoted as saying, "Everything in the PSE charts tells me that someone else was involved in the assassination—and that Sirhan was programmed through hypnosis to kill R.F.K."

The Jodie Foster–obsessed John Hinckley, Jr., appears to be another suspect for brainwashing. He was copiously dosed with mood-altering drugs, prescribed by a hometown psychiatrist, and was on Valium when he shot President Reagan on March 30, 1981. His father, John Hinckley, Sr., is a friend of George Bush. Another of the senior Hinckley's sons had a dinner date with Bush's son Neil on March 30. It had to be changed due to extenuating circumstances.

The other assassin who could have been mind controlled is Mark David Chapman. On December 8, 1980, Chapman pumped a revolver full of hollow-tipped bullets into the back of ex-Beatle, cultural icon, and peacenik John Lennon.

The first reaction of an arresting detective, Arthur O'Connor, who scrutinized Chapman, was that "he looked as if he could have been programmed." Chapman's behavior was described as "dazed."

British lawyer Fenton Bressler unfolds the entire scenario in his book *Who Killed John Lennon?* Bressler contends that Chapman came into contact with the CIA through the international auspices of the YMCA. That would explain why, when Chapman was able to choose any foreign city to do YMCA work abroad, he chose Beirut—a cesspool of spies, terrorists, and killers. Bressler wonders if Chapman was trained to kill in Beirut. Or at least "blooded," that is, desensitized to violence there. Mae Brussell insisted that the CIA maintained a training camp for assassins in Beirut. There's no hard evidence, but if you had to pick a place to train assassins, Beirut is as good as you'll get.

The official version of Chapman's motive is that he was a "deranged fan," that he harbored a paranoid obsession with John Lennon. Bressler establishes that Chapman was not a fan of John Lennon. Suddenly, a few months before the murder, he began to identify with Lennon, even signing his own name "John Lennon" on at least one occasion. Could an image of John Lennon, one wonders, have been deliberately stamped into his puttylike brain?

Could Hinckley—whose travels took him through a number of strange interludes, including membership in a neo-Nazi group—have been a similar victim? His identification with the Travis Bickle character in the film *Taxi Driver* suggests that Hinckley, like Travis, was an alienated loner. Could the Jodie Foster gimmick have been the clever plan of someone who shaped Hinckley's mind, opening him to suggestion with drugs, then programming him with a movie, like Alex in *A Clockwork Orange*?

Before drawing his gun to shoot at Reagan, Hinckley has said that he had hoped someone would stop him. As he drew his gun, he felt, "Now I have no choice." He said he felt "relieved" once the shooting was over. Like Chapman and Sirhan, he squeezed out bullet after bullet, then became preternaturally calm, as if his predetermined function was now complete.

There are also a couple of parallels between Hinckley and Patrick Purdy, the commando-geared gunman who slaughtered seven Vietnamese children in a Stockton, California, school yard in 1989. Both had flirtations with neo-Nazi groups. And both were heavily dosed with psychiatric drugs—mind-control drugs, by definition. Purdy strode coolly into that playground, pumping away at his AK-47, with the same glaze-eyed robotic demeanor characteristic of one-day spree killers. Many of those killers are dosed with mood-altering drugs, a fact little publicized when such tragedies occur.

Perhaps Hinckley and Purdy were the victims of psychiatry gone berserk, monsters manufactured by accident. Or perhaps they were deliberately programmed. Mind control is all very nebulous. Nonetheless, mind control is real, and no one seriously disputes that it is. Nor does anyone argue that under mind control, human beings can be made to do virtually anything, even take their own

lives. No one argues these facts, because everyone knows that they happened, on November 18, 1978, in Jonestown, Guyana.

The United States government has worked on perfecting mind control for a long time. The CIA says it cut off its program in 1973, without having succeeded. If the sleazy "Messiah from Ukiah," Jim Jones, could master the art of mind control, is it crazy to believe that the government, with its vast resources, would also succeed?

Many survivors of the Jim Jones experience believe it. And, what's more, they believe Jonestown is *where* the government succeeded.

Jonestown bloomed in the moral and spiritual abyss of the 1970s. Like countless cults cropping up in that decade of soul-searching in the dark, its members were said to be brainwashed—living proof that human beings were just so much wire and circuitry. Cult members were often kidnapped back by their families. The hired kidnappers were called "deprogrammers." They might better have been called "reprogrammers."

Jim Jones transplanted his cult from its church in downtown San Francisco to the jungles of Guyana. There he set up his own utopia, and christened it in honor of himself. His followers were mostly black, mostly women, almost all poor. Some were homeless until they found the People's Temple and its prophet/king, clad in shades that made him look like a Secret Service agent. Even Jones's adopted home base, Ukiah, in California's unspoiled north country, suggested paradise on Earth.

The paradise of Jonestown was really hell. Jones abused and degraded his followers. He forced them into slave labor with minimal rations of food. When Congressman Leo Ryan made a trip to Jonestown, investigating allegations of Jones's brutality, he and several reporters were murdered.

One of the most ghoulish horrors in American history followed. On Jones's command, his brainwashed followers killed themselves, more than nine hundred of them, by the particularly gruesome method of drinking cyanide.

Those are the events as recorded by most chroniclers of the Jonestown massacre—the facts as most Americans believe them. As we often find with grisly murders, assassinations, and prominent suicides, there are unanswered, upsetting questions.

On audio tapes of the Jonestown massacre, Jim Jones's voice is audible. At one point, he is heard shouting, "Get Dwyer out of here!" This "Dwyer" was Richard Dwyer. And who was Richard Dwyer? He was a twenty-year veteran of the U.S. Central Intelligence Agency.

After the killing of Congressman Ryan and four others at the airstrip outside Jonestown, an eyewitness saw Dwyer "methodically" washing his hands.

"I've been stripping the dead," Dwyer explained. "It's not a nice job." Then the CIA agent, under cover as an embassy official, produced the wallets and other effects of the five killed there. Dwyer had been shot in the leg during the attack, but he said his wound was "fine." He stayed behind, apparently returning to Jonestown.

When Joseph Holsinger read, one year after the massacre, about the CIA man's presence at Jonestown, he was mortified. Holsinger was an aide to Leo Ryan, who was his best friend and mentor. The shadow of the CIA over Jonestown stirred grim suspicions in Holsinger. He began to contemplate the same possibility a number of People's Temple defectors had feared ever since the massacre.

Jim Jones was already a Mansonlike icon of evil to the American public. Holsinger and the others suspected that the reality of Jonestown was a far darker, more terrible evil.

Contrary to the television-movie Jonestown scenario, which spawned innumerable "Kool Aid" jokes, many of the Jonestown dead received their cyanide by injection into their upper arms, an unlikely spot for a suicide shot. The first coroner on the scene, Guyana's top pathologist C. Leslie Mootoo, stated that only two hundred of the victims actually died by their own hands. All 260 children who died at Jonestown were murdered, he said. Mootoo found one seven-year-old who died when cyanide was forcibly squirted into the back of his mouth.

The death toll jumped from initial reports of about four hundred to the final 913 total a couple of days later. The official explanation

of the discrepancy is that bodies were stacked on top of each other. The skeptics' version is that hundreds of escapees were hunted down and slaughtered.

There were large quantities of psychotherapeutic drugs, including John Hinckley's favorite, Valium, found at the massacre site. The assassins of Leo Ryan were described as glassy eyed and methodical. The man charged with killing Ryan, Larry Layton, was said by his relatives to have lapsed into a "posthypnotic trance" as he became ever more absorbed by temple affairs. Layton's own father called him "a robot."

A CIA agent accompanying Jones. Murders, not suicides. Indications of a government cover-up. For Leo Ryan's aide Joseph Holsinger, the pieces were assembling to a shattering conclusion.

"(The) possibility is that Jonestown was a mass mind-control experiment by the CIA as part of its MKULTRA program," Holsinger said in 1980. An essay he'd received in the mail from a U.C. Berkeley psychologist, entitled "The Penal Colony," provided the final piece in the puzzle. "The Berkeley author of the article . . . believes that rather than terminating MKULTRA, the CIA shifted its programs from public institutions to private cult groups, including the People's Temple," Holsinger said.

Joyce Shaw, who spent six years in the temple but broke away before the move to Guyana, wondered if the mass suicide story was a cover for "some kind of horrible government experiments, or some sort of sick, racist thing . . . a plan like the Germans to exterminate blacks." Soon after Shaw quit the temple, her husband was killed in a strange railroad accident. Her father-in-law happened to be a friend of Leo Ryan, and that's how Ryan's investigation began.

There are eerie footnotes to the Jonestown conspiracy theory. They suggest that the conspiracy did not end with the slaughter in Guyana.

Far from a relic of 1960s' utopian naivete, Jones was for six years a Republican. He raised money for Richard Nixon. He was a Republican when he announced himself the reincarnation of both Jesus and Lenin, and led antiwar protests. His rightist ties extended to one of his closest advisers—a mercenary for UNITA, the CIA-supported Angolan rebel army.

In the early 1960s, Jones spent eleven months in Brazil, where, according to his next-door neighbor at the time, he "lived like a rich man." Why he was in Brazil—who knows? According to that same neighbor, "Some people here believed he was an agent for the American CIA."

The temple's lawyer was Mark Lane, who always seems to be around when events take a strange turn. Lane first became famous as the author of *Rush to Judgement*, a best-seller that spurred early doubts about the Warren Commission. He has since represented several unusual clients, including the conspiracy-stalking Liberty Lobby, publishers of *Spotlight*, and sponsors of the neo-nativist (if not neo-Nazi) "Populist Party."

Lane is also coauthor of a book explaining a conspiracy behind the assassination of Martin Luther King, Jr. He is the longtime lawyer for James Earl Ray, King's accused assassin (like Mark David Chapman, Ray pleaded guilty and was never tried; he claims he was tricked into pleading the case by his pre-Lane legal team).

A memo recovered from Jonestown files showed that Jones and Lane considered smuggling a star King assassination witness to Jonestown (when the memo was discovered, Lane denied discussing the possibility). There are other bits of weirdness about Lane. Did he know about the danger to Leo Ryan, yet fail to warn the congressman? How did Lane escape the massacre?

Another bizarre footnote: There have been attempts to repopulate Jonestown. Not with blacks this time, but with Dominican and Indochinese refugees. Billy Graham's evangelical group was behind the repopulation program.

Jonestown was not the only "Jonestown." In Guyana, at the same time Jim Jones presided over what was either a cult or a government experiment, self-styled "Rabbi" David Hill lorded over "Hilltown." His eight thousand–member Nation of Israel cult made the People's Temple look puny. Hill had power outside his own domain. Some people in Guyana's capital called him the "vice prime minister."

The spookiest Jonestown doppelgänger was Chile's Colonia Dignidad. The 7,500-acre camp was home to a cult founded by German Paul Schaefer, and to the torture chambers of DINA, the Nazi-trained Chilean secret police. In fact, Colonia Dignidad, a

slave-labor enterprise, was the concentration camp of Chile's fascist regime.

The American government running its own concentration camp at Jonestown—a brainwashing laboratory whose specimens spilled into public view. Unthinkable. No more unthinkable, though, than 913 people swallowing cyanide at the command of a lone madman.

One theory of Jonestown is that it was part of a "black genocide operation," intended to be one of many such programs to entrap, enslave, and eventually kill off black people.

In the game of American power, blacks are consistent losers. Many of those black political leaders with the most potential to alter that situation have been cut down. No conspiracy theories required: Effective black politics has been decapitated by violence.

Malcolm X was assassinated just as he was beginning to moderate his views on separatism, just as he was coming in from the political fringe. Martin Luther King, Jr., who never ran for office, was capable of changing the American system, and he did. He bridged society's gaps. When he was assassinated, he was beginning to preach about economic democracy that would unify the underprivileged of all races.

Civil rights leader Medgar Evars was also assassinated. King's mother was shot to death just days after King's widow stated that she believed a conspiracy killed her husband.

Huey Newton founded the Black Panther Party. Their violent public image to the contrary, the Black Panthers' most important achievements were in promoting community self-determination. Their free breakfast program for black schoolchildren was a model, and they started a private school that offered the quality education unavailable to inner city blacks in public schools. Newton was shot in an altercation with police and jailed for allegedly killing a police officer (long since passé, Newton was murdered on an Oakland street in 1989). Another Panther leader, Fred Hampton of Chicago, was gunned down by a gang of police who burst into his apartment at four in the morning.

The most recent death of an effective black leader came in August 1989. Mickey Leland, the Texas congressman who was the leading

congressional advocate of African hunger relief, was killed on a mission to an Ethiopian refugee camp. The small plane carrying Leland and fifteen others—and which had been scheduled to have on board another outspoken black congressman, Ron Dellums— apparently crashed into the side of a mountain near Addis Ababa. The search for Leland in Marxist-ruled Ethiopia was the largest of its kind ever conducted. The intelligence community was openly involved, sending U-2 spy planes to survey the country.

A couple of the killings on the preceding list were obvious conspiracies. Others are more doubtful. The question is, if any were conspiracies, why?

There seem to be government connections to the assassination of Martin Luther King, Jr. Accused killer Ray was not arrested until nearly a month after the fact, in England, of all places. Where a nickel-and-dime crook like Ray got the funds for his extensive trans- and intercontinental travels piques the interest of all conspiracy researchers.

The government's unusual behavior in prosecuting (and some would say, defending) Ray was also cause for concern. Only one witness, a chronic drunkard and self-avowed racist named Charles Q. Stephens, gave a positive make on Ray as the gunman. But he didn't "recall" that Ray was the man he'd seen until six weeks later. On the night of the assassination, when interviewed by a newspaper reporter, Stephens described the man he'd seen fleeing from the alleged sniper's nest as "a nigger."

Stephens' live-in girlfriend, Grace Walden, has said that he was nearly unconscious from booze that night and couldn't have observed much of anything. Walden had her own story. She had seen a white man—*not* fitting Ray's description—running from the scene.

Walden was committed to a mental institution the same day her boyfriend was taken into FBI protective custody. A court later found that she was committed illegally. Grace Walden was the witness Mark Lane and Jim Jones discussed smuggling to Jonestown, according to the memo found in Jonestown files.

Is there a systematic conspiracy to eliminate black leaders, to disable and discredit black activist groups? There are conspiratorial cadres, the Ku Klux Klan and others, who wouldn't be adverse to

that aim. The FBI formed its own conspiracy, COINTELPRO (short for counterintelligence program), which planted provocateurs in black activist groups, crippling them.

When Hoover ordered a COINTELPRO against white hate groups, it had a very different effect. Former G-man Wesley Swearingen says Hoover "just didn't like black people." The FBI actually formed its own chapter of the KKK and recruited two hundred members. The spectacle at one point featured an FBI agent promising "peace and order in America if we have to kill every Negro." Instead of weakening the racist movement, the FBI strengthened it.

In addition to wrecking black activist movements from within, the government has exercised official plans to squash civil disturbances with force. The Nixon White House "Operation Garden Plot" was originally aimed at racial uprisings. After the 1970 invasion of Cambodia, demonstrations erupted throughout the country. The government activated Garden Plot against college students. Following the Kent State killings and numerous clashes in California (where Governor Ronald Reagan lustily cheered the operation on) the antiwar uprising was critically maimed. Operation Garden Plot was still in effect as late as 1985.

Rex 84, a collaboration between the Defense Department and the Federal Emergency Management Agency, had a similar purpose. It provided for the president to declare martial law and round up Central American refugees into detention camps together with, presumably, domestic dissidents. One of Rex 84's authors was reportedly Oliver North.

Suffice to say, official conspiracies exist against minority groups, protesters, radicals, and activists. Whether they have secretly involved the systematic assassination of black leaders, whether they have entailed large-scale experiments in detention, mind control, and extermination, is the subject of conspiracy theory. The hypothetical purpose of such a large-scale conspiracy is a fact of social life in America: Blacks and other minorities remain the bulk of a massive economic underclass, a source of cheap labor, and a scapegoat for social ills like crime and drugs.

Traditional liberal analysis has it that the vicissitudes of eco-

nomics and an amorphous "institutionalized racism" are the real
roots of black economic subjugation. But the effort to find something more specific to blame is understandable. And in light of the
public record, wholly justified.

Effective black leaders are a threat to the status quo, and that is
motive enough for conspiracies to knock them off. Likewise, conspiracy theories surround the death of virtually anyone who poses a
threat to the power structure. Often with good cause. The official
explanations for many assassinations have more of a fairy-tale ambience than conspiracy theories. Conversely, many suspicious
deaths give the appearance of not being suspicious at all.

The death of Pope John Paul I, for example, was attributed to a
heart attack. Author David Yallop's best-seller *In God's Name*
argues that John Paul I's papacy was truncated at thirty-three days
by poisoning, not natural causes. The pope's plan to eradicate the
Vatican's global financial empire and expose the Masonic membership of high-ranking clergymen, Yallop says, aroused the wrath of
the Masonic-fascist Propaganda Due (P2) Lodge.

As early as 1952, the CIA was discussing how to "knock off key
guys" and make it look like natural causes, declassified CIA memos
have revealed. Heart attacks and cancer are preferred methods. CIA
director William Casey developed a brain tumor just as he was
supposed to make public his knowledge of the Iran-Contra affair.
Nelson Rockefeller suffered a heart attack *in flagrante delecto* with
his secretary. Two assassination plots against Gerald Ford would
have made Rockefeller president, but they both failed. Once Rocky
was no longer useful, he turned up dead.

Suicides are also popular, as are one-car accidents. Kennedy
haters have no trouble envisioning a heavy-handed Kennedy-
engineered conspiracy behind Chappaquidick and the death of
Mary Jo Kopechne. Other theorists take the same anomalous
facts—unusual dents in the car, time lapses in Ted Kennedy's
memory—to mean that Kennedy and Kopechne were victims: he
drugged, she murdered. Chappaquidick was final insurance that a
Kennedy brother would not be president.

Some researchers have told me that even journalist Jessica Savitch was the victim of a conspiracy. She was coming back as an investigative reporter, after cocaine-burnout, when she perished in a Chappaquidick-style plunge.

The most reliable method, at least for big jobs, is still the lone nut. Not one but two lone nuts took separate shots (or tried to— neither was very competent with a handgun) at Gerald Ford, who stood in the way of intelligence and oil overlord Nelson Rockefeller's ascendance to the Oval Office. One of the "nuts," Sarah Jane Moore, worked for the FBI and three other police agencies. The other, Lynette Fromme, was a member of the Manson Family, conspiracy theories about which are the subject of a later chapter.

Michael Milan, who claims he was a hit man for Hoover, says that he was offered a contract on Ford, but declined it as "suicide."

Then there is the long list of dead people connected with the Iran-Contra affair. Many of them may have had knowledge of an "October Surprise" deal between the 1980 Reagan for President campaign and the Islamic Iranian government. The deal is said to have delayed the release of American hostages until after Reagan's inauguration in exchange for arms shipments and other covert collaboration.

The list of Iran-contra/October Surprise casualties should be taken in the spirit as the hit parade following the J.F.K. assassination. Topping the charts is the aforementioned William Casey, who was Reagan's campaign manager in 1980. Amaram Nir, an Israeli officer who was his country's Oliver North, went down in a possibly sabotaged plane late in 1988. Fund-raiser Carl "Spitz" Channel died in a hit-and-run accident.

Arms dealer Cyrus Hashemi met his maker a surprisingly short two days after finding out he had cancer. Iranian foreign minister Sadegh Ghotbzadeh may have been the person who talked Khomeini into holding the hostages until Reagan was safely in office. A year later, he was tortured and executed on Khomeini's orders after plotting a coup. William Buckley, CIA Beirut station chief, was killed by Islamic fundamentalist kidnappers in 1985. There are reports that Buckley, too, knew firsthand of the Reagan-Iran deal in 1980.

My reaction, when I first began researching assassination conspiracy theories, was probably a typical one: "Doesn't anybody just die?" I've heard conspiracy theories for every dead person from J. Edgar Hoover to Lenny Bruce. My instinctive reaction was always if not to scoff, then at least to look askance. But far be it from me to dismiss any theory out of hand. I've only been able to study a few, and most in less than the detail I would have liked. Inevitably, when I do a little digging, I find enough strange circumstances to make me dizzy.

The average human mind can handle a few conspiracies; the concept of conspiracies by the hundreds is harder to accept. Still there are premises: People are killed, and their deaths lead to political changes. These political changes benefit a few people at the expense of the great many. There are murky circumstances around many such deaths. The conclusions one can draw from those premises often cross the threshold of belief.

Assassination conspiracy theories are easy to write off as fantasy conceived in trauma—the desperate imagination of disappointed idealists grasping for reasons why their dreams are as dead as their heroes. But there is an upsetting logic to those theories. The dyspepsia is worsened by the unreal quality "official versions" usually exude. Violence, murder, war, and terror have restructured America's social and political order over the past three decades.

Something is terribly wrong. No one can be blamed for asking what it is. We can blame only ourselves when we expect the answer to comfort us, and it does not.

# 12

# THIS IS YOUR GOVERNMENT ON DRUGS

*This is your brain on drugs.*

> Voice-over from an anti drug
> public service announcement on
> television, read while an egg is
> shown frying.

In 1931, Aldous Huxley published *Brave New World*, the story of a totalitarian government satiating citizens with drugs, to maintain their complacency. The novel, now familiar to tenth-grade English students everywhere, was set in the future. Suppose Huxley's future is now.

"I think it is no mistake that a majority of the drugs in this country is being deposited in black and Hispanic and lower-income neighborhoods across the country," filmmaker Spike Lee said, on an ABC "Nightline" show.

"The epidemic of drugs and violence in the black community stems from a calculated attempt by whites to foster black self-destruction," echoes Louis Farrakhan, head of the Nation of Islam.

"The theory is that the white establishment pushed heroin into the black community to divert young people from political action," explains Andrew Cooper, publisher of Brooklyn weekly newspaper *The City Sun*, "so they'd be zonked out and wouldn't be a threat."

The drug conspiracy theory is not peculiar to the African-American community. In varying permutations and degrees of

intensity, it is widely discussed. Senator John Kerry of Massachusetts would hardly endorse the rather rash pronouncements of Spike Lee or Louis Farrakhan. But he did "see a larger conspiracy here than met the eye." His committee's investigation concluded that CIA agents and U.S. government officials knew about and participated in cocaine smuggling by Nicaraguan contras in league with Colombia's cocaine barons. In the 1980s, when the contra war was flaring, cocaine suddenly became cheap and plentiful. Previously a status drug of decadent neo-sophisticates, cocaine emerged in smokable "crack" form, permeating inner cities as well as suburbs.

On the other end of the spectrum from Kerry is Lyndon LaRouche, who ascribes the international drug trade to British masterminds, secretly perpetuating the empire, with the full knowledge of the queen.

The truth is in there somewhere. Individual drug problems may be the fault of individuals, but despite current enthusiasm for persecuting "the casual user," America's drug problem appears to have been inflicted upon it.

At one level, most of us are vaguely aware of that fact. While not usually reported in the news media, the entertainment media—which speaks to far more Americans—have occasionally taken up the theme. I won't go through a filmography here. But one movie scene that said more than it probably intended cropped up in *The Godfather*. At a meeting of Mafia chieftains trying to plan how to handle the previously taboo heroin business, they agree to confine sales to black neighborhoods. "They're animals anyway," says one of the celluloid dons. "Let them lose their souls."

That was only a movie, of course. But it is hardly unthinkable that a real-life version of that conversation took place. It is only half true that the Mafia had a code of honor prohibiting it from trafficking in narcotics. Salvatore C. Luciana, a.k.a. Charles "Lucky" Luciano, was first arrested for heroin possession in 1915, when his criminal "family" was still known quaintly as the "107th Street Gang."

But the heroin business did not begin booming for Luciano, who innovated and dominated it, until after World War II. Luciano organized Sicilian gangs into a nationwide structure, and aligned

them with their Jewish counterparts controlled by the likes of Meyer Lansky and Bugsy Siegel. With this flourish of managerial élan, Luciano created the national organized crime syndicate—the Mafia, La Cosa Nostra, the Outfit, the Mob.

The immediate postwar period seems an ironic time for an increase in heroin traffic. At no other time since the drug was introduced did U.S. law enforcers have a better opportunity to wipe out the problem of heroin. Austerity inflicted by the war forced most junkies to go cold turkey, so demand was down. At the same time, supplies came up short. Shipping channels were impeded by the always inconvenient presence of torpedoes whistling through the water, and American customs security had been tightened. The intent was to stop spies and saboteurs from getting into the country, but heroin smugglers got caught in the net as well.

In China, opium operators found themselves face to face with Mao's rebel armies, which swept them away. In France, Corsican gangsters were the source of the heroin business, and many of them shortsightedly chose to collaborate with the occupying Nazis. Once the Allies liberated France, the Corsicans' wartime selection of associates did not sit well with their countrymen. They had a hard time reopening for business. In Italy, Mussolini carried out a personal vendetta against the Sicilian Mafia, which left that heroin stronghold in sorry straits.

After World War II, there were a scant twenty thousand addicts in the whole U.S.A., down from ten times that twenty years earlier. A mild tightening of the thumbscrews and heroin could have been, for all practical purposes, banished from the country.

Instead, the exact opposite happened. This entrepreneurial coup owed much to the amazing ingenuity of Luciano and his fellow mobsters. But he couldn't have done it without the help of his dear, dear friends in the United States government.

The military first bonded with organized crime in 1942. Unable to control sabotage of Allied ships on the New York waterfront, the Office of Naval Intelligence had what Oliver North might call "a neat idea." Gangsters already had their hooks into the New York docks. The naval spies decided to get them to help out. "Operation

Underworld," as the Navy called this little adventure, led them directly to Lucky Luciano. Doing business from prison, Luciano agreed to cooperate, and the government's first show of good faith was to have the underworld overlord transferred to a cushier jail, near Albany, New York. There he received military intelligence officers as visitors, and also met with colleagues like Lansky.

The military-Mafiosi joint venture extended overseas. General George S. Patton, the legendary blood-'n'-guts commander of the Seventh Army, sliced through Sicily like scissors through silk. Patton was a general of extraordinary martial dexterity, but the sixty thousand troops and countless booby traps in his path should have given him at least a few problems. His way had been cleared by Sicily's Mafia boss Calogero Vizzini, at the request of Luciano.

The mob and the U.S. military nuzzled closer once Allied forces secured Sicily and installed an occupational government. Needing to maintain law and order, but also needing as many of its own troops as possible for the remaining campaign through Italy, the occupying American Army appointed Mafia bosses—including Vizzini—mayors of many Sicilian townships. Gangsters became an American-backed quasi-police force.

The Americans used the gangsters to bust the burgeoning antifascist resistance in Italy. This seems paradoxical, because the Americans were fighting the Italian fascists and one would think they'd welcome a strong, indigenous resistance movement. The problem was, the resistance was loaded with leftists. Italian Communist Party membership swelled. These developments were far more alarming to the American occupiers than any fascists they might have to fight. The Mafia became willing warriors in the anti-Communist struggle, which seemed to supplant the not-yet-complete effort against the fascists who still ruled Italy.

The military literally let their Mafia henchmen get away with murder. Vizzini killed the police chief in Villaba, where, thanks to the Americans, he was mayor. In American-occupation headquarters, one of the best employees was Vito Genovese, who eventually inherited Luciano's New York operation. The Genovese crime family is one of New York's five families, among the most formidable mob syndicates in the country.

After the war, military intelligence sprang Luciano from prison

and had him deported along with a legion of his organized crime associates. From abroad, Luciano and Co. founded what might as well be called Heroin, Inc., an illegal multinational corporation.

Havana, Cuba, became Luciano's hub of operations. When Luciano himself was forced out of Cuba, he turned management chores over to Santos Trafficante, the Miami boss. Trafficante grew into one of the most powerful—maybe *the* most powerful— godfather in the country. When the CIA wanted to assassinate Fidel Castro, Trafficante was one of the mobsters it turned to. In 1979, the House Select Committee on Assassinations recommended Trafficante as one of the "certain individuals" in organized crime bearing investigation in connection with the John F. Kennedy assassination.

Between 1946, when Luciano set up his heroin shop, and 1952, the addict total in the U.S. tripled, then jumped to 150,000 by 1965, due primarily to the efforts of Luciano's new operation.

Six years later, that number had doubled and nearly doubled again, the addict population topping half a million. The epidemic is often attributed to the Woodstock generation and the proliferation of hedonistic hippies, but the CIA's partnership with opium-growing Laotian warlords probably has as much to do with it. The CIA's covert operation in Laos during the Vietnam War remains the largest it has ever staged.

The "Golden Triangle," Laos, northern Thailand, and Burma, is where seventy percent of the world's opium comes from. Much of the raw opium goes to Marseilles and Sicily, where Corsican and Mafia gangs have laboratories to turn it into heroin for sale by the Luciano-founded crime syndicate.

The CIA's own thinly disguised cover airline, Air America, flew raw opium in and out of Laos, as a way of financing the illegal Laotian war without going to Congress. Much of the heroin manufactured from the CIA-couriered base was sold to American servicemen in Southeast Asia, who developed a widespread heroin problem.

In the fall of 1990, a book called *Kiss The Boys Goodbye*, coauthored by intelligence expert William Stevenson and his wife Monica (a former "60 Minutes" reporter), documented how the CIA and the military quashed investigations into POWs left in

Vietnam after the war. Many of the POWs, the book says, were involved in CIA drug operations, which is why the government is none too eager to get them home.

Conservative billionaire H. Ross Perot was charged by President Reagan with scouting out leftover POWs. Frustrated, he told then vice president George Bush, "I go looking for prisoners, but I spend all my time discovering the government has been moving drugs around the world."

Those junkie GIs who did make it back stateside brought their jones to the home front, fostering the worst drug problem the country had, to that date, ever seen. The heroin plague led Richard Nixon to declare the first "War on Drugs." It was an interesting move for Nixon, because he was also responsible for the war on Laos.

These things always seem to come full circle.

A little more than a decade later, the CIA staged its second largest covert operation—propping up Afghan *mujahedin* guerrillas against Soviet invaders. Like the Laotians before them, the Afghans used opium as a financing tool. And the Americans were there.

Author James Mills spent five years tracking international drug traffic for his book *The Underground Empire*. He came away with that same observation.

"You do not have to be a CIA hater," noted Mills, "to trek around the world viewing one major narcotics group after another and grow amazed at the frequency with which you encounter the still-fresh footprints of American intelligence agents."

Heroin was not made illegal in the United States until 1924. Invented in the nineteenth century as a "nonaddictive" pain reliever to replace morphine, it was in widespread medicinal use until the country noticed that not every heroin consumer was using the drug strictly according to doctor's orders. The drug's real name is diacetylmorphine. "Heroin" is a brand name invented by its first distributor, the Bayer corporation.

In the early 1990s, heroin is back in fashion and appears more plentiful than ever. It's now used as a supplement to the drug that took the country by storm in the decade just past—cocaine.

Like heroin, cocaine started out as a legal drug. A popular pick-me-up, it was an ingredient in the soft drink that bears its name, Coca-Cola. Once outlawed, cocaine became the purview of gangsters. Heroin ran westerly, controlled by the Mafia, but cocaine filtered north, from Latin America. Once again, the United States government was there to help out. It was, as Yogi Berra might say, déjà vu all over again.

The CIA-contra-cocaine connection is a complicated conundrum. One of the biggest names in the business was Manuel Noriega, the former dictator of Panama, who, at this writing, is still in U.S. custody awaiting trial on drug charges, having been seized during the December 1989 U.S. invasion of Panama.

To comprehend the government's role in cocaine traffic, Noriega is useful as a kind of focal point. He was on the payroll of the CIA at the same time he worked for the Medellín Cartel for four million dollars per month. The Medellín Cartel is the Colombian cocaine syndicate, responsible for most of the cocaine that enters the U.S.A.

Noriega was also connected to George Bush, and through Bush to Oliver North. They used Noriega as a conduit for getting arms to the contras.

Bush, North, and other government insiders at the CIA and the National Security Council (which under Reagan got heavily into covert operations) most likely knew about Noriega's involvement with drugs. Revelations about Noriega, and about direct contra and CIA involvement with cocaine smuggling, found their way into the public record via a subcommittee of the Senate Foreign Relations Committee, chaired by John Kerry.

In 1986, Senator Kerry received information that the Costa Rican branch of a Miami-based shrimp company Ocean Hunter, widely regarded as a drug-running front, had received checks for more than $200,000 dollars from the U.S. government. The money was part of the "humanitarian aid" allocated for the contras by Congress. Wondering why the cash was channeled to this shrimp-and-dope outfit, Kerry went to the FBI asking for an inquiry. Instead, the FBI investigated Kerry himself.

According to FBI reports, North asked the FBI to investigate

Kerry, to find links between the Massachusetts senator and the Nicaraguan Sandinista government. The investigation was reportedly initiated by a crack FBI counterintelligence group usually employed to track foreign agents in the United States.

To North's distress, the agents did not find evidence to follow through with a full-scale investigation. North may have had reason to worry. The Drug Enforcement Administration had knowledge in the fall of 1986 that the flight crews making clandestine arms deliveries to the contras were flying cocaine into the U.S. on their return trips. When DEA agents confronted one of the pilots, he told them he had White House protection. He dropped North's name. The agents didn't pursue the North connection, dismissing the pilot's statement as "a bluff."

Accounts of secret testimony before Kerry's committee revealed that Felix Rodriguez, CIA agent and friend of George Bush, arranged a ten million dollar donation to the contras direct from the Medellín cartel. The cartel's chief accountant and money launderer (at least until he was arrested), Ramon Milian Rodriguez, testified to the donation. Milian Rodriguez is said to have conveyed $180,000 in campaign contributions from the cartel to Ronald Reagan's 1984 presidential campaign, and was invited to Reagan's inauguration as a gesture of thanks from the grateful candidate. It was Milian Rodriguez who made the monthly multimillion dollar payoffs to Noriega on the Medellín cartel's behalf.

The guns-for-drugs deals, many of which centered on the Costa Rican ranch of alleged CIA operative John Hull (who kept a private army of up to one hundred men) have been officially documented. Both Kerry's committee and the Costa Rican government uncovered the drugs-and-government conspiracy, yet the scandal has little resonance. In the middle of an inexorable flow of antidrug hysteria, the United States Senate found government officials smuggling drugs. The official House-Senate Iran-Contra investigating committee never touched the contra drug connection, and, therefore, the daily press ignored the story. The omission looks like nothing if not a deliberate cover-up. On the other hand, who knows if the cognitive dissonance induced by a government both fighting and favoring drug traffickers would have been too much for the American people?

The whole story might have emerged if the media had paid attention to an obscure case of dirty money and drug smuggling in California's Napa Valley, a plush area beloved for its vineyards and win-
eries. The story, which has enough intrigue to hook any audience,
has been covered by no media outlet other than a free semi weekly
called the *Napa Sentinel*, with a circulation of twenty thousand.
Mixed in with stories about the local Oktoberfest and "Volunteer of
the Year" were such headlines as "Drugs, CIA, Real Estate and Napa
Connections" and "Former Napan Linked to CIA Arms-Drugs."

As with the Collier brothers and their Votescam series in the
*Home News*, it takes an eccentric little local paper to touch such
torrid topics. The only other play the Napa "Drug Tug" case gets is
from David Emory, who has read all of the *Sentinel's* articles on his
Sunday night show and enriched them with his own uninhibited
speculations.

The story began in 1988, when a tugboat packed with hashish,
the "Drug Tug," was seized by federal agents in San Francisco Bay.
Subsequent investigations found that the fees collected by the Drug
Tug's captain were laundered through a Napa real-estate investment firm called "LendVest," which collapsed after the boat was
seized and Captain Calvin Robinson arrested.

"The Drug Tug—which made several trips before being seized—
was a transportation instrument used to ferry drugs from CIA-
appointed sources to CIA-designated drug brokers," wrote Harry
V. Martin, the paper's editor and author of the series. "The purpose
was to gain a source of clandestine financing to aid the *contra*
movement."

The *Sentinel's* stories disclosed a Möbius loop of links. According to Martin's stories: Robinson was connected to Thomas Smith,
a drug trafficker with ties to the Medellín cartel, and to the CIA
through Air America. The Drug Tug's up-front fifteen-million
dollar fee came from Panama, laundered through Costa Rica. The
Costa Rican laundry man was Kenneth Armitage, a wealthy En-
glishman on the lam for fraud charges. Armitage was later returned
to England, where he died in prison before coming to trial.

Armitage was also a business partner of Noriega. The Brit owned

an island off of Costa Rica used as a midway point for El Norte–bound drug shipments. To keep the island secure, Noriega funneled money into the 1982 Costa Rican elections. When the contra war started sizzling, the CIA touched down on the island, leaving weapons there which would later be funneled to the contras via Hull's ranch.

The Costa Rican government, investigating the CIA-arms-drugs operation, in 1989 reported that Hull and Noriega were also working for Oliver North at the National Security Council. North testified to the U.S. Congress that the president approved of everything he did. North was also working with George Bush, or so documents that have materialized through Freedom of Information Act releases indicate. North and Bush traveled together in 1983 to a meeting with Noriega.

Part of the Drug Tug scam was a counterfeit passport operation that let smugglers travel freely to the "drug island," according to Harry Martin's reporting. In 1990, Christic Institute chief counsel Daniel Sheehan, unaware of the Drug Tug case, made a prediction; news of the Noriega case had dropped from the headlines, but Sheehan predicted that when the case finally came to trial Noriega would be charged with little more than passport forgery.

The *Napa Sentinel* series is full of surprises. It draws Colorado mob figures into the Drug Tug scenario, and the outre personage of Christopher Boyce. A cellmate of Calvin Robinson, Boyce spied for the Soviets and ended up with his exploits glossied and glorified in a movie, *The Falcon and the Snowman*, in which he was played by Timothy Hutton. Boyce, according to Martin's stories, tried to enlist Robinson in a bank-robbing spree. Boyce escaped prison less than a week after Robinson was released, and the Drug Tug skipper may have sheltered the CIA turncoat in Santa Cruz.

Martin included plenty of historical support for his Drug Tug revelations. He wrapped up his series with a fifty-six–name "Who's Who in the Drug Tug Series" inventory. On the list, alongside Oliver North, Manuel Noriega, and Dan Quayle, is Lucky Luciano.

For government insiders, collaboration with the drug trade appears to have been a matter of convenience rather than an organized

conspiracy to somatize the population, or certain segments thereof. Still, it did and does have that numbing effect. America's thirst for instant gratification is quelled by drugs better than anything, with the possible exception of television.

Just as disseminating fire water to Native Americans insured the final victory of the white man, infusing American culture, particularly its economically lower branches, with heroin and cocaine has gone a long way toward keeping minorities and the poor out of the ball game.

Middle classes, too. Drug use, cocaine use especially, began as a middle-class diversion and infects placid suburbs, school yards, and executive boardrooms. As drug use in America has gone up, political involvement (measured by voter turnout) has dropped. Could be a coincidence. Nevertheless, drugs are an important element in the stupefaction of America.

The government officials who gave aid and comfort to drug traffickers were surely aware that the stuff was not cotton candy. I can see them justifying their involvement with the *Godfather* rationale: "They're animals anyway, let them lose their souls." Only this time, they're talking not only about blacks, but about everyone.

Opiates and coca derivatives are soul stealers, to be sure. The other popular strain of "illicit" drugs, hallucinogens, have had, at least ostensibly, the opposite effect. LSD and its fellow psychedelics politicized a generation.

LSD, which like heroin and cocaine was developed by corporate researchers (in the case of LSD, Sandoz Pharmaceuticals), was introduced to America largely by the CIA through its MKULTRA program (see the previous chapter). Like cocaine, it began as a luxury, a perk that came with membership in the ruling class. Henry Luce, *Time* magazine publisher and CIA mouthpiece, was among the first users, as was his wife, Clare Booth Luce. *Life* magazine, a Luce subsidiary, ran a lengthy piece by J. P. Morgan Company vice president R. Gordon Wasson, extolling the joys of psychedelics. In the early MKULTRA experiments, CIA agents ate LSD with enthusiasm, even if they often feigned detachment.

MKULTRA fed the drug to human subjects, both willing and unsuspecting, in prisons, hospitals, and university labs. The public record renders disingenuous the statement of former CIA director

and MKULTRA father Richard Helms: "We do not target American citizens."

Could the MKULTRA-related LSD programs have extended beyond the appalling instances of human experimentation that are fully documented? We've mentioned the theory that MKULTRA was never terminated, only transferred to "cult" groups that use mind control to train assassins. Did the CIA go even further than that, inundating American streets with LSD in an attempt to bring about some kind of societal transformation?

The whole idea smacks of Lyndon LaRouche's "New Dark Ages" conspiracy theory. LaRouche pegs such psychedelic pioneers as Aldous Huxley as part of the British establishment still ruling the world through occult techniques, manipulation of the drug culture most notably. A more plausible motive (realizing that "plausible" is a relative term here) would be the establishment's need to rip apart the fabric of progressive politics. The CIA, FBI, and various other intelligence organs were trying to do just that throughout the 1960s and before, placing provocateurs and informers inside all significant left-leaning political groups. If there was a governmental LSD conspiracy, it could have been trying to accomplish the same thing on a massive scale.

The book *Acid Dreams: The CIA, LSD and the Sixties Rebellion*, by investigative journalists Martin A. Lee and Bruce Shlain, contains the curious tale of Ronald Stark, the most prolific manufacturer of LSD in the late 1960s. The largest percentage of LSD in circulation, more than fifty million doses, came from Stark's laboratories, in those years that the youth movement was spinning out of control. Ronald Stark, as Lee and Shlain report, may well have been a CIA agent. He was chummy with European terrorists as well as diplomats, and bragged that the CIA tipped him to shut down his French LSD lab.

"Was Stark a hired provocateur or a fanatical guerrilla capable of reconciling bombs and LSD?" wonder the authors of *Acid Dreams*. They note that when Stark, a fugitive from drug charges involving his 1960s LSD operation, was finally brought back to the U.S. in 1982, he was imprisoned only briefly and then the Justice Department dropped all charges against him. Two years later, Stark died of a heart attack. Or should that read "apparent" heart attack?

*Acid Dreams* also records that on Richard Helms's command, most of the official documents concerning the CIA's romance with LSD were shredded due to what one official called "a burgeoning paper problem." That explanation has the same ring as the Defense Intelligence Agency's claim that their shredding of files on Lee Harvey Oswald was "routine."

"The use of LSD among young people in the U.S. reached a peak in the late 1960s, shortly after the CIA initiated a series of covert operations designed to disrupt, discredit and neutralize the New Left," Lee and Shlain comment. "Was this merely historical coincidence, or did the Agency actually take steps to promote the illicit acid trade?"

The first effect of LSD on the radical, progressive movement was catalyzing, invigorating. Its final effect was dissipating, destructive. What doomed the movement—one of the many factors—was the "delusions of grandeur" that charged it, fueled by LSD, say Lee and Shlain. "They wanted to change the world *immediately*—or at least as fast as LSD could change a person's consciousness."

In the end, it was impatience that led the progressive movement into trying to change the world by fiat, rather than through the organization, education, and strategic action that leads to deep changes in the system. LSD began as a spark and ended as a short circuit. And LSD, at least to some extent, came from the CIA.

"LSD makes people less competent," notes drug culture paragon William S. Burroughs, who wondered if the LSD craze was something other than what its adherents thought. "You can see their motivation for turning people on."

The irony of the LSD conspiracy, if it was real, is that while it wrecked the progressive movement, the social transformation it wrought was far larger than any narrow political goal. Whether on purpose or not, elements of American society were alchemically transformed.

Or is it so ironic? Perhaps that was the plan: like all conspiracies, a design of a few to induce a change in the masses—the secret agenda of a secret society.

# 13

# CIA: THE DEPARTMENT OF CONSPIRACY

*There exists in our nation today a powerful and dangerous secret cult—the cult of intelligence.*

VICTOR MARCHETTI and JOHN
D. MARKS, *The CIA and the Cult
of Intelligence*

The United States Central Intelligence Agency was created on September 18, 1947, when Harry S. Truman signed the National Security Act. Most of the debate over the act centered on its restructuring of the military. The Army and Navy were joined, the Air Force was created, and all three branches were placed under the secretary of defense, a new position. All but lost on the public, and Congress as well, was an equally unsettling concentration of power. The act brought the nation's numerous intelligence services under a single department. It seemed almost an afterthought.

Following the chaos of Pearl Harbor, the government was desperate to assemble some sort of clearing house for intelligence. Eisenhower himself bemoaned the "glaring deficiencies" of the manifold intelligence bureaus. Virtually every agency of the U.S. government has an intelligence wing. The Central Intelligence Agency was chartered to collect information from those diverse outfits, and pull it into a neat little package for the president. Hence the name, "Central" Intelligence Agency. The CIA was to be the central station through which all intelligence was routed.

The CIA was never meant to do its own spying. And it certainly wasn't meant to conduct clandestine operations. The original purpose of the CIA was to summarize and analyze the information turned up by other intelligence operations. It was a report-writing department.

Truman's intention appeared innocuous—to create a smoother running intelligence collation machine. But when he'd created the CIA's immediate predecessor, the Central Intelligence Group a year earlier, Truman celebrated by throwing a party at which guests were presented with cloaks, daggers, and black hats. Strange, for a bunch of supposed pencil pushers. Truman was a devoted Mason, and therefore accustomed to clandestine rituals and bizarre symbolism. Maybe he was just being funny.

Truman's possible true purpose notwithstanding, almost everything the CIA does today violates the terms of its creation.

The CIA's one loophole is a fuzzy phrase in the 1947 law. According to the bill signed by Truman, the Central Intelligence Agency would perform "other functions" at the discretion of the National Security Council. The language of the act is fairly specific. Those "other functions" relate only to intelligence. Nowhere does it mention clandestine operations. Even so, the "other functions" clause has been the rationale for what over the past more than forty years has become, in addition to a massive government bureaucracy, a fully functioning, government-sanctioned, secret society.

There is little doubt that Congress did not mean "other functions" to encompass all of the operations the CIA is known to have undertaken, and that it definitely was not intended to cover the things the CIA *may* have done (namely, the assassinations and dope dealing covered in the previous two chapters). When they were debating the National Security Act, some congressmen worried that a centralized intelligence operation could turn into a United States "Gestapo." Because of those fears, the agency has remained on the penumbra of government operations.

The CIA stays there for the same reason secret societies over the past few thousand years have kept their internal workings encrypted. Secret societies are secret because what they do offends popular morality.

There are many other American intelligence agencies besides the

CIA. Nor is the CIA directly responsible for everything its agents do. The agency is known to contract much of its touchier business out to semimoral mercenary types, who, even when their CIA obligations expire, still feel free to claim CIA affiliation as license to do almost anything. The agency probably is inclined to cover for them, lest past questionable endeavors be exposed. Then again, these lone operators are so easily written off as "renegades" that, when they do work for the CIA, they lend convenient deniability to illegal operations. The sophisticated use of covert agents is but one strategy the CIA shares with the archetypical, conspiratorial secret society.

The CIA keeps its very charter a mystery. No one on the outside knows the real purpose of the CIA, as set out in top-secret presidential directives, piled up over the years, which constitute the "charter." In 1968, the deputy director of the agency's "dirty tricks" department said (in what he thought were confidential remarks) that the CIA's charter "must remain secret . . . the problem of a secret charter remains as a curse, but the need for secrecy would appear to preclude a solution."

"We are not Boy Scouts," added one of the CIA's most storied directors, Richard Helms. Helms put his unscouting morality to work as the originator of MKULTRA, the CIA's mind-control project, which tested the brand new drug LSD on human subjects.

There is a long-standing regulation that any incident that might embarrass or expose the CIA is to be immediately reported to the agency's Office of Security, the CIA's internal police force meant to secure it from enemy infiltration. In reality, the Office of Security spends much time securing the agency from exposure to the public. That's what happened when a CIA employee, Frank Olsen, was slipped a dose of LSD without his knowledge. Olsen was a lab rat for a MKULTRA experiment. The bad trip drove him crazy and he leapt out of a New York hotel room window. The CIA denied for years that it had anything to do with his death.

Secret societies stay secret by draping their real affairs in myth. Some of the myth is beyond their control. Whenever something is secret, people are going to speculate about it. Some of the myth is deliberately concocted by the secret society itself, to mystify the uninitiated, or terrorize them. With all secret societies, it is difficult

to demarcate where the myths end and truth begins. Often, the two are commingled.

The CIA is no different. The catchall myth the agency whips up to garb its true designs is "national security." Exposing CIA activities, we're told, would endanger this "security," which is your personal security, by implication. The myth, more than a little self-aggrandizing, creates a mystique, a godlike importance for all the secret practices of the CIA.

As a rationale for too many CIA endeavors, "national security" is about as real as the cloaking device used by alien spaceships on "Star Trek." And it serves the same purpose, just as effectively.

The CIA is a deft, effective manufacturer of myth about itself. When the CIA's station chief for Greece, Richard Welch, was gunned down on his doorstep on December 23, 1975, the agency wasted little time grieving. Reflexively and with consummate cynicism, it turned the assassination into the perfect case for tightening its own security. The CIA's self-serving disinformation effort in the Welch affair was so sudden and smooth that one wonders if the CIA itself didn't know about the killing in advance. Welch's murder couldn't have come at a better time for the CIA. In the aftermath of Watergate, its secrets were exploding in Congress and in the press with the severity of an aneurysm. The agency needed to stop the hemorrhage.

Welch's identity had been revealed in *CounterSpy*, a magazine of investigative reporting on the CIA, cofounded by CIA dissident Philip Agee. *CounterSpy* made a practice of publishing the names of CIA officers, ferreting out the data from public records. The CIA was not pleased by this practice. What it didn't want the American people to know is what any interested citizen of a foreign country already knew: that the names of important CIA officers were readily available to anyone with the mild determination needed to discover them.

The Greek revolutionary "November 17" group had been planning Welch's "execution" long before his name was published. The assassins staked him out for months. But as soon as CIA headquarters got the news of Welch's killing, the agency's press spokesman phoned reporters (on "deep background" of course) to inform them of both the murder, and the *CounterSpy* article naming

Welch. The national press needed little prodding to make the link. Official hysteria was immediate. Eventually, Congress passed the "Intelligence Identities Protection Act," outlawing publication of CIA names.

It was all a myth. The CIA knew, in the summer of 1975, even before it shipped Welch to Greece, a nation in loathing of the CIA, that he was in danger there. Headquarters warned him not to move into the same house that several previous CIA station chiefs had occupied, but he moved in anyway. After his name appeared, along with his address and job description in the English-language *Athens News*, the CIA, if it were really worried, could have removed him from Greece, but it did not. Welch's killing had nothing to do with *CounterSpy* or any other publication.

But the CIA took the opportunity to rebuild the then-eroding fiction that public scrutiny of the CIA endangers not only national security, but the lives of individual men. Such propaganda only fuels more myth, of a type not as flattering to the CIA.

The conspiratorial demonology of the CIA, the myths that originate with ordinary people who feel the need to pierce the CIA's secrecy, are different from the propaganda myths authored by the CIA. Popular myths, seething from the zeitgeist, are not deliberate falsehoods. They grow to explain things that we can't understand. There is often far more truth to them, literal and figurative truth, than we'd like to suppose. The CIA myths explain evidence that is suggestive but not conclusive. Speculation—ranging from wholly reasonable, if startling, to utterly farfetched—must fill in the gaps. Hard facts have been spun into conspiracy theories about the CIA's still-secret machinations.

With good reason. Again, just because myths are myths doesn't mean they're lies. The CIA intersects again and again with other secret societies. Reagan's director of central intelligence William Casey belonged to the Knights of Malta, a Catholic order formed several hundred years ago along the lines of the Knights Templar, and other "holy" military fraternities (the Teutonic Knights were another).

John McCone, another of the CIA's most prominent directors,

was a Knight. William F. Buckley, "patron saint of conservatives" and a former CIA man, is a Knight, too, and a member of Yale's quasi-Masonic, elitist Skull and Bones. The most famous Bonesman hanging around these days is CIA director turned United States president George Bush.

Through Licio Gelli, the CIA also comes into contact with both the Knights of Malta and the Masons. Gelli was the founder of Propaganda Due, aka P2, the shadowy Masonic lodge that became, under Gelli's guidance, a worldwide fascist conspiracy. A 1987 indictment of 20 P2 members called the group a "secret structure [that] had the incredible capacity to control a state's institutions to the point of virtually becoming a state-within-a-state."

P2 has tried to set up a fascist countergovernment in Italy and is known to be behind a 1980 terrorist bombing that killed eighty-five people in a Bologna railroad station. At the time, it was Europe's deadliest terror attack. P2 surfaced again in connection with the Vatican banking scandal, and the murders and "suicides" that went with it.

Gelli, a real "joiner," is a Knight of Malta, which brought him into contact with Casey and Al Haig (yet another Knight). Casey was Ronald Reagan's 1980 campaign manager before becoming CIA director, and Gelli helped secure good press for Reagan in Italy. As a show of appreciation, Gelli was awarded a ticket to Reagan's 1980 inauguration gala, in the good seats.

There is also some speculation that George Bush may be at least an "honorary" member of P2, or an affiliated lodge. It would hardly be out of character. One of Bush's 1988 presidential campaign advisers, Philip Guarino, is definitely *Piduisti* (as members of the lodge are called). Guarino also worked for Reagan in 1980.

Gelli's CIA contacts helped him get P2 off the ground in 1966 (Gelli first became a Mason in 1963. It took a few years to get his own lodge). The CIA, according to its lapsed contract agent Richard Brenneke (more about him later), has financed the P2 organization since 1970 through a corporation called Amitalia, itself an offshoot of something known as the "International Fund for Mergers and Acquisitions," based in Panama.

The Masonic Grand Lodge of Italy ultimately suspended P2 for refusing to reveal the names of its members. Through the P2 mem-

bership roster, Gelli also brings the CIA into contact with another, better known secret society, the Mafia.

But that's not a new relationship. The best-known snuggle-up between the CIA and La Cosa Nostra came when the two joined hands in an attempt to knock off Fidel Castro, whose regime put the mob out of business in Havana, a plot that may have twisted into the assassination of President Kennedy.

The Italian government has long suspected that P2 is not Gelli's baby (bear in mind, many members of the Italian government belong to P2). The lodge, it is widely believed, is controlled by some outside power, with headquarters beyond Italian borders. Maybe the Mafia, some feel. Maybe even the Prieure de Sion, the apparently gnostic, proto-Masonic group that became the subject of all kinds of theorizing after the 1983 publication of *Holy Blood, Holy Grail*, the book that exposed its existence to an international audience.

Journalist Mino Pecorelli, himself a P2 member, wrote an article in 1979 naming the outside power pulling P2's strings. He named the CIA. Pecorelli had tried to blackmail Gelli before writing the piece. Shortly after it was printed, Pecorelli was killed as he sat in his car outside the offices of his magazine. He was shot twice in the mouth, a Sicilian Mafia way of saying, "Shut up."

The list of CIA types on the rosters of powerful secret societies seems endless. The Knights of Malta contingent included, conspicuously, General Reinhard Gehlen. Gehlen was the Nazi spymaster who turned around after the war to become, in effect, a founder of the CIA. His anti-Soviet Nazi espionage network was transferred virtually undisturbed to American intelligence. "He's on our side," said CIA director Allen Dulles. "That's all that matters."

According this honor to Gehlen, and other top Nazis, exacerbated the Cold War immeasurably, almost triggering World War III. The very act of signing Gehlen and his entourage of war criminals and stormtroopers was "a substantial escalation of the cold war," author Christopher Simpson points out. More important, Gehlen's intelligence reports systematically exaggerated the Soviet "threat," fueling American paranoia about the Soviet Union's military intentions and about domestic communist "subversion."

"The only intelligence provided by the Gehlen net to the United States," asserts Carl Oglseby of the Institute for Continuing De-

Nazification, "was intelligence selected specifically to worsen East-West relations and increase the possibility of military conflict between the U.S. and the Soviet Union." The effect of the decidedly undemocratic Gehlen "Org" on America's institutions of democracy, adds Oglesby, was to "weaken them incalculably."

Who knows how the influence of unrepentant Nazis shaped the philosophy and methods of the CIA? "Whatever the CIA was from the standpoint of law, it remained from the standpoint of practical intelligence collection a front for a house of Nazi spies," Oglesby says.

The CIA's involvement with Nazis didn't end with Gehlen, and led it into contact with another powerful secret society, the Order of the Death's Head, better known as the Schutzstaffel. The SS. The SS was more than the Nazi police force and terror unit. It was fashioned by its leader Heinrich Himmler to be an elite chivalric order. It had mystical rites, oaths, and internal rankings, or degrees—the trademarks of a secret society.

Hundreds, even thousands, of SS men became part of CIA operations after the war. Among the most notable was Otto Skorzeny, the hulking hero of numerous high-risk Nazi adventures, known in Germany as "Hitler's favorite commando." In the 1950s, Skorzeny worked for the CIA in Egypt. Skorzeny was sent ostensibly to train that country's security forces, to insure that Egypt would be safe from the Soviet threat.

Into the Egyptian "security forces" Skorzeny recruited about one hundred former SS men and neo-Nazis. Skorzeny's mucking about in Egypt eventually helped trigger the Suez crisis, one of the Middle East's bloodier wars. While the CIA was underwriting "Scarface" (Skorzeny's face bore a frightful duelling scar) Skorzeny's nazification project, it was also paying another former SS man to stave off the Soviets in the Middle East: Alois Brunner, Adolf Eichmann's gung-ho chief aide, said to be responsible for murdering 128,500 human beings.

It was Dulles who bestowed this congeniality upon Gehlen, Skorzeny, Brunner, and their Nazi ilk. Before World War II, Dulles's law firm did considerable work in Nazi Germany and showed a startling degree of indifference to Hitler's increasingly evident policies.

It was also Dulles, in all probability, who "rehabilitated" the pro-Nazi corporation International Telephone and Telegraph (ITT) into a South American host for CIA operatives in the early 1950s. In 1970, the CIA would secure Chile for ITT with a coup in which its elected president Salvador Allende was assassinated.

It was Dulles, after all, who once said, "An intelligence service is an ideal vehicle for a conspiracy."

Commies are bad, but, to committed Nazis like Skorzeny, Jews are worse. Once in Egypt, Skorzeny busied himself training the first Palestinian terrorist groups. Descendants of those groups still wreak havoc in the Middle East today.

The CIA also bumps into secret societies in the Far East. Through its Golden Triangle operations tied to international opium smugglers, the CIA also touches base with the "triads," an Asian secret-society equivalent of the Mafia.

Then there is the unlikeliest intersection of all.

The late Stephen Knight, a British investigative reporter who specialized in covering Freemasonry, believed Licio Gelli was working for the CIA's Soviet doppelgänger, the KGB. Although it is hard to believe a hard-line fascist like Gelli would sell out to the Soviets, he is said to have made a number of Communist contacts after World War II. He was a survivor first, a fascist second. Knight says that the KGB made a practice of infiltrating Freemasonry in a number of countries, because of its convenient blend of access to influential people and good cover.

The truth, probably, is that all of these organizations—Knights of Malta, Prieure de Sion, Freemasons, SS Nazis, Asian triads, even the KGB—bond with the CIA somewhere in the twilight zone of international intrigue.


On a somewhat lighter note, even the initiation rite—that is, the entrance interview into the CIA—has something in common with secret society initiations. It is common in secret societies—and in cults, not coincidentally—for initiates to be put through an ego-stripping process that usually involves revealing the details of one's sex habits. Pledges into Skull and Bones must lie naked in a coffin and recite their entire sexual histories. The mind reels at the concept

of George Bush or William F. Buckley stripping to their birthday suits, climbing into a coffin, and then reciting a litany of God-knows-what.

In any case, in 1972 former CIA officer Patrick McGarvey recalled that he was first welcomed to the CIA by being strapped to a lie detector machine and asked, "Do you still masturbate?" Stunned by the question, he was taken even further aback by his examiner's hot-tempered insistence that he answer. The questioner then proceeded with predictable follow-ups. For example, "Ever had a blow job?"

Prurient hazing aside, the CIA shares another trait with those secret societies with which it is so thoroughly enmeshed: money. Most secret societies are much more than social organizations. They are repositories of wealth as well as power.

The CIA maintains an impressive financial portfolio, which seems to serve a dual purpose. It bankrolls the CIA's many adventures and, through a network of "proprietary" companies, provides cover for clandestine activities.

Among the revelations in the Iran-Contra scandal was the fact that a CIA-run shrimp fishery, Ocean Hunter, was used as a drug-smuggling operation with proceeds going to the CIA-financed contras. The CIA also infiltrated Wall Street in the 1960s and 1970s through a thirty million dollar company called "Southern Capital." It has owned and operated airlines. Through a technology company called "Zenith Technical" in Miami, the CIA ran numerous operations against Cuba in the 1960s. The agency doesn't stop with its own companies either.

The CIA owned stock in ITT in 1970, at the same time it was staging the coup that led to the overthrow and assassination of Salvador Allende in Chile—an action that handed the South American country to ITT. Major oil companies are often inseparable from the CIA. In Venezuela, for example, according to investigative reporter Jim Hougan, "Exxon *is* the CIA." Smaller oil companies are, too. Zapata Oil, founded by George Bush, is believed by some to have been CIA connected.

Some executives look at fronting for the CIA as good business. Howard Hughes figured that if his company took CIA contracts, the CIA would be there to bail him out when he needed them. They

may not have been there for Hughes (that's another story!), but they seem to be there for a more contemporary group of big-bucks brigands: savings and loan executives.

The CIA's most recent venture into the universe of high finance may be its most costly ever, in terms of raw dollars. The collapse of the savings and loan industry appears to have been caused at least in part by CIA hijinks, and it may yet cost the United States taxpayers one trillion dollars to reimburse the lost, federally insured money. What's more, some corrupt S&L executives are said to have "get out of jail free" cards supplied by the CIA.

None other than the director of the FBI, William Sessions, testified to Congress that "looting" had more to do with the S&L failures than the abstruse economic factors that fascinate official analysts. Sessions didn't say who pulled off this massive looting operation, but a lone investigative reporter from Texas, where S&Ls were rolling into oblivion like so many tumbleweeds, followed the money for five years. Along the way, he bumped into an array of CIA operatives and their mobster pals.

Pete Brewton of the *Houston Post* listed twenty-two savings and loan institutions where evidence pointed to plunder by the organized crime–CIA nexus. The CIA immediately denied the *Houston Post* stories, saying "that would be a violation of U.S. laws, and we do not violate U.S. laws."

The CIA maintains deniability on many of its more outlandish escapades by using contract agents rather than its own full-time personnel. That was how, in its old rough-and-ready days, the agency used the private detective firm headed by superspook Robert Maheu, who was also Howard Hughes' alter ego. Maheu's firm took on assignments the CIA deemed too sensitive to handle. It was the inspiration for the television series "Mission: Impossible."

If the CIA was involved in looting the S&Ls, it used its contract agents to do the work. One of the contractors, Brewton reported, was Farhad Azima, a pro-Shah Iranian who headed one of the largest charter airlines in America, Global International Airways. The airline borrowed money from an S&L in which Azima was a major investor, then declared bankruptcy. Global was either a CIA proprietary, or a heavy contract client of the CIA. Some of Global's pilots also flew for the defunct Air America, known to be a CIA

company. One of Global's creditors was Southern Air Transport, a Miami company once owned by the CIA (the agency sold it to an ex-CIA lawyer), which supplied planes for shipping arms to Iran, and to the contras.

Global Airlines' biggest client was a company called "Egyptian American Transport and Services Company." (EATSCO), run by some of the same CIA men named by Daniel Sheehan as defendants in the "Secret Team" lawsuit—men who have been behind the darkest of the CIA's dark doings for thirty years: Ted Shackley, Edwin Wilson, Thomas Clines. According to Gene Wheaton, a private eye who once worked as an investigator at the Pentagon, EATSCO actually owned Fazima's Global Airlines.

Azima milked a Kansas City S&L called Indian Springs State Bank, according to Brewton's stories. Vision Banc Savings in Kingsville, Texas, was another CIA target, according to the Brewton series. It loaned millions for a failed Florida land deal to convicted money launderer Lawrence Freeman, a friend of Paul Helliwell—a CIA man from the agency's early days and an associate of William Casey. Brewton cites sources who told him that some of the money siphoned off by Freeman may have gone to covert operations.

Vision Banc Savings was owned by an alleged money launderer and occasional CIA contact named Richard Corson, Brewton's stories say. Brewton also reports that Freeman may have been a front man for Mike Adkison, who borrowed a total of one hundred million dollars from Corson's bank and five other Texas thrifts. Adkison, according to Brewton's reports, is reputed to be an international arms merchant who has sold arms to Iraq.

A Florida-based newsletter called *Money Laundering Alert* said in April 1990 that "a significant amount of money obtained through fraudulent means from a number of the nation's failed S&Ls were laundered through the accounts of CIA front companies . . . to fund covert operations."

Former CIA contract agent Richard Brenneke, the same man who testified that he had flown George Bush to a Paris meeting in 1980 to strike a preelection arms-for-hostages deal with Iran, told Brewton that money from S&L raids was being spirited to the contras. Reporter Stephen Pizzo said that in researching his book about the S&L plunder, *Inside Job*, he and his collaborators came

across the CIA "about a half a dozen times," but decided "that's not what we're writing about right now." They resolved to follow only the trails of mobsters (trails lengthy enough to consume any investigator's time).

"Who knows how many those [the CIA connections] would have linked to," Pizzo said. "We just don't know." Eventually, they wrote an article summing up their CIA-S&L findings for *Penthouse* magazine.

The savings and loan fiasco, if it unfolds the way Brewton's reports indicate, would not be the first time the CIA has exploited the banking industry. Christic Institute counsel Dan Sheehan says that Bank of America, which came close to collapsing in the 1980s, suddenly reversed its losses when the Iran-Contra scandal became public. The suggestion is that B of A was being looted for a contra war. Much better documented, however, is the saga of Australia's Nugan Hand bank, a CIA operation in every respect but its name. Under the agency's sage guidance, the Nugan Hand bank was a front for drug running, a laundry machine for money coming from the Shah of Iran and Ferdinand Marcos, and a channel for the CIA's covert funding of its preferred political parties throughout the world.

Nugan Hand met with a fate not unlike that of so many American S&Ls. More than fifty million dollars in debt, it folded. The fate of its titular owners was far worse than anything yet meted out to an S&L exec, however. Frank Nugan was shot to death, and Michael Hand disappeared.

Like all good secret societies, the CIA knows the ancient art of invisibility. The full story of the CIA-S&L affair may never come out. A former Justice Department prosecutor, quoted by Brewton, summed up the frustration of trying to apprehend the elusive CIA. "It's like trying to grab smoke."

Allegations against the CIA get wispier and wispier when puzzling over how the CIA performs the one duty dear to all conspiratorial societies, fomenting revolution. On the one hand, there's no question the CIA has been behind more toppled and subverted governments than could be catalogued here. Guatemala in 1954.

Chile in 1970. Grenada in 1984. Iran. Greece. The Dominican Republic. Cambodia. Nicaragua. And of course, Vietnam. Those countries make up a pitifully incomplete inventory of nations whose governments have been installed, overthrown, or undermined by the CIA.

The subject becomes more ambiguous when we explore the CIA's support for terrorism. Terrorists (as modern revolutionaries are called) have become the arch villains of American folklore. In popular parlance as prescribed by government and the media, a "terrorist" is by definition a hater of America, so it seems beyond belief that an agency as fanatical as the CIA is about protecting American interests and enforcing the American will would have anything to do with terrorism.

Part of that problem of perception has to do with the American definition of "terrorism." Somehow, terrorism has come to be firmly linked to left-wing insurgency, as if right-wing terrorism did not exist. Though the idea of terrorism as a leftist phenomena is certainly perpetuated by official sources, to say simply that the media or government propaganda invented this definition and made it stick would be too facile.

The meaning of terrorism comes down to the meaning of "us" and "them." "They" are the poor, blacks, foreigners, and so on. "We" are American mainstream, white folks with a little money in our pockets. The reason the "we" seem so eager to accept that terrorism is a threat only from the extreme left is that the extreme left threatens "us." Since communism was concocted, Americans have been indoctrinated with the notion that the Left wants to take away all the things *we* treasure so deeply. The right wing, conversely and more comfortingly, is primarily concerned with *them*—minorities, the poor, foreigners—and directs its violence away from us. Right-wing terrorism isn't very terrifying because it doesn't terrorize *us*.

At least, that's how we've been instructed to think.

Despite the American delusion of terrorism as a left-wing phenomena carried out by radical Marxists lauding the people's struggle as they bomb department stores and gun down tourists, the right-wing "Black International" is actually far more entrenched. The movement was founded by Skorzeny and other Nazis, includ-

ing "Butcher of Lyons" Klaus Barbie, and, perhaps most important, the enigmatic old guard Nazi financier François Genoud.

That conspiracy could not have formed, it's fair to say, without sustenance from the CIA. The CIA helped Nazis, Barbie among them, escape prosecution for war crimes. It used them as intelligence "assets," set them up with new lives and some of them with new identities. The right-wing terror network is still in evidence today.

Palestinian terrorist organizations are part of it. Their spark was lit by Skorzeny and his SS compadres backed by the CIA. Agency connections reveal themselves right up to the present. The CIA schmoozed with Ali Hassan Salameh, leader of Black September, mastermind of the 1972 Munich massacre at the Olympics. The agency was so keen to make Salameh an "asset" that it gave him an all-expense paid vacation in sunny Honolulu. Salameh's day at the beach came to an end when the long arm of Israeli vengeance got to him in 1979. But the Israelis waited to hit Salameh until they'd received clearance from the CIA.

Still more recently, as commandos backed by Iran and Libya were holding American hostages and staging suicide attacks against U.S. servicemen, a network of arms dealers based in the White House was arming Iran at the behest of CIA chief (and longtime intelligence agent) William Casey. That operation was the heart of the Iran-Contra scandal.


On December 21, 1988, just four days before Christmas, thirty-one thousand feet in the air over the countryside village of Lockerbie, Scotland, a Pan Am 747, whose nickname "Maid of the Seas" was painted across its cockpit, exploded. The passengers and crew, mostly Americans bound home for the holidays, were thrown into the air to their deaths, some of them still safety buckled into their seats. Several more people, residents of Lockerbie, died when the wreckage of the plane smashed in a blaze to the ground.

The bombing of Pan Am Flight 103 from London, originating in Frankfurt, was immediately pinned on Palestinian terrorists with links to the Iranian government. Not surprisingly to those initiated into the mysteries of terrorist conspiracies, the CIA showed up on

the scene as well. The CIA connection to the horrific mass murder received far less publicity than did the equally shadowy Arab–Iranian involvement. From reading most news accounts, even to this day, one could miss mention of the CIA completely.

The stories, cover stories, and theories about the bombing of 103 have become numerous. Undisputed, though not often discussed, is the fact that CIA agents were passengers on the plane. There were at least four, possibly five. Some accounts say eight. But they were there. What were they doing on board a civilian airliner, these obvious targets for assassination? That they would be targets is made more likely by the nature of their mission. They were returning from Lebanon, where, it is suspected by most who bother to check, they were working on some sort of deal regarding the American hostages held by pro-Iranian kidnappers.

They could have been part of an effort to buy the hostages' release. Bundled, large-denomination traveler's checks worth more than half a million dollars were found by two farm boys at the crash site. Or they could have been planning a rescue operation. Searchers found a diagram of what appeared to be a building in Beirut, with exact locations of two hostages marked.

The conspiratorial story is much more complex. It came out in a report prepared by a former Israeli intelligence agent working as an international private investigator for a firm called Interfor. Pan Am hired him to do the investigation, and, based on what he found, the airline subpoenaed from the U.S. government a whole set of material. Most intriguing, Pan Am alleged that the CIA possessed a videotape of the bomb actually being placed on board the plane. The Interfor report calls that tape "the gem" of the investigation.

The Interfor report was reported on the front page of the *Toronto Star* and several London newspapers, some of which led their own journalistic investigations of the bombing. In America, it made the rounds of the alternative press, written up in the *San Francisco Bay Guardian* and San Pedro, California's *Random Lengths*. My paper, the San Jose *Metro*, also made some mention of it. But in the daily press and on television, nothing.

The unfortunate CIA squad on board Pan Am 103 are actually the heroes of the Interfor report. That team, led by an Army major named Charles McKee—on loan to the CIA from the Defense

Department—had in fact been in Lebanon on a top secret, hostage-related mission, the report says. In their investigations, they zeroed in on a Syrian drug smuggler named Monzar Al-Kassar, who had connections high in the Syrian government. In fact, he was married to Syrian President Hafez Assad's niece.

Al-Kassar also had connections in other governments. Like many international drug traders, he also dealt arms and, as such, he was useful to the American Iran-Contra "Enterprise." Richard Secord and Albert Hakim paid Al-Kassar $1.5 million to ship small arms to the contras. Interfor said he was earlier the go-between between the French government and terrorists when a few French hostages were set free. According to the Interfor report, a mysterious "off the shelf" team of CIA agents lurking in West Germany, with their "control" at an unknown location not at Langley but in Washington, tried to use Al-Kassar for the same thing.

The McKee team found out about this other CIA operation. And they discovered that the other agents, in exchange for Al-Kassar's help, were protecting his drug-running routes. Incensed, the McKee team boarded Pan Am 103, for home.

Unknown to them, presumably, they picked the flight used by Al-Kassar for his drug smuggling. And on that flight, Al-Kassar's terrorist friends decided to use the CIA cover of his drug route to plant the bomb. West German police, with the help of Israeli intelligence, found out about it. They actually videotaped the bomb going onto the plane. When the CIA agents covering for Al-Kassar phoned back to their "control" to ask what to do, they were told, "Don't worry about it. Don't stop it. Let it go."

They did. 259 people died on the plane, eleven more on the ground.


Late in 1990, allegations surfaced in the Italian press that none other than the P2 Lodge was the real mastermind of the Pan Am 103 bombing, to cover up its own role in arms deals with Iran. I haven't seen that claim supported or corroborated anywhere, but it wouldn't be out of character for the P2. And it suggests a dizzying conspiracy theory: with P2 allegedly funded through an Italian corporation whose parent company was in Panama (recall Bren-

neke's allegations earlier this chapter), CIA man George Bush somehow connected to the P2, and that Panamanian parent company (according again to Brenneke) in existence right up through the end of General Manuel Noriega's reign. Suddenly, from the depths of international intrigue, the possible true motive for Bush's 1989 invasion of Panama creeps into light: to destroy records that could link the CIA, and even himself, however indirectly, to the mass murder aboard Pan Am 103. Of course, there's no evidence for any of that—just another demon raised from conspiratoriological hell.

Sometime after the crash, George Bush phoned Margaret Thatcher. According to Jack Anderson, the two leaders agreed that the investigation into the bombing would be "limited" in order to protect British and American intelligence interests.

Another stray fact worth noting about Pan Am 103: In addition to the CIA's McKee team, the plane was also carrying Bernt Carlsson, the U.N. negotiator with South Africa, who had just carved out a deal on Namibian independence. He was on his way back to New York to ink the pact. Needless to say, he never got to sign his name.

The Interfor report, when it's mentioned at all in the major media, is usually dismissed. The lone exception as of this writing is a December 1990 feature piece in *Barron's*, a Dow Jones–owned financial weekly. The *Barron's* article was quite thorough, with one glaring exception. It never mentioned the McKee team. The title of the piece, "Unwitting Accomplices?," is also an odd one, given that the story *did* mention CIA headquarters' alleged instructions to "let it go," when warned of the bomb—hardly "unwitting." Leaving out the McKee team story obscures one possible motive in letting the bomb go: to eliminate agents who had learned too much about the drugs-hostages-arms connection.

Other than *Barron's*, no news organization that I know has even bothered to check out the Interfor report's allegations, save consulting their intelligence sources, who, as expected, deride it as a "spitball," meaning a hodgepodge of fact and fiction with no value as intelligence. I doubt that much of what the Interfor report says will ever be seriously examined. It tells a tale that, even for a conspiracy theory, is one of the darkest ever spun about the CIA.

And its implications are even more daunting. If the report proved true, it would connect the bombing of Pan Am 103 to the Iran-Contra scandal; the bombing would become part of the Iran-Contra cover-up.

Iran-Contra, the real story, was costly enough without 270 lives added to the price tag. The Iran-Contra operators, particularly Richard Secord and Albert Hakim, were hooked up with "renegade" CIA operatives Edwin Wilson and Frank Terpil. Wilson and Terpil sold arms and explosives to Libya's Colonel Qaddafi. They were indicted, convicted, and imprisoned for it. Secord and Hakim were not. Nor was Ted Shackley, an almost godlike figure in spook circles. Shackley was Wilson's CIA supervisor. He had distinguished himself in Vietnam as a prime mover behind the near-genocidal Phoenix program, in which the CIA killed tens of thousands of Vietnamese civilians.

Shackley is author of a book, *The Third Option*, that advocates in no uncertain terms U.S. covert operations to control the politics of foreign countries. He is also widely believed to have been a leader of the CIA's Golden Triangle opium smuggling activities, which he angrily denies.

When Wilson and Terpil were caught arming terrorists, Shackley was allowed to quietly resign his CIA post. The CIA's deputy director at that time, who supported Shackley, was Frank Carlucci. After National Security Adviser John Poindexter was forced to resign when accused of masterminding the Iran-Contra cover-up, Carlucci got his job.

Iran-Contra and the Wilson affair got a lot of press, although their significance was never fully explained in the mass media. Less publicized are the CIA's strange encounters with characters like Licio Gelli and its darker weavings with the fascist terrorist cabal. Gelli is said to have conspired with "Black" terrorist Stefano Delle Chiaie to plan the Bologna train station bombing. The European Black International in which Delle Chiaie was a preeminent figure consisted of old and "neo" Nazis, including SS officers, and other elements of European fascism and anti-Semitism. Among its list of accomplishments, this same network was responsible for bombing a Paris synagogue just weeks after the train station bomb went off.

Delle Chiaie, as well as Gelli, had his own CIA friends. Both are

linked to the Mafia. No surprises there. But both are also tied in with the "Red International," that is, with international left-wing terrorism. In recent years, the two terrorist factions have become so close that the distinction is not much more than semantic.

In late 1990, around the time I was finishing this book, a story broke in Europe that put the CIA's connection to right-wing terrorism into focus. The story became a huge scandal in Italy, threatening to topple the Italian government. In America, it received limited play. The *Washington Post* ran an article headed "CIA Organized Secret Army in Western Europe." The *New York Times* offered its own summary of the affair, but did not mention the CIA.

The "secret army," European press revealed, was part of the CIA's "Operation Gladio," its Cold War project to organize the extreme right in Europe into an anti-Communist resistance. The German arm of the Gladio army was made up of former SS men. The Italian branch contained such sterling characters as Delle Chiaie and his P2 cohorts. The London *Independent* newspaper wrote that the killing of Italian prime minister Aldo Moro may have been carried out with the cooperation of these CIA-backed elements—namely, P2 members in the Italian government. Moro's kidnapping and execution were pulled off by the supposedly left-wing Red Brigade.

As early as 1969, the Black International held a summit conference in Barcelona, Spain, with good wishes from the country's fascist dictator, Francisco Franco. The summit was called to plan strategy for Yasser Arafat and his burgeoning cabal of Palestinian terrorists. Left wing? Or right wing?

The fact of the matter is, while it's easier to link the CIA to right-wing terrorism than to left-wing terrorism, the line between right and left is blurred beyond recognition. The alliance goes beyond their shared tactics of extreme violence aimed at oblivious civilians. Their new unity is known as the "Third Position," and its adherents rally around the slogan "Hitler and Mao united in struggle."

"Third position" interlocks explain some apparent anomalies. Klaus Barbie, CIA-backed Nazi war criminal, was represented at his 1985 Paris trial by left-wing lawyer Jacques Verges. Verges became famous for using the courtroom as his platform for lashing

out at Western imperialism. He married one of his most famous clients, Algerian bomber Djamila Bouhired, converted to Islam, and became a doctrinaire Maoist after traveling to China and meeting Chairman Mao himself. He is named in connection with many of the best-known "Red" terrorists. Yet he represented the most infamous Nazi war criminal since Eichmann, and has known François Genoud for four decades.

Left-right intercourse also explains why the hijackers of the *Achille Lauro* cruise ship demanded the release of Odifried Hepp, a prolific neo-Nazi terrorist then incarcerated in West Germany. In the early 1980s, Hepp planned and carried out attacks on several American army installations, NATO bases, and night spots where U.S. soldiers liked to hang out. Some of the attacks were attributed in the press to leftists. Sometimes, left-wing groups went out of their way to claim credit for the attacks.

Right and left lose their meaning in the swirling eddy of global insurrection. The connections are dazzling. They set the legend of the CIA in the same light as legends of secret societies from the Illuminati to the Hashishim to the Freemasons. They are committed not to national aims, nor to explicitly ideological ones. They are devoted only to their own subversive, secret agenda.

# 14

# SHOTS FROM THE BUSHY KNOLL

*Friendly fascism in the United States would not need a charismatic, apparently all-powerful leader such as Mussolini or Hitler. . . . The chief executive, rather, becomes the nominal head of a network that not only serves to hold the Establishment together but also provides it with a sanctimonious aura of legitimacy. . . .*

> BERTRAM GROSS, *Friendly Fascism*

Not since Adam Weishaupt founded the Bavarian Illuminati on May 1, 1776, has one man been at the pinnacle of such a massive pyramid of conspiracy theories as our forty-first president, George Herbert Walker Bush. No doubt about it; he has earned his way there.

If conspiracy theories came into some sort of vogue in the mid-1970s, with the Watergate mystery unresolved, the House Select Committee on Assassinations casting shadows on the Warren Report, Senator Frank Church displaying secret CIA death weapons on national TV, and Trilateral Commissioner Jimmy Carter in the White House, they seem even more apropos in the 1990s, with haphazardly gesticulating, sentence-fragmenting, broccoli-bashing, yet somehow sinister, Bush as chief executive. All the

elements that incited dark innuendo in the cynical 1970s have come to life in one man. Called everything from a "veteran of the Kennedy assassination," to a Rockefeller stooge, to head honcho of Dope Inc., Bush's case history is a conspiracy researcher's textbook.

Bush serves as a concentric point for the two circles that are the focus of most American conspiracy theory. He is a product of the Eastern Establishment who also functions smoothly in the Southwestern cowboy clan of oil and adventurism. It's sometimes said that Ronald Reagan's presidency marked a shift in power away from the Eastern Wall Streeters to the space-laser cowboys of Texas, Arizona, and Southern California. Away from nuclear deterrence and into Star Wars. Away from effete Trilateralism into Red Menace machismo.

The two wings of the ruling oligarchy have been struggling for predominance for a long time—at least since Barry Goldwater slugged it out with Nelson Rockefeller in 1964. Reagan, rather than marking a final transfer of power, may have been a transitional president in the process of melding the two sects into one unified body of overlords. Getting Bush into office seals the marriage with a salty kiss.

Bush was chief of the CIA under Gerald Ford. Before entering government, he was a Texas oil boss. His name came up in the aftermath of the J.F.K. killing. He belonged to the Council on Foreign Relations and the Trilateral Commission and is an initiate into an exclusive secret society with occult, if campy, rituals.

The Christic Institute posits Bush as a key coordinator of the Iran-Contra "enterprise." There is ample documentation that Bush lied about his involvement in the scandal. He was never "out of the loop" as he claimed. How deeply is Bush involved in drug trafficking? His perduring relationship, gone sour, with Panama's former dictator Manuel Noriega suggests he knows something about the narco trade that he could hardly be expected to tell.

As CIA boss, he covered up the assassination of a Chilean diplomat in Washington, D.C., and the terrorist bombing of an airliner that killed seventy-three people. As Nixon-picked chairman of the Republican National Committee, he stonewalled for his patron president up until the day before Nixon resigned. "I owed Richard

Nixon a lot, and as a matter of fact I still do," he shamelessly declared, in his 1987 autobiography.

A former CIA operative testified under oath that he piloted Bush to Paris in October 1980, where the then vice presidential candidate helped negotiate a deal with Iranian hostage holders—to keep holding hostages until Reagan was in office. As if hobnobbing with terrorists wasn't distasteful enough, fascists turned up in the infrastructure of Bush's 1988 presidential campaign—real live fascists of the same ilk imported by the CIA after World War II. They were part of the Republican "Ethnic Outreach" effort.

Right-wingers always wondered why Reagan picked Bush for vice president in 1980. The sunbelt-conservative cowboy and tweedy, bespectacled Brahmin made an asymmetrical pair. "The same people who gave you Jimmy Carter now want to give you George Bush," the hard liners warned when Bush was leading Reagan in the Republican primaries that year. In response to the pressure, Bush resigned from the Council on Foreign Relations, damning it as "too liberal," out of step with his newfound affinity for the radical right. He stayed on for a while on the Trilateral Commission, though.

Was Bush, like Carter before him, being groomed for the top job by invisible power brokers from the start? Though he would later derive unlimited mileage by invoking the malaise-laden spirit of Jimmy Carter to ward off Democratic opponents in the 1988 presidential campaign, the *L.A. Times* reported that in the 1970s Bush was bucking for a job in the Carter administration. Carter's national security adviser, Trilateral Commission founder Zbigniew Brzezinski, took a high profile role in Bush's 1988 campaign, advising on foreign policy. In 1980, his campaign was aided in no small measure by a group of disgruntled intelligence operatives known loosely as "Agents for Bush."

Once in vice presidential office, Bush flirted with a fast promotion. Curiously, Bush's son Neil had a dinner date with an old family friend the night that John Hinckley, with a .22 caliber bullet, almost facilitated George Bush's ascendancy to the White House. The old family friend was John Hinckley's brother, Scott.

Hinckley, as I mentioned in Chapter 10, was under the influence of mind-altering psychiatric drugs, and dabbled with neo-Nazi

cultism. We looked at the theory that he was a mind-controlled assassin. But what about the theory that he was a mind-controlled patsy, not unlike—the speculation goes—Sirhan Sirhan? In the NBC news special reports immediately following the attempt on Reagan's life, correspondent Judy Woodruff said on the air, with considerable certainty, that at least one shot came from an overhang above Reagan's limousine. Later she said that the shot came from *a Secret Service agent* stationed on the overhang.

A shot from that angle would explain how a bullet got into the president's chest, when Hinckley would have had to fire straight through a car door to hit him at that angle. Later, the shot in the chest was explained as a ricochet. John Judge, seizing on Woodruff's on-the-scene report, calls it "the shot from the Bushy Knoll."

Neil Bush, almost a decade later, leapt to national infamy in the savings and loan scandal. Allegedly, while a director of Silverado Savings and Loan in Colorado, he voted to approve loans for one of his business partners. Another received a loan from Silverado that was never repaid, contributing to the thrift's demise. Neil was also involved with a Colorado company called Sun-Flo International, a dehydrated foods maker that functioned as a money-laundering machine for known drug dealers. The company's founder, a convicted drug trafficker, is quoted saying, "Bush's kid is in my hip pocket."

George Bush was also entwined with Sun-Flo, hosting one of its consultants on a 1982 African tour. Thus, the vice president, in the words of the alternative newsweekly that reported the story (most dailies missed it), "unwittingly helped promote a firm run by a convicted drug dealer."

Bush's help may have been unwitting, but maybe not out of character. In the public eye, he's an amiable, if slightly twerpy, family man. In the underground information exchange, he's a cunning, ruthless spook with a secret agenda. The real George Bush, say the suspicious, lurks in the shadow cast by his thousand points of light. Not "kinder, gentler," but "a dangerous threat to world peace." One person, one president, but viewed through two different lenses.

In his own mind, who knows when George Bush first decided that his mission was to become president of the United States? In reality, his fate was fixed when William Casey convinced Ronald Reagan to select Bush as his 1980 running mate. Bush and Reagan had some contentious encounters on the primary circuit, but Casey, Reagan's campaign manager, was an old buddy of Bush. Four years earlier, Bush and Casey worked together to produce a special intelligence document whose purpose was to exaggerate the alleged Soviet "threat." The Reagan administration used the document as a basis for its rabidly anti-Soviet foreign policy, and increases in military spending at home.

William Casey was an intelligence agent from OSS days, a member of the Council on Foreign Relations, and a financial adventurer who rode the stock market like a bucking bronco. Legality and ethics not always his top priority, Casey was, by some accounts, apt to attempt a remodeling of public policy to suit his own prospectus. When Casey became director of the CIA, an inside joke developed that "CIA" stood for "Casey Investing Again."

With George's father, Prescott Bush (a World War I Army Intelligence agent) Casey cofounded a think tank in 1962 called the National Strategy Information Center, which got into trouble for financing publications issued by a CIA front company engaged in disinformation campaigns. Fourteen years later, Casey, dissatisfied with the CIA's modest estimates of Soviet military prowess (he was then on the president's Foreign Intelligence Advisory Board), got together with George Bush, then director of the CIA, to form a study group that would counter the conventional CIA wisdom.

The Bush/Casey group amassed evidence to support its predrawn conclusion that the Soviets were winning the arms race, and that the U.S. was malnourished by comparison. One of the study group's leaders was General Danny Graham, who went on to found High Frontier, the organization that effectively shaped Reagan's "Star Wars" policy.

The report cooked up by Bush and Casey's team served as a major rationale for the Reagan defense buildup. Who benefited

from the defense buildup? Defense contractors and the companies they do business with—many of the country's largest corporations. Who sits at the top of those companies? Some of America's richest people, whom I'll be introducing in the next chapter. They're sometimes called "the Establishment." The Bush-Casey report was a gift to America's most wealthy and powerful. At the expense of everybody else.

That Bush would be a loyal member and servant of the American ruling class is more than a matter of tradition, friendships, or family pride. Like so many of the elite and influential, Bush roots his power in private organizations that do business in dim corners, where the cleansing broom of public opinion cannot reach. Insulated from outside forces, the values and viewpoints formed in the cool remove of a secret society emerge fully formed into the light of politics. The public does not—and as far as the society's members are concerned, should not—understand where they came from, or their real motivations.

This is not to say that all members of a secret society conform to dogma. There is much dissent within societies, and sometimes war between societies. What their members share is a framework of belief, an image of themselves as an elect, a chosen people. To get into a secret society, they have been, quite literally, chosen. That framework guides the "brothers" to perpetuate their elite breed by any means available, and those means are plenary.

Bush belongs to Skull and Bones, a group "tapped" every year from Yale University's junior class. There are seven "Senior Societies" at Yale with long traditions of cornball cloak and dagger, college style, but Skull and Bones is the elite of the elite. Bush was a 1947 inductee. The society is more than just a glorified frat. It has a fat financial portfolio and a summer retreat on Deer Island available to Bonesmen for life. Most important, though, it provides a network of support and cooperation for some of the most powerful people in the U.S.

Bush is the second Bones president. William Howard Taft was the first. Other heavy-hitting Bonesmen include William F. Buckley; alleged leftist William Sloane Coffin; multinational business demigod Averill P. Harriman; Rhode Island senator John Chafee; one-time Nazi-sympathizer Henry P. Luce, who founded *Time*

magazine; and numerous top-of-the-heap corporate and legal figures. Massachusetts Senator John Kerry, who has been Bush's most dogged congressional pursuer on the Iran-Contra drug-smuggling trail, is also a Bonesman, oddly enough. McGeorge Bundy, an architect of the Vietnam War, is Skull and Bones too, as is Robert Gow, president of Zapata Oil, which was Bush's company in the 1960s.

It should hardly be a revelation that the roster of the CIA is speckled with Bonesmen. Besides Bush, a partial list would have to mention William Bundy, another Vietnam booster and vet of both the CIA and OSS. An enthusiastic proponent of "counterinsurgency" Bundy advocated preserving "liberal values" through "the use of the full range of U.S. power, including if necessary its more shady applications." Other Skull and Bones former intelligence agents include the aforementioned William F. Buckley, whose brother James is also a Bonesman and backer of CIA covert activity in Chile (though not CIA himself), and William Sloane Coffin.

The wife of a Bonesman once expressed her distaste for the society's clandestine fixation by calling it "a sinister unhealthy offshoot of the gentleman's code . . . a weird, CIA-like thing."

With headquarters in an iron-gated sanctuary, said to be adorned with skeletal remains of historical celebrities, the group's skull and crossbones insignia is explicitly Masonic, although I've never found a study linking Skull and Bones to the Masons. Its initiation rituals serve the purpose of all occult initiation rites: to break down the individual and build him up again as a member of the order.

Picture if you will George Bush lying naked in a coffin reciting his entire sexual history. The ritual, called "Connubial Bliss," (the naked-in-a-coffin part has never been confirmed) forces initiates to surrender their intimate secrets to the society, while at the same time encouraging that unbreakable male bonding of which sexual bull is so much a part.

The bond lasts forever. In 1985, when Bush was despondent about his political future, still languishing in Reagan's long shadow, a cadre of Bonesmen showed up at his residence and took him into a private room for a similar confessional. After reportedly baring his

insecurities, and receiving the unsparing critique of his comrades, Bush emerged rejuvenated. The future president, reconstructed in the Skull and Bones mold.


In the summer of 1988, well after George Bush had sealed the Republican nomination for president of the United States, the *New York Times* reported that a twenty-five-year-old memo had surfaced naming a "Mr. George Bush" as an agent of the CIA. This Mr. Bush, according to the memo, was passing information to the FBI about the Kennedy assassination.

Ten days later the *Times* reported that it was all a case of mistaken identity. The "George Bush of the CIA," circa 1963, was not the same George Bush running for president in 1988. The *Times* closed the case.

In November 1975, President Gerald Ford offered George Bush—the same George Bush who would later run for president, no doubt about it this time—the job of director of Central Intelligence. Bush, who'd been eyeing Ford's vice presidential nod for the 1976 election, suddenly scotched those ambitions and took the CIA job, to the bewilderment of some of his old friends. One Skull and Bones compatriot from Bush's class of 1947 asked him bluntly, "What the fuck do you know about intelligence?"

He knew enough to know his role: not so much the CIA's director, but its chief executive in charge of cover-ups. He took over the CIA in the midst of its most severe political crisis. Under attack from congressional committees, with former director Richard "The Man Who Kept the Secrets" Helms about to be investigated for perjury by the Justice Department, the CIA was in danger of finally facing its secret, saucy past in public.

Before Bush took office, he and outgoing director William Colby launched into a good-cop/bad-cop routine that ultimately bamboozled congressional probers. Using the conveniently timed assassination of CIA Athens station chief Richard Welch as a springboard, Colby dove into an all-out attack, charging critics of the CIA with wantonly risking the lives of hardworking, all-American agents. Meanwhile, Bush began a project of backslapping and hand clasping that ingratiated him with the CIA's adversaries on the Hill.

After a few months, the public mood had flipped from outrage at the CIA's dirty, sometimes deadly, tricks, to a groundswell of rally-round-the-boys, which cast Congress and the press as collaborators in league with terrorist assassins gunning for our men in the field. Or something like that. In any case, the propaganda gambit paid off. In early 1976, the Senate Intelligence Committee struck a hush-hush deal with Bush, agreeing to back off if Bush would only be so kind as to inform the senators, discreetly of course, of what the CIA was doing.

Bush put on a good show of holding up his end of the backroom bargain. He appeared before Congress almost once a week, on average, during his term as CIA director. But there was plenty he did not reveal. He stonewalled on the CIA's role in the Washington car-bomb slaying of a Chilean diplomat and in the aerial bombing of a Cubana Airlines jet that killed seventy-three people. Two anti-Castro Cubans were arrested for the airline bombing. One, Orlando Bosch, had been arrested just a few months earlier in connection with a plot to kill Henry Kissinger. The other, Luis Posada Carriles, turned up in 1985 working for the CIA in El Salvador. His immediate superior was Felix Rodriguez, George Bush's friend, the man who boasts of personally killing Che Guevara, then looting the corpse, and who is alleged in Senate testimony to have passed ten million dollars to the Nicaraguan contras from the Colombian Medellín cocaine cartel.

Bush also violated a direct order from President Ford to turn over documents that would have shed light on the CIA's use of the Drug Enforcement Agency as a cover for domestic activities, including MKULTRA, the mind-control operation. The CIA is barred by law from any clandestine or surveillance activities on American soil.

Bush's real job as CIA chief was to allow the agency to get back to the business of cloak and dagger without pesky congressmen getting in the way with all their whining and moaning about laws and ethics. To that end, he appointed some of the hardest of hardcore, old-guard covert operators to administer the CIA's "operations" division. Among them was Ted Shackley, long rumored to have been key in setting up the Asian Golden Triangle opium-smuggling outfit. Shackley's name became much more familiar a decade later. The Christic Institute, in its massive Contragate law-

suit, named him as a defendant, and alleged that he was the brains behind "The Enterprise," sometimes called "The Secret Team," an ongoing unofficial network of intelligence operatives deep into drugs and guns, assassination, and freelance counterinsurgency.

Shackley's associate Edwin Wilson was caught arming and training Libyan terrorists in September 1976. Wilson's "off-the-books" operation involved on-duty CIA agents, even though Wilson is now labeled a "renegade" CIA agent.

Bush's most famous acquaintance in the intelligence world would turn out to be Manuel Noriega, the Panamanian military man and $200,000 per annum CIA operative. Noriega would rise to the dictatorship of his country, develop a bad case of hubris, and turn his patrons against him. On December 20, 1989, President Bush ordered an invasion of Panama to get rid of Noriega and to "restore democracy."

During the 1988 presidential campaign, Bush's opponent Michael Dukakis ineptly attempted to make Bush's buddying up to the acne-scarred strongman a campaign issue. It probably should have been one. The U.S. government knew about Noriega's involvement with drug smugglers since the Nixon years, and Bush was claiming he had heard nothing about it until a federal grand jury indicted Noriega in early 1988.

According to a State Department official, the CIA had "hard intelligence" about Noriega's dope business by 1984. It's hard to believe that Bush, with his galaxy of CIA buddies and colleagues, was never told. Donald Gregg, Bush's friend since 1976, might have at least dropped a hint. A CIA man since graduating from Williams College, Gregg met Bush when they both worked at CIA headquarters.

Assigned to the vice president's staff in 1982, Gregg is alleged to have helped persuade Bush to use his office as a cover for a contra resupply program that involved switching planeloads of arms going out for planeloads of cocaine coming in to the United States. In his autobiography, Felix Rodriguez—named as a coordinator of the operation—denies that it ever existed.

These and many other murky circumstances led Noriega to boast that he "had Bush by the balls." Shrewd as the dictator was, Bush

turned out to be shrewder. The pretext for the 1989 Panama invasion was supposed to be Noriega's "declaration of war" against the United States (he never made such a declaration) and attacks against U.S. soldiers by the Panamanian Defense Force (which was trained by the CIA). The attacks appeared part of an American provocation program. Just weeks before the invasion, Bush authorized three million dollars for a CIA operation against Noriega. A candid U.S. military officer in Panama admitted that U.S. troops goaded PDF troops into attacking Americans. "It was an attempt to tick them off, so they'd do something," the officer said, of American soldiers' repeated forays into off-limits Panamanian turf.

The final twist of irony, if it can be called that, to Bush's Panamanian adventure is that the "democratic" government installed by the U.S. was corrupt from the get-go. The new head of the army was another CIA functionary, according to reports, and the new administration does nothing to rout police involved in all kinds of underhanded schemes. In fact, one prosecutor was suspended after fingering a police chief in a kidnapping plot. Bushian "democracy" marches on.

The Panamanian combat was the first time the current incarnation of the U.S. military engaged in all-out urban warfare. The soldiers didn't fare too well, despite the clandestine presence of the Stealth bomber. Unfortunately, they expended much energy and ammo shooting at each other.

In the Reagan administration and his own, Bush was involved with federal planning for martial law and roundups of terrorists and political dissidents, in league with Louis Guiffrida of the Federal Emergency Management Agency. Meld that fact with the Defense Department's surging enthusiasm for taking part in the ceaseless drug war—which appears more about rolling back individual liberties than curtailing drug use—and the scapegoating of inner city blacks for the nation's drug problem, and the Panama invasion looks unnervingly like a dry run for the domestic crackdown.

Just a thought.

CIA alliances and dalliances with dictators are just part of the complex constellation of contacts that codify into the George Bush

cabal. It's hard to pick the most apalling of these people, but seven good candidates arose from the Republican "Heritage Groups Council," which has worked for years in the Republican party and aided Bush's presidential campaign among ethnic groups. Among these unsavory characters: Laszlo Pasztor, a Hungarian Nazi collaborator who came out of the Arrow Cross party—one of many political organizations set up by the SS in Eastern Europe; Florian Galdau, member of the Romanian Iron Guard, another arm of the SS; Philip Guarino, an honorary American member of Italy's fascist-terrorist Masonic P2 Lodge; and Nicolas Nazarenko, who served in the German SS Cossack Division and who identifies Jews as his "ideological enemy."

Bush announced that criticism of these honorable men was nothing more than a political smear tactic, and he took no action against them. The Heritage Council was not a minor part of the Republican power base. According to one former chairman, it recruited eighty-six thousand volunteers to work for Reagan and Bush.

That group is my selection as Bush's worst association. Those of a more Birchian bent might select his Kissinger compadres, most notably Brent Scowcroft, his national security adviser, and Lawrence Eagleburger, deputy secretary of state. Both Scowcroft and Eagleburger refused at their confirmation hearings to make public the list of clients they had served while working for Dr. K's private "consulting" firm, Kissinger Associates. Potential conflicts of interest were abundant. Congress went ahead and confirmed the two anyway.

Scowcroft later surfaced in Peking, sent by Bush, toasting the Chinese leaders who had pulled off the Tiananmen Square massacre just weeks earlier. Bush's refusal to come down on China the way he did on, say, Panama, can be seen as a continuation of Henry Kissinger's China initiatives of the early 1970s. Bush was U.S. envoy to China back then, and people close to him say that, in that job and as ambassador to the United Nations, Bush simply took orders from Kissinger.

Maybe Bush's attitude toward China has at least a little to do with his brother Prescott, who works for a consulting firm involved in big business deals with the Chinese government. Said one U.S.

diplomat of Prescott Bush's relationship with the Chinese, "He was smart enough not to mention his brother's name, and the Chinese were smart enough to make the connection."

As I was wrapping up this book, Iraq invaded Kuwait and George Bush readied for combat once again. He spewed a slew of tenuous rationales for the massive U.S. buildup, but as can be expected when George Bush is involved, there was more to the story than presented for public consumption. On October 21, 1990, two and a half months into the "gulf crisis," the London *Observer* featured a special investigative report suggesting that Bush encouraged Iraqi dictator Saddam Hussein to attack Kuwait.

Earlier in the year, the *Observer* reported, Bush sent a secret envoy to meet with one of Hussein's top officials. The envoy told the dictator's confidant "that Iraq should engineer higher oil prices to get it out of its dire economic fix," wrote the English paper. The story appeared nowhere that I ever saw in the major American media.

Hussein took the envoy's advice, and moved his troops to the border of Kuwait. April Glaspie, the U.S. ambassador to Baghdad, told Hussein, "We don't have an opinion on inter-Arab border disputes such as your border dispute with Kuwait."

"The evidence suggests that U.S. complicity with Saddam went far beyond miscalculation of the Iraqi leader's intentions," wrote *Observer* reporter Helga Graham. The leaked documents on which she based her piece "have built up a picture of active U.S. support for the Iraqi President."

Two years earlier, Peter Dale Scott wrote an article for Pacific News Service detailing Bush's role in an international oil price-rigging scheme. The story was named one of the year's ten best "censored" stories by "Project Censored," an annual competition to recognize important stories that the big media skip, spike, or suppress. On the sands of Saudi Arabia, the petroleum president was at work once more.

On January 16, 1991, Bush ordered a massive bombing attack against Iraq. In the ensuing saturation media coverage of the war,

mentions of the Glaspie green-light to Saddam Hussein cropped up in passing but by and large there was little discussion of U.S. policy toward Iraq prior to the conflict.

My paper, *Metro*, was an exception. We ran a piece by *Village Voice* reporter Murray Waas detailing how Glaspie's attitude toward Iraq's "border dispute" with Kuwait was hardly an anomaly. In the months leading up to the invasion, administration officials repeatedly swore off use of force against Iraq. Secretary of State James Baker even went so far as to offer what sounded like a rationalization for Iraqi use of chemical weapons. He reported to a Senate committee Saddam Hussein's explanation that chemical weapons were his only deterrent against nuclear attack.

"I am not taking sides," said Baker—an astonishing statement in light of events that followed. "I am just stating that."

*Metro* also ran my little story about how Silicon Valley's original high-tech company, Hewlett-Packard, sold computers to Iraq knowing that they would be used in ballistic missile development. Numerous U.S. companies, I reported, sold military technology to Iraq right up until the international embargo came down after the invasion of Kuwait. German corporations were far worse offenders. Those companies under the jurisdiction of America's close ally were directly responsible for Iraq's chemical weapon-making ability.

Was Bush deliberately trying to get the U.S. into a war, to satisfy yet another cryptic agenda? Waas wrote off the Bushian pro-Iraq stance as a diplomatic blunder, albeit one of history's worst. Perhaps so. The Vietnam war was half-a-decade old when the Pentagon Papers leaked out to confirm what a sizable segment of the country suspected: the administration's public reasons for throwing the country into that war were simply sham.

Perhaps someday a "Pentagon Papers II" will appear, exposing how the country was fooled into the Persian Gulf war. I rather doubt it, however. Whatever his reasons for risking thousands of American lives (and taking thousands of Iraqi lives, including innumerable civilians) he is managing the war-propaganda well. The press is tightly controlled and seems to accept its bitter medicine with disturbing calm. Even enthusiasm. Meanwhile, Bush beats away on his theme of us against *him*, Saddam Hussein. It's the U.S. against a lone nut. How strangely fitting.

I'm sorry to admit that I've only skimmed the surface of the Bush file in this chapter. When I scanned a data base of newspaper articles from the years 1987 through mid-1990, the single largest subheading in Bush's entry was "investigations." In time, his life and career will be the subject of hundreds of books. As a Kissinger protégé, Nixon stooge, oil baron, CIA agent, Reaganite, Trilateralist, invader of foreign countries, coddler of fascists, family friend of a brainwashed assassin, president of the United States, and member of a secret society, there is no realm of conspiracy theory that cannot find a comfortable spot for George Bush. He is an *embodiment* of conspiracy. Maybe some of those future books will show that those eccentric, incredible theories were tinged with the flavor of truth, and the part he played in reshaping America will be illuminated a little bit brighter.

# 15

# JUST A GROUP OF CONCERNED CITIZENS

*In a subtle and civilized way they create an environment in which ideas are absorbed almost by osmosis and in which one draws the strength which comes from being with a group of individuals who form a community in this best sense.*

HENRY KISSINGER, singing the praises of his colleagues on the Council on Foreign Relations

The November 13, 1989, issue of *U.S. News and World Report* magazine contained an announcement that slipped quietly by amidst news of the fall of the Berlin Wall and the lifting of the Iron Curtain. Innocuously stated, it heralded an equally startling revolution. "After nearly a century," the magazine proclaimed, "the Rockefeller 'thirst for dominion' may be quenched."

The announcement was prompted by the sale of Rockefeller Center—legendary real-estate development in the center of Manhattan—to Mitsubishi, a Japanese corporation. Also sold was fifty-one percent of the Rockefeller Group, the company that coordinates the Rockefeller family's dazzlingly diverse holdings. The press recorded the transaction as evidence of Japanese encroachment into American affairs. Little mention was made of the long alliance between the Rockefellers, American industrial rulers, and

Mitsubishi, which plays a similar role in the Japanese corporate state. The press also failed to scrutinize the assumption that the Rockefeller organization is actually "American." In fact, it is global, and the guiding philosophy of the family in its business dealing is not nationalistic, but "one world."

Nor was it widely noted that while direct influence of Rockefeller family members over the day-to-day operations of the "domain" may have diminished with the sale, the organism fertilized and nurtured by the Rockefellers lives and grows. This being, with a mind of its own by now, is sort of a supersociety, on top of the society in which the average American lives. It goes by many names, most of them chosen by people not part of it: the American aristocracy, the faceless oligarchy, the power elite, the ruling class. The Establishment.

How powerful is this high society? What kind of influence does it have over our daily affairs?

Many of these people hold the highest positions in government and in big business. They sit on the boards of banks and control the money circulating around the world. They decide what gets manufactured, and how much. Educational institutions and mass media outlets are under their control, which means the information we receive—the very stuff of our thoughts—is also shaped by this elite, this "Establishment." This conspiracy.

America is arranged as a republican democracy in which elected representatives of the people make enlightened decisions through a consensus process. Because the American system is supposed to allow an equal voice for all, wealthy society is dismissed by many otherwise serious thinkers as having no undue influence over the governance of society at large.

For conspiracy theorists, there is no question that the ruling elite rules. American government as we know it is but a servant, indentured to this ruling system of which the Rockefeller clan is a central component.

The class is not just people; it is institutions: social clubs, prep schools, universities, "think tanks," councils, and committees; multinational corporations; Harvard and Yale; Exxon and Mobil; the RAND Corporation; the Council on Foreign Relations (CFR); the CIA—all temples of the ruling elite. The John Birchers

aren't the only ones who see these organizations as secretive conclaves of the world's most powerful people. David Rockefeller pleads innocence, calling the conspiracy theories "foolish attacks on false issues."

Defending one such organization, the Trilateral Commission, which he founded, Rockefeller said, "[F]ar from being a coterie of international conspirators with designs on covertly ruling the world, the Trilateral Commission is, in reality, a group of concerned citizens interested in fostering greater understanding and cooperation among international allies . . . in such an uncertain and turbulent world climate . . . we must—all of us—work together to help frame a foreign policy that best reflects the courage and commitment that are the cornerstones of this great nation."

Rockefeller's "We Are the World" rhetoric appears more than a little disingenuous with a perusal of the Trilateral Commission's membership list—which included, when Rockefeller made that speech, the president of Mitsubishi. "All of us," in Rockefeller-speak, means leaders of established corporate giants, along with academics willing to do the grunt work of preparing reports and papers to give the corporations a scholarly justification for existence.

The stock comeback to the conspiracy theory is to point out that, in reality, members of the alleged ruling class have a hard time agreeing on lunch, much less on strategy for global conquest.

One of the elite's superstars, Henry Kissinger, feuded with his colleagues on the CFR, particularly McGeorge Bundy, whom Kissinger regarded as something of an intellectual lightweight and closet anti-Semite. For that matter, George Bush, who reached the zenith of elite apsirations, resigned in protest from the CFR calling it "too liberal." Bush also turned in his Trilateral Commission credentials, feeling that association with the Rockefellers was becoming a political liability as he sought the presidency in 1980.

David Rockefeller has said he finds the charge that Trilateralists are of one mind "totally absurd." He has said that there is no such thing as a "Trilateral position" on issues. There is no "Trilateral conspiracy." The commission is merely a forum for discussion and has no power anyway.

"If 'conspiracy' means that these men are aware of their interests, know each other personally, meet together privately and off-the-record, and try to hammer out a consensus on how to anticipate and react to events and issues," writes sociologist G. William Domhoff, "then there is some conspiring that goes on in CFR, not to mention the Committee for Economic Development, the Business Council, the National Security Council and the Central Intelligence Agency."

There is no necessary contradiction between the fact of diverse opinion within the elite, and a conspiracy among the elite. The institutions of the elite "conspiracy" act like a blender, taking the jumble of opinions, personalities, and interests and stirring them into a smooth consensus. Forming a consensus from competing interests is the *purpose* of the Trilateral Commission, the CFR, and like bodies.

Furthermore, seemingly contradictory points of view within the Establishment are not as different as they might seem. On an obvious level, the membership of groups like the Trilateral Commission and the CFR is largely composed of businessmen. Funding comes from big business, businesspeople, and business foundations. It is therefore reasonable to conclude that, in general, these groups are not inclined to take up viewpoints which could be characterized as "antibusiness." The debate centers mainly around which policies are best for big business, not whether policies favoring big business are best.

The Rockefellerian apologia, that the goal of his commission is to promote a foreign policy "concerned with the most basic needs of the nation as well as its enduring aspirations," may well be sincere. But in Rockefeller's rarefied world, there can be little difference between the national interest and the objectives of international finance and trade. As Bill Moyers said, after shadowing Rockefeller for a week, "In the world of David Rockefeller it's hard to tell where business ends and politics begins."

Beyond the relatively simple requirements of self-interest, there is something else about the elitist worldview that bonds the Establishment together—the guiding philosophy of "management." "The peace and prosperity of the Trilateral world is not threatened

by aggressors, spendthrifts, socialists, or other human types—only by problems," explained one of the rare mainstream journalists to write about the Trilateral Commission at any length.

To the Trilateralists (and I'm using that term more or less interchangeably with "elitists," etc.), the world is a perpetually pumping machine in need of constant adjustment. Their purpose is to make these adjustments. They don't view themselves as "a coterie of international conspirators" because the way their world works "makes conspiracy redundant" (to quote Moyers again), with power wielded through handshakes and luncheons.

Since the system is set up for the good of all, the managers are not rulers, but servants. Servants have no power. There is no such thing as power; there is only the system and its managers. When Rockefeller waves off talk that he and his Trilateral pals are running a global conspiracy with himself as "cabalist in chief," he is sincere. At the same time that he was flying all over the world—never worrying about customs, passports, or the other formalities of international travel—greeting Communist premiers, lunching with despots, striking deals with oil sheiks, Rockefeller probably saw himself as nothing more than a "concerned citizen" trying to do his best for the system—a system with an elite group of managers at the controls.

The elite's conspiracy of shared belief leads to a conspiracy of action. The Trilateralist conspiracy theory got its most public airing during the administration of President Jimmy Carter. Carter portrayed himself as a political outsider, not a false picture as far as Washington was concerned, but he was a member of the Trilateral Commission and it was at the Rockefellers' knee that the Georgia peanut farmer learned his foreign affairs.

During the 1976 presidential campaign, Hamilton Jordan, Carter's top adviser, was heard to promise, "If, after the inauguration, you find Cy Vance as Secretary of State and Zbigniew Brzezinski as head of national security, then I would say that we failed. And I'd quit."

Brzezinski was David Rockefeller's operative who did the scut work to organize the Trilateral Commission in 1972. Cyrus Vance

was one of the most respected "commissioners," a Wall Street lawyer, Johnson administration official, and director of IBM, Pan Am, and the New York Times Company. After the inauguration, Hamilton Jordan was appointed Carter's chief of staff. Vance was named secretary of state, and Brzezinski became national security adviser. Jordan did not quit.

Twelve years later, when George Bush, another former commissioner, was scoring heavily in his presidential campaign by comparing his opponent Michael Dukakis to Jimmy Carter, Brzezinski popped up again—in Bush's camp. He endorsed Bush and advised him during the campaign on foreign policy matters. The press and public made little note of this irony, and never scrutinized the Trilateral connection behind it.

In its own literature, the Trilateral Commission lists "collective management" of global "interdependence" as its objective. Although Rockefeller may insist that he wields no real "power," and here in the United States his name rarely appears in the news, citizens of other nations have some difficulty with his demure attitude toward his own world position. In some countries, particularly in Latin America, where loans from Rockefeller's Chase Manhattan Bank propped up tyrannical regimes, his mere presence causes riots. Rockefeller's 1986 visit to Argentina set off the worst domestic uprising that country had seen in years.

Lobbying by David Rockefeller and Henry Kissinger influenced Jimmy Carter to allow the deposed shah of Iran into the U.S. for medical treatment. Carter's decision touched off the seizing of the American embassy in Tehran. The subsequent 444-day hostage crisis mutated American politics, allowing Reagan and establishmentarian George Bush to assume the country's top two elected posts.

It is one of the many paradoxes of American conspiracy theories that Rockefeller forces would put Carter in office, then help to depose him four years later. Perhaps David Rockefeller is right; the alleged conspiracy doesn't work as smoothly as imagined by those who launch "foolish attacks" on Trilateral integrity. Or perhaps the Trilateralists simply saw a better opportunity with Ronald Reagan as figurehead and Establishmentarian George Bush as deceptively obsequious second banana. The Reagan administration

turned out to be as thoroughly shot through with Trilateralism as Carter's. But that is a matter for later in the chapter.

The Trilateral Commission was founded in 1972. David Rockefeller raised the idea for the new roundtable group at a meeting of an older one, the Bilderbergers.

Named for the Bilderberg Hotel in Holland where the group held its first get-together in 1954, the Bilderberg Group is a traveling convention of the world's richest people who gather to talk about how to get richer. The Bilderbergers are more secretive than the Trilateral Commission, perhaps with good reason. Their president until the mid-1970s was Prince Bernhard of the Netherlands. The Bilderbergers thought it best that he resign when his name surfaced in the Lockheed bribery scandal.

Apparently, Lockheed, one of globe's biggest multinational military contractors, paid the prince millions to convince the Dutch government to buy its planes. The Lockheed affair, which involved several multinationals in a web of bribery, spying, and other sordid affairs, shed at least a little light on the dirty dealings of big business. "Respectable" corporate executives stood exposed as no better than mobsters—worse, because they committed crimes on a worldwide scale. Those activities may well be the sorts of things hashed over in the cozy confines of the Bilderberg.

All the Bilderbergers are American and European. Letting in Japanese elites is a Trilateralist innovation. While it was hatched at a Bilderberg meeting, the Trilateral Commission owes an equal debt to its more direct predecessor, the Council on Foreign Relations (CFR), perhaps the most elite of elitist think tanks.

The CFR sits in a building called the Harold Pratt House at 68th Street and Park Avenue in Manhattan. Initiates of elite society wander in and out: presidents, chiefs of staff, secretaries of state, directors of Central Intelligence, industrialists, financiers, media moguls, academic authorities. Solar plexus of the conspiracy, the CFR was incorporated on July 29, 1921, after two years of planning by some of America's most influential people. At least, they

thought they were influential until they went to the Paris Peace Conference of 1919.

Edward M. House, President Woodrow Wilson's close adviser and power behind the throne, organized one hundred of the crustiest members of the upper crust into a group called "the Inquiry," which met secretly in New York, putting together Wilson's strategy for the peace conference. To their horror, Wilson snubbed their carefully composed counsel. They watched in blushing disgruntlement while European leaders had their way with the American president at the negotiating table.

Thomas W. Lamont, an official of the Morgan Bank and the U.S. Treasury, was particularly perturbed. He took his concerns to his aristocratic British counterparts and the idea that later became the CFR began to coalesce. Morganites already had an elite foreign policy group of their own, the Round Table.

CFR members pepper U.S. government employment rolls. When CFR mainstay John J. McCloy (sometimes called the "chairman of the Establishment") was personnel chief for the secretary of war, he admitted he did most of his recruiting off the CFR roster.

The CFR's membership swelled to more than two thousand by the 1980s, but it still admits just five percent of applicants and recruits many members out of the government. Late CIA director William Casey was rejected on his first try, even though he was a well-heeled Wall Street speculator. But in 1973, when he became an undersecretary of state, the CFR sent Casey an invitation and he joined.

Casey's background in the intelligence community probably didn't hurt him in the CFR's eyes. CIA directors John McCone, Richard Helms, William Colby, and George Bush were all CFR members. Traditionally, the CIA has drawn its top agents from the same social circles where the CFR finds its members. Pipe-puffing Allen Dulles, the CIA's most storied director and a Warren Commission member, dates back to Edward M. House's "Inquiry" group. The CIA counts on CFR members to front for its cover organizations, and CIA officials feel comfortable revealing the touchiest information at CFR meetings.

It was within the catacombs of Harold Pratt House that American policy makers were first introduced to the idea that nuclear war

could be "winnable," so uninhibited is the Establishment in its search for new and more efficient world management techniques. The CFR has its own publishing house and, in 1957, it hit the best-seller list, not that it needed the money. The best-seller was *Nuclear Weapons and Foreign Policy* by Henry Kissinger. "Limited nuclear war is in fact a strategy which will utilize our special skills to best advantage," wrote the young German scholar. "Our superior industrial potential, the broader range of our technology and the adaptability of our social institutions should give us an advantage." Dr. Strangelove on the CFR.

Kissinger's scary opinions are made more so by his origins. Long before he became Richard Nixon's national security adviser, Gerald Ford's secretary of state, or Lyndon LaRouche's personal Lex Luthor, Kissinger was a protégé of Nelson Rockefeller, who mentored the young professor and supported him financially. In the Nixon administration, when Kissinger was making a public show of disassociating himself from Rockefeller—Nixon's personal enemy—he was sneaking documents out of the White House to Rockefeller's estate.

Nixon and Rockefeller were arch rivals. Tricky Dick hated the "Eastern Establishment," which he thought looked down its elevated nose at him. So how and why did he get Henry Kissinger on his side? Or was the Big K a Rockefeller mole all along, guiding Nixon's foreign policy in the CFR-Trilateral "One World" direction it eventually took?

Just as the Establishment is at the center of conspiracy theories, the Rockefeller family is at the center of the Establishment.

"The Rockefeller family is the most powerful family in the United States," writes sociologist Holly Sklar, an authority on Trilateralism. "Rockefeller power lies in the many interlocking corporations, financial institutions, foundations and leading individuals they control."

The Rockefeller strategy of owning a piece of everything is typical. Interlocking corporate directorates are rampant among the Establishment, giving further appearance of a conspiracy.

Sklar wrote a decade before the Rockefellers unloaded Rockefeller Center, Radio City Music Hall, and fifty-one percent of the Rockefeller Group on Mitsubishi. Nonetheless, the list of Rocke-

feller investments was and still is impressive. In the 1970s, when Nelson Rockefeller became vice president, the family portfolio included Exxon, Mobil, Standard Oil of California, Standard Oil of Indiana, Eastern Airlines, the Chase Manhattan Bank, Metropolitan Life Insurance, and several of the nation's largest philanthropic foundations. Nelson Rockefeller tried to soothe conspiracy panic when he was appointed vice president. "We have investments, but not control," Rocky told the Senate committee confirming him. "I hope that the myth or misconception about the extent of the family's control over the economy of this country will be brought out and exposed and dissipated."

Rocky had run for president twice already, in 1964 and 1968. His lust for the high office was no secret. So in 1974, when, in the aftermath of Watergate, Nelson Rockefeller became an appointed vice president to an appointed president—the famed "heartbeat away"—even the sober minded could be forgiven for wondering if maybe there was something to those Rockefeller conspiracy theories after all. When two separate assassins came a bullet away from putting Rocky in the Oval Office, they could be forgiven once again. If not for a couple of jammed pistols, Nelson Rockefeller would have fulfilled his dream of becoming president—without winning a single vote.

The Rockefellerian elite is generally referred to as the "Eastern Establishment." It is centered on Wall Street and nurtured in New England prep schools and Anglophilic Ivy League universities. As we saw earlier, the Eastern Establishment is the bane of anti-Communists, who see the Rockefellers aiding and abetting, in fact, masterminding, the international Communist conspiracy. Under President Reagan, the Council on Foreign Relations, the Trilateral Commission, and the rest of the Eastern Establishment was usurped by a more hard-right, uncompromising, intellectual and financial elite based in the South and West. The Trilateralists, who always advocated absorbing the Soviet bloc into the capitalist New World Order (it was the Third World that was never invited in), slipped into the shadow of Stanford University's Hoover Institute, the intellectual hub of anticommunism and right-wing theorizing.

As it happened, the Rockefeller crew had the last laugh. With George Bush as president, the Communist countries have been subsumed into the "free" world and talk of a "New World Order" is uninhibited.

Much of the financial backing for the Southwestern Establishment—sometimes called the "Cowboys," as opposed to the Eastern "Yankees"—came from Texas oil barons. This was the same Southwestern Establishment involved, as we saw a few chapters back, in a scenario allegedly behind the assassination of President Kennedy. But the cowboy/Yankee division is not that simple.

The overlaps and interlocks between the two factions stretch across the oil business into the CIA, which draws its upper echelon agents from the CFR, yet spent decades enforcing the raunchy anticommunism of the Southwesterners. The blend became smoothest in the Reagan years, when William Casey ran the CIA. He slithered in and out of the two spheres—detesting the "Eastern Establishment" while making a fortune on Wall Street, the Establishment's breast, and sitting on the CFR. The "Reagan Doctrine" of interventionist foreign policy, of which Casey was operational manager, was debated within the administration between Secretary of State George Schultz, former president of the multinational construction company, Bechtel Corporation, and Trilateral Commissioner Casper Weinberger, Reagan's defense secretary.

If we need further proof that George Bush is the ultimate conspiracy president, note his easy transition between the cowboy and Yankee cliques. He literally claims two homes, one in crusty New England, another in tobacco-stained Texas. He comes from an aristocratic Connecticut family and, with his father's financial backing, made his first name for himself in the oil-sodden circles of Houston wealth. In the CIA, he was equally at ease with rootin'-tootin' Bay of Pigs–hardened Cubans like Felix Rodriguez, and their Williams College–educated tutors like Richard Helms and Donald Gregg. Disunity between the Northeastern and Southwestern elites may have once been a mitigating factor against total takeover by elites of the political system. But Bush brings the two camps into one tent.

The confluence of interests between the "Yankees" and the "cowboys" comes down to one thing: power. Which is more or less

synonymous with money, because money is the most important tool with which humans control other humans. The "Establishment" conspiracy theory sees the raw pursuit of power by the wealthy as the only real motive for the conspiracy. Just as one Kennedy assassination theory points to the Southwestern Establishment, another pins the crime on the Rockefeller set.

The difference becomes almost semantic as the conspiracy theory becomes increasingly all consuming. The idea of powerful elites who conspire to control the masses is what Neil Wilgus calls the "Illuminoid" theory, the theory that sees secret societies behind all the major events of political history.

"If the Illuminati begat the Round Tablers who begat the CFR who begat the Bilderbergers who begat the Trilateral Commission, then perhaps," writes Wilgus, "this is the ultimate answer to the Kennedy and other assassinations."

Could it be that David Rockefeller's "group of concerned citizens" can trace its heritage back hundreds, maybe thousands, of years? We've already seen how the CIA functions as a secret society, how the CFR feeds the CIA, how the universe of elite elements can coalesce in one limited conspiracy—the J.F.K. assassination—with incalculable sociopolitical, economic, and even psychological effects. Is there any noumena behind these phenomena, or are they simply phantoms? Do the shadows of history play tricks on the eye?

Peter McAlpine's witty little volume *The Occult Technology of Power*, purporting like a modern version of *The Prince* to be a how-to handbook for the power elite, draws the same connection as did Wilgus's work.

"Perhaps the most accurate overview of our intelligence community can be achieved by visualizing it as a 'nationalized secret society,' " says the book, written in the first person as if by a master conspirator to his son, about to inherit the covertly controlled empire. "Our predecessors, in their struggle against the old order of kings and princes, had to finance secret societies such as the Illuminati, Masons, German Union, etc. out of their own pockets. . . . How much easier it is for us, inheritors of a fully developed state-capitalist system! By appealing to 'national security' we are able to finance and erect secret societies of a colossal scope."

Contemporary American conspiracy theories tend to downplay the secret society angle. European conspiracy theories pay secret societies much more attention. But the archetype is there. The CIA and the Trilateralists both fit the model. There have been secret societies forever, it seems, and they still exist today. Maybe they are nothing but coincidentally similar groups that sprout from time to time in response to the pressures of each particular historical time and place. Or perhaps the "technology of power" has been "occult" since early civilization, when humans first began to control nature and those most important creatures of nature—other humans.

# 16

# FROM MYSTERIES TO MASONRY

*The true student does not speak of the work
he is engaged in nor of his experiences, or
the degree of his development other than to
his master.*

Rosicrucian secrecy oath

The meaning of "secret society" has become somewhat foggy over
the centuries. Ancient secret societies were politically and reli-
giously subversive. If their existence was uncovered, they would be
wiped out.

More modern secret societies often don't bother to keep their
membership rolls secret. Freemasonry, for example. Few Masons
are shy about revealing their allegiance. They wear their Masonic
pins and rings proudly. Anyone who wants to spend the time at a
good library can find voluminous Masonic books spelling out rituals and Masonic etiquette in detail. The same is true for the
Rosicrucians, the "Order of the Rosy Cross," who claim an Egyptian heritage. One latter-day Rosicrucian order offers its secrets by
mail order in magazine classified ads.

So what's the big secret? In the summer of 1988, the Masonic
Grand Lodge of New York took out an advertisement in the *New
York Times* asking just that question: "Why do some people still
think Masonry is a secret society?" This was followed by text
explaining the pure-hearted purposes of the Masonic order, "the
oldest and largest fraternity in the world." The appearance of this
advertisement cum apologia was something of a curiosity in itself.

The exact origins of Freemasonry aren't one hundred percent clear. The standard account is that the society metamorphosed out of medieval labor guilds. How a union of bricklayers could become haven to freethinking professors and philosophers is still mysterious. Freemasonry on the continent was very much a spiritual endeavor. Not exactly atheistic, it was not explicitly Christian either. Lodge activity included speeches and research into the nature of man as a moral being, and the furtherance of human fellowship. The motto of the French revolutionaries—"Liberty, Equality, Fraternity"—was the Masonic motto.

At the same time that lodges were pondering how mankind might be made free and equal, they were also elitist. In England, Masonry took a different direction from its continental counterpart. The royal family and the aristocracy was largely Masonic.

In America, Masonic lodges don't have the aristocratic airs their European counterparts retain. Typically American, they're largely places to strike up business contacts rather than ruminate on the perfectability of human nature. Nonetheless, how many Americans know that sixteen American presidents were Masons? Couldn't it be possible that the social contacts they made in their lodges, and the beliefs passed on through Masonic rituals, had some influence over their presidential decision making? For George Washington, and the other Masonic founding fathers, they did. They went so far as to base the urban design of Washington, D.C., on Masonic mystical principles.

The average person isn't aware of those principles. Nor do many understand them. Even reading about Masonry in books is not equivalent to the experience of being initiated. All secret societies have some kind of ritual that must be experienced to be understood. Membership may be public knowledge, beliefs may be recorded in books, activities may on occasion be advertised, but the secret of a secret society is the shared experience of the members.

These days, secret societies have as much in common with social clubs as with the cults and mystical orders that are their ancestors. The classically fashioned secret society is an association of true believers. Usually, a "grand master" rules the society with absolute authority. The society itself is as repressive as the social order it opposes. Some societies have taken their fanaticism to extremes.

The Russian Skoptski, or Castrators, are the best example of devotion to the esoteric cause. The members castrated themselves in order to more readily attain enlightenment.

Few secret societies get that carried away. But, throughout history, clandestine groups, hidden cabals, and secret societies have been accused of manipulating events and shaping the social order. The Bavarian Illuminati were thought to have fomented the French Revolution. The Knights Templar, precursors of Freemasonry, became Europe's controlling bankers and landlords in the Middle Ages, until they were accused of practicing the black mass and worshipping a disembodied head known as "Baphomet." The authorities exterminated them.

"The world is governed," said Queen Victoria's prime minister Benjamin Disraeli, "by very different personages from what is imagined by those who are not behind the scenes." Disraeli, no paranoid, was nonetheless a firm believer in the power of secret societies over political events and the course of history. Adolf Hitler held a similar belief. He may well have been the tool of such societies himself. The Nazi party and the SS, in particular, were patterned after secret societies. The occult motivations of the Nazis is a touchy topic, not widely discussed among academic historians—which means, of course, that this book will cover it extensively in the next chapter.

Secret societies have indeed had an unseen hand in shaping the world, probably since the beginning of recorded history and definitely since the dawn of the modern era. Has the truth been hidden for thousands of years? Have the few who comprehend this secret knowledge been using it to control the world? Or have the initiates been the oppressed ones, guarding the truth from the power mongers who are threatened by its existence? Either way, truth is concealed. Ordinary people meander through life with delusions, and no understanding of the human predicament.

The history of conspiracy theories, then, is the history of secret societies. The history of secret societies is the history of conspiracies. And that is the history of civilization itself.

What follows does not claim to be a comprehensive history of secret societies. By the very nature of secret societies, that history can never be written. If it were, what might it reveal? The fanaticism

and paranoia basic to human nature, or the greatest conspiracy, the *only* conspiracy in the history of the world: the conspiracy against truth.

"Illuminati" has become like a secret society brand name. When a Bavarian professor named Adam Weishaupt founded a meta-Masonic order by that name on May 1, 1776, he had every intention of changing the world. His legacy instead has been a voluminous library of literature not by him but about him, from anti-Semitic tracts naming Weishaupt as the pawn of a centuries-old Jewish plot, to acid-tripping novels with the Illuminati as metaphysical secret agents, sort of a gnostic SMERSH.

According to assorted scribes, the Illuminati are behind the French Revolution, the Bolshevik Revolution, the American Revolution, the pope, the Kennedy assassination, Charles Manson, the Rockefeller dynasty, the New Age movement, UFO visitations, and the Universal Price Code. The odd inscription "57 Varieties" on Heinz Ketchup has been called an Illuminati code phrase. And if you ever see the word "fnord" in the *New York Times*, watch out. You'll know the Illuminati are on the scene.

The Illuminati saga has understandably become a favorite of freaks—hate groups on one extreme, dorm-room Dungeons and Dragons devotees on the other. For John Birchers, the Illuminati are "the conspiracy above communism," an enemy to be suppressed. For the pop philosophers, "Illuminati" is a game, a puzzle whose pleasure is in the solving, not in the solution.

In actual fact, the existence of the Bavarian Illuminati was a minor scandal of the late eighteenth century. The group plotted ambitious political stratagems. As far as the general public knew, its influence was stifled in 1790 when the Bavarian government outlawed the group and seized its records. That fourteen-year time span gave the Illuminati opportunity to infiltrate governments and in some way tie itself to the French Revolution. If that were the society's only achievement, the Bavarian Illuminati would be a force for social transformation. Whether the Illuminati's influence extended further, possibly into perpetuity, has been the subject of much debate, speculation, and fantasy.

Weishaupt, founder of the Illuminati, was a law professor at the University of Ingoldstat in Bavaria and was accepted into Freemasonry in 1774. Weishaupt had been taught by Jesuits, had some Jewish background, and supported the Protestant cause for a while, but finally got fed up with all religion. He'd studied paganism while a student and drew up a plan for a secret society modeled on pre-Christian mystery cults.

Weishaupt's godfather was librarian at the University of Ingoldstat. He stocked books of a freethinking bent condemned by Jesuits, who had held a tight rein until then on the parameters of intellectual debate in Bavaria. Weishaupt was just twenty-six when he was appointed to his professorship, a chair that had been held for ninety years by Jesuits.

In the same year, 1775, Weishaupt joined the "Lodge Theodore of Good Counsel," a somewhat radical Masonic organization in Bavaria. Like most continental Masonic lodges of the day, the Lodge Theodore devoted its proceedings to dissertations on the attainment of human happiness and perfect morality. During the Enlightenment, we often forget, rational thought and mystical practices were not yet divorced. Science, philosophy, and mysticism were all one discipline. Masonic lodges were the laboratory.

Weishaupt was one of the Lodge Theodore's most rambunctious members. He rejected established authorities and believed man should live in an enlightened state of nature, free from restrictions imposed by European society. His political program was to alter civilization to make his utopia possible. He founded the Illuminati, alternately known as the "Order of Perfectibilists," out of his annoyance with the limitations of Masonry. But he knew he needed Masonry, and he believed in it. The Illuminati was not a breakaway from the Freemasons, but a secret order above the Masons. Masonic lodges were Weishaupt's recruiting grounds. Once an initiate had mastered the tenets of Freemasonry, through its ritual "steps," he was (unknown to himself) a candidate for induction into the Illuminati.

Weishaupt was inspired by the Jesuits, the Catholic order whose teachings he rebelled against but whose structure he admired. The same intellectual discipline demanded by Jesuits was

requisite for all Illuminati. Only when each new member was thoroughly versed in the principles of each stage of "illumination" would he be ready for initiation into the higher mysteries. Some never were. Only when members climbed to the top of the staircase of degrees were they told the true purpose of the Illuminati: world revolution.

The Illuminati began with five members. Within eight years, the order had franchises throughout Europe and, by some estimates, four thousand members. The society had agents inside parliaments and aristocracies and had infiltrated Masonic lodges all over Europe—and at the same time was itself infiltrated by police. When informers exposed an Illuminati scheme to overthrow the Hapsburg dynasty in 1784, the government began its first crackdown on secret societies.

Some writers maintain that Weishaupt was a nonviolent revolutionary. This seems doubtful now—or, if he was, his followers were not. The Comte de Mirabeau, an instigator of the French Revolution, is reported to have been an Illuminist. Illuminati pamphlets, rife with esoteric symbolism, were strewn through the streets of revolutionary France.

"Illumination" is the objective of most secret societies. Mysticism is the belief in and practice of transforming one's consciousness through meditation, yoga, intensive study, drugs, sex, sacrifice—any form of ritual whose purpose is to produce a direct experience with the sacred. The "sacred" is just another way of saying "reality" or "the truth." Secret societies are not religions per se, but they all hold some concept of a higher truth.

Weishaupt's Illuminati aimed to induce not merely the personal transformation of its initiates, but the transformation of the whole human society. A quintessential conspiracy—a quintessential conspiracy theory.

Weishaupt based his Illuminati on ancient mysteries, goddess-worshipping cults that flourished in Greece and Rome. The mysteries of antiquity were not as rabble-rousing as Weishaupt's brainchild. For adherents, they were refuge from corrupt society, offering freedom in their festivals and belonging in their rituals. And, most of all, transcendence of the one dire inevitability that faces all of us: death.

The sacred secrets of the mysteries were the secrets of life and death. In the view of religious scholar Hyam Maccoby, human sacrifice was a commonly practiced sacred ritual among early Jews and Christians. The sacrificial priest was a "sacred executioner," who brought death to one victim for the greater good, or rebirth, of the tribe.

The Old Testament, says Maccoby, carefully covers up the history of human sacrifice among the Hebrew tribes. The New Testament, in a rather startling reversal, rejoices in sacrifice.

Interviewed by Patrick Tierney in his book *The Highest Altar*, Maccoby explains how he broke a "biblical code," revealing the numerous murder stories in the Old Testament as ritual sacrifices. The most obvious example is Abraham's sacrifice of Isaac, his son, at the command of the god Yahweh. The biblical story contains a deus ex machina allowing Abraham to spare the boy. Other versions of the story, from Jewish oral tradition, have a bloodier end. Furthermore, he says, the biblical story contains no criticism of a child sacrifice. Abraham was unnervingly placid about Yahweh's rather extreme request, as if children were sacrificed all the time.

For the sacrifice, Abraham was blessed by Yahweh, becoming the father of an entire people. Through death, a rebirth. In some versions of the story, Isaac himself is resurrected. Tierney notices "how similar [the Abraham myth] is to the many child sacrifices at the origins of other religions." He lists Greek, Mayan, and Dogon tales in which killing and rebirth of children are acts of primal creation.

The killing of Abel by Cain is usually taught as the "first murder." Cain had been offering vegetable sacrifices to God, while Abel's animal sacrifices netted much greater results. So, according to Maccoby, Cain turned around and sacrificed his own brother. As a reward for this supreme offering, Cain is given his own city, which he dubs "Enoch" after his son. Cain's descendants become musicians, artisans, and livestock breeders, "inventions typically ascribed to godlike culture heroes in every primitive society," writes Tierney. By his sacrifice, Cain was rewarded; humanity was rewarded by the civilization he founded. Death, and rebirth.

The mystery schools were filled with sacrificial rites, real and symbolic. Cultic rites often entailed eating the body of a sacrifice, or consuming a communal meal with food substituting for a god's body. Sound familiar? The Last Supper fits the pattern.

For the ancient mystery cults, death and rebirth were "the basic idea of an initiation ritual." Mystery cults were the earliest secret societies. Not really religions, the way religions are defined today, they were ritualized groups devoted mostly to the worship of the Great Goddess and the Fertility God in all their permutations. The names of gods changed from culture to culture, but ancient religion was richly cross-pollinated. Mythical personalities were nearly indistinguishable. Sacrifice was an important part of the mystery rituals. There are conspicuous similarities between modern secret societies and their ancient forebears.

This is not to say that secret societies are bastions of "that old-time religion," human sacrifice. Rituals of *symbolic* death and rebirth are common. Masonry's most important myth is one of human sacrifice: the murder of Hiram Abiff, godlike architect who built the Temple of Solomon. To be admitted to the Masonic "third degree," a member acts the part of Hiram in a playlet of this ritual killing, after which the initiate is reborn as a "Master Mason." Under one interpretation of Masonic mythology, Hiram is an incarnation of Osiris, the Egyptian god of resurrection. In one rite of Masonic initiation, the novice lies down in a casket. In Egyptian mythology, Osiris was murdered by being shut in a casket.

It is worth noting that the Temple of Solomon—the most sacred of Masonic symbols—appears not to have been a monument to Yahweh, the Hebrew god, but to the heaven goddess Astarte, of whom Solomon is identified as "a follower." The goddess figure was also known as Isis, Ishtar, Demeter, or Ashtaroth, all of whom had mystery cults devoted to their worship (under Christianity, Ashtaroth became a demon, and male). To the Greeks, Osiris was Dionysius, god of renewal—and of wine—who had a cult of his own. Either the original Masons deliberately concocted myths modeled on these ancient archetypes, or the Freemasons are the latest stage of secret society evolution beginning in the earliest civilizations.

One theory suggests that raising Lazarus "from the dead," one of

Jesus's many "miracles," was actually a death-rebirth initiation rite. The entombment of Lazarus was his rite of passage, and his resurrection by Jesus was the final stage of his initiation. Taken literally or not (and not all early Christians did), the tale of Jesus's own crucifixion describes a death-rebirth ritual.

Jesus is the most important historical figure of the past two thousand years. He is the most enigmatic figure as well. There is no small question as to whether such a person actually lived, and, if so, what kind of person he was. Although his era was tense and active, politically and intellectually, no contemporary historian mentions him except for a writer named Josephus—but most scholars believe that the mentions of Jesus in Josephus's work are forged interpolations.

There are two possible explanations for the absence of a Holy Paper Trail. First, Jesus never existed—he is a purely fictional character. Second, and more likely in my view, is that historical writings about Jesus have been censored to insure that no extant information could contradict the "official" biography of Jesus that gave the Church a rationale for power. Under either scenario, the story of Jesus holds many dangerous secrets.

As sage a source as Saint Augustine acknowledged that the "true religion" existed long before Jesus appeared, "from the very beginning of the human race," in fact. Christianity, he said, was a continuation of this primeval tradition. If Jesus was real, he was an adherent of the "true religion." If he was made up, then his story would likely be another in a long line of allegorical stories meant to convey the principles of this religion of creation, of life and death.

The story of Jesus, in its broad outlines, matches many myths that came before. Lloyd Graham, in his bluntly titled book *Deceptions and Myths of the Bible*, points out that what he calls "the pagan and mythic nature of the Christ story" repeats the Greek myth of Hercules. Both were born of virgins, sons of gods, called "savior," and died martyr's deaths. Graham also sees similarities between Jesus and Bacchus, who incidentally was the god figure to a breed of mystery cults. The specific historical source for the Jesus myth, says Graham (who contends that Jesus is a fictional charac-

ter), was the Indian legend of Krishna. Graham maintains that there are no less than sixteen "Christs" who predate Jesus, whose stories could have been rewritten as the New Testament Gospels.

Among these resurrected gods was Attis, whose cult was one of the most well attended of the Greek mysteries. Patrick Tierney notes that the Attis cult had a stronghold in the town of Tarsus. That town of Tarsus was home to Saint Paul, the ideological founder of Christianity. The death and resurrection of Attis also reverberates with Christlike connotations. Attis was supposed to have died and been resurrected around the time of the spring equinox, for example, just like Jesus. The time between death and rebirth was three days, just like Jesus. The festival of Attis includes a "communion meal."

According to Tierney, the Jesus story is out of sorts with Judaism of that era, which was repulsed by human sacrifice. But "it fits perfectly with the cult of Attis."

Another mystery idol, the bull god Mithras, shared something with Jesus: a birthday. Both were born on the winter solstice. The cult of Mithras was popular among Roman soldiers.

Just because his story fits a pattern of age-old mythology doesn't mean that Jesus was not a real person. In 1966, *The Passover Plot* became a best-seller with its case that the real Jesus was a political revolutionary who orchestrated the last few weeks of his life, including his own crucifixion, to fulfill Old Testament prophecies.

In 1983, another book, *Holy Blood, Holy Grail*, took that argument much further. The authors of that book, Michael Baigent, Richard Leigh, and Henry Lincoln, make a case that Jesus did, indeed, plan the whole thing. Traditional lore has it that a few of Jesus's key disciples made their way to France following the crucifixion. Among them were the mysterious Joseph of Arimathea—a wealthy landowner said in the Bible to be a "secret disciple"—and Mary Magdalene. Evidence supports the view, the book contends, that Magdalene was a mystery cultist, or former cultist, who became Jesus's wife. They base this opinion on passages from the scripture itself, including Mary Magdalene's display of spousal obedience at the resurrection of Lazarus, her brother. That would make him Jesus's brother-in-law.

The crucifixion itself, the *Holy Blood, Holy Grail* authors argue,

was staged. Jesus may have survived it. His surprisingly quick death and removal from the cross (under Roman custom, crucifixion victims were denied burial, left to rot on the cross) indicate that the crucifixion of Jesus was not routine. More unorthodox, the Roman governor, Pontius Pilate, discharged the body to the care of Joseph of Arimathea, the "secret disciple." The crucifixion itself, reading between the biblical lines, took place in a private garden far from public view. Could Pilate, a corrupt thug, have been bribed to participate in this contrivance?

Legend also has it that when Joseph and Mary escaped to France, they brought with them "the Holy Grail," whatever that may be. Baigent, Lincoln, and Leigh theorize that "Holy Grail" is actually a mistranslation of a word that means more precisely, "royal blood." In other words, the Holy Grail is the bloodline of Jesus—the heirs to the throne of Israel. Jesus had a rightful claim to that throne. In the Gospel according to Matthew, he is described as a descendant of King David and King Solomon.

The Holy Grail in popular lore is usually described as the cup from which Jesus drank at the Last Supper, but there's no more evidence for that claim than for any other. Historical genealogist Noel Currer-Briggs identified the Grail with the Shroud of Turin (a strange sheet imprinted with a quasi-photographic likeness of a crucified man, the shroud has until recently been passed off as the burial cloth of Jesus).

In the early Grail Romances, which were widely condemned by church authorities, who spotted the pagan heresy immediately, the Grail is a cup of plenty. Food, drink, and eternal life are the rewards to anyone who can grasp its meaning. The Grail is a fertility symbol, a life giver. Death and rebirth.

Whatever the Grail is, it is a secret. Given the symbolism-drenched, allegory-thick description of the Grail in epic poems from the Middle Ages, the Grail is as much an experience as a physical object. The Grail Romances describe it as a cup or a stone, but also as a series of visions and a riddle—"Whom does the Grail serve?" Evidently, the Grail represents some sort of secret knowledge that must be experienced to be comprehended.

The Holy Grail is forever associated not only with Jesus, but with King Arthur—yet another mythical icon who fits the bill as a

"Christ." The earliest Grail Romances were Arthurian tales spun by Chretien de Troyes in the twelfth century. In these poems, the Grail has no Christian connotations. That came later. Those who dwell on such arcania tend to agree that the Grail myth is pagan, not Christian, and has ancient origins.

In Chretien's poems, the Grail is guarded by a group of knights called Templars. It seems likely that these were the same Knights Templar who appeared out of nowhere in the Holy Land sometime early in the twelfth century, claiming to be a tiny band of "poor knights" numbering just nine. Over the following two centuries, these "poor knights" encompassed Europe with their banking/real-estate empire, backed by their own military might.

The Templars were founded in the city of Troyes, Chretien's hometown and home to the count of Champagne. Esoterica and mysticism flourished in the count's court.

King Phillippe of France, on Friday, October 13, 1307, ordered the destruction of the Templars. The knights were arrested, tortured, and burned at the stake. The entire operation took seven years. It concluded with the Templar grand master, Jacques DeMolay, roasted alive on a spit. Phillippe's motive was probably money, but there was more to it. The Vatican sanctioned the operation even though the Templars were knights of the Church.

Among the charges of heresy brought against the Templars was their worship of a severed head. The Grail myth, according to Arthurian historians, evolved from pagan Celtic head-hunting cults that worshipped severed heads. To the Celtic tribes, chopped-off heads brought fertility and protection from enemies. From the death of the choppee came life.

The Grail myth, in which the Grail is an experience of truth, is also decidedly gnostic. Gnostic gospels tell of Jesus faking his own crucifixion. He laughs as some anonymous poor sap is nailed up in his place. The Islamic holy book, the Koran, also contains this ghoulish "substitution" scenario. On the docket of indictments against the Templars was the allegation that they shunned Christianity in favor of infidel Muslim beliefs.

Despite the barbecuing of their grand master, it is highly likely that the Templars were not totally eliminated. Survivors went underground, coming under the protection of Scotland's bad-boy

king Robert Bruce. From there, the Templars preserved their heritage by forming a secret society. At the time, it was secret in every sense of the word. The metamorphosis of the Templars is much debated, but with each new study seems more and more plausible. There are too many similarities between the Templars and the society that eventually took the name "Free and Accepted Masons." Freemasons.

Freemasonry in American history is not hard to spot. George Washington was an avid Mason. His funeral in 1799 was a major public event, and featured full Masonic honors. As president, Washington had been sworn in by a Masonic grand master. When the cornerstone of the Capitol building was laid in 1793, the ceremony was unabashedly Masonic. When the Marquis de Lafayette, a Mason, made his historic visit to the young United States in 1825, he was welcomed by lodges from city to city. Masonic banquets in his honor were widely covered by the press.

The great seal of the United States is gorged with Masonic symbolism, from the "eye in the pyramid" to the "Novus Ordo Seclorum" banner announcing the dawn of a New Age. Benjamin Franklin was inducted into Freemasonry in 1731. He belonged to the first official American Masonic lodge. Franklin's travels brought him into contact with other secret societies. On trips to England, he'd often drop in on the Friars of St. Francis of Wycombe, otherwise known as the "Hell Fire Club." The "club" was the creation of Sir Francis Dashwood, a notably decadent aristocrat and occultist who was a member of the British parliament. Dashwood also belonged to a Druidic cult (though he would be expelled).

As a visitor to the Hell Fire Club, Franklin likely took part in the strange goings-on there. Dashwood was something of a porn buff. His secret society was a cover for sex orgies and, according to some accounts, Satan-worshipping Black Masses with a naked woman serving as the blasphemous altar. In the years leading up to the American Revolution, Franklin and Dashwood worked together to come up with a nonviolent way to smooth over differences between the colonies and Dashwood's friend, King George III.

Their efforts came to nothing, of course, but the participation of Masons in the war for American independence didn't stop. Almost every one of the signers of the Declaration of Independence was a Mason. The U.S. Constitution was also framed to fit Masonic precepts of liberty, equality, and fraternity.

Masons fought on both sides in the revolutionary war, which helps explain why the British lost. Surely the mighty British Empire could have suppressed a poorly armed colonial rebellion if it had so chosen. On the battlefield, and in the generals' quarters, the unwillingness of British Masons to slaughter their colonial brethren, with whom they were sworn in fraternity, weakened British resolve. Masons who took other Masons prisoner would not hold them long. In that sense, the American Revolution was not merely a rebellion of disgruntled taxpayers against their colonial lords, but a rebellion of Masons against the established social order. The "Novus Ordo Seclorum" that would be the American republic was the result.

After the revolution, as the republic developed, Masonry enjoyed an era of what historian Ronald Formisano called "an uneasy legitimacy, even as it attained an unparalleled prominence and acceptance."

The explosion came in the 1820s, when Masonic membership grew well into the thousands, with hundreds of lodges cropping up throughout the colonies. Formisano, while doubting that Masonry was a "political conspiracy," acknowledges that Masons "did occupy many more positions of leadership in government and in publishing relative to their numbers than did the rest of the population. . . . Masonic activity, like church activity, was a way of aiding a political career."

As the Masons accrued political power, their arrogance swelled. They flaunted their power, taunted critics, and flouted the law. In the fall of 1826, Masons in upstate New York caught wind of a local newspaper publisher's idea for a book "exposing" Masonry. They embarked on a program of intimidation to stop the book. Finally, they kidnapped and probably murdered one of the aspiring authors, William Morgan, who disappeared (no body was found). There was a long string of trials, but a tight cover-up prevented any Masons from receiving more than light penalties.

The Morgan affair was one, albeit the most egregious, of many incidents in which Masons displayed contempt for laws and norms governing noninitiates. Anti-Masonic backlash left Masons chastened. Within a decade, the lodges had either curtailed their political agitating or had taken it underground.

Roughly 160 years later, on February 11, 1988, Masons were in the White House again. High officials of the Washington, D.C., grand lodge were in the Oval Office to honor Ronald Reagan, who, like presidents Ford, Truman, Franklin Roosevelt, Harding, Taft, Teddy Roosevelt, Garfield, Andrew Johnson, Buchanan, Polk, Andrew Jackson, Monroe, and, of course, Washington, was a Mason.

With all this Masonic activity in disturbingly high places from the very dawn of our beloved nation, it's only natural to think that at least some of what went on in the secret chambers of the Masonic temple had an influence over what happened in government. If the framers of the Constitution applied their Masonic education to affairs of state, why wouldn't their successors do the same? Right-wing conspiracy theorists have no doubt of it. F.D.R. in particular is singled out as an Illuminatus—more than a mere Mason. F.D.R., according to some sources, belonged to another secret society known as the Ancient Arabic Order of Nobles and Mystics, in which he supposedly held the title "Knight of Pythias." The Comte de Mirabeau—Illuminati and force behind the French Revolution— had also been an adept of the "Ancient Arabic Order," as had Francis Bacon, who founded his own school of philosophical Masonry. It was F.D.R. who ordered the pyramid and eye insignia onto the dollar bill. More importantly, it was F.D.R., with his New Deal, who first introduced socialism into the American economy.

Socialism, as we saw in our chapters on the Birchers and conservatives, is looked upon as the first step toward one world government. The ultrarightists, many fundamentalist Christians, and some even further right see socialism as nothing short of a conspiracy guided by the ultimate "Illuminatus," the Angel of Light, Lucifer himself. The "one world government" would be a world united under the rule of the Devil.

Some of these theories, as usual, get lost in the stratosphere. I

blame that more on the effects of secrecy than on the fanaticism of the conspiracy theorists. When government is zippered shut with secrecy to begin with, and an unusual number of powerful people in the government belong to a secret society, speculation becomes difficult to keep in check. Indeed, it should not be kept in check. Freewheeling, independent thought is the only real antidote to secrecy's chief weapon, propaganda.

In any case, while secrecy in itself is destructive, its aims don't have to be. The ideals of liberty, equality, and brotherly love are laudable enough. There are worse beliefs on which to base your country. On the other hand, if the secret societies' goals are so benign, why all the cloak and dagger? Because the goals are not always benign.

Soon after the Civil War—a war in which brother fought brother, real brothers and Masonic brothers—a group of southern Freemasons and like-minded non-Masons got together to form a new secret society. The purpose of the society was to preserve the Southern way of life shattered by the confederacy's defeat. The new society was not officially Masonic, but it incorporated Masonic-style initiation rites, symbols and argot words. These founders were not a bunch of stereotyped Southern yokels. They were sophisticated and educated. For the name of their society, they went to classical Greek and took the name *kuklos*, which meant "circle."

The name was soon Americanized, taking the pronunciation "Ku Klux." Then they mixed in some Templarism, fancying themselves a chivalric order, defending the old white South. They called themselves Knights of the Ku Klux Klan.

Not even Freemasons themselves know much about the beginnings of their fraternity. The most common explanation is that the society grew from stonemason guilds of the Middle Ages. Researcher John J. Robinson rebuts that claim. The labor guilds were meticulously Christian, he writes. The Freemasons were heterodox from the start, requiring only a belief in a nonsectarian Supreme Being.

The temple from which the Knights Templar get their name is the Temple of Solomon, Freemasonry's most important symbol. In

their mythology, they claim a direct descent from its architect. The temple itself sat on Mount Moriah, a low hill in Jerusalem, where, according to tradition, Abraham sacrificed (or almost sacrificed) his son. The very "rock of ages" where the human sacrifice took place was housed in the temple. Remember that the temple itself was probably a tribute to the goddess Astarte, to whom Solomon's erotic "song" is a paean.

According to Robinson, the new secret society created by the Templars set to work immediately. In 1385, there was a nationwide peasants' uprising in England. Appearing spontaneous, the revolt was too widespread and too well coordinated to have been anything but a planned conspiracy. Rumors floated through the country of a "great society" organizing the rebels. The society's existence was confirmed, but its connection to the revolt was unclear; as unclear as the connection between the Bavarian Illuminati and the French Revolution four hundred years later.

In *Holy Blood, Holy Grail*, Baigent, Leigh, and Lincoln find a great society that they posit as the guiding hand behind both the Templars and the Masons. This group called itself the Priory of Zion (*Priuere de Sion*). It is a real society, and it had something to do with the French Resistance in World War II. The three authors trace its existence back to 1099, and its original headquarters to an abbey on Mount Zion, right outside Jerusalem. They were set upon their quest when investigating the mystery of Rennes-Le-Chateau. In 1885, a country bumpkin priest named Sauniere took over an abbey in a small town in the south of France, Rennes-Le-Chateau. Quite by accident, he discovered in the church a secret "treasure." The "treasure," whatever it was, made him rich, but the treasure was not money.

Sauniere also found encrypted documents, which, when deciphered, stated that the treasure belonged to Dagobert II, a seventh-century French king of the Merovingian dynasty who was assassinated by agents of the pope.

Without recounting the entire book-length argument of *Holy Blood, Holy Grail*, here are its conclusions: The Merovingian dynasty was the kingdom created by the heirs of Jesus upon their arrival in south France—the Merovingian kings were direct descendants of King Solomon, and of Jesus; the Priory of Zion was

created to preserve the Merovingian bloodline—the Holy Blood which is also the Holy Grail; the Templars were agents of the Priory of Zion—guardians of the Holy Grail, a secret truth tracing back to the Temple of Solomon and before, to the earliest days of humanity on earth.

If the Freemasons are descended from the Templars, and the Illuminati from the Freemasons, then the conspiracy theorists are not far wrong with their ravings about a transmillennial line of Illumined ones leading back to the Garden of Eden.

Of course, there can be no single, unimpeded conspiracy over thousands of years. But there have been secret societies for that long, and many of them claim a heritage going back that far. There's a feeling, in secrecy, of being different, of being in possession of something sacred no one else has. There is a feeling of power. That is why secret societies, though ostensibly religious, mystical, or simply social, are by their nature political.

"When linked, secrecy and political power are dangerous in the extreme," notes ethicist Sissela Bok. But has there ever been power without secrecy? Until we find a regime that holds power while allowing full and free publicity, then power itself is "dangerous in the extreme."

# 17

# CONSPIRACY NATION

*Every thing secret degenerates . . . nothing
is safe that does not show how it can bear
discussion and publicity.*

LORD ACTON

Anyone who has seen *Raiders of the Lost Ark* has a notion of the
ties between Nazis and the occult. That flick and its second sequel,
*Indiana Jones and the Last Crusade*, in which Nazis scour Europe
in search of the Holy Grail, have some relation to reality. The Nazis
did perform strange excavations in France looking for mystical
relics—presumably the Grail, or maybe Templar treasure. Even
people who don't like cartoony adventure movies may be vaguely
aware that the swastika was an ancient magic symbol signifying
light, which the Nazis reversed to symbolize darkness.

Nazi preoccupation with mythology is good Saturday matinee
fare, but the origins of nazism in Germany's occult underworld are
not usually looked upon as a legitimate topic for study by historians
of the Second World War. On the one hand, we have the sweeping
but wholly conventional poli-sci analysis à la William L. Shirer's
*Rise and Fall of the Third Reich*. On the other, there's the psycho-
historical outlook typified by *The Psychopathic God* by Robert
G. L. Waite, which attempted to explicate nazism with reference to
Hitler's fifty percent deficit in the testicle department—a new twist
on the lone nut theory.

Academic minds tend to force the most irrational phenomena
into the frame of reference found in a college bookstore: politics,

economics, sociology, and, of course, abnormal psychology. All such approaches seem almost designed to isolate Nazi Germany from the continuum of history and confirm that it can't happen here. This is a comforting notion, conducive to detached, scholarly analysis of the role of secret societies peopled by true believers, whose motives were not only irrational but antirational, which falls outside the spectrum of temperate discourse on modern history's darkest period.

I'm not arguing that Germany's rotting economy, its stratified class structure, the impotence of its Weimar government, or even the mental and genital abnormalities of the Nazi führer have no place in understanding the Nazis. They have a big place. But without the highly organized, perversely passionate, subterranean occult movement that gestated in Germany around the turn of the century, all of those elements could not have congealed into nazism.

More than a political party, the Nazi party was very much a cult. Like most demagogic religious sects, its rank and file was spellbound with the courage of demented convictions, and its leadership was financed and supported by powerful people whose main interest was accumulating more power. The finely tuned machine of brainwashing, fanaticism, and secrecy is perfect for that purpose.

Germanic occultists, like the Ku Klux Klan, were in love with religious warriors, holy knights. They were disgusted with even-keel, post-enlightenment rationalism, which cut man off from his spiritual nature and turned him into a timid species of accountants and clerks. The Middle-Ages were their romantic ideal. Squalor, plague, ignorance, and malnutrition—endemic to the Middle Ages—meant nothing to these incipient Nazis. All they cared was that spirituality in those days was transcendent. Templars and Teutonic Knights were their heroes. In this German version of medieval mythos, the Grail was the pure blood of prehistoric gods, and it was carried by only one race, the Aryan. Everyone else was subhuman, Jews and nonwhites especially. The holy knights, according to this lore, were guardians of the Aryan bloodline. Aryans, the occultists believed, were descended from a race of giants who ruled earth long before recorded time. The supercivilization had a Great Fall. Only Aryans perpetuate the holy heredity.

Jorg Lanz von Liebenfels and Guido von List, two Austrian mystics, were the ideological grandfathers of nazism. Lanz formed, in 1900, a society called the Order of New Templars (ONT). The ONT, and the societies that evolved from it, ultimately the Nazi party, was a core for industrialists, lawyers, publishers, and other powerful individuals who needed a means to consolidate control of German society. Their security at the top of Germany's power structure was threatened by insurgent communists.

The ONT published *Ostara*, a magazine chronicling the eternal war between godlike Aryans and the bestial subhumans. Comic book paintings of luscious blonde bombshells in the clutches of furry ape men adorned its pages. The psychosexual subtext of these quaint racial theories was difficult to miss. Among the readers of *Ostara* was a young Austrian painter and fan of the occult, Adolf Hitler.

Eight years after Lanz founded his New Templars, List started a group he called *Armanen*. He took the swastika as the *Armanen* emblem. In 1912, the two societies merged to form the *Germanen Orden*, direct forerunner to the Nazi party. While Hitler was still watercoloring postcards in Vienna, this coven of wealthy occultists was incubating the racial, nationalist, quasi-pagan theory that would become law in the Third Reich.

In 1918, members of the *Orden* started a new secret society, called *Thulegesellschaft*, the Thule Society. The legend of "Thule" was a variation on the Atlantis myth. Thule was supposed to be a nation of superbeings with a utopian civilization. It flourished until 850,000 years ago, when it was wiped away by a cataclysmic flood. The flood itself was symbolic of the "Fall," but the Thulians—or Atlantians—had brought it upon themselves by mating with creatures of a lower race.

The Thulists appropriated this tale from the writings of Madame Blavatsky, "theosophist" housewife-turned-guru who created a cult in nineteenth-century New York City. Blavatsky's writings are gospel to more recent "New Age" groups. The Thule Society adapted Blavatsky to their own prejudices. The supermen, they believed, were forerunners of the Aryan race. The subhuman creatures became Jews. To overcome their own debased nature and become supermen once more, the Aryans must overcome the Jews.

Like apocalyptic movements for millennia before them, the Thulists were fervently messianic. Unlike many of their precursors, they weren't happy waiting for the messiah to appear. They went out and found him.

In 1913, Hitler moved out of Austria, settling in Munich for what he said in *Mein Kampf* were "political reasons." Actually, he was avoiding conscription—a draft dodger. Nonetheless, he ended up enlisting with enthusiasm in the German military. Though a commoner and a private, Hitler received preferential treatment at every stage of his military service. Perhaps he was an intelligence officer. He may already have been an agent of the Thule Society. After a prolific stint as an anticommunist informer, in which he sent scores of his army pals to their executions, he was sent to university anticommunism seminars paid for by the Thulists. He joined and eventually took over the German Workers Party, which was founded, funded, and controlled by the Thule Society.

In 1919, Hitler met Dietrich Eckart, a drunkard, drug addict, small-time playwright, and socialite. Despite his character flaws, Eckart had a powerful mind and a powerful personality to go along with lots of money. He published an anti-Semitic magazine and belonged to the Thule Society's "inner circle," the members most involved in the Thule's political program.

"Their meeting was probably more decisive than any other in Hitler's life," writes Wulf Schwarzwaller in his biography, *The Unknown Hitler*. "Eckart molded Hitler, completely changing his public persona." Under the occultist's tutelage, Hitler transformed from a temperamental painter, who spent more time pigging out on coffeehouse cake than at his easel, to a shrewd, forceful orator—a dangerously persuasive propagandist.

From his deathbed in December, 1928, Dietrich Eckart issued a command to his fellow adepts of the Thule Society: "Follow Hitler!" he implored. "He will dance but it is I who have called the tune. Do not mourn for me. I shall have influenced history more than any other German."

Hitler's 1941 pogrom against occult groups is often mistakenly taken as evidence that the occult was at best an incidental influence

on nazism. The crackdown, in all likelihood, was damage control following the famous flight of Rudolph Hess, one of Hitler's closest confidants. Hess, for reasons still not entirely clear, stole a plane and made a solo flight without Hitler's knowledge to Britain, where he was captured. One story has Hess lured there by British intelligence in a plot masterminded by Ian Fleming, the spy who later turned writer and created James Bond.

Hess belonged to the Thule Society. Reportedly, the British intelligence service was interested in what he knew about the occult's hold on Hitler and the Nazis. Fleming allegedly wanted Aleister Crowley to act as the interrogator. Crowley is undoubtedly the most notorious occultist of the twentieth century. His secret society, the *Ordo Temple Orientis*, attracted, as so many of these groups do, people from the top of society in any country where it set up shop. Crowley himself was terribly decadent. A happily heroin-addicted, bisexual Satan worshipper, he asked people to call him "The Beast 666." Crowley believed that he was literally the antimessiah of the apocalypse. Or at least he wanted people to believe that he believed he was.

Crowley was also an intelligence agent. He claimed to have worked for the British Secret Service in the First World War. He may have been working for Germany as well. He renounced his British citizenship and took openly pro-German positions, even writing pro-German propaganda. Though British intelligence officials denounced him, he was not prosecuted and developed (or continued) a relationship with the British government between wars, feeding information to MI6 (one British spy outfit) about German occult activities.

The Nazi government may have been based on occult principles, but it was not the only government with an interest in every secret thing.

"We find it difficult to admit that Nazi Germany embodied the concepts of a civilization bearing no relationship at all to our own," note Louis Pauwels and Jacques Bergier. "And yet it was just that, and nothing else, that justified this war."

Pauwels and Bergier wrote *Morning of the Magicians*, a book that aroused a fracas in the early 1960s by finding occultism seething beneath every layer of modern life, particularly in the Nazi era.

While I'm not sure I endorse their view that "nothing else justified this war," their point is well taken: The war against the Nazis was not only a war for territory, money, or even power. It was a war to decide whether a "humanist" or a "magical" view of the universe would dominate planet earth. "This truth was hidden from us by German technology, German science and German organization, comparable if not superior to our own," says *Morning of the Magicians.* "The great innovation of Nazi Germany was to mix magic with science and technology."

Both the American and Soviet governments wanted a taste of that toothsome mix. Once Hitler was safely beaten, they competed fiercely for the services of Nazi scientists. The U.S. seems to have been more successful, winning commitments from Nazis like Wehrner Von Braun, rocket scientist and SS major once described by Allied intelligence as a "potential security threat." The government cleansed Von Braun's wartime record, brought him into America, and put him to work on projects that culminated in the Saturn V rocket—the booster that lifted Neil Armstrong and the Apollo 11 crew to the moon.

Von Braun was the most famous of the Nazi scientists imported after the war. Most were described by the government as "ardent Nazis," but those pejoratives were scratched from their files. Operation Paperclip (so named because secret files on the scientists were denoted by a simple, everyday paperclip) employed seemingly supernatural German expertise to construct the American war machine. The Paperclip Boys were the plasma of the military-industrial complex.

Meanwhile, the newly formed CIA was busy recruiting SS spymaster Reinhard Gehlen and "Hitler's favorite commando" Otto "Scarface" Skorzeny. Under cover of U.S. intelligence, these two and their minions did more than anyone to keep the ideals of the Third Reich alive, and pave the way for a Fourth Reich. Gehlen manipulated intelligence information to portray the Soviets in the worst possible light. With his CIA collaborators, he started the Cold War and kept it going.

While Gehlen played the U.S. government—and American public opinion—like a flute, Skorzeny globe-trotted. He established

Nazi power bases in South America that nurtured the continent's many dictatorships.

Skorzeny did a similar favor for the Middle East. Gamel Abdel Nasser came to power in Egypt with help from Skorzeny and an elite corps of former SS storm troopers. Always the good Nazi, Skorzeny never gave up on the twisted dream of wiping out Jews. He set up the earliest Palestinian terrorist groups, trained them, and sent them on commando raids into Israel. Without the American-backed entrepreneurship of this disfigured Nazi, the Middle East would probably be a much more stable place than it has been for the past four decades.

From the Order of New Templars to the Thule Society to the SS, the CIA, and the PLO, the intersection between government and secret societies continues to make our world an uncertain, terrifying place. The Nazi conspiracy rolls on.

Nazi Germany, impregnated with occultism, was a state founded in conspiracy, by conspiracy, for conspiracy. A relatively small group of people with hidden motives, using propaganda, mind control, and terror, carried out a plan to take over a country and the world. The German secret societies succeeded in conjuring up a massive social transformation, at a staggering cost in human lives. The ever-present, grim irony of secret society revolutions, nowhere more evident than with the Nazis, is that the great transformation, while it may overturn governments, makes conditions secure for the hidden powerful. Secret society revolutions happen when the secret oligarchy feels threatened.

The Thule Society was a magnet for rich businessmen and aristocrats, who provided it with considerable financial wherewithal to carry out its ambitious conspiratorial schemes. Without funding from big business, German and international, the Nazis never could have sprung from the Thulists' loins. "It is even partly true that Hitler was able to sell an evil idea like anti-Semitism simply because he had the support of wealthy contributors," say the authors of *Who Financed Hitler*. Nazism was occultism, but it was also fascism; it carried out Mussolini's dictum "Fascism is corporatism."

Craven Jew-hater Henry Ford, inventor of the automobile company if not the automobile, was such a doting patron of Hitler's that the führer once offered to import some shock troops to the U.S. to help "Heinrich" run for president. Alfred Rosenberg, the Nazi party's sinister mystic laureate (his extreme racial theorizing was found by the Nuremburg tribunal to be so instrumental in nazism that he was hanged), was friends with petroleum magnate Henri Deterding—managing director of Royal Dutch Shell and one of the world's richest men. Almost every major industrial concern in Germany, oil companies, agricultural firms, banks, and shipping companies, made sizable donations to Heinrich Himmler's *Schutzstaffel*, the SS, the Nazis' elite corps, which itself was fashioned as a secret society.

I. G. Farben, the gargantuan chemical cartel, was one of the new Reich's stolid financial supporters. There was plenary profit in nazism for Farben, and all of Hitler's corporate investors. The cartel's contributions were especially egregious. It manufactured Zyklon-B, a poison gas, for use in the gas chambers. Auschwitz was a slave-labor camp for an on-site Farben factory. I. G. Farben and its associated companies were among the passel of Nazi corporations that did business with the most powerful Wall Street law firm of the 1930s and 1940s, Sullivan and Cromwell. Their chief contact at the firm was an attorney named John Foster Dulles, who became secretary of state in the Eisenhower administration.

"Sullivan and Cromwell thrived on its cartels and collusion with the new Nazi regime," say the firm's chroniclers. In 1933 and 1934, when the Nazi's brutal course was obvious, Dulles led off cables to his German clients with the salutation "Heil Hitler." In 1935, he scribbled a screed for *Atlantic Monthly* dismissing Nazi state terrorism as "changes which we recognize to be inevitable." Dulles's brother, Allen Dulles, was also a partner in Sullivan and Cromwell. He later founded the CIA and recruited thousands of Nazi SS men into the new "department of conspiracy." Much to Foster's consternation, he never met Hitler, while little brother Allen was granted that thrill.

Sosthenes Behn met Hitler, too. Behn was the founder of International Telephone and Telegraph (ITT) and virtual inventor of the multinational corporation. He met Hitler in 1933, the first Ameri-

can businessman to receive an audience with *der Führer*, while striking up deals with German companies. At the same time, he filed classified reports on their activities to the U.S. government. American spy or not, Behn allowed his company to cover for Nazi spies in South America, and one of ITT's subsidiaries bought a hefty swath of stock in the airplane company that built Nazi bombers.

Behn recruited Nazis onto ITT's board. His closest Nazi friend, Gerhard Westrick, visited New York at Behn's expense in 1940— when the Nazis were conquering Europe without much resistance. The agenda of Westrick's visit: to talk American corporate leaders into forging a German-American business alliance. These sorts of activities could easily be dubbed treason on Behn's part, but by 1944 and the Allied liberation of France, he was celebrated as an American hero. Allen Dulles—who supplemented his legal income as a U.S. intelligence agent—appears to have been the magician behind this miracle rehab, helping Behn set up his relationship with the U.S. military. Later, Dulles was an originator of the idea that multinational corporations are instruments of U.S. foreign policy and therefore exempt from domestic laws—a theory that has been a secret government policy since the mid-1950s. Behn also gave money to Himmler's SS.

The Nazis were able to weld corporatism to occultism seamlessly, which may say something about the similarity between the two. "The oligarchs of agricultural kingdoms wrapped themselves in witchcraft. . . . As industrial capitalism accumulated power and wealth the old mysteries were replaced and dwarfed by the new mysteries of high finance, market manipulations, convoluted and lucrative legalisms, pressure-group politics, and a labyrinth of new bureaucracies," writes Bertram Gross.

But it also says that for the Nazis, the occult served both idealistic and pragmatic purposes. Himmler was immersed in occultism, but though he believed the stuff, he also used it as a method of mind control. When he began the corps, he needed a large membership to consolidate power. He recruited about sixty thousand. Membership was literally for sale to the wealthy, and "honorary" membership was available for as little as a mark per year. There was no way to unify such an unwieldy legion, so once the SS had established

itself as the most powerful faction of the Nazi state, Himmler purged his rolls of anyone ideologically impure, or racially suspect (members had to draw up a family tree going back more than a century to prove their pure Aryan, non-Jewish, lineage). He also banished or killed all the SS homosexuals he could spot, and there were quite a few.

The SS was still absent a coherent ideology to bind its remaining members in strict obedience. Himmler found one in his own neo-pagan beliefs. He renovated Wewelsburg Castle, a Westphalian fortress, and made it his own Camelot. He installed an oaken round table where the twelve "knights" of his inner circle would gather for initiations and rites. Like all cult leaders, Himmler was skilled in using ritual and esoterica to strip away the individuality of his followers. Whatever humanity the SS soldiers possessed was subsumed by their mission to exterminate "lower races" and stand guard over the Reich. The storm troopers became robots programmed to kill.

Himmlerian mind control didn't die when Himmler bit his cyanide capsule. While real live Nazis like Skorzeny and Gehlen frolicked about the world causing merry mischief, their younger admirers kept the occult spirit of nazism alive in right-wing hate groups and Satanic cults.

The popular image of right-wing "neo-Nazi" groups as Neanderthal thugs is somewhat misleading. The rank-and-file skinheads may be a little on the slow side, but the movement's leaders tend to be voracious readers, researchers, and theorists, after a fashion. Just as they are, perhaps correctly, the subject of conspiracy theories, they've developed anti-Jewish, anti-Masonic, Illuminati-style theories of their own that display an unsettling level of detail—all in the tradition of Thulian master-race paganism.

White Aryan Resistance chieftan Tom Metzger—a regular on "Geraldo"-style daytime talk shows—is anti-Christian as well as predictably anti-Jewish. He and his skinhead disciples call themselves pagans, and adhere to the ancient Germanic religion. They find affinity in the "Christian Identity" religion, which began in England in the nineteenth century and now flourishes in cornfield

churches of the Midwest. The Identity churches are only "Christian" in the sense that they count Jesus as an Aryan. White Europeans, they say, are therefore the true biblical "Jews," and the "race" that calls itself Jewish is really a conspiracy of subhuman imposters.

Unlike the conspiracy theorists profiled in the first part of this book (with the possible exception of Lyndon LaRouche), Nazi and neo-Nazi groups use their conspiracy theories, like Himmler, as a technique of control, to mobilize a group to a common goal, to move people to actions they might not otherwise carry out. More brazenly occult variations on the same theory turn up in Satanic cults.

The Manson family was portrayed in the mass media as a group of crazed hippies, of flower children gone mad. In the mass mind, Charles Manson is associated with the political left—ironic for a Hitler-worshipping racist. Like Hitler, who learned his oratorical skills at the knee of Dietrich Eckart, Manson picked up his powers of persuasion in the occult underground of San Francisco circa 1967. His "I am Christ, I am the devil, Christ is the devil" rants could have been lifted from sermons by Robert DeGrimston, British émigré and leader of the Process Church of the Final Judgement.

The Process, which may have had Manson as member, was a Satanic cult that sprung up in the 1960s and sputtered out by the early 1970s. But does it still exist? Maury Terry's book *The Ultimate Evil* makes a case that the Process didn't die. Instead it faded away in a Satanic diaspora, forming offshoot cults that link into a loose nationwide conglomerate of dope dealing, S&M porn, and ritual murder. The Son of Sam killing spree that terrorized New York in the late 1970s was Terry's focus. He alleges that the murders were carried out by a conspiracy of cultists based on Long Island with connections across the country. One of the Sam murders, Terry contends, was committed by a character called "Manson II," famous among Satanists as the occult underworld's top hit man, a friend of Charles Manson himself.

The Tate-LaBianca murders, crimes that won the original Manson his infamy, may not have been random "Helter Skelter" slayings, according to Terry and to Manson biographer Ed Sanders.

They appear to have been murder for hire. But who would hire Manson and why? Could it have been the same people who hired Manson disciple Lynette "Squeaky" Fromme to shoot President Ford? Namely, someone in the U.S. government, according to Michael Milan, who says he was once a hit man for J. Edgar Hoover.

Here we get into the grayest of conspiratorial speculations, foggy even by the standards of conspiracy theory. Contentions that the intelligence community is somehow aligned with Satanism, using cults as indoctrination for mind-controlled robot assassins, are backed up by only gossamer strips of information. Milan's claim that the Manson family "took the contract" on Ford; Maury Terry's implication that New York police may have been in on the Son of Sam murders (taken together with known facts about the CIA's infiltration of big-city police departments); and the name of the drug dealer who led the Matamoros death cult, the nasty devil worshippers who murdered a med-school student in a Mexican shack a few years ago, allegedly turning up in the address book of downed contra pilot, Eugene Hasenfus, a CIA contractor.

The most curious case, to my mind, is that of Michael Aquino, another frequent talk-show guest who bears an uncanny resemblance to Mark Lenard, Mr. Spock's father on "Star Trek." Aquino founded and leads the Temple of Set, an offshoot of Anton LaVey's Church of Satan, which was the first Satanic church ever to receive tax exemption. The Temple of Set takes a dour turn on LaVey's dime-store pseudopagan buffoonery. Unlike LaVey, Aquino never sought publicity. He got it anyway, when he was accused of molesting children at a military day care center on San Francisco's Presidio base.

Aquino was never tried on any charge, and he vehemently denies any crimes. He sued the city of San Francisco for defamation of character after an investigation failed to turn up any evidence that he or his "Temple" was involved in child molestation. Aquino is nonetheless an odd bird with thought-provoking connections.

Aquino is always careful to distance himself publicly from nazism, but he is so fascinated by Hitler and Himmler that he once made a pilgrimage to Wewelsburg Castle, the site Himmler planned as home to his mystical order. He carried out some form of black

magic ceremony there, amidst the SS relics. When the Presidio scandal became news and Aquino's name surfaced, the Pentagon denied that he was in the Army. This was in 1981, at the same time that the Army was granting Aquino his Top Secret security clearance. In reality, Aquino is an Army specialist in psychological warfare. He wrote an article on "MindWar" and PSYOPS (psychological operations) and their use in controlling mass populations. America's failure in Vietnam, he believes, was a failure to apply the effects of "MindWar."

In the conspiracy theory, the epidemic of Satanism across America stems from the U.S. government deploying MindWar against its own people.

**"S**ome things are secret because they are hard to know, and some because they are not fit to utter. We see all governments as obscure and invisible." So declared Francis Bacon, founder of his own school of Masonry, and of the inductive "scientific method." Bacon didn't issue that utterance with any intention of condemning government secrecy. The governance of men, he believed, was necessarily a secret affair. People are incapable of understanding what government does. And some things that government does, it is best that the governed never know.

When governments are involved in terror and murder, it is not hard to understand why they keep secrets from their people. Nor is it surprising that Francis Bacon, given his immersion in secret societies, would feel the way he did. If Bacon's reasoning holds true, it might be better to have no government at all.

A government that is obscure and invisible will inevitably, like the Nazis, be a government based on conspiracy. The very act of keeping government secrets is a conspiracy.

Secret government—and by Bacon's cold logic, all governments are secret—divorces everyone in society except the secret keepers from any genuine understanding of the circumstances that govern their own lives. Conspiracy theory is an attempt by a few minds to reclaim some understanding.

In this part of the book, I've tried to piece together as many slabs and slices of information that I could find to support the kinds of

conspiracy theories that got me interested in the subject. These are American conspiracy theories, many with long historical roots, but, nonetheless, distinctively contemporary conspiracy theories. These are theories born in a country too big and diverse to govern, but permeated totally by government. A country whose basic ideal is individual freedom, where daily life is dominated by authority. From the runaway power of the presidency to the tyranny of workplace management, liberty is strangely difficult to come by. We've substituted the multicolored spectacle of consumerism for control over our own lives, and we're supposed to think that because we have so much stuff available for purchase we have the freedom to choose. But you can't fool everyone. Conspiracy theorists may not always be right, but they are not fooled.

The information in this section is not supposed to be an argument for any particular conspiracy theory, although there seem to be plenty in here. I've been trying to present a *way of thinking* about a society where information is controlled, ergo, understanding is impossible. Conspiracy theories are a guide to life in a strange and threatening America: a conspiracy nation.

# *Conclusion*

# THE THRESHOLD OF BELIEF

*Every government is run by liars and noth-
ing they say should be believed.*

I. F. STONE

*We go around in circles in the night and are
consumed by fire.*

GUY DEBORD, Title of his
last film

The Firesign Theatre, a surreal comedy ensemble popular on
college radio stations a long time ago, once made an album called
"Everything You Know Is Wrong." The Firesign Theatre may have
been right.

All the anomalies, all the horrors, all the conspiracies that we've
just journeyed through—can they be true? Is the nation really that
malevolent? That insane?

I hope not. But the point is, we just don't know. We all have our
belief systems about the world. Whatever doesn't fit into our systems, we ignore. I look at the foregoing trip through the conspiracy
nation in the spirit of Charles Fort. Fort believed that there are
phenomena that conventional science is not able to explain; I look
on conspiracy theories as the stuff that conventional political science refuses to deal with.

The science and philosophy of Charles Fort is ethereal stuff.

251

Conspiracy theories are about politics—the reality of day-to-day life. Surely the truth of who, or what, governs America should be accessible. People created this nation. People run it. Someone, somewhere must know what's going on. Why can't everybody? Conspiracy theories begin with that very question. The truth is being kept from us.

In *Friendly Fascism*, a book describing what can only be called a conspiracy between big business and big government to rule America, Bertram Gross makes it a point to declare, "[T]here is no single, central conspiracy." Perhaps not. There is no council of twelve running the world, no Illuminati board of directors that plans every war, every election, every fluctuation in the economy, every piece of legislation.

There are, however, many councils, many boards of directors. In most contemporary American conspiracy theories, there is no "single central conspiracy." Instead, there is power and powerful people who will do anything to keep their power. Power is a fact of life in America, but most Americans are far removed from it. Secrecy is power's chief tool. Government seems distant, yet somehow domineering. We are increasingly isolated from one another—stuck in front of computer and television screens, prisoners behind windshields. There is a frustrating feeling of disconnection to modern American life. Are our lives really absurd? Or are we just being deceived? Conspiracy theories try to put the pieces back together.

W hat if AIDS was deliberately created? Biological warfare by the American government against its own people. Such experimentation would hardly be unprecedented. From the LSD MKULTRA experiments (see Chapter 10) to the 1950 spraying of infectious bacteria onto San Francisco from Navy ships, various government agencies have exhibited no reservation about trying out new chemicals and toxins on U.S. citizens. Some of these literally sickening experiments were instigated by ex-Nazi doctors. The government brought over biologists as well as rocket scientists from the Third Reich. Former government lawyer John Loftus, in his book about imported SS war criminals, *The Belarus Secret*, speculates that

Lyme disease may be the result of one ex-Nazi–inspired biowarfare test.

Why not AIDS, then? Or does it cross the threshold of belief to suppose that our government, even one isolated element of it, could commit such an atrocity?

The conspiracy theory of AIDS sees the disease as a vast eugenics exercise, not that it would take Nazis to dream up a eugenics program. Back in 1904, the philanthropic Carnegie Foundation, founded by founders of the American industrial system, bankrolled eugenics experiments at a bioresearch lab in Cold Spring Harbor, New York. The American preoccupation with weeding out "inferior" humans continues to this day, in softer forms. The IQ test was first administered by scientists (and I use the term loosely) whose initial interest was identifying "the feebleminded."

AIDS's proclivity for hitting the underprivileged and marginal members of society is hauntingly reminiscent of the "great pellagra cover-up" in the early twentieth century. No one I've heard of suggests that pellagra—a fatal disease rampant until the 1930s—was deliberately created. It almost might as well have been. The real cause of the disease, malnutrition, was discovered in 1914, but ignored. In 1917, a national commission announced that the disease was hereditary, attributable to the same bad genetics that, in the minds of government eugenicists, caused the poverty of most of the disease's victims. Not until the Depression hit, and the previously well-off found themselves in dire financial straits and therefore susceptible to malnutrition, was the disease finally brought under control.

What, then, is the truth about AIDS? Much government-sponsored research is secret. The rest is esoteric, understandable only by other scientists. Public comprehension of science is scant, depending entirely on third-party interpreters and "experts," who have agendas of their own. Not only is general scientific knowledge therefore minimal, more importantly, few people understand how science works. We think we're getting objective truth, when what we're really seeing is a political, acerbically personal process involving billions of dollars, reputations and egos, and belief systems that censor large slices of fact and theory. Is AIDS the result of a

demonic scientific experiment? Who knows? I tend to doubt it myself. But could it be? Of course it could, because if it were, no one in a position to do anything about it would believe it.

The process of everyday politics also looks strangely like a conspiracy. Despite the presence of cable television cameras in the Senate and House of Representatives, few meaningful decisions are made in public. Legislative votes are public, of course, so there is a degree of accountability, but coalitions are made in private, and deals are cut in closed meetings. Presidential decision making is absolutely unencumbered by public scrutiny.

In 1989, just a month or so after the Tiananmen Square massacre of prodemocracy demonstrators in China, President Bush sent two envoys secretly to meet with the Chinese government, to reaffirm American-Chinese ties.

The envoys, probably not coincidentally, were two former employees of Henry Kissinger, National Security Adviser Brent Scowcroft and his deputy, Lawrence Eagleburger. Kissinger's "consulting" firm has extensive business ties to China. When Bush was ambassador to China, it was said that he did almost nothing, leaving the driving to Henry, as it were. Bush's own brother has a "consulting" business link to the Chinese government.

When reporters, in an uncharacteristic display of indignation (perhaps more at being left out of the story than at the predictable breach of trust) challenged Bush, he uncorked an impassioned defense of his right to do business in secret, a theme he has hit upon repeatedly during his presidency.

Bush is hardly unusual among presidents in that regard. But when business like Bush's China mission takes place in secrecy, can so-called conspiracy theorists really be blamed for surmising that the whole thing was a Kissinger scam? Kissinger's clients include the world's largest corporations. What does that say about the apparent conspiracy? The Bush cronies' covert China junket appears as one more installment of the ongoing conspiracy of the wealthy, powerful, and very, very private against the average person.

The number of people who can find out firsthand what goes on inside the presidential administration, in Congress, the halls of

academe, research labs, and corporate boardrooms is tiny. The rest of us must rely on the communications media, news, and entertainment. News has *become* entertainment. Television is the main source of news, and the only real purpose of *any* commercial television program is to deliver an audience to advertisers.

The programs and the advertisements become indistinguishable, both serving the purpose of massaging the viewer into the mood to consume. If there were no such thing as official U.S. government propaganda, America would still be in the grip of the most powerful propaganda apparatus in human history: the advertising industry. Advertising is not usually thought of as propaganda, because it has no obvious political slant. All the better to brainwash you with. In fact, advertising sells a political ideology as fully developed and as potent as anything pushed by Joseph Goebbels. The ideology is consumerism.

There are two types of propaganda identified by Jacques Ellul, whose book *Propaganda* is a definitive work on the subject. There is propaganda of integration (sociological propaganda) and propaganda of agitation (political propaganda). Advertising is both. It presents a coherent set of values and standards, which serves the purpose of molding (integrating) disparate "propagandees" into a coherent group with shared ideals—in this case, the equation of happiness with consumer products. And it "agitates" its targets into performing specific acts for the benefit of the political system—namely, purchasing things, an act without which industrial capitalism, our political system, would perish.

Conflation of advertising and propaganda spawns USC professors Ian Mitroff's and Warren Bennis's book title, *The Unreality Industry*. The advertising and entertainment industries have teamed up to instill America with a culture based upon outright falsehoods and manipulations of fact. We worship celebrities whose public personas bear little relationship to their real identities, then we purchase products designed to make us identify with the artificial celebrities. The process perpetuates until we're living in a mirage. Or perhaps it's more like a hologram because the illusion is deliberately created.

What becomes of our own identities in this haze of consumption? We lose them, as we submerge ourselves into the mass culture.

Striving to create ourselves in the images presented to us by advertising, we lose touch with reality.

Isn't there one branch of the media devoted expressly to the truth? Aren't newspapers and television news programs still devoted to letting us know what's really going on in our world?

Forget for a moment that all major news media are beholden to advertising for their existence. Forget that about twenty national and multinational companies own the bulk of America's newspapers and magazines. Reporters rely so heavily on "official sources" for their news, and are so slavishly credulous of the information those sources feed them, that otherwise "respectable" news media are easily infiltrated by the CIA. In one particularly infamous incident, *New York Times* correspondent C. L. Sulzberger, nephew of the paper's owner, reprinted a CIA press release, called a "briefing paper," verbatim under his own byline.

The CIA infiltrates and even operates newspapers in the capital cities of numerous foreign countries, and disinformation appearing in those papers often "blows back" into the American press. One CIA-planted story, linking Italy's Red Brigades to the Soviet KGB, was used by author Claire Sterling in her book *The Terror Network* to support her conspiracy theory that the Soviet Union was the hidden hand behind international terrorism. Her book and its KGB conspiracy theory was scooped up by Reagan's first secretary of state Al Haig (another Kissinger protégé), who used it to justify administration policy in Central America.

The Reagan administration also ran an "Office of Public Diplomacy," which, despite its soothing nomenclature, had as its true purpose a propaganda campaign to persuade and pressure major news organizations to provide favorable coverage of the Nicaraguan contras and defamatory coverage of the then-ruling Sandinistas. The propaganda campaign worked, and, lest anyone protest that "propaganda" is too strong a term for the Reagan administration's program, authors Martin Lee and Norman Solomon have uncovered internal White House memoranda using exactly that word.

If everything you know is wrong, how do you know what's right? There are no final answers—only questions. Conspiracy theorists ask those questions. They are intellectual outcasts, often

social outcasts. But they are not aberrations. In a society woven together by propaganda and "unreality," whose own government and economic establishment operates in secrecy, there will always be conspiracy theorists. Eventually, we all may be.

The night that I sat down to write this concluding chapter, Meir Kahane was gunned down outside a Manhattan hotel. I wasn't particularly saddened by his death. Rabbi Kahane was the founder of the Jewish Defense League, an anti-Arab racist who led a movement to drive all Palestinians out of Israel, a religious zealot and theocratic fascist. Despite his repulsive qualities—or probably because of them—he was one of the most visible, widely quoted, frequently interviewed Jewish political leaders in the world outside of the Israeli government (though for a short time, Kahane was a member of the Knesset). His murder was more than another in New York's homicide wave of 1990. It was a political assassination.

There had not been, to my memory, an assassination of a political leader on American turf since the killing of John Lennon ten years earlier. Those loath to count the ex-Beatle as a "political leader" would have to look even further into the past. Even after writing this book, I still, somewhat naively it turns out, expected extensive coverage of Kahane's assassination on the evening's newscasts. I wanted to know who killed Kahane; whether the assassin belonged to any significant organizations; what significance there was to the timing of Kahane's murder, coming as it did with America and perhaps Israel preparing for war against Iraq; what kind of trouble had Kahane been stirring up recently; what happened to his security, which I assumed must have been tight. And a long list of other questions, none of which I saw so much as a comment upon the night of Kahane's killing. Why not?

Maybe the problem was me. Kahane was a hated man. It's perfectly plausible, especially in crazy old New York, that some angry Arab would pick up a gun and blow his head off. Was I being paranoid in asking those questions? Frustrated at the impoverished news coverage, had I become infected with the twisted anger of a conspiracy theorist?

If a conspiracy theorist is someone who sees the world dogmat-

ically, a single conspiracy behind everything, then I've never been
one and, after wallowing in conspiracy theories for more than two
years, I'm still not. There are plenty of conspiracy theorists who fit
that description, and the dogmatist is the popular stereotype of
conspiracy theorists—the "large number of Americans who . . .
have taken to an extreme the desire to find connections between
events. . . . They don't react to new information and ideas by adapting. They try to squeeze the world into their systems." Paranoids.
Simpletons.

I went into this project suspicious of all stereotypes. There had to
be more to conspiracy theories than nuttiness. I've come away
believing that there is. As I watched the thirty-second reports on
the assassination of Kahane—the highlight of each being a gory
shot of blood-smeared New York pavement—I wondered how the
questions I wanted asked were any more simplistic than what I was
seeing on television.

What I've come to believe is that the seeming "paranoia" of
conspiracy theorists is not necessarily the result of some underlying
mental dysfunction or of stupidity. The conspiracy theorists I interviewed for this book, with almost no exceptions, were nothing if
not highly intelligent.

The dysfunction is with American society, maybe even civilization as a whole. The structure of civilization itself requires mass
adherence to faith in the institutions that built civilization and make
it run. The institutions are innumerable: science, politics, communications, education, arts, government, business—it all comes
down to a faith in authority.

We have to believe the institutions are functioning in our best
interests. We have to believe what the people within those institutions assure us to be true. If not, we're sentenced to a life on the
edge, filled with frustration, indignation, confusion, and perhaps
what society calls insanity.

The conspiracy theorists I encountered question our authorities,
and, because they do, they skirt the fringes of society.

Anthropologist Jules Henry took it for granted that "our civilization is a tissue of contradictions and lies." He used the term
"sham" for the everyday deceptions we need to survive in this
corrupted society. Henry argued that mental illness, a concept of

which he was highly skeptical, is simply the refusal to accept that "sham is reality." In the case of conspiracy theorists, that refusal starts with questions, and often concludes in a highly developed worldview that is incompatible with the "sham."

Henry would have understood conspiracy theorists well. "Sham gives rise to coalitions because usually sham cannot be maintained without confederates." In other words, to keep civilization afloat requires a conspiracy. "In sham," Henry goes on, "the deceiver enters into an inner conspiracy against himself."

Conspiracy theorists resist joining the "inner conspiracy." They can't lie to themselves, like Colin Wilson's "outsider" who "cannot live in the comfortable insulated world of the bourgeois, accepting what he sees and touches as reality." The more they strip through the sham, the madder they appear.

"I anticipate a geometric increase in madness," says Jules Henry, "for sham is the basis of schizophrenia and murder itself."

To understand conspiracy theorists, I now believe, is to first understand that civilization is a conspiracy against reality.

# *Notes*

## INTRODUCTION

Bertram Gross quote: *Friendly Fascism*, p. 5.
*New York Times* assassination editorial appeared 1/7/79.

## CHAPTER 1

Thornley and Oswald's relationship in Marines and after: my interviews
with Kerry Thornley; Thornley, *The Dreadlock Recollections*. Thornley testimony to the Warren Commission in *Hearings before the President's Commission on the Assassination of President Kennedy, Vol. 9.*
Thornley *Affidavit*, 1/8/76. "Oswald, as Only a Marine Buddy Could
Know Him" by Kerry Thornley; series in *Men's Digest*, 1965 (no
months on my copy). Thornley, *Oswald*; "Outfit eightball" quote
from *Oswald*.

Thornley's reaction to J.F.K. assassination: *Affidavit*.

"Breeding experiment" quotes: my interviews with Thornley.

Landlady snickering quote: letter from Thornley to me.

Bob Black on Thornley: *Rants*, p. 201.

Bowling alley birth of Discordian Religion: my interviews with Thornley.

*Principia Discordia* first published on Jim Garrison's Xerox machine:
Wilson, *Cosmic Trigger*, p. 165.

"Poor man's *Ugly American*," quote: *Affidavit*.

Thornley in New Orleans, Bourbon House incident: *Affidavit*. Garrison's suspicions; "second Oswald": Garrison, *On the Trail of the
Assassins*, pp. 74–78. Calls Thornley an Oswald "look-alike": ibid.
p. 274.

Weisburg asks for touched-up photos: "Photo Touch-Up Charged" and
"Weisburg Admits 'Touch-Up' Letter; Denies Connection" by Tom
Raum, *Tampa Times-Tribune*, 11/27–28/68.

"Was Thornley an agent . . .": Garrison, op. cit. p. 77.

Thornley denies he's a CIA agent: "Deputies Arrest Thornley on Fugitive
Warrant," by Tom Raum, *Tampa Times-Tribune*, 2/22/68.

"As luck would have it . . .": Garrison press release, 2/21/68.

"very funny . . .": *Affidavit*.

Thornley travels to Mexico: Thornley's Warren Commission testimony.

Oswald in Mexico: Summers, *Conspiracy*, chapter 19; Groden and Livingstone, *High Treason*, photos.

Thornley's alleged New Orleans intelligence connections: Garrison, op. cit. pp. 72–73.

Bannister, Ferrie, and Oswald: Summers, *Conspiracy*; Groden and Livingstone, *High Treason*. Note: Material on the relationship among these three turns up in just about every book about the Kennedy assassination.

Thornley meets Bannister: *Affidavit*.

Thornley's relationship with Lifton: my interviews with both; *Affidavit*; Epstein, *Counterplot*.

Roselli says CIA "killed . . . president": *Affidavit*.

"Gary Kirstein" recollections: my interviews with Thornley, and his letters to me; *Affidavit*; Thornley, *The Dreadlock Recollections*.

"Did the Plumbers Plug J.F.K., Too?": Thornley refers to this article in his introduction to *The Dreadlock Recollections*. He says it was published in a newspaper called *The Great Speckled Bird*, but he gives no date of publication.

Attacked by men in ski masks: *Cosmic Trigger*, pp. 152–54.

Thornley quotes on mental programming, his mother, Vril Society, and Nazi breeding experiments are all from my interviews.

"Nazi Connections to the J.F.K. Assassination," by Mae Brussell. *The Rebel*, 11/22/83.

Discordian philosophy: Wilson, *Cosmic Trigger*; Hill and Thornley; *Principia Discordia*.

Concluding Thornley quotes: interview.


## CHAPTER 2

Background material on News Election Service from research, including interviews, compiled by me and summarized in my article, "Compute D'Etat" in San Jose *Metro*, 9/28/89.

The Colliers' Votescam theory and peregrinations in pursuit of: Collier and Collier, *Votescam*; my interviews with Ken Collier.

"There isn't one single person in public office who earned their way there . . .": my interviews with Ken Collier.

Dade County election: *Miami Magazine*, July 1974, reproduced in *Votescam*.

Background on the Colliers: "The Great Vote Fraud Conspiracy" by Mike Clary, *Miami New Times*, 6/29/88.

The Colliers' *Spotlight* articles were reprinted in one special supplement, *The Stealing of America*, 8/84.

*Home News* articles are reproduced in *Votescam* and described in "The Great Vote Fraud Conspiracy."

The Colliers' book proposal: *Votescam*.

"It was a random thing . . .": KAZU-FM, Carmel, California, interview with Ken Collier, May 1988.

"What do they do?": ibid.

Staffing of NES: my interview with Paul Hain, former NES official.

The Colliers' suspicions about "master computer": my interviews with Ken Collier.

NES conceived: "Networks Plan Nov. 3 Vote Pool," *New York Times*, 6/8/64. "Many television executives . . .": ibid. "Master tally boards . . .": ibid.

NES performance: "News Media Pool to Speed Returns," *New York Times*, 11/1/64; "News Media Pool Sets Vote Marks," *New York Times*, 11/4/64.

Erroneous data in 1968 election: "Vote Computers That Failed are Under Analysis," *New York Times*, 11/7/68; "Nixon Popular Vote Lead Is Increased," *New York Times*, 11/8/68.

"Nixon has more power now . . .": my interview with Ken Collier.

Computers tabulate fifty-four percent: Hoffman, *Making Every Vote Count*.

"If you did it right, no one would ever know": "Electronic Elections Seen as an Invitation to Fraud," *Los Angeles Times*, 7/4/89.

Voter turnaround estimate belongs to the Colliers.

Bush wins New Hampshire despite bad polls: "New Hampshire Confounded Most Pollsters," *Washington Post*, 2/18/88.

The Colliers' Sununu theory: *Votescam*.

Shouptronic background: *An Election Administrator's Guide to Computerized Voting Systems, Vol. 2*, ECRI Report, 1988.

Naegle quote from my interview with him.

Shoup fined and sentenced: "Counting the Votes" by Ronnie Dugger, *New Yorker*, 11/7/88.

"We had to get Reagan elected . . .": ibid.

Forty percent figure from my interview with computerized voting entrepreneur Robert Varni.

"heap of spaghetti code . . ." and "shell game": "Machine Politics" by John W. Verity, *Datamation*, 11/1/86.

The Colliers' videotape alleged chad-related vote fraud, sue Republican National Committee: interviews with Ken Collier; "The Great Vote Fraud Conspiracy"; *Votescam*.

"He acted without jurisdiction . . .": testimony of Kennety F. Collier before U.S. Senate Judiciary Committee, 8/6/86.

The Colliers' allegations about Scalia and Nixon, and "He never invoked that as a reason for Watergate": interviews with Ken Collier.

NES as a CIA operation related to Kennedy assassination: my interviews with Ken Collier.

Jim Collier's stomach tumor: "The Great Vote Fraud Conspiracy."

"It's not even a quest . . ." and "Ultimately, it might come out . . .": my interviews with Ken Collier.


CHAPTER 3


LaRouche's formative years, Trotskyism, Operation Mop-Up: "Politics and Paranoia: The Strange Odyssey of Lyndon LaRouche" by Frank Deane and Randall Rothenberg, *The Nation*, 8/16/80; King, *Lyndon LaRouche and the New American Fascism*, chapters 1–5; my interviews with LaRouche.

"seating arrangements of the French National Assembly . . .": "Secret Agent Man" by James Ridgeway, *Village Voice*, 10/13/87.

"The problem with most conspiracy buffs . . .": my interview with LaRouche.

The clearest statement of the "moral imperative" appears in Kant's *Critique of Practical Reason*.

"promotion of scientific knowledge . . .": my interview with LaRouche.

"Wherever populations have become more rational . . .": LaRouche, *There Are No Limits to Growth*.

SDI as "my proposal": my interviews with LaRouche.

LaRouche's condemnation of the empiricists appears in almost every book or major article he has ever written.

"irrational hedonism": *There Are No Limits to Growth*.

"Henry's career . . . as a tool of Chatham House . . .": my interviews with LaRouche; LaRouche's British conspiracy theory is his central theme, stated most explicitly in *Dope, Inc.*, as well as in interviews and in almost everything he has ever written.

For a more complete history of the Templars, Masons, etc., see Chapter 16. "The leading controllers of the opium war . . .": *Dope, Inc.*, p. 61. See also chapter 9 of *Dope, Inc.*, in which LaRouche's "investigating team" explains how "the entire world drug traffic has been run by a single family since its inception" and how "the family religion" is the gnostic "Isis Cult." See Chapter 16 of this book for a history of mystery cults and secret societies.

"Who's the conspiracy theorist . . . ?": my interview with Odin Anderson.

LaRouche's network of organizations and holdings: *The LaRouche Cult: Packaging Extremism*, an Anti-Defamation League Special Report, Spring 1986.

*Executive Intelligence Review*'s scooping propensity is acknowledged even by Dennis King, LaRouche's fiercest journalistic adversary. See King, *Lyndon LaRouche and the New American Fascism*, p. 161, for King's account of how *EIR* got the scoop on the Iran-Contra affair.

". . . we are able to think better . . .": my interview with LaRouche.

The "Get LaRouche Task Force" hypothesis is stated most succinctly in the introduction to and Appendix A of *Railroad!* by LaRouche's rather misleadingly named "Commission to Investigate Human Rights Violations" (the "commission" is concerned exclusively with violations of Lyndon LaRouche's rights). The Boston trial received national press

coverage. Copies of numerous newspaper accounts are in my possession, but for the curious reader's, and my own convenience, widely
reported facts will be attributed to this LaRouche-produced book, a
straightforward account of LaRouche's legal ordeals consisting mainly
of reprinted court documents and FOIA releases (copies of many FOIA
documents, including most of the important ones, are also in my files).

"The government got caught . . .": my interview with Anderson.

North-Secord memo: "North Memo Reveals Other Intrigues," *Philadelphia Inquirer*, 3/10/88.

Government informers as actual perpetrators of the crimes is LaRouche's
central defense, which he was prohibited from using at his subsequent
trial in Alexandria, Virginia, the trial at which LaRouche was convicted
following the Boston mistrial. See *Railroad!* for a full account.

LaRouche and North competing for cash: "Search for Dollars Links
LaRouche, North, "*Lowell* [*MA*] *Sunday Sun*, 7/12/87.

LaRouche accuses Kissinger of organizing frame-up: my interviews with
LaRouche.

Kissinger letters to Webster: *Railroad!*, pp. 546, 548.

"Politics of Faggotry" flyer: King, *Lyndon LaRouche and the New American Fascism*, p. 140.

Webster memo asking for investigation: *Railroad!*, p. 550.

"We opposed it because it stank . . .": my interviews with LaRouche.
"You don't . . . start shooting up Jesuits": ibid.

Nancy Reagan as "an idiot," President Reagan as "pussy whipped":
"Secret Agent Man."

Kissinger as LaRouche's adversary and LaRouche's allegation of Kissinger's "land scam operation": my interviews with LaRouche. Also
from my interviews, Grateful Dead as a "British intelligence operation," and ultimate purpose of "this Satanism business."

Episcopal canon alleged by LaRouche to visit "Mineshaft" club: "The
Indictment of LaRouche's Enemies," *New Federalist*, 2/17/89. *New
Federalist* is LaRouche's successor paper to *New Solidarity*, which was
closed by the government. LaRouche didn't write the cited article, but
given the nature of the LaRouche organization it's quite certain that
nothing he'd denounce makes it into his paper.

Confrontation with Nancy Kissinger recounted in Johnson, *Architects of
Fear*, p. 191.

Masturbation prohibited: "Politics and Paranoia" by Deane and Rothenberg.

LaRouche's attitude toward sexuality is explicated in *Lyndon LaRouche and the New American Fascism*. LaRouche recognized that "personal life" and sexuality in particular were the greatest obstacle to total political commitment, according to his hostile biographer Dennis King. LaRouche sought, often using brutal techniques, to deprive his underlings of their sexual identities, or any sexual opportunities, promising to "take your bedrooms away from you," King, p. 25.

"Another word for it: New Age . . ." and LaRouche's comments on conspiracy: my interviews with LaRouche.

Judge's speculation that LaRouche is "put up by the Rockefellers": my interviews with Judge.

LaRouche's meetings with foreign leaders are recounted in *Lyndon LaRouche and the New American Fascism*.

For Carter's connection to the Trilateral Commission, see Chapter 15.

LaRouche's CIA and administration contacts: "The LaRouche Connection" by Dennis King and Ronald Radosh, *The New Republic*, 2/6/84.

LaRouche's anti-Bush campaign: *Lyndon LaRouche and the New American Fascism*, pp. 124–25.

"very much involved" with beam weapon: my interviews with LaRouche.

Dinner with NSC aide and use of Mitch WerBell: "The LaRouche Connection" by King and Radosh.

LaRouche's group was sued by *U.S. News and World Report* for impersonating the magazine's reporters.

Souter, Rizzo relationships with LaRouche: "David Souter and Lyndon LaRouche" by James Ledbetter and James Ridgeway, *Village Voice*, 9/18/90.

Boston jury agrees that government may have been involved in fraud to discredit LaRouche, takes straw poll: "LaRouche Jury Would Have Voted Not Guilty," *Boston Herald*, 5/5/88.

## CHAPTER 4

All of the material on William Bramley comes from my interviews with him. Some quotes are taken from his book, *The Gods of Eden*, and are so noted in the text. See also my article "Alien Notion," from San Jose

*Metro*, 6/21/90. Also, for more on secret societies, see Chapter 16 of this book.

All John Keel quotes are from *UFOs: Operation Trojan Horse*, his definitive book. Charles Fort catalogued lights in the sky in *The Book of the Damned*.

Roswell incident, absence from Project Blue Book: Randle, *The UFO Casebook*, pp. 5–11.

Robertson Panel: Good, *Above Top Secret*, pp. 335–39.

UFOs as psychotronic technology: Vallee, *Messengers of Deception*, p. 21.

"I AM" movement and fascism: ibid. pp. 192–93. William Dudley Pelley led the "Silver Shirts," and American fascist party before World War II. Pelley, who was interned by the government during the war, was also a mystic who helped two of his students, Guy and Edna Ballard, found I AM. After the war, Pelley started an occult group called Soulcraft, which also included George Hunt Williamson (aka Michel d'Obrenovic), a contactee. Pelley's own difficult-to-obtain writings are said to contain oblique references to UFOs. Pelley also associated with another contactee, George Adamski. The ideology of this cadre was standard "master race" stuff, with the twist that the "master race" are aliens who have left their descendents on earth. The "star children" turn up in the canons of various "New Age" groups and cults.

CHAPTER 5

"There's hope . . .": my interviews with John McManus.

Welch as dictator: In section eight of *The Blue Book of the John Birch Society*, Welch explains that the society is to be "monolithic" and under the "complete authoritative control" of one man, Robert Welch. By the way, Welch's family business survives as a leading grape juice bottler.

John Birch's bio: Vahan, *The Truth about the John Birch Society*, pp. 13–16.

Welch's education, business, fascination with Birch: "Salesman of the Right," *New York Times*, 4/1/61; Dudman, *Men of the Far Right*, p. 67; *The Truth about the John Birch Society*.

Birch's parents support JBS: "Birch Parents Support Society," *New York Times*, 4/2/61.

NOTES

Origins of Birch Society: *The Truth about the John Birch Society,* chapter 2; *Men of the Far Right,* chapter 5.

*The Politician* likened to *Mein Kampf:* "The Americanists," *Time,* 3/10/61.

Welch's allegations about Eisenhower, others: quoted from *The Politician* in *Men of the Far Right,* and *The Truth about the John Birch Society.* Welch also called Eisenhower's brother, Milton "a communist" and speculated that Milton may in fact have been Ike's "boss."

Goldwater's reaction to *The Politician: The Truth about the John Birch Society,* p. 85.

Characterization of Welch and descriptions of his monotonous, irascible speaking style rely on Schomp, *Birchism Was My Business.* Author was one of the Birch Societry's few paid staffers. Also, "Coast Reaction Mixed on Welch," *New York Times,* 4/14/61.

"most heated public controversy . . . since McCarthy": *The Boston Traveler,* quoted in *The Truth about the John Birch Society,* p. 41.

Walker controversy: "Walker Resigns from the Army," *New York Times,* 11/3/61; "Birch Unit Ideas Put to U.S. Troops," *New York Times,* 4/14/61; *Men of the Far Right,* chapter 4. For Walker's role in Kennedy assassination scenario, see Chapter 10 of this book.

NAM censures Birch Society: "Birch Council Member Denies Censure Vote," *New York Times,* 4/14/61.

"We should use a rifle . . .": "Salesman of the Right," *New York Times.* "If you measured . . .": my interview with McManus.

Birch concentration in Idaho: "John Birch Society 'Wages War for Minds' in Idaho," *Idaho Statesman,* 3/24/85; in Oklahoma: "Still Keeping Watch," by Mike Easterling, *Oklahoma Gazette,* 4/26/89. Total Birch membership: "Area Man Leads Birch Society 'Youth Movement,' " *Norfolk Virginian-Pilot,* 2/2/85. Summer camps: "Swimming, Campfires and Anti-communism," by Ron Grossman, *San Jose Mercury-News,* 9/18/89.

"We've got truth on our side . . .": my interview with McManus.

"Early in our history . . .": Bunzel, *Anti-Politics in America* p. 41.

Origins of the Know-Nothings: Bennet, *The Party of Fear,* pp. 105–16. Buntline as founder: Coates, *Armed and Dangerous,* p. 26.

"There is abundant proof that a foreign conspiracy . . .": "Startling Facts

for Native Americans Called Know-Nothings," pamphlet published in New York, 1855, p. 66.

Jack Chick comics are available through Amok Books; for background on Jack Chick, see Johnson, *Architects of Fear.*

Know-Nothings in elected office: *Armed and Dangerous,* p. 28.

"advocating the largest freedom . . .": "Address of the Executive Committee of the American Republicans of Boston to the People of Massachusetts," 1845, p. 11.

". . . a conspiracy above communism . . .": my interview with John McManus.

"why the Communists . . . celebrate May Day.": ibid.

Allen quote on Adam Weishaupt: *None Dare Call It Conspiracy,* p. 80; a brief history of the Illuminati is in Chapter 16 of this book.

Welch's ideas about Illuminati, and rejection of term "Supercom": "And Some Ober Dicta" by Robert Welch, 1976, pamphlet mailed in Birch Society copies of the book *Wall Street and the Rise of Hitler.*

"marketplace of ideas . . .": "A Member of the CFR Talks Back" by Zygmunt Nagorski, *National Review,* 12/9/77.

"The reality of socialism . . .": Allen, *Say No to the New World Order,* p. 21; How the *Insiders* built the Soviet Union is the theme that runs throughout *None Dare Call It Conspiracy* and most of Allen's writing.

McManus radio interview on KGO-San Francisco, 11/26/90.

Bertrand Russell called "British pro-Communist socialist," ADA called "Fabian Socialist": Smoot, *The Invisible Government,* p. 121.

"Our Jewish members were very upset . . .": my interview with McManus. List of anti-Semites in Birch Society from Anti-Defamation League of B'nai B'rith, *Extremism on the Right.* The former employee critical of Birchian anti-Semitism is Schomp, author of *Birchism Was my Business.*

"No one has anything to fear . . .": my interview with McManus.

## CHAPTER 6

Pat Buchanan made his "anti-Christian" accusation on an episode of the Cable News Network program *Crossfire* in August, 1988.

"I'm not a conspiracy theorist . . .": my interview with Ted Temple.

"The growth of big government . . .": Sorman, *The Conservative Revolution in America*, p. 144.

Willard Givens is quoted in Stormer, *None Dare Call It Treason*, p. 123.

NEA as friendly to Soviet totalitarianism: Reed, *NEA: Propaganda Front for the Radical Left*.

"The real goal . . .": McManus, *The Insiders*, p. 18.

Jesse Helms's rant: *Congressional Record*, 12/15/87.

Reagan's early political career as GE spokesman is summarized in Wills, *Reagan's America*, and Dugger, *Reagan: The Man and His Presidency*; Reagan's key speeches are reprinted in *Reagan Speaks*, including the "evil empire" speech.

Bush as having "more input into policy" than Reagan, Schultz as "errand boy for the commercial establishment," and "follow the money": my interview with Howard Philips.

Irvine's connections to ACWF, WACL: Anderson and Anderson, *Inside the League*, pp. 86, 157; AIM's crusades are carried out in its twice-monthly newsletter "AIM Report," which often includes preprinted postcards addressed to corporate sponsors of programs AIM doesn't like, allowing AIM readers ease in participating in pressure campaigns; the anti-"Shootdown" effort started in "AIM Report" of January (Issue A), 1990. Irvine in that issue finds it very incriminating that the NBC censor to whom he complained about "Shootdown" "acknowledged that he read *The Nation*." Irvines's comment about major TV networks "ill-equipped to screen out . . . propaganda inimical to our country's interests" is from the "AIM Report," January 1989, Issue B.

For other Irvine connections, see "Accuracy in Media" by Louis Wolf, *Covert Action Information Bulletin* #32. Before Irvine, AIM was run by Abraham Kalish, a former employee of the U.S. Information Agency, the government's department of propaganda.

## CHAPTER 7

Material on David Emory and Judge is based primarily on my interviews with them.

Mae Brussell's career, threats against her, her death: "All Things Con-

spired" by John Whalen, San Jose *Metro*, 11/17/88. "Conspiracy Theorist Mae Brussell Dies," by Ann W. O'Neill, *San Jose Mercury-News*, 10/5/88. "In Our Hearts" by John Judge, *World Watchers International*, Fall 1989.

Mae Brussell and *The Realist*: Brussell's second and third *Realist* articles were published in 1974. The second was titled "The Senate Committee is Part of the Cover-Up," and detailed alleged martial law plans cooked up by the Nixon administration and known to, but concealed by Senator Sam Ervin's Watergate investigating committee. (This allegation doesn't seem so outlandish in light of its echoes more than a decade later during the Iran-Contra hearings when Texas congressman Jack Brooks tried to ask about Oliver North's role in drawing up a plan to suspend the constitution. Brooks was silenced by committee chairman Sen. Daniel Inouye. For more on North's plan and other martial law scenarios see Chapter 11.) Brussell's third *Realist* piece was "Why Was Patricia Hearst Kidnapped?" Krassner's refusal to publish Brussell's footnotes to the "Patricia Hearst" article, and financial disputes, severed the relationship between Brussell and *The Realist*.

"I'm an existentialist," quote, "candidate is selected" quote from Mae Brussell radio interview, KPFK Los Angeles, 3/2/88. Nazis: "The Nazi Connection to the John F. Kennedy Assassination," by Mae Brussell, *The Rebel*, 11/22/83.

Emory on guns from "One Step Beyond" broadcast, KFJC, 10/22/89. Emory tape titles from *The Dave Emory Archive Cassette Catalog*, Archives on Audio, P.O. Box 170023, San Francisco, CA 94117 (1990).

Tom Davis quotes: from my interview.

## CHAPTER 8

Because Garrison did not answer my written request for an interview, and on the phone his secretary told me he was "too busy" to talk to the press, I've reconstructed a narrative of Garrison's career and his case against Clay Shaw from the sources below; most contain overlapping information (although their points of view differ greatly), which is why in most cases I haven't listed individual citations.

Epstein, *Counterplot*; Flammonde, *The Kennedy Conspiracy*; Garrison, *On the Trail of the Assassins*; James and Wardlaw, *Plot or Politics?*; "The Case of Jim Garrison and Lee Harvey Oswald," by Gene Rob-

erts, *New York Times Magazine*, 5/21/67; "The Garrison Commission on the Assassination of President Kennedy," by William W. Turner, *Ramparts*, 6/67; "Is Garrison Faking?," by Fred Powledge, *The New Republic*, 6/17/67.

Jack Martin described as "full of that well-known waste material . . .": James, *Plot or Politics*, p. 48.

Martin allegations about Ferrie, characterization of Ferrie as CIA contractor, eccentric: op. cit.; also Groden and Livingstone, *High Treason*; Summers, *Conspiracy*.

Ferrie as amateur cancer researcher: Flammonde, *The Kennedy Conspiracy*, p. 19.

Killing of Aladio del Valle: Groden, *High Treason*, p. 118.

"I continued to believe that Shaw had participated . . .": Garrison, *On the Trail of the Assassins*, p. 250.

Garrison sculpts Russo's testimony: Flammonde, *The Kennedy Conspiracy*, p. 302.

Helms admits Shaw was "CIA contact": Garrison, ibid., p. 251. Marchetti confirms: Groden, *High Treason*, p. 161.

Bethell documents: Flammonde, *The Kennedy Conspiracy*, p. 198; Garrison, *On the Trail of the Assassins*, p. 48.

James Wilcott told the HSCA that Oswald was recruited by the CIA to act as a double agent against the U.S.S.R. Wilcott, a former CIA finance officer, said he handled funding for the Oswald/Soviet mission. Summers in *Conspiracy* (pp. 129–30) notes that Wilcott's story turned out to have some holes, and Wilcott later teamed up with CIA dissident Philip Agee in an anti-CIA campaign. However, Summers notes, "just as most of Agee's allegations are accepted as authentic, there may be some nugget of fact [in Wilcott's story]." Summers also speculates that Wilcott may have been still working for the CIA, in which case his story could be seen as disinformation, perhaps to lead the HSCA down the wrong path.

Helms on Oswald's "dummy file": Groden, *High Treason*, p. 93.

HSCA calls FBI's reaction to Marcello threat "deficient": Summers, *Conspiracy*, p. 259.

Garrison dismisses allegations of mob connections: *On The Trail of the Assassins*, 287–88.

CHAPTER 9

Biographical information on Daniel Sheehan from Rashke, *The Killing of Karen Silkwood*; "The Law and the Prophet," by James Traub, *Mother Jones*, 2–3/88; "Where Have All the Idealists Gone?," by Connie Matthiessen, *Utne Reader* 10–11/86.

Christic lawsuit: *Affidavit of Daniel P. Sheehan*.

Forty thousand dollars per week figure: "The Law and the Prophet."

One million dollar sanction against Christic Institute: "Christic Institute Fights for Its Existence," by Frank Provenzano, Detroit *Metro-Times*, 2/28/89; "Targets of Contra-Conspiracy Suit Awarded $1 million," *San Jose Mercury-News*, 2/4/89.

Reactions of defendants to Christic suit: "The Law and the Prophet."

CHAPTER 10

For a good summary of Kennedy's Vietnam withdrawal plans and their postassassination reversal, see Prouty, *The Secret Team*, pp. 4–19. The author of the book, Lt. Col. L. Fletcher Prouty, was a "briefing officer" serving as informational liaison between the CIA and the Pentagon. As such, he was privy to the country's most sensitive information, and authored many of what were eventually published as "The Pentagon Papers." (Prouty points out that most were not "Pentagon" papers at all, but an attempt by the CIA to deflect responsibility for the war away from itself to the Pentagon.) On October 2, 1963, Defense Secretary Robert S. McNamara responded to Kennedy's stated desire to get out of Vietnam with a report stating, "It should be possible to withdraw the bulk of U.S. personnel by [the end of 1965]." No sooner was Kennedy dead than McNamara and his operatives set to work on a "vastly different" report for President Johnson, calling for "major increases in both military and (United States Operations Mission) staffs," as well as operations in Laos. This second report was the first of the "Pentagon Papers" published by the *New York Times*. Prouty coined the phrase "Secret Team" (later appropriated by Daniel Sheehan) to refer to the lifetime, inner-circle members of the intelligence community and defense establishment. Near the close of his book (p. 416), he remarks, "While the echo of those shots in Dallas were still ringing, the ST moved to take over the whole direction of the war and dominate the activity of the United States of America."

Domhoff's comments: "The Cult of Conspiracy," by Tai Moses, *The Sun* (Santa Cruz, CA), 1/26/89.

"It was a different world . . .": my article "Theories on an Assassination," *Worcester Magazine*, 11/23/88.

Secord involvement in Desert One: "The General and the Blonde Ghost," by Ron Rosenbaum, *Vanity Fair*, 1/90. This is an interesting article, interviewing both Secord and the reclusive Ted Shackley, but it perpetuates the odd myth that Vietnam and, in fact, the whole history of CIA and "secret team" malfeasance for the past thirty years are "the tragic legacy of J.F.K.'s Camelot." In light of Prouty's statements above, this curious canard is ironic in the extreme.

Lifton found a plethora of discrepancies, foremost among them that, according to eyewitnesses, the coffin that carried J.F.K.'s body into the Bethesda autopsy room was an ordinary metal shipping casket, not the ornate, expensive ceremonial casket in which his body was loaded onto Air Force One. If Lifton's eyewitnesses are reliable, the body must have been stolen at some point, which leaves wide open the possibility of alterations—a proposition for which Lifton amasses considerable evidence.

Johnson, creating the Warren Commission, also declared that if rumors of a foreign conspiracy were not quelled, the U.S. could be thrown into "a war which could cost 40 million lives." Summers, *Conspiracy*, p. 408.

Nixon in Dallas on day of assassination: Scott, *The Dallas Conspiracy*. Scott cites Earl Mazo and Stephen Hess, *Nixon: A Political Portrait* (New York: Popular Library, 1968), p. 296. Scott notes that Nixon's business likely involved the Pepsi bottling plant planned for Arlington, Texas. If so, says Scott, he would have almost certainly been doing business with Great Southwest Corporation, of which more later in this chapter. The implication that Nixon's presence in Dallas on the two days leading up to the assassination, and, indeed, the very morning of November 22, 1963, is significant may seem farfetched, and it may be. But why, then, did Nixon later deny having been in Dallas on those dates, making him as Groden in *High Treason* quips, the only person of his generation *not* to remember where he was when Kennedy was assassinated?

Nixon death threats: "Guard Not for Nixon," *Dallas Morning News*, 11/22/63.

Trowbridge Ford's comments and background: my interviews with Trowbridge Ford.

"I believe that a full exposure . . .": "From Dallas to Watergate: The Longest Cover-Up," by Peter Dale Scott, *Ramparts*, 11/73.

Nixon, Rebozo, mob links: ibid.

Nixon possible meeting with Murchison: Groden, *High Treason*, p. 243, citing Penn Jones, Jr., *Forgive My Grief* (Rt. 3, Box 356, Waxahachie, TX 75165), vol. 4, p. 114.

H. L. Hunt's death squad: Hougan, *Spooks*, p. 55 (Hougan notes that Hunt denies this allegation, blaming it on a CIA operative out to smear him); Groden in *High Treason* notes that just an hour after the J.F.K. assassination, Hunt was flown from Dallas by the FBI to Mexico, where he stayed for a month. Groden on p. 203 reports Hunt's financing of *Krushchev Killed Kennedy*.

Murchison connections: Groden, *High Treason*, pp. 243, 262–63. Hoover connections: Scott, *The Dallas Conspiracy*, chapter 6.

Marina Oswald and Murchison: Scott, *The Dallas Conspiracy*, chapters 3 and 10. General Walker and German neo-Nazis: ibid., chapters 1 and 4.

Hunt tries to persuade Nixon to pick Ford: Groden, *High Treason*, p. 262; Cabell brothers: ibid., pp. 262–63.

Sturgis plants Cuban conspiracy story: "From Dallas to Watergate."

E. Howard Hunt in Mexico: Summers, *Conspiracy*, pp. 418–19, citing Tad Szulc, *Compulsive Spy* (New York: Viking Press, 1974).

Witness deaths: Penn Jones, Jr., in his book *Forgive My Grief*, cited above, first formulated the "mysterious deaths" theory, calling attention to what appears to be an unusually high rate of untimely demise among witnesses to the assassination and possible participants in a conspiracy. The list of deaths has been oft amended and repeated. I've taken mine from Groden, *High Treason*, chapter 7, simply for the sake of convenience.

Oil companies and Vietnam: Scott, *The Dallas Conspiracy*, chapter 9.

Garrison on Permindex: *On the Trail of the Assassins*, pp. 89–90; *Nomenclature of an Assassination Cabal* was written by William Torbitt, which was a pseudonym for a Houston attorney named David Copeland, now deceased. Re. Permindex, see also Flammonde, *The Kennedy Conspiracy*; "Who Told the Truth about J.F.K.," by Jay Pound, *Critique* #21/22.

Kennedy vow to smash CIA: Groden, *High Treason*, p. 355. Kennedy's true sentiments toward the CIA came to light during the hearings of the

House Select Committee on Assassinations. Prouty, in *The Secret Team*, recounts how Kennedy came to the presidency with strong CIA support, even reappointing Allen Dulles as CIA director. But after the Bay of Pigs, he felt he'd been double-crossed. According to Prouty, Kennedy maintained a public show of support for the CIA while in private he plotted against it as he realized that he could not control the intelligence behemoth.

Hoover's friends with underworld ties: Nash, *Citizen Hoover*, pp. 109–13; Messick, *John Edgar Hoover*, pp. 209–11. An example of Hoover's curious links was industrialist Lewis Rosenstiel, who was directly associated in congressional and New York State legislative testimony to the mob's financial overseer Meyer Lansky, and political and gambling boss Frank Costello. Arthur Samish, a liquor industry lobbyist sent to jail for tax evasion, was another mutual friend of Hoover and Lansky.

Interpol, Nazis and Hoover: Foomer, *Interpol*, pp. 49–54. Hoover first joined Interpol in 1938, when the organization was taken over by Nazis. During World War II Interpol was dormant. When it was revived it may or may not have been free of its Nazi links. See Anderson, *Policing the World*, pp. 41–42. Anderson sees "no convincing evidence" that the post-war Interpol was Nazi-influenced, but he does quote from another book, Omar Garrison, *The Secret World of Interpol* (London: Ralston Pilot, 1976). "Several of the committee which reconstituted (Interpol) in 1946 had worked with the Nazis. Four out of seven of Interpol's presidents since the restructuring in 1946 may reasonably be considered carriers of the police state germ."

"Once we decide that anything goes . . .": Moyers, *The Secret Government*, p. 44. Moyers, who could hardly be called a conspiracy theorist (in the same paragraph, he notes, erroneously, that "most of us" dismiss suspicions of conspiracy in J.F.K.'s death—in fact, polls consistently show the majority of Americans *accepting* a J.F.K. assassination conspiracy theory), also marvels at (p. 54) "how easily the Cold War enticed us into surrendering popular control of the government to the national security state."

CHAPTER 11

Robert F. Kennedy conspiracy theories come from a number of sources, notably, Robert Kaiser, *RFK Must Die!* (New York: E. P. Dutton Co., 1970), William Turner and John Christian, *The Assassination of Robert*

*F. Kennedy* (New York: Random House, 1978), and many others. My job, however, was made very easy by a quick look back in the files of my own paper, San Jose *Metro*, for an article, "Unanswered Questions," by Andy Boehm (12/15/88), which is the best summary I've seen of the R.F.K. assassination theories. I also relied on Ted Charach's 1973 documentary film *The Second Gun*, which is in my possession on videotape.

MKULTRA, origins and effects: Marks, *The Search for the "Manchurian Candidate"*; Lee and Shlain, *Acid Dreams*; Bowart, *Operation Mind Control*.

Hinckley on Valium: "Hinckley's Psychiatrist Prescribed Disastrous Treatment, Doctor Says," *Miami Herald*, 5/19/82 (with sidebar "Valium Can Cause Rage, Expert Says").

Chapman "could have been programmed": Bressler, *Who Killed John Lennon?*, p. 17. Other details about Chapman, including possible YMCA/CIA connection, from throughout the same book.

Hinckley hoped someone would stop him, felt "relieved": "Hinckley's Psychiatrist Prescribed . . .": op. cit.

Purdy on psychiatric drugs: "A Report to Attorney General John K. Van de Kamp on Patrick Edward Purdy and the Cleveland School Killings," State of California, 10/89.

CIA agent Dwyer at Jonestown: "CIA Agent Witnessed Jonestown Mass Suicide," by Rick Sullivan, San Mateo *Times*, 12/14/79; Dwyer is listed in *Who's Who in the CIA*, p. 152. Dwyer "stripping the dead": Kilduff and Javers, *The Suicide Cult*, p. 176.

Holsinger's story comes from his address to a forum entitled "Psychosocial Implications of the Jonestown Phenomenon," held in San Francisco, 5/23/80.

Statements of Dr. Mootoo, evidence of Jonestown murders: "Coroner Says 700 in Cult Who Died Were Slain," *Miami Herald*, 12/17/78; "Some in Cult Received Cyanide by Injection, Sources Say," *New York Times*, 12/12/78; "Hundreds Were Slain, Survivor Reportedly Says," *Los Angeles Times*, 11/25/78 (from Associated Press).

Death toll jumps: "Question Linger about Guyana," by Sidney Jones, *Oakland Tribune*, 12/9/78.

Layton "a robot": "Cult Reportedly Got Assets from Layton," *Los Angeles Times*, 11/26/78.

Mind control drugs at Jonestown, mentioned in Holsinger's talk, op. cit.; Holsinger quotes, ibid.

"some kind of horrible government experiments . . .": "Cult Defectors Suspect U.S. of a Coverup on Jonestown," by Bella Stumbo, *Los Angeles Times*, 12/18/78.

Jones as Republican: "Jim Jones Was a Republican for 6 Years," *Los Angeles Times*, 12/17/78. In Brazil: "Jones Lived Well, Kept to Himself During Mysterious Brazil Stay," San Jose *Mercury* (date missing from my clipping).

Jones and Lane consider smuggling assassination witness: "Memo Discusses Smuggling Witness into Guyana," *New York Times*, 12/8/78.

Jonestown resettlement: "Resettlement Plan Set Up by Relief Groups," San Francisco *Examiner*, 2/18/80. Hilltown: "Hill Rules Cult with Iron Fist," Cleveland *Plain Dealer*, 12/4/78. Colonia Dignidad: "West German Cultist Concentration Camp in Chile," by Konrad Ege, *Counterspy*, 12/78.

King assassination conspiracy theories: Blumenthal and Yazitian, *Government by Gunplay*; "The Conspiracy to Kill Martin Luther King," by John Sergeant and John Edginton, *Chicago Reader*, 3/2/90.

COINTELPRO against white hate groups: "Vigilante Repression," by Ken Lawrence, *Covert Action Information Bulletin* # 31.

Operation Garden Plot and Rex 84: "Blueprint for Tyranny," by Donald Goldberg and Indy Badhwar, *Penthouse*, 8/85; "Variations on a FEMA," by James Ridgeway, *Village Voice*, 11/14/89; "The Take-Charge Gang," by Keenen Peck, *The Progressive*, 5/85; "Meese-ing with Civil Rights," San Jose *Metro*, 3/28/85.

CIA discusses "how to knock off key guys" with cancer: "CIA's Bizarre Ideas for Assassinations," San Francisco *Chronicle*, 4/2/79.

The Jessica Savitch theory, which usually raises a few eyebrows, is not uncommon among conspiracy researchers. It was relayed to me by John Judge.

Sarah Jane Moore working for FBI: Blumenthal, *Government by Gunplay*.

Ford assassination allegations: Milan, *The Squad*, pp. 285–90.

The list of "October Surprise" allegedly strange deaths comes from Honneger, *October Surprise*, pp. 283–92.

## CHAPTER 12

Black leaders on drug conspiracy: "Talk Grows of Government Being out to Get Blacks," by Jason DeParle, *New York Times*, 10/29/90; "Many Blacks Blame Drug Woes on Conspiracy among Whites," by Howard Kurtz, *San Jose Mercury-News*, 1/1/90 (from *Washington Post*).

John Kerry's opinions on drug conspiracy: my interview with John Kerry.

The best source I have found for a quick summary of the Mafia's early involvement in drugs is in McCoy, *The Politics of Heroin in Southeast Asia*, the definitive work on U.S. government involvement in the drug trade up to 1970. Figures on heroin demand and addict population, pp. 16, 17. Lucky Luciano's heroin entrepreneurship, pp. 18–27.

McCoy's book contains Air America material, but also appeared in a book called *Air America* by Christopher Robbins. However, when a movie of the same title appeared in 1990 (with Mel Gibson), Robbins condemned it in the *New York Times* (8/28/90) as a "half-baked . . . conspiracy theory." As the media-criticism publication *Extra!* noted (11/12/90), "Robbins wasn't always negatively disposed toward the film: he had unsuccessfully petitioned the Writers Guild for a screenwriting credit." As a movie tie-in, a new edition of Robbins's book came out. "Without explanation," *Extra!* observes, "the new version of the book omitted numerous passages about CIA support for dope smugglers that appeared in Robbins's original 1979 text."

Re *Kiss the Boys Goodbye*, it is worth noting that coauthor William Stevenson is author of *A Man Called Intrepid*, perhaps the most highly respected book on intelligence ever written by an intelligence outsider. William Webster cited the book in the confirmation hearings for his current job, director of the CIA. Stevenson's point of view, while thorough and objective, has always been basically prointelligence, so for him to coauthor a book like *Kiss the Boys Goodbye* is truly astonishing, and has to make one think.

Afghan drug connection: "Afghan Rebels and Drugs," by William Vornberger, *Covert Action Information Bulletin* #28.

"You do not have to be a CIA-hater . . .": Mills, *The Underground Empire*, p. 1142.

John Kerry investigation: my interview with John Kerry; Noriega-contra-CIA links; "Made for Each Other: The Secret History of

George Bush and Manuel Noriega," by Murray Waas, *Village Voice*, 2/6/90; "Noriega Has Achieved Least-Favored-Strongman Status," by John M. Goshko, *Washington Post National Weekly Edition*, 3/7/88; see also Cockburn, *Out of Control*; "Is North Network Cocaine Connected?" by Vince Bielski and Dennis Bernstein, *In These Times*, 12/10/86; "Three Committees Track Down Smuggled Drugs, Not Smoking Gun," by Dennis Bernstein and Robert Knight, *In These Times*, 8/5/87.

Drug Tug case: *Napa Sentinel* series ran from 8/4/89 to 10/6/89, with numerous follow-up articles since, including one dated 10/13/89, just a week after the series was supposed to have ended, entitled "It Doesn't End."

History of LSD: Lee and Shlain, *Acid Dreams*; Marks, *The Search for the Manchurian Candidate*. Ronald Stark story appears on pages 279–88 of *Acid Dreams*. Speculation that LSD may have been a CIA tool to destabilize the New Left, ibid., p. 285; Burroughs quote, ibid., p. 282.

## CHAPTER 13

Origins of the CIA: Kilpatrick, *The U.S. Intelligence Community*, pp. 45–48; Corson, *The Armies of Ignorance*, pp. 289–91; Prouty, *The Secret Team*, pp. 98–104; Bledowska and Bloch, *KGB/CIA: Intelligence and Counter-Intelligence Operations*, pp. 6–16.

Truman's cloak-and-dagger party: Bledowska and Bloch, *KGB/CIA*, p. 8.

"Other functions" clause: Prouty, op. cit.

CIA charter "must remain secret . . .": Marchetti and Marks, *The CIA and the Cult of Intelligence*, p. 305.

"We are not Boy Scouts . . .": Powers, *The Man Who Kept the Secrets*, p. 159.

Olson incident: Marks, *The Search for the Manchurian Candidate*, chapter 5.

Richard Welch affair and CIA response: Agee and Wolf, *Dirty Work*, pp. 79–105 (this anthology devotes several articles to the Welch assassination, including a full transcript of a "communique" from the "November 17 Revolutionary Organization," which actually "executed" Welch, in which the assassins tell exactly how they planned and carried

out the killing—the group issued this communique in response to the vast disinformation campaign surrounding the Welch affair).

Knights of Malta: "Their Will Be Done," by Martin Lee, *Mother Jones*, 7/83.

Licio Gelli and the P2 Lodge: Yallop, *In God's Name*, pp. 129–39. 1987 indictment: Honneger, *October Surprise*, p. 231.

Bologna bombing: ibid., p. 139. Christie, *Stefano Delle Chiaie: Portrait of a Black Terrorist*, pp. 109–12.

Gelli as Knight of Malta: Baigent, Leigh, and Lincoln, *The Messianic Legacy*, p. 360 (authors note that "confirmation is now impossible" of Gelli's Knighthood, but note that his closest associate in P2 is a Knight, so it seems unlikely that the ubiquitous Gelli would neglect to join). Note that Knight of Malta Al Haig, according to the LaRouche intelligence network, played some role in actually founding P2. Gelli, incidentally, was arrested on various charges in Switzerland in 1982. He escaped capture and at last report was said to be living somewhere in South America.

Gelli at Reagan's inauguration: Yallop, *In God's Name*, pp. 359–60. Gelli relayed his offer of help to Reagan through Philip Guarino, a member of the Republican National Committee and of P2. See following note.

Guarino works for Bush: "The Republican Party and Fascists," by Russ Bellant, *Covert Action Information Bulletin* #33; speculation that Bush is a P2 member comes from Honneger, *October Surprise*, p. 240. Honneger says that her mysterious "Informant Y" told her that Bush was inaugurated into the P2 in 1976.

Mino Pecorelli killing: Yallop, *In God's Name*, p. 310.

Gelli and CIA: Yallop, *In God's Name*, pp. 131–32; Brenneke's claim that CIA funded P2 through Amatalia is from *L'Europeo*, 8/25/90. I do not have an original copy of the article, but I do have a handwritten translation that I first heard read by David Emory, 12/17/90.

Gehlen as Knight: "Their Will Be Done." The Knights awarded Gehlen their Grand Cross of Merit, the top honor a Knight can receive.

"He's on our side . . .": Simpson, *Blowback*, p. 53.

"substantial escalation of the Cold War . . .": ibid., p. 54.

Oglesby comments on Gehlen: "The Secret Treaty of Fort Hunt," by Carl Oglesby, *Covert Action Information Bulletin* #35.

CIA's recruitment of SS men: Simpson, *Blowback*; Loftus, *The Belarus Secret*; Infield, *Secrets of the SS*, chapter 15.

"An intelligence service is the ideal vehicle . . .": Wise, *The American Police State*, p. 187.

Skorzeny in Egypt, training terrorists: Infield, *Skorzeny, Hitler's Commando*, pp. 212–17.

Alois Brunner on CIA payroll: Simpson, *Blowback*, chapter 16. Brunner murders 128,500: ibid., p. 249.

Nazi links to Dulles law firm: Lisagor and Lipsius, *A Law Unto Itself*, chapter 8.

Dulles and ITT: Hougan, *Spooks*, p. 425.

CIA in the Golden Triangle: McCoy, *The Politics of Heroin in Southeast Asia*. See notes to previous chapter for numerous citations.

Gelli and P2 linked to KGB: Knight, *The Brotherhood*, chapter 27.

Skull and Bones: "Secret Society," by Steven M. L. Aronson, *Fame*, 8/89. Aronson also reveals that the Skull and Bones headquarters, seen only by initiated Bonesmen, contains "a little Nazi shrine." More on Skull and Bones in the next chapter.

CIA lie-detector exam: McGarvey, *CIA: The Myth and the Madness*, p. 161.

CIA proprietaries: Borsage and Marks, *The CIA File*. Ocean Hunter: Cockburn, *Out of Control*.

"Exxon *is* the CIA": Hougan, *Spooks*, p. 437. A Venezuelan subsidiary of Exxon called Creole was actually founded and operated by the CIA, and eventually consolidated operations with its parent company in Venezuela, thus making the CIA and Exxon indistinguishable in that country.

Speculation that Zapata is CIA linked: "Bush's Boy's Club: Skull and Bones," *Covert Action Information Bulletin* #33. Zapata was an offshore drilling company based in Houston, started by Bush. For more on Zapata, see "The Mexican Connection" by Jonathan Kwitny, *Barron's*, 9/19/88. Kwitny describes Bush's illegal involvement in an oil venture with Jorge Diaz Serrano, one of the most important figures in Mexican politics (he helped write the Mexican constitution), who in 1983 was convicted of defrauding the Mexican government of fifty-eight million dollars while in charge of Mexico's government-owned oil monopoly.

Hughes and CIA: Drosnin, *Citizen Hughes.*

CIA and S&L scandal: *Houston Post* articles by Pete Brewton (note that Brewton's series is ongoing): "S&L Probe Has Possible CIA Links," 2/4/90; "A Bank's Shadowy Demise," with sidebar "Azima No Stranger to Texas Business," 2/8/90; "Lindsay Aided S&L Probe Figure," 2/11/90; "Loan from Texas Thrift Weaves a Tale of Deceit," (note that this article connects the demise of Silverado Savings and Loan, which implicated George Bush's son Neil, to alleged CIA operatives); "Attorney Linked to S&L Crisis Has Ties to CIA, Mafia Figures," 4/4/90; "FBI Points to Insider Fraud as Big Factor in S&L Crisis," 4/12/90.

Other sources on CIA/S&L connection: (note that most other sources rely heavily on Brewton's articles) "Bankrolling Iran-Contra," by John Whalen, San Jose *Metro*, 2/22/90; "Did CIA Raid the S&L's," by Joel Bleifuss, *Los Angeles Reader*, 4/27/90; "Ripoff Savings and Loan of Colorado," with sidebar "Did They Get a Free Toaster, Too?," by Brian Abas, Denver *Westword*, 4/18/90; "S&L Crisis Tied to Mob," by Dave Armstrong, San Pedro *Random Lengths*, 3/15/90; "The Great S&L Robbery," by Dave Armstrong, *Ramdom Lengths*, 4/12/90; "Savings and Loan Sharks," by John Whalen, *Metro*, 5/24/90; "Consensus of Silence?," by Joel Bleifuss, Detroit *Metro Times*, 5/23/90; "Loan Star State," by Joel Bleifuss, *In These Times*, 5/2/90; "Beltway Bandits," by David Corn, *The Nation*, 5/7/90; "The Mob, the CIA and the S&L Scandal," by Steve Weinberg, *Columbia Journalism Review*, 11–12/90; "Cash and Carry: The Banks and the CIA" with sidebar "Who's Spookin' Who? A Cast of Characters," by Paul Muolo and Stephen Pizzo, *Penthouse*, 10/90. See also Pizzo, Muolo, and Fricker, *Inside Job: The Looting of America's Savings and Loans* (book doesn't cover CIA connections, but it's the definitive work on organized crime involvement in the S&L scandal, which appears to be just one step removed from CIA involvement).

Nugan Hand Bank: Kwitny, *The Crimes of Patriots.*

A good history of CIA's foreign intervention is Blum, *CIA: a Forgotten History.*

"Black International," name: Sterling, *The Terror Network*, p. 1. Sterling's book promotes the thesis that the Kremlin is the prime mover behind world terrorism. It became the Bible of the Reagan Administra-

tion's terrorism policy. Ironically, on the first page, Sterling acknowledges right-wing terrorism, but dismisses it as a subject she simply chose not to focus on.

Skorzeny, Barbie, Genoud involved in founding right-wing terrorist movement: "Killers on the Right," by Martin Lee and Kevin Coogan, *Mother Jones*, 5/87.

Skorzeny and Palestinian terrorism: Infield, *Skorzeny: Hitler's Commando*, pp. 212–17.

Ali Hassan Salameh: Livingstone and Levy, *Inside the PLO*, pp. 110–12.

Pan Am 103 bombing and CIA connection: much information comes from the Interfor report itself, most of which is in my files, and Johnston, *Lockerbie: The Tragedy of Flight 103*, chapters 4 and 10; characterization of Interfor report as "spitball" is from Emerson and Duffy, *The Fall of Pan Am 103*, a book that, though it contains much useful information, appears to be based almost exclusively on unnamed intelligence and law-enforcement sources and so can't be considered reliable with regard to CIA involvement.

Other sources on Pan Am 103/CIA connection: (most based heavily on Interfor report) "Lawmaker Links Arms Dealer to Bombing of Pan Am Jet," by Frank Greve and Aaron Epstein, *San Jose Mercury-News*, 11/4/89 (first public mention of Interfor report); "Pan Am Blames CIA for Airline Bomb Plot," by John Picton, *Toronto Star*, 11/12/89; "CIA Downs Jet to Protect Drug Pipeline," by Erick Anderson, San Pedro *Random Lengths*, 11/15/89; "Flight 103: The Other Story," by Erick Anderson, *San Francisco Bay Guardian*, 11/6/89; "The Bombing of Pan Am 103," by Jeff Jones, *Covert Action Information Bulletin* #34; "Unwitting Accomplices?," by Maggie Mahar, *Barron's* 12/17/90.

There are interesting parallels between the Pan Am 103 bombing and the crash on December 12, 1985, of an Arrow Air charter jet carrying 248 American servicemen and eight flight crew members (all 256 died), in Gander, Newfoundland. Though a terrorist group claimed immediate credit for bombing the plane, the official cause was listed as "ice on the wings." However, recent revelations suggest that "ice" may have been the Lee Harvey Oswald of this murder. In fact, it appears the plane was bombed. Furthermore, Arrow Air turns out to be a CIA airline (if not owned by the CIA, it was regularly used by them), which shipped arms to the contras as part of the Iran-Contra affair. The cover-up of the

bombing, then, would become part of the Iran-Contra cover-up, as would the Pan Am 103 bombing if the Interfor report is credible. See "Crash, Burn, Cover-up," by Joe Conason, *Details*, 12/90; possible bombing was revealed on ABC News *20/20* of 10/13/89.

The allegation that P2 was behind the bombing was read over the air by David Emory, 12/17/90. I don't have a copy of what he was reading.

Bush phones Thatcher: "The Bombing of Pan Am 103"; Bernt Carlsson on board: ibid.

Secord-Shackley-Wilson connections: see Chapter 9.

Gelli and Delle Chiaie: Christie, *Stefano Delle Chiaie: Portrait of a Black Terrorist*, pp. 110–13, 162–63.

Operation Gladio, media coverage and involvement in Moro killing: "Press Clips: Gladio Tiding," by Doug Ireland, *Village Voice*, 11/27/90.

"Black International" summit: Sterling, *The Terror Network*, p. 115.

Links between left and right terrorists, "third position": "Killers on the Right". Jacques Verges background: ibid. Odifried Hepp background, connection to *Achille Lauro* hijackers: ibid.

## CHAPTER 14

"I owed Richard Nixon . . .": Bush's autobiography *Looking Forward* quoted in "A Bush Bestiary," by Joe Conason, *San Francisco Bay Guardian*, 12/14/88.

The former CIA operative is Richard Brenneke. A transcript of his testimony is in my files. Brenneke was later tried for perjury for making his accusation against Bush. He was found not guilty.

Bush resigns from the CFR: Silk and Silk, *The American Establishment*, p. 220.

Bush wanted to work for Carter: "A Carter Connection?," by Don Shannon, *Los Angeles Times*, 5/7/88.

Intelligence operatives in Bush campaign: "Agents for Bush," by Bob Callahan, *Covert Action Information Bulletin* #33.

The Neil Bush–Scott Hinckley dinner date was widely reported. It is noted in Honneger, *October Surprise*, p. 244. Honneger notes a series

of odd circumstances around the Reagan assassination attempt, including the fact that Hinckley once belonged to an American pro-Khomeni "Islamic Guerilla Army."

Neil Bush's involvement with the Silverado Savings and Loan failure was a major story in 1990. A good summary, including Bush (both Neil and George) and Sun-Flo appears in "S&L Crisis Tied to Mob," cited in Chapter 13 notes; see also, "Neil Bush's Insider Deals," by James Ridgeway, *Village Voice*, 10/2/90.

Casey convinced Reagan to choose Bush: "Agents for Bush," by Bob Callahan, *Covert Action Information Bulletin* #33.

"Casey Investing Again": from a *Newsweek* article of 10/10/83 cited in Johnson, *Shootdown*, p. 115.

Bush/Casey study group: "Agents for Bush."

Skull and Bones: "Secret Society," by Steven Aronson, *Fame*, 8/89; "Skull and Bones," *Covert Action Information Bulletin* #33; Rosenbaum, *Travels With Dr. Death and Other Unusual Investigations*, pp. 375–395.

William Bundy quote: ibid.

"a sinister, unhealthy offshoot . . .": "Secret Society."

Skull and Bones initiations: ibid.; "Yale Society Resists Peeks into Its Crypt," by David W. Dunlap, *New York Times*, 11/4/88.

Bush confesses to Bonesmen: "Bush Opened Up to Secret Yale Society," by Bob Woodward and Walter Pincus, *Washington Post*, 8/7/88.

"Mr. George Bush of the CIA" memo and subsequent denial: " '63 Bush CIA Link Reported," *New York Times*, 7/11/88, and "Doubts Are Raised in Report on Bush, '63 Memo Seen as Case of Mistaken Identity," *New York Times*, 7/21/88.

"What the fuck do you know . . .": "Company Man," by Scott Armstrong and Jeff Nason, *Mother Jones*, 10/88.

Bush/Colby strategy: ibid.

Crimes allegedly covered up by Bush at CIA: ibid.

Felix Rodriguez and Che Guevara: Rodriguez, *Shadow Warrior*.

Violation of Ford order: "Bush: Covering Up for the CIA," by John Kelly, *San Francisco Bay Guardian*, 12/14/88.

Bush appoints Shackley: "Company Man."

For more on Christic Institute's lawsuit and "The Enterprise," see Chapter Nine.

The best concise summary of the widely reported relationship between Bush and Noriega that I have seen is "Made for Each Other," by Murray Waas, *Village Voice*, 2/6/90. Among other salient details, Waas notes that in 1988, when the Reagan administration was calling for Noriega to resign, Bush told Noriega that he could stay in office until May 1989. Noriega took this as a signal that the U.S. government's call for him to step down was not sincere.

Bush's office in arms-for-drugs operation: "The Dirty Secrets of George Bush," by Howard Kohn and Vicki Monks, *Rolling Stone*, 11/3/88. Rodriguez denial: *Shadow Warrior*.

"Bush by the balls": "The Dirty Secrets of George Bush."

Three million dollars for anti-Noriega operations: "New CIA Plot Reported to Overthrow Noriega," by Robin Wright, *San Francisco Chronicle* (from *Los Angeles Times*), 11/16/89.

"It was an attempt to tick them off . . .": "Flawed Intelligence Let Noriega Escape," by John M. Broder and Robin Wright, *San Jose Mercury-News* (from *Los Angeles Times*), 12/21/89. Almost a year to the day after that *Los Angeles Times* story ran, the *Times* ran another story, "Some Blame Rogue Band of Marines for Picking Fight, Spurring Panama Invasion," by Kenneth Freed, 12/22/90. The story describes "a pattern of aggressive behavior" by a supposedly free-lance group of marines calling themselves "The Hard Chargers," who intentionally provoked Panamanian soldiers. Though the "Hard Chargers" are predictably labeled "rogue," and the entire story was denied by the Pentagon, it could serve to further confirm that the invasion was planned well in advance. Bush simply needed a pretext to put the plan into action.

New Panama government's corruption: "Panama Is Still Besieged by Corruption," by Jack Anderson, *San Francisco Chronicle* (syndicated column), 6/25/90; see also "Press Clips/Jingo Bells," by Doug Ireland, *Village Voice*, 1/2/90. Ireland points out that Panama's American-backed president Guillermo Endara "served for 10 years as a top aide to Arnulfo Arias Madrid, who was three times elected (and three times deposed—by the U.S.) as president of Panama. Arias . . . was identified in 1940 as a 'fascist' by U.S. intelligence reports, which said he had 'reached some understanding with the Rome-Berlin axis.' " Ireland further notes that Endara's former boss, while president, "promulgated racial laws, including one expelling all West Indians. His support came

from 'the oligarchies with fascist tendencies' and from the new antiblack class."

"Heritage Council": "The Republican Party and Fascists," by Russ Bellant, *Covert Action Information Bulletin #33*.

Scowcroft and Eagleburger's Kissinger ties: "Nominee Discloses Consulting Income," by Jeff Gerth, *New York Times*, 3/9/89; "Scowcroft Tells of Private Income," *New York Times* (from Associated Press), 3/15/89.

Took orders from Kissinger: "Company Man."

Prescott Bush's business with China: "Firm That Employs Bush's Brother Stands to Benefit from China Deal," by Jim Mann and Douglas Frantz, *Los Angeles Times*, 12/13/89.

Bush and Iraq: "U.S. Oil Plot Fueled Saddam," by Helga Graham, London *Observer*, 10/21/90.

Peter Dale Scott story: "Project Censored," by Craig McLaughlin, *Syracuse New Times* (from *San Francisco Bay Guardian*), 7/27/88. The article states that Peter Dale Scott "filed a December 21, 1987 Pacific News Service Story that alleged that Vice-President George Bush, a former Texas oilman, actively promoted the Iran-Contra drugs-for-arms deal . . . to stabilize falling oil prices by developing a pricing agreement between the United States and other oil-producing countries, Iran included."

Bush pre-war policy toward Iraq: "How America Lost Kuwait," by Murray Waas, San Jose *Metro*, 1/24/91.

Hewlett-Packard sells to Iraq: "The H-P Connection," by Jonathan Vankin, San Jose *Metro*, 1/24/90.

## CHAPTER 15

Rockefeller sale to Mitsubishi: "Philanthropy for the 21st Century," *New York Times*, 11/5/89.

Rockefeller's defense of Trilateral Commission: "Foolish Attacks on False Issues," by David Rockefeller, *Wall Street Journal*, 4/30/80.

Kissinger/Bundy feud: Silk and Silk, *The American Establishment*, pp. 218–19.

"If conspiracy means that these men . . .": "Who Rules America," by G. William Domhoff, in Horowitz, ed., *Corporations and the Cold War*.

In the world of David Rockefeller . . .": *Bill Moyers Journal*, Public Broadcasting System, 2/7/80.

"The peace and prosperity of the Trilateral world . . .": "The Grey/Lurid World of the Trilateral Commission," by Richard Brookhiser, *National Review*, 11/13/81.

Carter and Trilateralists: "Jimmy Carter and the Trilateralists: Presidential Roots," by Laurence H. Shoup, in Sklar, ed., *Trilateralism*.

Hamilton Jordan quote: reprinted in *Trilateralism*, p. 89.

Vance and Brzezinski background: "Who's Who on the Trilateral Commission," by Holly Sklar and Ross Everdell, in *Trilateralism*.

Collective management of interdependence: "Trilateralism: Managing Dependence and Democracy," by Holly Sklar, in *Trilateralism*.

Anti-Rockefeller demonstrations: Sklar, *Reagan Trilateralism and the Neoliberals*, p. 11.

History of the Bilderbergers: "Bilderberg and the West," by Peter Thompson, in *Trilateralism*.

Lockheed scandal: Hougan, *Spooks*, chapter 13.

History of the CFR: Schulzinger, *The Wise Men of Foreign Affairs*, pp. 2–3.

CFR membership: "An Elite Group on U.S. Policy Is Diversifying," by Richard Bernstein, *New York Times*, 10/30/82.

Casey rejection and subsequent joining of CFR: Woodward, *Veil*, p. 19.

Other CIA directors on CFR: *Trilateralism*, p. 173.

CIA reveals touchy information: Marchetti and Marks, *The CIA and the Cult of Intelligence*, p. 267. Discussing a speech to the CFR in 1968 by CIA Clandestine Services Chief Richard Bissell, Marchetti and Marks note, "When the agency has needed prominent citizens to front for its proprietary companies it has often turned to Council members."

Kissinger on "limited" nuclear war": Kissinger, *Nuclear Weapons and Foreign Policy*, pp. 174–202.

Kissinger sneaking out documents: Hersh, *The Price of Power*, p. 479.

Sklar on Rockefeller family, family's investments: *Trilateralism*, pp. 53–55.

Rockefeller's quotes from his testimony at confirmation hearings.

"If the Illuminati begat . . .": Wilgus, *The Illuminoids*, p. 142.

"Perhaps the most accurate overview . . .": McAlpine, *The Occult Technology of Power*, p. 50.

## CHAPTER 16

Urban design of Washington, D.C., based on Masonic principles: Baigent and Leigh, *The Temple and the Lodge*, figure 36 and p. 262.

Russian Skoptski: Daraul, *A History of Secret Societies*, chapter 8.

Templar as bankers: Robinson, *Born in Blood*, pp. 74–77. Robinson says that the term "banking" doesn't quite fit the Templars. He prefers "financial services." But the Templars took money for deposit, loaned money for a fee, issued paper money, and maintained trusts, according to Robinson. While they may not have been "bankers" in the strict, twentieth-century meaning of the word, it seems to me an appropriate description.

Disraeli quote: this is the conspiracy buff's favorite quotation, cited in numerous sources. I culled it from McAlpine, *The Occult Technology of Power*.

History of the Illuminati: Robison, *Proofs of a Conspiracy*; Wilgus, *The Illuminoids*; Wilson, *Cosmic Trigger*; Howard, *The Occult Conspiracy*; Johnson, *Architects of Fear*. The strange bit about Heinz's "57 Varieties" is in Adams, *The Straight Dope*, pp. 196–97. "Fnord" in the *New York Times* is from Robert Shea and Robert Anton Wilson's novel, *The Illuminatus! Trilogy*, intended in jest, of course. Isn't it?

Comte de Mirabeau: Howard, *The Occult Conspiracy*, p. 64.

Hyam Maccoby's views on human sacrifice in the Bible, explication of Cain and Abel story: Tierney, *The Highest Altar*, chapter 21.

Rituals of mystery religion: described throughout Burkert, *Ancient Mystery Cults*; Howard, *The Occult Conspiracy*, chapter 1.

Masonic "third-degree" initiation is described firsthand in Campbell-Everden, *Freemasonry and Its Etiquette*, pp. 222–33; see also Baigent and Leigh, *The Temple and the Lodge*, pp. 124–31.

Abiff as Osiris: *The Occult Conspiracy*, p. 15.

Solomon's temple as tribute to Astarte: *The Temple and the Lodge*, p. 126; Solomon is identified as a "follower" of Astarte at 1 Kings 9:4–5. Note also that Tyre, home of Hiram, was a center of goddess worship. At 1 Kings 3:3, Solomon is said to follow Yahweh, "except that he offered

sacrifice and incense on the high places." Howard, in *the Occult Conspiracy* (p. 8), says that the "high places" were traditionally used for sacrifice to the goddess figure. 2 Kings 23 tells how the priest Hilkiah destroyed all the goddess shrines throughout the kingdom, and how King Josiah "desecrated" the high places "which Solomon king of Israel had built for Astarte" and for several other pagan gods.

The Lazarus theory is from Baigent, Leigh, and Lincoln, *Holy Blood, Holy Grail*, pp. 338–44.

Parallels to Jesus: Graham, *Deceptions and Myths of the Bible*, pp. 287–90.

Cult of Attis in Tarsus: Howard, *The Highest Altar*, pp. 441–42.

Jesus as political revolutionary: Schonfield, *The Passover Plot*.

Grail as Shroud of Turin: Currer-Briggs, *The Shroud and the Grail*.

Grail myth as pagan, early "Grail Romances": *Holy Blood, Holy Grail*, pp. 285–303; Matthews and Stewart, *Warriors of Arthur*, pp. 19–21.

Troyes as center of occultism, origin city of Templars: *Holy Blood, Holy Grail*, pp. 87–88.

Destruction of Templars: Robinson, *Born in Blood*, chapter 9; Baigent and Leigh, *The Temple and the Lodge*, chapter 3.

Grail and Celtic head-hunting: Stewart, *Warriors of Arthur*, p. 61.

Jesus substitution on the cross in Gnostic gospels: *The Second Treatise of the Great Seth*, in Robinson, ed., *The Nag Hammadi Library*, p. 365 (this book identifies Simon as the one who actually "bore the cross on his shoulder" and presumably was nailed up in Jesus's place); in Koran: 4:157.

Melding of the Templars into Scottish Freemasons under the protection of Robert Bruce is the theme of both *Born in Blood* and *The Temple and the Lodge*.

Franklin and the "Hell Fire Club": *The Occult Conspiracy*, pp. 78–80.

With regards to the Masonic origins of the U.S., I have always found it ironic that fundamentalist Christians claim that our founding fathers were devout Christians. Christian conspiracy theorists—Joseph Carr, for example (author of *The Lucifer Connection* and *The Twisted Cross*)—see Masonry as an arm of a satanic conspiracy. If Masonry is satanic, then the U.S. is a satanic country.

Masons in the American revolutionary war: *The Temple and the Lodge*, chapter 18.

American Masonry circa 1820s: Formisano, *The Transformation of Political Culture: Massachusetts Parties, 1790's–1840's*, chapter 9.

Reagan Masonic ceremony: *Born in Blood*, p. 325.

Roosevelt in "Ancient Arabic Order": *The Occult Conspiracy*, 92–93.

Ku Klux Klan, Masonic origins: *Born in Blood*, p. 328.

Peasant's revolt backed by "Great Society": ibid., chapters 1–2.

"Secrecy and political power . . .": Bok, *Secrets*, p. 106.

## CHAPTER 17

Nazi myths of Aryan origins: Sklar, *Nazis and the Occult*, chapters 2–3.

Order of New Templars and subsequent proto-Nazi occult groups: ibid.; Howard, *The Occult Conspiracy*, chapter 5.

*Ostara* magazine and psychosexual racism: *Nazis and the Occult*, pp. 17–19.

List adopts founds *Armanen*, adopts swastika: ibid., p. 22.

Thule Society, myths and origins: ibid., chapter 4; *The Occult Conspiracy*, pp. 124–28; Schwarzwaller, *The Unknown Hitler*, pp. 54–55.

Hitler as intelligence agent, possible Thule connection: *The Unknown Hitler*, pp. 52–55.

Dietrich Eckart's character, influence on Hitler: ibid., 56–60. "Follow Hitler! He will dance . . .": ibid., p. 60.

Hitler's crackdown on occultists as cover-up of Hess flight: *The Occult Conspiracy*, p. 137. Hess, Ian Fleming, and Aleister Crowley, their relationship to British intelligence: ibid., pp. 133–37.

"We find it difficult to believe . . .": Pauwels and Bergier, *Morning of the Magicians*, p. 179; "This truth was hidden . . .": ibid., p. 180.

Operation Paperclip is chronicled in Bower, *The Paperclip Conspiracy*.

Wealthy financiers of the Thule Society: Pool and Pool, *Who Financed Hitler*, chapter 1. "It is even partly true . . .": ibid., p. 2. Hitler and Henry Ford: ibid., chapter 3. Rosenberg and Deterding: ibid., p. 319.

"Sullivan and Cromwell thrived . . .": Lisagor and Lipsius, *A Law unto Itself*, p. 125. Dulles using "Heil Hitler" salutation and writing pro-Nazi article for *Atlantic*: ibid., p. 132.

Sosthenes Behn's Nazi links, arranging of Westrick visit: Sampson, *The Sovereign State of ITT*, chapter 2; Hougan, *Spooks*, chapter 12.

Himmler's recruitment of SS members and subsequent purge: Hohne, *The Order of the Death's Head*, pp. 156–62. Wewelsburg Castle: ibid., pp. 172–74.

Multinationals as instruments of foreign policy: Hougan, *Spooks*, p. 427.

"The oligarchs of agricultural kingdoms . . .": Gross, *Friendly Fascism*, p. 54.

For an excellent overview of contemporary American neo-nazism, see "The American Neo-Nazi Movement Today," by Elinor Langer, *The Nation*, 7/16/90. Background on the Identity Church: "The Identity Movement and Its 'Real Jew' Claim," by Michael D'Antonio, *The Alicia Patterson Report*, Spring 1988.

Background on Manson's satanism: Sanders, *The Family*, chapter 3.

Process Church: Terry, *The Ultimate Evil*, chapter 9. Terry's book has the thesis that the Process was the ultimate force behind the Son of Sam murders; see also Lyons, *Satan Wants You*, pp. 88–92.

"Squeaky" Fromme hired to kill Ford: Milan, *The Squad*, pp. 285–90.

Michael Aquino and possible military links to satanic mind control: *Satan Wants You*, chapter 9; Raschke, *Painted Black*, chapter 7.

Bacon quoted in Bok, *Secrets*, p. 172.


## Conclusion

"no single, central conspiracy": Gross, *Friendly Fascism*, p. 58.

AIDS as biowarfare conspiracy theories are quite prevalent: see Rappoport, *AIDS Inc.*, chapter 26, for an overview; see also "Is AIDS Non-Infectious? The Possibility and Its CBW Implications," by Nathaniel S. Lehrman, *Covert Action Information Bulletin* #28.

Loftus speculation on Nazi link to Lyme disease: Loftus, *The Belarus Secret*, p. xvii.

For background on eugenics-origins of IQ testing, see Chorover, *From Genesis to Genocide*.

Pellagra cover-up: ibid., p. 47.

Bush envoys sent to China: "Earlier Secret Trip was Made to China," by Owen Ullmann, *San Jose Mercury-News*, 12/19/89.

Sulzberger prints CIA press release: Lee and Solomon, *Unreliable Sources*, p. 116.

CIA blowback in Sterling's book: Woodward, *Veil*, pp. 130–31.

Internal White House "propaganda" memorandum: *Unreliable Sources*, p. 135. The memo is addressed to Pat Buchanan, the syndicated columnist who was then Reagan's Director of Communications, from someone in the State Department's "Office of Public Diplomacy." The OPD was, despite its obfuscating name, a full-blown domestic propaganda operation, which the General Accounting Office concluded in 1987 was engaged in "prohibited, covert propaganda activities." The subject of the memo to Buchanan is " 'White Propaganda' Campaign." "White" propaganda means the undisguised placement of government propaganda in the media. For example, op-ed pieces in the *New York Times* signed by government officials (or, as in the example noted in the memo, contra leaders). "Black" propaganda is the covert placement of propaganda; for example, keeping "legitimate" journalists on a secret CIA payroll would be a "black propaganda" operation.

"large number of Americans . . .": Johnson, *Architects of Fear*, p. 12.

"Sham gives rise . . .": Henry, *On Sham, Vulnerability and Other Forms of Self Destruction*, p. 123.

"I anticipate a geometric increase in madness . . .": *ibid.*, p. 124.

"cannot live in the comfortable, insulated world . . .": Wilson, *The Outsider*, p. 15.

# Bibliography

## Note on the Bibliography

This bibliography contains full citations of books cited in the notes or consulted in preparation of this book. The notes section contains only abbreviated citations. Not listed here are the many articles from newspapers and periodicals from which I drew information. Those are cited in full in the notes. Also not listed are the interviews I conducted. Those from which I took direct quotations are cited in the notes. Others remain as background.

Adams, Cecil. *The Straight Dope*. New York: Ballantine, 1986.

Agee, Philip and Lewis Wolf, eds. *Dirty Work: The CIA in Western Europe*. Secaucus, NJ: Lyle Stuart, 1978.

Allen, Gary. *None Dare Call It Conspiracy*. Rossmoor, CA: Concord Press, 1972.

_____. *Say "No" to the New World Order*. Seal Beach, CA: Concord Press, 1987.

Anderson, Jon and Scott Anderson. *Inside the League*. New York: Dodd, Mead and Co., 1986.

Anderson, Malcolm. *Policing the World*. Oxford: Clarendon Press, 1989.

Anti-Defamation League of B'nai B'rith. *Extremism on the Right: A Handbook*. New York: Anti-Defamation League of B'nai B'rith, 1988.

_____. *Hate Groups in America*. New York, 1988.

Ashe, Geoffrey. *The Discovery of King Arthur*. New York: Henry Holt and Co., 1985.

Bagdikian, Ben. *The Media Monopoly, Second Edition*. Boston: Beacon Press, 1987.

Baigent, Michael and Richard Leigh. *The Temple and the Lodge*. New York: Arcade, 1989.

Baigent, Michael, Richard Leigh and Henry Lincoln. *Holy Blood, Holy Grail*. New York: Dell, 1983.

_____. *The Messianic Legacy*. New York: Dell, 1989.

Bain, Donald. *The Control of Candy Jones*. Chicago: Playboy Press, 1976.

Balsiger, David and Charles Sellier. *The Lincoln Conspiracy*. Los Angeles: Shick Sunn Classic Books, 1977.

Bennett, David. *The Party of Fear*. New York: Vintage Books, 1990.

Bennis, Warren and Ian Mitroff. *The Unreality Industry*. New York: Birch Lane Press, 1989.

Birmingham, Stephen. *America's Secret Aristocracy*. New York: Berkley Books, 1990.

Black, Bob and Adam Parfrey, eds. *Rants and Incendiary Tracts*. New York: Amok Press, 1989.

Bledowska, Celina and Jonathan Bloch. *KGB/CIA: Intelligence and Counter-Intelligence Operations*. New York: Exeter Books, 1987.

Blum, William. *CIA: A Forgotten History*. London and New Jersey: Zed Books, 1986.

Blumenthal, Sid and Harvey Yazitian. *Government by Gunplay*. New York: New American Library, 1976.

Bok, Sissela. *Secrets*. New York: Vintage Books, 1984.

Borosage, Robert and John Marks, eds. *The CIA File*. New York: Grossman Publishers, 1976.

Bowart, Walter. *Operation Mind Control*. New York: Dell, 1978.

Bower, Tom. *The Paperclip Conspiracy*. Boston: Little, Brown and Co., 1987.

Bramley, William. *The Gods of Eden*. San Jose, CA: Dahlin Family Press, 1990.

Bressler, Fenton. *Who Killed John Lennon?* New York: St. Martin's Press, 1989.

Bunzel, John. *Anti-Politics in America*. New York: Vintage Books, 1970.

Burkert, Walter. *Ancient Mystery Cults*. Cambridge, MA: Harvard University Press, 1987.

Calic, Edouard, ed. *Secret Conversations with Hitler*. New York: John Day and Co., 1971.

Campbell-Everden, William. *Freemasonry and Its Etiquette*. New York: Weathervane Books, 1978.

Chorover, Stephan. *From Genesis to Genocide*. Cambridge, MA: MIT Press, 1980.

Christie, Stuart. *Stefano Delle Chiaie: Portrait of a Black Terrorist*. London: Refract Publications, 1984.

Coates, James. *Armed and Dangerous: The Rise of the Survivalist Right*. New York: Noonday Press, 1987.

Cockburn, Leslie. *Out of Control*. New York: Atlantic Monthly Press, 1987.

Collier, Kenneth and James Collier. *Votescam*. Unpublished manuscript.

Commission to Investigate Human Rights Violations. *Railroad!* Washington, DC: Commission to Investigate Human Rights Violations, 1989.

Corson, William. *The Armies of Ignorance: The Rise of the American Intelligence Empire*. New York: Dial Press, 1977.

Curran, Douglas. *In Advance of the Landing: Folk Concepts of Outer Space*. New York: Abbeville Press, 1985.

Currer-Briggs, Noel. *The Shroud and the Grail*. New York: St. Martin's Press, 1987.

Daraul, Arkon. *A History of Secret Societies*. Secaucus, NJ: Citadel Press, 1961.

Drosnin, Michael. *Citizen Hughes*. New York: Bantam Books, 1986.

Dudman, Richard. *Men of the Far Right*. New York: Pyramid Books, 1962.

Dugger, Ronnie. *Reagan: The Man and His Presidency*. New York: McGraw-Hill, 1983.

Ellul, Jacques. *Propaganda: The Formation of Men's Attitudes*. New York: Vintage Books, 1983.

Emerson, Steven and Brian Duffy. *The Fall of Pan Am 103*. New York: Putnam, 1990.

Epstein, Edward Jay. *Counterplot*. New York: Viking, 1969.

Erickson, Paul, ed. *Reagan Speaks*. New York: New York University Press, 1985.

Flammonde, Paris. *The Kennedy Conspiracy*. New York: The Meredith Press, 1969.

Foomer, Michael. *Interpol*. New York: Plenum Press, 1989.

Fort, Charles. *The Book of the Damned*. New York: Ace Books, 1941.

Furneaux, Rupert. *Ancient Mysteries*. New York: Ballantine Books, 1978.

Garrison, Jim. *On the Trail of the Assassins*. New York: Sheridan Square Press, 1988.

Good, Timothy. *Above Top Secret: The Worldwide UFO Cover Up*. New York: Quill, 1988.

Graham, Lloyd. *Deceptions and Myths of the Bible*. New York: Citadel Press, 1975.

Greider, William. *Secrets of the Temple: How the Federal Reserve Runs the Country*. New York: Touchstone, 1987.

Groden, Robert and Harrison Livingstone. *High Treason*. Baltimore: The Conservatory Press, 1989.

Gross, Betram. *Friendly Fascism*. New York: M. Evans and Co., 1980.

Harris, Robert and Jeremy Paxman. *A Higher Form of Killing: The Secret Story of Chemical and Biological Warfare*. New York: Hill and Wang, 1982.

Henry, Jules. *On Sham, Vulnerability and Other Forms of Self-Destruction.* New York: Vintage Books, 1973.

Hersh, Seymour. *The Price of Power.* New York: Summit Books, 1983.

Hoffman, Lance. *Making Every Vote Count.* Washington, DC: George Washington University, 1988.

Hohne, Heinz. *The Order of the Death's Head.* New York: Ballantine Books, 1971.

Honey, Martha and Tony Ayrigan. *La Penca: Report of an Investigation.* Washington, DC: The Christic Institute, 1988.

Honneger, Barbara. *October Surprise.* New York and Los Angeles: Tudor Publishing Co., 1989.

Horowitz, David, ed. *Corporations and the Cold War.* New York: Monthly Review Press, 1969.

Hougan, Jim. *Spooks.* New York: Bantam Books, 1978.

Howard, Michael. *The Occult Conspiracy.* Rochester, VT: Destiny Books, 1989.

Infield, Glenn. *Secrets of the SS.* New York: Jove Books, 1990.

_____. *Skorzeny: Hitler's Commando.* New York: Military Heritage Press, 1981.

James, Rosemary and Jack Wardlaw. *Plot or Politics?* New Orleans: Pelican Publishing House, 1967.

Jensen-Stevenson, Monica and William Stevenson. *Kiss the Boys Goodbye.* New York: Dutton Books, 1990.

Johnson, George. *Architects of Fear: Conspiracy Theories and Political Paranoia.* Los Angeles: Jeremy P. Tarcher, Inc., 1983.

Johnson, R. W. *Shootdown: Flight 007 and the American Connection.* New York: Penguin Books, 1987.

Johnston, David. *Lockerbie: The Tragedy of Flight 103.* New York: St. Martin's Press, 1989.

Jones, Alexander, ed. *The Jerusalem Bible: Reader's Edition.* Garden City, NY: Doubleday and Co., 1968.

Keel, John. *Disneyland of the Gods.* New York: Amok Press, 1988.

_____. *UFOs: Operation Trojan Horse.* New York: G.P. Putnam's and Son's, 1970.

Kilduff, Marshall and Ron Javers. *The Suicide Cult.* New York: Bantam Books, 1978.

King, Dennis. *Lyndon LaRouche and the New American Fascism.* New York: Doubleday, 1989.

Kirkpatrick, Lyman. *The U.S. Intelligence Community: Foreign Policy and Domestic Activities.* New York: Hill and Wang, 1973.

Kissinger, Henry. *Nuclear Weapons and Foreign Policy*. New York: Council on Foreign Relations, 1957.

Knight, Stephen. *The Brotherhood: The Secret World of the Freemasons*. New York: Dorset Press, 1986.

————. *Jack the Ripper: The Final Solution*. Chicago: Academy Chicago Publishers, 1986.

Krause, Charles. *Guyana Massacre: The Eyewitness Account*. New York: Berkley Books, 1978.

Kwitny, Jonathan. *The Crimes of Patriots*. New York: Touchstone Books, 1988.

LaRouche, Lyndon. *The Power of Reason: A Kind of Autobiography*. New York: New Benjamin Franklin House, 1979.

————. *There Are No Limits to Growth*. New York: New Benjamin Franklin House, 1983.

Lee, Martin and Bruce Shlain. *Acid Dreams*. New York: Grove Press, 1985.

Lee, Martin and Norman Solomon. *Unreliable Sources: A Guide to Detecting Bias in News Media*. New York: Lyle Stuart, 1990.

Lifton, David. *Best Evidence: Disguise and Deception in the Assassination of John F. Kennedy*. New York: Carroll and Graf, 1988.

Lisagor, Nancy and Frank Lipsius. *A Law unto Itself: The Untold Story of the Law Firm Sullivan and Cromwell*. New York: Paragon House, 1989.

Livingstone, Neil and David Levy. *Inside the PLO*. New York: William Morrow and Co., 1990.

Loftus, John. *The Belarus Secret*. New York: Paragon House, 1989.

Lyons, Arthur. *Satan Wants You*. New York: Mysterious Press, 1989.

Mader, Julius. *Who's Who in the CIA*. Berlin: Julius Mader, 1968.

Malaclypse the Younger. *Principia Discordia*. Port Townsend, WA: Loompanics Unlimited.

Marchetti, Victor and John Marks. *The CIA and the Cult of Intelligence*. New York: Dell, 1975.

Marks, John. *The Search for the "Manchurian Candidate."* New York: Dell, 1979.

Matthews, John and Bob Stewart. *Warriors of Arthur*. London: Blandford Press, 1987.

McAlpine, Peter. *The Occult Technology of Power*. Port Townsend, WA: Loompanics Unlimited (reprinted from Alpine Enterprises, 1974).

McCoy, Alfred W. *The Politics of Heroin in Southeast Asia*. New York: Harper and Row, 1972.

McGarvey, Patrick. *CIA: The Myth and the Madness*. Baltimore: Penguin Books, 1972.

McManus, John. *The Insiders*. Belmont, MA: John Birch Society, 1983.

Messick, Hank. *John Edgar Hoover*. New York: David McKay Company, 1972.

Milan, Michael. *The Squad: The U.S. Government's Secret Alliance with Organized Crime*. New York: Shapolsky Publishers, 1990.

Miller, Nathan. *Spying for America*. New York: Paragon House, 1989.

Mills, James. *The Underground Empire*. New York: Dell, 1987.

Moldea, Dan. *Dark Victory: Ronald Reagan, MCA and the Mob*. New York: Penguin Books, 1987.

Moore, Alan and Bill Sienkiewicz. *Brought to Light*. Forestville, CA: Eclipse Books, 1989.

Moyers, Bill. *The Secret Government*. Washington, DC: Seven Locks Press, 1988.

Nash, Jay Robert. *Citizen Hoover*. Chicago: Nelson Hall, 1972.

Ouides, Bruce, ed. *From: The President: Richard Nixon's Secret Files*. New York: Perennial Library, 1990.

Pagels, Elaine. *The Gnostic Gospels*. New York: Vintage Books, 1979.

Parfrey, Adam, ed. *Apocalypse Culture*. New York: Amok Press, 1987.

Pauwels, Louis and Jacques Bergier. *The Morning of the Magicians*. New York: Dorset Press, 1988.

Pizzo, Stephen, Paul Muolo and Mary Fricker. *Inside Job: The Looting of America's Savings and Loans*. New York: McGraw Hill, 1989.

Pool, James and Suzanne Pool. *Who Financed Hitler?* New York: The Dial Press, 1978.

Powers, Thomas. *The Man Who Kept the Secrets: Richard Helms and the CIA*. New York: Alfred A. Knopf, 1979.

Prouty, L. Fletcher. *The Secret Team*. Englewood Cliffs, NJ: Prentice-Hall, 1973.

Rand, Ayn. *Atlas Shrugged*. New York: New American Library, 1959.

Randle, Kevin D. *The UFO Casebook*. New York: Warner Books, 1989.

Rappoport, Jon. *AIDS, Inc. Scandal of the Century*. San Bruno, CA: Human Energy Press, 1988.

Raschke, Carl A. *Painted Black*. San Francisco: Harper and Row, 1990.

Rashke, Richard. *The Killing of Karen Silkwood*. Boston: Houghton Mifflin Co., 1983.

Ravenscroft, Trevor. *The Spear of Destiny*. York Beach, ME: Samuel Weiser, Inc., 1973.

Reed, Sally D. *NEA: Propaganda Front for the Radical Left*. 1984.

Robbins, Christopher. *Air America: The Story of the CIA's Secret Airlines*. New York: Putnam's, 1979.

Robinson, James M., ed. *The Nag Hammadi Library*. San Francisco: Harper and Row, 1988.

Robinson, John. *Born In Blood: The Lost Secrets of Freemasonry*. New York: M. Evans and Co., 1989.

Robison, John. *Proofs of a Conspiracy*. Boston: Western Islands Press, 1967.

Rodriguez, Felix and John Weisman. *Shadow Warrior*. New York: Pocket Books, 1989.

Rosenbaum, Ron. *Travels With Dr. Death and Other Unusual Investigations*. New York: Penguin, 1991.

Sampson, Anthony. *The Sovereign State of ITT*. Greenwich, CT: Fawcett Crest, 1974.

Sanders, Ed. *The Family: Revised and Updated Edition*. New York: Signet, 1989.

Scheflin, Alan and Edward Opton, Jr. *The Mind Manipulators*. London: Paddington Press, 1978.

Schomp, Gerald. *Birchism Was My Business*. New York: MacMillan, 1970.

Schonfield, Hugh. *The Passover Plot*. New York: Bantam Books, 1967.

Schulzinger, Robert A. *The Wise Men of Foreign Affairs: The History of the Council on Foreign Relations*. New York: Columbia University Press, 1984.

Scott, Peter Dale. *The Dallas Conspiracy*. Unpublished manuscript, 1971.

Scwarzwaller, Wulf. *The Unknown Hitler*. New York: Berkley Books, 1990.

Shackley, Theodore. *The Third Option*. New York: Dell, 1988.

Shea, Robert and Robert Anton Wilson. *The Illuminatus Trilogy*. New York: Dell, 1988.

Shoup, Laurence and William Mintier. *Imperial Braintrust: The CFR and U.S. Foreign Policy*. New York: Monthly Review Press, 1977.

Silk, Leonard and Mark Silk. *The American Establishment*. New York: Avon/Discus Books, 1981.

Simpson, Christopher. *Blowback*. New York: Weidenfeld and Nicholson, 1988.

Sklar, Dusty. *Nazis and the Occult*. New York: Dorset Press, 1989.

Sklar, Holly. *Reagan Trilateralism and the Neoliberals*. Boston: South End Press, 1986.

Sklar, Holly, ed. *Trilateralism: The Trilateral Commission and Elite Planning for World Management*. Boston: South End Press, 1980.

Smoot, Dan. *The Invisible Government.* Boston: Western Islands Press, 1965.

Sorman, Guy. *The Conservative Revolution in America.* Chicago: Regenery, 1985.

Sterling, Claire. *The Terror Network.* New York: Holt, Rinehart and Winston, 1981.

Stormer, John. *None Dare Call It Treason.* Florissant, MO: Liberty Bell Press, 1964.

Summers, Anthony. *Conspiracy.* New York: Paragon House, 1989.

Sutton, Anthony. *Wall Street and the Rise of Hitler.* Seal Beach, CA: '76 Press, 1976.

Terry, Maury. *The Ultimate Evil.* Garden City, NY: Dolphin Books, 1987.

Thornley, Kerry. *The Dreadlock Recollections.* Unpublished manuscript, 1984.

―――. *Oswald.* Chicago: New Classics House, 1965.

Tierney, Patrick. *The Highest Altar: The Story of Human Sacrifice.* New York: Viking, 1989.

Tudhope, George. *Bacon-Masonry.* Mokelumne Hill, CA: Health Research, 1989.

United States Senate. *Hearings Before the Subcommittee on Terrorism, Narcotics and International Communications,* 1988.

U.S. Labor Party Investigating Team. *Dope Inc.: Britain's Opium War against the United States.* New York: New Benjamin Franklin House, 1978.

Vahan, Richard. *The Truth about the John Birch Society.* New York: MacFadden Books, 1962.

Vallee, Jacques. *Messengers of Deception.* Berkeley, CA: And/Or Press, 1979.

Welch, Robert. *The Blue Book of the John Birch Society.* Belmont, MA: Western Islands Press, 1959.

―――. *And Some Ober Dicta.* Belmont, MA: American Opinion, 1976.

Whyte, William. *The Organization Man.* Garden City, NY: Doubleday/Anchor, 1957.

Wilgus, Neil. *The Illuminoids: Secret Societies and Political Paranoia.* Santa Fe, NM: Sun Books, 1978.

Wills, Garry. *Reagan's America.* New York: Penguin Books, 1988.

Wilson, Colin. *The Encyclopedia of Unsolved Mysteries.* Chicago: Contemporary Books, 1988.

―――. *The Outsider.* Los Angeles: Jeremy P. Tarcher, Inc., 1982.

Wilson, Robert Anton. *Cosmic Trigger: Final Secret of the Illuminati.* Phoenix, AZ: Falcon Press, 1986.

Winrod, Gerald. *Adam Weishaupt: A Human Devil.*

Wise, David. *The American Police State.* New York: Random House, 1976.

Woodward, Bob. *Veil: The Secret Wars of the CIA, 1981–1987.* New York: Pocket Books, 1987.

Yallop, David. *In God's Name.* New York: Bantam Books, 1985.

# INDEX